Prime Time
Love and Desire and Hate

Prime Time

Love and Desire
and Hate

Joan Collins

SMITHBOOKS

Prime Time First published 1988
Copyright © 1988 by Gemini Star Productions Ltd

Love and Desire and Hate First published 1990
Copyright © 1990 by Gemini Star Productions Ltd

This edition published in 1992 for
Smithbooks, Canada, by Cresset Press,
an imprint of Random House UK Limited
20 Vauxhall Bridge Road, London SW1V 2SA

ISBN 0–88665–213–8

Printed and bound in Great Britain by
Mackays of Chatham PLC, Chatham, Kent

Prime Time

PRIME TIME

For every actress
who has ever suffered the slings and arrows
of outrageous fortune
that are such a part of all our lives . . .
and for Daddy, who was
such a part of mine.

ACKNOWLEDGEMENTS

I would like to thank . . .

Michael Korda and Nancy Nicholas, my editors, for their encouragement and wonderfully constructive criticism . . .

Irving Lazar, for believing I could do it . . .

Cindy Franke, who tirelessly deciphered my complicated shorthand with accuracy and devotion . . .

And Judy Bryer, for her loving support.

Part One

1

Chloe Carriere strode swiftly through the Heathrow departure lounge, trying with little success to escape the inquisitive lenses of the familiar throng of paparazzi. As photographers and reporters buzzed around her, several businessmen waiting for flights lowered their morning newspapers to stare at one of Britain's most famous and sexiest singing stars. 'How long will you be in Hollywood, Chloe?' demanded the hack with acne from the *Sun*.

Chloe smiled, increasing her pace. Her sable-lined trench coat billowed gracefully around her newly slimmed figure. She had spent a gruelling week at a health farm in Wales trying to erase the combined ravages of Josh, a demanding six-month tour of the provinces, and her first acting role in a BBC docudrama about women in prison. It had brought her down to fighting weight, and now she looked and felt great – better than she had in years.

'What kind of a part are you testing for?' grinned the one with the green teeth from the *Mirror*. 'Is it a new television soap opera, then?'

'I don't really know too much about it yet,' she hedged. 'Other than that it's based on a best-selling novel called *Saga*.'

'Do you want the part?' asked the one from Reuters with the adenoids and the bulging Adam's apple.

Did she want the part? What a stupid question! Of *course* she wanted the damn part. After more than twenty years of singing gigs in Britain, Europe and the States, she ached for it but she answered the questions casually: *if* she was lucky enough to be chosen for the role of Miranda Hamilton, it could turn her career around, make her a big name, maybe even a superstar. But she didn't want these little bastards – and those bigger bastards – waiting in Hollywood to look her over to know just how much she cared, how desperately she needed this role, particularly when she was only one of four or five actresses who were testing for it.

Testing for it! Demeaning, but what the hell. She knew this business was no fairy godmother. She had been up and down in it, up and then down again, for years. Seven hit records in two and a half decades. A fixture in the Top Ten, then suddenly now in 1982 she couldn't even make *Billboards* Top 100. Twenty-five years of performing, but still surviving, and still sane, thank God. She gave the reporters and the photographers a smile and a friendly wave as she reached the departure gate and as they snapped a few more frames for good measure, she hoped the photographs would be kind in tomorrow's tabloids.

In the first class comfort of the British Airways cabin she relaxed, accepted a Buck's Fizz from the smiling steward, then changed her mind in anticipation of the forthcoming scrutiny of studio moguls, asking instead for Evian water. She waved away cashew nuts and caviar, accepted the *Herald Tribune* and the *Daily Express*, removed her cream kid boots and belt, reclined her seat to its maximum and thought about this irresistible role.

Miranda Hamilton, in *Saga*. A story of intrigue, corruption, betrayal, ambition and lust, set against a background of great wealth amidst the opulent estates, luxurious yachts and ultra-modern skyscraper offices of Newport Beach, California. A tale of men and women who loved and hated with passions larger than life. The book had been on *The New York Times* best-seller list for six months, and now they were casting for the television series. According to Chloe's agent, Jasper Swanson, they had already cast several familiar television names for various roles, but had not yet found their bitch-goddess villainess Miranda. The network wanted a glamorous manipulating bitch, a rotten-to-the-core heartless tramp, a deviously ambitious but sexily elegant woman of the world, a female so mean and gorgeous that every man watching would either want to make love to her or give her a taste of her own medicine, and whom every woman would either envy or emulate if the show was a hit. The actress who would play her could be catapulted to ephemeral television fame, glory and the eventual megabucks that went with that success.

But Miranda Hamilton *couldn't* be the average Hollywood blonde bimbo. She had to be at least forty, preferably closer to forty-five. Survivor of three or four marriages and three or four dozen affairs, she had borne three or four children, owned three or four estates scattered throughout the world, had three or four million dollars' worth of jewels; not to mention two or three hundred million dollars in the bank. The actress picked for this plum part would certainly have to have enough in common with Miranda to be believable to the audience. They would have to hate her, and they would have to love her. Not an easy combination to achieve. She had to be a bitch, but she had to be vulnerable. She had to have fire, but she had to be warm. She had to be dominating, yet men must feel they could be the one to dominate her. And last week the producers, dynamic Abby Arafat and his partner, the equally dynamic Gertrude Greenbloom, had come up with the idea of testing Chloe.

Chloe had attracted Abby Arafat's interest at a cocktail party at Lady Sarah Cranleigh's Eaton Square flat. Just returned from a tour of Scandinavia, Chloe, unable to decide whether to reconcile with her husband, Josh, in L.A., had lingered for a few days in London, where the other person dearest to her heart lived.

She felt there was little hope of patching things up with Josh. There was no question that she had been a loving, faithful wife to him. Yet he seemed unable to control his sexual drive with other women. He was lukewarm with her, whined if she wasn't around, yet nagged her if she was. He was a man who had almost ruined his career with his volatile temperament so much so that record companies had been cancelling contracts, and his tours were drying up. Often he would sulk for days, refusing to talk to Chloe, locking himself into his personalized state-of-the-art recording studio and mixing his own records hour after hour, day after day, week after week blocking out everyone else around him.

The day before she had left, walking past his bathroom she saw him masturbating over a copy of a men's magazine. It had nauseated her, but she had not let him know she had seen him. If he could become aroused by a picture in a cheap magazine, why couldn't he make love to *her* properly any more? It had been weeks – no – months now since they had. Ever the optimist, she had hoped things would be different after this last separation. Obviously she had been wrong.

Chloe sighed as she came out of her reverie as the 'fasten seat belt' sign came on. Carrying her beige crocodile Morabito overnight bag, she walked to the plane's cramped toilet. Why, she wondered, with so much effort expended on design, are the toilets not big enough even to brush one's hair without fracturing an elbow? She slipped off her Gianni Versace cream silk blouse and skirt and pulled on a blue velour track suit. She ran a comb through her luxuriant black curly hair and removed her makeup to let her skin breathe, then slathered moisturizer on lavishly – flying ruined her complexion, there was no doubt about that – and strolled back to her seat.

Although aware that several of the women passengers had noticed the transformation and were checking her for cracks, Chloe didn't care. She had little vanity about her looks. She thought she looked fine without makeup, casually dressed. Not for her the elaborate lengths to which many female entertainers went to prevent the world from seeing their real faces. She smiled as she thought of her co-star in the BBC TV play she had just finished. Pandora would arrive in a full, light, makeup at six every morning, completely done, even to false lashes, and wearing one of her many Kanekolan wigs which she possessed in several styles. Pandora King was a seldom-out-of-work American actress who had been appearing in supporting roles in series and movies of the week for the past ten years. Although the public never really knew her name, they always recognized her attractively foxy face and glamorous, auburn hair. She would be swathed in her mink of the day, which she had in all colours, and would then disappear into her dressing room for three hours. Her makeup box was the size of a compact car and contained every device known to drugstore and cosmetic counter, from plastic fingernails to vaginal jelly. Only God and her makeup man knew what she did in that room, because when she surfaced she looked little different from when she went in.

The two women had spent an amusing lunch hour going through the contents of Pandora's 'box', as she called it, on a rare day when Pandora's frosty attitude towards the world, and especially towards other actresses, had thawed slightly.

Chloe wondered if a question one of the journalists had asked was true: was Pandora also testing for Miranda? If so, Pandora herself would be the last person to reveal *that* bit of news to Chloe. She believed in giving nothing away, particularly information of a professional kind.

Arriving at Los Angeles Airport ten hours later, Chloe was whisked by limousine to the endless freeways of Los Angeles.

She grimaced as she observed the repetitive and unattractive streets and boulevards. Grey smog hung heavily over the city, stinging her eyes and throat, even though the windows of the Cadillac were closed and the air-conditioning turned on full blast.

Chloe had spent a great deal of time in the past two decades living in L.A., but she still disliked the look of the city. It was so ugly, almost sordid in places, and people seemed to exist solely on hamburgers, doughnuts and diet sodas judging by the number of establishments that were selling those substances. New health clubs, gyms and fitness centres sprouted like mushrooms. She counted sixteen new ones. The residents obviously needed them to balance their ruinous eating habits.

Rows of faded buildings, their signs proclaiming the delights of 'Yoghurt City', 'The Popcorn Palace', and 'Chuck's Chilli Dogs' passed. Chloe sighed. Nothing had changed in the six months she had been away, there just seemed to be more smog.

She snuggled deeper into her sable-lined coat, shivering although it was seventy degrees. She was in Los Angeles, coming home to face Josh hoping to salvage something from their years of magic together.

When the limousine came to the end of the interweaving freeways, turning right onto the straight Pacific Coast High-way at Sunset Boulevard, Chloe relaxed, loosened her coat and opened the window to feel the cool sea breeze on her face. She loved the ocean, the mystery and power of it. She never tired of watching the greenish grey flatness of the Pacific crest into thick fierce white waves, as she sat on the beach for hours.

When they had first bought the house in a secluded part of Trancas Beach, beyond Malibu, she and Josh spent early mornings and most evenings walking along the caramel sands dodging the tide, talking about everything under the sun, laughing at the baby sandpipers, breathing the salty pure air, so different from the smoggy atmosphere that passed for oxygen in the city. They had been so happy that Chloe thought that no married couple could ever have been as obviously passionately devoted to each other. But that was then, and this was now, and it was time to find out if he had changed his tune in the six months they had been apart.

He was watching the box as usual, slumped in his favourite comfortable armchair. They kissed abstractedly, lovers whose lust for each other had lost its lustre. He was dressed in rumpled navy blue cords and V-necked cashmere sweater. His black hair was untidy and flecked with grey and although he had known she was coming home, he hadn't bothered to shave, and she felt his splintery stubble against her soft cheek.

'I brought you some special honey at Fortnums. It's new – from Devon – they say it's wonderful.' He ignored her, his body loose and relaxed as she hugged him tightly.

Was it too late she wondered, as she held the face she had adored for so many years between her hands and kissed his cool lips. In spite of his waning interest in her and his womanizing, she still couldn't believe this was happening to them. *Why* was he turning off her? After six months apart, why did he make no effort? Not even a pretence of delight in her homecoming, he didn't even bother to stand up. What had she done to make him so indifferent? Even before she went on tour, there had been too many moments in bed, their usual arena of compatibility, when she had had to coax him to make love to her. She felt like a cheap tart. Was this what ten years of marriage did to a man's libido? she wondered bitterly, as she pressed her body seductively close to his. She felt nothing. Not a bump, not a lump, not a twitch. This from a man who had a worldwide reputation as a great lover. Maybe still did. But not with her.

She turned away, pretending to busy herself with a pile of mail. Hot tears pricked the back of her lids and her throat felt constricted. How long could this continue? It was a farce. Without comedy.

'Your agent called,' Josh said coolly, turning up the volume on the TV. Eyes glued to Clint Eastwood, 'Call him back, says it's *important*.' The last word sounded almost like a sneer. She ignored his tone, smiled too brightly. Went to the antique wooden bar to fix a forbidden vodka and ice. The health farm had said no liquor for at least a week. To hell with them.

She called Jasper from the bedroom, not wanting Josh to hear. The slightest thing set him off these days. She wanted to try and keep the peace as long as she could.

'Dear heart, I'm so glad you called,' Jasper sounded pleased. 'It's looking good for "Saga", looking very good indeed for you, dear.'

'Wonderful.' Chloe smiled, the vodka giving her a buzz.

'They will probably shoot six or seven days a month in Newport Beach,' she heard Jasper saying. 'The rest of the filming will be at one of the studios. Possibly Metro, may be Fox.'

'That's great, Newport is beautiful. Will they be shooting on any boats?'

'Yes, yes, dear.' Jasper was often impatient with his clients' desire for details. 'Listen to me, Chloe, on the twenty-fifth you're on display. Abby and Maud Arafat are giving one of their casual little dinners, just twenty or thirty of the most important people in this town. They want you there, dear girl. Best bib and tucker on. You have twelve days to prepare so get out your new Bob Mackie. I *hope* you lost all that bloat at the fat farm, dear, bellies don't look good in Macks.'

'Yes, Jasper, I lost every ounce,' she said obediently. 'I won't let you down. I promise.'

'You better not, dear, this one's a biggie, believe me. Could make you HUGE, dear, really huge.'

'I know, Jasper, I know.'

She knew what a casual little dinner for twenty or thirty meant. There were no casual little dinners in Hollywood any more. Every meeting in La La land was business. Whether spoken or unspoken, potential deals simmered beneath the surface of even the simplest lunch. A gathering of twenty or thirty of the town's finest citizens at an important producer's house was often the equivalent of a summit meeting in Washington.

Knowing Abby and his partner, Gertrude Greenbloom, who would unquestionably be present too, Chloe surmised that the three or four other potential candidates for Miranda would also be attending. She knew she was only included as the lucky result of a recent fortunate meeting in London.

The slit of Chloe's black silk Valentino skirt had been just high enough to glimpse a firm, elegant thigh. Her chiselled features had a look of abandon, her hair was an aureole of black curls, and her figure was slim but voluptuous.

Abby had downed two martinis, and holding back had never been his forte. 'How would you like to play Miranda? I hear you could do with a job and you've certainly got all her attributes from where I stand.' His eyes scanned her face and body like a laser beam.

Chloe laughed. 'Abby, you know I'm just a saloon singer.'

Although she was aware that Hollywood's search for 'Saga's' leading roles was a hot show business topic, she was too canny to be taken in by Abby's pitch, and yet – and yet – why not? Singing had not been satisfying her for some time. The young Stevie Nickses and Pat Benitars had more appeal to the public today than a forty-year-old singer, and God knows touring was becoming more and more gruelling. Maybe settling down again in California with a steady job would bring her and Josh closer together.

'Streisand said that, Garland said it, so did Liza.' Abby smiled approvingly as he surveyed her. She certainly was a gorgeous-looking woman, five feet six to his six feet two, but in three-inch black satin Maud Frizon sandals she met his eyes with ease. 'They thought they were just singers too.'

'I'm not really an actress, Abby. I just did one play for the Beeb, that's all.' She sipped her Kir while surveying him through a forest of real eyelashes. 'I did get good reviews, though. I'm sure you read them.' She smiled a catlike beam, that was one of her stocks in trade.

He started to melt. Abby was that rare Hollywood phenomenon, a producer who actually *liked* and admired actresses. He puffed on his cigar, scrutinizing her from top to toe. She had class – there was no doubt about that. And beauty, sex appeal and glamour.

'Who cares about acting? It's presence, charisma, pulling power, that's what we need for Miranda. Most of the old-time screen greats couldn't act their way out of a McDonald's hamburger bag. Look at Hayworth, Grable, Bardot, Ava Gardner. None of 'em could *act*, for Christ's sake, but they had *it*. And I think *you've* got *it*, kid, in spades – so let's give it a whirl. Come to California and we'll test you, honey. You'll be great, I know you will.'

'Let me think about it, Abby – truly I will consider it.' Chloe suspected that Abby's pitch, enthusiastic as it was, was probably equally strong to the other actresses he was considering. 'Doesn't Miranda have to age from twenty to some ancient age? Mind you, I could probably play that,' she joked.

'Yes, yes,' Abby said eagerly. 'That will be in the four-hour movie of the week we shoot before the series starts. When first we see the young Miranda she's eighteen, and a virgin.'

'Oh, no *way*!' cried Chloe with a chuckle, 'I couldn't look eighteen!'

'Of course you could.' He laughed at her protestations. 'We've got Lazlo Dominick doing the lighting. He could make Bette Davis look twenty, for Christ's sake. You've got the aura, you've got the looks and the sex appeal. I think you've got the talent. Test for us, sweetheart, please, you won't be sorry.'

'All right, Abby,' Chloe had agreed. 'All right. I'll test but I warn you I'll be terrified.'

'Wonderful,' Abby had wheezed. ' Olivier's always terrified – sign of great talent. You'll hear from us next week, sweetheart, and don't be frightened – you'll be terrific. I can feel it in my bones.'

'So who else is testing?' she asked Jasper a mite too casually.

'Some of the suggestions are *insane*. Simply *mad*.' Jasper laughed. 'I know it's a peach of a part, dear, and this town has gone wild about the casting. There hasn't been anything as exciting since Selznick was searching for Scarlet O'Hara. But listen to the other contenders.'

'Who are they?' Chloe's voice wasn't casual now. She needed this information.

'Sissy Sharp – now we all know she hasn't had a hit in years, needs the part badly. Wonderful actress. Zero sex appeal but she is an Oscar winner, of course.'

'I know,' Chloe said ruefully. 'I was there, Jasper, remember? I sang the award-winning song. Whatever was it called?'

'Who cares?' Jasper said testily. 'Nobody remembers the names of who won *last* year, let alone fifteen years ago! Sissy is hungry, dear – hungry as hell for that role. Hungry enough to test, but she's pretending she's not interested in TV, only the big screen, and they don't give a fuck about her these days. However, the good news is that Abby and Gertrude don't think she's right.'

'She's not looking too good these days, is she?' said Chloe. 'I don't mean to be bitchy, but I saw her on "Lifestyles" last week; she looked well ravaged, like a fugitive from Belsen.'

'Diets like an anorexic teenager,' Jasper said bluntly. 'She's crazy, she thinks she constantly rejuvenates herself with all those fad diets – not to mention the surgery. She must have had her face and her tits lifted at least three times in the past five years.'

Chloe shuddered. The idea of a knife near her body terrified her.

'Then we have Emerald,' said Jasper smoothly. 'Now *she* is definitely a contender, Chloe, and don't underestimate her.'

Emerald Barrymore. No star had ever been bigger. Not Brando, not Kelly, not even Monroe. And no one had sunk to the depths she had. Drugs, alcohol, men and scandal, all had contributed to her downfall.

'She has been the subject of more front page headlines than you have had hot dinners, my dear,' Jasper continued. 'But *what* a survivor. The ultimate, and the public adore her.'

'And she is still a major star.' Chloe heard a reverence in her voice that the mention of Emerald's name often caused.

'So's Kim Novak, dear,' said Jasper snidely, 'and she can't get a job either. Emerald really needs bread now. She's been desperate for cash ever since her last lover fleeced her. She wants that part desperately, and she's using all her influence.'

'Who else, Jasper?'

'Rozalinde Lamaze. Lamaze is somewhat of a slut, as we all

know,' purred Jasper in his smoothest, English tones. 'But the public love her – especially males. They would all like to fuck her tiny brains out. She's possibly a little too Latin, too ethnic for Miranda, but she has a huge fan following, even though her last three films didn't even recoup their negative costs.'

Chloe took a gulp of vodka. This was indeed tough competition. Why she was even included with this group she couldn't imagine. She realized television was constantly searching for new, fresh faces – maybe that was the reason. She was virtually unknown in America now. She'd been gone so long from the charts. She could be a new face yet!

'Help!' Chloe gulped the last of the vodka. 'Jasper, I'll be the *last* of that group the producers would want.'

'Nonsense,' the old man countered swiftly. 'You actually have most of the attributes needed for the role. There are several other actresses Abby wants to test, but I assure you that Meryl Streep, Jackie Bisset and Sabrina Jones will not be interested, even though there will be a great deal of fanfare about them being considered. Now get some rest, dear. Don't worry and remember *always*: Think positively. Banish those negative vibrations.'

He hung up, leaving Chloe trying to 'Think positively,' but still thinking her chances were slim. In the living room Josh still sat glued to the tube, oozing 'negative vibrations'. She poured herself another vodka. Some of his mates were on 'Hollywood Squares', so he *shhsshd* Chloe as she tried to tell him about her conversation with Jasper. She wanted him to cheer her up, joke with her as he used to, but he was like stone. Tears filled her eyes as she walked into the bathroom and turned the taps on the big marble Jacuzzi tub. It had been built for the two of them. Now Chloe lay there alone, the bubbles tingling her flesh, staring out into the beauty of the ocean and the cresting waves, as she wondered if she could make it work with Josh. How many more separations and reconciliations would it take before she stopped fighting for their marriage and gave them both their freedom? This had been their second separation in as many years. She remembered the first one two years ago . . .

14

2

For eight years they had reigned as one of show business's happiest and most successful couples. But in the past year as Josh's last three singles had plummeted, Josh's behaviour had become so outrageous and intolerable that she had to get away from him, hoping that a trial separation would make him see reason – make him see what he was losing by losing her.

Raindrops slid across the windows of the first-class railway carriage taking her to Scotland.

It was a bleak January day. Sleet scudded onto the roofs of identically dun-coloured houses as Chloe's train approached the suburbs of Edinburgh. Everything looked as grey and dismal as she felt. Sheep huddled together for comfort, and the sodden meadows seemed to echo her misery.

As she poured the last of the Liebfraumilch into a thick British Rail glass, her feeling of guilt was quickly replaced by a feeling of security as the wine warmed her.

She was getting away from it all. Getting away from Josh. From his lies, his drinking, his drugs and his philandering.

Getting away from her stepdaughter, Sally, a wilful Beverly Hills brat, whose blazing love for her father was matched by an equally blazing dislike for her stepmother.

Chloe could never understand why Sally hated her so much. God knows she had bent over backward to be as good a stepmother as she could, understanding only too well what effect it must have had on the little girl to watch her own mother's slow death from cancer. But in spite of her attempts to fill the maternal void in Sally's life, she only seemed to hate her more.

Sally was nearly eight when Chloe had married Joshua Brown in 1972. A scrawny, sullen-looking wisp with mousy braids, her grape-green eyes dominated a tiny, strangely adult face. She seemed to magically appear from around corners surreptitiously whenever Josh and Chloe were cuddled up on the couch watching TV, eating the lavish high teas they loved of brown bread and butter with the crusts cut off, covered with honey, being particularly cosy and affectionate with each other.

Silently the tiny child would stand, unnoticed by the lovers staring stonily at their newlywed happiness. Josh had not been an affectionate father to Sally, so Chloe was not taking anything away from her. But in Sally's mind Chloe was the rival for her daddy's love. Her jealousy for her stepmother turned to hatred as the years went by, and Sally grew to realize that the more she misbehaved and insulted Chloe, the more attention she received from her father.

Their houseman, Roberto, had addressed Chloe as Mrs Brown the first week of the marriage, as they were discussing menus. Sally, who had been engrossed in a comic book, suddenly whirled violently on the frightened Filipino and screamed, '*Don't* call her Mrs Brown! There's only one Mrs Brown, and that's my mother!'

Sobbing, she ran to her bedroom, locking the door, oblivious to the entreaties of everyone except Josh, who, summoned from the recording studio, arrived and finally placated the hysterical child with cuddles and as much fatherly affection as he could.

When Josh first married Chloe, to appease Sally he started to get the little girl involved in his music. She lapped it up. She took guitar lessons at eight, trumpet lessons at nine. She already played the piano, and had started singing lessons at five. Josh discussed many aspects of his music with her. Although so young she was a stern, knowledgable critic: he had a certain respect for her ideas and opinions, and she worshipped him.

God knows there had been enough romping and giggling and wrestling and climbing on Daddy's knees and cuddling in the eight years since Chloe and Josh had married. Sally did it to distract her father from Chloe – she did everything she could to antagonize Chloe. Often she succeeded.

Chloe had tried from the beginning to conceive a child with Josh. She felt a baby would make their life together complete. But try as they might, it didn't happen. Chloe went to the top gynaecologists all over the world. There seemed to be no physical reason why she couldn't conceive; they should 'just relax and keep trying', was the advice given.

She had thought that if only she could have given Josh a child, their marriage would have been better, but she knew why she couldn't. Even though her doctors said she was perfectly fine physically, she knew that something had gone wrong when she had given birth to Annabel. Chloe had been in labour for twelve hours, nearly out of her mind with pain, and the post-natal care she had received in the clinic had been minimal.

Chloe had never told Josh about her baby. At first she was afraid he would disapprove because she had given her away, then, as time passed, she thought it best to keep the truth from him as the realization she could not have another child might have been blamed on Annabel's difficult birth.

Chloe had been twenty-one when Annabel was born. With the resilience of youth she recovered quickly from the ordeal, but the physical scars left by the pain of the difficult delivery and the anguish of having to give up her baby – her beautiful little Annabel, so close to Sally in age, but so different from her in temperament – would never disappear.

Now it was too late. Annabel had been brought up by Chloe's brother and his wife in their little terraced house in Barnes. And nobody ever suspected. Nobody. Not the slimy Fleet Street reptiles, nor the staff at the clinic. Annabel herself didn't even know, Chloe thought sadly, lighting a cigarette in defiance of the 'No Smoking' sign. No one other than her brother and sister-in-law knew about her secret child and the deep devotion she had for her.

She realized that Annabel had become almost an obsession with her – and Sally noticed it. The chant of 'Not *another* special present for your niece! Anyone would think she was *your* kid,' made Chloe flinch.

As Sally approached her teens and became aware of Chloe's thwarted desire for a baby she often needled her with it. 'You're *barren*, aren't you?' she gloated at Chloe one day as they lay by the pool trying to tan under a sun almost obliterated by a thick pall of smog. Sally was studying Elizabethan history. 'Just like Henry the Eighth's daughter Mary. Barren!' She chortled gleefully, 'Barren, barren, BARREN!' and dived into the pool, drenching the novel Chloe was reading. Eventually Chloe gave up all pretence of friendliness, and their relationship became a minor battlefield.

One spring when Chloe and Sally were in Paris, where Josh was playing at the Olympia to packed houses, Chloe had gone to Galéries Lafayette to shop, and Sally, her instinct telling her this was another chance to antagonize her stepmother, had cajoled Chloe into taking her too. Chloe picked out matching shirts and sweaters for her nephews, and then carefully chose a Christian Dior burgundy coat with a velvet collar and hat, and a matching dress, for Annabel. She was off to London to visit her brother, and was filled with excitement at the prospect of seeing her daughter. Sally, now that she was a teenager, was wearing a collection of tattered rags that were the 'in' thing in Beverly Hills prep schools this year. She had sneered at Chloe's choice. 'Square – *yuuck* – what a *nerd* Annabel must be,' she said, examining a pile of socks in bright neon colours and stuffing a couple of pairs into the pocket of her oversized jacket while no one was looking. No matter that her father could have bought her a crate of socks – Sally loved to do the forbidden.

Annabel was a typically well-behaved, nicely-brought-up English schoolgirl, the complete opposite of Sally. She had loved the outfit. She was charming, delightful and shy. After lunch as she and Chloe had walked along a leafy English lane, she confided in her 'aunt' that she too wanted to be a singer one day, and had started taking guitar lessons as well.

'But you're so young,' demurred Chloe. She wanted something better for her daughter than the tough life that she had chosen.

'Oh, Auntie Chloe, I love the guitar and I love singing. I love it so much.' The girl had jumped up and down, her cheeks flushed, her deep green eyes sparkling.

'I play your albums all the time, Auntie Chloe. I *love* how you sing. I've never told you this . . .' She blushed and looked away.

'What, what, darling?' Chloe's throat tightened with the effort of holding back the tears. This darling girl, this sweet lovely child was her own and only baby. If only she could be with her. But she couldn't. Stop it, Chloe, she told herself. Don't rock the boat, let's not have a True Confessions here, it will wreck everyone's life – especially Annabel's.

She listened carefully as the girl breathlessly confided her secret hero worship and admiration for her 'aunt'.

'When I grow up, Aunt Chloe, I want to be just like you,' she chirped, her little face alive with animation. 'I just hope I can sing only half as well.'

'Oh Annabel darling, oh, baby.' Chloe couldn't stop her tears now as she knelt in the Sussex lane and hugged her daughter to her fiercely. 'Darling Annabel, I will do anything I can to help you, I promise I will.'

'I'm so proud you're my aunt.' Annabel wondered why Auntie Chloe, normally so cool, was drowning her in tears. It was embarrassing, but grown-up people were often weird.

The sudden acceleration of the train jolted Chloe back to the present. She sighed, removing her dark glasses, which had not protected her from stares of recognition from waiters and several passengers. She looked a wreck. Two bottles of wine each evening, followed by sleepless Seconal-filled nights and a difficult tour, did not for beauty make. A week at the fat farm would take care of that. The health farm was her yearly saviour. With luck, she would look five years younger again. Her cheekbones would emerge from her cocoon of bloat, her turquoise eyes, no longer dimmed with inevitable red threads of too much vodka, would brighten again, and the waistbands of her clothes would regain a comfortable ease.

She sipped her wine, trying not to feel bitter. Sally would be thrilled she was away. She could have her father all to herself. Perhaps they could share a joint and listen to his latest single, turning up the volume so loud that the labrador whined and sought refuge in the wine cellar. Oh, they were so alike, father and daughter, two peas in a pod. Both Scorpio, both selfish, scornful, beautiful and arrogant. He was forty, she was sixteen, and they understood each other perfectly. Their close relationship made her longing for her own daughter only more intense.

3

In 1964, to have given birth to an illegitimate child would have wrecked Chloe's blossoming career. She was just beginning to make it as a singer, moving up from working-men's clubs to 'Top of the Pops' with new jazzed-up renditions of old Cole Porter standbys had taken her barely five years. Five years of fierce determined dedicated work on her voice, of studying Ella Fitzgerald for the phrasing, Sinatra for the nuances, Peggy Lee's husky sensual overtones. She managed to instil sexuality and meaning into the most mundane lyrics.

Every night since Chloe was still in her teens, waiting on tables, singing the occasional song when they would let her, she had gone to sleep, no matter how exhausted, to the sounds of one of her three favourite performers lulling her into the dreamless eight hours necessary for the maintenance of her second-best asset, her face – hours spent applying and reapplying lipsticks, eye shadows, brow shapers, analysing – re-structuring with cosmetic witchery a pleasing proportion of wide innocent eyes, upturned nose, slanting cheekbones and full lips into a seductive exotic face that would not have been out of place in the fashion magazines.

She accepted any one-night gig up and down the length

and breadth of Britain, watching, learning, imitating and discarding. Eventually her talent and burning ambition to succeed turned her into a passable and popular singer, famed for her sensuality and elegance.

She had no time for men. Certainly those she met in Leeds, Glasgow or Birmingham were so doltish that rejecting their advances required little effort. But there was the occasional crooner on the same tour. Usually married, usually on the way down, whereas Chloe was – she knew it – on the way up. There was the occasional young drummer with the band and the occasional saxophonist or clarinet player, and once even the Maestro himself, the leader of the band. But all in all they were a sorry lot and in no way conformed to Chloe's ideals.

She had observed Susan, her best friend since school, now married to Chloe's brother, Richard, weighed down with the responsibility of shopping, cooking, cleaning and taking care of a toddler while pregnant again. Susan was already losing the bloom of youth and vitality that had made them the two most popular girls at school. No man was worth it, thought Chloe, worth the effort, worth the pain. And no one *had* been – until she met Matthew Sullivan.

Matt was a newspaperman. He worked for the *Daily Chronical* as a show business journalist, interviewing has-been American stars who were flocking to London to peddle their fading wares in the thriving British film industry of the early 1960s. He drank whiskey, flirted with anything in a miniskirt and told outrageous jokes. He was a half-Irish, half-Jewish rogue, charm personified, cynical, hard drinking and careless about with whom he dallied. More often than not he could be found propping up the bar at any Fleet Street pub regaling his mates with anecdotes, rather than in his family nest in Shepherd's Bush with his plain wife and their twins. His reputation as an inveterate womanizer, wastrel and life-of-the-party raconteur was well known to everyone. Except Chloe.

With fame and success on her mind, and men low on her list of priorities, Chloe, bright-eyed, full of life and twenty-one years old, was performing at the Cavern, a dingy but extremely popular disco in downtown Liverpool, much publicized recently for discovering four local lads known as the Beatles.

She had met Matt several times before at clubs up and down the less salubrious parts of northern England. He was writing about the rock scene, as his readers were interested in many of the new groups like the Beatles, the Stones, the Animals, Herman's Hermits. Chloe had been aware of his interest in her the last time they met, although he had been with his wife. They had all gone for drinks to an after-hours drinking club. Chloe was with her current clarinetist, Rick. But her interest in him was on the wane. Rick knew, and was already casting his eyes to pastures new.

Matt made Chloe laugh with juicy gossip and outrageous jokes. When she stopped laughing, she found him staring at her. Their eyes locked; he was giving her a clear message. She found herself blushing as he gestured to the dance floor.

Vic Damone was singing – something mellow and sultry. The smoky club had an aura of sexuality. Bodies swayed together, warm – sweating – moist. Matt held her confidently. Not the usual groper, she thought gratefully, although his arms around her were possessive. He had the assurance that came from knowing he was attractive, desirable, and could probably have any woman he wanted.

His arms tightened as the music slowed, their bodies moulded even closer. She was aware of his excitement now. She was also aware of hers. An unusual feeling for Chloe, to want a man. To really desire him. She shivered, gazing into his black eyes again. His message was clear. She felt a total melting new to her, and it frightened her. Mesmerized, she continued gazing into his eyes, holding him closer to her until his wife tapped him on the shoulder to tell him the babysitter had to go by twelve-thirty and they must leave.

Matt telephoned three days later. He was back in Liverpool again, minus wife. Did she feel like a drink at the Cavern after the show?

Chloe didn't hesitate. She had found herself thinking too often about his face, his hard body, his black hair – his heavy-lidded black eyes, his aggressively curved mouth. Goodbye, Rick.

Matt was pleasant and funny at the club, but they shared no meaningful looks. Chloe began to wonder if she had imagined the physical yearning he had conveyed to her last time they had met, as she asked him back for a coffee.

When they arrived at her digs she asked him to be as quiet as possible as they climbed the rickety stairs. Her landlady didn't approve of nocturnal gentlemen callers, often a good excuse for Chloe to get rid of overly ardent swains. This time she didn't want that excuse. She wanted Matt.

When Chloe awoke the next morning, he was gone. She felt unbelievably, glowingly wonderful. She had experienced indescribable sensations last night. He had stayed until dawn, and every minute he had been with her, Chloe fell more passionately in love with him.

At least it felt like love, she ruminated, running her hands over her body that still felt his caresses. She stretched deliciously. Was six or seven hours of the most heavenly lovemaking she had ever experienced love? If not, it was better than anything Cole Porter had ever written about. At this moment, she couldn't, didn't ever want to think about anyone but Matt. She felt vibrant, full. At twenty-one, she felt like a woman.

Annabel was conceived in London on the fine spring bank holiday weekend when Matt's wife and twins went to visit her mother in Bognor. Matt had an important article on the Beatles to finish. He asked Chloe if she wanted to stay with him for the weekend. She couldn't resist. She had fallen heavily for the irresistible combination of Irish charm and Jewish wit and wasn't about to lose any opportunity to be in his arms again for the whole weekend.

She could smell May blossom in the air as she rang the bell of the shabby front door in Shepherd's Bush. In spite of herself, her breath caught in her throat when he came to the door. Although he was eighteen years older than she, Matt was an impressively handsome man. His black hair, touched with feather streaks of grey, curled carelessly around his face. His black eyes devoured her as she embraced him.

'Oh, darling, darling, I've missed you – how I've missed you,' she breathed huskily, holding his body close to hers.

'It's only been a week, love, you couldn't have had time to miss me with that ball-breaking tour you've been on. Come in, come in – the neighbours will see us.'

In the tiny front parlour he poured two generous helpings of whiskey into mismatched glasses and gestured to Chloe to sit down on the well-worn velveteen sofa. In a window, a yellow canary swung in its cage, the tray encrusted with droppings. Ash trays were full of butts, files of discarded newspapers and magazines littered the floor. Take-out pizza mouldered on a table next to an ancient typewriter, seven or eight half-empty mugs of congealed coffee were scattered around, and, she observed with a pang, on the piano reposed a large colour photo of a plain woman and a pair of plain twins. Chloe pretended not to notice that.

'Matt, oh, Matt! It's so wonderful to see you again.' She felt incredibly excited. She couldn't take her eyes off him, couldn't keep her hands off him.

'You look good, kid, you look fine.' He squeezed her arms playfully and stroked the back of her neck, which sent shudders over her body. She wanted him now – wanted him badly. But he was not ready yet.

'Ciggie?' he asked, lighting two Lucky Strikes and handing one to her.

'I'll share yours,' she breathed, remembering the last time.

He took a puff of his cigarette, inhaled slightly and leaned towards her. With their lips slightly parted, hers soft and moist, new petals on a rose, his cool, yet sensual, they kissed – a kiss as soft as butterfly wings. She felt the acrid smoke filter into her mouth. She could feel, taste his lips, his tongue. He exuded a masculine smell of cigarettes, whiskey, faint sweat, but his breath smelled sweet to her. The taste of lust was in his mouth. His blazing black-fringed eyes gazed into hers as his tongue lazily traced the outlines of her mouth. She saw his pupils dilate with desire. His hands softly touched her blouse, caressing the outlines of her full breasts. He looked into her eyes the whole time, mesmerizing her, the fire in his eyes equalling the fire inside both of them.

'Oh, darling, darling,' she breathed. 'I want you so much.'

'Not yet, baby, not yet.' His experience made him able to hold back. She was so eager, just a kid in spite of her sophisticated songs, panting like a puppy, dying to feel him inside her. He could afford to take his time. He knew the longer he made her wait, want him, desire him totally, the better it would be for them both.

He played her like a Stradivarius. Slowly, with infinite patience, he unbuttoned her blouse and brushed first his fingers, then his mouth, against her eager nipples.

Finally, when her clothes were off, he laid her gently on the sofa, tracing a pattern of ecstasy all over her body with his tongue. She felt the hardness of him inside the corduroy of his trousers. She tried to free him, but he wouldn't let her.

Chloe thought she would die of pleasure. The only part of him he allowed her to touch was his mouth. He teased her clitoris with his tongue until she exploded. Every part of her body was afire with an intensity she had never felt before. She had never known a man to take this much time to give this much pleasure with his lips, his tongue, his fingertips.

When she felt she would go mad if he did not put himself inside her, when his touch made her dance to another orgasm, when she begged him, cried, pleaded, 'Please darling, Matt, darling, *now*, I *want* you now! I want you! Please!' only then did he tear off his clothes and fuse his body with hers.

It was a night unlike any Chloe had ever experienced. She had only known musicians and singers, whose chief aim was to get her pants off as quickly as possible, get themselves installed inside her immediately, pump away for a few minutes in a quick frenzy and then collapse. At best it had

26

been only moderately exciting. She had never even approached the heights of rapture she did with Matt.

Hours later, she was limp, replete, surfeited, yet still wanting more of him as he carried her up to his tiny bedroom. There in the dark, he held her tightly, spoke to her lovingly, longingly, as he made love to her throughout the night. She clung to him, passionately whispering over and over how much she adored him, needed him, wanted him.

Unfortunately he no longer wanted or needed her six weeks later, when she informed him she was pregnant.

Chloe's obsession with Matthew had grown so much in the two months she had known him that she was now consumed by sexual passion. She could not stop thinking about his dark eyes, his body fusing with hers, his hands on her flesh, his lips bringing her to the heights of desire.

She knew his faults. Faults! There were few redeeming qualities in his character other than his extraordinary gift for lovemaking. He lied. She knew he lied all the time – to his wife, obviously, and to Chloe too. It was a way of life to him. Lies tripped more easily from his tongue than truths. Too much time spent in Fleet Street, no doubt. But she forgave him. She forgave him everything once he was in her bed. She could not get enough of him – but she saw him so rarely. Five times all told, including that incredible weekend. Five magical, wonderful nights that left her glowing, but the following day miserable with longing and the need for more of him.

But she was not to have more of him. That he made clear to her in his bluntest manner. He did not love her. He was completely honest about that, at least. He desired her sexually, he adored making love to her, but he knew himself only too well. He was nearly forty years old, he had no intention of ending his marriage; if Chloe left him, there would be other nubile young bodies around, other fish to fry. He had plenty of options, and there was no way he could accept Chloe's having the baby.

27

In Chloe's naïveté she couldn't believe that he had made love with her so passionately and not fallen in love with her. She found it impossible to come to terms with his callousness. She cried herself to sleep for months on end.

She thought it a crime to abort their baby, their love child. Atavistic primal female instincts made her want to keep it. In spite of his denial and his dismissal, she went through to term, and in January of 1964, in a nursing home in Plymouth under an assumed name, she gave birth to a baby girl she called Annabel – it had been her grandmother's name.

She had made one difficult decision; now she had to make another. She knew she could never keep the baby. She had to earn her living, and the only way she knew how was by singing on the road again. No life for Annabel.

Chloe's brother, Richard, and his wife, Susan, agreed to bring the baby up with their own two. They explained to the neighbours that Annabel was the daughter of Susan's cousin, sadly killed in a car crash in Australia. No questions were asked by the neighbours, and soon Chloe went back to work with a vengeance. She sang for her supper up and down the length and breadth of England, Ireland, Scotland and Wales. And in seven years she had risen to the top of her profession.

Chloe was an exciting singer of popular and standard songs, a performer who gave audiences more than their money's worth. And her indisputable talent, coupled with her undeniable sex appeal, enthralled audiences and critics alike. She had risen to the top in Britain, and now America was starting to make tentative overtures to her. She was considering an offer to play Las Vegas the night she first saw Josh.

4

Chloe never stopped loving Annabel. Throughout the years, whenever she saw another woman with a baby, she felt pain, and bitterness that she couldn't see her lovely little girl growing up. Susan and Richard sent photographs regularly, which only made her feel worse as she saw the sweet little face, dark-eyed, like Matt's, curly-haired like Chloe, laughing out at her from brief moments captured in time. On the pebbles at Brighton beach, in the family garden, standing with Richard and some of his friends dressed in cricket clothes outside a pub, Richard proudly holding the little girl on his knee. Annabel with her favourite doll, Annabel with a kitten, Annabel with her new best friend, Annabel with her brothers and sisters. And growing . . . all the time growing up. Without her real mother.

Chloe kept a scrapbook of her child. Lovingly she pasted in the mementos, the photos, all the tiny notes in a childish scrawl that dutiful Susan had made the child write. Chloe sent her gifts from all over the world, and always received a grateful letter. Toys, clothes, books, souvenirs. Wherever she toured, Chloe was passionate about buying something wonderful or unusual for Annabel.

She hadn't wanted to see the show. Having just finished a forty-city singing tour, she felt and looked exhausted. The realization had dawned on her that twenty-nine was no longer nineteen. Now she needed eight full hours of sleep every night, otherwise, goodbye face. She snapped open her compact in the warm darkness of the theatre, glanced hastily at her almost flawless complexion, then looked back at Josh on stage. In spite of herself, she smiled. God, he was gorgeous!

Chloe had been instantly attracted to Josh. A surge of sexual excitement and interest she hadn't felt since Matt.

Joshua Brown was the show business king of 'swinging London'. Thirty years old, he was a brilliant, talented cock o' the walk and an enfant terrible. By virtue of his exceptional looks and innovative style, the West End was at his feet, and Chloe was no exception.

Thousands of men watching her sing her sultry songs had lusted after her, and now she was experiencing this feeling herself – lusting after the performer onstage. Why Josh Brown of all people? This physical stirring she hadn't experienced for years. She revelled in it. She let herself bask in it. Sat back and drank him in.

Her enormous turquoise eyes widened with admiration at the athletic feats Josh performed. He was playing a 1920s silent movie star, a Douglas Fairbanks-type character. He leaped and danced about the stage and into the auditorium for nearly three hours, performing stunts of such virtuosity and sheer daring that the cheering audience gave him ovation after standing ovation.

The following week Chloe went back again to see the show for the second time in three days. This time, instead of being in the seventh row, she had deliberately chosen front row centre. She had gone alone.

That's the man I will marry, she thought, her eyes never leaving his handsomely saturnine face, his powerful body. At the curtain call, when he stepped forward from the rest of the cast to receive a solo ovation and her palms were raw with clapping, she willed him to meet her eyes.

He bowed to the waves of applause, lapping it up, obviously loving his audience, his thick black hair fell over his tanned forehead, he was six feet tall, with a devilish face, and he personified masculinity, charm, humour and sex appeal. You name it, he had it. She could see the perfectly developed muscles of his chest ripple through his white cambric shirt open to the waist, and through his tight black trousers she could see the outline of his sex. A power bulge indeed. The cuffs of his shirt were ruffled and she noticed strong hands, hands she wanted to feel on her body. She thought about the rumours she had heard about him. Supposedly not only difficult, but the biggest philanderer in London. Well, in this business, unless you were Julie Andrews the gossips wagged their tongues constantly. Maybe it was true, maybe it wasn't. Right now she didn't care. All she felt was an unbelievable physical and metaphysical attraction.

His eyes met hers finally. They looked at her appreciatively. A clear message of interest was shown, an imperceptible nod of his head, and she was winging her way giddily backstage to his dressing room. A fourteen-year-old with a crush on Elvis.

Perry, Josh's valet and man Friday, offered her a drink as she waited expectantly in the shabby anteroom, halfheartedly looking at faded portraits of Edmund Keane and Henry Irving that decorated the peeling yellow walls. She heard him humming opera – was it Verdi? *Aida*? Could this musical-comedy singer, composer, matinee idol, jack-of-all-show-business-trades aspire to the higher level of opera? Before her question could be answered, the scruffy green velveteen curtain was flung aside and he stood there. She knew immediately he was meant for her. Forever, a voice inside her said. *Forever*. His presence overwhelmed her.

'I've loved all of your records.' He wasted no time in flattering her. 'Especially "I've Got a Crush on You". We

31

play it all the time, don't we, Perry?' His energy was a force Chloe could almost taste.

The young man smiled admiringly at Chloe as he motioned to a stack of LPs. 'Sinatra, Ella, and *you*, Miss Carriere. They've always been the young master's faves.'

'Thanks,' murmured Chloe, more than overcome, yet trying to act the cool sophisticate. Why, oh why did she feel, in front of this man, so weak, so *feminine*, so – let's face it, dear, said the voice inside, horny? Just plain horny. Celibacy at your age is a bit much, don't you think? Go *get* him, girl!

'I don't suppose you're free for a bite of supper?' Josh asked diffidently. They both knew the answer to that.

During dinner at a restaurant in Soho they laughed and joked. He regaled her with stories of the ill-fated tour of his show and the disasters that had befallen it before it hit the West End to become the biggest musical hit in England since *Oliver*. There was no question as to where the evening would end. He had a little flat in Fulham. She had a little flat in Chelsea. They tossed a coin for it. He won.

She had thought that no man could ever surpass Matt in her bed. She had attempted a few halfhearted affairs in the past seven years, but after a while decided it wasn't worth it. She would rather be in bed with a book, or playing cards with friends, than rolling around the sheets with a stranger, trying to simulate a lust she couldn't feel. So she hadn't bothered. Idly she had thought she had probably become frigid since Annabel's birth. Luckily she was wrong!

With Josh, she was turned on even before he touched her. His curved sensual mouth brushed her lips in the elevator going up to his flat. An experienced kisser, a gentle kisser – a man who knew women, who truly liked them – she could tell by his lips, by his hands tangled in her curls, no question about that. She felt his passion building as the ancient elevator shuddered to a halt. Slowly their lips parted from each other.

Apart from the furnishings in his bedroom, very dark plain furniture, *very* large four-poster bed, the only out-of-the-ordinary feature was a large mirror on the ceiling, attached to chrome-and-mirrored posts at each corner of the bed, incongruously covered with a blue candlewick bed spread.

'A gift from the Empire Hotel in Las Vegas,' he laughed, as she looked at it quizzically. 'I broke the house record there last year. They asked me if I wanted a diamond-studded Rolex, but I said I preferred the bed, so they shipped it over. It's fun.'

I bet it is, thought Chloe.

Five hours later, limping to the cramped untidy kitchen for a sustaining drink, she knew just how much fun it was. Her legs felt as if she had worked out for three hours at the gym. He certainly was a wonderfully exciting lover, but oh, what fun he was to talk to as well. In between bouts of lovemaking, which at the very least equalled anything she had experienced with Matt, they talked, laughed and joked. They were so easy with each other. After hours of exploring each other's bodies with lips, tongue, fingers, she had to beg him to take her. He had kissed and teased her until she was at a pinnacle of ecstasy, thinking she would die if he did not enter her. The buildup of desire made her body feel as if it were one enormous battery – a million nerve endings waiting to be ignited by his body.

When he finally started to make love to her, the sensation was so exquisite that neither of them was able to hold back. Within seconds, they simultaneously reached a plateau of such intensity that Chloe almost fainted. Afterwards, as he held her tightly against his warm, muscular chest, stroked her black curls, damp now with the sweat of their bodies, she knew that he was the one. The man she had always known she would meet one day. Her forever man.

She knew in her soul that this could be the start of something big. And it was. They were perfect for each other. The perfect couple. They had everything in common. Their courtship was swift, their marriage three months later an occasion to rejoice. They were both extremely popular, so they had a huge flashy show business wedding at the

Dorchester, attended by everyone from Peter Sellers to Sir Lew Grade, and for their honeymoon they went to Capri where, when they weren't swimming and sunbathing, they spent most of their time in bed.

From the start Josh insisted on being totally honest with Chloe. He had told her about his many girlfriends, confessed he had never been able to be faithful to a woman for longer than a few months, but he was going to have a damn good try with Chloe. He was thirty now – time to grow up at last. He even told her about the tiny amounts of white powder he occasionally had the need to sniff to get through the exhausting show. She didn't care. She loved him. Love would conquer all. Marriage would be forever. They were ecstatically happy together, in spite of his precocious daughter who lived with them. Although, as in most marriages, the physical side became less important with time, they had tremendous camaraderie and rapport. They laughed, loved, argued, worked together. The perfect couple, everyone said. Chloe thought their bond was of iron and she worked at the marriage, worked at their love, and it flowered and prospered.

They hated to be apart. They needed each other's support, each other's presence. Often at parties the hostess became annoyed as Josh and Chloe, who had spent all day and night together, would sit together on a sofa laughing, holding hands, engrossed in each other, ignoring the rest of the guests. Their communication was total, their commitment to each other complete. Their only area of dissent was his cocaine habit. Sometimes he wouldn't touch the stuff for months on end – then, when the pressure of work became too much, he would be at it again.

'I've been doing it since I was eighteen, for Christ's sake,' he would say angrily. 'It's never hurt me yet.'

'It's a *killer*, Josh.' Chloe always became excited and angry whenever she caught him taking it. She had seen the ravages coke, smack and speed had caused several musician friends on tour. She hated it. It destroyed lives.

Josh made no promises to stop – only to cut down. For now,

that would have to suffice, Chloe realized. After all, he had given up all the women. No one was perfect. Least of all herself. And they had a good marriage. A wonderful marriage. Eight years of wedded bliss. She was a lucky woman.

Then one day, she came home to the sickening truth of his infidelity.

She had told him she was lunching at the Polo Lounge with a girlfriend and then would go shopping on Rodeo Drive. By this time they had bought a beautiful airy beach house in Malibu as well as a little town house in London. They managed to combine life on both continents with comparative ease, taking the best of what each had to offer.

After lunch, walking out to the forecourt of the Beverly Hills Hotel to get her Mercedes, Chloe decided that the heat was so intense she could not face a trip to Rodeo Drive. Besides, her period was five days late – maybe this time she and Josh had at last made the baby they wanted so much, and at thirty-seven her biological clock was running out of time fast. She decided to head for home.

She let herself into the sunlit house quietly. There was no sound from Josh's rehearsal room, where even through the soundproofed doors she could often hear the muffled sounds of his eight-track as he endlessly mixed his next single, hoping for a new hit. Sally was at school, the housekeeper at the market.

She kicked off her shoes and walked over the soft blue carpet to their cool bedroom. What she saw there made the bile rise in her throat.

Josh had insisted on keeping the mirrored canopy from Las Vegas, had shipped it back from London. On that bed, underneath the mirror, lay a very young blonde girl. Her legs were spread-eagled, her long yellow hair fanned out on Chloe's blue satin sheets. Her eyes were open, staring up into the mirror with fascination.

Kneeling over her, his black curly head between her legs,

was Josh. He was doing things to the girl that were causing her to spasm with delight as she watched herself. His strong muscular hands were caressing the young girl's breasts, his thumbs massaging her nipples. Chloe knew by the movements of his body, by his deepening moans low in his throat, how much he was enjoying this.

The girl was young, fifteen or sixteen, and inexperienced; Chloe noticed that her hands, although clutched around Josh's thick penis, were not stimulating him as she knew he liked. Motionless, she stood watching the sickening tableau, the two of them so intent that they did not notice her. With horror, Chloe realized the girl was coming, her husband's head thrusting faster between the child's thighs as she bucked and moaned with pleasure.

Chloe could not stop the cries that involuntarily rose from the depths of her being. The girl screamed, and Josh turned to her, shock and horror on his face. Chloe couldn't move. In a dream she watched as the girl ran whimpering into the bathroom, as Josh picked up his terry-cloth robe and almost too casually put it on after a few minutes. The girl, now in blue jeans and T-shirt, darted sobbing out of the bedroom.

Then Chloe ran into the bathroom and wept.

Later that night Josh begged her to forgive him. 'I'll go down on my knees, Chloe,' he sobbed.

'You were on your knees this afternoon, you *bastard*.' Chloe's throat was raw from screaming at him, her eyes swollen almost shut with tears. 'In *my* bed, you pig. You disgusting pervert. *Our* bed. How? Why did you need to do it? What did I do wrong?' She couldn't stop weeping. Couldn't bear the betrayal, the disloyalty.

'Nothing, Chloe, nothing. Christ, I don't know why, Chloe. I'd been to the bar down at the beach with the boys, had a few drinks – you *know* how it is – Chlo – '

'Yes, I *know*. I *know*.' She couldn't keep the screech out of her voice as she opened drawers and closets, throwing clothes into a suitcase blindly. 'The boys, the boys – you've always got to be one of the boys, haven't you? You *bastard*.' She tried to slam the case shut. 'Is THAT why you need young girls?'

She had to get away – away from him. She couldn't bear to be near him.

Hearing the row, Sally came into the bedroom to watch. This was better than a TV sitcom.

'Bugger *off*,' her father had yelled, one of the few times he had ever raised his voice at her. Chloe knew the reason why, and it disgusted her even more – it was sick, perverted. She had recognized the blonde girl as a school friend of Sally's. Sally had set the whole thing up. She knew her dad liked young 'grumble', as he and his musician friends called it when there were no women around to call them male chauvinist pigs – 'grumble and grunt', English rhyming slang for a particular part of the female anatomy. The girl probably had a crush on Josh. It must have been easy for Sally to arrange. She knew her father very well, knew his weaknesses. After all, he was only a man. Men were weak – Sally knew that already.

Josh continued trying to stop Chloe from leaving, but everything he said only angered Chloe even more. 'Fuck you, Josh. Fuck you! Fuck you!! *Fuck you!!!*' she screamed, as she snapped the lid shut on the Vuitton case. 'You *disgust* me! And I can't be with you any more – ever again.' She wished she could stop weeping. 'Get yourself to a shrink – you need help.'

'Babe, babe, please listen – I couldn't help it. Christ, Chloe, I'm a *man*, you know – sometimes a man needs to . . .'

'Needs to what?' She turned to him, her turquoise eyes blazing with fury and hurt. 'Screw a teenager? Make a groupie come? You make me sick, Josh. Sick to my stomach.' She started to leave the room but he grabbed her arm and held her tight. His eyes were soft, sad – almost filled with tears. He never cried. He was a child of the Second World War years. You hardly ever cried, however much you hurt.

'I know I'm a shit, babe, but I love you. Remember that, Chloe. I've always loved you. I want you – you're my woman and you always will be. Remember that, when you sleep by yourself in an empty double bed.'

She began to interrupt, but he stopped her. 'I *know* you, Chloe. You're not a bed-hopper, you don't go from man to man, you won't find another man who loves you like I do. All right – so I made a mistake. A bad one. Lots of men make mistakes. You found this one out. It's terrible, I know, Chloe . . . but don't leave me, Chloe – please, please *don't*, darling.'

She sobbed uncontrollably, sobbed as he tried to take her in his arms, kiss her sodden cheeks, but she wouldn't, couldn't let him.

She pulled away. The thought of his arms around that young girl . . . his mouth, his tongue – how many other girls had there been? She felt sick. She couldn't bear to be near him. Couldn't bear his hands on her ever again, his mouth on her mouth . . . The thought of his mouth on the girl . . .

She pulled away from him, dragging the heavy suitcase with her. She ran to the front door, climbed into her silver Mercedes and, blinded by tears and the rain that fell from the Malibu sky, she drove off into the wet California night.

Chloe immediately accepted a six-month tour of the English provinces to try and forget him. But it was not easy to forget a man you had loved with such passion. But the pain started to fade. Josh continually called her. He pleaded. He begged her to forgive him. He cried, he cajoled, he sent gifts and bombarded her with roses, with messages of love undying and adoration. Until she melted and eventually forgave him. Would he have done the same for her?

That had been the first time she had caught him.

The last time had been a year ago. When she discovered this second infidelity she was so hurt and confused that she had gone on a drinking binge. Vodka healed. When she came to after a week of debauchery, she decided to go to a health farm in Scotland to recuperate.

Now, together again after a six-month absence, seeing his

indifference, how distant he was, she finally admitted to herself that the marriage was over. As she watched the bath bubbles slowly going flat, she thought how sad it was, how terribly sad. There had been so much that was good between them. So much love – so much investment in laughter and fun.

That was all gone now. She had to get her mind on to other things. She had to think about her career – think positively, as Jasper had said. She *had* to get that part. Miranda –Miranda Hamilton. She needed it now more than ever.

Part Two

5

Sissy Sharp sank back onto her nest of pink satin and lace pillows and impatiently pushed away the head of the blonde young Adonis from between her legs.

'Who?' Sissy screamed into the phone, her tiny boobs bouncing. 'Luis who? He's not *right* to play my husband, for fuck's sake. You promised me it was going to be Pacino or Nicholson or that English actor – what the fuck is his name, Finney something or other – and now you tell me I'm playing opposite some fucking unknown Mexican grease-ball?'

The vehemence of her yells caused the blond Adonis, whose name was Nick, to rise sulkily from the bed and skulk into a corner, where he slouched angrily in a pink art deco armchair covered with protective plastic and glared at her with ill-concealed fury.

He had been giving head to the bitch for over an hour, had her close to coming at least twice, and each time the phone rang and she picked it up. Picked it up! While his tongue was playing a concerto on her clit. This time it was her fucking agent talking about some new actor to star opposite her. Why not him?

Nick wasn't screwing Sissy for love – nor even a modicum

of lust. Sissy's skinny frame, lack of frontal development and penchant for pills did not inspire him to great cocksmanship. But as the current teenager's TV delight, he was more than anxious to break into movies before he hit the advanced age of thirty. Screwing Sissy Sharp, the ageing good old girl next door, was Nick's entrée into the world of feature films. He hoped.

It had been Sam's idea. Sam Sharp had been married to Sissy for seventeen years, during which time they had convinced the American public that they had one of Hollywood's happiest marriages. Sam's preference for his own sex was well known in Hollywood circles, as was Sissy's sexual appetite for men twenty years her junior; but true to the Hollywood tradition of never sullying the images of their most prominent citizens, no publication had even hinted at anything un- toward in the Sharp marriage. They went their merry way, a picture of marital togetherness in the eyes of their public, while continuing to compete for the favours of the young studs who proliferated in Hollywood.

Sam and Nick worked at the same studio, where Sam had been starring in movies for thirty years. He regularly made seven hundred and fifty thousand dollars a picture, and many of the aspiring young actors on the lot.

Nick was in his second TV season, riding high. As the star of a fast-paced sitcom in which he played an undercover cop, he had teenagers in heat over his blond hair and perfect face and body. He was on the cover of every TV magazine and supermarket scandal sheet, and his love life – a succession of gorgeous starlets and models – was well chronicled. But career advancement was uppermost in his mind. The trans- ition from TV hunk to motion picture star was tough, particularly when the powers that be considered Nick's acting ability low on his list of assets.

He knew Sissy always made sure she had casting approval of her leading man, and of any female performer who might conceivably overshadow her. She was starting her new movie in two weeks. Rumours on the street had it that everybody who was anybody had turned it down. No well-respected leading men wanted to star opposite a has-been like Sissy. But it could be Nick's big chance.

He'd allowed Sam to chat him up in the commissary one lunchtime. He'd allowed Sam to invite him to his mammoth motor-home dressing room and to share a bottle of Dom Perignon after shooting. He'd allowed Sam to unzip his jeans and expertly suck his cock. He had not allowed Sam to kiss him on the mouth. Nor had he touched any part of Sam's body himself. He closed his eyes and imagined a beautiful girl was giving him head. Men were not his scene. But he was ambitious, and he needed to get invited to the Sharps' mansion in Bel Air for dinner one night. He had been – about three months ago.

And he met Sissy at last. She looked pretty good for forty-four: skinny and bejewelled, the lines of discontent and envy not apparent behind the heavy makeup until you got close. Really close. Which Nick intended to do.

He had been seated on Sissy's left during dinner. The table was crowded with the usual overdressed dinosaurs that the Sharps surrounded themselves with socially. Median age fifty-five, thought Nick. Not an attractive woman in sight. Unless you counted Lady Sarah Cranleigh, fifty if she was a day, so covered in frilly lace, pearl necklaces, ringlets and ruffles that all that was visible was a double chin and a pair of laughing eyes.

Known in England for her penchant for young men, Lady Sarah was having a delicious time in Los Angeles. Daily trips to the Santa Monica beach yielded her a quota of gorgeous young studs of a quality hard to find in Britain. Her latest conquest, who was barely nineteen, was seated next to her, in utter confusion as to which of the three golden forks he should use on his artichoke.

Nick found Lady Sarah extremely amusing, but quite unfanciable. A true Rabelaisian character, she was devouring her food with gusto, at the same time giving the beach boy a grope and rubbing one ample, satin-covered knee against Nick's. In contrast, Sissy, ever conscious of her weight, age and appearance, was picking at her food, her tiny birdlike hands reaching often for the Venetian goblet of champagne discreetly refilled by the butler.

Nick had concentrated his considerable magnetism and charm on Sissy, aware that, at twenty-nine, he was perhaps a bit too old for her taste. He noticed her locking eyes with Lady Sarah's beach boy, who was probably more her type.

Abby Arafat, one of Hollywood's most prolific producers, was talking about his latest project, a miniseries that would spin off into a series.

'It will make *Gone With the Wind* look like a B feature,' he boasted. 'The budget is going to be twenty million, we'll be shooting in London, Paris, the Caribbean and Newport Beach, and with Deane directing and the right actors to play Miranda, Sirope, Armando and Steve, we're gonna blow the ratings through the roof. I know we will.'

'What is this property called?' asked Lady Sarah, delicately wiping up the last of her artichoke butter with a large piece of French bread and signalling to the butler for more champagne.

'The biggest goddamn blockbusting novel since *Taipan*,' bragged an excited Abby. 'You must have heard of *Saga* —it's been on *The New York Times* best-seller list for six months now. Cost us two million for the rights, but what the hell! Everyone wants to play Miranda: Dunaway, Streep, Streisand. What a part! It's the greatest goddamn woman's role since Scarlett O'Hara. Miranda Beaumont Duvall Hamilton. God what a role – a real Emmy getter.'

The attention of the table had left the artichokes, and Abby had his audience.

'For Steve, we want a major male star.' He looked knowingly at Sam.

Sissy pricked up her ears. As hound smells fox, so she smelled a potential part for herself.

'I didn't know you'd bought the rights to that book, Abby

darling,' she trilled sweetly across the table to him, cursing silently that she had not seated him on her left instead of the blond TV star, who was obviously after only one thing – her body. Sissy was convinced that most men who met her desired her body. She had a loyal coterie of sycophants and yes-men who assured her constantly how gorgeous and desirable she was while gleefully tearing her to pieces behind her back.

'I just *loved* that book – I couldn't put it down, could I, Sam?' She smiled at her husband who dutifully chimed in on cue. The Sharps were completely in cahoots with each other. They cared very much about their careers. Strongly supportive of each other in this respect, they cared not at all about each other's sexual flings.

The fraction of a second Sam caught Sissy's eye was enough for him to realize she wanted that role.

'So who *is* going to play Miranda?' Sam asked casually.

'Who? Who? Aha, that is going to be *the* question from now on.' Abby sat back complacently and lit a cigar despite the fact that the first course was not yet cleared and he knew Sissy loathed cigar smoke. He leaned confidentially across the table to Lady Sarah, who was far more interested in exploring Nick's thigh than hearing this boring Hollywood gossip. Really trite. So unlike London small talk. No one would ever dream of discussing his business affairs at a dinner party in England. But Americans were so crass, particularly Californians. She glanced at the young blond boy who looked totally baffled by the prospect of having to dismember the small but perfect squab just placed in front of him. She couldn't wait till dinner was over and she got him into her bungalow at the Beverly Hills Hotel. Meanwhile there was nothing to do but feign interest and enjoy the cuisine, which was not bad – not bad at all. She took a large bite of squab, oblivious to the juices that dropped onto her slightly soiled Emmanuel dress and leaned towards Abby.

'Who – *do tell* – who is going to play the female lead?' she lisped eagerly. Abby drew on his cigar, aware of the interest he had created and milking it for all it was worth.

'Streisand's agent called this morning. But it's no good – as good as we could photograph her, Barbra's no beauty, and no chicken either. And if there's one thing that Miranda has to be, it is *gorgeous!*' He stabbed his squab for emphasis. 'This role is too important. We can't give it to Streisand, star that she is. Miranda is a beauty – a raving beauty – and only a beautiful actress is going to play her. Maybe Brooke Shields.'

'Forget her, Abby. Her mother's a pain in the ass,' chimed in Arthur Van Dyk, executive vice-president of MCPC, the Makopolis Company Picture Corporation, one of the few remaining major studios in Hollywood. Founded by a shrewd Greek immigrant in 1911, it had reached its zenith in the thirties, forties and fifties, thanks to the business acumen of its chairman, the austere Stanford Feldheimer, who had taken the studio into television production in the late fifties with great success. 'Besides,' he went on, 'she's too young. Brook could never age up to forty or forty-five.' Sam and Sissy exchanged a fleeting glance. Although she was loath to admit her true age, nevertheless for the right role Sissy would play age sixty –or kill her grandmother.

'What we're *really* going to do – to create maximum excitement and controversy about the four hour miniseries – is to ask the public to vote for who they think could play Miranda,' said Abby smoothly with the confidence of a man whose mistakes would be paid for with other people's money.

'The public will eat it up. Great, heh?' He looked to Lady Sarah for approval. Like so many Californians, he had a healthy respect for the British aristocracy. Weren't they all related to the Queen?

'But suppose the public decides that they want Barbra Streisand or Brooke What's-her-name or other equally unsuitable people – what then?' asked Lady Sarah, bored to tears by it all, but trained in the subtle art of polite dinner-table conversation. One hand held a squab leg, the other rested on the crotch of the beach boy.

'Unknowns. We test unknowns. Dozens of them,' crowed Abby, spearing his squab triumphantly.

'And' – he winked – 'we'll test established stars too. Great publicity. Can you imagine? We test Bisset, Streep, Lamaze! Christ, the publicity will be *dynamite*.'

Sissy's blood froze. Lamaze! They were thinking of testing that Mexican cooze! Were they mad?

For fifteen years Rozalinde and Sissy had been one of Hollywood's favourite feuds. The thought of Rozalinde Lamaze even being considered for this plum role infuriated Sissy so much that she choked on her champagne. To control her anger she started to return the attentions of Nick's wandering fingers on her Bob Mackie beaded thigh, but her mind was elsewhere.

She wanted that role. She realized how it could revive her flagging career. All the couture clothes, the jewels, the flattery, the lavish Bel Air mansion and the ever-present sycophants could not disguise the fact that she was no longer young, no longer 'hot', no longer considered for the top movies, which now mostly starred nineteen-year-olds or the hot triumvirate of Fonda, Streisand and Lange. She tossed down another glass of champagne and gave Nick what once had been a golden smile but was now a rictus grin.

A dazzling miniseries, which would automatically spin off into a successful weekly series! It was too good to be true. She needed it, and she would do her damnedest to get it. God knows films of a decent calibre were becoming harder and harder to come by these days. Hardware films like the James Bond series, *Superman* and *E.T.* were the box-office blockbusters now. Or teenage horror and comedy films, made on low budgets and designed for the high school and juvenile college crowd, starring unknowns who looked as much like real movie stars as Lassie. The writing was on the wall. The glamorous romantic love stories she had made a career of in the sixties and seventies were finished, she must move with the times.

It was a similar fate for Sam. The epic adventure stories he had made his forte in the fifties, sixties and seventies had run their course, and now were popular only with TV audiences. His last three features had been huge flops. Young audiences of today were not interested in a leading man nearly half a century old. O.K. for Newman, Redford and Nicholson – they were special. Different. Elevated super megastars. Sam was of the old school – the Cary Grant, Robert Montgomery, William Powell school of acting. Dry wit, innuendo, subtlety, glamour, romance and adventure. The kids today didn't want it. God knows, they were the only people supporting the cinema. Older folks stayed home to watch TV. And by older, that meant anyone over twenty-eight. It was too expensive to go out at night. If they had babies they had to get sitters, then buying dinner out, even if it was only hamburgers, parking and the tickets could cost close to fifty bucks for two. So stay home, watch the hot new TV shows like 'Starsky and Hutch', 'Charlie's Angels' and 'Dallas', and see their favourite stars of the sixties and seventies – like Sam Sharp – in the movie reruns on their own TV in their own living room.

Sam was astonished at how well his movies did in the TV ratings. The network put them on regularly in prime time opposite the rival networks' hottest shows, and invariably the Nielsen ratings proved Sam's popularity with the public. His TVQ, although he had never made a product specifically for the medium, was one of the hottest.

Although the networks and television producers always denied it, a TVQ was a popularity contest in which actors on TV were graded according to their likability quotient with the public. The public, amidst enormous secrecy, was secretly polled to name its favourites, as it was considered 'unconstitutional' by the Screen Actors Guild to base hiring on the public's opinion. Nevertheless, the policy continued and those with the highest TVQ received the highest salaries. And the best parts.

Abby had made Sam a top secret hard-to-refuse offer to star in 'Saga'. Fifty grand an episode, thirteen episodes at least, this year, and if the show was a hit, the network would guarantee twenty-three episodes next season. That was a cool million plus a year. Sam had been thinking about it but hadn't told Sissy yet.

He would play the patriarch of a large fashion manufacturing and designing family who lived in Newport Beach. They would shoot in Newport for several weeks, at least two or three times a season – a prospect most appealing to Sam, who adored the ocean and owned a ninety-five-foot sailboat. His character, Steven Hamilton, would have a devoted wife, two feuding ex-wives, and six children – a boy and a girl by each ex-wife, and a boy and a girl by the present one.

He would work a minimum of two days a week and a maximum of four. No more than ten hours of shooting a day. He would have perks galore. Approval of cast, director, scripts, his own stand-in, double, and full-time valet and cook at the studio, paid for by the company, a wardrobe of clothes made by his tailor, Doug Hayward of London, whom the studio would fly over twice a year for fittings. He would keep the clothes, naturally. There was also to be a chauffeur-driven Cadillac with smoked windows to drive to and from the studio, and his own makeup man and hairdresser to put on his pancake and his auburn toupee in the privacy of his luxurious motor home.

Yes, a veritable cornucopia of goodies. Certainly better than most actors were receiving in TV today. He was definitely considering it. Definitely. Too bad his father wasn't alive to see how big he had got. Not John Wayne, of course, but big.

Sam lay on the tan suede Saporiti couch quietly trying to watch a video of a John Wayne movie.

John Wayne. 'A "real man",' his father used to tell him on the Saturday afternoons when they would go to the cinema in Tulsa, where he had been born and raised. 'That's a *man*, son. You watch how he walks and talks. He don't take no shit from no one, boy. That's what a real man is like. He's the boss – the chief, the breadwinner everyone takes real good notice of him, you see.'

Little Sam nodded gazing in awe at the huge black-and-white cowboy up on the screen. John Wayne was a massive person, and the screen made him even more so. In fact, he did not look unlike Sam's own father, Hank. A towering granite-faced cowboy-looking man, who chewed tobacco and spat it on the sidewalk, and who got drunk with the boys in the bar every Saturday night. After he had a fight with one of them he went back to his tiny two-bedroom house, woke up Lizzie, Sam's mother, who was petrified of him, and without preamble, foreplay, kissing or hugging, fornicated with her with such grunts and groans and thumps and moans, that Sam's young ears heard everything. Heard his young mother's cries of 'Oh, no, Hank, no, not tonight. I've got the curse.' Heard his father's hoarse whiskey-thickened voice tell her to 'shut up and raise yer nightgown, woman. I don't want to look at it, I just want to get me piece in it.' Heard the stifled cries of his mother, then heard his father cursing, 'Look at this, look what you've done to me, woman. Look at this blood. You're a filthy woman, and the Good Lord will punish you for having such filth between your legs.'

Sam heard the slap, heard his mother's weeping long after his father's snores shook the house. He'd go sit with her in the kitchen, where, sobbing quietly to herself, she tried to hold ice on her swelling eyes.

'Don't cry, Mama – please don't cry,' begged the little boy, holding his mother close.

'I'm not crying, dear.' She tried to curb her tears as she held Sam close to her warmth and rocked him to her bosom. These were the tenderest moments in young Sam's life.

When Lizzie's second pregnancy was in an advanced stage, two or three weeks from delivery, Hank came home one night considerably drunker than usual.

In spite of the doctor's warning not to, he tried to have sex with Lizzie, who, after fighting him off, managed to escape next door to the sanctuary of their neighbour's house. Sam lay in his cot, scared for his mother, but relieved that tonight he wouldn't have to hear the usual panting and moaning. Suddenly, his door was pushed open and his father stood there, silhouetted against the dim yellow light.

'Wake up, son,' snarled the huge man. 'Wake up, I want to show you something.'

Terrified, Sam pretended to be asleep.

'Wake up, I said,' yelled his father. 'Wake up, you little pisser.'

He pulled all the bedclothes off Sam with a yank of his massive hand. Through half-closed eyes, Sam saw what his father held in the other hand. His ten-year-old senses screamed danger, but he still pretended to sleep. Anything rather than having to look at that huge red *thing* his father grasped.

'Wake up, son.' Hank's whiskey breath came closer to his son's face. 'I want to show you what a real man is like.

'Asleep are yeh – well you won't sleep much longer now, sonny boy. I'm going to teach you the facts of life.'

His huge hand lashed out. Sam jumped up to crouch, cowering, on his bed. He couldn't believe what his father was doing. His massive thing, as big as a hose pipe, red and swollen, was in his father's hand, and he was pulling it, pulling it hard.

'See, boy, this is a cock, boy. Look at it. This is what John Wayne and all of us *real* men have got between our legs. Let's see what you've got down there, son.' With his other hand he grabbed Sam's flannel pyjamas. 'Well, look at that, I declare.' He almost fell over laughing. 'That's not a cock, boy, that's more like a little thimble, something your mother would use to sew with. *This* is a cock, boy, and if a man is not ramming it into some woman, then he's doing *this* with it.' Sam watched in horror as his father jerked his hand harder and faster across himself until the boy thought it would burst. As he thought that, it did, and he watched in horrified amazement as his father let out what sounded like a wolf howl and slumped against the wall.

A few years later, a boy named Bobby took him into the boys' bathroom after school hours and, proudly bringing out a rather large thirteen-year-old penis, suggested to Sam that if Sam touched it, he would do the same for Sam. For the first time in Sam's short life, he experienced sexual fulfilment, as both boys came together. He found it to be an experience of such excitement that he and Bobby met there twice a week for the next two years.

Even when Sam became a fully grown man of twenty, his penis never came even close to the size of his father's. He thought he was not a 'real man' like John Wayne and his father, because, he realized reluctantly, he liked 'doing it' with boys. Well, maybe he couldn't be a 'real man' by his father's standards; but he soon had a chance to be a 'real star'.

Sam was a solid actor, one on whom the movie company could always rely. Not overly exciting, sometimes a little dull. Sam had played some of the most solid citizens since God, starting off with George Washington and including Abraham Lincoln, General Eisenhower and Franklin D. Roosevelt. American heroes all. Fine upstanding gentlemen to boot. To some of the audience Sam *was* the President, so many had he portrayed.

Sam had interspersed these parts with lighter roles, for which he had been nominated for an Academy Award, though none had won. Four perma-plaqued certificates attesting to his Oscar nominations were displayed on his library walls, along with framed photos of him and Sissy with Nancy and Ronnie, Gerald and Betty, Rosalyn and Jimmy, and Jack and Jackie. A testament to almost but never. His agent had said the role of Steve Hamilton would be a shoo-in for an Emmy. It wasn't an Oscar, but it wouldn't be just a nomination this time. This time he'd have a real honest-to-goodness gold-plated statuette, almost as good as the kind he had craved all those years as he'd sat in the Santa Monica Auditorium, heard his name announced in ringing tones, and lost out with monotonous regularity to Jack Nicholson, Al Pacino, Ben Kingsley and Dustin Hoffman.

He was slightly bitter about never having won an Oscar, especially since Sissy had received one. Hers was prominently displayed on a red-and-gold boulle table in their marble entrance hall. She kept it there, she said, because the gold in the figurine matched the gold inlay of the table so well. He knew better. She kept it there so that every damn person who came to the house couldn't fail to see it. Naturally it had been stolen a couple of times being in such an accessible place, but each time Sissy just called the Academy and they sent her another. One of the statuettes had been recovered, but Sissy, instead of sending it back to the Academy, kept it. It resided in a rather less obvious place, on a shelf opposite the bidet in her bathroom. Now it appeared she had not one but two Oscars. Bitch. He frowned. He didn't often think of his wife of seventeen years as a bitch, although to many people she most certainly was.

He was loyal to her, they had an excellent marriage, but she could be an impossible cooze. This morning she had insisted on involving him in a fashion layout she was doing for a syndicate of European magazines. Running her hands through his hair – goddamn it, how he hated having to stick his hairpiece on by himself – using him as a backdrop for her newest Norells and Blasses. When he informed her he had a one o'clock call, she had pouted sulkily, as though they were the loving couple the public imagined.

Now that she realized the potential in the role of Miranda, if he accepted Abby's offer to play the lead he would have to do his husbandly duty and try to get her a test.

He groaned inwardly. She could be the grande dame diva to end them all, but still, she was his wife. He was a loyal husband. He would try to use his influence. Otherwise, his life could become unpleasant.

Sissy had a way of doing that to people.

Sissy and Sam's party broke up early, as all the best (and worst) Hollywood parties always do.

In spite of the general public's opinion that Hollywood was a place of fun, brilliance and glamour, filled with outrageously extroverted, gorgeous people, deliciously dressed and participating in scintillating conversation, the opposite was true. The truth was that Hollywood in the 1980s was dull. The glamour girls and boys of the thirties, forties and fifties no longer existed. It was a business town now, run by company men.

Paparazzi and reporters clustered outside Sissy and Sam's home, waiting to snap the stars and celebrities who were leaving, were aware of this lack of star power today. That was why, when a star like Emerald Barrymore, attended an event, flashbulbs exploded and the paparazzi knew they would make money tonight.

Calvin Foster waited quietly by himself, his heart pounding, but his demeanour expressionless. He would see *her* tonight. His idol, his queen: Emerald.

He was a slight young man with dirty blond hair and an absolutely forgettable face; people who met Calvin never seemed able to remember him – not even the paparazzi, with whom he spent hours, carrying a Nikon and pretending to be one of them. Only his eyes, cold, pale grey and secretive, would have attracted attention if anyone had looked closely. He knew that, which was why he usually wore mirror sunglasses.

He licked the sweat congealing on his upper lip.

The photographer from the *American Informer* was complaining that all the women had worn furs or wraps to the party and there wasn't a decent cleavage shot to be had.

'When Emerald comes out she'll have on a great dress, you'll see,' volunteered Calvin, the excitement of this thought electrifying him.

'Shit – she ain't here, she's in South America or somethin',' replied the *Informer* guy.

'She's not here?' gulped Calvin. His information was usually flawless.

'Nope,' said the *Informer*. 'Her picture went over schedule. She ain't due back till next week.'

Calvin felt emptiness engulf him. He hadn't seen Emerald

for over two months now. It was true, she had been in South America recently making some low-budget adventure film with some unknown Spanish actor. The pang of disappointment was so intense that Calvin couldn't disguise it. He jabbed his fist in the air with frustration. The other paparazzi looked at him curiously as he loped off to his car, his camera bag flapping against his potbelly.

No Emerald! Damn. Damn. Damn . . .

He had been deprived of a glimpse of her beauty, her one-of-a-kind sexual glamour. No one else had it, had ever had it, like Emerald. She of the emerald eyes and the sea-green gowns. She of the golden curls and the tremulous upper lip. Emerald, the survivor of torrid love affairs with James Dean, John Garfield and Gary Cooper, among others. Close friend of Monroe, Garland and Clift – Hollywood survivor par excellence. Survivor of Valium and vodka, aspirin and anisette, casting couch and death. She'd looked them all in the face very often and said, 'Fuck you'. Survivor of two car crashes, one of them fatal to her husband, the other to her fiancé, six marriages, two abortions, nine miscarriages, fifty-seven mediocre movies, three Academy Award nominations, more than one hundred lovers, not all of them male, not all of them white, and numerous smear campaigns to blacken her name, starting with the one during the McCarthy era, when she was only a teenager and in no way interested in communist plots. . . .

Star of stars, oh, how he loved her, wanted her, needed her! Calvin felt the familiar heat in his loins as he slid behind the wheel of his green Chevrolet – green in honour of Emerald. Her face was everywhere in his room. He must hurry home to her.

6

There are two kinds of people in this world, decided Rozalinde Lamaze, gazing into her magnifying mirror in the harsh north light: those who screw, and those who get screwed. And last night, she thought gloomily, she was a front-runner in category number two.

Luis Mendoza made no pretence of being in love with her. If his prowess in the bedroom was anything to go by, she was just a receptacle for his well-formed cock. So what *was* the problem? Was she losing her charms? She studied her face in the magnifying mirror, peering closely with her shortsighted eyes to get a better view. She sighed and applied Dr René Guinot's moisturizing cream for mature skin with even more abandon to the threadlike lines that were starting to appear beneath her chocolate-brown eyes.

She was a plumpish, short, pretty woman of thirty-six, who, with the expert application of myriad cosmetic devices, exotic outfits and a number of cleverly arranged postiches and nun's hair wigs, was regularly transformed into the fantasy woman of every truck driver and construction worker from Hoboken to Hollywood.

A million men had fantasized about Rozalinde Lamaze as

they reached for their wives to take their conjugal rights, thoughts of Rozalinde's tawny limbs locked around them arousing their minds and their cocks. A million schoolboys had awakened from erotic dreams with the guilty evidence of their nocturnal fantasies of Rozalinde's creamy skin, taut tits and glistening lips – a sticky little mess on their pyjamas, which would be hastily rinsed under the tap before Mother discovered it.

For fifteen years now Rozalinde had thrived on her image as a saucy, sexy Latin American goddess. It was an image that had brought her much money and many men, both of which she had used with a voracious Latin appetite.

But was she fading now? She frowned as she thought of last night, then quickly stopped as she caught sight of the furrows in her magnifying mirror. She was a study in beiges and browns. Pollen-coloured skin deepened to a dark amber on her body, for she had kept her face from the sun as much as possible in the past several years. She had observed the skin disasters of women who littered the beaches and pools of Southern California like shipwrecked debris.

Her hair was as dark a brown as possible without veering to black. Her eyes were chocolate almonds and her nipples . . . She slipped the silk pareu she was wearing off her shoulders to her waist to observe the perfection of her perfectly formed, delicately tanned breasts with their thick brown nipples.

As she looked, she imagined Luis's lips on them last night, licking them to a fever before he entered her, and then a quick thrust or two and it was over. He had rolled off her, reached for a cigarette and turned his back and *gone to sleep*! He had used her like a *puta* – a whore. Her mother had been a *puta*. Some people thought of Rozalinde as one.

Unconsciously her hand reached for and cupped her left breast. It was still oily from Dr Guinot's nourishing lotion, and the sensation was decidedly pleasant. As she caressed herself, she saw in the magnifying mirror her brown nipple hardening until it looked like a bud about to burst. In spite of her anger and sexual frustration from last night, Rozalinde felt her breathing sharpen.

To watch herself caressing herself in the privacy of her luxurious marble bathroom was a good deal more thrilling than the wham-bam-thank-you-ma'am that Luis had served her last night without a thought for her satisfaction. Angrily, she stroked herself more sensually. What would they think now, those millions of men who had lusted after her for all these years, if they could see her like this?

Suddenly she paused in the middle of arousing herself in the mirror. She left the dressing table and, stalking to her closet, took out an exquisite white ermine cloak. Throwing it on the bathroom floor she lay on top of it and looked into the mirrored ceiling of her bathroom.

She feasted her eyes on a sight most men in America would harden for. Amber skin, plump but exquisitely firm arms and legs. The face and hair were not so good, but with her shortsightedness, she neither saw nor cared; and running her hands over her own body, using the moisturizer of Dr Guinot at two hundred dollars an ounce (an extravagance indeed), she made herself come as only she knew how to do with exquisite pleasure. She moaned, gazing at herself in the mirror as she climaxed. It excited her tremendously, and Luis was forgotten. The narcissistic pleasure she took in her body banished other thoughts. Even the ringing of the telephone did not stop her delicious frenzy. Once, twice, four, five times – the divine agony. Finally, exhausted and infinitely more satisfied than she had been for weeks, she rolled over, threw the fur wrap on the chair and answered the phone.

'How was it?' It was Polly, her agent and best friend.

'What a *disaster!*' Rozalinde was almost screaming as she reapplied the precious moisturizer to the sensitive skin under her eyes. 'That bastard could barely get it up, and when he finally did, it was all over in two minutes. *Cabrón!* What a *putz!*'

'No no no, you little idiot,' Polly said exasperatedly. Did

Rozalinde ever think about *anything* except sex? 'How was the *meeting*, dummy? Did you make a good impression on Abby and Gertrude?'

'Oh, that – oh yeah.' Rozalinde slumped back in her cream satin chair, admiring her left breast as it escaped from her kimono. She grabbed a cigarette and tried to concentrate on her career, which had always come in second to her primary interest.

'Did you discuss the part with Gertrude or Abby?' Polly enunciated her words carefully, realizing that her friend and client's attention was more concentrated on her woeful sexual fling with Luis than on an exceedingly important role.

'Oooh, yes – I did – I did make a good impression. Gertrude thinks I'm wonderful!' She beamed. 'She loved me in *That Girl from Acapulco*.'

Polly groaned. 'The character you played in that turkey was about as much like Miranda Hamilton as Juliet is to Blanche du Bois.'

'No, no – I forgot. She saw *The Mistress* – the one I did in London.'

'Ah, good, good, you were *great* in that, honey, great.'

'Thanks.' Rozalinde squinted, peering closely into the mirror as she found yet *another* line beneath her chocolate-coloured eyes. Did they *never* stop arriving?

'Did she mention the test, honey?'

'What?' asked Rozalinde.

'The test – the test for "Saga".'

'Yes, she sort of did.' Rozalinde was vague. She had sampled two of Luis's fine Mexican joints last night, and her mind was still hazy. The professional in her suddenly snapped back to attention. 'Don't fret, Polly. Don't worry. I have an idea, *querida*. I have *every* intention of getting that part, and I *will*. I want it, and what Rozalinde wants Rozalinde *gets*.'

'Good girl.' Polly knew that when Rozalinde was motivated nothing could stop her. She could be tough and strong as an ox when her mind was focused on something other than sex.

In fact, when it was focused on sex she was usually stronger. 'So what's your plan, honey?'

'Why *can't* you get me a fucking test for fuck's sake!' screamed Sissy Sharp over the phone to her agent.

'If you can't even get *me* a test, Dougie, I swear I'll go to the Morris office. I mean it, Doug! I truly mean it. First you get me this – this lousy, Luis Mendoza, to play opposite me in this piece of shit film.' She started coughing and her ever-watchful butler hastily filled her plastic patio glass with more white wine.

'Then I hear that everyone in town, I mean *everyone* except me, is testing for Miranda. You better do something fast, Dougie. I want that role. Otherwise I'm defecting to the Morris boys.'

She slammed down the phone and glared into the black onyx pool where Sam was doing his usual forty laps. Part of her observed the rippling muscles of his admittedly well-shaped fifty-year-old back as he butterflied down the length. She wished she was in as good shape as he was. Maybe that's why they wouldn't test her. Too old. They thought she was too old. And I am, she thought sorrowfully to herself, allowing a tear to course down her overly tanned leathery skin. Forty-four. Shit. Even though her public relations people constantly told everyone that she was thirty-eight, the town knew the truth. Everyone always knew the truth in this town: how old you were, how much you made, how greatly in demand you were. They all knew. Jungle drums. No secrets.

Fuck this town, she told herself. There had to be a way to test! Had to. She poured more wine and stared at Sam's muscles until the phone rang. Sam had said he was going to do his best to get her a test, but he was not being assertive enough. She had to try, herself, subtly. She picked up the phone as it rang again.

'Sissy, darling, have you heard the news?' purred her friend and confidante, Daphne Swanson.

'What news?' growled Sissy, knowing full well it had something to do with *her* part.

'They're going to test Chloe Carriere for the part – can you *believe* it, darling? A *singer* playing Miranda, and British to boot. It's too too hilarious!' Her well-modulated English diction trilled off into gales of girlish laughter.

'Who told you?' barked Sissy, rage enveloping her to such an extent that she seized a handful of Sam's cashew nut-and-raisin health mix and, throwing caution to the winds, shoved it in her mouth. She would do penance for that later, she realized – she would have to make herself do one hundred extra sit-ups. The nuts contained more calories than she usually ate all day. Sissy prided herself on weighing ninety-eight pounds. Many people said it made her look younger. Most thought she looked like a cross between a sparrow and a hawk.

'Johnny told me, darling,' said Daphne, complacently munching a Godiva chocolate at her end of the telephone. She had no weight worries. Red-haired, zaftig, and at sixtyish still active in the sack. Two of her old suitors, Frank Tillie and Richard Hurrel, still were regular nocturnal visitors to her house. She was a lady at peace with herself. Her son Johnny filled her in on all the town's gossip, some of which he got directly from his agent father, Daphne's ex-husband, Jasper Swanson. 'Can you *believe* it, darling?'

Sissy ground her teeth and stuffed some more health mix in her mouth. 'Why her?' she sniffed. 'She's not an actress. She's a saloon singer and she's British – why would Abby want her?'

'Certainly not to screw her.' Daphne laughed. 'But even you must admit she's quite attractive, darling.'

'Abby told me he was maybe going to test Bisset, Candy Bergen, Emerald, and maybe Sabrina Jones – what else have you heard? Who else?'

'Well,' said Daphne, lowering her voice and her body into her imported downy-soft eiderdown comforter from Ireland,

and dipping again into the Godiva chocolate box, 'Johnny told me that Rozalinde Lamaze is *very* interested in testing.'

'That Mexican trash basket,' sneered Sissy. 'She would be useless – hopeless. She has no class at all. What does Abby say? Have you talked to him yet?'

Daphne's mornings were always spent on the phone where she became *au courant* with every piece of news, gossip and scandal from L.A., New York and London. Truly the eyes, ears and mouth of Hollywood, she was thinking of turning her expertise into something lucrative. She would, of course continue to impart this information free to her friends, but she was considering an offer to write a gossip column in a trade paper.

'Of *course* I did. But, darling, his lips are sealed tighter than Tut's tomb. Other than Jackie, Candy, Emerald and Sabrina, he will *not* tell me who else is testing.'

'Well, they've already announced *them* in the trades, so that's no news. I thought Abby told you *everything*, Daphne,' Sissy said accusingly.

'He does – but, darling' – she lowered her voice – 'he says he needs a star name for Miranda, so he wants the press to get really hot on this. He talks to Liz Smith and Suzy every day, darling. I'll put in a good word for you, poppet. I promise. I'll remind him you've got two Oscars.' She giggled.

Sissy replaced the receiver and stared stonily at her husband, who emerged smiling and wet from the pool. He laughingly ruffled her hair, which irritated her. 'You'll do anything to get that part, won't you, honey?' he joked.

'Anything,' said Sissy grimly, 'absolutely anything, Sam. I'd even fuck you for it.' They both laughed hollowly.

The amazing thing about Sissy was that, like Rozalinde Lamaze, when she put her mind to something – really went 100 per cent for it – she usually got what she wanted. She had wanted Sam all those years ago, and she had got him, even though he had seldom shared her bed even in the early days. She had wanted fame and success, and she had achieved those too.

Now the role of Miranda was her top priority and she would pull out all stops to get it.

7

Luis Mendoza slammed the door of Rozalinde's house. Her three Persian cats rubbed themselves against his ankles as he crossed the garden. He kicked them away. Luis hated animals and children. In Luis's life, only two things were important – beautiful women to make love to and Luis himself. As far as narcissism went, he made Rozalinde look like Mother Teresa. Whereas she was shrewd enough to see herself objectively as a commodity, he saw himself as simply the most handsome, most talented, most *macho* man in the world.

'The male Bo Derek,' his new manager, Irving Klinger, had assured him last month as Luis had scrawled his almost illegible signature across the all-encompassing management contracts in which shrewd Irving had arranged that 40 per cent of all Luis's earnings would go to him.

'The sex symbol of the eighties!' cried his new press agent, Johnny Swanson, an enthusiastic and brilliant manipulator of talent, which he brought to the attention of the world's media for only 5 per cent of the talent's earnings.

'The most superb man in the world!' Rozalinde had confided to Suzy after their first date five weeks ago. He hadn't really fancied Rozalinde – being Mexican too, she reminded him of his sisters. He adored blondes, but Luis Mendoza was nobody's fool. To be romantically linked with Rozalinde Lamaze was good for his image. When you were the middle son of a poor Mexican family, and from the time you could toddle had fought for pieces of tortilla with nine brothers and sisters, you grew up crafty and clever or you didn't grow up at all.

Luis Mendoza had done what most twelve-year-old boys in Tijuana did for a living. He parked cars for tourists, cleaned their car windows for the five or so pesos he was lucky to get, and sold matches, or gum, or straw bags if he had been really lucky and managed with some other hungry boys to break into a warehouse to steal a couple of cartons.

By the time his mother died he had secretly saved a thousand pesos, the equivalent of approximately eighty-four dollars, which he kept in an old sock at the back of a cupboard. It was 1968. Things were happening in the United States. Senator Robert Kennedy had just been assassinated. Luis had heard the news on the radio. The Who, a rock group from somewhere in England, were taking America by storm. A beautiful Latin girl called Rozalinde Lamaze smiled invitingly at him from billboards and newspapers all over Tijuana. She was twenty-two, ten years older than Luis, but his adolescent manhood grew hard at the thought of her juicy lips and plump round thighs. She was a girl you could dream of screwing, unlike the beautiful cool North American blondes who were beyond his reach even in his dreams.

He wanted it all, even then. He wanted to go to the United States and become a big rock star like the Beatles and make love to gorgeous women like Rozalinde, and the other one – the classic blonde, Emerald Barrymore.

One day he would have fame, success and money and make love to Rozalinde and Emerald and all the rest of the gorgeous creatures he glimpsed in the pages of the men's magazines he scanned at the newsstand. Of this he was sure.

He had been his mother's favourite. '*Guapísimo*' she would

murmur, running careworn hands through his abundant black curls. '*Niño mío.*' She snuggled Luis close to her skinny frame, bloated constantly with pregnancy, and whispered endearments to him to the jealousy of the rest of her brood.

Carmelita poured the love she had once had for Luis's father into the handsome young boy – the love of a beautiful young Mexican girl who year by year grew older and uglier while her husband no longer had any use for her except as a household serf and receptacle of his occasional lust. Year by year the family increased until the frail mother, worn out at the age of thirty-seven by the birth of ten children, the poverty of her life, and the lack of love from her husband, expired peacefully in her sleep. Carmelita gave Luis her strength. She gave him pride in himself. She made him believe that he could be a king – a god – a star. These hopes and dreams she whispered to young Luis throughout his formative years, building him up, making him believe in himself, giving him the inner strength and resilience he needed to survive.

When she died, three days before his thirteenth birthday, Luis wept for the last time in his life. Now he must follow the path his mother had prepared him for.

With his thousand pesos tucked safely into his worn sneakers, and wearing one of his three T-shirts, jeans and a ravelled sweater, he tried to cross the Tijuana border into the States one cold February night. Unfortunately he chose a time when immigration was on the rampage against wetbacks. Caught by a patrol guard, he ended up spending a night in jail with a bunch of drunken derelicts, pimps and thieves, who promptly relieved him not only of his precious thousand pesos but also of his virginity. For a macho Latin lad to be disgraced and abused by foul-smelling drunks and lecherous queers, to the jeers of the other vermin who inhabited the cell, was an indignity so barbaric that Luis had nightmares about it for years. He had never liked the company of men particularly. His father's treatment of his long-suffering mother had always disgusted him. Eventually his disgust for his own sex had turned him into a loner who loved and needed the company of women.

Thirteen-year-old Luis returned to the family home the following week a sadder and wiser boy. One year later, on his fourteenth birthday, he boarded a train to Mexico City with the money he had again managed to save. He never saw his family again.

Luis was tall for his age and immensely strong and agile. His looks were such that women of all ages were his for the asking. Since the night in jail, he had made it his business not only to make love to as many girls and women as possible but had developed a peculiar passion for sadistically beating up any boy he even suspected was homosexual. He developed an aversion to all forms of homosexuality that bordered on the psychotic.

By the time Luis was fifteen, he was working as a waiter in a Mexico City nightclub. By the time he was twenty, he was part of the band, singing Latin American ballads and oozing so much raw sex appeal that staid Mexican matrons groaned with ecstasy at the sight and sound of him. By the time he was twenty-two, he had conquered Mexico as Cortez had never dreamed of doing.

He was the most famous and successful singer of romantic ballads in the country. In Spain and Italy too, his records outsold those of Julio Iglesias, and his face and body endorsed everything from jockey shorts to aftershave lotion.

Adolescent girls wept when they saw him on television. They huddled for hours outside the entrance to his grand apartment in Mexico City for a glimpse of him. Luis Mendoza fever swept Latin America. At twenty-four he started making movies and became even more popular. Latin America was at his feet. But North America, the America he strived to conquer, wasn't interested in him.

'Latins have never made it big on the screen,' said Abby Arafat, the arbiter of taste at MCPC Studios.

'What about Valentino?' argued Irving Klinger. 'And Ricardo Montalban, he was big in movies too.'

'Yeah, but he was a has-been until "Fantasy Island". And Valentino was Italian.'

'Look at Fernando Lamas, Cesar Romero, Tony Quinn,' persisted Irving.

'People don't want to know from spics,' spat Abby, inspecting perfectly manicured nails. 'Pacino and Travolta may look a little greasy, but the world knows they're Italian, right? And Italians are O.K. So are the frogs and the limeys. But spics! There's never been one that could make it in the movies unless it was character roles. Men resent a guy who's a Mexican getting the girl. They think he should be parking cars or pumping gas.'

'I'll tell you what, Abby,' said Irving. 'I'll test the kid in Mexico City. I'll pay for the fucking test myself, and I'll eat my fucking hat if you don't think he's got the greatest potential since Brando.'

Irving rarely backed losers, and Luis Mendoza arrived in Hollywood one month later, on a warm April day. He had a three-picture deal in his pocket and he expected Hollywood to be at his feet.

When he left Mexico City, hopeful of never seeing it again, he was besieged by weeping fans, harassed paparazzi, and reporters, whom he brushed off with his usual charming civility. He arrived in Los Angeles wearing a white Armani suit, dark glasses and a tan. As he moved swiftly through Immigration and Customs, there was not even a hum of interest from passengers and airport personnel.

He was one of the biggest stars in the world in Latin America, but no one seemed to know or care in California.

The going in Hollywood proved tougher than Luis had ever imagined. They snubbed him; the goddamn fucking Hollywood *pigs* ignored him. Oh, he knew why, well enough. Because he was to them just a greaseball, a goddamn Mexican wetback. What an insult. He had a legitimate green card; he was here under the auspices of the American government. He had a movie contract. Why were they so

70

disdainful of him? Even Lamaze, that cooze, had insulted him last night. He had only screwed her because Irving said they would make a hot twosome from which he would get publicity, which might make him more popular with the American public. Sure, oh, sure. What he realized bitterly was that it was better for her career than for his to be a gossip item.

Eventually Irving got him a starring role in a picture. It meant playing opposite that over-the-hill bag of bones Sissy Sharp, but it was an American feature film at last, even though the script was lousy.

He looked in the mirror and arranged his tousled black curls more artlessly. Richard Gere, eat your heart out! Here comes Mendoza. In terms of looks and sex appeal, Gere was zero compared to Luis. He was on his way now. Nothing could stop him.

Sabrina Jones lay on the beach and looked into the camera with an enchanting smile. The camera loved her. Everyone loved Sabrina.

She was America's newest golden girl. And golden she was. She had been renamed Sabrina by a shrewd network executive who had adored Audrey Hepburn in *Sabrina Fair*. When she had walked into his office three years ago, she was immediately given one of the three leads in a new cops-and-robbers TV series. She didn't even have to test. Her five-foot eight, one hundred-ten-pound body was honey-tanned and flawless. Her tawny blonde hair, the envy of every actress in Hollywood, was thick, shoulder-length, and fell into natural waves and curls without the necessity of hot rollers. She was clad in a golden mesh evening gown, which skimmed her sensational body. As she lay on the sand gazing into the camera lens the photographer shook his head in awe. There hadn't been anyone this gorgeous in town since Ava Gardner had hit it. She was sheer perfection. Those eyes! Those legs! Those breasts!

In 'Danger – Girls Working', Sabrina zoomed to immediate TV superstardom. Instead of asking, as most overnight TV successes do, for more money and more perks, she had been perfectly content to stay in the series with the other two girls, accepting the reasonable increases in salary her eager bosses bestowed upon her. She was never demanding, never difficult. She loved the series, loved the crew, adored Patty and Sue Ellen, her co-stars, and had a wonderful life. She even liked giving interviews and posing for stills – a press agent's delight.

Sabrina was that rare creature, a truly happy actress, happy with her life, happy with her career, full of joie de vivre and love. A secure and loving family had given her a solid foundation for life, but at twenty-three, there was one thing that had eluded her thus far – megastardom. Well, testing for 'Saga' could change all that, now that her series had finished.

She turned and gave the photographer her most seductive gaze. He gulped again, clicked and immortalized her for her fiftieth magazine cover.

Sue Jacobs, her agent, was waiting for the photo session to end. 'Get yourself dressed and then let's go someplace quiet for a drink,' Sue said, brushing past the crewmen who were still ogling Sabrina. 'We've got lots to talk about.'

'How about the Polo Lounge?' Sabrina said. 'I just love the Polo Lounge.'

Clad in a raw silk Brioni jacket, a black silk shirt and black pants, Luis strolled into the Polo Lounge and stopped dead in his tracks as he came face to face with the most beautiful girl he had ever seen in his life.

Long, blonde hair, perfect golden skin, sweet innocence in her eyes, she was in deep conversation with an older woman. Luis didn't even pause, he made straight for their table.

'Señorita,' he said, waving away the waiter, 'allow me to introduce myself. Luis Mendoza, at your service, señorita. You are simply the most beautiful woman I have ever seen in my life. I am stunned by your beauty. Would you share a bottle of Dom Perignon with me, señorita – please?'

It was not an original approach; he had used it before, but due to his magnetic looks he was seldom turned down. Few women could resist being called the most beautiful woman in the world. Sabrina Jones was no exception.

'It would be my pleasure.' She smiled at him invitingly, to the annoyance of Sue, who was in the middle of trying to convince Sabrina to take a three-picture deal at Universal instead of testing for 'Saga'.

Half an hour later, Sue toddled home muttering, 'Cock, cock, that's all they think about today.' She had realized after observing the way they gazed at each other that the force of their mutual attraction was too strong to fight. She was right.

The next day Luis arrived on the set exhausted. He felt as if he had already put in a full day's work. The crew bustled around him, setting up the lights and equipment for his big love scene with Ms Sissy Sharp. His Latin temperament was tickled by the 'Ms' that Sissy insisted upon. Who was she but some over-the-hill hag, obviously so ashamed of her femininity that she couldn't be called Mrs or Miss. 'Ms' indeed. A smile crossed his handsome face as he thought of last night and Sabrina. Sabrina. What a name. What a dame. He felt his balls tighten at the thought of her. Sabrina Jones, *the* female sex symbol of the eighties. So gorgeous, so sexy, so young – every man's sublimated desire.

But not his – oh, no, indeed. No sublimated desire existed for Luis Mendoza. Sabrina was his – she belonged to him now. His Latin pride swelled at the thought of her firm tanned body close to his. They had made love for hours, their physical attraction for each other so mutual and strong that sex became ecstasy. Experience had taught him what turned a woman on, but with Sabrina lovemaking was so natural, so free, so *loving*, he didn't need any tricks. Maybe he thought he was truly in love for the first time in his life. Luis woke from his daydream with a smile as the assistant director called him to rehearse. Sissy was waiting. She looked chic. Hard and chic. Probably women all over America would copy what she was wearing in this scene. She was a clotheshorse and about as fuckable as – Luis sought the metaphor, then burst out laughing – a horse! That was what she looked like. A racehorse in drag.

Sissy frowned at him. She was a total professional, and she hadn't been in this business since she was sixteen years old without knowing it inside and out. She loathed Luis. Detested everything about him. Certainly he was handsome, and not a bad actor, but she disliked foreigners in general. That included Jews, Germans, French and Italians. About the only non-Americans she tolerated were the British, but there were so many of them around now, it would be like not accepting smog. They were there, like it or not.

She sighed and tried to smile at Luis, who strolled over cockily as the director called for a rehearsal. With thoughts of testing for 'Saga' whirling around in her mind, she had difficulty remembering her lines.

'Stop it, Sissy,' she said to herself sternly. 'You are a star – a professional. Behave like one.'

She *had* to have that goddamn part. Had to!

8

'The search is on!' blazed the front page of the *American Informer*. 'Biggest talent hunt since *Gone With the Wind*,' screamed *USA Today*. 'Who will play Miranda?' demanded *Newsweek*, which had photographs of Sabrina Jones, Jacqueline Bisset, Emerald Barrymore, Raquel Welch, Chloe Carriere and Rozalinde Lamaze splashed across its 'People' section.

Sissy was having another one of her turns. Screams of pent-up rage, long-suppressed feelings of self-doubt, were released in a frenzy of hysterics. She lay on her velvet coverlet with the three heraldic S's intertwined in elaborate Gallic gold embroidery in the middle and sobbed her heart out. Not, thought her unsympathetic maid, Bonita, that she had a heart at all, coldhearted bitch. Bonita bustled about dispensing Kleenex, aspirin, vodka and a stream of comforting Spanish words, while her mistress thrashed about on the coverlet, her big black mascara tears falling onto the lavender velvet.

Sam, downstairs in the study, listened with a mixture of concern and indifference. Concern, because he knew what playing Miranda could do for her career, which was definitely on a downward spiral in spite of the many movies-of-the-week she was offered by the networks, and this cheapie potboiler she was making with Luis Mendoza. Indifference, because he was finally becoming fed up with her constant hysterical, demanding and selfish outbursts.

Was she going through early menopause perhaps? he wondered, clicking a channel on his remote-control TV. She had certainly looked like hell recently – thin as a rail, dark as a prune, and with skin of the same consistency. He stopped his clicker at Channel 13 and admired the roguish looks and physique of the young Rod Dimbleby in a syndicated rerun of an old series. He certainly had what it takes in every department. Even his five-year-old rerun showed the twenty-four-year-old fledgling actor's promise. He was definitely gorgeous and charismatic. Sam felt a twinge of desire, remembering their passionate encounter in his trailer on the lot a few days before.

Sure, he realized that Rod was only doing it as a favour given for a favour gained. He wanted the role of Sam's second son in 'Saga' and would at this moment turn every trick in the book he could.

Sam was aware that he could hardly enthral for long a young man of Rod's obvious heterosexuality and sex appeal – nevertheless, he was interested enough to tell 'Saga's' casting director, Dale Zimmerman, that Rod was right for the second son.

'*Saaam!*' screamed Sissy from her boudoir, arousing him from his reverie. 'Come here, *Saam!*' Her voice rose to a crescendo of despair. Sighing, he clicked off the TV and loped into his wife's purple sanctuary. She was sprawled in her mauve negligée across the bed gazing with horrified fascination at the six photographs in the magazine.

'*Look*,' she shrieked, her frizzed blonde bouffant hair standing on end around her tear-bloated face. 'Spic *bitch*, how could she ever be considered for *my* part?' She hurled the magazine to the floor and pressed the number 5 button of her automatic dial phone.

'Hello,' said the clipped voice of Daphne Swanson.

'Did you see *Newsweek*?' hissed Sissy. 'Did you *see* it? I can't believe that spic slut is *actually testing*! Is it true? Tell me it's a lie, Daphne, for God's sake.'

'I'm sorry, darling,' breathed Daphne, and in spite of her close friendship with Sissy rather enjoying her misery. 'It *is* true. I don't know what she must have done to Abby – but I spoke to him ten minutes ago to confirm it for my new column. It's true, darling. She's testing. I'm *so* sorry.'

She smiled in spite of herself. As a former actress, she sympathized with the gruelling in-fighting that one had to be involved in to crawl up the ladder of fame and success. Such miserable bedfellows really. She was delighted she'd given it all up. None of the Swansons were actors any more, but they were definitely Hollywood's in crowd.

Daphne and Jasper Swanson had been stars of the British silver screen following World War Two. When this electric twosome was imported to the USA in the late 1940s, Daphne, red-headed and reckless, launched herself into a series of sizzling affairs, in some part to emulate a notorious raven-haired English duchess whom she greatly admired.

Among those with whom she had cuckolded the hapless, handsome Jasper were: Richard Hurrel, the prominent attorney, of whom it was said he bedded only major stars or the wives of close friends; Lawrence Huntington, the celebrated Scottish Shakespearean actor, who on arriving in Hollywood proceeded to cut a sexual swathe through the ranks of the young and beautiful, the like of which had not been seen since the heyday of Errol Flynn; and Frank Tillie, the witty, peripatetic producer of radio soap operas. It was to Daphne's great credit that thirty years later two of the men were still her lovers.

Jasper Swanson's smouldering sensuality fired the lusts of a million Yankee virgins, and his CinemaScope career was off and running. Off and running in another direction flew the dainty Daphne. Frank, Lawrence, Richard and occasionally – very occasionally – Jasper shared the delights of her connubial bed until eventually (or was it by design?) she became pregnant and a son, Johnny, entered the world on a warm Christmas day in 1952, screaming his lungs out. Nearby, a doting father, and three more-than-doting godfathers stood. Hollywood money was on Frank Tillie but no one actually knew for sure who Johnny's father really was.

When the boy was fifteen his mother, Daphne, was playing the part of the mistress of King Charles II in a boisterous Restoration comedy at MGM. It would be her last American film, even though at forty-five she was still lusty, red-haired, sexy and delectable, with a rapier wit to augment her charms. But this was 1967 and full blown forty-five-year-olds had not yet come to vogue. Johnny, however, thought otherwise. Deflowered one dusty sunlit lunch hour on the Metro backlot by his mother's stand-in, Cathleen, an equally lusty, if not so tasty, forty-two-year-old, Cathleen taught him the infinite pleasure of the flesh, taught him how to please a woman as only an older woman was bold enough to demonstrate. How to kiss, to fondle – to caress. Cathleen was a fine teacher and Johnny an excellent pupil. He continued these fascinating studies, unbeknownst to his mother for the remainder of his school holidays. He dallied with Cathleen, who with a true generosity of spirit introduced him to the likes of Deirdre, thirty-six, Maureen, thirty-nine, and Kate, forty-one. Lovely ladies all, and more than willing to play sexual coach to this precocious, erotic fifteen-year-old lad already equipped with the endowments of a fully grown man.

So Johnny had been well spoiled by these ladies, and when he came to manhood, sex was only exciting for him with mature women. Many a budding starlet and bright eyed secretary had batted their eyelashes at handsome Johnny, but to no avail. With girls under thirty he couldn't even be bothered to get it up.

Daphne didn't exactly disapprove. Johnny dutifully came to dinner three times a week at her home, either before or after his current dalliance, and so there was, thank God, fat chance of her becoming – *quel horreur* – a grandmother, even though she was over sixty.

*   *   *

Daphne turned and smiled at Richard Hurrel, lying like a beached whale on her Irish linen-and-lace pillow cases. He was panting. A night with Daphne usually left him wondering if his heart would last through the next day. Even after thirty years of intermittent fornication, she was still the hottest number he'd ever had, and he'd certainly had a few, and still had, even at the age of sixty-three.

Her tumbling red-curls – out of a bottle or not, he neither knew nor cared – creamy Irish skin, never abused by the California sun because, as she said, 'I refuse to look like a crocodile' and abundant Rubensesque curves, coupled with a zest for life unsurpassed by many a third her age, made Daphne quite a woman. A constant parade of faithful lovers who kept coming back for more proved it.

Richard was glad of the phone break. She had been about to make a morning onslaught on him, and he knew his heart couldn't take it this time. He bounded out of bed with as much agility as a man his age could muster and, watched appreciatively by Daphne out of the corner of her eye, staggered into her marble bathroom.

'Darling,' Daphne hissed into the phone, 'I know the truth. I know why Lamaze is testing, but it *must* be between us.'

'Why? How? What did she do – *fuck* the old fart? You know that's impossible, Daphne. If it wasn't, I would have tried.'

'I can't talk now,' said Daphne as Richard came into the room shaving himself with the portable shaver he always kept in his briefcase. 'Let's meet for lunch – are you free?'

'Yes, of course, yes,' said Sissy, mentally cancelling her lunchtime exercise session.

'One o'clock, Ma Maison – I'll book.'

Sissy slammed down the receiver and burst into tears. 'I'm the only actress in town who's not been announced to test,' she wailed to Sam. 'It's so humiliating . . . I could kill myself,' she sobbed as she rocked in his capable homosexual arms while he whispered comforting brotherly words in her ear.

'You'll get your test, darling. I promise you. I've spoken to Abby, I know you'll get it and soon as the network approves.'

'But suppose they DON'T!' sobbed Sissy. 'Then I'm truly fucked.'

Calvin's heart pumped fit to burst. She had *smiled* at him! Emerald Barrymore had actually smiled.

She looked past the diehard fans and the rest of the eager paparazzi pressing in on her in the parking lot of Ma Maison and smiled at *him*. He was sure of it!

When Emerald had emerged from Ma Maison, clutching the arm of that old Italian actor Vittorio somebody, Calvin's breath had caught in his throat. His hands trembled so violently that he had difficulty in adjusting the focus on his camera. She was so sexy, so beautiful, so lushly undulating, so free. He almost swooned with excitement when she turned and when, for a fraction of a second, her emerald eyes made contact with his flat grey ones. Then the other photographers got in his way, pushing, shouting, yelling, '*Emerald, Emerald,* here, here, Emerald. Turn to me, *please*, Emerald! I love you, Emerald. Emerald, just one more! Please!' She had posed and preened for the appropriate amount of time, tossing her golden curls, enjoying the attention, then jumped quickly into her limo, a glimpse of perfect leg and golden ankle-strap shoe leaving an indelible memory on his mind.

Calvin thought about the first time he'd heard of Emerald. At sixteen he had a crush on a pretty blonde girl called Jenny. Everyone at high school said that Jenny was the image of Emerald Barrymore, the big Hollywood movie star. Calvin had not been aware of Emerald up to then, as he was a staunch John Wayne – Randolph Scott fan. Calvin's awkward shyness had appealed to Jenny; after he plucked up the courage to ask her she agreed to go out with him. On their first date they went to a movie to see her favourite star – Emerald Barrymore – in *The Princess and the Pauper*.

Emerald's beautiful Technicolor face appeared on the screen, and Calvin saw the resemblance immediately. He watched her voluptuous body, clad in seductive nineteenth-century underwear – white frilly bloomers, tightly corseted waist with blue rosebuds embroidered on the bodice – and felt his adolescent cock harden. As Emerald's magnificent powdered white breasts spilled out of her lacy camisole, close enough to touch, Calvin could contain himself no longer. His sweaty, trembling hand began to inch up Jenny's thigh. She pushed him away. He tried again, nature driving him. She pushed him away again. He became more aggressive. He had heard that Jenny let other guys do it. Why not him?

Finally Jenny had enough of his insistent groping. She got up. 'Creep!' she hissed, as she left the theatre.

Alone, sitting in the dark, he watched Emerald's vermilion lips fill the screen and felt his cock burst in his pants.

He started spending a great deal of time locked in his bedroom, his heart pounding, his palpitating cock in one hand, a photograph of Emerald from a magazine in the other.

His infatuation with the screen goddess grew, as did his collection of her photographs, which now almost covered all the walls of his room. Eventually he plucked up courage to write to her. Within a week the dutiful studio fan-mail department sent him a glossy eight-by-ten of Emerald wearing lace décolletage, her tumbling blonde tresses beautifully backlit, the photo inscribed in green ink 'To Calvin, affectionately, Emerald'.

Calvin, unaware that her secretary wrote the inscriptions on Emerald's photos, was overcome. Three months later he sent in another request for a picture. This time it arrived in colour – Emerald in a long green satin dress slit to the thigh, her blonde hair shorn in a twenties bob, a cigarette dangling smokily from her carmine lips, eyes half-closed, sheathed in mystery. 'To Calvin, with all my love, Emerald' was scribbled across one milky thigh.

Calvin was never the same again.

Calvin carefully tore the 'People' section from *Newsweek* – 'Who will play Miranda?' screeched the heading – and analysed the photographs of the six beautiful women.

Saga had been America's best-selling novel for months now, rivalling *Valley of the Dolls* in sales and popularity. Miranda was a peach of a part. It could not possibly go to any of those five sluts. To Calvin, all women except Emerald were sluts. A great role like Miranda should be – must be – was destined to be – played by the greatest of all actresses, Emerald Barrymore. *She* was the only woman who could play Miranda. Emerald Barrymore, superstar, his idol, his love. No one must get in her way.

He picked up the *Hollywood Reporter*.

'Who has the inside track to play the part of Miranda Hamilton in "Saga"? *Tout* Hollywood is talking about Rozalinde Lamaze. This columnist believes she is the only actress right for the role,' glowed Hank Grant.

Calvin placed the periodical carefully on top of his desk. He took out a fresh white pad, a new ballpoint pen, and wrote carefully at the top of the page: 'Project Miranda.' Number One: Eliminate negative factors.

He believed in planning. He was going to make sure Emerald got that role.

When Rozalinde wasn't working, she lay around her house all day wearing nothing but her ex-husband's pyjama top and a torn, stained silk bathrobe. Both had seen better days, years, actually, but it was hard for Rozalinde to throw anything out. The bathrobe had adorned her lush body in *Latin Lover*, a film made in the golden Technicolor days of the late sixties when she was a big star – which she would be again when she got the part of Miranda.

Just the night before, she had been given a lecture about her image by her sister, Maria, who was very socially attuned – much more so than Rozalinde.

'Look at Sissy,' Maria had commanded as the two women sat on Maria's fern-filled patio watching 'Entertainment Tonight' and sipping Margaritas.

Sissy appeared on the TV screen in the lobby of the Hilton on her way to a charity gala for the Princess Grace Foundation, attended by the cream of the Hollywood crop. The families of Sinatra, Stewart, Peck, Douglas and Moore were well represented. Sissy was a vision in black Balenciaga with the yellow diamond necklace from the estate of Merle Oberon clasped around her stringy neck, and Sam was clasped to her left arm as she gushingly told the interviewer how thrilled she was to support this great cause.

'You should be there, it's good for your image,' Maria nagged, but Rozalinde, busily eating taco chips and guacamole, laughed, 'Why? I don't need that sort of thing. In fact I hate it.'

No, Rozalinde thought, when she became Miranda, then she would start socializing again. Meanwhile, she lay on her unmade king-size bed amidst the crushed cushions stained with the residue of last night's makeup and littered with orange peel, trade papers and nail paraphernalia. She had vainly attempted to give herself a manicure, but had dumped that in favour of an intriguing movie that had just started on Channel Z. Curling up like a kitten, sucking an orange with gusto, Rozalinde was barely recognizable as the divine diva beloved throughout North and Latin America. The phone rang several times, but she ignored it. What was an answering service for?

Rosa, her maid and also an aunt once or twice removed, knocked respectfully on the door. 'What do you want?' Rozalinde snapped petulantly, her eyes pivoted to the planes of Montgomery Clift's profile as he clasped Elizabeth Taylor.

'*Por favor, señorita.*' In spite of Rosa's being distant family, Rozalinde insisted on monarchlike respect. Rosa was weighed down with an ivory tray, a gift from a Far Eastern admirer, on which reposed Rozalinde's brunch: *hueveos rancheros* covered with hot sauce, half a dozen Oreo cookies and a diet Coke.

'What's the problem?' Rozalinde sighed, glued to the couple as the camera lovingly made an eighty-degree slow pan around their rapturous faces. 'If only I could be photographed like that,' she sighed, and then remembered that she just had been in the new photos she had had taken for Miranda.

'The service called,' Rosa wheezed, thankfully depositing the heavy tray and catching her breath. 'They say they have had several nasty calls.'

'So what!' snapped Rozalinde. 'I'm a star, not everyone can

adore me.' Rozalinde's eyes never moved from the television screen.

Rosa looked frightened. 'But *señorita*, the service say, they say thees man, he want to kill you.' There, she'd said it. Her obligation to the fat cow was done. Eat your Oreos and *hueveos rancheros, puta*, and gain another three pounds.

Rozalinde drank the Coke from the can, ignoring the wine glass Rosa was always instructed to bring. Her eyes left the screen long enough to feast upon the steaming plate of eggs.

'Who is he, this man?'

'The service, they don't know nothing. They only want to warn you. Maybe we should call the police. He sounds like a crazy man. He calls six or seven times.'

Rozalinde shrugged again. 'The usual crap. Don't worry.' She turned back to Liz and Monty only to find Shelley Winters's young but already pudgy face filling the screen.

'But Miss Angelica, she away, and I go off tonight to see my gran'son. Are you sure you are fine alone here?' Not that she gave a damn, but she didn't want to get fired for lack of solicitude.

'Yes, yes, yes.' Impatiently Rozalinde spooned up her eggs. 'Now go away, Rosa, and leave me alone. I want to *relax*. Can't I ever relax, damn it?'

Silently Rosa left, cursing the cow. What a pig. It was bad enough when she had two or three men a week and lay in bed half the day moaning and groaning like a bitch in heat; but now men were *out* and lovely little innocent Angelica was *in* – for how long, God knows. Now Rozalinde lay in bed longer and her moans were less frantic, more like the purring of a satisfied cat.

She knew what they did. Overcome with curiosity about the moans and screams of ecstasy, she had crept up the stairs one afternoon and applied a practised eye to the keyhole. At first it was difficult to make out what was happening in the dim light; eventually she realized that the two women had stuck their faces into each other's most private parts and were licking and kissing each other with enthusiasm. No crevice seemed to be unexplored, and their bodies, shiny with sweat, bucked in multiple orgasms. This Rosa had only read about in the pages of Spanish *Cosmopolitan*, her favourite magazine, and she was deeply shocked and became quite faint, needing a large brandy before feeling fit enough to prepare dinner.

Her mistress was sex-mad, there was no doubt about that. A sex-mad slut. What the public saw in her Rosa could not fathom.

The following day, Rozalinde was over the moon. She'd done it! She was going to be tested! Along with five or six of the most important actresses in Hollywood. The photographs had worked. She was a genius, and so was the photographer.

She pranced around her bedroom in a paroxysm of joy as she planned the outfit in which she would lunch at Ma Maison. It was to be a celebration. A triumph of sheer cunning and audacity over established stars like Sissy Sharp, who, she knew through the grapevine, was not yet on the test list, yet desperately trying to be.

She considered the advantages of her grey silk Adolfo, very Washington working woman, against a new Saint Laurent burgundy bolero with cream silk blouse and skirt. Perhaps rhinestone buttons were a trifle much for Southern California at high noon, so she discarded both of them and decided to revert to type. It had made her millions, after all. She threw on a striped orange-and-white off-the-shoulder cotton peasant dress, several rows of chunky coral beads, and a wide-brimmed straw hat heavy with spring flowers.

In the hall she paused to tuck a celebratory white gardenia behind her lustrous brown curls, and with a gay 'See you later, Rosa,' to the maid, jumped into her red Mercedes convertible and sped off down Benedict Canyon towards Melrose.

The man in the green Chevrolet followed her.

Ma Maison on a sunny Friday in early June was jumping. At the round table in the centre of the patio dining area sat 'The Boys'. Although the cast of characters changed weekly, today most of the main protagonists were present. Richard

Hurrel, having recovered from his heavy night of love with Daphne, looking dashing in a brown blazer and a brown-and-cream Cardin shirt with white collar and brown silk tie. It set off his snow-white hair and deep tan. He felt pretty good. Daphne usually had a rejuvenating effect on him – made him look and feel young again. Frank Tillie was regaling the group with hilarious stories of the latest antics of the gay male lead on one of his top seven soap opera series.

Johnny Swanson sat listening with admiration and amusement to the man who, some people surmised, could be his real father.

At the entrance, seated at a small table for two, sat Sabrina Jones and Luis Mendoza, who in a short time had fallen madly in love. They were truly a dazzling couple. Sabrina had a day off, as did Luis. She was ravishing as usual in a simple white cotton shirt and a khaki mini skirt, that showed off her long, tanned legs to perfection. In her ears were tiny gold-and-diamond studs, a recent gift from Luis; around her waist she wore a thick tan leather belt with an elaborate enamel and gold buckle.

Luis wore cream linen pants and a dark blue shirt, open to his waist to reveal a smoothly muscled tanned chest. Several golden chains of various lengths and thicknesses, upon which dangled the talismans of superstition and virility beloved by Latin American men, glinted in the afternoon sunshine.

They were engrossed in each other – he swimming in the jade depths of her eyes, and she in the bottomless black of his.

'They seem *so* in love,' sighed Lady Sarah Cranleigh, spearing the last of her asparagus, careless of the melted butter dripping onto her Victor Edelstein floral silk blouse.

'Bullshit,' sneered Sissy, observing them from three tables away. 'Take my word, Sarah, Luis Mendoza lives for one thing and one thing only – and that's himself.' She reflected with faint nostalgia on their two-night stand during the location shooting of their movie. Brief it had been, but exciting. Luis was a thrilling lover and had been able to supply for an hour or two the sexual ecstasy she craved, but seldom received, from the post-adolescent, lackadaisical beach boys she usually sampled in bed.

But she had better things to discuss than the love life of Sabrina and Luis. She was irked that Daphne had brought along her undeniably amusing house guest, Lady Sarah. It was difficult to plot and plan with that overdressed lump of lard guzzling everything in sight. Lady Sarah had already devoured two rolls of French bread and four pieces of garlic toast with her asparagus hollandaise and was now deftly stealing croutons from Daphne's spinach salad.

Throwing pride and caution in the direction of La Cienega Boulevard, Sissy plunged in at the deep end. 'How did she do it, Daphne?'

'Darling, I never would have believed that the trash basket could be so smart,' said Daphne, spearing a crouton hastily, ahead of Lady Sarah's eager fork.

'Well, what? What did she do?' Sissy almost screamed, downing her vodka and Evian water and trying to remain calm.

'She went to Hana, spent thousands, poppet – absolute *thousands*, having a series of photographs taken of herself as Miranda. Brilliant photos they were, too, of course. You know Hana's work, he's the absolute best. He actually made her look nineteen. I mean, he had to put a mohair blanket over the lens, but, my God, he *did* it.'

'Brilliant,' agreed Sissy through gritted teeth, cursing Rozalinde's cleverness. Why hadn't she thought of that? Come to think of it why didn't her fucking PR people think of it? Four grand a month plus expenses, and they couldn't even keep her name out of the fucking *National Enquirer*. She made a mental note to fire them and hire Rogers & Cowan.

'One photo was of her as a teenaged Miranda – she looked eighteen, I swear.'

'Impossible,' snapped Sissy.

'Not with Hana's lighting, duckie. He took other photos of her looking twenty-five, thirty-five, that was easy – because of course she is thirty-five.'

'Oh, really,' sneered Sissy angrily, stuffing a large mouthful of garlic toast in her mouth. 'She'll never see forty again and you know it, Daph.'

'Will you *listen*?' Daphne snapped. 'Then forty-five, then fifty-five, and – listen to this – in the last one of the set she has been made up to look *eighty*, and that's what really sold Abby on the idea. He was so impressed with the presentation, he promised her agent, who just happens to be my ex-husband, darling, that he would definitely test her.

'And, petal' – Daphne fished in her capacious handbag and brought out an eight-by-ten envelope which she slid over to Sissy – 'one of my sources managed to get hold of the photos. I thought you might be interested. Oh, but don't look at them *here*, dear.'

Sissy snatched the brown manila envelope from her friend and stuffed it into her large Chanel bag. She glared at Daphne, who smiled blandly and looked around the restaurant, nodding at various acquaintances. Lady Sarah stared at Sissy with ill-disguised contempt. What a rude woman. In England she would simply not be invited anywhere.

As soon as she got home Sissy inspected the photographs. In spite of herself, she felt a grudging admiration for Rozalinde. She looked luminously young and fresh in the early photos, even if Hana had used his encyclopaedia of camera tricks to make her so. And the brilliance of her attitude in the photos of Miranda at forty-five verged on sheer genius. It was a clever scheme, and there was no question in Sissy's mind that Rozalinde had leaped ahead in the Miranda Hamilton stakes.

It was so expertly simple, so obvious, so fucking clever, *goddamn* the bitch! Sissy knocked back another vodka. Bloody brilliant. It was, yes, brilliant, admit it. She, who had been in the business for twenty-seven years, should know how gullible people were. With enough chutzpah and assertiveness in this town, one could rule it easily. This round went to Rozalinde, but Sissy was not about to go down for the count just yet.

A life-sized nude of Sissy reclining on an eighteenth-century chaise à la Madame Récamier took pride of place above the grey suede couch in the combination gym and screening room.

As Sissy performed her morning workout to the music of Bob Dylan, she admired the soft angles and curves of this more than flattering picture of her painted fifteen years ago by a then unknown, but now much in demand, artist. The painting had the look to which Sissy aspired. Unfortunately, hard as she tried, the more she strove for the physical perfection of the portrait, the more it evaded her.

She was becoming dangerously anorexic-looking. Even her best friends were daring to criticize her. Her face, pulled taut from a recent trip to Rio and Dr Pitanguy, was thin and gaunt, although there wasn't a line or wrinkle upon it. Somehow, instead of making her look more youthful, it seemed to age her. Sissy, with the blessed shortsightedness of early middle age, seemed not to notice. She clapped her hands with glee when she saw on her doctor's scale that her five-foot six-inch frame was down to ninety-seven pounds. She had to peer at the number with one of the thirty pairs of spectacles she left in every place where she could possibly need them.

'Perfect, perfect. Now I can wear the Grès for the test, and I won't look fat,' she cried to no one in particular. She was testing for Miranda next week. Her husband had done it for her. The big pitch, and Abby had been unable to say no. Neither could the network. Sam was playing the male lead in 'Saga'. They could hardly not test his wife when he was so insistent. Of course she'd get the part. How could she not? After all, she was an Oscar-winning actress, star of some of the most successful films of the past fifteen years, and married to the leading man of the series. How could they not? The competition was negligible. She could beat them all, and she would – she had to!

Rozalinde Lamaze – no way. A trashy tramp, a lightweight, in spite of the amazing photographs. She was a workingman's wet dream – an ageing sexpot. She couldn't be a serious contender. Emerald Barrymore? Certainly she was a legend in her own time, superstar, supercelebrity, but she was nowhere *near* the actress that Sissy was. She couldn't approach her for talent, and she was years older. Her applause and accolades had always been for her private life, which was far more interesting than the movies in which she had starred. That was what the public loved about her best – her men, her scandals, her suicide attempts. She was a tabloid celebrity, larger than life, she would overpower the rest of the cast. Surely the network were wise enough to see that?

The only fly in the ointment was that damned Chloe Carriere. She *was* a definite threat, no question about that. Sissy grudgingly had to admit that she was ideal for the role. She had the right look – that mixture of innocence and evil that everyone who discussed the part felt the actress who played it had to suggest. And she was a new face, even though she was nearly forty – and everyone *loved* a new face. Sam tried to assuage Sissy's fears by saying that even if the network and Abby insisted on Chloe, *he* would then insist on Sissy playing ex-wife number one; he had made the network agree to that at least.

But Sissy knew that Sirope was not the plum part. Ex-wife number one was a dullard. A flaccid Goody Two-shoes role. It was Miranda Hamilton, wife number two, she wanted to play. Oh, how she wanted that role! The bitch. The wicked one. The manipulator, seductress, traitress, cunning, cool, yet with a heart of gold that she knew was buried in the pages of the 'Saga' script. She could almost taste the character. Perhaps if she lost another pound?

It was the day of Abby and Maud Arafat's intimate dinner for all the contenders and they were all rather concerned about it.

What to wear? What to wear? Chloe wondered what could she don that would knock 'em dead tonight?

Tonight, the producers – Abby and Gertrude – would see all their main contenders for the role together in one room.

91

Comparisons could be odious, Chloe knew. Although she usually had no difficulty in choosing her outfits, tonight she was in a lather of indecisiveness. She had shopped feverishly for two days, systematically haunting Rodeo Drive and Sunset Boulevard boutiques. What facet of Miranda should she best exploit for this party?

The bitch? In that case, her high-necked black satin Valentino gown with a lace jacket sparkling with black-beaded jet bows and matching jet-and-crystal earrings should be the one.

The seductress? Ungaro's red chiffon, cut to the clavicle in front and to the tenth vertebra at the back. Clouds of red chiffon fanned seductively out from her knees to the floor, and matching red satin sandals with heels so high she could barely walk completed the ensemble. Sexy – yes – perhaps too much so.

But perhaps she should just be herself, Chloe Carriere. Yes, why not? She would be just Chloe tonight. She would wear an old favourite, a gown she had worn several times before and felt at ease in. Cream silk jersey, cut on the bias, draped Grecian style over one tanned shoulder, leaving the other bare. She selected a forties faux diamond clip to fasten the draped fabric at her waist and small Bulgari diamond studs as her only jewellery. She would carry a cream enamel-and-rhinestone-studded Judith Leiber minaudière in the shape of a rabbit in her hand – a present from Josh on her last birthday, and a good luck mascot to boot. Luck! She needed it tonight.

Birthdays! She shuddered as she sat at her dressing table and swiftly applied myriad cosmetics to her face. She would be forty years old this year. Forty!!! It seemed so incredibly ancient. She couldn't believe her life had flown by so fast, her youth passed so soon. All those years so swiftly gone.

'It's not over yet, kid – not by a long shot,' she admonished herself as she applied Dior lip gloss with a practised hand. 'There's life in the old girl yet.' She brushed out her thick curly hair, sweeping it to one side with a tortoiseshell comb.

Slipping cream grosgrain sandals, little more than tiny straps of ribbon, onto her silk-clad feet, she surveyed herself from every angle with a critically objective eye. In her three-way mirror she looked more than beautiful. She looked fabulous. Radiant. Everything was perfect tonight, except one thing was missing. Her man.

Chloe consulted her diamond Boucheron watch. He was late. Josh was recording again. He'd warned her that he might be late. The mixing of his new album was at the critical stage. Since it was already late for delivery, he *had* to get the last track finished, and he wanted it to be perfect. It was vital because this album was critical to his waning career. It had to be at least a minor hit, or, Josh knew, this time his career would be over. At his age, it *was* over as far as most of the kids who bought albums were concerned anyway. They simply didn't care about someone old enough to be their father strutting his stuff on TV video or stage. Offers for Josh to tread the boards in New York or London were thin on the ground too. He was slipping fast, careerwise, and no one was more aware of it than he and Chloe.

The irony was that it had taken him years, decades, to become a star. The climb up had been much more difficult than the slide down. It crossed Chloe's mind that maybe, just maybe, he might be playing around again, but she dismissed the thought quickly. She had been absolutely final about what steps she would take if he started screwing underage bimbos again. No ifs, no buts, no maybes – she would divorce him instantly.

Forget. Forget all those times she had caught him. He had promised, hadn't he? Said that now that he was over forty he thought it undignified to pull young 'grumble'. Told Chloe he really cared, wanted the marriage to work. He'd promised, hadn't he? The limo was waiting. He *was* mixing his tracks. It was party time. She sprayed herself with *Bal à Versailles* and left for Abby and Maud's party in an optimistic mood and a cloud of fragrance.

It definitely was one of Tinsel Town's more up-market

parties, Chloe realized, as the polite young man with 'Chuck's Parking' embroidered on his red jacket opened the car door for her and she glimpsed the front hall of the Arafat mansion awash with true Old World Hollywood glamour.

No photographers, either unofficial or official, were allowed inside or outside the house. This was a sure sign of social superiority. Not even George Christy from the *Hollywood Reporter* had been invited. The more important the party, the less press was the golden rule of Hollywood. Premieres, publicity parties, launches, wrap parties, the more press at those the merrier, but on this occasion the press was conspicuous by its absence.

The entrance hall was vast. Polished grey marble terrazzo imported from Montecatini was barely visible beneath the hems of the designer gowns of the women and the impeccably creased black trousers of the men. The seventy-five dist-inguished guests who sipped Cristal champagne or Perrier water ignored the lacquered eggshell walls on which hung more than fifteen million dollars' worth of paintings. They had seen it before; industry talk was far more entrancing.

An eclectic group of paintings ranging from Renoir to Fischl was displayed to perfection on walls which had been sanded a dozen times and then had seven coats of lacquer applied to create a flawless matt finish. The guests also ignored the black onyx Corinthian columns placed at four-foot intervals throughout the hallway on top of which reposed priceless Roman marble busts from the fifth and sixth centuries.

Chloe, however, could not quite ignore any of it. She found it fascinating. She had never seen such opulent grandeur. She and Josh, although they had been on the Hollywood scene for years, had not been invited to this house before. Abby and Maud Arafat believed in putting their money where their friends could see it. Their home was clearly meant to look like that of a multimillionaire megaproducer. And see it they certainly could. Chloe gasped at the gorgeousness of the decor, the obvious value and beauty of the art. She accepted a glass of champagne from one of thirty liveried servants and strolled into the living room. The room was at least seventy-five feet long, dominated by a Picasso that was unfamiliar to Chloe. It was obviously from his blue period and portrayed two of his great sterile-looking athletes on the beach. The windows were over fifteen feet high, elaborately draped in cobalt blue brocade, heavy with fringe and tassels. The doors to the garden were open, and Chloe wandered onto the terrace. There, on a lawn so thick and green it resembled cut velvet, stood eight of the most exquisite and valuable Henry Moore sculptures in the world. Chloe was amazed that they should be placed so casually on the lawn.

Some of the guests were chatting on the lawn; it was a balmy California night with a light breeze blowing from the coast. Chloe thought about the letter she would write to Annabel describing the scene. She wrote to her at least once a week, describing with care interesting events that had happened, and places she had visited. In return she received little notes, for which she was grateful. Annabel, her baby. As usual, as soon as she started to think about her daughter, Chloe became sad. She took a gulp of champagne. 'Stop it, Chloe,' she said to herself. 'This is business. Concentrate on it. Sparkle, girl – sparkle.' So who was there? She couldn't help notice that all the main contenders for Miranda were there, in the full flower of their elaborate toilettes.

Sissy Sharp had opted for red. Reagan Red, she trilled to all who were aware of the friendship, now, alas, long lapsed, that had existed between Nancy and Ronald and Sissy and Sam when Ronnie was president of the Screen Actors Guild, and Sam one of its officers. Sissy exaggerated the depth of the friendship, dropping the Reagan name with unerring consistency. She and Sam had, in fact, recently returned from a state dinner for the President of Yugoslavia, not one of Washington's top affairs, but newsworthy enough for a one-liner in *USA Today*. She had regaled everyone who would listen with amusing anecdotes about the doings of Nancy, and the funny sayings of 'Dutch'.

Rozalinde Lamaze, escorted by a languid stud, wore gold lamé from Lina Lee. Rozalinde looked satisfied, the stud, tired.

Rozalinde and Chloe exchanged glances, nodding brief hellos. Chloe thought the other woman's outfit looked cheap, but that Rozalinde herself was a remarkably attractive woman who certainly did not look her age. With her luxuriant dark hair caught at the side with a gardenia, and her vivacious smile, Rozalinde looked sexily gorgeous and no more than thirty.

There was a flurry of excitement when Emerald Barrymore arrived. She was Hollywood's child. A major star since age three, she still managed to create excitement wherever she went. Not a decent movie under her belt in ten years, but her aura of stardom glowed undiminished.

No one loved a star more than those who lived and worked in Hollywood, and Emerald was soon surrounded by sycophants and worshippers, none of whom, however, was prepared to offer her a decent job, save for a guest stint on an episodic TV show or perhaps a supporting role in a miniseries.

She had arrived late, as usual, being unable to decide which one of her five fabulous necklaces to wear. Her jewellery was legendary, more so because people thought she had never bought a single piece of it herself. This was actually not true. She had bought most of it herself, jewellery was a passion with her – but she wanted the public to think she was always being showered with gifts by her many lovers, and her press agent worked hard on this image.

She was with her latest husband, Solomon Davidson, a New York suit manufacturer, out of his league but determined not to show it. She sported a cabochon emerald the size of a golf ball on her engagement finger and was wearing an ankle-length sable coat – even wholesale, as Soloman had managed to buy it, the $100,000 price tag was steep. The coat was a mite too long for Emerald's five feet two, but for what she lacked in stature she made up for in hair. Back-combed to within an inch of its life, her fine blonde hair stuck out in dangerous punk-style spikes. She was sheathed in a silver Norell and looked, Chloe had to admit, glorious – a true superstar.

The two contenders whom everyone agreed would turn Miranda down even if they were offered the role, chatted amicably. Jacqueline Bisset and Meryl Streep were far too involved with the cinema to sacrifice their careers for a part in a TV soap opera. The general consensus was that Abby and his partner Gertrude Greenbloom, as co-owners of a studio and the creators of so many great films, were demeaning themselves by turning to TV. Snobbery was still rife about the relatively young medium – so far, in 1982, very few major stars had done a series. Those who did were looked down upon by their peers. Chloe didn't care. She was not a snob – TV or movies, it didn't matter. She needed a good job – and this was the one she wanted.

A few pretty young girls with names like Sharon, Tracey and Cindy wandered around with the fixed desperate smiles of those who feel they're out of place, but realize it's good for their careers to be there. They were starlets under contract to MCPC, outfitted in beaded dresses other stars had worn in last year's movies.

The old guard clung together, as usual: Edie and Lew Wasserman, Mary and Irving Lazar, Janet and Freddie de Codova, and Billy and Audrey Wilder. How many parties had they attended throughout the decades? How many studio heads, how many up-and-coming actors, how many hot young directors had they seen come and seen go? Still they always seemed to enjoy themselves, and the fact that they were there tonight made it an 'A' party.

Chloe felt confident, even in her two-year-old Bruce Oldfield. 'Better under than over, m'dear,' Lady Sarah had always told her. Lady Sarah, of course, had not listened to her own advice to underdress, and was festooned with ropes of pearls the size of garbanza beans, mauve organza flounces and taffeta bows bouncing in her red curls as she chatted with Sissy. Chloe nodded to Sissy, who gave her an icy smile. They had never been friends, had little in common.

As the dinner hour approached, Chloe started to become nervous. Josh had promised to be with her tonight. She needed his moral support. It was nerve-racking enough to be at a huge formal Hollywood banquet, not to mention attending it alone. She nervously sipped her champagne, then put it down, realizing she was getting slightly high. She looked at her watch again. Ten to nine. Dinner was bound to be announced any minute. She was supposed to be seated at a table with Josh. It would be embarrassing if he didn't come. She crossed her fingers, willing him to arrive.

Another contender for Miranda, but in everyone's opinion a rank outsider because of her youth, lurked uncomfortably on the terrace, wishing she could go home.

'It's ridiculous,' said Sabrina Jones to Johnny Swanson, her press agent. 'I *know* I'll never get this part. I'm too young.'

Johnny agreed. Twenty-three was much too young to play such a conniving woman of the world. 'I'm sure Abby wants you to play one of the daughters. He knows a great hype and since you're so hot, your name means more interest in the columns.'

'Mmm,' Sabrina said. She was miserable. She missed Luis, but Johnny had told her she couldn't bring him here. Too much emphasis on sex – not enough on career.

Chloe moved over to Sabrina and Johnny. The young man was friendly; he was witty and attractive, and, strangely, he seemed to want to pay more attention to Chloe than to his beautiful young client. Chloe enjoyed talking to him – he made her laugh in spite of her nervousness.

Johnny Swanson liked Chloe, had in fact fancied her for some time. She appeared to be in a daze, he thought. Was it because Josh wasn't with her? He felt sorry for her, but he admired how she was handling it. Lady Sarah approached and asked him to dance, her tongue too close to his ear for comfort. He disengaged himself in distaste. God, what a mass of amorphic flesh and frills! She didn't attract him in the slightest, even though she was the age he liked. 'No, my little honeybunch,' he said firmly. 'Dance with the stallion in yonder corner who is giving you the once-over. My shoes aren't made to shuffle tonight, sugar.' Lady Sarah raised pencilled auburn eyebrows. 'Honeybunch' indeed! She looked at the stallion, Alex. Mm, not bad, not bad at all.

Johnny moved away to continue studying Chloe. She was not easily had – the grapevine knew that. The boys lunching weekly at Ma Maison knew all about the sexual proclivities and preferences of 'The Available 400', as they were called. Exchanging this information gave them many a clue as to what each lady preferred in bed. Johnny knew that Chloe's marriage had held up pretty well, but tonight it looked to be on its last legs. She was here alone. None of the boys had heard of her ever having an affair. A faithful wife was a rare bird in Hollywood. Particularly one who looked as good as Chloe. A one-man woman, faithful and around forty – just his type! She was leaning at the bar now, temporarily alone, sipping champagne, a frown between those ravishing turquoise eyes. She looked sad. Her façade was starting to crack.

'Champagne gives you nightmares,' he cracked. 'Hot milk's better for you. But then I suppose it depends on what you're doing in bed.'

Chloe smiled faintly at his boyish charm, tried to banter back. 'I hate hot milk,' she said. 'Reminds me of my childhood.'

Before Johnny could continue his verbal foreplay the butler announced that dinner was served. The guests started to drift in from the marble hall, the manicured velvet lawn, and the Louis Fifteenth drawing room, and into the ballroom. The ceiling of the ballroom looked as if it had been painted by Michelangelo. Angels flew in formation against an azure sky with scudding white clouds. On the walls were eighteenth-century sconces in which beeswax candles burned. There was no electric light; only the hundreds of candles on the walls and on the ten tables which were set up symmetrically around the ballroom. In the centre of each table reposed a Lalique bowl in which white roses, calla lilies and tiny fairy lights had been artfully arranged by Milton Williams. Liveried footmen helped the guests to find their tables.

Just as Chloe was in despair about Josh, he appeared at her side. 'Hi, babe,' he whispered, squeezing her arm and brushing his soft lips against her cheek. She smelled the faint aroma of tequila, and also the stronger smell of dope. 'I didn't let you down, kid. I'm here – good old reliable.'

'Darling, I'm so glad you came. I was getting worried.' She smiled, touching the face she cared for so much.

'You knew I wouldn't let you down, Chloe.' He wavered a fraction, and she knew he was high on something. His words were almost imperceptibly slurred. No one but Chloe would know he had been drinking or drugging; he was an expert at covering up, a true pro.

She did not reproach him. He had come to the party after all. For her. Don't make waves, Chloe, her inner voice said. He's here. He does love you. Be thankful.

The guests looked surreptitiously at their watches. It was ten-thirty. At ten forty-five it would be considered correct to split. Two and a half to three hours was the usual length of time guests stayed at a Hollywood party. Then they wanted to go home – watch Carson or a video, read a script, call a broad or smoke a joint. Few, other than those actors who arose at six to film, actually went to sleep at eleven, but it was such a perfect excuse to leave. There were so many parties – to stay longer than three hours would be a waste of time. Silver fork tapped against crystal goblet, and Abby had the guests' attention.

'Tonight is an important occasion for MCPC pictures,' said Abby, revelling in the crowd's fickle attention focused on him.

'Our new show, "The Great Conspirators", has been very successful on network.' Knowing looks were exchanged. A flop, everyone *knew* it was a flop, even at nine o'clock on

Tuesday night when its only rivals were miserable sitcoms with appalling ratings. 'The Great Conspirators' was the most dismal of failures, but Abby, a smart mover and shaker, was on to his next announcement, glossing over failure with practised skill.

'I'm thrilled you're all here tonight, my dear friends, partners and co-workers.' His eyes swept the room, meeting bland smiles, slight attention and fidgets.

'Get on with it, luv,' muttered Lady Sarah, plump beringed hands tracing circles on the thighs of the hot young man she had pulled at the bus stop on Santa Monica Boulevard that morning.

'As you all know, TV is here to stay, and we're staying with it.' Since the majority of his guests were motion-picture people, reaction was minimal. They still couldn't take television seriously. It was a medium for selling soap – for fading stars, and up-and-coming performers.

'We' – he nodded his head to his partner Gertrude who smiled encouragingly – 'have decided to make *the* most exciting prime time long form series of the 1982/83 season. Of the next *ten* seasons, in fact, so successful do we think it will be!

'We have bought the book *Saga*, which as you know is the best-seller to end all best-sellers and we will start shooting the four-hour miniseries in three months, to be followed immediately by the series.' He paused triumphantly to sparse applause. The guests were looking at their watches. 'We are still in the process of casting, but we have some very exciting announcements to make. The part of Steve Hamilton, the patriarch – a man of the people, a man of substance, integrity and true grit – will be played by America's favourite hero, Sam Sharp.' Applause, applause. Sam was popular. He stood and made a self-deprecating bow, the kind that had endeared him to the American public for a quarter of a century. Sissy smiled a razor smile tinged with wifely pride.

'For the role of Miranda, the Scarlett O'Hara of the 1980s, we have narrowed our choice down to these five fabulous ladies. Please stand up, Miss Sabrina Jones.' Weak applause. In spite of her moderately successful series no one knew her here. They would when her college movie was released. So far she was just hype. Sabrina looked flushed and embarrassed. Johnny gave her hand a comforting squeeze, wishing he could fancy her, but she was far too young.

'Miss Chloe Carriere!' Lukewarm applause. As Chloe took her bow in front of Hollywood's finest, she realized that she was not accepted by them at all. Certainly they would see her show in Las Vegas if they happened to be there. But she was of no real interest to them. She was just a singer. An English vocalist. Not famous. Not young. Not established. Just another performer.

'Miss Rozalinde Lamaze.' More enthusiastic applause, a few murmurs of appreciation, as her bare thigh showed itself throught the slit of her gold lamé skirt. Rozalinde had starred in many films that had made much money at the box office. She had been hot – could be again – so the applause was warm and almost sincere.

'Miss Sissy Sharp.' Lots of applause, particularly from those who aspired to President Reagan's friendship. Sissy's flat eyes glittered triumphantly. If reaction of her fellow guests was the criterion, she was a shoe-in! She milked it for all she could – aware that they all were pretending to love her tonight.

'And finally, Miss Emerald Barrymore.' Vociferous, frenzied applause. Emerald was extremely popular, and her recent self-confessed struggle with drugs, her triumphant rehabilitation and physical metamorphosis, had touched the sympathy of the town. What difference did it make that she hadn't made an American movie in ten years? She was a survivor. A star with a capital S, and she would remain one for the rest of her life, even if she never worked again.

Josh squeezed Chloe's hand supportively. She squeezed his back and smiled. She saw by his pupils that he had been at the coke again. How long this time, O Lord? she thought. How long before his habits catch up with him and he goes off the rails and stabs me in the back again?

10

Calvin never made it to college. Not only could his parents not afford to send him, but his grades in high school were so bad that no self-respecting university would even consider his application.

At eighteen he decided to leave the sleepy Utah town where he had grown up and head west. California was his goal, and he felt that there he would eventually attain his ultimate dream: meeting Emerald Barrymore, his idol, in person.

He didn't find it difficult to get a job. His needs were simple, and he was prepared to work hard. He found work as a packer and loader at Thrifty Drug Store on Canon Drive in Beverly Hills. Soon he was promoted to stock clerk, and finally after five years he was allowed to deal with the public when he graduated to junior clerk behind the counter of the photography department.

There he daily came into contact with many stars of TV and movie screen. Some of them even left their 'happy snaps' to be developed, and once he had found some casual photographs of Emerald at a backyard barbecue at the home of superagent Sue Jacobs.

He bided his time. One day she would come in and he

would serve her. They would become friends and then, who knows, perhaps lovers. All he had to do was wait.

When Josh was recording in L.A., he stayed in a room at the Beverly Wilshire. Watching the women on Rodeo Drive was his usual afternoon ritual, then trying to 'pull' them. It was like big-game hunting or gambling, really – a fascinating game he never tired of. It bolstered his ego, and he needed that. He knew he was in a dance of death with Chloe but he couldn't help himself. It had become a sick obsession, and he knew it. In the ten days since the Arafats' party he had been snorting more cocaine then ever.

He'd woken up today at about 3 p.m. with a hangover as usual. Perry, his valet and Man Friday, had brought him the same breakfast he always had when Chloe wasn't around – a glass of Perrier and fresh lemon juice with three Alka-Seltzers fizzing in it, a cheese danish warm with butter and blueberry jam, and half a gram of coke on a silver salver next to a fresh, neatly rolled hundred-dollar bill. The coke cleared his head. He had thought he would work today on the lyrics for the new song. But after three hours he gave up – ideas eluded him. He couldn't find words, let alone a tune, no matter how much he snorted.

He adjusted his telescope and, leaning on the penthouse windowsill, focused it on the south end of Rodeo Drive. It was just after lunch, and women and girls of all ages and sizes were spilling out of nearby restaurants – the Bistro, the Bistro Gardens and La Scala – strolling down the elegant street, indulging in the Beverly Hills woman's favourite sport: shopping.

Josh became interested as he looked at a thirty-five-year-old Chinese woman and her teenage daughter. They were waiting to cross the road, headed for Bonwit's. They looked around vaguely. Out-of-town from where? Hong Kong? Singapore? Not important. He grew hard as he looked at the pubescent girl's tiny nipples under her T-shirt. Her mother's were nice too. A pair of tiny Oriental porcelain dollies. He nodded to

Perry. Perry was no slouch at picking up women. Over the years of soliciting for Josh, he had racked up a 75 per cent success ratio, and he had a smooth line of chat.

'See the chink and the chinkette, Perry?' Josh said. 'Get 'em.'

From across the street where she was about to enter the St Laurent Boutique, Chloe stopped as she saw Perry approach two Chinese women. She felt a wave of nausea as she realized that Josh was up to his old tricks again. She could almost read Perry's lips and see the bemused, expression on the women's faces as he chatted them up.

Disgusted, she turned to cross the road to the parking complex. Forget the new dress for their party tonight – they had decided to celebrate their tenth anniversary in spite of their problems.

Where did she go wrong? Was Josh just a conniving faithless philanderer, had he always been a philanderer, all through the first eight years? Had she been blind? Could he never be faithful? Or was he just bolstering his male ego? Was it because his career was on the wane, because he was frightened of getting old. Or was it drugs? Did cocaine cause him to behave in this sickening way? A forty-year-old man with the morals of a seventeen-year-old slum boy. She had wanted to understand, to forgive, but she couldn't any longer. Yes, things were looking up for her career, just as his was on the wane. But she couldn't let him destroy her now – destroy her ego along with his. How dare men think they are the only ones with a fragile ego. What presumption made them feel that women had no claims to one?

In the early months of their marriage, she had put her own career on hold. She had busied herself with newfound domesticity: cooking for her man, shopping for his favourite foods, filling his closet and hers with outfits in which they could relax around their sprawling estate in Malibu. One of their favourite pastimes was to ride around the countryside – he on his Arabian stallion, she on her favourite English mare.

They would often ride through the dunes at dawn after a night of partying or abandoned lovemaking.

She collected records for him. He had a supercilious dislike for the efforts of Tom Jones, Rod Stewart and even Mick Jagger, all of whom he had at various times been likened to, so Chloe kept her antennae out, searching for long-lost recordings of Billie Holiday, Fats Waller and other greats of the past. Josh could listen to them all day.

He loved being cuddled as she caressed him, calling him endearing names, holding him like a baby. His eyes closed, his black tousled head would nestle between her breasts, a smile of satisfaction on his face. Her fingertips would trace a pattern across his body, touching him skilfully here, there, everywhere. Sometimes, wickedly, her expert fingers touched him intimately transforming his soft innocence into her shaft of pleasure.

He never failed to thrill her. In all of their years of marriage she never tired of the feel of his thighs between hers, his tongue exploring her mouth, his muscular hands palpating where she liked it most, always bringing her to fulfilment.

'I want you so much, babe,' he would whisper into her hair. As they entwined, all of his customary crudeness of speech disappeared in the act of love with Chloe. With her Josh became a tender, demonstrative, affectionate lover. No one was more amazed by this transformation than he – he who had never given a damn for any of the women from his indiscriminate past. For Chloe now only endearments issued from his lips. Terms of love, sweet talk, tender, loving, sincere. Chloe loved it. She loved him so much. Forever. It could only be forever.

'Stop it, Chloe,' she said to herself, thoughts of their lovemaking now hopelessly interwoven with thoughts of him fucking the two Chinese women she had seen being escorted by Perry to the Wilshire. 'Stop it *now*, girl. It's over. You know you have to end it. It's finished. It's been finished for years.'

She drove her silver Mercedes back to Malibu, her eyes

stinging with salty tears that coursed down her face. She had to get ready for the party tonight. Their anniversary party. She felt numb. Was this what a broken heart felt like?

It was four o'clock when she got home. Pop music blared from the kitchen where the Mexican staff was preparing a feast for the party. She walked to the beach and stared bleakly at the ocean. Her marriage was cracked. Josh didn't love her. She had subordinated her career, encouraged his flagging one. She had tried to breathe new life and respectability into his hell-raising image; he had not responded to her care. He was a wastrel and an ingrate.

Deny it as he might, he was a slipping, ageing rock star. It didn't matter that he still looked sexy, tough and confident with his tumbling black curls, tinged faintly with grey – and only the tiniest hint of a gut, which he dieted and sweated off before each tour. No, the fourteen-year-olds *knew* he was hitting forty when they saw his face on an album cover, no matter how much retouching from the experts. Their eager hands picked at the new Michael Jackson or Rick Springfield album, ignoring Joshua Brown – he was yesterday's news, their mamma's idol.

'We can't all be young forever, darling,' Chloe had soothed and comforted him as he raged at the injustice of it, his insecurities mounting as his hair line receded. Try as she might, Chloe could no longer assuage Josh's self-doubt with her love. It wasn't enough for him any more. He needed fresh game to stalk. New pussy. The chase. Ah, the thrill of the hunt! He never tired of it now.

Although Josh had been notoriously successful with women, he had tried to be true to Chloe during their marriage. Chloe, loving, caring, demonstrably sexy, gave him neither reason nor motivation to stray in the early years of their marriage. But a stiff prick no conscience hath, and now he needed more reassurance that he was up to it twice, thrice, sometimes four times a session. He became petrified by his waning sexuality, a normal thing for most men his age. He

107

had to prove himself again and again – perhaps not the same way as when he was a kid on tour with groupies – but certainly he needed to feel he was still desired by other women. His sexual interest in Chloe waned. Her all-consuming love began to smother him. Sure he loved cuddles – 'the goodies' he called them – adored lying close to her as she caressed him, sang to him. She even sang *his* hits! Clever girl. He loved that. But she was too damn clingy, to damn wifely-womanly-motherly. She was smothering. Suddenly he wanted new game to hunt.

He thinks I'm his goddamned mother, she fretted, as she strode the Malibu sands in a flowing white cotton Laize Adler. Her painted toenails crunching and popping the seaweed that encrusted the shore, she puffed nervously on a cigarette, a habit she had quit a year ago.

'Damn him!' she thought two hours later as she lay back in the black marble Jacuzzi, so often the scene of their love-making. Only last week he had 'taken' her there as she lay mesmerized listening to Lena Horne wailing 'Love me or leave me'. It had been the first time other than an occasional 'duty fuck' in six months that they had made love joyously and spontaneously. Covered with bubbles they had embraced each other in the hot foaming Jacuzzi. It was almost like the old days. Almost.

That had been a week ago. Remembering that once they felt deprived if they had not made love once in the morning and once at night, at least, Chloe felt bitter sadness at the thought of him with the two Chinese women. What was he doing with them? She couldn't bear to think about it.

Love dies, passion erodes. The opposite of love is not hate – it is indifference. She groaned inwardly, trying to think about tonight's party, wishing she could feel indifferent towards Josh instead of this jealous sexual angst. She loved him still, she could not help herself. Oh stop it, girl –get it *together* now, get out of the bath. Think about the damn guests. Could she cancel the party now? Impossible. Half of them were home in Beverly Hills preparing their toilettes, painting their faces and nails, having their chauffeurs spit-polish the Silver Spirit or the Porsche. No, she must brazen it out tonight. There were problems with Josh's recording session, she would tell the guests with a smile. He's still at the studio. Deadlines. You know how it is. They would nod wisely. Of course they knew how it was. They were all in the business so they knew only too well.

Rozalinde Lamaze and Johnny Swanson were the first to arrive. She had dressed casually – tight white leather pants were tucked into seven-hundred-dollar Fabrizio cowboy boots inlaid with turquoise leather; her turquoise silk cowboy blouse was slashed to the navel; around her neck cascaded the spoils of some long-forgotten Navajo tribe, a silver, turquoise and mother-of-pearl squash-blossom necklace. A silver belt encircled her twenty-three-inch waist, and several turquoise rings adorned her dusky fingers.

Johnny and Rozalinde had been friends for years, relying on each other for 'escort duty' when no one more exciting was on the horizon. Johnny was twenty-nine to Rozalinde's thirty-six and six feet to her five feet two. He was good-looking and slim in a suave boyish way, and his cutting wit gave him a special brand of charm. For one so young, he had more than a way with both words and women. 'If it moves, fondle it,' was his motto. His prowess as a 'stick man' preceded him, along with his colourful family history.

Rozalinde rearranged her silver neckwear and surveyed the room. Featured tonight were several bit players in both her life and Johnny's. But Eureka! There he was again, fat old Abby Arafat. The man who held the key to her future. She oozed beguilingly over to Abby, voluptuous hips performing a melody of their own as she played the game of 'Oh I'm bored – I've got *sooo* many movie offers but nothing turns me on. What shall I *do*, Abby darling?' She didn't want him to know she was eager for Miranda, although she had agreed to test. She who plays it the coolest shall win the first prize. American phrase much in vogue recently.

Abby chomped on his cigar and half-listened with amusement as he surveyed the other woman he was going to test for Miranda. That Chloe. She was beautiful and charismatic. His eyes narrowed as he watched her in a clinging white silk Azzadine Allaia dress, her black curls tumbling artlessly, and the definition of a well-formed breast visible as she threw back her head and laughed with Alex Andrews. Where was her hubby, Abby wondered? Why wasn't he keeping an eye on this hot number?

Alex Andrews was the latest hunk in town. Gorgeous, young, sexy, blond, virile, intelligent, he possessed every one of the qualities necessary for big screen appeal. However it just wasn't enough to be gorgeous and young, etcetera, today, mused Abby. That had been sufficient in the thirties, forties and fifties to guarantee movie stardom; then in the sixties, those attributes almost became impediments to an actor's career. Were Dustin Hoffman, Michael Caine and Jack Nicholson gorgeous and young? No. They were actors, artists, thespians who had perfected their craft. They had charisma as well as talent. Intelligence as well as interesting looks. In the eighties you have to have it all. The public was too demanding. Gorgeous, young and sexy were minor requirements. Essential were talent, personality, intelligence and uniqueness.

Alex, studying hard with his acting coach, strived to acquire all these. But tonight he was working in a different way on Rozalinde, flashing his hooded hazel eyes in her direction, turning to give her a fine view of his twenty-five-year-old black-leather-covered buns. Alex was a pure soul, a cowboy from Indiana, with all the accompanying naïveté. 'The great open spaces are in his head,' quipped Johnny, ever vigilant to spot an upstart trying to break into the rarefied ranks of the 'in' crowd.

Johnny was totally accepted everywhere in Hollywood: at A parties, B parties, orgies, stuffy charity affairs he was ever welcome. He wasn't an actor, and he was from a fine family, even if no one was quite sure who had sired him. But Alex was an outsider. A climber. All curls and cock. No family. No background. He had far to go, even if his agent claimed that he had the part of Steve's son on 'Saga' all but sewn up.

Alex chatted eagerly with Rozalinde, trying to spark her feminine interest in him. He realized that although she was a big star, and he the male equivalent of a starlet, they were both playing the same game. He felt she was hungry. He could sense her sexual hunger in the way her round brown eyes admired the contours of his high-cheekboned face. Her plump, beringed fingers had started to flutter gently, skimming over his black silk shirt. A delicate butterfly touch. Little did he know she wasn't thinking of him. Rozalinde had Angelica on her mind. God forbid this crowd should ever find out she was a dyke. She'd be finished in this town. Men could get away with being gay; it was a man's world, let's face it – but a woman – a sex symbol be a lesbian? Perish the thought. She'd never get another job.

Abby Arafat moved smoothly through the crowd, talking to everyone. Smiling, nodding, charm personified, he was fully aware of his power tonight. Who wouldn't be? He had the crème de la crème of the acting profession at his feet, all dying to play one of the six or seven wonderful roles in 'Saga'.

Abby mourned the long-gone era of the true movie stars. The Hedy Lamarrs, Ava Gardners, Lana Turners and Rita Hayworths. Nubile, tender wisps of sixteen or seventeen summers plucked from high school or the cosmetic counters of the local drugstores, adored and worshipped for a few years by an adulatory yet fickle public who soon glorified another new face. That same public was unaware that the stars they paid homage to were merely the products of a slick studio build-up. Many of them were plastic models, with no heart, no guts, no reality – robots who lived by the studio's rules and behaved themselves. So they should, thought Abby. Do what the studio said. Enough already with these coozes with brains, these Glenda Jacksons, Vanessa Redgraves and Shirley MacLaines. They thought they had ideas. They

111

wanted to produce, to direct, to have a say in their work. They couldn't be manipulated, cajoled or flattered.

None of *them* would ever play Miranda, or even Sirope. He wasn't even considering them. He needed a dame with oomph – vulnerable, soft, beautifully dressed, who oozed sex appeal – all those qualities that were unfashionable in these emancipated days of 1982. A woman of sensitivity and sex appeal who appealed to the basics in a man. A woman like . . . Chloe. His eyes glimpsed her curves again through the silky stretch fabric of her gown. Her sultry face, knowing, yet young-looking. Why not Chloe? He chomped on his cigar. Sure, she's really a saloon singer, but who says singers can't act? Look at Streisand, Minelli, Cher. On second thought, don't, he groaned. Streisand gave him heartburn.

He moved to where Chloe was talking animatedly to Johnny. She knew she was giving off good vibes tonight. She was amusedly aware of her power over men who were attracted to her aura of vulnerable little girl, but one who knows the ropes. Several men at the party were vying for her attention as she fumed inwardly over Josh's nonappearance but desperately tried not to show it. She knew what she wanted to do, what she *had* to do for the sake of her self respect. Dump him. End the marriage. Get the part of Miranda and ta-ta, Josh.

'Great party, Chloe,' Abby intruded, reeking of cigar and goodwill. Johnny melted away. He had nothing to gain from chitchatting with this ancient relic of Hollywood about whom his dear mother Daphne often fondly reminisced. Aware that his dear mother had bedded half of Hollywood, Johnny was shrewd enough not to let it bother him – in fact, he joked about it, so that Daphne's escapades in bed became part of his own repertoire of anecdotes. Often he recounted a tale of Mummy and a swain with minor embellishments at the exclusive men-only Friday lunches at Ma Maison.

Suddenly Chloe saw her husband stumble in through the Aztec-carved front door. He was supported on each side by an Oriental female, and the crowd engulfed him in a shower of bonhomie as he disappeared towards the bar. He was drunk – very drunk. Probably stoned, too.

'Darling,' Chloe cooed, pressing her silken body close to his. 'You're just a tiny bit late, darling. Did the session go well?' She managed to combine wifely concern with womanly understanding, while squeezing his cheek hard.

'Yeah, babe, went late, real late.' He pinched her perfumed ivory cheek gently. He wasn't about to tell her about his afternoon at the Beverly Wilshire. He realized he'd made a mistake. A bad one. He hadn't fucked the Orientals, although they clung to him like lint. As his head cleared and the room came into focus, the realization of the magnitude of his mistake in bringing them here hit him. Christ, if Chloe should suspect, she'd be bloody furious! She didn't seem to be.

'Why don't you have a quick shower and freshen up, *darling*?' Chloe used her sweetest tone, aware of forty pairs of potentially gossiping eyes viewing their reunion. Rumours were already rife that Josh had started catting around – and he and Chloe were after all, on their third reconciliation in less than two years. Everyone knew Josh possessed a roving eye, and many people were surprised that Chloe had kept him by the home fires all these years. 'A leopard never changes its spots,' observed Abby sagely. 'Never.'

After Josh's arrival the party proceeded smoothly. A tiered mocha cake from the X-Rated Cake Shoppe, featuring a couple in pink-and-brown icing suggestively entwined, was served. A trio of singing telegramettes arrived and sang 'Happy Anniversary' while stripping to approving cheers from the crowd. Toasts were drunk to the happy couple who had survived ten years of marriage, a record by many Hollywood standards. Chloe watched Josh, with impassive eyes that hid her pain as she realized it was finally over. Goodbye and farewell to her 'forever marriage'. There was no use prolonging the agony. She glimpsed his tongue playfully teasing the ear of one of the women he'd arrived with, saw her

113

stroke the bulge in his jeans, observed his hand try to sneak up the skirt of the other. Saw – and died inside.

Sally saw it all, too, and, daughterly devotion aside, felt sorry for her father. But she did enjoy seeing Chloe squirm. She could read the pain in her eyes. She saw the glances Chloe stole at Josh. She realized how it must hurt her to watch him with the two women. She didn't care. Maybe they would get a divorce and she would never have to see Chloe again. 'Miserable old cow,' she said, downing a beer and throwing back a tequila after it, as she had seen her father do.

Chloe circulated among her guests, laughing, charming, playing her part. Josh stayed at the other end of the stadium-sized living room, surrounded by his buddies and the two women. As he drank more, he became more raucous, more aggressive and, Chloe noticed, more unattractive. An ageing, greying, middle-aged rock star trying to remain young. It was pathetic. He had been smoking dope and drinking tequila – he looked out of it. He looked over the hill, tired and unsuccessful. 'He's wrong for you, darling,' Daphne whispered. 'Wrong, wrong, wrong. He's a lout, and a drunk and a wastrel.' And a loser too, she thought, behaving like this in front of everyone.

Chloe was beyond humiliation. The embarrassment of seeing her husband in her living room with those two strange women, his obvious fascination with this Chinese mother-and-daughter act, made her ill. She felt as if she were observing everything in slow motion. One of the waiters continuously refilled her glass with champagne. She floated through the room, watching everything objectively, not caring any more about anything or anyone. She realized that Abby had left. She was thankful that a potential boss was not a witness to her humiliation. As for the other guests, she simply didn't give a damn what they thought.

'Where's the wife? Where is she then?' Josh suddenly called out, whirling on the tinier of his tiny strumpets, slapping her hands away from where they were toying with his chest hair.

'C'mon, Chloe, give us a song,' he bawled, grabbing Chloe's hand in his bear grip and pulling her over to the piano.

'No, Josh, no.' Chloe tried to pull away from him. 'No duets tonight. I can't. Don't do this, Josh, please.'

Josh seemed oblivious to her distress. He shrugged and beckoned to the teenage Chinese girl, who came to his side with a sly Oriental smile.

Chloe desperately wished everyone would leave. Finally, as if reading her thoughts, they started to go.

Rozalinde threw back her sixth Bailey's Irish Cream and smiled at Alex. 'Let's get out of here, honey pie. It's a bore,' she murmured. 'Got wheels?'

'Sure, sure,' Alex said happily. His manager had lent him his Cadillac, not wanting his latest client to be seen at an important party in a clapped-out Mustang. Alex realized that leaving this party with Rozalinde Lamaze was quite a coup. Even if she was a decade older than he, she was a big star. He hoped there would be paparazzi outside the house, ready to take a happy snap for the *National Enquirer*. He made a mental note to have his press agent call Army and Hank tomorrow, to give them the exclusive scoop about this new hot twosome. Maybe even Liz Smith or Suzy would run it in New York. What would the folks in Indiana think!

Johnny hadn't scored tonight. Not that it bothered him. Scoring was too easy in this town. By the time a good-looking guy was twenty-nine he had usually scored so much easy pussy that, if he didn't start playing the marriage-and-divorce game, only challenges could excite him. Chloe Carriere, for instance, was quite a challenge, and Johnny thought he might throw down his gauntlet for her.

Calvin, from his hiding place, outside the house, saw Rozalinde leaving the party with Alex. He sneered to himself. What a slut! Hanging on to a stud at least ten years her junior, stroking his long blond hair, fondling him in places that Calvin knew were dirty. Filthy whore! She was scum.

Where was Emerald? Why wasn't she at this party? Many others of importance seemed to be. He had been told she was coming, but perhaps Chloe hadn't invited her – out of jealousy, no doubt. A jealous British bitch. They were all jealous of Emerald – she was so ravishing, so sweet. Vulnerable yet glamorous. None of these over-the-hill spic sluts or limey cows was in her league. None of them was fit to lick her size three satin-shod feet. She was the Queen. The Goddess. The Best.

He looked at his watch. Twelve-thirty. He saw that the Mexican tramp and the stud toy-boy were locked in an embrace in the front seat of a Cadillac.

An unaccustomed excitement suddenly engulfed him as he watched the couple fondling each other. Even though he despised Rozalinde, watching her hands roam over Alex's body aroused Calvin tremendously. As Alex finally disengaged himself from Rozalinde's hot hands, put the car in gear and moved into the highway, Calvin followed in his green Chevrolet.

After the guests had left, Chloe confronted Josh. 'This was the last straw tonight, Josh. I want a divorce, and I mean it this time. How dare you bring those women to our house?'

'No, babe, please, *no*. Chloe, I love you, you know I do. It's always been you, babe. Always, you know it, babe.' His words were erratic.

'Oh, stop it, Josh – you sound like a broken record. I can't take your cheating any more.' She tried to keep the pain out of her voice. It hurt to swallow, her throat was so constricted. He had wounded her too many times now with his playing around. She had tried to pretend to herself it didn't really matter, it was just sport fucking – nothing serious. Had tried many times to forgive him. But tonight she had run out of forgiveness. 'I *won't* stand for it any more, Josh,' she said wearily. 'We've come to the end of the road. You know we have. We *must* divorce, or I'll go mad, because I think YOU are, Josh.'

'No, Chloe, no. I can't make it without you,' he had begged her, gone on his knees, tears streaming down his face. He used every trick in his book to persuade her not to end their marriage. But bringing up old times only made her think of old injuries and convinced her more than ever that the marriage was over. The Oriental women were the end. It was intolerable. Whether or not he had made love to them made no difference. The fact that he *wanted* to was enough. In front of their guests, at their anniversary party, he had humiliated her terribly. Insulted their marriage. Disgraced them both. 'This isn't *love* any more, Josh!' she screamed, all control suddenly evaporating. 'It's war – it's sick – it's horrible. The whole goddamn party saw it, and I *won't* stand for it. It's an *illness*, Josh.'

She'd drunk a lot of champagne. Now it released her, released the pain. She locked the bedroom door, took two Valium, ripped off her clothes, letting them lie on the floor, and, without removing her makeup, fell into a dreamless slumber.

Josh zoomed down the Pacific Coast Highway at 75 mph in his Cadillac convertible. He didn't notice the police car behind him. His stereo was turned on full blast to his latest track, and he had just taken a swig of tequila from his leather Gucci flask. The booze and the joint he had smoked earlier were making him feel slightly better. Chloe would eventually come to her senses. She had to. He needed her. They were the forever couple, weren't they?

Then as the flashing lights of the police car pulled in front of him and the sound of the siren finally penetrated his consciousness, he realized that he was in more trouble.

He woke up covered with sweat. His black silk shirt was sodden, his grey slacks oozed moisture. Where the hell was he? His bewildered brain waves tried to connect. Was he in jail? But for christsake, why? How dare they put him, Joshua Brown, superstar, behind bars. He started sweating even more; he needed a snort badly. He reached into his pocket for the leather pouch in which he kept his paraphernalia – the brown cube of 'downtown', the glass phial of 'uptown', the solid-gold razor blade, the platinum straw. Gone. Frantically he felt in his other pockets and then scrabbled on the filthy floor. 'Hey, you mother-fuckers,' he screamed, the tendons standing out on his neck. 'Bring me back my stuff, you shit-eaters!'

A black guard appeared, opened the hatch and looked at him coldly. 'Shut your mouth, junkie, or we shut it for you,' he spat, and slammed the hatch shut.

Josh started to tremble. He hadn't had a fix since . . . when was it? Two or three o'clock this morning – after Chloe had gone to bed and left him alone. It was now – he looked at the clock on the wall outside his cell – 9 a.m.

Shit. He started to tremble violently, waves of nausea rocking him. He threw up into a bucket, then, weakened and disoriented, fell back onto the filthy bunk again. Staring at the ceiling and walls encrusted with the graffiti of a thousand derelicts, he dropped off to sleep. The pain in his head and chest faded as his dreams took over. He was a star once more. A superstar. Caesar's Palace in Vegas . . . the London Palladium . . . Olympia in Paris. He had packed them to the rafters all over the world. Standing room only. Josh Brown, the most charismatic English performer the world had ever seen. He could have had any woman he wanted, and he did. But eventually he wanted only one – only Chloe. And he wanted it to last forever. The others never mattered. Why couldn't Chloe realize that? He loved her – he would always love her. He groaned.

He was allowed one phone call from jail. He called his agent, who immediately sped down to the county court with bail money. Josh was released in a blaze of bad publicity.

In the days that followed, Josh tried to contact Chloe, but she insisted the marriage was finished and she wanted out. With a heavy heart, he moved into the Beverly Wilshire, and she sent his belongings over with Perry. Chloe filed for divorce two days later on the grounds of irreconcilable differences.

Josh threw himself into finishing the album while he consumed huge amounts of tequila and cocaine and made frantic love to as many under age girls as he could. When the album was nearly finished, his agent called and told Josh he had an interesting job for him. He could and should go back into the theatre. A major English impresario wanted him to write and star in a musical version of *Cyrano de Bergerac*. It was a wonderful opportunity, one he had wanted for years, for the theatre had always been his first, his true love.

Two weeks after he and Chloe separated, Josh packed his bags and left for London.

Part Three

11

They sat in the number one booth at the Polo Lounge drinking Dom Perignon and exchanging information.

Solomon Davidson, Sol to his many acquaintances, was telling Chloe about the events at the end of his recent marriage to Emerald. Sol and Emerald had indulged in a rapid tabloid-style romantic affair, culminating after a few months in a quick engagement, a short marriage and a fast separation last week.

'Why did you wear that colour?' he asked her accusingly, eyeing her jade-green Halston dress.

'Why – don't you like green? Don't tell me you're superstitious?' Chloe murmured, as she sipped her champagne, watching him with amused eyes.

Solomon, bon vivant and friend to the stars, and Chloe had been good friends for years. They had laughed and joked through many evenings together, and Chloe was sorry to see him still clearly obsessed with Emerald.

When Emerald divorced for the fifth time, she had immediately turned her sea-green eyes, the light in them undimmed, even though she was approaching her half century, in Sol's direction. Oh, lucky man! Oh, foolish and vain man! She had eventually crucified him on the altar of the trash magazines. He had been made to look like a bumbling fool – a poor peasant not fit to slip a bangle on Emerald's slim wrist.

Poor Sol, who revelled in his role as confidant and gofer to the famous, lost both his credibility and his lady to the snide sniggerings of supermarket pulp. But he had swallowed his pride, picked himself up, dusted himself off and ventured back into the Los Angeles social scene again.

'I want her back,' Sol confided to Chloe. 'I still love her.'

Chloe sympathized. Joshless now for over a month, she had shed many tears and soaked many pillowcases every night as she yearned to have him beside her.

Emerald read Army Archerd's column with growing concern: 'Chloe Carriere, one of the main contenders for the coveted Miranda role in "Saga", and Solomon Davidson, Emerald Barrymore's soon-to-be ex, had more to discuss than the heat wave in the Polo Lounge last week. Is that the love light in their eyes?'

She threw down the paper, lit a Sherman with a green malachite lighter, and with remarkably steady hands inserted it into a pale emerald holder.

Chloe was a parvenu, a Johnny-come-lately. She didn't belong. First of all, not only was she British, but she was not even an actress. She was a singer – a singer who had a couple of hits in the sixties and seventies, and then faded out. Now she had reemerged as a more-than-serious contender for her, Emerald's, role. When Emerald first heard that Chloe was testing, she thought it was a joke. Now the joke was turning out to be a serious threat not only to her part, but to her nearly-ex-husband. Not that she wanted Sol, but she didn't want Chloe to have him either.

Emerald crunched the pale emerald holder between her tiny, perfectly capped teeth. It was essential to her career that she get this role. She was no longer hot in movies. She needed this part badly. Doing this commercial in Australia was not a great career move.

In spite of her many marriages, her drinking problem and a penchant for carelessly throwing away her hard-earned cash on her friends and husbands, she was a true child of Hollywood, and it still loved her. She had thrived in the era in which she had grown up, became Hollywood royalty, and the ultimate symbol of survival. Many of her contemporaries had succumbed to drugs, drink, suicide or illness. How much of it caused by career failure, no one could know, or even guess.

Marilyn Monroe. Poor Norma Jean – she had never believed in herself, and it had destroyed her. Emerald and Marilyn had studied at the Actors Studio together. Milton Greene, their feisty mentor and glamour photographer par excellence, brash, knowledgeable, and crafty, had guided both their careers simultaneously in the early sixties. The girls had been close friends. Shared gowns, men, and laughs. Emerald had been devastated when Marilyn had died.

James Dean – Jimmy – darling Jimmy – her first lover. No matter that Pier Angeli, Ursula Andress, and countless others were on his fishing line that long hot summer of 1955. She had given herself to him – totally. Emerald Barrymore, eighteen years old, gorgeous, sexy, idol of millions of youngsters, had allowed James Dean, moody, unpredictable and intense, to take her much-discussed virginity.

She had adored him passionately until his death a few months later. A shortish period of mourning – after all she was only eighteen – then she was in love again. This one was more dependable, and the studio breathed a sigh of relief when they married. A young actor, up-and-coming. Unfortunately for Emerald, he was not able to come up often enough to satisfy her. And when she discovered him in bed with another man, he had to go. Divorce, more tears, more mourning. Then into her life came Stanley O'Herlihy! How destructive can one man be to himself? Maybe Irishmen have a death wish, but Stanley carried it to new heights. He was short, middle-aged and ugly, with a thirst for whiskey and women that was practically unquenchable. Writing was the driving force of his life, and he devoted most of his waking hours to it.

He was fifty to her twenty when they wed for the first time. His lovemaking left a lot to be desired: two bottles of Irish whiskey a day did not a stallion make. After brief, unsatisfactory couplings he would retire to his desk and his fountain pen and write far into the night, leaving his radiant young bride alone and unfulfilled. He gave her a vibrator for her twenty-first birthday, with a sarcastic note. She took it to the studio and her latest leading man showed her what to do with it – and him!

For some reason, Stanley's obvious lack of interest in her charms captivated Emerald further, making her more determined to make him love her. He had told her he had never truly loved a woman in his life, and that if he did, she would certainly not be the one, as she was nowhere near intellectual and intelligent enough for him, but the more he insulted her, the more besotted with him she became.

Twice she left him in frustrated rage for younger, handsomer, wealthier and more caring men – men who satisfied her sexually, who complimented and praised her, who wanted to marry her. But they were never enough for Emerald. They represented only convenient arm decorations and temporary sexual passion – they meant nothing.

She yearned for Stan O'Herlihy, who, knowing a good thing when he saw it, allowed Emerald to move back into his life time and again. She put up with his drunken rages, his foul Irish temper and his indiscriminate fornication with the trashiest of waitresses and prostitutes, women he seemed to find far more exciting than he did her. He craved kinky sex: threesomes, orgies, S and M. She put up with it until finally after two marriage and divorces and ten years of on-again, off-again connubial non-bliss, Stanley drove his Porsche into a tree, instantly killing himself and the black prostitute with him.

Emerald mourned long and loud. It was 1970; she was at the peak of her beauty and sexuality, yet now she couldn't get arrested as far as movies were concerned. Studios considered her a celebrity, no longer a serious actress, in spite of having made fifty films. After decades of success suddenly she was considered box-office poison.

In Hollywood, socially she was still the crème de la crème, but to new hot young directors and producers she was yesterday's news. She was, after all, well into her thirties, even though her smashing blonde beauty showed none of the wear and tear expected.

Eventually Emerald philosophically accepted that Hollywood had turned its back on her and she went to live in Italy. There she learned the language, starred in some low-budget but compelling Italian and French programme fillers throughout the decade, married a couple of times, travelled, spent every cent she earned, and waited for the day when she would return in triumph to Hollywood.

Now as she sat in her Sydney hotel room, watching the sunset behind the façade of the beautiful white opera house shining off the harbour waters and reading a week-old copy of *Daily Variety*, she knew she *must* pull out all the stops to get this part. She would call in every one of her markers. She would do anything to get it. *Anything*.

A week later, back in her Hollywood apartment, she reclined on soft green towels and let Sven do his damndest to her vertebrae. 'God, vat kinks,' he said, enthusiastically pummelling her with firm Scandinavian hands. Emerald's eyes were alight in her middle-aged, still-beautiful face. More than four decades a star and now reborn, thanks to the miracles of South American plastic surgery and a Midwestern alcohol-and-drug rehabilitation clinic. She had lost more than thirty pounds in the past year thanks to a restrictive diet of zucchini, broiled chicken and Evian water. A major consumer of alcohol all her life, she had completely cleaned out her system of the poisons and toxins that had accumulated over the years, and was now determined to conquer the new and exciting world of prime time TV.

She balanced a pale green phone on the pillow. 'You know I'll test,' she said. 'I don't have any false pride about that, darling.' Her agent, Eddie De Levigne – a diminutive elflike figure who had been around since the days of Swanson, and whose legendary career and monetary accomplishments for his clients always paid off so handsomely that his nickname in the business was Fast Eddie – was pleased. Emerald was a smart cookie. The smartest thing she'd done recently was to fire the Morris boys and hire him. In this town where fledgling actresses become prima donnas in less time than you could say, 'Who won last year's Oscar?' her attitude was refreshing. Throughout her bouts with alcoholism and drug addiction and her mistakes with men, Fast Eddie had waited in the wings for her to come to her senses so that he could pick up her pieces and put them together again, as only he knew how. He was an agent in the proper sense of the word, not a faceless grey-flannel-suited cipher like so many of the boys at the conglomerates. Fast Eddie cared – and he got results.

Sven finished kneading her back, packed up his equipment and left. With a groan of pleasure, she strolled, unselfconsciously naked, into her mirrored closet to survey her dozens of green outfits.

Emerald almost exclusively wore green, and, occasionally, white. For films she wore other colours, but in private life, all she ever wore was pistachio green, grass green, pea green, olive green. Every imaginable shade of green hung in the hundred feet of her spacious walk-in closet. She selected a mint-green Ungaro blouse with matching gabardine culottes, clasped her everyday emerald pendant around her reconstructed throat and left for Eddie's office to discuss strategy.

Fast Eddie did not mince words. Although Emerald was at the moment his favourite client, he always called a spade a spade. 'This Carriere dame is the favourite kid,' he rasped. 'No doubt about it. I talked to Gertrude today and she gave it to me straight. Abby loves her, so does the network and they always have the final say, as you know.'

'Shit.' Emerald sat up straight, her gorgeous eyes flashing. 'That English nobody. How *can* they prefer her to me? I'm a *star*. She's a nightclub singer. What can we *do*, Eddie?'

'The best we can, kid, the best we can,' said the little man wisely, frowning through his massive spectacles. 'Listen, kiddo, we've just gotta persevere. I've told 'em you're the best, the biggest star, the most gorgeous and the most talented. I'm gonna give 'em all I can, kid, and you've gotta help me.'

'Oh, I will, you know I will, Eddie darling.'

'Give 'em your best shot on the test. You're a damn fine actress, kiddo, in spite of all your rotten movies, and your stupid marriages.'

Emerald winced. True, the critics didn't love her, but the fans did. They adored her. Producers and directors loved her too, but didn't give her jobs. They gave them to Anne Bancroft, Sally Field and Jessica Lange. 'Saga's' Miranda Hamilton was the key to a whole new career for Emerald, and she was determined to get it.

The network, Abby, and Gertrude finally decided on a date to test their finalists for Miranda. Scripts were sent. Wardrobe women went on the hunt for costumes. Early nights for the five actresses became de rigueur. The town waited for the results eagerly.

The day of the test dawned to uncharacteristic California weather. Rain in great grey sheets had bucketed down on the highways and boulevards all night, leaving the Los Angeles area sodden and drab.

Chloe was awake at 5 a.m. She gazed with alarm at the six-foot waves pounding the foundations of her Trancas house and wondered if, as usual, the hills around Malibu Canyon had collapsed under the weight of the rain and become impassable. What then? Maybe she could make it over the Ventura freeway and cut through to Hollywood Boulevard via Franklin Avenue. She wasn't due at the studio until seven-thirty. Throwing on an old chenille robe and snuggling her feet into oversized bunny slippers, she went down to the kitchen. As she waited for the coffee to percolate and the Highway Patrol to answer the phone, she inspected again the call sheet for today's test.

There they all were, the final *six* names that had been approved by the network, by Abby, and by Gertrude.

So Pandora had managed to get a test, too, Chloe mused. Or was she going to play the other ex-wife? Either way it was not a bad idea. She had a sharp, dark, foxy face, was a good actress, the right age – oh, dear, more competition for Miranda.

As she sipped coffee, then showered she mulled over her chances compared to the other five actresses.

Sabrina Jones was no competition. Everyone including Sabrina knew she was wrong. She was a red herring. A publicity shill used by Abby to garner media coverage and hype the public's interest.

Pandora King? She would probably get the other role of the first wife, since according to the call sheet she was testing for both roles. She was a respected actress, but a second-stringer, and always would be.

Rozalinde Lamaze? Too ethnic. Whatever the networks might say, however much the producers denied it, it was doubtful that this very important leading role would go to Rozalinde, because of her Mexican origin. It wouldn't gel with the Anglo-Saxon feeling and look that Chloe knew Abby and Gertrude wanted for the show.

Chloe's main competitors were Sissy and Emerald – she had absolutely no doubt about that. Sissy was the better actress, plus being married to Sam would give her a strong edge. But Emerald was still such a megastar that Chloe was surprised she had agreed to test. Still, what the hell – they were all only actresses, weren't they? Bakers must bake, painters must paint, and actresses must act. That was their life.

Ah, well, may the best woman win, she thought as she dressed in jeans, a flannel plaid shirt of Josh's, and her

Burberry raincoat that had seen many a rainy day in the provinces of England. She drove her silver Mercedes swiftly through the pouring rain without encountering anything other than the occasional stalled car. Highway Patrol had managed to keep Malibu Canyon open, thank God. Huge men, sweating in spite of the freezing rain, shovelled the sliding mud as it threatened to cover the Pacific Coast Highway. Once on the Hollywood freeway, she relaxed and put the tape of the scene that she had committed to memory into her tape deck.

The English-accented voices, hers and that of Lawrence Dillinger, her acting coach, filled the Mercedes. Chloe listened objectively. Would she be too British for the network? There seemed to be no foreigners on prime time TV right now except Ricardo Montalban, and he was a character actor. The darlings of the tube were all-American as apple pie and very *young*. Charlie's Angels were all in their twenties – and the Dallas Dollies were certainly a lot younger than the group who would assemble on stage five today.

True, Suzanne Pleshette, Stefanie Powers and Angie Dickinson had all starred in prime time shows recently. They were close to, if not over, forty, but they were also 100 per cent American. Chloe wondered for the umpteenth time if her British accent would hamper her chances.

She rolled down the window as she approached the guard at the studio gate. He wore a clear plastic cover over his policeman's hat, and barked at her in an unfriendly way, 'Name?'

'Carriere,' said Chloe. 'I'm here to test for "Saga".'

'Oh, yes – report to makeup, Stage Five.' He peered into Chloe's face, letting raindrops drip from his visor down her neck. 'Don't I know you? Didn't you used to be Chloe Carriere, the singer?'

'I still am,' said Chloe calmly, having endured this type of conversation with strangers for the past six or seven years.

'Well, I'll be damned,' said the cop, smiling now. 'I used to *love* your records, Miss Carriere – played them all the time

131

when I was in high school.' Chloe winced. *High school!* The man was at least forty-five judging from his weatherbeaten face; he was *older* than her high school!

'How do I get to Stage Five?' she asked, politely cutting him off before he had a chance to get effusive.

'Turn left at Ladies' Wardrobe . . . see that cross light? . . . then make a right at Stage Seven and then another right past the Administration Building and you'll run right into it. Good luck, Miss Carriere.' He saluted her goodbye and Chloe, obeying the five miles an hour speed limit, drove to Stage Five.

She parked in a visitors' parking space as a young girl with waist-length blonde hair ran eagerly up to her. 'Hi, I'm Debbie, the trainee second assistant director on "Saga", if you'll just follow me, I'll show you to your dressing room, they're not quite ready for you in makeup yet.'

In a seven-by-seven foot shoe box called a dressing room Chloe regarded the lilac satin peignoir in a clear plastic bag hanging on one of the metal hooks hammered inexpertly into thin, cracked plywood. A pair of satin shoes dyed to match was placed carefully on the one piece of furniture, a brown couch. Next to the shoes lay two envelopes of Caress panty hose, one Beige Glow, the other Tawny Tan, and three pairs of rhinestone earrings of various sizes. They winked at her in the light from the flyspecked lightbulb hanging shadeless from the ceiling of this cell. There was a tiny dressing table with a cracked mirror in which she could see herself only if she hunched down two feet. There was a rickety chair, and covering the yellow-and-black linoleum a threadbare rug with 'Property of MCPC Studio' stencilled on it in fading black.

What a dump, thought Chloe à la Bette Davis, hanging her raincoat on the other hook behind the door. But you've seen worse, she said to herself. *Much* worse! The English provinces – nothing could ever be more disgusting than that rat hole infested with cockroaches she had dressed in while appearing at the Alhambra Theatre, Basingstoke, in 1968. Compared to that, this was a palace.

Too restless to just sit, Chloe stared out of the tiny window. She found she could almost see into the window of the large trailer with 'Makeup' stencilled in lipstick red on the door. She wished she could see what was going on in there.

Makeup was a hive of activity. Although it was already seven-thirty, Sabrina's face was not yet finished, Ben was applying peach blusher on her lids and cheeks, while Barry, the third assistant, fretted in the doorway.

'How much longer, Ben?' he asked the bearded giant with the delicate fingers.

'As long as it takes, Barry.'

'And how long is that – pray?' Barry fumed. Ned, the first A.D. would jump on him if the actors weren't ready on time. Today with all these divas and old-time stars coming in to test, it was an assistant director's nightmare. He realized that a one-and-a-half-hour makeup and hair call, which when discussed at the production meeting had seemed ample time to get each actress ready, was not nearly long enough. The youngest and most beautiful of all, Sabrina – every time he looked at her he swallowed hard, she was so gorgeous – spoke to him sweetly.

'I'm ready now, Barry.' She flashed him the world's most breathtaking smile and Barry inwardly swooned. Having just recovered from a year-long crush on Jackie Smith, which had caused him many sleepless nights, he did not want his eager heart to plunge again. Barry continued to worship from afar.

Robert Johnson, the actor known as 'A.N. Other' on the call sheet, had been hired today to play opposite all six of the leading ladies. He had been a minor TV star in the fifties in Steve McQueen's TV series 'Wanted: Dead or Alive', and his conversation was peppered with references to 'Steve and I', as in 'When Steve and I went cycle racing in 'fifty-two . . . When Steve and I went sailing . . . When Steve and I pulled those broads in Acapulco. . . .' He leaned against the door, trying, unsuccessfully to engage Sabrina in some sexual eye contact.

Sabrina wished that this good ole boy would stop un-dressing her with his hot eyes, but she was too polite to say so.

She smiled pleasantly as he rambled on about his adventures with Steve.

In the next chair sat Rozalinde, her hair in soft pink rollers, a black-and-white-striped cover over her shoulders, while Nora, the other makeup person, deftly applied frosted eye shadow to her lids. Nora did not approve of frosted eye shadow. It looked common, and it caked into the crinkly crevices of the eyelids of anyone over twenty-five. Certainly it looked wonderful in the current Revlon ads, on their eighteen-year-old models' flawless baby skins, but on Rozalinde it looked hard and old.

Rozalinde held a hand mirror while she applied lashings of thick black mascara. She hummed gently to herself along with the samba music from the radio she had brought along. She had also brought boxes of chocolates for all the hair and makeup crew and a magnum of champagne for the director of photography, which she had given him with a kiss and a sly 'Now, darling, you promise you'll give me the key light only directly *above* the camera, *yes*? And don't forget the eye light too, darling.'

Lazlo Dominick, who had lit every top actress in Hollywood since Fay Wray, knew all the tricks in the book. He winked at her and agreed. He would have lit her that way anyhow, but the champagne was a nice thought, so perhaps he might give her a little more care than the others. He whistled inwardly when Sabrina Jones, dressed in a pale peach satin négligé, drifted onto the set. What a looker, he thought as did the rest of the crew, who all stood a little taller and watched their language. Sabrina's innocence, freshness and niceness brought out the best in men. The director, another old Hollywood hand, Marvin Laskey, discussed the scene with her and tried to put her at ease. Since she was already at ease, secure in her beauty, fully aware that since she was completely wrong for this part she would not get it, Sabrina gave him her dazzling smile and her full attention.

'They're ready for you in makeup now, Miss Carriere,' said

Debbie brightly. Chloe walked the ten yards from the tiny shoe box to the vast shoe box that housed the makeup department. The rain had stopped, and a rainbow shimmered in the lightening sky. A good omen, she thought as she stepped into the room. The first person she bumped into was Rozalinde.

'Chloe – *chica* – Chloe, how are you doing?' Rozalinde noted that Chloe didn't look bad, considering her face was totally nude of makeup, and she had pulled her hair straight back. She looked severe, somewhat sexless. No wonder Josh had strayed, thought Rozalinde.

Chloe tried to be polite as she slid into the black leatherette chair and let Ben examine her face. She observed that even though everything was muddy from the rain, Rozalinde was wearing high-heeled black strappy sandals through which her toenail polish showed chipped and discoloured. She recalled Sissy's sneering at 'the Mexican trash basket', and smiled to herself.

'Hurry *up* for Christ's sake. We're late enough already,' Sissy yelled to her chauffeur. Harry merely shrugged. If they were late, it certainly wasn't his fault. He had been told to be at the Sharps' Bel Air Mansion at eight and he had been there on the dot. Madam had appeared at eight twenty-five, cursing like a truck driver, expecting him to get her to the studio in the pouring rain in five minutes. Well, he wasn't about to risk life and limb to do it – neither his nor the old cow's. He kept to the 35 mph speed limit and to his usual careful driving in spite of her furious shrieks to get a move on.

Having read and reread the call sheet the night before, she had hardly been able to sleep, so enraged was she that there were now no less than *six* actresses testing. SIX!! It was ridiculous. Although she had used every contact she had in this town to get this test, she was filled with bitter rage that she was actually lowering herself to do it.

'Do you realize how *demeaning* it is for me to test –especially with that Mexican slut in the running?' she had spat at Sam as he relaxed in his armchair attempting to watch a ball game on TV.

'Yes, dear, I do,' said Sam, imperceptibly pressing the up volume on his remote. 'But you wanted to test, Sissy. You used enough pressure on Abby to get this test. You can't back out now, dear. You will look foolish.'

One thing Sissy Sharp did not relish was looking foolish. She glared at her husband, who was totally involved in the Lakers' game, and flounced off the bed in quest of an early night; but sleep eluded her in spite of three Valium and eventually a Mogadon taken in desperation at three o'clock. She tossed and turned all night, her mind in a whirl about the test and her competition. At half past six she eventually nodded off.

Bonita, her maid, had brought a spartan breakfast on a white wicker bed tray into her bedroom promptly at seven. '*Buenos días, señora,*' Bonita whispered, drawing the drapes to reveal the sodden palm trees, which dripped relentlessly over the six-acre estate.

Sissy mumbled, turned over in bed and, ignoring the glass of hot water with lemon juice and the sliced pineapple, continued to sleep.

Only when Sam, leaving for his twice weekly squash game, woke her for the second time did Sissy jump out of bed, overturning the wicker tray onto the Porthault sheets and screaming blue murder at everyone in sight, including her Pekingese dogs, Edwards and Lowell.

Now, swathed in a new sable cape, with matching crêpe de Chine blouse, gabardine trousers and polished boots, an Hermès silk scarf covering her hair and immense Raybans covering her bloodshot eyes, she perched on the edge of the backseat of her Rolls and yelled at the driver to hurry.

'Yes, your name?' said the cop at the gate. Sissy glared at him venomously through the smoked glass of the Rolls.

Peasant, didn't he go to the cinema? If she got this part, he would be fired immediately.

'Ms Sissy Sharp, testing for "Saga",' said Harry deferentially, with a wink at the cop. Sissy gritted her teeth. Harry was in the firing line now.

'Oh, of course. Hi, Sissy.' The cop smiled familiarly, waving them on.

Sissy gave her dressing quarters a sharp inspection. Knowing that most TV actors are given cubbyhole dressing rooms or tiny trailers, she had insisted on borrowing her husband's lavish motor-home, supplied by the studio, for the test. It was fully furnished with a bed, a stove, a television set and a makeup mirror surrounded by flattering pink lights.

Sissy had been used to making films in the days when stars were given the delicate treatment they expected – treated like hothouse orchids, fawned over by everyone. The age of television had spawned a new bunch of overly young and eager, or over-the-hill but grateful stars, who didn't care a hell of a lot if they had to dress in a garage, they were so thrilled to be working. Then, if their show became a prime time hit, they became excessively demanding. They would then insist on every sort of perk from a cellular telephone to a private sauna, and, in the case of some female stars, on days off for their menstrual periods, and breast feeding privileges for the infants they often insisted on bringing to work with them.

Each season, network executives observed with a mixture of dread and greed the rise to stardom of obscure actors or actresses. Eager to work initially for a reasonable salary, they soon become complaining, dissatisfied autocrats who, believing their own publicity, wield their newly gained power over the studio, the producers and the network. The networks liked to create stars, but not superstars. 'The bigger the stars, the more the public loves 'em, the bigger the monsters they all become,' Abby said ruefully. This happened a couple of times each season. The public's obsession with new fresh faces on the box guaranteed that new TV stars were born each year.

'We've *got* to keep them in their place, dammit,' cried Gertrude. 'I *insist* that we make everyone on "Saga" equal – equal salaries for all.'

137

'Impossible,' Abby interjected. 'We've got young kids and established stars. You can't give 'em all equal salaries – don't be a fool.'

'Well, we must *try* to keep equality in other things then,' said Gertrude implacably. 'There will be no fancy-shmancy dressing rooms, Abby. No free gowns, no unlimited phone bills. No privileges other than the privilege of working for *us* on "Saga".'

'Try it, Gert.' Abby smiled cynically. 'Just try it, hon. It'll never work, you know it. We've already set a precedent with Sam Sharp. He's getting a godamn limo, a massive motor-home, Doug Hayward flying from London to make his fucking suits. It's a wonder we don't have a unit cocksucker in his contract to keep him happy on his lunch hour. God knows what else. Do you *really* think our other stars aren't going to want the same?'

'Sam Sharp is a highly respected motion picture star. He has *earned* his place in the sun,' insisted Gert. 'He has a "favoured nations" clause in his contract. No *one* can get a salary within fifteen thousand of his.'

'Yeah, we're not paying him peanuts, thanks to you, Gert,' said Abby, angrily lighting his third cigar of the day. 'Thirty-five grand an episode for a new show for an over-the-hill actor is *steep*, baby, it's *steep*.'

'Abby, the character of Steve Hamilton is highly important to the success of "Saga". You *know* that,' Gertrude said stiffly. 'If he is not the quintessential patriarch with inbred qualities of leadership and a dynamic force, *we have no show*. In Sam Sharp we have all of these qualities. They are built into his character throughout the years of playing all of those fine Yankee gentlemen. Plus of course his TVQ is tremendous. His last three films did at least a Nielsen forty share in prime time.'

'Yeah, and bombed at the box office,' said Abby flatly.

'He's a major star,' insisted Gertrude.

'He's a has-been,' sighed Abby.

'We *need* him,' persisted Gertrude.

'O.K., O.K. Maybe you're right, Gert. Maybe he *is* a star, but he's also a fucking faggot. How are we going to keep *that* out of the garbage magazines?'

'Very easily,' said Gertrude. 'Since he has pulled the wool over the public's eyes for thirty years, there is no reason he cannot continue to do so. *Particularly* if we cast Sissy as Miranda.'

'What? Sissy? That shrivelled cooze? Oh, c'mon. She's *wrong*, the wrong woman for Miranda. I'm only testing her as a favour to Sam. She could never play Miranda. Miranda is sexy, feminine, voluptuous. Sissy's too – too – ' he fumbled for the word.

'Hard?' asked Gertrude.

'Yeah. Hard, ball-breaking hard. She lacks – '

'Sex appeal?' murmured Gertrude.

'Yeah. Miranda's gotta have tons of the old SA.'

'She's a brilliant actress, Abby,' said Gertrude.

'Yup – in the right role, tremendous. I don't deny that, but I don't know many guys who would want to get it up for her.'

'Well, let's think about her for Sirope, then?' said Gertrude.

'Sirope! For Christ's sake, the woman's supposed to be the fuckin' Virgin Mary. She's Ingrid Bergman before Rosselini, Doris Day with Little Red Riding Hood thrown in. We need a *saint* for Sirope. And there ain't many saints in this city, particularly forty-year-old ones.'

'Let's try her,' said Gertrude with a wheedling smile. 'I think she'll be wonderful. A bitch playing a saint – it's inspired casting, Abby.'

'Oh, God, Gert. She's all wrong.'

'Abby, Abby – what can we lose? She's a fabulous actress, she still looks good – she's got that tired angelic look. A bit of a pain, I admit.'

'A *bit*?' Abby threw in. 'I know ten directors who would rather direct the shark in *Jaws* than work with her. But O.K. O.K. – O.K. – if you think it could affect the Sam Sharp situation. We shall test. She's testing for both parts.'

'Right?' said Gertrude, knowing she'd won. 'It's the test that counts, don't it, Abby?'

Sissy had decidedly mixed feelings about testing for both Miranda and Sirope. She couldn't decide whether the network was paying her a compliment or hedging their bets. She sat on the brown suede sofa in Sam's motor-home, looking at the bottle of Dom Perignon in an ice bucket, the six-ounce can of Sevruga caviar and the Lalique dish containing grated egg, brown bread and finely shredded onion.

'Welcome to a star, Love, Abby and Gertrude' was written on the gilt-edged card. A Baccarat vase full of white lilies and cream roses reposed on the mahogany coffee table with another note: 'Rooting for you my darling, Your Sam.'

She grimaced. *Why* did he always send her lilies? They were only for funerals. God knows she had told him often enough she detested them, even told his florist, but still they arrived on every occasion where floral tributes were appropriate. Lilies and cream roses. How boring!

The orchid was much more attractive – a cymbidium in a plain stone pot. The card simply said, 'Kill 'em'. It was from Robin Felix, her new agent – a man who knew very well how to keep his clients, and his temper, unlike her ex-agent, Doug. Sissy as a client was a lucrative proposition, but sometimes, without a doubt she was simply the most difficult of any female stars Robin had ever handled. However, he felt she had the inside track to the role of Sirope – which he knew she was right for, and he was going to be right there when the big TV bucks came rolling in.

'Ready for you, Miss Sharp.' Debbie was deferential as she knocked at the door of the motor-home. Sissy was the only actress testing today occupying one. The others were all in the egg boxes. 'Can I get you something to eat or drink?'

'No, thank you, my dear,' said Sissy grandly. 'I never eat or drink before a performance. Just see that the prop man puts a bottle of Perrier water and a packet of Dunhill cigarettes next to my chair and make sure that chair is right next to the one of the lighting cameraman, Mr Dominick.'

'Right away, Miss Sharp,' chirped Debbie, scampering away.

Sissy entered the makeup room by one door as Rozalinde exited the other. Ben was putting the finishing touch to Chloe's face. She looked radiantly exciting. This was a completely different face from the pale, washed-out visage of this morning. Witchy, bitchy, sexy, exotic, yet soft – Ben had done his work well, although Chloe had the basic beauty to let his craft express itself.

She looks common, thought Sissy, who believed any woman weighing over one hundred pounds, with a chest measurement of more than thirty-three inches, common. Common and overweight. The ladies nodded briefly and then ignored each other as De-De, the body makeup girl, dabbed 'Beige Blush' pancake onto Chloe's cleavage.

When Chloe finally walked onto the set at ten-thirty, her palms were sweating. Sabrina and Rozalinde had finished their tests and had left. The crew was taking a coffee-and-doughnut break. Robert Johnson came up and smilingly reintroduced himself.

'Last time we met was at a party at Steve's, when he was married to Ali. I was the guy that went on the cycle race over the Trancas dunes with him. You were cheering us on like crazy – remember?'

Chloe didn't, but she made all the right noises.

The director came in to discuss the scene.

Chloe half-listened. She had her own ideas about this character – definite ones. And she was going to play it her way.

Pandora King strolled into the makeup room to give Chloe a quick hug and an effusive 'Hello, darling!' Pandora was sharp, a good trouper, with no side to her. Except for her enormous makeup case, which went with her everywhere, she was just like a rather acerbic woman next door.

'Darling, darling, we *must* have lunch and discuss this

insanity. I'm testing for both roles – isn't it a riot?' She laughed, showing strong white teeth and too much gum. Even though she hadn't been made up yet, she wore a light layer of base, lip gloss, blusher, eye liner, and a tousled blonde wig. She was not a beautiful woman, but she made the best of herself and would never be caught dead without her face on. 'Ready, Miss Carriere?' Debbie popped her head around the door. 'As soon as you're dressed, they'd like you on the set.'

Chloe stood in the centre of the magnificent set, feeling more relaxed. Milton had staged the scene much the way she had envisioned it. Now it was time for her to perform to the ultimate. Robert stood behind the camera ready to give her lines off. 'O.K., ready, darling?' asked Milton. 'Yes, fine. I'm ready.' Ben dusted her cheeks with a puff, Theo fluffed out her thick dark curls, Trixie fussed with the lace around her shoulders, Hank brought a tape measure to her nose and called out a number, Lazlo held a light box to her face and called instructions to a shadowy figure twenty feet up in the gantry. Big John and Reggie rearranged lights behind her head.

'O.K., Chuck, take it down a tad,' called Lazlo to the figure in the gantry.

'Right,' called Chuck. Now they had all left. Now Chloe was alone with the camera to record her emotions, her passions. Alone even though seventy-five men and women stood idly by observing her – judging her. Alone. It was time to show them.

'Aaaaand – *Action*,' yelled Milton.

' "I never loved you, Steve," ' said Chloe to Robert calmly, feeling the fire of Miranda building inside her. She remembered the last time she had talked with Josh. *The last time.* She used the emotion that came welling out of her. ' "To me, you were someone to be used, because you always used me. Someone who could get me what I wanted – what I needed." '

' "I don't believe you, Miranda," ' said Robert quietly, with dignity.

' "It's true, Steve. As God is my witness, it's true. How could I love you when I *knew* you killed Nicholas?" ' Her eyes were filling with tears now. Real tears. She felt her throat aching, and she had to use her actor's control to stop the tears from carrying her away.

' "That's a damn lie and you know it." '

' "Oh, no, Steve. I have the proof. You see, I was there that night, when you thought you were alone with Nicholas." ' Chloe took a step towards the camera and started to build her intensity. Her nerves felt raw. For two pages she gave the scene everything she could, every nuance, every emotion. Her experiences in life added to her fire. She berated Robert, scorned him, declared that her love for her dead lover, Nicholas, would never end, and that she would hate Steve until her dying day and would do anything to destroy him. Throughout the scene, she thought of Josh. It was Josh she was pouring out her heart to. Josh who had destroyed a part of her that was hollow now, empty – miserable. She thought of how she had loved him with such passion, of how she could love him again if only . . . if only . . .

When she finished the scene, sweat was dripping down her robe and tears down her face. Milton yelled out in delight, and several crew members broke into spontaneous applause. 'And *print*! That was fabulous darling, absolutely *fabulous*. We don't need another one, you're *great*.'

'Check the gate,' yelled Hank.

'It's O.K.,' the operator, Bill, said. 'Thank you, darling, thank you,' Milton enthused. 'You were wonderful, you brought tears to my eyes.' He bent his head and whispered, 'I hope you get it.'

Gratefully Chloe walked off the stage. Her coterie of helpers had deserted her and gone off to attend the next testee. She got out of the lilac negligee herself, combed her hair free of the sticky hairspray and ripped off the false eyelashes. As she finished dressing, she saw through the mirror that Emerald and Co. had arrived.

*　　*　　*

143

Emerald never travelled light, never alone, and never on time – a reaction to her childhood as a baby star, when she had had to get up at five each day and live her day by the call sheet. When she was thirty, her contract finally expired after twenty-seven years of living by the clock. Emerald vowed she would never do it again.

Today she was forty-five minutes late, which for her was almost punctual. She looked great. Her blonde hair was freshly bleached, framing her chiselled, newly tucked face, and her figure was as curvy as it had been in the fifties. Behind her marched a battalion of her troops: her personal assistant and man Friday, Rick Rock-Savage, her manager and agent, Lulu Pierce, and her public relations man, Christopher McCarthy. Lulu was large and nasty, and Christopher was small and sweet. Together they balanced each other out. Christopher's main job was fending off the dozens of calls and inquiries that still came into his office each week for Emerald's availability to do interviews, talk shows, attend openings, appear at charities and attend premieres. Public interest in her had never waned, although she could not get a decent movie job in the States.

Emerald greeted everyone in makeup and hair like an old friend; she had worked with them all through the years, and they adored her.

'I *want* this job, Ben,' she said seriously to the bearded giant. 'Make me look better than any of them.'

'I'll try, darling. I'll do my very best,' said Ben, looking at her with professional objectivity.

'How was the English girl's test?' asked Emerald a mite too casually.

'Oh, er, good. She was very good.' Ben didn't have the heart to tell her that Chloe had been great; it could affect her performance. 'But I gotta tell you, darling, we had a gal in here this morning prettier than Lana in her heyday. We can't beat *her*, 'cause she's just a baby, but I guarantee we'll beat the others.'

'I need this job, Ben.' Emerald looked into her old friend's eyes. 'Do your damnedest for me, you hear?'

She smiled the dazzling smile that had graced a thousand magazine covers and sank into the black leather chair.

12

For the six women, the following days were not easy. Only Sabrina banished thoughts of the role from her mind. She had been offered a feature movie in which she would play a seventeenth century virgin transported by time warp to a modern day college campus. She was more interested in that. The part would pay her two hundred thousand dollars, and could make her a major movie star. Then she would be ready to play opposite Al Pacino or Richard Gere, she hoped. She was continuing with her acting classes, while her nights were filled with love and Luis.

'TV is for old actors,' she confided to Sue, her agent. 'Movies are where it's *at*, and that's where I wanna be!'

Each of the six women had her own individual method of getting through the agonizing waiting period, since it was going to be at least three weeks before the network executives made their decision.

Pandora went to Las Vegas to visit her current boyfriend, a young Bortsch Belt comedian, where she spent her time in bed with him or engrossed at the blackjack table.

Chloe stayed at the beach house. She took long walks along the coast, contemplating her future if she failed to get the part. The marriage with Josh was over. Lawyers had taken over the question of the divorce settlement. When necessary, she and Josh spoke by phone; the conversations were like those of casual acquaintances. He told her about his new record; he said he was working hard on the new scenario for his London play.

After dinner she went straight to bed, restlessly switching channels, comparing herself to Farrah, Jackie, Cheryl, Stefanie and Angie, which only made her more depressed.

One day Johnny Swanson called to invite her out. What the hell? she thought. He seems like a nice guy. Who cares if he's years younger than I am? The older woman-younger man couple is all the rage these days.

Johnny came to the beach house in a black Porsche 911 Turbo. Of course he *would* have a black Porsche, thought Chloe. It was the ultimate phallic symbol. As she climbed in and looked around the sleek car, she was amused by the way Johnny had fitted it out like a mini-office. Next to the driver's seat was the latest-model cellular phone with automatic dialling for twenty-five numbers. A microphone above the sun visor assured Johnny that he could always hear and be heard on the phone, even while going through tunnels. A highly complex stereo system with four speakers installed in strategic spots amplified Chloe's own mellow voice as she heard a recording of herself singing, 'From This Moment On'.

She smiled, flattered in spite of herself. He certainly knew how to charm. He'd then put on her own favourite recording – an old album of Cole Porter and Gershwin classics. He was definitely very classy, very smooth, and as she looked at his profile, blond hair artfully curling over a black polo neck, very attractive.

In the back of the car was a small TV set, attached to the back of one of the seats, and a well-stocked bar plus a miniature fridge.

'Drink?' offered Johnny, turning left on the Pacific Coast Highway.

'No, thanks – it's illegal in the car,' Chloe replied,

remembering Josh's recent trouble. 'The police are tough on you if you're caught.'

'No sweat, sugar, my uncle's the chief of police down here.' Johnny laughed. 'Here have one of these instead.' He offered her an expertly rolled joint.

'No, I don't. Thanks,' said Chloe, feeling rather old-fashioned. In spite of her years around musicians and rock stars she still hated druggies.

She hadn't been out on a 'date' in a long time – since before Josh – over ten years. She felt strange. Strange and archaic. Johnny didn't seem to be fazed that she didn't want a toke, and he chatted amiably until they arrived at a picturesque restaurant nestled in a tiny street behind Topanga Canyon. The owner knew him well, greeting him effusively, and Johnny seemed at home there, even knowing the names of most of the waiters.

Throughout dinner Chloe felt herself warming to him. Despite his brash exterior he was delightful. Witty, charming, lively, handsome – a veritable cornucopia of male goodies. His sense of humour reminded her of Josh – a youthful Josh. So he was young – so what? thought Chloe, feeling abandoned and young herself after they had drunk two bottles of champagne. Twenty-nine wasn't *that* young.

Arm in arm they walked into the cool California night. 'Look – stars. Maybe the world is coming to an end,' Johnny said. 'I haven't seen stars in California for years.'

'Where's the smog? L.A.'s not L.A. without it,' Chloe laughed. She felt ebullient, as if a weight had fallen from her shoulders. She liked Johnny more and more, even though she knew his reputation with women. Well, she was a mature adult now, not a naïve young woman as she had been with Josh. She was not going to be hurt, whatever happened.

This they would play by *her* rules.

As the black Porsche pulled into her driveway, she invited him in for coffee.

'Never touch it,' said Johnny, as he opened the door in his

gallant English public-school manner. 'I'll take a cognac though. Or an Armagnac if you have it.'

They sat before the flickering fire, sipped Armagnac and talked. She had turned the lights off, and through the big picture window the sky was filled with a million stars. They started exchanging pieces of the jigsaw puzzle of their lives that might one day, if their relationship progressed, form a complete picture.

His lips eventually touched hers, and she found herself responding. His mouth was insistent, seductive, sweet. His hands touched her face, then fluttered to the buttons on her silk blouse. It had been a long time since Chloe had been caressed. It was all too sweet, all too tender.

She tried to draw back as a vision of Josh came to her.

This was wrong, wrong, wrong. Johnny was too young for her. It was too soon after Josh. She wasn't ready. He would tell the boys at Ma Maison. He would boast about her. *Josh*, her inner voice screamed silently. Josh, oh, Josh, I don't want this. I don't. I want you. She tried to put the brakes on, then realized how ridiculous it was. A forty-year-old woman acting like a girl. Necking like an adolescent. Smooching as though she were sixteen again. 'No, I can't. I'm sorry, I just can't, Johnny.' She pushed his tender, insistent mouth away, and his hands, which were expertly but gently pulling on her skirt now.

'Why *not?*' His voice was hoarse; he became more insistent. He kissed her again and again. He seemed to know where she wanted to be kissed and his lips were there, turning her into a furnace against her will.

She had no answer. She felt weak. She wanted him. She hadn't been with Josh for months now. This, their third separation, looked as though it would be their last. She certainly wasn't in love with Johnny, but he was attractive and she found him sexually appealing.

Why not? She felt surges of desire building within her. She wanted him to take her now. She felt the hunger of her sexual need.

149

Suddenly it didn't seem worthwhile to fight him any more. Go with it, she thought. To hell with tomorrow. To hell with Josh. To hell with what people think. With thoughts of Josh filling her head and her heart, she let Johnny Swanson take her to bed.

During the difficult weeks of waiting, Emerald went on a social whirl. Ever popular, she accepted every party, every luncheon, every premiere. She emptied her diminishing bank account on dozens of new outfits. Her business manager despaired, but she smiled deliciously and continued to spend.

Sissy punished her body religiously. She lost three more pounds on a magic new diet of Chinese seaweed, rice cakes and kiwi fruit. She spent her mornings jogging, doing yoga and exercising, and her afternoons on the phone with Daphne and Robin Felix, her agent, discussing her chances.

Rozalinde Lamaze spent a great deal of time in her sunny little kitchen indulging in two of her favourite pastimes: cooking and watching soap operas on Channel 8, the Spanish station. At the moment she was preparing refried beans and rice, which smelled delicious. She couldn't wait to devour them with her young niece, Angelica, and later devour Angelica. The two of them sat in the breakfast nook eating beans and rice as, enthralled, they watched Lolita Lopez, great Mexican star of the fifties, emoting in 'Mis Niños y Mis Hombres', a favourite of the Spanish speaking community of L.A.

Rozalinde was happy just pottering in her house. She was a simple woman at heart. Simple in everything but sex. She had become bored by the sexual embraces of her numerous lovers over the past few years. The weight of their thick bodies, their heavy breathing, their sweating hot flesh, their smells of alcohol and tobacco had started to repel her.

Recently, each time she had let a man make love to her, she had tried to feel *some* sort of excitement and had felt nothing.

150

When she failed to respond, she impatiently sent them away, finding sensation with her fingers. That too, soon began to pale. When Angelica, her cute little eighteen-year-old niece, came to stay, she found to her delight that they had a lot more in common than a love for refried beans and Channel 8 soap operas.

These days nothing could compare to the enthralling nights she spent exploring and being explored by the delicate body of the young Angelica.

When Chloe's agent called and said that Dionne Warwick had suddenly been taken ill and couldn't perform at the Las Vegas Empire Hotel, Chloe jumped at the opportunity to fill in for her. She would be getting away from Johnny, who was pestering her now, wanting what she didn't have to give him. She realized that her attraction to him was diminishing more rapidly than she even dreamed was possible. What had been for her a minor fling to get her over Josh had meant more to him, and he was insistent on seeing her more than she wanted to see him.

'Singing again will get your mind off the waiting, duckie,' said Jasper soothingly.

'You're right, Jasper, this waiting's too much even for my nerves of steel,' Chloe said gratefully.

'Can you leave the day after tomorrow?' He sounded anxious. 'Be ready for a nine o'clock show.'

'What?' gasped Chloe. 'Jasper, I know we're both British and can do anything, of course, but *darling*, I haven't rehearsed. I haven't even sung a note since the last tour ended.'

'That was only two months ago, my dear,' Jasper chimed in smoothly. 'If you can take the company plane from Burbank on Thursday at one o'clock, you can be rehearsing in the Copa Room at three. You can sing your little heart out for four hours. Surely that's enough for a silver-throated talented nightingale like you, my love?'

'Bullshit, Jasper!' Chloe smiled in spite of herself. 'Actu-

151

ally, though, it could be rather exciting; at least it will give me something to do to take my mind off that bloody *test*.'

'Good girl, clever girl.' Jasper's voice was soothing. 'I have the hotel over a barrel moneywise, darling. Not quite what Dionne was getting, naturally, but forty-five grand a week, how does that grab you, my love?'

'It will keep the wolf from the door and help me at Valentino for a while.' Chloe was mentally going through her wardrobe. 'O.K., Jasper, I'll see you at the airport. I must pack now.'

Chloe filled her suitcases swiftly and efficiently. Twenty years on the road had enabled her to pack what was necessary in minimum time. She surveyed her rack of beaded evening dresses critically as she skimmed through other racks, selecting and eliminating with an expert eye. She packed a red bugle-beaded Bob Mackie slit to the thigh, with a 'Merry Widow', also beaded in red, and another in black lace. A silver lace and nude chiffon Nolan Miller, accented on the broad padded shoulders with exquisite appliquéd flowers, went in along with a sleek black silk jersey Chanel, the flute-shaped sleeves trimmed in black fox. A white lace Valentino dotted with pearls and rhinestones, his masterful cut accenting the simplicity and purity of the long, slightly fitted gown, completed her selection of stage gowns. Chloe surveyed them while waiting for her maid to bring her black wardrobe skips and tissue paper.

Next she surveyed her two racks of short, informal evening outfits, dresses and suits that she changed into after the show, when she would either go out to dine or cut a swath through the casinos of the Vegas strip. Three Saint-Laurent suits and three Bruce Oldfields, two or three Versaces, one Donna Karen, and her favourite dress, a black lace point d'esprit, designed by herself and made by Freddy Langlan. Was that enough for two weeks? God forbid she should ever be seen offstage in the same outfit more than once. Suppose Sinatra was performing at Caesar's? Barbara would certainly be there, too. Las Vegas was a small community. They would all be at the same parties every night. Be prepared. Better too much than too little.

She hastily picked out two more short dresses, a Karl Lagerfeld and an Anthony Price and gave instructions to Manuela to pack the correct accessories, which were neatly stored in appropriate boxes under each dress. Chloe was exceedingly organized about her clothes. Each outfit she considered an investment, and she took great care of them.

She scooped up an armful of assorted sweaters, shirts and skirts, threw them on the bed and went to her jewellery drawers. An entire chest of small drawers contained her extensive collection of costume jewellery. Not for her the responsibility of real jewels. With the exception of her sapphire-and-diamond ring and a diamond Boncheran watch, she only wore faux jewels. Her collection was fabulous, extremely expensive, and much admired.

Manuela had finished packing the theatrical gowns and accessories in the black skips, and was now filling her burgundy ostrich suitcases.

Johnny had called this morning murmuring something about meeting Richard Hurrel at the gym, then lunching with 'the boys' at Ma Maison.

As Chloe rolled her hair and rapidly applied makeup, she tried to ring him at the gym. He was not there. Ma Maison expected him at one-thirty. She left a short message with his secretary.

'Where you going?' Sally appeared at the door without knocking as usual. She was sporting a new punk hairdo and her usual sarcastically belligerent attitude.

'What are you doing here?' Chloe asked as evenly as she could.

'I'm picking up some more of my things. Dad bought me an apartment in the Wilshire Towers. I'm decorating it myself.' She fingered one of Chloe's Gallé vases carelessly.

'I'm doing it modern, of course. State of the art. High tech.'

'How nice,' said Chloe pleasantly, wishing the girl would leave and stop touching her things.

Sally's hair had been shaved two inches above her ears, and what was left had been dyed into jet-black and silver stripes and sprayed with a lacquer so strong that seven- and eight-inch spikes stood up all over her head. Her lipstick was purple, as was her eye paint. She wore an incredible outfit – a purple vinyl skirt, barely covering her pubis, silver thigh-high leggings over silver crocheted tights, and an immense lavender mohair sweater which almost covered the skirt. Around her neck was a five-inch statue of Christ on the Cross attached to a tarnished silver chain, and she appeared to have pinned what looked like black bats in her hair. From one ear hung a black rubber snake, the kind sold at toy stores for fifty cents, in the other was one of Chloe's most expensive Dior rhinestone earrings. She seemed high, although it was barely 11 a.m.

'Where are you off to then?' Sally opened and closed the drawers of Chloe's lingerie cabinet, picking up and discarding some of her stepmother's most intimate apparel as she spoke.

'Vegas.' Chloe gritted her teeth in disgust, determined not to rise to the bait that Sally always threw at her.

'Got a gig then?'

'Yup, two weeks at the Empire.' Chloe concentrated on combing out her hair, observing Sally opening her bathroom cabinet and casually inspecting the contents. She seethed but she could hardly throw a teenager into the street.

'Oh, well, I suppose you better get on with your singing career,' Sally said with a sneer. 'It doesn't look like you're gonna get the part, does it?'

Chloe was calm as she finished her face, ever determined not to let this snotty kid girl get to her. 'Why do you think that, Sally?'

'It's in the trades today, haven't you seen it yet?'

'No. Why don't you tell me what it said, dear? I have a plane to catch.'

'It's in Army's column – he said that Rozalinde Lamaze is a shoo-in.' She left the room and returned with the paper. 'Here.'

Chloe glanced at it briefly, her heart sinking.

'It's just conjecture,' she said briskly, checking in her Hermès alligator bag for her lucky mascots.

'Sure,' Sally grinned, revealing a small diamond inserted in her front tooth. 'Well, good luck in Vegas then, Chloe. See ya.'

Chloe noticed that Sally had appropriated a vial of Valium, a mauve chiffon scarf and four silver bracelets before she left.

'Limo's here, Miz Carriere.' Manuela buzzed her. 'He's comin' up now for the bags.'

'Send him up,' said Chloe. 'I'm ready.' And with a deep breath she walked swiftly down the stairs.

Rozalinde read the piece and smiled. Her new press agent had proved his point.

She had agreed to sign with his firm at three thousand dollars a month if they got her into Army Archerd's important trade column within the week. Well, they had done it. They were worth the three grand. She called her business manager and told him to send the cheque.

She glanced at the other side of her bed. It was empty. Angelica had gone to visit her sick mother in Mexico City for the weekend. Three days to work on a tan, thought Rozalinde, luxuriating in her crumpled flowered sheets. And who knows, maybe I *will* get the part. God knows she had said enough Hail Marys, confessed to sins she could barely remember, and lit an extra thirty candles to the Virgin Mary and baby Jesus last Sunday in church. If religion and superstition could guarantee it, she should get Miranda.

Calvin read the item in the gossip column again and again. Cold rage gripped him. What kind of people were these Hollywood morons? Didn't they know a true star when they saw one? How could they *possibly* pass over the most beautiful, talented actress in the world? How could they even *consider* that trumped-up Spanish tart, Rozalinde? It was an outrage. A slur and an insult to Emerald.

Calvin was out every night now with the amateur and professional paparazzi, who hung around outside Spago, Morton's and Chasen's like a pack of wolves, whenever they heard through the grapevine that a party, an opening or a premiere was going on.

He had seldom been disappointed in the past two weeks – Emerald was having one of her social bouts. Desperately insecure about the results of the test, she was hitting the high spots of Tinsel Town with a vengeance.

Emerald had gradually started falling off the wagon. She was furious with herself for her lack of willpower, but she simply couldn't help it. She needed to forget about that damn test. Forget how much she needed that part. Forget the fact that in spite of her mansion and the fabulous jewels, she was almost flat broke. Forget she was well along in her forties and not good marriage material after so many failures. She threw herself into social life with gusto, yet was completely unaware of the slight sandy-haired pale-eyed man who watched her every movement. Each restaurant, each party, each opening she attended, Calvin was there, looking through his lens at Emerald, holding his breath at her beauty, capturing her flesh, her blonde loveliness forever with each click of his shutter.

His room was now a positive shrine to her. Every wall was covered with posters from her films. More than two hundred plastic frames contained her image, many of the pictures taken by him. Huge scrapbooks also filled with her pictures were piled in the bookshelves, along with seventeen of the books that had been written about Emerald's movie career and her even more exciting private life.

He even had one of the Emerald dolls that had been so popular with every little girl in America in the early 1930s when she was a baby star and a box-office champion. The doll was three feet high, with big round sausage-shaped flaxen curls and huge green saucer eyes fringed with thick auburn lashes. The little painted mouth formed a perfect Cupid's bow, and tiny porcelain hands had fingernails that were painted pale pink. The doll had come in a white carrying case, complete with three changes of costume, from a lime-and-white striped bathing suit with a tiny rubber cap and a miniature terry-cloth robe to a frilly green party frock. There was also a little green enamel mirror with comb and brush which could be used to comb the Emerald doll's curls.

Sometimes Calvin sat and did his doll's hair. He would talk to her as he manipulated the nylon curls with his rough hands. 'You *are* Miranda, my lovely girl,' he would croon to the painted face as he turned the curls around his fingers. 'No one, but *no one*, can be her except you.' Lovingly he would change her clothes, pausing often to examine and stroke the smooth, sexless body of the doll. He would put the tiny cotton socks on her perfect feet, then the little black patent-leather Mary Jane shoes.

He loved this doll. But he loved the real Emerald even more.

13

Rozalinde glanced again in the rearview mirror of her BMW. It seemed stupid to be paranoid about this car that appeared to follow her from La Scala to her home on the summit of Mulholland Drive. The car pulled ahead of her and vanished around a corner at high speed. Stupid, but all the same, the voice of reason warned her, as she drove up the long, winding canyon: 'Watch out, *querida*.'

John Lennon's sweet voice poured forth 'Imagine' from her tape deck. She thought about his death – so recent, so sudden, so . . . It could happen to *me*, she thought – it could happen to any of us. To Robert Redford, with his notions about solar energy and conservation. Or to Jane Fonda, with her radical ideals and impossible exercises. To anyone some fanatic became phobic about. To *her*, for no reason at all except that she was a star. She shivered, despite the warmth of the car, as she drew up outside her Mulholland mansion.

Why did I buy a bloody mansion? she asked herself as she sat in the car staring at the ominous outlines of her home. And *why* wouldn't I even consider having a bodyguard? Everyone was getting one these days.

The house looked like something out of Edgar Allen Poe on

this windy night: a grey stone façade, thick black clouds, winds of 50 mph. There was a Santa Ana blowing, and the palm trees swayed violently in the gale. Strange objects – birds? leaves? debris from some unknown holocaust? scudded around the house. Her house. Wrested from the fangs of a money-crazed ex-husband and his ravening Beverly Hills lawyer. Court fights, acrimony, tabloid headlines. Thanks to some brilliant legal manipulations, eventually it became *her* house. Was it worth it, though, this big pile of pewter-coloured brick ersatz nineteenth century, with the latest twentieth-century plumbing?

She cut the engine. It was suddenly still. The wind had dropped with characteristic California suddenness. It was a silent night all right, but far from holy – a silent and venomous night. She felt suddenly fearful.

Calvin sat in the attic observing Rozalinde's hesitation from the tiny window.

He heard her close the car door – her footsteps had a deceptively casual sound – and insert her key into the front-door lock. He heard her call out halfheartedly, 'Rosa, are you back?', proving she had given her housekeeper the night off. The door closed. She was inside. Inside the house with him. Just the two of them, he thought, locked in together. . . .

Soon the TV clicked on in her bedroom. He heard her flushing the toilet as he crept down the stairs and put his ear to the bedroom door.

'Hi, Angelica.' She was talking on the phone. 'I know this is crazy, but I'm spooked tonight.' Calvin smiled to himself. 'I miss you, *querida mía*. Come home to me soon.'

Rozalinde was smiling as she hung up the receiver and popped a chocolate into her lush mouth. As Calvin pushed open the door of her sanctuary, she looked up, startled.

'What do you want?' Suddenly her voice was a dry rasp. The pupils of her beautiful brown eyes dilated to points of fear, and her hands brought the creased comforter up to her body as if she could protect herself with it.

Calvin could sense the animal terror in her as he stood at

the door. He felt himself controlling the situation. Controlling her with his presence.

'Nothing,' he replied slowly. 'I don't want anything at all.' He stood very still, taking in the surroundings. Everything was pink. She sat cross-legged, a crumpled pink comforter pulled up to her waist, a flimsy silken wrapper barely concealing her abundant body. Behind her dark nimbus of curls were piles of pillows embroidered with sayings: 'A hard man is good to find'; 'Happiness is having you for a friend'; 'I come alive at five'. Stuffed animals cluttered the bed, even an old Snoopy.

Calvin jumped as he felt a silken ghost brush his legs and saw a white Persian cat spring off its mistress's bed. The cat crouched under the dust ruffle, peering out. The two of them stared at Calvin with eyes of dread.

Rozalinde swallowed. She thought of what she had read in magazine articles about rapists. How to talk them out of it, be assertive. The stories she had read had said to be ballsy, tough, let him know she was stronger than he, that he could not get the better of her.

'Get the fuck out of this room, you creep!' she shouted in a voice that called upon all of her acting ability. 'How *dare* you come in here? You're trespassing. I'm calling the police.'

Frantically she tried to remember where she had put the panic button. Bel Air Patrol had been absolutely specific when they installed the latest fail-safe burglar alarm. First and foremost, they had instructed her, *always* turn on the alarm when leaving or entering the house. She realized she had ignored that advice tonight, as she had ignored the second warning: *Always* keep the panic button on your person while in the house. When activated, it would send a signal straight to police headquarters, and help would arrive within eight minutes. So they said. She knew it was more like fifteen or twenty minutes because she had pressed the panic button by mistake a couple of times. She *must* keep this maniac talking! Where, oh *where* was the damn panic button? she cried silently to herself.

One hand clasped her robe around her throat as the other crept beneath the rumpled sheets, magazines, pillows and scripts in search of the alarm.

She looked at her bedside table. The pink marble top was obscured by the paraphernalia of her bedtime pastimes. A half-empty wineglass, two coffeecups with congealed contents, an apple with one bite out of it, piles of letters, fan mail, photographs of herself, baby oil, ashtrays overflowing with butts, even, she noticed, a roach. What she would give for a puff now!

This wasn't, *couldn't* be happening to her! Suddenly, she caught sight of the panic button, half hidden under the pile of mail. Time to talk. Time to deal with this madman – for he looked mad, his face soaked with the perspiration that flowed down his forehead, his eyes dilated. He's even more frightened than I am, she told herself – but it didn't help.

Calvin licked his lips. He could taste the warm salt of his sweat. The bitch was talking. It was hard to understand what she was saying, the pounding in his head was so intense, like a hammer. Her lips were moving but he couldn't hear her. As she spoke, her robe parted more. He glimpsed her breasts, her navel, and that other thing. The thing that disgusted yet excited him. Her hand stroked a stuffed teddy bear. He wanted her hand to stroke *him*, but at the same time the thought repelled him. He loathed her femaleness. Hated her moist red mouth, her high, brown-tipped breasts. As she talked, her hand was moving to the bedside table. What was the bitch doing? She had something in her hand, now what was it. A radio? A tape recorder? She continued talking to him. Smiling, looking pleased with herself. Bitch. Cow. Whore. She almost looked as if she were tempting him as she sat on her satin sheets, robe open, stroking her bear and trying to smile.

Suddenly he heard her words: 'You know you're quite a good-looking guy. What's your name, honey?'

Honey! She was calling him 'honey'! What kind of disgusting slut was she? When a man breaks into her room she calmly invites him to seduce her! She was a slut, a tramp. That the network were even *considering* her for the same part as Emerald was an abomination. *She* was an abomination, he told himself. He walked towards her slowly. The pounding started in his head again. He saw only her actions – her seductive smile, her calm voice. As he came close to her her smile faded. A whimper escaped her.

'Don't hurt my face, please,' she said in a feeble, little-girl voice.

'Your face?' The fact that she cared so much about it made him want to smash into it. 'What face?' He picked up a large bronze statue and brought it down with all his force on her upturned, pleading face.

'No, please, no!' Blood streamed from her forehead. 'I'll do anything. You can take me, do what you want, but please, please don't kill me, don't, don't, I beg you.'

'Whore!' he screamed as his hands encircled her white throat, slippery now with her blood. 'Bitch!'

The cat jumped fearfully away, its back arched as it tried to get out of the room, but the door was closed.

When Calvin had finished with her he gazed at her voluptuous nude body splayed on the satin comforter. In spite of himself the urge to ravish her was so strong that he hated her even more for this feeling she aroused. She was stretched out in such a way, her blank celluloid stare and limp flesh curiously erotic, that he could not help himself. The white cat cowered in fright, low yowls emanating from its throat as it watched Calvin perform the ultimate horror. As Calvin finally drew away from the still body he heard police sirens in the street.

By the time the police reached the house he was gone. Only the white cat hiding under a sofa was witness to what had happened.

Chloe stared horrified at the headline: 'ROZALINDE LAMAZE SLAIN – RAPED.' She put down the paper, shaking her head in

disbelief: Rozalinde dead, horribly murdered. It was unbelievable. What was even more horrible was the message
scrawled obscenely in lipstick across the body: '*You won't be the
last.*'

Chloe shuddered, pushing away the poached eggs and
grapefruit juice the hotel waiter had placed before her.

The TV set was tuned to the local Las Vegas news
programme. She switched channels with the remote to hear
more. After every programme there was another news flash
with more reports about Rozalinde's death. Clues, inside
information, close friends and family, fans with tear-stained
faces talking to the TV cameras about their dead darling.

Chloe was genuinely upset. Although she had not known
Rozalinde well, the woman had been a guest at her house only
a few weeks ago. She wished she could call Josh to talk about
it. He had always been her best friend. They had always been
able to laugh, to cry, to discuss everything. . . . But Josh was
now the past. She looked at the Cartier clock next to the
rumpled burgundy sheets. Not rumpled by passion – just by
yet another sleepless Las Vegas night.

It was 1 p.m. It would be 9 p.m. in London. Even if she did
call Josh – which she shouldn't anyway, her lawyer had
forbidden it – he would be out. He'd be down at one of his
haunts, the wine bars in Chelsea or Soho, hanging out with
the boys, his drinking and womanizing buddies. No doubt
he'd contacted them all again, started up where he'd left off
before he married Chloe. He'd be buying them champagne,
getting drunk, telling jokes – and all the boys would be
hanging on to his every word, after all, he was a star. He loved
the camaraderie of his own sex, the jokes about women, the
drunken anecdotes.

Forget Josh, she sighed to herself as the phone rang. It was
Johnny Swanson with the latest Hollywood gossip. He
wanted to talk about Rozalinde's murder. 'They found a book
of matches, apparently from some bar in downtown L.A.,
someplace Rozalinde would never go. Must be the killer's.'

'How do you know?'

163

'Uncle Van. He's a buddy of the L.A. Chief of Police. He says they'll find this nut case soon.'

'I hope so.' *You won't be the last.* It had an ominous ring to it. Chloe shivered.

'Anyway, sugar pie, I miss you, and I'm thinking of you,' said Johnny affectionately, not mentioning the evening of fun and frolic he had indulged in the previous night with a sultry Brazilian actress in town overnight to plug her new movie. 'I'll be up to see you next weekend, sugar, O.K.?'

'O.K., Johnny, I'll look forward to that.' She sat on the rumpled bed and looked at her heart-shaped face in the mirrored canopy above it. Would it always remind her of Josh? *Damn* him!

She picked up the phone and gave the hotel operator a London number. Time to talk to Annabel. Darling Annabel, her baby, who always made her feel so good. . . .

Rozalinde's sister Maria held the wake at her Beverly Hills mansion. Maria had married a successful movie producer, Emmanuel Siegal, taking immediately to Beverly Hills like a duck to water. The wake lasted five days. Chasen's catered continually at a cost of over ten thousand dollars. Chuck Pick supplied valet parking from noon to midnight, three hair-dressers from the Beverly Hills Hotel were in constant attendance, servicing Maria, the young, grief-stricken Angelica and a host of Rozalinde's cousins and aunts who appeared from Mexico, Acapulco and downtown Los Angeles.

Practically every major producer, director, agent and star in town came to pay homage to the woman at whom they had often sneered when she was alive, although, to be fair, they had grudgingly admired her indisputable spirit and the box-office pulling power that had made millions of dollars for many of them.

Rozalinde would have been proud to know who attended her wake. Many of the same people who would barely have crossed the commissary to say hello to her in life cried crocodile tears and mouthed platitudes about her. Despite her on-screen success, Rozalinde had never been socially accepted. There had been something a little tacky about her. Certainly truck drivers, blue-collar workers and college kids had adored her, but in spite of her sister's efforts, she had never made a social impact. Not that she needed to. Her richly varied sex life and her career had been all-consuming. She had merely shrugged when Maria had tried to get her more socially committed.

As the turnout at Rozalinde's wake showed, Hollywood still loved to mourn its celebrated dead in style, as though to make up for the long-gone wonderful parties of the thirties, forties and fifties; with each decade, Hollywood's sparkle had dimmed. Nevertheless, a carnival atmosphere prevailed in the Siegals' antique-filled yellow living room featured only last month in *Architectural Digest*. Manny had never stopped moaning about the cost, but he wasn't moaning now, Maria said to herself, proudly watching Hollywood's famous at her groaning buffet.

Comedian Buddy Bridges, with a week off between Vegas dates, was a daily visitor, regaling everyone with a stream of patter so blue that he would not dare to do it on Carson, or even in Vegas. The word had spread that the Siegals' was *the* place to be – that week.

Even Sissy, crocodile tears, crocodile shoes and matching handbag, went to the wake. She made her entrance complete with tiny pillbox hat with point d'esprit veil, on Friday evening, the day before the funeral. She had been informed by Daphne, who had hung out at the Siegals' daily, receiving the juiciest gossip she had obtained all year, that '*tout* Hollywood' was there. Indeed it was, and Sissy had herself a productive time culminating in a discussion with Menachem Golan of a possible three-picture deal with Cannon.

The funeral at Forest Lawn was a frantic mix of hysterical fans, munching junk food and snapping stars with their Instamatics, and eager paparazzi, heedless of the immaculate grass and flower beds, pushing and shoving for their respective tabloids. Sweaty cops, boiling in ninety-degree heat, tried

165

to keep order. A small group of soberly clad mourners, Rozalinde's closest friends and family, attempted to retain dignity in the face of the pandemonium. Four burly TV camera crews pushed heedlessly through the gaping crowds, their cables tripping up those too busy gawking to look where they were going. A few blocks down the tree-lined boulevard, four TV trucks manned by efficient technicians recorded the scene for the jaded appetites of their nightly news viewers. The only thing that mattered to them was getting the best footage. To that end, people were pushed, lawns were mangled, tempers frayed. Celebrity funerals rated at least fifteen or twenty seconds on prime time news and garnered good ratings, particularly if there was an interview with a major name.

Chuck Waggoner, anchorman from CBS News, an old and experienced hand, had covered most of the major Hollywood funerals of the past twenty-two years. He looked serious and trustworthy wearing a sombre grey suit, as he stood to the side of the chattering crowd, while the cortège and coffin came slowly out of the church and up the hill to Rozalinde's green and sunny final resting place. It was her wish not to be cremated. She had been shocked when the loveliness of Marilyn Monroe was incinerated nearly twenty years ago. Although barely seventeen at the time, she had told Maria that when she died she wanted to be buried in a beautiful sunny place, Maria had remembered, and as the big oak-and-bronze nine-thousand-dollar coffin was lowered into the ground, and cool earth covered it, she wept for her little sister who had loved the sun so much.

Calvin, wearing a Universal City T-shirt and bermudas, and sucking on a frozen Kool-Aid, stood outside the church with the rest of the paparazzi and fans. He was filled with a strange joy, a feeling of euphoria. He smiled and chatted with the other photographers, who were a bit surprised at the gregariousness of this usually reticent little man.

He felt almost godlike. He had done it! He had paved the

way for his idol to get the part. Surely the network would pick her now! Emerald. His goddess.

He pretended to photograph the other stars as they drew up in their mourning clothes, posing briefly for the photographers. Sabrina Jones came with Luis Mendoza. They looked stunning together, arm in arm, both dressed in charcoal grey. Her blonde unteased unpinned unbleached hair blew in the warm Pacific breeze. Luis's curls fell darkly over his forehead, accenting his brooding Latin eyes. The photographers surged forward to snap them. Calvin stayed back. He was waiting for *her* to arrive. He knew she would. And she did.

Emerald looked exquisite clad in a silk jersey dress of such a dark green it was almost black, a demure inch below her knees; she wore black hose with seams and a large black straw hat on her platinum hair. She was escorted by Sol, hastily summoned from New York for escort duty. Sol was more than happy to oblige, as the torch he carried for her still burned brightly.

'You'll get that role, Emerald my love,' whispered Calvin to himself. 'Miranda *is* you! Only you can play her.' If only she could know what he had done for her, he thought. But he wasn't finished yet. . . .

Sissy watched the news coverage at six o'clock, grudgingly admiring Emerald's stunning yet sober outfit. She sneered at Luis, Latin-smooth as ever. What a prick, she thought, sipping Perrier and chewing a sliver of lemon peel.

She had just finished her massage. Her skin felt taut and tingly. She was always relaxed after Sven's hard Scandinavian fingers manipulated her bony frame.

A few years ago Sven's hard Scandinavian cock had manipulated her too. It had been an erotic experience, especially exciting since her door had been left slightly ajar and she knew that Sam was on his way back from the studio and might discover her at any moment, flat on her back on a portable massage table, covered with baby oil, legs in the air, a large blond Swede installed between them.

That had been the first and last time Sven had gifted her with the pièce de résistance of his famous Swedish massage. Not that he wasn't good at it, but Sissy preferred toy-boys, and Sven, at thirty-seven, was too old for her taste.

'The best stud in town, dear, is the silent Swede,' Daphne had confided to Sissy at Ma Maison one day at lunch, as they became nostalgically drunk on champagne supplied by Patrick Terrail while celebrating one of Daphne's many birthdays. 'Ten years ago, dear, more or less, I never remember dates, we had a little thing, or rather a big one.' She giggled as Patrick poured more champagne and threw in a strawberry for good measure.

'Darling heart, he was divine, truly divine, and what is more, he doesn't *talk*, no ceaseless chatter about business, politics or *golf*!' The dreariness of masculine conversation had never appealed to Daphne. Masculine company was important, men were important, too, for their proper functions, which for Daphne, were money and sex, but she preferred the company of her own sex to share her most intimate thoughts, and the thing she adored perhaps even more than sex – gossip!

The fact that Daphne had now been able to parlay her considerable talent for the innuendo, the whispered secret, the rumoured affair into a lucrative syndicated column had also given her some new influence in town, which she was beginning to relish.

Now, snuggled in a white terry-cloth robe from the Ritz, Sissy read Daphne's latest column. She owned a selection of terry-cloth robes taken from every major hotel in the world, a habit she had developed when the studio picked up the tab.

'Vivacious and free-loving Rozalinde Lamaze will be sorely missed by her scores of loyal friends and millions of fans. Our town honoured the sexy flame-haired spitfire at the fabulous mansion in the heart of Beverly Hills of her sister, Maria, and brother-in-law, Emmanuel Siegal. Emmanuel told me confidentially that Dustin Hoffman will definitely play Toulouse-Lautrec in his remake of *Moulin Rouge*, which Manny will film in Paris next spring. His lovely and grieving wife, Maria, confided in spite of her sadness that they were looking forward to their vacation on the Côte d'Azur at the fabulous Voile D'Or Hotel, where they would be meeting their good friend Adnan Kashoggi on his gorgeous boat, *Nabila*, and attending Lynn Wyatt's annual birthday bash. And reed-thin, divine-as-ever Sissy Sharp, elegant in Bill Blass black, lamented the loss of the talent and beauty of Rozalinde. Sissy had just returned from a sneak preview of her new picture, *Lady Be Bad*, which opens nationwide next week, and is tipped to be a big one.

' "Luis Mendoza will be a major star after this film is released," confided the ever-generous Sissy.

'They sure don't make 'em like Sissy any more. A true star in the old Hollywood mould. Glamorous, talented and considerate. And one of the leading contenders for the most coveted and talked-about role of Miranda in "Saga".'

Sissy reread the article, pleased that Daphne had been so kind to her. That's what friends were for. She picked up her Sony cassette recorder and left a message for her secretary to send a basket of orchids to Daphne.

And then there were three, she mused. Three actresses who would be right for Miranda Hamilton.

Poor old Rozalinde, you will not be missed by me, she thought spitefully.

The amateur British bitch and that talentless, passé Hollywood celebrity ex-baby star, Emerald, were her only remaining competition. There surely could be no contest in the minds of the powers that be at the network that she, Sissy Sharp, acclaimed actress and Academy Award-winning star, was the only right choice to play Miranda.

14

The day after Rozalinde's funeral Emerald woke up feeling sad. She had liked Rozalinde, who, although younger, had been a close friend in the early seventies.

Emerald remembered the smouldering summer when they both had found themselves staying at the Byblos in St Tropez. Emerald was between husbands and recuperating from filming in Spain during which she had not only fucked her two leading men but also the lighting cameraman – a good trick that guaranteed to get a girl great closeups. Rozalinde was on the prowl, taking her pick of the dozens of tanned, gorgeous young men who strolled the beaches, bistros and discos looking for distractions.

The two women had fun together. Emerald's sexual appetites were not as eclectic as Rozalinde's, but when Rozalinde, flushed from lovemaking with some Gallic stud, regaled her with the stories of her exploits, she would get hysterical with laughter as they ate croissants and drank café au lait on Emerald's tiny balcony overlooking the Mediterranean.

Emerald had been her idol since she was a schoolgirl in Mexico, and it thrilled her to have her idol right there.

Emerald enjoyed playing the sophisticated older woman, dispensing advice and wisdom with the breakfast croissants. 'There's nothing wrong at all with having a passion for men. I've loved a few myself, but I married or lived with most of them. Your mistake, my darling, is you're just too open about it.'

'I know.' A crown creased Rozalinde's pretty face. 'I hear what they have called me sometimes. The Mexican Open! What an insult! Did they call Errol Flynn or Warren Beatty such names? They loved women like I love men. Oohh! Look at him!' Rozalinde suddenly leaned over the crimson bougainvillaea to observe a young man bouncing on the hotel diving board. He had rippling muscles, a deep tan and a more than respectable power bulge. 'Mmm, *very* nice. What do you think, Emerald?'

'Sure is, why don't you go get him?' Emerald laughed. 'And I will see you at the Tahiti for lunch.'

When they met at lunchtime, Rozalinde, as always, had caught her prey. She was twenty-six years old, gorgeous, and a movie star, few red-blooded males could resist her.

Emerald sighed, remembering those days. She was sad. When she was sad only two things could cheer her up – shopping or a visit to Bekins.

She phoned good old Sol, and he drove her to a large ugly building on Western Avenue. Emerald had told him about Bekins Storage but he had never been there with her.

The staff knew her well. 'Good afternoon, Miss Barrymore,' the man at the desk said respectfully. 'Everything is ready for you.'

In an ancient freight elevator they ascended to the third floor and walked down corridors lined with cardboard, metal and wood crates and containers of every possible size.

'Here we are,' said the guard as they came to a large padlocked door. 'Shall I leave you, Miss Barrymore?'

'Yes please,' said Emerald.

The man left, bowing deferentially.

Sol couldn't believe his eyes. The room was lined with

dozens of cardboard dress cartons. The lids had been removed and the contents were revealed, glittering and sparkling in the harsh California light.

Emerald's dresses. Her costumes. Every outfit she had ever worn onscreen and off was stored there, each carton neatly labelled. 'Isn't it wonderful, darling?' Emerald's eyes lit up with an ecstasy that was almost evangelical. 'Aren't they beautiful?' she whispered as she caressed silks, chiffons, satins, ginghams, every possible fabric ever created.

Sol nodded, amazed. Emerald had mentioned that she kept a 'few things in storage', but the extent of her collection was incredible.

'Look darling, look, my first movie,' she breathed.

The box was labelled '*Little Miss Marzipan*. 1940. Columbia'.

Emerald took out some of the tiny spangled dresses, almost in a trance. 'I was six years old,' she breathed. '*Six* years old.' She sighed. 'Look, here I am with Mr Douglas and Miss Goddard. Look, wasn't I *adorable*?' She took out a few eight-by-ten stills from a cardboard folder taped to the inside of each carton and showed them to Sol. She had indeed been a little cutie – her hair a mass of golden curls, chubby dimpled cheeks. Cupid's-bow mouth. In the photo she wore the frilly white spangled dress she now held and stroked. Her mind drifted back over forty years as she gazed at the smiling faces of Melvyn Douglas and Paulette Goddard, who had played her aunt and uncle.

'They wanted me to be a musical star in that, and I *was*,' she said softly. 'I sang and danced, and no one could ever *believe* I was only six years old. They thought I was a twenty-five-year-old midget, can you *believe* it, Sol?' Her laughter rang out, and, looking at her, Sol could almost see the tiny sweet little girl she had been.

'Miss Goddard was *so* wonderful to me,' whispered Emerald. 'She showed me how to put on eye shadow and rouge. She used to let me use her perfume. It was so strong, so sexy. "Je Reviens" it was called. She had it sent from Paris, bottles of it. She even gave me my own little bottle.'

'Do you still have it?' asked Sol, his brash New York manner slightly subdued by this new strange Emerald.

'Of *course* I do.' She flashed her jade eyes. 'Look, come with me.' She took him into the next room, which was filled with smaller cartons similarly labelled. She opened the first one. It contained dolls, teddy bears, tiny tap shoes.

'Look!' Triumphantly she retrieved a tiny navy blue bottle, empty now. She held it to her nose and sniffed deeply.

'I can still smell it. "Je Reviens". I wore it for ten years after that. Paulette, I mean Miss Goddard, was *so* kind to me. I loved her, really.'

She went back into the first room to a carton labelled, '*Daisy Did It*, Fox. 1951'. Out came crinoline gowns like those then worn by teenage prom queens. 'Janet Leigh and I were the stars of that.' She carefully opened the manila envelope. 'Look at this *coverage*! We made the cover of every single fan magazine at least three times in 1951. Look Sol, *look*! Every teenage girl in America wanted to look like us.'

Sol looked at the two blonde smiling girls wearing sneakers and shorts, windblown at the beach, and another shot of them in matching strapless formals standing beside a young Robert Stack.

'See, I even made the cover of *Life*.' She showed him a black-and-white cover of a laughing young Emerald kneeling in a white two-piece bathing suit on the beach, head thrown back, yellow hair blowing, not a care in the world.

'There's another one – *Look* magazine – now *that* was *hard* to get on. Milton Greene took this picture.' A serious, pouty young Emerald gazed thoughtfully from the cover of *Look*, wearing a chaste high-necked blouse and a thick leather belt that gave the illusion of an eighteen-inch waist.

'Jesus, why do you keep all this stuff, Emerald?' Sol was confused. A man of simple tastes, he was of the disposable generation – if you don't use it, throw it away. He thought it strange that Emerald kept all this. 'It's junk, honey.'

'Junk? Junk! You stupid son of a bitch! This is Hollywood history! No one has this, *no one*. Mary Pickford, Gloria Swanson, Greta Garbo, Joan Crawford, Liz Taylor, Lana Turner, *none* of them kept their things, none of them cared enough about this wonderful business of ours to keep their clothes, their accessories, for posterity. Do you realize what this will all *mean* to film historians in a hundred years, Sol?'

Sol nodded, humouring her. He couldn't understand the fascination of a bunch of out-of-date gowns and old movie magazines and stills. Who'd want 'em?

'1962. Look, Sol. I made *"Les Amies de Montmartre"* in Paris. It was my first French film. With Alain Delon. He was unknown then, of course. I was the star. I was the biggest star in France then. Wasn't I gorgeous?'

'You still are, hon,' said Sol, gazing· in fascination at a 1960s copy of *Paris Match* where Emerald, teased platinum hair, high white boots, a black micro-miniskirt and fishnet stockings, was leaning on the balustrade of the Pont-Neuf over the Seine next to a glowing-faced dark-haired beautiful young man whom Sol recognized as the young Alain Delon.

'I played an English rock star.' Emerald laughed. 'Just look at the stuff we wore then. I bought it all on Carnaby Street and King's Road. Oh, it was such *fun* in those days, Sol. The Parisians hadn't seen anything like my clothes. I wore the shortest miniskirts in Paris – in the whole of France, in fact. Look!' She brought out a hanger on which hung six or eight small skirts made of leather, felt and denim. Each one of them was no longer than thirteen inches and contained only about half a yard of fabric.

'Jesus, you wore those?' Sol swallowed. 'They must have seen your cooze every time you crossed your legs.'

'Sol, really. I had matching *panties*, look!' Under each skirt hung a pair of pants the same colour as the skirt. 'With Courrèges flat high-white boots, I looked like a teenager, even though I was nearly thirty. See.' She shoved another bunch of eight-by-ten glossies into his hand. 'London and Paris in the swinging sixties. *God*, did we have fun.'

There was Emerald with Brigitte Bardot on the quay in St Tropez, both of them in gingham shorts so short that the cheeks of their round brown derrières were almost revealed; there was Emerald sitting with Belmondo in Paris, wistfully sipping coffee at a Left Bank café. Emerald had a long blonde fringe and she wore a French beret. There was Emerald in London with Mick and Bianca, and John Lennon at a Bob Dylan concert, both of them in identical flat black leather caps and granny glasses, and with Michael Caine, Terence Stamp, and England's most famous model, Jean Shrimpton, dining at Club del Aretusa. They all looked young and eager and joyful. 'The sixties,' Emerald sighed fondly. 'The best of times and the worst of times for me.' She picked up another batch of photographs.

'Here's me and my Lord.' She laughed showing him a formally posed black-and-white wedding picture. 'Lord Lichfield took the pictures. Princess Margaret came, so did the Duchess of Argyll and the Duke of Westminster. All the English aristocrats came. The crème de la crème of England. It was at St Mary's church in Mayfair. I was Lady Haverstock for, oh, at *least* two or three years.'

Sol laughed. Emerald always joked about her many marriages, filled with delight and expectation as each nuptial day approached. She always started out as a devoted, dutiful wife, until her expectations were unfulfilled and the husband turned out to be a human being after all. None of Emerald's six marriages, other than to O'Herlihy, had lasted longer than three years, but, ever the optimist, she continued to walk blushingly down the aisle.

'Didn't you marry *twice* in the seventies?' queried Sol.

'Yes, the English lord and my Italian count – "the cunt", my friends all called him.' Emerald smiled and went to a carton marked 1971, which was filled with lacy, flowery garments – floating sleeves, embroidery, and ethnic trimmings. 'In 1971, I became La Contessa Calimari for seven and one half magic months – which I spent mostly lying in the sun in Franco's marble villa in Ibiza, while he cruised for

175

young boys. And when I say young, darling, I mean *young*. He married me as a cover-up. Let's face it, an American movie sex goddess is about the best cover-up you could have for a practising Italian homosexual. We were annulled. The Pope did it, of course.'

'Of course,' Sol said. 'Who else?'

'Sol?'

'Yeah, hon.'

'I don't know why I'm doing this. I never brought anyone here before. Maybe you think it's strange, but' – her voice started to break, but she controlled it – 'it's all I *have*, really.'

'You got *me*, hon. If you want me, of course,' said Sol, who would have remarried her in a flash if she'd have him.

'No, Sol. You're sweet, but this place, these boxes of possessions, *they* are my real life, Sol. They are more real than any of the men, any of my marriages. This is the *real* Emerald Barrymore. This warehouse is where she lives.'

She sat down on one of the cartons, sobbing violently. Sol felt helpless. She had never opened up like this to him before. Emerald Barrymore, Movie Queen Supreme for over forty years, had a heart just like any other broad. He didn't know what to do.

Up to now, theirs had been a friendly marriage and divorce based on physical attraction and convenient availability. Emerald often needed an escort. She liked going out, was bored being 'walked' by gay men friends. For Sol, it was a dream come true when he finally met the gorgeous girl whose picture he had pasted on the wall of his locker while he fought the Koreans. But that dream had lasted considerably less time than her others. She had worn his Van Cleef and Arpels emerald-and-diamond wedding ring for only three months. But thank God, they were still friends. Now he could be the strong shoulder she needed to cry on.

And cry she did. 'If only I could have had children,' she sobbed, as mascara ran down her cheeks in blue rivulets. 'Sol, I wanted to have kids more than anything in the world, when I was thirty.'

176

'What happened?' he said, stroking her fine platinum hair, the roots showing greyish brown.

'Between the abortions the studio insisted I have and the damn fucking *pill* – too many years on that goddamn pill, Sol, that's what happened. I stopped when I married his lordship. I really wanted to give him an heir, someone to play with Princess Margaret's son when they grew up.'

She dabbed her wet lashes with a tiny hanky trimmed in lace. Sol didn't know anyone else who carried a hanky, let alone a lace one.

'So, go on, hon.'

'I got pregnant by his lordship three times in two years. I lay flat on my back, hoping, but each time I lost it. Finally his mother gave him an ultimatum. Emerald can't have children, get rid of her. You must have an heir to the title. Well, anyway by that time, I was bored to tears with that "Hooray Henry" British horsey crowd, but I was sad. I was so sad, Sol.' She blew her nose on the tiny hanky violently.

'So then?' asked Sol. He couldn't believe what she was telling him. She never had confided in him during their marriage.

'Oh, so then, I bought the dogs!' she laughed hollowly. 'I had the dogs, and I got fucked a lot, and I fell in love a lot, and I got engaged a lot, and I kept getting pregnant, and I kept losing them until my gynaecologist took me into his office the day before my fortieth birthday, by which time I'd been pregnant *eleven* times in ten years, and told me I could *never* have a child, and to stop fooling myself. Forty was too old anyway.'

'Nonsense,' Sol said kindly.

'For motherhood,' Emerald said bitterly. 'I was an aged primipara every time I got pregnant. Cute, isn't it? An aged primipara! Ugh! So I got rid of all the equipment.'

'What equipment?' Sol was bemused.

'The *female* equipment, darling. The tubes. All the stuff that makes you moody and unpredictable twelve or thirteen times a year, and which arrives unexpectedly as you've put on a

177

new white skirt and you're sitting at a formal dinner with the Ambassador of God-knows-where and the host is a gay, so you know you can't find a tampon in *his* bathroom, just Vaseline and amyl nitrate.'

She smiled sadly. 'So that's when my career packed up. My gyno must have told *tout* Hollywood I was no longer a *real woman.*' Anger crept into her voice. 'No more offers for poor little Emerald. And I still had my "fabulous" life style to support. That's when I did the pornos.'

'They weren't *pornos*, for Christ's sake, Emerald. They were fuckin' *art* films, and you know it.'

'To you they were art films. To me they were pornos.'

'So you showed your tits,' he argued.

'And my ass, too.'

'You got a great ass, kid,' he said, affectionately squeezing it, wondering if she might consent to a quickie among the crinolines.

'They *were* great photos though, weren't they, Sol?'

'Yeah, oh, yeah, babe.' He remembered, as had thousands of men, her revolutionary pose for the exceedingly serious yet erotic Italian film *L'innamorata.*

'There's the picture, Sol. It's five years ago now. Do you think I look any different?'

She was holding up an eleven-by-fourteen colour photo from *L'innamorata.* She wore a Gestapo officer's hat set at a rakish angle on cropped blonde curls, and a black Nazi uniform, the jacket of which was open to reveal a medium-sized but perfect bosom.

It was a sensational photo, more so because Emerald had been forty-three years old at the time. It had got her the cover of *People*, *Newsweek* and a spurt of new movie activity, mostly in Spain, Germany and France.

'Now you know why I must play that part in "Saga", Sol. I *swore* I'd never do TV, swore it on Momma's grave, but time is running out, and my only assets are my face, my body and my fame.'

'You're still beautiful, hon, beautiful,' Sol soothed.

'I have exactly two hundred and fifty thousand bucks in the bank, which, with *skimping*, will last me a year, if I'm clever. I have the house in the hills. . .'

'That's worth a couple of mil,' Sol said, 'easy.'

'Maybe *one*, tops.

'I have furs galore, loads of fabulous jewels; if I sell those then maybe I can get by for another year, and then what? *Then what*, Sol? What does Emerald Barrymore do for an encore?'

'Marry me again, sweetheart. Marry me.'

'No, I can't. I'm sorry but I don't love you, honey. You're adorable, funny, sweet, but I *must* feel passion. I've always had to feel passion, and I can't pretend. You know it, and I can't fake it.'

Amidst the paraphernalia of Emerald's forty-year career, they gazed at each other sadly. 'Now you know why I *have* to have that part, Sol,' she said, gripping his hand. 'I've been an actress for forty years. I don't know how to do anything else. I *want* this role, I want acceptance in this town by my peers. I want the money, the fame, the magazine covers again, Sol. If I don't get them, I'm on the scrap heap forever. I'm too tired. I'm too old . . .'

'No, hon, you're not.'

She stopped him. 'If there's one thing I know, it's Hollywood. Yes, I'm still a star to the public, but everyone in the business, every goddamn producer and agent in this whole stinking, rotten town thinks I'm a washed-up has-been, Sol, and it's not going to stay that way. I'm going to play Miranda if it kills me. I'm going to do everything I can, and I'll be a *real* bloody star again! I can't and I won't settle for anything else.'

He nodded sadly. It was only too true. 'Let's get the hell out of this place, kid,' he said.

15

Nothing had changed in Las Vegas, Chloe realized, as she surveyed her companions in the casino elevator. Fat thighs in tight shorts, shrivelled old ladies whose hair had been permed so often it looked like grey-blue cotton wool, hookers and businessmen. Chloe never failed to wonder at the beefiness of the Vegas visitors. Maybe they ate too many milk shakes and doughnuts, too many snacks. Certainly the fattest were the ones who drank diet soda with their food. A woman sucking an ice-cream cone dripped it onto Chloe's suede shoes, and she grimaced.

Her suite at the Las Vegas Empire was as lavish as ever, even though the 'damask-and-silk' hangings on the wall and windows were 100 per cent polyester, and felt like glazed cardboard to the touch, and the 'velvet' sofa was hard as a rock. The black acrylic bathtub with ersatz gold taps was wide enough for two; it had a thin black plastic pillow at one end, in case two wished to sample the delights of the Jacuzzi. She sat on the eight-foot-wide burgundy crushed velvet-covered bed and looked up at her lonely reflection in the bevelled mirrored ceiling. She remembered the last time she and Josh had played the Empire, how they had shared this suite, the shiny black tub, the same bed, watched themselves in that same mirror. . . .

Josh always loved looking at their two bodies entwined together on wine-coloured sheets, her ivory legs encircling his bronzed ones. He was never more aroused than when they were together in Las Vegas, and he took her sometimes three or four times a day, his ardour fired by the sight of their bodies in the mirror. She sighed as she removed her De Fabrizio suede pumps. Stop thinking about Josh, she admonished herself. Stop thinking about what was. Get yourself together, girl – you've got a show to do.

In a cramped motel room in downtown Las Vegas, Calvin unpacked his canvas holdall and regarded the contents. There it was. The knife. Its flat bluish metal reflected his flat bluish eyes, which gazed blankly out the window at the high blue Nevada sky. They didn't see the bare sandy vista shading into the distance, interspersed with a few sickly palm trees and shaggy bushes. All they noticed was the sign that dominated their view. A huge billboard announced:

CHLOE CARRIERE
JULY 16–27
$20 EARLY SHOW $25 LATE SHOW
For show reservations call 732-8800
THE LAS VEGAS EMPIRE
AMERICA'S #1 ENTERTAINMENT SPOT

Slowly Calvin picked up the phone and dialled 732-8800. Under the name John Ryan he booked a booth for the following night. It was time to get her.

Later that evening, as Chloe sat in the dressing room, her hairdresser fixing white sequinned flowers in her dark hair while she painted her face with trembling hands, thoughts of Josh tormented her. She could hear the crowd out front, laughing at the opening act – Shecky Greene.

She remembered four years ago, in this same dressing

room, begging Josh to stop taking the drugs that were destroying his career and their marriage. The bouquet of medication he needed for support had become a nightmare. He usually awoke at four or five in the afternoon and got a vitamin shot for his voice from the local Vegas quack. Then he took three uppers, a large snort of coke and a Coca-Cola. He'd stop at the crap table for a couple of hours if Chloe was having a massage or a manicure. If she was around, he'd want to have sex. In spite of his drugging, he was still incredibly virile. He was her husband, and she adored him in spite of everything. An hour before their show he would get another shot for his voice, swallow a decongestant with codeine, two uppers, and take another massive snort of coke. Just before he went on stage he took a Dilaudid, a legal drug twice as powerful as heroin. His beautifully tanned and muscular body in a white silk shirt open to the waist and black pants showed off his tremendous sex appeal. He still had 'it' for the female Las Vegas patrons. Old and young, they found him wildly attractive. After the show, in which he sang for the first forty minutes, she for the second forty, they then harmonized and vocalized together for fifteen more minutes. They gazed into each other's eyes, singing ballads, love songs and point numbers with sophistication and sexy undertones that drove the audience wild. Afterwards, his trusty doctor took his blood pressure, and if it was over 140 gave him a pill to come down, after which he'd take another snort of coke. Fortified by the applause, by the onstage empathy and rapport with each other, they then received visiting friends, acquaintances and business associates in their dressing room with the mirrored bar and wood-burning fireplace.

Later they would go to dinner with friends in the Rib Room; then he would hit the tables until dawn. Before he went to sleep, Josh took two Quaaludes, a blood-pressure pill and a Demerol.

It was too much. Much too much. She had lectured him long and often, but he maintained he was not addicted, he could handle it, he needed it to work. 'Cut the crap, Clo,' he'd say. 'It's not hurting me.'

The extraordinary thing was, it didn't seem to – then. But gradually his habits began to erode his performances, then his life.

The owners of the Vegas casinos soon got the message. He was becoming irresponsible, unreliable. Slowly the Vegas gigs, the years of the big money – seventy-five, one hundred grand a week – started to drift away, and then they had to start doing the tours. Oh, those tours! Numbing. Soul-destroying. Milwaukee, New Haven, Idaho, Atlanta, Connecticut, Kansas. Weeks, months of one-night stands.

It was a killer. It had killed his career and their marriage. Now she only had herself to take care of. She looked at her face, finished now. The matte complexion, the fuschia-gloss lips, the smoky eyes. A black lace over nude chiffon Bob Mackie original, clung to every contour of her thoroughly toned body. She looked in fighting form.

The band was playing her intro now. She heard applause for the well-known songs – *her* songs.

It was time to perform.

Although Chloe hadn't played Vegas for four years, her opening was a huge success – she still had many fans. To her surprise and delight, Sammy and Altovise Davis, Milton and Ruth Berle, and Steve Lawrence and Eydie Gormé had shown up the first night to wish her well. Pandora had been there too. Her romance with the young comedian was on the wane. He spent more time at the tables than he did with Pandora. She was philosophical.

'Honey, romance is like a bag of groceries, the more you put in, the heavier it gets.'

Chloe laughed as the two of them lay by the pool at the Empire the next morning, watching the constant action.

'Another ship will cross my horizon, honey,' Pandora drawled, rubbing Bain de Soleil on her slender legs. 'Men are like buses; if you wait long enough, another one will come along.'

'The way you look, darling, it won't be long either,' said Chloe, admiring her friend's slim body in her white maillot.

'Phone for you, Miss Carriere,' trilled a tiny page as he plugged a phone into an invisible outlet and handed it to Chloe.

'Hello, darling, it's Jasper,' he said in his impeccable English accent. Chloe smiled.

'Hi, Jasper, what's happening?'

'I think you're the number one front-runner for Miranda, my pet. I spoke to Abby and Gertrude this morning. They *and* the network feel that you gave the best test. They feel certain that they want you for Miranda.'

'But they're not completely sure yet, right, Jasper?'

'Right, petal. You know how it is. So stay calm, dear, do the show, and I'm sure by the end of the week we'll have a firm answer.'

'Good.' There didn't seem much else to say.

'Oh, and Robert Osborne has you as his lead item in the *Reporter* today, said that you were the main contender for Miranda. Just thought I'd let you know.'

'Thanks, Jasper, keep in touch, love.' Chloe hung up feeling elated.

Pandora was deep in conversation with the straight half of the magic act that was currently breaking all records at the hotel. 'You know The Great Geraldo, don't you?' she breathed, her eyes alight with new found interest.

The Great Geraldo inclined his head with European gallantry, revealing dyed black roots and an inch of flab hanging over green Ralph Lauren trunks.

'*Enchanté, madame.*'

'Excuse me a second, I'm going to buy the trades.' The Great Geraldo bowed in gallant Continental fashion, as Chloe, avoiding oiled mahogany bodies, walked into the cool darkness of the lobby.

She was indeed the lead gossip item in the *Hollywood*

Reporter: 'Abby Arafat and BCC network seem to agree that the perfect choice for Miranda Hamilton on Abby's new series, "*Saga*", is Chloe Carriere, now headlining *sans* Joshua Brown at the Las Vegas Empire until July 27th. Catch her if you can, folks: this gal is hot!'

Chloe was pleased. This was no public relations plant. She didn't have a press agent. Maybe the item was true.

> *'It had to be you*
> *It had to be you*
> *I wandered around*
> *and finally found*
> *somebody who* – '

Chloe was in good voice, relaxed and confident. The nerves of the first few nights had evaporated, and she was surprised at how much she was enjoying this gig.

She looked radiant in a silver lace Nolan Miller gown. The spotlight sparkled on the tiny rhinestones scattered on it, and her face seemed to reflect the glow. The house was packed. The audience liked her, and appreciative applause greeted the end of each number.

In a back booth, huddled alone with an unaccustomed whiskey to bolster his courage, Calvin watched her every move.

Bitch. Where did she get that confidence? How *dare* she flaunt herself in that gown, that silken dress so sheer that the audience could see the outline of her breasts and twat. She was an English whore; she would pay dearly for it. He swallowed the whiskey, feeling the unfamiliar taste burn his throat. He stared at her malevolently as she came down into the audience singing her signature tune, 'Everyone's Gotta Love Someone', weaving gracefully through tables full of polyester-clad tourists who reached out to touch her radiance. She took their hands, looking warmly into their faces, sharing her joy with them.

'Cunt.' His lips tightened as his hand tightened on the knife in his pocket. His fingers itched to slash the bitch's face. He groaned. He was getting hard. Why did this happen now? When he hated this woman so much, why did his body betray him?

He tried to distract himself by observing the faces of the audience, eyes glued to her glittering feline figure as she threaded her way through the packed tables in the moving spotlight.

'Get a load of the guy in the booth,' Jake Walker whispered to his partner, Hank Gillis.

A plainclothes security man, with fifteen years in the casino business and ten years as a state cop behind him, Jake prided himself on his instincts. But Hank wasn't listening to him. Jake nudged his partner again.

'Ssh!' Hank hissed. He was mesmerized by Chloe, gazing at her as she slowly advanced through the audience. Maybe she'd reach out and touch him. Oh, boy! 'Shut up, Jake, I'm in love,' he said.

Chloe was getting closer now. She paused at a table of excitable Japanese tourists. '*Everyone's gotta love*,' she breathed clasping the hands of a young Japanese girl, who blushed with excitement.

Calvin's breath caught in his throat. He'd planned it brilliantly. This booth was next to the exit. One quick move, and even before the blood could come spurting out of her throat, before anyone realized what had happened, he would be in the casino mingling with the crowd. It was almost midnight on a Saturday, and the room was packed. He could disappear easily into the crowd. He was disguised in a red wig and horn-rimmed glasses, which he intended to dispose of later.

She was edging nearer. Would she come to him? Yes, of course she would. Last night he had observed both her shows. She always performed to the last row. The time was nearly ripe. The knife was burning on his lap. His hands were soaking wet as he wiped them on the red linen napkin. Red, the colour of the blood that would soon be splashed all over that silver dress. He hadn't had an erection like this for a long time. He groaned. He needed relief.

Chloe was so close now, he could almost smell the scent she wore. It was pungent, musky – in spite of himself he liked it.

All eyes were on her except for the pair that was fixed on Calvin.

As Jake watched him with instinct honed by years of experience, he knew something was very wrong with this man. '*You gotta love, love, love . . .*' Chloe sang, thrilled by the love and happiness the audience brought to her and she gave back to them.

'*Love, love, love,*' the audience sang back happily. All except Calvin, his eyes glazed, and face sodden with sweat. Jake watched his eyes, then his hands, waiting for any move that would tell him his suspicions were correct. When Chloe was only yards away Calvin's hand reached for the knife. Jake moved into the booth next to him. Calvin froze.

Jake flashed his badge. 'Freeze, motherfucker,' he said, as, with expert pressure on the man's hand, he extracted the knife. It was certainly a lethal weapon, a deer-hunter's knife, eight inches long, five inches past the legal limit. Sharp as a bayonet.

'This is a concealed weapon. You planning on going hunting?' he snarled to the trembling Calvin, as Chloe sang her way past the booth on her way back to the stage. Terror gripped Calvin. Sweat dripped from his brow onto Jake's hand, which held his wrist in a vicelike grip. No one noticed the two men. All eyes were on Chloe's undulating figure. As thunderous applause rang out, Jake's attention was moment-arily distracted.

With an animal cry and a madman's sudden strength Calvin whipped his left arm into Jake's face, leaped over the table and sprinted towards the exit.

'Stop him!' Jake yelled to the uniformed guards at the entrance. 'Stop that man!'

Calvin screamed in frustration and pain as the hefty guards grabbed him and tussled him to the ground. His wig fell off, his glasses crashed to the floor. Chloe's reprise was forgotten as the audience, distracted by Calvin's screams, got up to see what was happening.

Chloe froze in fear as the chattering crowd thronged around her, pushing her in their panic. The same people whom she had enthralled only seconds before now shoved her out of their way. As she started to move up the steps to the stage, she lost her footing and tripped. A hand reached out from the crowd to steady her and helped her onto the stage. The band was playing another tune now, the bandleader having signalled the orchestra to play something upbeat.

'Are you all right, Madame?' Chloe looked gratefully into the eyes of a tall, dark man, who put his arm around her protectively.

'I'm fine . . . no, I'm not. I . . . I feel faint. What's happened, do you know?'

'Come with me,' he said, leading her backstage, past gossiping barebreasted showgirls in ostrich feathers who were oblivious to the commotion out front.

In her dressing room, Chloe sat on the couch as he poured her a glass of water. Then, silently, he half-filled a brandy snifter with cognac and passed it to her.

'Do you know what happened?' she asked again.

'Drink, don't talk. Drink the brandy,' he commanded.

Chloe felt a surge of gratitude to the stranger who obviously understood how disoriented she was and wanted to help.

'Oh, God,' breathed Chloe. 'What was that man *doing*? Who was he?'

'I don't know.' Chloe recognized an accent. French, Italian? She couldn't tell.

'Thank you for helping me. Please excuse me, I'm a bit rattled.'

'Understandably so, Madame. May I introduce myself? I am Philippe Archambaud, *à vôtre service*.' He made a slight but formal bow and gave her a smile that enhanced his attractiveness.

'Las Vegas is a long way from France.' Chloe felt better as she sipped the brandy, felt it warming her.

'I'm here on a working vacation, to experience and write about what we call "The American Scene". I'm doing a series of articles for *Paris Match*.'

A *journalist*! Chloe groaned inwardly. She never trusted journalists. They were her *bêtes noires*.

Her maid came in and said the police would like to talk to her. Philippe stood up. 'I shall go now.' Philippe pressed her fingers swiftly to his lips. '*Tout à l'heure, Madame Carriere.*'

'*Au revoir, et merci*,' Chloe said, admiring his physique, his impeccably cut dark suit, beautifully knotted, subtle tie, and noticing that he had written something on a book of matches which he now put into her hand.

'I shall be here for the rest of the weekend. If you would like, perhaps we could have a coffee together. If you are free, of course.'

He bowed again, in the manner of a cultivated Frenchman, and left her dressing room as two policemen entered.

The interrogation was short. Although the officers seemed sympathetic, there was an edge to their concern that made Chloe feel almost guilty, as if the incident had been her fault. She was glad when they left. There was nothing she could say to help them. She had only seen the man for a second or two. She had no enemies.

Her maid bustled about. Would madame like another drink, a cigarette? No, madame would not. Madame knew what she needed tonight.

She felt lost, lonely, cold. She wanted to be close to someone. She picked up the match book that Philippe had left, and looked at it. 'Philippe Archambaud. Room 1727'.

What an attractive name. What an attractive man, she thought. And opening her handbag she put the card firmly inside.

She would spend the night as she had spent the last forty nights – alone.

Part Four

16

Chloe looked at her watch. This was the day. Jasper Swanson had promised to call her with the news as soon as Abby called him. It was three o'clock. He should be back from his Friday lunch at Ma Maison. It's gone to Sissy, thought Chloe, staring at the ocean. Better accept the offer to tour Europe for three months. It was preferable to doing episodic TV guest shots on 'Charlie's Angels' and 'Policewoman', both of which she'd politely declined in the three weeks since she had been back from Vegas. Were they *ever* going to make a decision? It was almost the end of summer. 'Saga' would start shooting in two weeks – what were they waiting for?

She pulled on a black one-piece swimsuit and a white terry-cloth robe. To hell with waiting. To the ocean – a long swim, a glass of iced tea, then off to the Bill Palmer Salon to have Tami give her a manicure and Dino give her a new coiffure. *Forget* about Miranda! The phone rang. Twice. Three times. She picked it up on the fourth ring.

Chloe heard Jasper's excited tone. 'You have it, my love, you have it!'

The excitement in his voice infected Chloe. 'Oh, Jasper, I can't believe it! Are you sure? Are you positive?'

'Yes, yes. Of course I'm sure, my love. The network *adored* you. They said there really was no contest. Your test was by far the most exciting. Gertrude said you *are* Miranda!'

'Oh,' bubbled Chloe, 'Jasper darling, you're a magician. How could they have chosen me over Emerald, who is such a huge star . . . and Sissy, such a great actress? I simply can't believe my luck. Why did they wait so long?'

He laughed. 'They received a million dollars' worth of publicity by stringing it out. Dear girl, the network isn't stupid, you know. You have a quality, Chloe. You may not even understand what it is. If you start to realize what it is, and if you start to analyse it, you may lose it, so don't think about it, that's my advice, dear.'

'What do you mean?' asked Chloe. The enormity of what had happened was just beginning to penetrate.

'I mean you have got *star* quality, toots.' His British voice became more serious. 'Abby and Gertrude knew it right after your test. They just had to convince that bloody-minded network that you were the right woman for the part.'

'And they did. Oh, God, Jasper, I'm so excited I could scream! We must celebrate.'

'All right, we'll hit the town tonight. Put on your best bib and tucker.' Jasper had been in the business for nearly thirty years but he had rarely heard a performer so happy to get a job. 'Spago, Chasen's, Ma Maison – what is your pleasure, Milady?'

'Oh, all of them!' Chloe laughed. 'Spago for champagne, Chasen's for chilli and Ma Maison for dessert.'

'You're on, toots.' He added knowingly, 'Now you must watch out, my love. Watch out for the woodwork people – the ones who didn't want to know you before, who will try to become your best friends now. You will be *swamped*, dear, with new "best friends".'

'I will watch out, darling, of course I will. By the way, how much will I be getting?'

He paused. 'Weeell, my love, that's a teeny bit of a

problem. I mean, let's face it, we *know* you're a cabaret star. For a singer you're quite big.'

'Bottom-line it for me, Jasper darling.'

'Fifteen an episode.'

She was astonished. 'Fifteen! Oh, Jasper, that's *peanuts*. I don't mean to sound ungrateful but I know that Sam Sharp is getting fifty, why only fifteen for me?'

'My dear, you know this business. They want you, but as far as the U.S. of A. is concerned, you're an unknown.'

'I just sold out the house in Vegas,' remonstrated Chloe.

'For goodness sake, Chloe, be reasonable! After all, we are *both* British. We know you did well in Vegas, but they've got ten other cast members to pay. You are not a star yet. Oh, by the way, they've cast Sissy as the other wife, Sirope.'

'Sissy! How odd, when she tested for Miranda. Why?'

'Well, Abby needs star power for this role. And Sissy needs a decent job. That is why they can't pay *you* what you deserve, dear. Sissy is still a star, and she will be paid like a star. In this town, my love, a star is a star is a star.'

'O.K. You know how much I wanted this part. And I'm certainly glad I got it. But what happens if I become a big star too, Jasper? Will I get a rise?'

'My love, the sky will be the limit then, no question about it, I'll see to it that they triple your salary if you get a high TVQ, I promise you, my love. *Triple* it.'

'Fine.' Chloe beamed. 'Then I accept. Not that there was any question, really. You knew I would.'

'That's my girl. You've always been smart, Chloe. My limo will pick you up at eight. Don't forget, watch out for the woodwork people.'

'I won't forget, Jasper, I promise.'

'No – no – no! I can't believe it!' screamed Sissy to her agent. 'How dare they give it to that no-talent saloon singer? How *could* they?'

In spite of herself, large black tears rained mascara from her eyes. She clutched a towel around her nonexistent breasts and signalled to Sven, the Swedish masseur, who had been doing his best with the kinks in her neck, to bring her a cigarette.

'Shit! Shit! Shit!' she screamed in frustration and rage as she sat up on the portable massage table inhaling smoke deeply into her lungs. Screw cancer, she thought to herself bitterly. 'I'm finished, *ruined* by this foreign *cow*.'

Sven lit a Camel and stoically sat studying the latest issue of *Body Building* he had taken from his briefcase. His calm Scandinavian features betrayed nothing of the pity he may or may not have felt for Sissy – sad sight that she was, with her overtanned skin, overdieted body, and overdyed hair, sobbing in rage on the telephone.

'How can I hold my head up in this town ever *again*?' she yelled to Robin, her hapless agent, on the other end of the phone. 'How? Tell me?'

Robin was obviously trying to placate her because she remained silent for a while. 'Well, I'll think about it,' she muttered. 'That wife is nowhere near the role that Miranda is, but if I did accept, of course they *would* build the show around me more, wouldn't they?'

She listened again, dragging heavily on her cigarette. Sven observed the lines etched deeply above her thin lips, the result of thirty cigarettes a day, which no number of face-lifts could erase.

'Forty thousand an episode? Hmmmm.' She was getting visibly calmer. The lines in her face softened a little.

Sven looked up from his magazine.

Sissy finished her phone call with an 'I'll think about it. I promise I will. Call me tomorrow,' and hung up. She smiled. The deep wrinkles and the bitterness in her face seemed to vanish. When she smiled she lost ten years, and could look almost girlish. 'Come here, Sven,' she commanded in a husky, sensual voice.

The beauty of Sven was that he was terribly discreet and definitely heterosexual. None of the ladies who had partaken of his munificent Scandinavian charms had ever had a cause for complaint. He aimed to please, and he did. He also never passed up an opportunity. If the lady wanted it, he could and would supply it. In spite of his total lack of interest in Sissy as a person, her body or her sexuality, Sven uncapped a bottle of baby oil and, slowly removing the towel from her body, commenced work on the famous pièce de résistance of his repertoire.

When Sue Jacobs had told Sabrina that she hadn't been cast for any of the roles, Sabrina had been pleased, and signed for a new movie immediately.

But Emerald, Miss Tricky One, was something else, and she had to be placated.

Emerald was upset when she had lost Miranda to Chloe – very upset indeed. She had spent one entire morning weeping alone in her bedroom, her hysteria mounting along with her insecurities, then called Eddie back.

'Why Chloe? Why not *me*?' she demanded. 'Who is she anyway? Can she act? Is she a megastar? I *still* am!' she yelled, looking closely into the superstrong magnifying mirror to see if the tiny scars from her jaw job were visible.

Fast Eddie sighed. The bigger the star, the harder they fell, and the more difficult it was for them to accept it.

'They *loved* your test, kiddo. Abby and Gertrude thought you looked fantastic, and your performance was great – magic, kid.'

'Terrific!' spat Emerald, catching sight of yet another line under her wide green eyes. 'But Eddie, dear – if it was so fucking magic, why didn't I get the fucking part?'

'Chloe fits the role better, that's all, kiddo. They wanted a new face, they always do.' Eddie was right. They wanted someone they hadn't seen for years with their morning coffee in every gossip column and on their TV screens with another newsworthy scandal, marriage, engagement or divorce. It was obvious that the American public, although they still admired Emerald, found her a larger-than-life character. They could never dissociate the persona of Emerald

Barrymore, superstar, from the character she played. This was Abby, Gertrude and the network's opinion. Anyway, Emerald would off-balance what they wanted to be an ensemble piece.

Eddie tried to explain this to a furious Emerald, but in the middle of the conversation, Emerald hung up on him with a harsh 'Fuck you and your fucking agency! Eddie, I'm firing you!'

Emerald took a deep breath and a long, harsh look at her own assets. She still possessed beauty and sex appeal, and she was famous. She hired the best agent in town – Jasper Swanson – who, never one to let a star fall by the wayside, immediately found her a low-budget movie in Australia. It was directed by the very hot, very up-and-coming young black filmmaker Horatio George Washington.

'Australia? Again? Why not?' Emerald said. 'I want to be as far away as possible from Chloe Carriere when she becomes a star.'

17

Perry brought Josh his breakfast along with a copy of the *Hollywood Reporter* which he had thoughtfully highlighted in red for his master to read.

CHLOE CARRIERE TO PLAY MIRANDA IN SAGA

Josh, in L.A. to record a hopeful new single, read the piece with a mixture of elation and sadness.

She'd done it. His little Chloe had the role she craved. He wanted to congratulate her, send her her favourite roses and lilies, a little note. He picked up the phone to call Perry, but then out of habit punched in their private number at the beach house. It hadn't changed.

She answered on the third ring.

'Chlo, I'm so happy for you, luv. I just heard the news. Congratulations.'

'Thanks, Josh.' Chloe couldn't keep the happiness out of her voice. He had called – and in spite of her denial to herself, she still cared. 'It's sweet of you to call.'

She had heard it in his voice. He cared too. In spite of his other women, his boozing, his drugging, his newfound bachelor freedom, his voice brought such happy memories flooding back. He wanted to see her, wanted to hold her close to him again.

'Well, I'd like to buy you a bottle of champagne, luv. I don't suppose you're free for dinner tonight?'

She hesitated for a moment, then, 'Yes, I am. I think I'd like that, Josh. Where shall we go?'

Possibly as a result of her getting the part, Josh and Chloe reconciled again, for the fourth and – Chloe hoped – final time. Her lawyer had groaned in annoyance, saying he had never in thirty years of practice known a woman who changed her mind as often as she. Josh had said he was definitely going to go to a shrink and solve his problems.

For the last two weeks everything had been more or less rosy, thought Chloe as she surveyed herself objectively in a tiny spotted mirror in what was laughingly called a star's trailer.

Ben had done a good job. Good old Ben. Discreet makeup, excellent hairstyle, chic, *non*-Hollywood. Simple black Chanel suit, expensively elegant enough to make the other actresses clothes look like those of a hausfrau. It was Chloe's own suit. Last week she had categorically rejected in disgust the studio's safe little tweed suits with mink collars and rhinestone buttons. Asserting her dramatic rights, she had requested a high-fashion look. All the actresses on most of the other prime time soaps wore silk blouses, gabardine trousers or skirts. For evening scenes, they dressed in low-cut silk jersey dresses with spaghetti straps from Holly's Harp or Strip Thrills. Chloe was determined to create a look that no other actress had featured since the glamorous days of Dietrich, Turner and Crawford.

She had stressed the glamour image in all her interviews. 'I am *not* the woman next door,' she insisted over and over again. 'Miranda is a mysterious woman of the world, and that's what I shall look like. She wears couture clothes and lives a jet-set lifestyle.'

There had been some flak at the front office when Abby and Gertrude heard about the way she wanted to portray Miranda, but after viewing some tests, they were ecstatic.

'Gorgeous, she looks simply gorgeous,' glowed Gertrude, congratulating herself for having had the strength to reject Sissy's frenzied pleas of longtime friendship, reminders of all the things *she* had done for Gertrude when they had been starting out in New York together a century ago.

'Fabulous. I *love* her. She looks mean and bitchy and evil, but underneath it there's something about her that you can't help liking,' Abby said.

'You're right, and she's a good actress too,' said Bill Herbert, 'Saga's' executive producer. 'She'll be big, very big. What are we paying her, Abby?'

'She's a steal, a *steal*.' Abby was excited. A bargain always appealed to him. 'Only fifteen grand an episode, and by looking at these tests she's worth at least twice that.'

'Don't let her get too full of herself,' warned Gertrude, ever the pragmatist. 'This is an ensemble piece, remember, everyone's equal.'

'Bullshit,' said Abby, getting to the point as usual. 'She and Sam will be the stars of "Saga" – I can see it.'

'Any actor or actress is dispensable,' Gertrude continued. 'Don't let us *ever* forget that, fellows. If we do, we let the inmates run the asylum. Look what happened to the movie business!'

They all took a moment to think regretfully about how the movie business had been disrupted by upstart actors and actresses who had started their own production companies, taking over the reins and the power. Redford, Beatty, Reynolds, even Goldie Hawn, had taken off and, in control, were calling themselves producers. And, of course, some of them had become successful, which made it even worse.

'Well, it'll never happen in TV,' Abby broke the silence.

'Oh, yeah? What about Lucy? She owned a frigging *studio*, for Christ's sake! How about Mary Tyler Moore?'

'Mary was a figurehead. Her husband was the power. TV is safe. Actors act, producers produce, directors direct, and that's the way it's going to be in *my* company, all the way down the line. On "Saga" no one is more important than the producer and the product.' Abby was adamant. They nodded in agreement.

'Run those rushes again,' he ordered. They watched earnestly as Chloe's face filled the tiny screen.

'She's got it,' breathed Gertrude. 'I just hope she doesn't realize it too soon. Once she does, we won't be able to hold her back.'

Chloe walked onto the set of 'Saga' exuding a confidence she did not feel. She was exhausted; she had spent half the night, when she should have been preserving her looks for the camera that never lies, in screaming arguments with a drunkenly abusive Josh.

His new single, 'Rainbow Girl', instead of gliding slowly but surely up the charts, as he and his advisers had predicted, had failed to make even the Top 100. It was received coolly by DJs from Coast to Coast.

His hopes of making a three-minute video of the song, an innovation still in its infancy, had been dashed when Polygram's president brushed him off. 'I gotta be brutally frank: The rock-video market is aimed at kids – and by kids we mean eleven to twenty.' He shrugged. 'Josh, these are the *children* of your fans, y'know what I mean?' he added, with a hint of malice.

Josh had taken his hurt out on Chloe, and now sat in front of the giant TV in their 'playroom' off the master bedroom drinking brandy from a tumbler and flipping channels every few seconds. The volume was on full blast, and the constant changing of the channels was driving Chloe mad.

She tried not to get rattled as she busied herself with the myriad details she had to attend to before going to work the first day on what was probably the biggest career move of her life.

She puffed furiously on her twentieth cigarette, trying to study dialogue already committed to memory. Her hair was wrapped in a towel while the conditioner worked, and she tried with shaking hands to give herself a manicure.

She had dieted and exercised for weeks now, and was down

to a fighting weight of one hundred and ten pounds. Ideally she would have wanted to rinse out her hair, dry her nails and fall asleep by nine o'clock with a glass of wine, which beat sleeping pills *any* time. That would give her eight solid hours of beauty sleep before she had to arise at five to get to the studio by six.

Perfect. Simply perfect. To make this break work for her, she had to be prepared. Mentally, physically and emotionally. TV was a tough, competitive arena. There were several prime time bitches out there, waiting for Chloe to come out of her corner; they were sharpening their claws, ready for battle. 'I'll chew her up and spit her out in little bits!' one of her TV rivals had sneered to Daphne Swanson, who couldn't wait to print it in her column. 'After all, I *am* ten years younger and four inches taller.' Chloe had smiled at the insecurities of this actress, obviously terrified she was going to slip in the ratings. The truth was, Chloe planned to give them all a damn good run for their money. She would make Miranda unforgettable. She hadn't spent the past twenty years of her life singing to and observing the jet set in their natural habitat without getting a head start on the character of Miranda. Witty, scintillating, glamorous and naughty – Mirandas were everywhere in the *haut monde*, the international jet set.

'Chloe, Chloe, when's dinner for Christ's sake?' Josh yelled from the playroom, interrupting her reverie.

'Well, darling,' she placated, 'you said we didn't need a live-in cook any more after Manuela left. Can't you find something in the fridge?'

The old row about having a live-in housekeeper was about to start. Chloe disliked cooking, and certainly did not intend to learn on the eve of her new job. Josh had always tried to instil a bit of old fashioned prefeminist guilt in her by insinuating that a 'real woman' always cooked. His mother cooked. His sister cooked. Even Sally cooked. Why couldn't she?

'What kind of a wife *are* you?' He was still clutching the

brandy bottle as he lurched into the room. He tried to smile in a winning way – the way that always warmed her heart.

'Ha, indeed, and what kind of a husband are you?' She tried to banter with him. 'Don't start, Josh, darling, please,' she said calmly, trying to ignore him as she unwrapped the towel from her hair.

He grabbed her, twisted her around to face him. The brandy was strong on his breath and his pupils were dilated. Her heart sank. Brandy and cocaine. A bad mix. He was out of it. She had seen it before, and it was not a pretty sight.

'I've got to rinse this off. It it stays too long on my hair, the hairdresser won't be able to work with it tomorrow.' She shook herself free and escaped into the shower.

'I don't care. I want dinner, and then I want you.' He loomed in the doorway, yelling over the noise of the shower. 'C'mon, Chlo, let's open up a coupla can of beans and fry some eggs like the old days. Chloe, c'mon, luv.' His tone had changed to flirtatious charm, hinting of romance, a prelude to what had once been their mating call in his voice. In spite of herself she found him exciting. In spite of a six-o'clock makeup call and first-day nerves, the residue of their long-time passion still stirred her.

She stepped out of the shower and wrapped herself in a terry-cloth robe. What the hell. She returned his embrace. Two poached eggs and a can of beans didn't take long to fix, she decided. If we make love, he'll fall asleep instantly, and then I can get some rest. . . .

Afterwards she snuggled against him trying to recapture old feelings of satisfaction and comfort, and longing for sleep. But he started complaining again. He moaned about his career being on the wane while hers was taking a turn for the better.

She let him ramble on about his frustrations with show business, about the unfairness of a record industry that failed to appreciate his talent, and about the stupidity of his fickle fans.

'Darling, please go to sleep,' Chloe mumbled, her glass of

white wine having done the trick. 'I've *got* to sleep, Josh.'

'Damn it, Chloe, you don't *give* a shit, do you?' he accused. He sat up in bed, snapping on the lights and the TV at the same time. 'You just care about yourself and *your* bloody career, not about mine. You're a selfish bloody bitch.'

There was no stopping him. Chloe closed her eyes, trying at least to rest them, and resigned herself to a bumpy night. Finally she went to the chilly, narrow bed in the guest room.

The final separation was easier than Chloe had expected. She had returned unexpectedly one day from the studio and found him making love to another fifteen-year-old girl. They were in the Jacuzzi, no less, using *her* foaming bath oil and with *her* favourite Lalique champagne glasses balanced on the edge of the tub, massaging each other with *her* one hundred and fifty-dollar-an-ounce body lotion.

She couldn't even be bothered to fight any more. Numb with pain, shock and disappointment, she locked herself in the guest room, swallowed two Valium and went to sleep in spite of Josh's night-long crying outside the door.

There was a limit to anyone's endurance, and Chloe had reached hers. The next day she called her lawyer. It was the end – absolutely. Reluctantly he agreed to take on the case again.

Josh didn't fight her. He moved to his favourite suite at the Wilshire. Tactful Perry arrived, quickly packed twenty suitcases of clothes, tapes and electronic equipment, and Josh was out of her life. 'No sweat, babe,' Josh said with a smile, as he kissed her goodbye – kissed eleven years of their life goodbye.

'Still mates, O.K., Chlo? We'll always be mates, won't we?'

She nodded dumbly. Her throat hurt with the effort of trying to stop the tears from running down her cheeks. Damn him, how dare he be so cool, so casual, so chummy. Would she *ever* get over him completely?

She slammed shut the heavy Aztec-carved doors and walked out onto the balcony. It was a sensational beach day.

Seagulls swooped, joggers jogged, the cobalt seas washed the seaweed-encrusted shoreline. A perfect Trancas Sunday. She was alone: her marriage ending, a TV career beginning, big things ahead. But she was now forty, an age considered scrap-heap ten or fifteen years ago. Thank God for Jane Fonda's changing so many people's attitudes about ageing women. They should build a shrine to her.

But today she felt her age. Felt old, washed-out, sad.

Sunday stretched ahead emptily. So, for that matter, did Monday, Tuesday and the rest of the week. The months and years seemed to lie ahead of her with nothing to fill them, except 'Saga'. Was a TV career that important to her? So many of her recent years had been dedicated to just being with Josh. He had filled her life, fulfilled her for much of the time, too. And now it was truly over. Dammit, *why* couldn't she stay happily married? Not for her the bed-hopping and assignations that filled the lives of so many of her acquaintances. It didn't thrill her. Her thrill was being with one person. All she wanted was one guy. One faithful man to be with, to share her life with. Why couldn't she have it?

So now what? She had the TV series, but she did not have – would never have – what she wanted most. A child. A baby to hold and hug and be Mummy to. A bit late now, sneered her inner voice. Your biological clock has ticked itself out. Her baby, Annabel, her best-kept secret, was now a long-legged, independent eighteen-year-old, living happily in London with an equally independent boyfriend, blissfully unaware that the famous Chloe Carriere was her mother. Chloe wrote to her every week, called her as often as she could, and thought about her every day. Annabel suspected nothing. Chloe felt such love for the tomboyishly beautiful girl so like herself at the same age. Independent, enthusiastic, ambitious. God, she prayed she wouldn't get hooked on a man like Matt or Josh.

'Good to see you, Auntie Chlo,' Annabel beamed, whenever they saw each other. She was always rushing somewhere, long auburn hair flowing, guitar thrown over her shoulder, off to some rendezvous to play her music with her friends. 'Must dash, luv, see you *soon*, promise.' Oh, yes, Chloe's sister-in-law sympathized with her, but if Chloe had been stupid and ignorant enough to get pregnant by Matt in the days when it was such a stigma, she must now bear the consequences for her actions. Besides, Annabel was Susan's child – legally adopted, much loved. And no one would ever know the truth.

Part Five

18

In late autumn of 1982 'Saga' went on the air. Sam Sharp played Steve Hamilton, the gruff, manly patriarch of the Hamilton clan. Chloe played Miranda Hamilton, his silkenly sexy ex-wife. Pandora King played the cool, sophisticated Judith Hamilton Stevens, ex-wife number two, and Sissy Sharp played Sirope, the saintly current Mrs Hamilton.

With assorted young actors playing a variety of sons, daughters, nephews and nieces, mistresses and lovers, within six weeks the ensemble soap opera became the biggest hit of the 1982–83 season. And Chloe Carriere was well on her way to becoming the household name that everyone had predicted.

'It's a total bummer,' confided Larry Carter, as they sat in the studio commissary at a quiet corner table. He ate an Abby Arafat Sandwich, while Chloe munched on sliced apple and avocado to keep the pounds off.

'I mean, how do you think I feel taking over from Alex? It's a break, I know, but, hell, he's one of my best friends.'

'Yes, but he didn't conform to the system, darling,' said Chloe. 'He bucked the system, Larry. You know he was always giving interviews, knocking the show, making fun of it on Carson and Merv. They won't stand for that. You know it.'

'True,' he said gloomily.

'Saga' had been on the air for one and a half seasons. It had become a gargantuan hit, greater than any other prime time soap opera in history. It had catapulted Chloe to stardom and fame she had never believed was possible. Now there were Miranda Hamilton dolls, Miranda Hamilton makeup, Miranda Hamilton T-shirts, greeting cards, and even car-bumper stickers with 'Let Miranda Live!' – referring to the courtroom scene in which Miranda had pleaded for her life after being wrongfully accused of killing one of her many lovers.

Magazines were clamouring for Chloe, so were gossip tabloids desperate for any skeleton in her cupboard to reveal to their readers. She started with diet and beauty magazines, fan magazines and fashion spreads. But soon graduated to interviews in *People*, *US* and foreign publications like *Paris Match* in France, *Holá* in Spain, *Oggi* in Italy, and the *Sunday Times* magazine in England. After that she started getting covers. Over an eighteen-month period, she was on the cover of more than two hundred magazines worldwide. 'Saga' had done great things for Chloe and for its other stars. All except Alex Andrews.

He had played Steve and Sirope's evil son, Cain, in the first thirteen episodes, but he had become deeply embarrassed by some of the clichéd dialogue and situations his character was involved in. He had started to bad-mouth the show in every interview he'd done, and he talked disparagingly on the set and in the makeup room about how stupid TV viewers were to be interested in such a puerile piece of crap.

It didn't take long for his bad-mouthing to reach the ears of Abby and Gertrude. He was called on the carpet in their palatial suite of offices – offices which could easily contain the living spaces of all the actors' trailers in 'Saga' – and told to cool it or else he would be replaced.

'We simply will *not* tolerate disloyalty to our show.' Gertrude's normally high colour dramatically increased, and her normally placid voice had turned shrill.

Abby said little. His huge bulk seemed totally in proportion with his massive imported black onyx desk, bare except for a colour photograph of him and Maud with President Nixon, one of his closest friends. It was tacitly understood that Gertrude was the spokesperson for the show when dealing with difficult actors, the schoolmarm telling off the naughty little boys and girls. Spank their bottoms, scold them sternly, and tell them to run away and behave. Alex was embarrassed. At twenty-three, he considered himself intellectually superior to both of these doddering relics who knew absolutely nothing about art, whose idea of cultural fulfilment was watching a Bertolucci movie at Sue Mengers's house. But he was also an actor who had to eat, and he had not bank-rolled himself sufficiently to relinquish the role of Cain.

Gertrude's diatribe lasted twenty minutes, in spite of three phone calls from a panic-stricken Ned who needed Alex back on the set.

'So don't let it happen again,' hissed Gertrude, her face now as flame-coloured as her frizzed red hair. 'We're a family here – a happy, productive family. We support each other, we *don't* bite the hand that feeds us.'

'Yes, Gertrude, of course. I'm sorry, it won't happen again,' he promised, hating his hypocrisy.

'Well done, Gert,' Abby said after the actor left, tail between his legs. 'Mustn't let them get away with it.'

'We never will,' she said strongly.

Two weeks later, while in New York for the weekend, Alex found himself drinking with some newly acquired Actors Studio friends at the Russian Tea Room. They were all unemployed, all secretly jealous of his prestige and the bread Alex was making, but they goaded him about what crap 'Saga' was, told him it was demeaning for a serious actor to be on it.

'The worst thing I have *ever* seen, it's an insult to the

intelligence,' said the small wiry-haired actress with a cast in one eye whose lack of talent and looks guaranteed that she would remain unemployed in her chosen profession forever. 'Doncha get sick to your stomach when you have to say those ridiculous lines?' said Tiger Lily, a beautiful Oriental actress who was having a tough time getting a job performing in anything other than porno films.

'The acting is the pits, man. The motherfuckin' pits,' groaned Mack, who washed dishes at Sardi's at night and auditioned in vain during the day. 'Quit! Become a *real* actor, man. Cut the crap. Come and live in New York where the action is, where an actor can have respect for himself. Where real talent is appreciated. Get back on the boards, man – the theatre. The real thing . . .'

Gertrude was in the middle of watching 'Saga' when the call came in.

'Fuck you – fuck your motherfucking shit show – it stinks. *You* stink. Let me out!' screamed drunken Alex.

She wasted no time. Without taking her eyes off the screen and Chloe's lovely face, while making a mental note to tell the hairdresser that Chloe's fringe was getting too long, she dialled Abby's house.

The news was on the street by the next afternoon. Alex had been dropped like used Kleenex. His scenes had been cancelled and new scenes with other actors substituted. A scene was written in which everyone wondered about his disappearance, then discovered that he had gone to Australia on a quest for his real father.

Two weeks later, Larry Carter was cast to replace him.

There was no explanation to the viewers as to why Cain had a different face, was ten years older and spoke with a British accent. His hair, dyed black, was the only concession that the producers made to the public. Such was the popularity of 'Saga' that viewers bought it without a murmur, and the show continued from strength to strength each week.

Her message service called Chloe with a wake-up call at 5

214

a.m. 'Good morning, hon, it's five o'clock. Are you up?' said the sympathetic voice of Gloria.

'Mmm, yeah – I am.' Chloe groaned, glancing at the digital clock on the bedside table. She slipped out of bed and into her lavish bathroom/dressing room, where she plugged in the electric coffee-maker which sat on top of a small fridge next to her 'Who Says Life Begins at Forty?' mug. She did ten minutes of fast sit-ups and push-ups while the water heater and her bath was running, and she watched the news on CNN. Twenty minutes later, scrubbed, showered and shampooed, and wearing a comfortable velour track suit, she jumped into her Mercedes and drove to 'The Factory', as the cast and crew affectionately called the studio.

MCPC Studios was a dull grey windowless building on the less attractive part of Pico Boulevard in Los Angeles. It bore about as much resemblance to the public's idea of a movie or TV studio as a prison did to a nightclub.

In her tiny dressing room, Chloe switched on Channel 5 to watch the local news, listened to the messages on her answering machine, and, sitting before the lightbulb-framed mirror, applied her TV makeup with swift, practised strokes. She preferred doing her own makeup when it was feasible. It was a little bit of time she had totally to herself – the only time she would have during the long twelve-hour day ahead.

Theo, her hairdresser, put hot rollers into her thick, dark curls, as she studied the scenes for the day. Debbie, the second assistant, brought her breakfast on a Styrofoam plate, with plastic fork, paper napkin and apple juice in a can, the whole covered by aluminum foil. At seven o'clock she went down to stage 11 for the first rehearsal of the day. Gina, her secretary, arrived with a clutch of eight-by-ten fan photos, and they discussed Chloe's schedule of social events and interviews for the next two days.

Today they were shooting a party scene in which all the cast were present. Sissy and Sam huddled together in a corner as usual, talking their heads off privately. For a married couple whom everyone knew had no sex life they certainly spent enough time gazing raptly into each other's eyes and having in-depth conversations. Today both wore designer jeans and plaid shirts and great wads of Kleenex were tucked into their collars to protect the clothes from the orange makeup the TV cameras required. Sissy's behind was so flat now, it looked as if it had been cut off by a bacon slicer. Her thin blonde hair was uncombed. It had suffered from the strong TV lights and from constant setting with hot rollers of the past seasons so she now wore a soft blonde wig while shooting.

Chelsea Deane, Chloe's favourite director, was directing this episode. The thirty-fifth. There were only nine episodes left before the end of the year. Ratings couldn't have been higher, nor could the spirits of everyone involved in the show. ' "Saga", Prime Time Hit Show,' the assistant directors cheerfully answered the stage phone, which rang constantly. There were eighty extras today, dressed in 1920s costumes for a costume ball. Three cameras were being used for the opening shot of the London mansion in which Sam, as Steve Hamilton, and Pandora King, as Louise, the third Mrs Hamilton, stood in the doorway to greet their guests. The crew sat around desultorily gossiping, munching bacon-and-egg sandwiches or doughnuts, sipping coffee. There was a hum of conversation as the actors rehearsed the first scene of the day. Chloe, Pandora and Sam usually referred to the script while they rehearsed, as they had not yet memorized their lines. Sissy was always word perfect, not only with her own lines but with everyone else's too. Woe betide any actor who dried. She had no patience and would blow her top.

After rehearsal Chloe went back to her dressing room. A heavily beaded gold flapper dress that had been designed for her by Rudolpho, Saga's resident designer, was hanging in the wardrobe.

'God, this is heavy,' she gasped, as Trixie, her dresser, helped her into it. 'It must weigh at least twenty pounds.'

'Thirty,' said Trixie laconically laying out long chandelier earrings, diamanté bracelets and golden shoes. 'We weighed it. It's broken two hangers already.'

'Great,' said Chloe. 'My shoulders already feel like I've been pulling a plough.'

'You must suffer to be beautiful,' deadpanned Trixie, as they heard the sound of Sissy yelling down the corridor, 'Trixieee, where the hell *are* you?'

'Ah, the dulcet tones of our divine diva.' Trixie smiled and winked at Chloe. 'Maybe I'll catch that skinny ass of hers in the zipper. That'll *really* make her yell!' Sissy was generally detested by cast and crew alike, but seemed oblivious to it.

In the hairdressing room, Theo combed out Chloe's hair and fixed golden ostrich feathers into it on a tight beaded band across her forehead. In the next chair sat Larry, while the other hairdresser, Monica, applied a layer of black pancake makeup to the bald spot that had started to appear recently on his scalp.

'Great, huh?' said Larry ruefully. 'My only consolation is that Prince Charles has one too.'

'And he's younger than you,' Chloe teased.

Larry grimaced. At thirty-five he was playing twenty-five, and it was becoming more difficult. He had to watch his weight constantly, as did all the actors to maintain their youthful appearance for the camera that never lied. Most of the crew gained several pounds each season, due to the long, boring hours and the ever present trestle table loaded with snacks and coffee that the producers laid on for them all day long. But the camera added five to ten pounds to an actor's appearance, so the cast tried to keep away from the junk food that was always on display. Often, however, at the end of the day all willpower lapsed, and to Pandora's and Chloe's dismay their tight-fitting costumes now and then would have to be let out in the waist or hips. This never happened to Sissy, however. Dieting was her religion.

'Ready, Chloe?' chirped the ever cheerful Debbie. 'Stage eleven, mush, mush, woman.'

On the stage, eighty extras were being organized by Ned

the first assistant director, as Chelsea Deane painstakingly rehearsed a scene in which Chloe and her latest lover, played by Garth Frazer, arrived to greet Pandora and Sam.

It was a short scene but difficult to shoot because the extras, or 'atmosphere' as they preferred to be called, had to move around in front of the principals without blocking the camera when the actors spoke their dialogue. The extras had to look animated, talk and laugh, yet were only allowed to mime so that the sound operator would pick up only the principals' dialogue.

After five takes Chelsea yelled, 'Cut and print.' The performers sat in a semicircle in their green director's chairs amidst a tangle of cables and arc lamps, relaxing for the eight to fifteen minutes it took to relight the scene for each of their close-ups. Theo and Ben fussed around Chloe's hair and face and Trixie worried about the bugle beads that kept falling off Chloe's bodice. She tried to sew them back on but finally gave up with a sigh. 'I don't think it'll show on camera.' Chloe tried to remain cool, calm and collected even though at 10:30 a.m. the temperature outside was hovering in the mid-nineties and the studio wasn't much cooler. According to the weather expert Doctor George on Channel 7, it was due to hit a hundred today.

Chloe felt her face sting under the heavy makeup. The strong lights washed out the performers' features to such an extent that excessive makeup was necessary to give definition to their faces. Sissy sat fanning herself with an antique fan she was convinced had once belonged to Lily Langtry. Garth, Chloe's TV lover, sat next to her, sweat pouring down his orange-tinted face.

Garth Frazer had blond, thinning hair and was only five feet nine, short compared to the other actors, most of whom were at least six feet. He had to wear high lifts inside his shoes, which gave him a curiously tipped-forward look, as though, if pushed, he might tumble over like Humpty-Dumpty. Chloe surreptitiously inched her chair away to escape his breath. Garth had obviously indulged the previous night in a fine Italian dinner laden with garlic. Little thought had he given to the fact that he would be locked in passionate embraces today with Chloe. But the more she moved her chair away to escape his breath, the closer he leaned, explaining to Chloe, as if she didn't know, the finer points of the scene they were going to perform.

Chloe was amused by his pomposity as he informed her what *her* motivation in their scene should be. Certainly he had been the star of two or three reasonable Movies of the Week, and had done a fairly respectable long-form series on prime time, but Lord Olivier he was not. She was beginning to resent his condescending attitude towards her and the rest of the cast and crew.

'I know you've only been acting for three years, darling.' He smiled, revealing the most awful capped teeth she had ever seen. How much longer could she tolerate this buffoon? Her 'beauty crew' – Trixie, Theo, De-De and Ben – sat nearby, observing, containing their amusement. Gina came over with a pile of mail to try to help Chloe escape as he droned on.

'So you see, darling, *that's* how I see Miranda and Charles's subtext in the scene, don't you agree?' said the blond actor earnestly.

'Mmmm, yes, of course,' mumbled Chloe. She knew her character better than he knew his, and she certainly knew her lines. He had been having serious trouble with his dialogue for the last four episodes. This was becoming a problem, as they were falling behind schedule. It cost them money, and if there was one thing the producers hated it was spending extra money. But Garth was seemingly unconcerned; he was a boorish puff-ball, a conceited egoist, in short, a fairly typical example of a mediocre prime time TV actor who had hit it lucky and whose success had gone straight to his head.

Mumbling 'Excuse me,' Chloe let Gina lead her away.

Several hours later the time had come to do their love scene. Chloe groaned inwardly.

'Ready for you, Chloe,' said Ned, as Ben packed Max Factor powder onto her face to stop the shine.

'O.K., my darling, let's go for one, shall we?' said Chelsea, still as hearty as a sailor on leave.

The lighting cameraman instructed the gaffer to move the lights more to the left. The sound man instructed the boom operator to adjust the proximity of his mike to the two actors because he was picking up too much echo. The camera assistant whisked a tape measure up to Chloe and Garth's noses and did some computations in his head, which he jotted down. Trixie fussed with Chloe's beads, Theo fussed with the feathers in her hair, which were starting to moult and fall onto her eyelashes. Ben outlined her lips for the fifteenth time that day with peach lip gloss. Bobby, the second makeup man, with a sigh of resignation mopped Garth's face with a wet chamois dipped in witch hazel, then mopped it with Kleenex before adding a thick coat of powder.

One of the secretaries from Bill Herbert's office arrived on the set with her entire family from Arkansas. They stood, mouths agape, directly in Garth's eyeline. One of them fiddled with an Instamatic camera, and they whispered loudly among themselves with excitement.

Chloe signalled to Ned to have them moved, but before it could be done Garth blew his top.

'Get those people out of my eye line, *please*,' he yelled. 'What is this, feeding time at the fucking zoo?'

'Calm down . . .' Chloe started to say.

'We're trying to do a goddamn scene here, not be stared at like monkeys in the motherfucking zoo, for Christ's sake.'

In unison the crew silently raised their eyes to the heavens. They had been suffering Garth's overbearing airs and graces in silence for months. Sissy they tolerated. Sissy was a big star, a central part of this show, their bread and butter. Garth had no such clout. This was basically Chloe, Sissy and Sam's show, in spite of the constant insistence by Abby and Gertrude that it was an ensemble piece.

Garth's makeup man once more attended to his sweaty

face, and Chloe wondered if he was on coke. She had never seen so much sweat.

'O.K., kids, let's 'ave a go, shall we?' Chelsea Deane was calm on the surface, but seething inside. This ignorant poofter was getting to him. 'What a no-talent numbnuts,' he had confided to Chloe the previous week, after directing a scene in which Garth blew his lines no fewer than eight times.

'I know, I know, darling, he's a pain. Why they cast him instead of Colin Bridges I'll never know.'

She and Chelsea exchanged glances of understanding. 'O.K., kids, *action!*' Chelsea stood next to the camera watching intently as Chloe and Garth started the scene. Garth immediately blew his first line.

'O.K., we go again,' said Chelsea, as the beauty crew trotted in to mop up. Ned called for the red light. The third camera assistant brought in the clapper board. 'Thirty-three take two,' announced the second man. 'Rolling.'

'Action!' yelled Chelsea.

'I love you, Miranda,' breathed Garth/Charles as he gently bent his blond head to Chloe's dark one. They were seated together on a chaise longue in the Hamilton mansion.

'I've never loved anyone as much as I love you.' Chloe felt nausea assail her at his garlic-laden breath.

'Oh, Charles, why do you say one thing, yet mean another?' Chloe moved her head away as far as she could without getting out of the careful lighting setup. There was a pregnant pause. Chloe tried to fill it with a girlish sigh. Garth had dried again.

'Sorry about that, love,' he said calmly. 'Heat's got to me.'

Chloe gritted her teeth. Trixie and Gina threw her sympathetic looks. The crew tried not to look affected.

'Thirty-three take fourteen,' cried the camera assistant briskly, as he snapped the clapper board exceedingly close to Garth's nose. The crew were seething inwardly now, and they felt sorry for Chloe, who was extremely uncomfortable. It was over a hundred degrees on the set. The heavy beaded dress, the moulting ostrich feathers, this ghastly actor with his awful breath and the sweat that poured from his brow onto her upturned face were a nightmare. Chloe had had enough. She had really had her fill this time.

They finally finished the master scene and after Chelsea covered it with medium shots and close-ups, Chloe went to her dressing room and called Gertrude's office. 'I need a meeting with you, now,' she said. 'And it can't wait.'

After seeing the abysmal rushes, Abby and Gertrude realized they had to find a new love interest for Chloe, and soon. She had rebelled for the first time in three and a half seasons. She told them she needed a strong, assertive man for her character to play opposite, a really macho man with strength, masculinity and sex appeal. They knew she was right.

An emergency meeting was called with Bill Herbert, Chloe and Jasper Swanson in attendance. Sitting in Abby's oak-panelled office they discussed the possibilities. Who was available, who wasn't. Who would do TV, who would think it was demeaning.

'Burt Reynolds,' suggested Chloe optimistically. 'There's a real man, and his movies haven't done well recently.'

'Ha!' said Abby. 'He's features, honey, *features*. He won't do TV.'

'Timothy Dalton,' suggested Jasper, ever one to get a fellow Englishman a job.

'Timothy who?' rasped Gertrude. 'Never heard of him.'

'He's good. He's an excellent Shakespearean actor. He's going to be hot,' insisted Jasper.

'Well, not on "Saga",' said Abby. 'I saw him in that Mae West film years ago. Nah – next.'

'You'll be sorry,' said Jasper. 'Timothy's going places, he'll be big.'

'Let him be big somewhere else,' said Gertrude. 'We need a macho guy with a name.'

For two frustrating hours they played the casting game. Then Jasper played his ace. He'd been waiting for the right moment. The moment when Tom Selleck, George Hamilton,

Robert Wagner, James Farentino, Alain Delon, Michael Landon, Peter Strauss, Martin Sheen, Jeff Bridges and Gregory Harrison had all been considered and, for one reason or another, dismissed.

'How about Luis Mendoza?' he suggested.

Luis sat across from Jasper at Ma Maison twiddling his thumbs. It had been three years since his movie with Sissy, a bomb if ever there was one. The producers couldn't even sell it to cable TV. Movie offers since then had been thin on the ground for Luis. If it hadn't been for his passion for Sabrina, he would have gone back to Mexico, where he was a superstar and his records still outsold Julio Iglesias's. In spite of his looks and his belief in his talents, Hollywood refused to take a singing Mexican seriously. He had hired the best public relations firm in town to promulgate his image as a serious but sensual actor. He had fired Milton Klinger and hired Jasper Swanson as his agent. He had been considered for movies with Bo Derek, Kim Basinger and Kathleen Turner – but he had had no firm offers.

He was now thirty-two and, with his black lustrous curly hair and slanting, heavily lashed brown eyes, handsomer than ever. He and Sabrina were the most beautiful and photogenic couple in Hollywood; the paparazzi went wild whenever they went out publicly, which was not often. They preferred to stay at the beach making love, lying in the Jacuzzi that was fitted into the deck outside their house, drinking wine and talking about their future.

Recently, though, the charms of Sabrina had begun to pall for Luis. Sabrina, gorgeous and loving as she was, had become a tiny bit boring. Occasionally, to his horror, he found that he was unable to respond to her amorous advances. Pretending headaches, exhaustion or lines to learn, he would retire to his study, where he sat pondering why his libido, of which he had always been justly proud, seemed to be deserting him. He recalled hearing the macho men of his youth discuss their *amigos* who 'couldn't get it up'; now he, too, seemed to be joining their ranks. Although it had only happened a couple of times in the past month, it was enough to turn Luis's hot Latin blood cold.

In the nearly three years he and Sabrina had been together, he had been more or less faithful to her, which for a Latin man was unusual. They had made love at least once or twice a day. Now his equipment was letting him down, a fate worse than death.

Preoccupied with his troubles, Luis was barely listening to Jasper.

'I think you should do a series,' Jasper was saying as he expertly slipped the band off a Davidoff cigar, lighting it with a kitchen match from a Victorian silver box he carried.

'A series? *Ay, mamá*, I was offered a series last month. The stars would be me and a talking car. No, thanks.'

'I don't mean *any* series.' Jasper was impatient. 'I'm talking about "Saga", the series of the moment, the hottest show in town.'

'So what? It's already cast with Sam and Sissy – ugh!' He grimaced remembering their ill-fated movie and even more ill-fated short-lived affair.

'What do you think of Chloe Carriere?' asked Jasper, puffing on the huge cigar with enjoyment. At his age, a cigar gave more comfort and pleasure than sex.

'Chloe Carriere, she's a dish, a bitch too, I hear.' Luis laughed. 'I hear she cuts off her leading men's balls and fries them for breakfast like *huevos rancheros*.'

'Not true, Luis,' said Jasper gravely. 'Not true at all. Chloe is actually a very nice girl who has become a victim, of sorts, of her own publicity.'

'But she's gone along with it, hasn't she?' persisted Luis.

'Dear Chloe, she is a wonder, I'll admit,' laughed Jasper. 'She's waited a long time for this break, so she's making the most of it. To get to the point, Luis, Abby Arafat and Gertrude have made us an offer that is hard to refuse.'

'What is it?'

'Two years on "Saga" with an option for a third. Twenty-five thousand an episode for the first year, forty thousand for the second, and the third negotiable, of course.'

'Hmmm, I can make more than that on a tour of Spain in a month,' said Luis.

'Luis, old boy' – Jasper was more serious now – ' "Saga" is a hot show this year, next year too. If they're lucky, they may even go to six or seven years. Chloe Carriere is a hot actress. They want you for her lover, husband, boyfriend whatever. This will make you the household name in America you've been dying to be. Let me tell you something, old boy, about the film scene. Nicholson and Redford find it hard to get the right roles and stay up on their movie pedestals today. TV is making the stars now. Take this part, Luis. Make every woman in America cream in her knickers when you come on the screen, and you can write your *own* ticket in two years' time. Look at Selleck – he made it on TV, and now he's got more movie offers than he can handle.'

Luis considered the Englishman's advice. It was true. TV was where it was now. With a few exceptions, there were no big movie stars any more. TV stars were the current royalty of show business, invited to the White House, curtsying to the Queen, on the covers of major magazines.

'Maybe I should do it. Let me think it over.'

'Do that, old boy. You have twenty-four hours to make up your mind; then they will go in another direction.'

Luis frowned. 'Don't threaten me.'

'I'm not, old boy. I'm not. I simply believe this is a major career move for you.'

'I told you I'll think about it,' said Luis.

It didn't take Luis long to accept the offer, and a few weeks later, locked in a passionate embrace with his new on-camera lover, Chloe, it didn't take him long to become a macho man again. He felt his manhood rising against the filmy chiffon of her nightgown. They were entwined under lilac Frette sheets on the set. Dozens of men and women barking orders and busying themselves with the thousand and one duties necessary before the camera could roll on the love scene unfolding in front of them milled around the bed. Luis started to sweat, something he normally didn't do. How *could* he be aroused by Chloe? She was far too old for him, and he hated her crisp British manner. She seemed always to be secretly laughing at him, and although she was friendly and charming, he hated her coolness and her lack of deference towards men in general.

Chloe looked startled at the feel of Luis's normally lackadaisical cock twitching against her thigh.

She looked into his eyes as they lay together while the camera assistant brought the measuring tape to each of their noses, and gave Luis a conspiratorial wink. Luis managed a weak smile as he willed his defiant member to subside.

Why, for God's sake, why now with Chloe? Why not with soft, adoring, gorgeous young Sabrina?

'O.K., kids.' Chelsea Deane beamed his cockney charm. 'I'm givin' you a lot of space here to really 'ave a go at it. I really want you to melt those TV screens. We've got a lot of leeway, so let me see if all the stuff they write about you in the papers is true, eh, luv?' He grinned at Chloe and she smiled back. Chelsea had a great sense of humour, something sadly lacking in most of the producers and directors of the show. He and Chloe insulted each other outrageously on the set, sometimes joking and kidding around until the crew broke up and Chloe had to go to her dressing room to try to recover from the giggles.

'*Aaand* action!' shouted Chelsea.

After the passionate love scene was over, there was silence from the crew. Trixie gave a terry-cloth robe to a stunned Chloe. Luis had been amazing. His ardour, inflamed by his sudden inexplicable desire for Chloe, had almost caught her up in the passion of the moment.

'Blimey, kids, that was *hot!*' said Chelsea admiringly. 'Print it – we don't even need coverage. Hey, Luis, you were great, man. Like just great!' Proudly Luis accepted compliments from various crew members and retired to his trailer as lunch was called.

Debbie Drake, the pretty young second assistant director, brought him his usual chef's salad, iced tea, and apple pie with ice cream. 'Anything else you want, Luis?' she said brightly, standing silhouetted against the bright California noonday sun in the doorway of his trailer, her taut breasts outlined by the simple white T-shirt she wore. She had a cute rear end enhanced by faded blue jeans. Her face, unadorned by makeup and framed by long blonde hair caught up in a ponytail, was pretty in a wholesome all-American way.

'Yes, *querida* – I want you,' he said huskily, giving her the benefit of the famous dark eyes that had caused maidenly hearts to flutter throughout Latin America.

'Oh,' gulped Debbie, having witnessed the love scene earlier. Oh, well, uhm, why not? she said to herself. Let's see if it's true what they say about Latin lovers. With a sharp kick of her sneakered foot, she pushed the door of his trailer shut and, pulling her T-shirt over her head, joined Luis on his sofa bed.

The following week Luis fucked Pandora. Although he had never been interested in older women, Pandora's brisk manner, coupled with a truly magnificent bosom, captivated Luis's imagination. His conquests seemed to improve his ardour for Sabrina. He found himself able not only to have some of the most interesting lunch hours he had ever had, but also to achieve new heights of passion with Sabrina. It was clear it couldn't last. All of a sudden Luis Mendoza was having his cake and eating it too.

19

In a weathered house on a small cul de sac in Santa Monica lived Sam Sharp's very good friend, Freddy.

A designer of ladies' clothing, Frederick Langlan was not in the class of Bob Mackie or Nolan Miller – his Hollywood gowns were in the seven-hundred-dollar price range rather than the seven thousand – but he had a loyal show-business clientele of not only wealthy but frugal women, but also of young TV starlets on the way up who wanted to look fabulous but couldn't afford Bob, Nolan's or even Neiman-Marcus's prices. Wives of B-picture actors on a tight budget but with a full social schedule, girlfriends of studio executives, older actresses who did occasional guest shots on 'Loveboat' and 'Magnum' and wanted to look their best, all were habitués of Freddy's rococo salon by the sea.

He painstakingly designed an 'original' Frederick Langlan for each one, an original that bore more than a passing resemblance to the exquisite creations of Valentino or Jacqueline de Ribes in the current issues of French or Italian *Vogue*.

To the ladies, it didn't matter. They were secure in the fact that there was no chance of the catastrophe that had happened recently at a Beverly Hills charity ball. The wives of two of Saga's producers, who had each blown nine thousand dollars on a gorgeous Galanos gown appeared at the ball wearing the same dress. If looks could kill, Mr Abby Arafat and Mr William Herbert would have been widowers. Hollywood chuckled with delight when the *Beverly Hills Tatler* ran front-page photos of the two women side by side wearing the identical dresses.

As they waited for Freddy, Sabrina Jones and Daphne Swanson sat in cosy chairs in his anteroom flipping through the *Beverly Hills Tatler* and laughing at the photographs of the two women.

Freddy drew aside the silver lamé curtains to his anteroom and swept in, followed by a cloud of pale grey organza and a torrent of the latest gossip.

'My dears, have you *heard* about Emerald's new boyfriend?' he said, giggling, as he lowered the neckline an inch and a half on Sabrina's creamy silk jersey to reveal more of her fabulous bosom, a sight guaranteed to get her, if not into the 'People' section of *Time* magazine, at least into the 'What the Stars are Wearing' in the *Beverly Hills Tatler*.

'I thought she was still seeing Solomon. Who is it?' Daphne interrupted her inspection of a box of Cadbury's milk chocolates which Freddy's flight steward friend had brought him from England. Daphne prided herself on being the first to know who was sleeping with whom – often stale news by the time the couple in question finally did it. With her network of spies in every restaurant, studio, boutique and hotel between Palm Springs and L.A., she usually knew, before the fact, the first time the eyes of potential lovers locked.

'My dear, it's *too* camp,' Freddy said through a mouthful of the pins with which he was outlining Sabrina's bosom. 'You *know* she's doing that movie in Italy?'

'Yes, yes.' Daphne impatiently lit a Dunhill, ever true to all things British.

'Of course we all know it's a turkey, if I ever heard of one, and she's playing opposite that has-been Italian star, what's his name?'

'Fabiano Frapani.' Sabrina whispered the name reverently. A has-been indeed! The greatest actor ever to come out of Italy. So what if he was pushing sixty – with talent like his, who cared?

'Weell,' said Freddy slyly, enjoying drawing out this scrap of gossip. 'You *know* who's directing, don't you?'

'Ouch!!' He had inadvertently pierced Sabrina's priceless left nipple with a pin.

'Oooh, *sorry*, dear, mustn't tamper with the merchandise. Do you want me to kiss it better?' he giggled, though both women noticed he was somewhat less effervescent than usual.

'It's all right, go *on*.' Even Sabrina, usually bored by gossip, as those who live their lives to the full mostly are, was intrigued by tales of Emerald's escapades. Almost three generations had now been titillated by them, yet interest in her private life still persisted.

'Horatio's directing, right?' Daphne was offhand. Although she knew who was fucking whom, minor details like who was directing whom usually escaped her.

'Yes indeedy. Horatio George Washington.' He stopped, becoming involved with the extent of the slit in Sabrina's skirt.

'To the thigh or to the crotch, dear? What do you think?'

'The thigh, please. I'm *not* Cher.'

'So what about Horatio George Washington?' Daphne was impatient. 'He's married to Edna Ann Mason, they just had a baby. Oh, dear, I *must* send her flowers.'

'Dear, he and Emerald have been at it like rabbits ever since they met when she went down under nearly three years ago.'

'How do you *know*, Freddy?' snapped Daphne, annoyed that her sources from Italy had not filled her in on this one.

'It's been in the English papers. Dempster's column, as a matter of fact. Now you've *got* to believe Nigel Dempster, haven't you, darling?'

'Not necessarily,' Daphne snapped. 'How do you know this for an actual fact?'

'Sorry, dear, can't reveal me sources.' Freddy leaned back on his heels, surveying the perfection of Sabrina in his copy of a Halston. 'We all know Emerald has always liked a touch of the tar brush, and Horatio *is* a famous coloured man, isn't he?'

'Black,' corrected Daphne. 'We say "black" now, Freddy dear, not "coloured".'

'Black, shmack, he's no more *black* than you and me, dear,' sniffed Freddy. 'More the colour of those chocolates, I'd say. But that doesn't matter at all. I think the fact he's married makes it a bit, well – '

'Tacky, darling?' finished Daphne.

'Yes, I suppose.'

'Well if the American papers get wind of this, *if* it's true, of course,' said Daphne, unzipping her dress and struggling into her organza, 'she will be in a lot of trouble with Middle American backlash.'

'I don't understand,' said Sabrina during the conversation as she threw on a faded denim shirt. 'He's married to Edna. *She's* white, *he's* black, no one cares about that, so why should it be such a scandal if Emerald sleeps with him? I mean DCOL: *It Doesn't Count on Location*, right, Daphne? Isn't that what you told me once?'

'Absolutely,' said Daphne breathing in for dear life and pressing her sides over her rib cage as Freddy attempted to zip her into the new dress. 'Dammit, Freddy, why did you make it so *tight*?'

'Duckie, face it, you've gained,' said Freddy, patiently opening up the seam.

While Freddy worked, Daphne explained. 'Edna is a, well, *proper* actress. I mean no one is really interested in what she does and with whom she does it. She could stand naked on the Empire State Building jerking off King Kong and it wouldn't even rate a mention in the trades, let alone the tabloids. She's too boring, too good, too mumsy. So the fact that she's married to a black director, even if he is only milk-chocolate-coloured does *not* interest the public. Edna is Edna. Solid, dependable, dull. But Emerald is Emerald, and *everything* she does, even if she sends back an overdone steak at Hamburger Hamlet, is of enormous interest to the public because of her *charisma*, darling. . . . *Aaah*, that's better, Fred.' Daphne breathed a sigh of relief as Freddy finally managed to do her up.

'Telephone, Meester Langlan.' The maid came in tentatively, in awe of Sabrina's beauty and Daphne's assertiveness.

'Who is it? I'm busy.' Freddy was fussing with the frills around Daphne's still appealing cleavage. Daphne was determined to outdo Lady Sarah in the frills department at next week's gala dinner in aid of cancer research. Her gown was an exact copy of the latest Zandra Rhodes.

'Eet's Meester Smeeth,' the maid said hesitantly.

Daphne looked knowingly at Sabrina.

''Scuse me, dears, be right back.' Freddy disappeared into his tiny cubicle of an office.

'Now you *know* who Mr Smith is, don't you, darling?' Daphne said smugly.

'No,' said Sabrina. She was wondering if she should take out a full-page ad in *Reporter* and *Variety* when the sequel to her college movie was released. Her press agent wanted her to, so did her agent, but her boring business manager said she couldn't afford it. What a drag. She was making over two hundred thousand a movie, and he said she couldn't *afford* a measly nine hundred bucks for an ad to enhance her flourishing career. Where did all her money go, for goodness' sake? she wondered. Nobody in Hollywood ever seemed to have the 'fuck-you' money they all craved.

Her rented furnished house at the beach cost three thousand a month, the cost of which she shared with Luis. Her car was leased. She had few good clothes; those she had were made by Freddy, who always gave her a good deal because she was the freshest, most beautiful of all his clients. Where *did* the money go? Her reverie was interrupted by

Daphne's whispering, 'If you don't know who Mr Smith is, I shall tell you dear.'

Sabrina neither knew nor cared. Her interests were mainly limited to her career and Luis. Both were full-time jobs, especially Luis, who seemed distracted these days. They certainly weren't making love as often as they used to.

Daphne went on, 'He's Sam Sharp, of course. They've been having a thing for *years*.'

'Oh.' Sabrina looked at Daphne, who was obviously pleased with imparting this bit of spice to one of the few who didn't know about it. 'How interesting.' Golly, she was bored by gossip.

'What's going on?' said Freddy to Sam, who almost never called during Freddy's work hours. They met, when possible, twice a month in Freddy's art deco-filled apartment above his shop.

'I haven't been feeling well, Freddy, and I'm working late. I can't make it tonight. Thought I'd let you know because we're on location and the damned cellular phone doesn't work when we get beyond a twenty-five mile radius of L.A.'

'Never mind, poppet,' said Freddy, slightly relieved to be on his own tonight. Now he could meet that pretty young sailor who was on leave for a week, and who drank at the King's Head in Santa Monica every night. They had locked eyes a few times, and Freddy thought it time to move in before the others did. 'Next Tuesday, O.K.?' Sam asked.

'Of course, luv.'

'Later, then.' Sam was terse on the phone. Terror at the possibility of his gay lifestyle being discovered became stronger with each passing year.

After Sam hung up on Freddy, he stretched and surveyed himself in the bathroom mirror of his luxurious trailer, which was now proceeding at a brisk clip down the Ventura freeway.

Not bad, not bad at all. He was fifty-three now, a vigorous, athletic, macho-looking fifty-three. If only he didn't feel so weak . . . maybe it was time for a checkup.

20

'What do you think of them?' asked Emerald shakily. The diamond and emerald bracelets winked on their dull black velvet bed.

'Beautiful, simply beautiful,' Vanessa Vanderbilt breathed. 'I must have them. How much?'

'Well, a bargain at thirteen thousand,' Emerald said tentatively. 'Don't you think?'

Thirteen thousand dollars. Vanessa mentally calculated the profit she could make from Emerald's bracelets. 'Too much, luv. Nine thousand, take it or leave it.'

And Emerald had to take it. It had been nearly three years now since she had failed to get the role of Miranda. In that time things had gone from bad to worse. Everyone knew who she was, but as usual no one wanted to employ her. She still spent money as though it was 1957 and tried to live the way she had then.

But it wasn't 1957. She was no longer in her twenties and America's favourite sweetheart, with suitors galore, a lucrative contract and money to buy enough gems to fulfil all her girlhood fantasies. It was 1985, and in spite of the face-lifts, the liposuction and the celebrity, she was in big trouble.

The six films she had made in the past three years had been worse than B. They were F – F for Failure. Emerald would now go anywhere for a movie. Anywhere she would be paid at least twenty-five thousand, they would agree to pay for an expensive suite at the best hotel near the location, anywhere she would be assured of five hundred a week in expenses, anywhere she would get to keep her wardrobe.

She didn't care if the movie was good, bad or indifferent. She had to keep up her lifestyle; she could not drop her standard of living.

Although she had traded her Beverly Hills mansion for a smaller house, it was still a little jewel in the hills of Beverly, but it cost. It cost her every penny she made. Unable to cope alone, without a steady man in her life, she took solace in vodka. Lots of vodka. Vodka with orange juice in the morning, vodka with ice on the set in a water glass; then bottle after bottle of Dom Perignon throughout the afternoon and night, whether she worked or not. And then after dinner, 90 proof Armagnac. Her drinking pattern would make strong men reel.

As the movies got worse, she hid her pain with other substitutes. The occasional odd joint at first. Then the snort. The blessed white powder that gave her such a lift. That made her feel young, successful, full of life and love again, but it was expensive, and she was now selling her jewellery to get it.

Vanessa Vanderbilt sounded tougher than she looked. Underneath her hard business exterior, she was generous and sympathetic. But dog will always eat dog, as Daddy had taught her. Only the most cunning survived in this world. There was no room for compassion in business. 'There's a bunch of fuckin' barracudas out there, me luv!' Daddy had instilled this dogma in her from the time she was four. 'Watch that little arse of yours *all* the time, darlin', otherwise the sharks will have it for their tea – mark my words.'

Vanessa, dutiful daughter, did just that, soon becoming more cunning and manipulative in business than Daddy ever

235

had. Oil-rich sheiks, Arab arms dealers, superstar entertainers, American politicians – Vanessa knew many, and she used them before they used and abused her.

'*Everyone's* a user. Don't ever forget that, my little love,' Daddy had said. 'If they're not a user, then they're a loser, and you're bloody well better off not havin' doin's with 'em, darlin'.' Thus spake Luke Higgins, the oracle of Petticoat Lane, as he cheerfully dispensed cockles and whelks from his stall every Sunday, worked in his secondhand furniture shop Monday to Friday, and Saturday taught his brood of eager kids the facts of life. Every Saturday morning in his cluttered shop off Petticoat Lane, across town from the Elephant and Castle, where Vanessa attended the local comprehensive school, Luke Higgins wheeled and dealed. This enabled Vanessa to grow up not only knowing the value of a pound, but also that of a dollar, a yen, a franc and a rouble.

Perhaps 'fence' was too strong a word for Luke, as he managed to stay a hair's breadth away from the law by dealing only in property stolen from another country. Interpol, although often hot on a scent, never managed to trace it to Luke, who was in his own words 'a crafty bugger' who always looked out for number one. Possessing a streak of Robin Hood's philosophy, he was a good-looking cheerful chap with ginger wavy hair, matching moustache, and rippling muscles in his wiry body, and he always gave the poorer of his clients a break when they needed to sell something legitimately. But to those from Italy, France and Germany, who passed their stolen goods to him, he showed no mercy.

The jewellery, cameras and other objects he received were the fruits of petty thievery on the French Riviera or ski resorts of Gstaad and St Moritz – also minor baubles that ladies had not bothered to put into their safes when they locked away their forty-carat diamond rings and half-million-dollar diamond necklaces. This was daytime jewellery, fun jewels: gold chains, Cartier or Piaget watches, one-carat diamond earrings, the odd charm bracelet. So wealthy were these women that they usually didn't even report these losses to their insurance companies, since it would only increase their premiums. A five-thousand-dollar Bulgari gold chain can easily be replaced, so can a Cartier watch – and it's *so* much fun to do it.

Through Luke's capable hands had passed some up-market, not overly expensive merchandise, which he managed to dispense via dealers in the antique markets of Portobello Road, Bermondsey and Kensington.

Luke had an enjoyable life, a pretty Jamaican wife who adored him and didn't give him a lot of lip like some of those uppity black women from Nigeria and Uganda. In return, he was a good father, a good provider and an excellent teacher, and his four children learned well from him.

Vanessa broke away from the family fold at eighteen to become a model. Having seen photographs of a gloriously elegant Gloria Vanderbilt in American *Vogue*, and becoming intrigued with all that her family represented, she changed the name Higgins to Vanderbilt, Vera to Vanessa. Higgins was too evocative of the East End to suit the lifestyle she craved.

In the 1960s Vanessa, a bubbly cocktail of her father's red curls and Irish charm and her mother's warm brown Jamaican skin, black eyes and sweet personality, became a minor success as a model, but a major one on the London social circuit.

Modelling was soon behind her, as she accompanied princes, rogues and rock stars on their travels. A diamond earring here, a Buccellati bracelet there, mink coats and fox wraps galore, Vanessa was in heaven. The Jet Set life was hers. Gloria Vanderbilt, watch out, she mused, here comes Vanessa Vanderbilt snapping at your heels.

She was courted and admired and made love to by wealthy and powerful men, but none of them ever fell in love with her. She sailed in their yachts, cruising in extravagant 180-foot vessels. She drove in their Ferraris, their stretch Mercedes, their antique Bentleys. She pocketed their crisp dollars,

237

pounds, or francs and shopped – as much as her heart desired. Vanessa was desirable, an alluring toy for rich men to play with. Year after year she flaunted her pert milk-chocolate body on luxury yachts in Portofino and Monte Carlo, basked by the pools in marbled villas in Marbella and Sardinia, grazed the boulevards of the Rive Gauche, Fifth Avenue and Rodeo Drive in search of ever more outrageous clothes to add to her vast wardrobe. She was a happy woman. So happy in fact that she celebrated this happiness with her favourite pastime – eating.

Vanessa would rather make a reservation than make love. Often during the act of love, she would think excitedly about the snack she would order after this tiresome tussle was finished. As the rich and powerful of the world buried their heads and their members in her fragrant alcoves, aroused by her moans of esctasy, they never imagined that her lust was not for them, but for food.

Usually Vanessa kept a little snack next to whatever bed she happened to be occupying – perhaps a biscuit tin with a picture of the Queen on it, full of Mars Bars or Swiss milk chocolate, on which she would happily munch afterwards, while her lover lay spent beside her. Soon, as she ripened like a watermelon in the noonday sun, she started to lose her lovers. The Americans went first, then went the English, then the French left. Soon the Italians and Germans lost interest, until eventually the only men left who desired her were Arabs.

Vanessa didn't care, so happy was she with her life of luxurious opulence and the friends she still had in abundance. Friends of both sexes adored her. She was fun, the first to make fun of herself, including her battle with the bulge.

In vain Vanessa tried to diet. Jane Fonda videotapes littered her rooms, but she had absolutely no willpower. She simply could not resist caviar with sour cream, veal chops with pommes frites, *mousse au chocolat*, everything delicious – not to mention the wines that accompanied her feasts and the liquor-filled chocolates, mints and savouries that followed.

To her current *beau*, an Arab sheik, she was manna from

238

Allah. A Western woman who loved to eat was as rare as teeth on a hen in London. Most of the 'models' and starlets he entertained ate like birds. Vanessa was more than just a hearty eater. She matched him in gluttony.

'Another baby lamb,' he would roar with delight as they squatted on the floor of his suite at the Dorchester Hotel, while his personal chef from Kuwait prepared delights from the Sinai desert, desserts the like of which could not be found in any cosmopolitan restaurant in the western world.

Vanessa leaned her plump little cheek on Samir's big plump shoulder, and, spooning pâté into a piece of pita bread, popped it affectionately into his mouth. It was so wonderful. Such a wonderful life. Samir was so generous with money and presents, so attentive when she needed him – which was not often, as she was far happier eating and shopping. Unlike many Arabs, he had charm, manners and, thanks to a Harvard education, the cutest American accent.

Sex bored her, and she found 'The French Way' positively repugnant. The only way she could tolerate it was to pretend she was eating an ice-cream cone. When Samir had to go to Kuwait, he left Vanessa in his permanent suite at the Dorchester with a generous supply of money and his company's American Express and Visa cards made out in her name.

She heard about his murder on breakfast television news in bed one morning as she devoured her fifth croissant with raspberry jam and Devonshire cream.

Things did not go well for Vanessa after that. Since she was not mentioned in Samir's will, his money and estate went to his three wives and eleven children in Kuwait. All that Vanessa possessed, apart from clothes and jewels, were two company credit cards. Her father's teachings having had good effect, she immediately went to the Bond Street antique shops and art galleries and bought as many objects of value as she could until the credit dried up. Although she still had a pretty face, Vanessa's weight now hovered around the two hundred pound mark; she no longer appealed to any of the eligible rich or powerful men in London or Europe. They preferred their women sleek, like their boats, their planes and their automobiles. Pretty butterballs with cheerful personalities did not interest powerful, eligible men, not even as temporary arm decoration. For the occasional one-night stand, maybe – but most of the men of her acquaintance were not interested by Vanessa sexually at all.

Vanessa had to face the unhappy fact that her days of using her looks to earn a living were over.

She was thirty-two. She had enjoyed La Dolce Vita to the hilt. Now it was time to go legit.

She started selling her own jewellery and the paintings and objects she had acquired after Samir's death. She had an abundance of items from fourteen years of grateful donors. Her father gave her a few pieces and she started attending auctions and estate sales in England. She had a clever eye both for a bargain and a good jewel, and in three years she had built her travelling jewellery emporium into a lucrative business. Often she did business with many of the men she had bedded, and since she was such a likable and loyal friend, her business prospered, and now she was on a trip to L.A.

'Would you like the box?' Emerald asked Vanessa. Looking at the red leather Cartier container with the embossed gold edging, Vanessa nodded. 'Yes, but I'll wear them,' she said, scribbling a cheque. 'I like them so much, I'm keeping them for myself – temporarily, that is.'

Emerald looked longingly for the last time at her bracelets. She loved them. She adored all her jewels. If a man wasn't buying them for her, she bought them for herself. Now they were going. And no one, it seemed, would be buying any more for her. Ever.

After selling her bracelets to Vanessa, Emerald headed for a bar she knew in West Hollywood. She ordered vodka stingers. Five in a row.

The barman looked at her curiously. She looked vaguely familiar, but he knew better than to engage in conversation with anyone who obviously had a lot of problems in life. This woman looked as if she had more than most. Obviously she had been quite a looker in her day. Now the blonde hair had grey roots and hung in uncombed snarls around a face devoid of makeup, but in which he could see vestiges of what might once have been aristocratic cheekbones, a sculptured nose and luscious lips. Her eyes were hidden behind tinted glasses, and she wore a shapeless tweed jacket and sweatpants that hid her body. On her feet were scuffed high-heels. She smoked Luckies, lighting each one from the last, rejecting offers of a light from the men who occasionally looked at her, perhaps catching the animal scent of her former glory. She stared straight ahead, barely moving except to lift the glass to her pale mouth.

Draining her fifth stinger, Emerald motioned shakily to the bartender for another.

'Lady, I think you've had enough, don't you?' The bartender tried to be kind. He had observed her coming back from the ladies' room. This broad could hardly walk.

'I'm fine. Give me another,' she snapped.

'I can't, lady. I'm sorry.'

'Screw you, buster!' snarled Emerald.

'Look, lady, there's a law in this town. I can't serve drinks to a person who's obviously had too many. I don't want to lose my licence.'

'Fuck your licence,' mumbled Emerald, getting up from her stool and lurching to the door. 'Fuck your licence and your crappy bar.' She looked around the bar at the dozen men staring at her. None of them recognized her. 'Fuck you, all you bastards,' she exclaimed and, slamming the door, staggered onto Olympic Boulevard.

The next day, when she came to, she pulled herself together, and went to visit Daphne Swanson.

'To be frank, love, I need a job – any job. I'm not proud. I'm down to my last few trinkets. I sold my favourite bracelets

241

yesterday, the ones Stanley gave me for our wedding. You know how much he meant to me.'

'I know, dear, I know. I remember it well, even though it was thirty years ago.'

'Twenty-eight,' said Emerald crossly. 'And I was only twenty.'

'Of course,' Daphne agreed smiling inwardly. Why did they all try and lop off the years when the town knew to the month what year they were born – and to the thousandth how many bucks they had in the bank?

'You know everything that's going on, Daphne. There must be *something*, somewhere, coming up that I would be right for. I mean, I *am* Hollywood royalty.' She laughed lamely.

'I know, duckie, you were – I mean of course you are,' soothed Daphne. 'But dear heart, you must realize that movie stars of your generation are, well, a bit *passé*.' She bit into a marron glacé, grimaced at the sweetness of it and fed it to the Pekingese nestled close to her on her pink down comforter.

Emerald bit a hangnail and lit up a Lucky Strike. God, she'd love a drink. She'd love a snort, too. What time was it? 11 a.m. Oh, well, it was 7 p.m. in London – cocktail time, civilized time. Her friends in Eaton Square and Chelsea would be drinking martinis now, or champagne.

'Do you want a drink, dear?' asked Daphne, reading her mind.

'Oh, I don't think so yet ... well, maybe just a Bloody Mary.'

'I'll join you,' said Daphne, graciously coming down to her level. 'Then we'll have lunch at the Ivy. Burt Hogarth is lunching there today.'

'What is Burt doing these days?' asked Emerald.

'Darling, *really*! I know you've been away, but don't you know anything that's going on in this town?'

'No,' said Emerald vaguely. 'I've been in *Italy* for the past five months, remember.'

'You'd better wise up, dearie, or get off the merry-go-round,' said Daphne, accepting the Bloody Mary from her maid. 'This is 1985, dear. If you want to stay in this business, you better get into television fast, because *that* is where it's all happening today. Even Burt Hogarth knows that – that's why he's doing TV after all those hit movies.'

Emerald drank her Bloody Mary, feeling the quick buzz vodka always gave her, the false sense of hope and optimism it inspired.

Daphne continued, 'Burt Hogarth is producing a prestigious and *very* ambitious series, darling. Not the usual potboiler schlock. It's called "America: The Early Years". I think the title tells the story, dear. I know they are casting now, major names, darling, major. They've already signed Sir Geoffrey Fennel and Olivia Grosvenor from the National Theatre – remember her Juliet? God, she was wonderful! But if Burt could see you, see how good you still look . . .'

In fact, Daphne didn't think Emerald looked good at all. The face-lift had not been much help, though her glamour was still there under the bloat, the bags and the grey roots. Having read the script, Daphne realized that actually Emerald might be a long shot for the part of Evelyn, the lusty, adventurous pioneer woman who comes from the old country to a new frontier town in the America of the 1880s. Against all odds she makes herself and the new town a force to be reckoned with throughout the nation. It was going to be the most important new series on prime time for the 1985–86 season – the most talked about series, in fact, since 'Saga'.

The fact that Burt Hogarth, film *Wunderkind*, was taking a temporary leave of absence from his dazzling film career as writer, producer and director of seven worldwide box-office blockbuster movies was a major and unprecedented event for television. Already all the rival networks were concerned enough about 'America: The Early Years' to be approaching top talent from both film and theatre to prepare projects to pit against it.

'So, shall we lunch or shall we not, dear?' Daphne asked. Emerald nodded. Daphne picked up the phone and made a reservation.

'Now go home and change into something glam and sexy, darling,' Daphne instructed. 'I'll meet you at one and you'll work your magic on Mr Hogarth. He'll be entranced, I'm sure of it.'

It hadn't worked out quite that way. Emerald had gone home and taken several Valium washed down with vodka to calm her nerves. In her muddled state, remembering Daphne's 'Glam and sexy, darling,' she had chosen a highly unsuitable lime-green lace cocktail dress, too *décolleté*, too short, simply too much, in fact.

She was late, as usual, as she pulled up outside the Ivy, and instead of hitting the brake, her foot slipped onto the accelerator, smashing her Mercedes into the open door of Abby Arafat's brand-new maroon-and-black Rolls-Royce Corniche – all in full sight of the amused lunch bunch and a couple of cops.

When her agent, Eddie – she'd come back; he'd known she would – finally bailed her out, the media had a field day. Her secret life of drugs and booze was openly discussed in newspapers, on television and in every drawing room and office in Los Angeles. Tongues wagged, and what they said was not complimentary.

'You've fucked up royally, kiddo,' said Eddie in no uncertain terms. 'You have blown your career. No studio, no network, no producer will ever touch you now.'

Emerald wept. She couldn't help it. Forty years of stardom! Is this how it ended? 'I'm not a lush, Eddie, I'm not an addict either, you know I'm not,' she sobbed into a lime-green hanky.

'Do I?' He looked cynical as he peered at her through his giant magnifying spectacles. 'You certainly looked like one, kiddo, when I sprung you from that vile prison.' He shuddered at the thought of seeing Emerald in her ridiculous short lace dress, facing the harsh California sunlight and hordes of press and paparazzi. 'You looked the pits, woman!'

The photos had not been pretty. They had made the front page of every tabloid from Tokyo to London – a weary disillusioned, bloated and blowsy woman looking older than her fifty years. Over the hill. Used up. No use to anyone any more.

Calvin had been in gaol for nearly three years. Most prisoners doing time for possession of a deadly weapon were paroled sooner, but Calvin had blown his chance for that by his uncooperative behaviour and attacking a guard who tried to have sex with him. He sat in his cell and reread the article in *The American Informer* for the umpteenth time.

'As Chloe Carriere soars to superstardom on the hit prime time show *Saga*, so the sad, once superstar, legendary actress Emerald Barrymore fights the twin battles of depression and dope. Picked up for drunken driving in Hollywood last month, the once-beautiful star is now practically destitute and unable to get a decent job in Tinseltown. How different would her life have been if *she* had won the coveted role of Miranda? Chloe Carriere now queens it in Hollywood while Emerald Barrymore is a broken woman.'

His Emerald. *His* beautiful, indestructible Emerald, was being ruined by this English bitch! He looked at the calendar again. The date was engraved on his memory. 24 April, 1987. That was the day he finally would be paroled. Soon after that the bitch would die!

Burt Hogarth studied the clippings his assistant had placed on his desk.

Certainly the woman looked awful. In that short low-cut dress she looked ridiculous. Booze and drugs had finally caught up with her as they do with everyone who abuses them. Her skin was stretched too tightly across her neck and her cheeks were bloated, but there was an undeniable strength beneath the vulnerability there – a softness underneath the tacky veneer that appealed to him. 'Let's test her,' he said to his assistant.

'*Test* her!' The young man looked at Burt in amazement. 'You can't *test* Emerald Barrymore, she's a superstar – a

245

legend in her lifetime, even if she's the town joke this week.'

'She tested for "Saga", didn't she?' Burt knew his Hollywood like a great white hunter knows the plains of Africa. ' "Saga" is schlock, we know that, but she wanted it. Badly, I hear. That was three years ago, and she's done nothing decent since. From what I hear she's hungry.'

'Maybe we should take a look at that "Saga" test?'

'No. I want to shoot my own. As far as I'm concerned, Emerald Barrymore is an over-the-hill ageing *ex*-star who *could* be right for this role, and if she is, it will be the best thing that happened to her since Rin-Tin-Tin rescued her from the train track. So get her fucking agent on the phone and set up the test. The network is trying to ram Angie Dickinson down my throat, but as much as I like Angie, she's not right. So we test Miss Barrymore, and hope for the best.'

'*Another* test! Oh, Eddie, why? I mean, I've made fifty-two fucking films for Christ's sake. I tested for "Saga" and lost. Can't they look at *that* test?'

'No, kiddo,' Eddie said coldly, looking straight at her. He was tough with his clients when they got out of line, hence they respected him all the more apart from Emerald. No client had ever left him was his boast, but he had dropped several.

'The "Saga" test was over three years ago, dear. Hollywood has a short memory. As far as the network shooting "America" is concerned, you are a convicted drug addict and a drunk.'

'No, that's not true!' cried Emerald.

'It's the truth that hurts, kiddo. Face it, my dear, you were the family favourite of the forties, the flavour of the decade of the fifties, the sexpot of the sixties and seventies. But it's 1986 now. You've been around a long time. It's time to get your act together or get out of the rat race.'

'I love this business. It's my *life*,' cried Emerald.

'Good. Then test,' said Eddie bluntly. 'Test and you'll get the part. Trust me.' The tiny man suddenly smiled a rare

246

smile. 'The ironic part, kiddo, is that the network is throwing all of its biggest guns into "America", they are going to pit it head to head against "Saga" next season. They're sick and tired of having "Saga" the number one prime time show week after week. This is war, toots, total war.'

'I've always loved a battle.' Emerald smiled, beginning to feel more like her old self.

'I know you do, duchess, and one of the things that is going to make this battle even more interesting is that if the series succeeds – which it will, of course – you will be Chloe Carriere's main rival on television. "The Battle of the Bitches"! I can see the headlines now.' His elderly eyes twinkled mischievously behind the huge glasses.

'I thought you adored Chloe, Eddie.'

'Of course, kiddo. I *do* adore her. She's my friend even if she isn't my client. She's made it big, and it hasn't changed her. I wish she could be happier in her personal life, though. I think she's still carrying an ember for her ex. That's the trouble with all you girls.' He looked scoldingly at Emerald. 'Unless you have a man in your life, you don't seem to be complete.' Emerald shrugged. 'But competition is healthy, kid. Makes the juices flow. Emerald Barrymore versus Chloe Carriere. For this event *I* want to have a front row seat. And so will the public, I guarantee it.'

21

Chloe awoke at six o'clock. It was still dark outside, and 'cold and damp', as Lena Horne sang about California. She went down to the kitchen to make a strong cup of Nescafé with three teaspoons of honey for energy. She showered, jumped into jeans, T-shirt, shirt, sweater, jacket, scarf and woollen hat. Despite what the world thinks, it really is *icy* in California in the early hours. Since the temperature changed between from forty to eighty-five degrees during the day, she always dressed in layers.

The teamster driver waited for her in his minibus for the seventeen minute drive to the studio. While he drove, she tried to study the scenes for the day, a total of eleven pages of dialogue – mostly a diatribe by Miranda.

After more than three years, the dialogue had begun to bear a dreadful similarity to the dialogue of last week's episode, and those of the weeks and months before. The actors were the same, the sets didn't change, only the costumes were different, which represented the only proof that this was another episode.

In her tiny shoe box of a trailer, identical to those of the other ten actors, the make-up man had laid out the tools of his trade. The trainee A.D. brought her another cup of coffee. She turned her radio to FM KJLH (Kindness, Joy, Love and Happiness – *the* survival station) and to the songs of Al Jarreau and Lionel Richie she applied her makeup while studying lines, drinking coffee and eating an orange.

At seven a.m. Debbie the second assistant director, summoned Chloe to the set. Half made up, hair in rollers, script in hand, lines still fuzzy and only half-learned, she, with Sissy and Sam blocked the first scene of the day.

Then it was panic and rush to finish hair and makeup and run lines with Ostie the dialogue coach.

Trixie, the wardrobe assistant, entered the trailer carrying six outfits in plastic hanger bags and a large Neiman-Marcus shopping bag full of shoes and purses.

'Rudolpho thinks you should wear the black, but the director says that the set's too dark, and you'll fade into the woodwork, so I brought the red for the first scene, hon.'

'O.K.' Chloe squinted at her face in the three-way mirror. Losing a pound or two wouldn't hurt. Weight always went straight to her face, and then her cheekbones disappeared.

'What do you want for lunch?' Debbie popped her head in the door. Chloe grimaced. Lunch! How could she know at 7 a.m. what would titillate her at one in the afternoon?

'Give me a tuna on rye and apple juice, darling,' she said, turning to Trixie, who was rummaging through a four-foot-high black chest of drawers – Miranda's jewel box – which stood on the floor.

Pearls, diamonds, rubies, emeralds and gold baubles trickled through her fingers.

'I think the Chanel pearls would look hot with this outfit,' said Trixie, critically laying them on the elegant suit. 'Or do you want to wear that Kenneth Lane gold chain?'

'Anything you say, luv,' agreed Chloe. She trusted Trixie's excellent taste in accessorizing the nine or ten outfits she had to wear each week.

'How about the Givenchy earrings? They look fabulous.'

'Don't you think they're too big?' said Chloe distractedly, working on her lashes.

'Hon, nothin's too big for "Saga", surely you know that!'

After Chloe put on the tight red suit, Trixie stood back surveying her handiwork and tugged at Chloe's skirt, which was beginning to feel uncomfortably binding around the waist.

'Got a little extra there today, huh?' Trixie was used to her female stars' fluctuations in weight. Even two pounds made a difference when each outfit was fitted like another skin.

'Thanks, darling. You're not exactly Twiggy today either.' They smiled at each other, used to the banter that kept them sane at 7 a.m.

Chloe bumped into Pandora on the short walk to Stage Two. Pandora was wearing a grey flannel Thierry Mugler suit, the shoulders of which were so exaggerated that she looked like a football player. Her red wig was styled in a 1940s page-boy, and she wore fuchsia lip gloss and gold eye shadow. She looked hard and chic.

'Hi, there. What did you think of the show last night?'

Pandora was a friendly soul with no axe to grind with anyone. She was no great shakes as an actress, but she was sweet and professional, and knew that she was lucky to be pulling down twenty-five grand an episode in one of the hottest shows on prime time.

'I thought your courtroom scene was excellent – really good.' Chloe never praised unless she meant it.

'Thanks, honey, it was a well-written scene. What did you think of *her*?' She gestured towards Sissy, already sitting upright in her director's chair, Kleenex folded down the neck of her turquoise suede dress, smoking the first of her eternal cigarettes through a holder and dispensing a stream of invective to all who came her way. 'Watch out, someone got out of bed on the wrong side today,' Pandora said.

'What else is new?' Chloe laughed.

Sam stood on the set sipping coffee from a Styrofoam cup and chatting to the crew. He was popular with all of them, making genuine efforts to communicate, to joke, trying to make up for the bitchiness of his wife. The crew felt sorry for him. 'No wonder he's a fruit,' Maxie, the teamster, muttered to Chloe one day. 'With a cow like that for a wife, I'd like boys too.'

Like everyone else, Chloe despised Sissy and adored Sam. She gave him a peck on his heavily made up cheek, which was becoming alarmingly thin these days, she noticed.

He was not looking well. His normally luxurious brown moustache looked unkempt and bedraggled. The thick brown toupee he always wore looked strange and lopsided, as though it was too big for him. Maybe it was because he was in pyjamas and a dressing gown and made up to look ill that he didn't look good. They were shooting a scene in which Sam/ Steve was in a coma in a hospital bed, while his three wives, one current and two ex, stood around his bed, willing him to live.

'Here's your coffee, darling.'

'Hi, Vanessa.' Chloe smiled at her new personal assistant.

Since stardom had been hard to handle with just a secretary, she had started to look around for a personal assistant to help her with the hundreds of requests for interviews and personal appearances, to sift through the thousands of pieces of fan mail and to read some of the torrent of scripts that were sent.

Vanessa Vanderbilt had become vaguely bored with her jewellery business. Fine jewels at the price she could afford to pay were not easily available these days, and Vanessa had been looking around for something more stimulating. One day she and Chloe had found themselves seated next to each other on a flight from London after one of Chloe's visits with Annabel. Chloe complimented Vanessa on her beautiful emerald-and-diamond bracelets, and Vanessa replied that they were for sale. Surprised and thrilled, Chloe wrote out a cheque for twelve thousand dollars, in defiance of her business manager, and slipped Emerald's lovely jewels on her wrists. The two women toasted the transaction with champagne, and after the third glass started to let their hair down. They discovered they had tremendous rapport. They laughed, told intimate stories of their lives, and found they were soul sisters. Before the plane landed, Vanessa had agreed to a trial run of three months as Chloe's personal assistant. So far it had been a success. The two women got along like a house on fire, much to the envy of Sissy, who could never bear to see happy business relationships around her, particularly between two women. She was unable to keep any assistant, and few of her domestic staff, longer than a few months.

'O.K., let's try a rehearsal,' called Ned, the first A.D.

The four actors walked onto the 'Saga' set. Sam stripped off his dressing gown and gratefully lay down in the bed. Thank God he had nothing to do in this scene except groan. He felt he could do that realistically enough. Last night had been ghastly. Sissy had been in one of her more vile moods. Her jealousy of Chloe was fuelled each day by various items in magazines or gossip columns. Last night her fury was released when she read the piece in Army Archerd: 'Chloe Carriere's career goes from strength to strength. The hottest female on TV has been signed to produce and star in her own miniseries "Ecstasy" in conjunction with Hammersmith Productions. Shooting will commence in London and Madrid during Chloe Carriere's third hiatus from "Saga".'

'Damn that woman!' Sam barely had the strength to duck as Sissy threw the trade paper across the room with such force that the tropical fish swimming lazily in their five-thousand-dollar aquarium, tastefully set into the polished granite above the authentic wood-burning fireplace, hastily disappeared behind their painted rocks.

'Damn that bitch. *Why*, why does she get her own fucking miniseries? What's *wrong* with my agent?' she railed, pouring a generous shot of Smirnoff into a Lalique tumbler.

Sam lay on a tan leather sofa quietly trying to watch a video of a John Wayne movie and feeling weak and ill.

* * *

252

Now Sam lay in a hospital bed on Stage Two, feeling worse. During a break in the shooting the three women couldn't stop talking about an item in today's Army Archerd column about 'America: The Early Years'. The columnist waxed enthusiastic about the new prime time series and the excitement in the industry about Burt Hogarth's masterminding of it.

'I heard he was interested in Emerald Barrymore for Evelyn,' said Pandora, tolerating Theo combing out her red wig for the umpteenth time.

'Really!' sneered Sissy, dragging on her cigarette holder, with brown birdlike hands tipped by scarlet claws that matched the slash of her thin lips. 'Are they going to be able to get her out of bed and off the bottle long enough to *get* her in front of the cameras?' She laughed maliciously.

Pandora and Chloe ignored the remark, but Sam managed a weak smile. He was not feeling good. He *must* find time for that checkup.

'Now, now, honey,' he remonstrated to his wife. 'You know Emerald's had a run of bad luck. Let's hope she gets that part. She's a nice gal. She needs it.'

Hmmm, Sissy calculated to herself, if Emerald *did* get it, there might be some advantages. Emerald might knock that snotty British bitch off the front pages and the magazine covers. Chloe's success was beginning to become more of an irritant every day. Chloe was becoming an obsession with Sissy. An obsession of hate. Only one person felt that hate more strongly.

Calvin lay on a rough grey blanket in his cell trying not to listen to the disgusting conversation of his cellmates. They were talking about sex as usual. That was all they ever talked about. Occasionally baseball or football was discussed, now and again a new inmate would cause a brief flurry of interest, but basically every man in that gaol was obsessed by one subject. Sex.

Calvin's cellmates were discussing in intimate detail the merits of the current *Penthouse* pinup. The woman's legs were spread wide, showing a view only a gynaecologist usually saw. The men were turned on. Calvin knew what would happen next. After three years he knew only too well. They would do things to each other, pretending it was the woman in *Penthouse*. Sometimes they would do it to Calvin, even if he resisted. He knew that. It had happened the first day he arrived in this gaol. With sickening regularity it had continued. Calvin was not classically handsome, but he was reasonably young, had fair skin and a firm body. The rest, the men's imaginations took care of.

Prison was a seething cauldron of the suppressed sexual desires of nine hundred potent men cooped up in the prime of their life with nothing to do except fantasize about sex.

Calvin tried to feign sleep but it was no good. Kolinsky, the big twenty-three-year-old Pole with the dark hair, bad teeth and huge thing, came over to him.

'C'mon now, Calvin, old buddy. Time to have a good time with yer ole friend here.'

Calvin knew if he rebelled he would get beaten. The guards turned a blind eye. Sometimes they themselves sampled some of the tastier young 'virgins' first. As he braced himself for Kolinsky's onslaught, he blanked out his mind until all he could think about was his hatred for Chloe Carriere, how she was to blame for this, and that he only had fifteen more months of this horror.

22

Since her final split with Josh, Chloe's love life had become a topic of great interest to the supermarket tabloids and gossip columns, and they printed every bit of dirt they could on her.

More than a casual chat with a man at a party, and she was reported to be having an affair with him. More than two dates with the same man, and she was engaged. More than six, and elopement and marriage were imminent. Since her split with Josh she hadn't been serious about anyone. She and Johnny spent the occasional night together now and then and dated on and off, but it was not a deep relationship. He had plenty of women on his string. With the AIDS threat hovering uneasily on the horizon, she was not about to risk her life for a casual encounter, however attractive that encounter might be. Three years of stardom and celebrity were beginning to take their toll. She was becoming snappy, irritable and uninterested in anything except 'Saga'.

'You need a man, dearie,' observed Daphne at lunch one day. 'A *good man*.'

'Yeah, and they're hard to find around these parts,' Vanessa added.

Chloe, tight-lipped, was drinking Perrier on the rocks and picking at her cuticles.

Daphne was insistent. 'You don't look happy.'

'I don't need a *man* to make me happy,' snapped Chloe, lighting a cigarette and wearily signing another autograph.

The table at which she sat with Daphne and Vanessa was in a corner of the studio commissary, but it was still the focus of all eyes. Fans came in droves to do the studio tour. The top draw was a visit to the 'Saga' set. It didn't matter that the actors were filming scenes that required concentration. Abby and Gertrude, realizing they had a gold mine in 'Saga', allowed tourists to roam free on the lot and provided a friendly studio tour guide to accompany them.

'You know, Vanessa, I don't mean to be paranoid but do you see that woman with the Instamatic over there?' Chloe said. Vanessa looked over to where a nondescript woman, dressed in a drab pants suit, sat looking around the commissary, too often her eyes returning to Chloe.

'What about her?' asked Vanessa.

'She gives me the creeps. I *swear* she's press. I've seen her here several times. She was even lurking on the set listening to me talk to Annabel on the phone last week.'

'You're joking?' Vanessa was alarmed. She was very protective of Chloe.

'No. She was hanging around by the coffee machines chatting with the craft service guys and the teamsters. I thought she was a hairdresser from the cop show on the next sound stage; then I saw her make notes in a book. Check her out, Van.'

'O.K., Boss Lady,' said Vanessa. She glanced at the woman, who looked away quickly. Chloe was right. She did look like press. British press, too, probably from one of the scummier daily rags.

Magazines and tabloids had now printed every major and minor detail of Chloe's past life ad nauseum. They had interviewed her school friends, teachers and co-workers. Rick, her old lover from her provincial days had sold his kiss-n-tell memoirs of their 'stormy affair' to the *Sun*, and reporters constantly called Richard, Susan *and* Annabel for any scraps of trivia on Britain's by-now most famous actress. Chloe lived in terror of the press discovering that Annabel was really her daughter. One of the gutter tabloids had gone to Somerset House, the British register of births and deaths and printed her birth certificate so that none of their readers could have any doubts how old she was. What was to stop them snooping around and finding out that on 15 January, 1964 a baby girl, father unknown, mother, Chloe Carriere, age 21, had been born in a nursing home in Plymouth. Chloe often thought about how it would upset Annabel's peacefully happy life.

She hated the fact she was becoming cynical and paranoid, but the relentless onslaught on her personal life, by both the media and the fans, had clouded her normally sunny disposition. The work was hard. Just the act of keeping her hair, makeup and clothes pristine twelve hours a day, while the crew sweated in T-shirts and sneakers, was an effort.

It was tiring to smile all the time at the fifty or sixty visitors a day who plucked up courage to speak to the Queen Bitch in person. God forbid she slough one off. Every fan lost was multiplied a hundredfold in viewing audiences, scolded Gertrude. 'Offend one fan, and they'll tell ten friends who'll tell ten more.'

'Be nice to them on the way up,' warned Jasper. 'You may be the flavour of the month now, but they'll all be there waiting on the way down – and there *will* be a way down, luv. That's for sure. Every actor has his shelf life. With some – the Cary Grants, the Katharine Hepburns – it's fifty years or more. With others – *especially* TV stars – it can be fifty months, or weeks, even days. The public is . . .'

'Fickle! I know, Jasper. You've told me a million times. I *know* they are.'

'Good girl. Remember it now. Don't become big-headed.'

'I won't,' she almost screamed. 'I'm just trying to be *me*.'

She had no time for men in her life. On a rare day off she was involved in interviews and photograph sessions. And fittings with Trixie and Rudolpho took hours of thought and concentration. She had to know lines, have script conferences, have a weekly manicure and pedicure, she had to exercise regularly, she had to have facials, keep up with current fashion trends. All in all, there wasn't enough time in the day even to read a newspaper or get a decent night's sleep, let alone get involved with a man.

'If only the public realized what a bloody hard grind this so-called glamour job is,' sighed Chloe, acknowledging the signal from Ned that her fifty minutes for lunch was up.

Lunch gave her indigestion. Everything was always rush, rush, rush. By the time she left the set, exchanged the beaded décolleté gown or some other fashionable outfit for a track suit, walked to the commissary, waited for a tuna salad and Perrier to arrive, exchanged a few stories with Vanessa and Daphne, who sometimes came by, it was time to return to the set. 'Heigh ho, heigh ho, it's off to work we go. Just like the Seven dwarfs.' Vanessa laughed.

'I think, dear, you need a man, for therapeutic reasons if nothing else, and I happen to know just the one. Perfect for you, and *very* handsome, darling.' Daphne never let up; she kept pushing the subject each time they had lunch together.

Vanessa giggled. She adored romance and intrigue. 'Who is he, anyone we know? I'd like her to get laid too. She's becoming a pain in the neck to me.' Vanessa smiled at Chloe teasingly. She adored her, even though they sometimes clashed. And Vanessa had become indispensable to Chloe for social arrangements, business meetings, clothes problems. Vanessa was Chloe's confidante and doer – a far cry from her days as an Arab potentate's mistress, but more interesting certainly.

'Laid! What's that? I can't remember that experience. Isn't it something mortals do?'

'Next Saturday night, darling, dinner *chez moi*.' Daphne loved playing Cupid. 'This man is French, and he is seriously sexy.'

'Oh, an import!' Vanessa beamed at Chloe. 'Someone who hasn't fucked all your friends. Ain't *that* good news?'

*   *   *

Chloe recognized him as soon as he walked into Daphne's living room. Although she hadn't thought about him in more than three years, she remembered the chemistry she had felt that awful night in Vegas. She shuddered. She still had nightmares about that.

Philippe Archambaud smiled his Alain Delon smile, revealing perfect teeth. He looked romantically Continental in a dark blue suit and a conservative tie, in sharp contrast to Daphne's beau, Richard Hurrel, who was a sartorial disaster in a cyclamen blazer with matching ascot, and to Luis Mendoza, who hadn't really bothered, because when every woman in America wants your body, all you need is a black silk shirt, tight white pants, and a tan. Philippe was handsome, tall, with brown wavy hair, dazzling eyes. He was also quiet. Not your actual comedian, thought Chloe, after enduring his rather pedantic discourse on French politics during dinner.

She remembered Josh's colourful English charm – how he had entranced her with his wit and humour. There had been so much passion and togetherness between them in the first seven or eight years. Where had it gone wrong? Why? Forget about it. She pushed those thoughts from her mind and concentrated on Philippe. Yes, he was extremely handsome. Yes, he was exceptionally charming. Yes, he certainly paid her attention and was very flattering. And why should he not be? She was at this moment the biggest female star on TV. For how long, of course, no one could predict. . . .

'When can I see you again, Chloe?' Philippe's hand traced a tiny path down her spine. She suddenly felt the remembered stirrings of desire – absent now for so many months. 'Tomorrow?' His eyes – what colour were they? Grey? Green? Blue? Chameleon eyes – they sent a clear message of ardour. In spite of herself she was interested.

'Well, tomorrow is Sunday. I have *tons* of dialogue to learn, a new script to study, and . . .'

'Darling!' Vanessa interrupted, reddish curls bouncing, cleavage brimming over her creamy antique lace blouse. 'No excuses, I think you should take him to the beach house,' she whispered through gritted teeth, her tiny satin pumps giving Chloe a sharp dig in her shin.

'And Richard and I will come too. Don't *worry*,' said Daphne joining in as she saw Chloe start to demur. 'I know you don't have staff on Sunday and you *hate* to cook. Richard will stop at Nate 'n' Al's tomorrow and get their Scottish smoked salmon, bagels and cream cheese. We'll have a picnic on the beach. Won't that be fun, dear? Just like England.'

Richard groaned. At sixty-five he felt a mite too old for picnics on the beach, let along hopping down to Nate 'n' Al's on Sunday with the Beverly Hills jet-setters. But Daphne was the boss in their relationship, so he tried to muster a smile.

'All right,' said Chloe, seeing Vanessa's enormous smile. 'We'll *all* have a picnic.'

'With champagne!' Daphne added.

'*Naturellement*,' Philippe said with a smile that was definitely beginning to affect Chloe. 'I will bring it.'

'Dom Perignon,' Vanessa warned. 'One *only* drinks D.P. on a picnic.'

'Of course, it will be my pleasure.' He bowed slightly, his eyes not leaving Chloe's.

Here we go again, she thought.

It was a short, fast courtship, Philippe's physical charms captured Chloe so quickly she didn't know what had hit her. For a woman who had always insisted on wit and conversation in her relationships with men, suddenly it didn't seem to matter this time.

They started seeing each other every weekend, then every other night, then every night. Soon he had moved many of his things into Chloe's houses at the beach and in Beverly Hills. After a couple of months they decided it was foolish for him to waste money renting an apartment he hardly used, and he moved in.

Philippe still wrote stories for *Paris Match*, *Jour de France* and an occasional article for *Oggi* or *Tempo*. That kept him reasonably busy during the day. Since he was good with figures and a dab hand at analysing the stock market, Chloe let him invest some of her money. He did so well and made her such consistent profits in the market that finally she fired her business manager and let Philippe handle her finances full time.

'Darling, he *is* adorable, but he is, well . . .' Vanessa tried to warn her friend a few weeks after her whirlwind affair with Philippe had begun.

'Dull? Boring? Opinionated?' Chloe laughed. 'I *know*, Vanessa. I'm not so stupid. I realize that he isn't Einstein. I don't know what it is – he seems to have my number, though.' She thought of last night and the passion they had shared until she had wearily risen at five to leave for the studio.

'Well, whatever it is he's doing to you, it seems to be doing you good,' said Vanessa. 'You haven't looked so well in a long time.'

Chloe blushed. Her nights, mornings and afternoons with Philippe had been amazing. The man was a fountain of energy. When he wasn't making love, he wanted to hold her in his arms, stroke her hair and tell her how wonderful she was. It was unusual for a man of thirty-nine to be so openly affectionate. And Chloe *liked* it, and liked him. More and more.

She still thought about Josh. Occasionally he phoned her from England or wherever he was. The first play he had done had been a disaster. Then he had disappeared for a year, and she had no idea where. One rumour was that he had emigrated to Australia, another that he was living with a pair of seventeen-year-old twins. Writing music. Entertaining in piano bars, men's clubs. Finally, out of the blue, he'd called her.

'Hello, Chloe, my little love. How are you?'

She couldn't believe the way her heart still fluttered when she heard his voice. Like a stupid schoolgirl, she scolded herself, after their short but sweet conversation.

He told her he'd been working in Australia, touring the

outback. There was no mention of teenage twins. And she didn't ask. He was working on cruise ships now. It was fun, he said. He had a lot of fans still. Middle-aged matrons and their paunchy escorts who remembered the young Joshua Brown of the 1960s. Remembered his songs. Gave him the applause he craved. He was off to sing his way around the Caribbean for the next few months on another cruise ship.

'Is it really fun?' Chloe had asked, feeling in some bizarre way guilty about her own immense success and his slide down the ladder. 'Are you enjoying it, Josh?'

'Sure, it's great,' he lied. 'All the fun of the fair, darlin'. Lots of booze, lots of laughs, lots of birds.' Chloe couldn't suppress a wince. The thought of Josh with another woman in his arms still gave her a jolt.

'*Hopeless*! You're hopelessly old-fashioned and out of date,' said Vanessa after Chloe recounted her conversation with Josh. 'I don't think you really know anything about men, do you, Chloe?'

Vanessa, having spent eighteen years studying the species, was somewhat of an expert and was often amazed by Chloe's romantic naïveté.

Chloe changed the subject. Talking to Josh had rattled her. She wanted to hear from him again. Their divorce still wasn't final. It had been dragging on for two years now. Her lawyer kept trying to get her to sign the final papers. Then, when Josh disappeared, even his own lawyer couldn't find him.

Philippe was now pushing Chloe to get the divorce finalized. He wanted to marry her, but Chloe wasn't at all sure. She was mad about Philippe physically; it was almost as if he had put a spell on her. But the communication she had shared with Josh was missing.

Perhaps she expected too much, she told herself, as she drove down drab Pico Boulevard to MCPC Studios. Oh, well, you can't have it all. You *can*. You can. You can, her inner voice whispered back. You *can* and you *should*.

'Saga's' success had been so immense and extraordinary that

262

every TV company and network had jumped on the band-wagon to imitate it. One rival network had put out an imitation, 'Abraham's Family', a near-clone of 'Saga', another had tried with 'Arizona Empire', but both had fluttered briefly and then expired.

'Imitation is *still* the sincerest form of flattery,' beamed Gertrude at a meeting with a worried Abby. 'We have nothing to fear, Abby. Just look at our ratings.' She was right. 'Saga' had consistently been one of the top five shows for the past four seasons. Saga clothes, Saga jewellery, Saga dolls, Miranda and Sirope dressed in tiny facsimiles of Rudolpho's beaded gowns, were everywhere. The world was aglow with Sagamania. The world loved Chloe and Sissy. And Sam and Pandora. They loved them all. Saga bedspreads, plates, candles, shoes, blouses and ties – department stores bulged with them.

'About the only goddamn things they haven't put the Saga name on are condoms,' laughed Pandora to Chloe on the set as Christopher, the diminutive public relations man, approached Chloe with the blueprint of the new advertisement for two Saga perfumes she, along with Sissy, would endorse.

One would be called 'Wicked' and feature Chloe looking provocative on the package. The other would be called 'Woman', and would feature Sissy looking as warm and sincere as her talent would allow.

In the four years the show had been running, Sissy had indulged in two mini face-lifts, one eye job and a breast implant. She still dieted relentlessly and looked like a hawk in real life, but she was a good enough actress to breathe life into the saccharine role of Sirope. She personified Mother Earth: sweet, long-suffering and kind, putting up with the problems of her TV children and the machinations of her TV ex-husband, Steve. Chloe, on the other hand, personified the wicked, manipulating, sex-hungry bitch.

The public had taken the two women to their hearts, never

quite sure if they were in reality the characters they played on the screen.

'You're sitting in my chair,' snapped Sissy to Chloe.

'Oh, sorry,' said Chloe eying the three empty canvas chairs that Sissy could have parked her scrawny behind on if she had chosen.

What Sissy did choose to do was to needle Chloe and the rest of the cast at every possible opportunity. With her newfound success, she had become impossible. Even faithful Sam, who had been loyal to her for years, found it hard to swallow her arrogance. She was rude to the crew, who loathed her. She was envious and spiteful to the cast, refusing to rehearse, abusing any actor who forgot his dialogue, and never deigning to read off-camera lines even for Sam. She hassled the producer to get better story lines for herself, she changed her dialogue constantly, confusing the other actors, and then became furious with them because they couldn't understand what she was doing.

Recently she started snorting a line of coke first thing in the morning to get her through the tedious days, another line at lunchtime, and one more halfway through the afternoon. At home each night she complained bitterly to Sam about the fact that the lighting cameraman preferred Chloe and Pandora to her, that the director was an untalented ruffian, her trailer not as big as Sam's. Sissy overreacted to the merest slight. Cocaine was turning her into a paranoid schizophrenic. If the public that admired her so much had known the truth, she would have been standing in the unemployment line on Sunset Boulevard.

'So what do you think of the new script?'

Chloe was surprised Sissy bothered to ask her opinion. She never had before. 'It's O.K. What do you think?'

'Trash, fucking trash. They keep writing like this, we'll be off the air next season.' Sissy was nervously running her fingers up and down her satin-clad thigh. 'Doris, bring me a cup of coffee – for Christ's sake, *hurry up.*'

Chloe felt sorry for Sissy. She couldn't really hate a woman whose insecurities were so obvious, and she often defended her while the rest of the cast tore her to pieces and mocked her. It didn't really help, because Sissy hated Chloe more than anyone else in the show.

If Chloe made the front page of *USA Today*, Sissy would scream at the network public relations people until they got the same coverage for her. In fact, the women got an equal number of national magazine covers. With a show as hot as 'Saga', the magazines knew a good way to sell copies was to put Sissy, Chloe or Pandora on the cover.

'Oh, did you see this?' Sissy had a glint in her eye as she passed Chloe the latest copy of the *American Informer*.

'CHLOE CARRIERE IN LOVE CHILD MYSTERY,' the headline blazed.

Chloe almost fainted when she read it. She pretended a casual glance, aware of Sissy watching her with a glint in her eye.

'Interesting, isn't it?' Sissy smiled her cobra smile. 'Any truth to it, Chloe *darling*?' She attempted a confidential girl-talk tone, which Chloe found even more offensive than her bitchy needling. 'You can tell *me*.' She leaned closer and Chloe saw the deep crow's-feet under her eyes and around her lips that even three face-lifts hadn't managed to erase.

'The usual pack of lies, Sissy – you know that.' She couldn't resist a dig. 'You remember the story they had about Sam being gay a few months ago? Ridiculous, isn't it?'

Sissy's jaws clamped shut and her flat grey eyes gave up their pretence of charm. 'Doris, where's that fucking coffee, for Christ's sake. Hurry it up.'

Chloe moved away. The story she had dreaded had finally appeared. She saw Sissy display the tabloid's cover with waspish glee to several of the crew and groaned inwardly.

At home Chloe studied the tabloid article with mounting horror.

'SECRET LOVE CHILD CHLOE HASN'T SEEN IN 20 YEARS', blared the headline. 'Chloe Carriere – superstar of the soap opera "Saga" has a secret that will haunt her to her grave. Twenty-one years ago she gave birth to an illegitimate child. The *Informer* can exclusively reveal that this young girl, Annabel, lives happily in the English countryside with Chloe's brother, Richard, and his wife, Susan, unaware that her real mother is television's most famous bitch.'

'Oh, my God – Annabel!' She threw the offending scandal sheet on the floor and picked up the phone with a shaking hand.

'Hello, Daphne – Daphne, darling, I didn't wake you, did I?'

'No, no, of course not, dear, I'm wide awake. What's happening in your life?' Daphne pushed Richard aside, and brought out the tape recorder she kept next to the bed.

It was not often that she received a call for help from Chloe. Chloe received so much unfavourable personal publicity that she rarely bothered to do anything about it except shrug it off.

'Have you read the *Informer* yet?' Chloe asked desperately.

'Yes, dear, I have.'

'It's a bunch of lies, Daphne, you *know* that.'

'Of course I do, dear. Everyone in town who reads that revolting garbage knows it.' But they love it, Daphne thought, everyone reads it at their executive desks, at their hair-dresser's, or borrows it from their maid, avidly reading the lies and innuendo about everyone else. 'Stop it, Richard,' she hissed. Being rejected had excited him more than usual, and he was exploring Daphne's abundant thighs.

'Daphne, people are actually beginning to believe all that stuff about me being a bitch. I don't mind that but this story is terribly upsetting for my niece.'

'I know, dear, I know it's a pack of lies. Ignore it, you're bigger than all of them, don't you ever forget it.'

'I always ignore it – maybe that's the trouble.'

'So what can an old friend do, dear?' said Daphne, having slapped Richard away and tried to settle him comfortably in the crook of her arm like a big floppy doll.

'Tell them to print a retraction as soon as possible.'

'I'll do what I can for you, I promise, dear,' said Daphne,

her attention distracted by Richard's halfhearted administrations as she hung up.

Chloe picked up the vodka and poured a generous slug into her orange juice as the phone started to ring. She let the answering machine pick up, listened, heard the nasal tones: 'Hello, it's Mike Russel here from *The News of the World*. I'd like to speak to Miss Carriere about . . .'

Wearily she switched it off. Tomorrow this American tabloid story would be in all the English papers. Annabel would see it. Uppermost in her mind was how she would react. Her darling Annabel, who thought of Chloe as her aunt. What would she think? How would she feel, knowing she had been lied to all her life? She had to be devastated.

Whatever her reaction, Chloe had to see her face to face. *Now*. There was no putting it off. She had to tell her the truth.

She called Gertrude. 'You've read the story?'

'Yes, of course. Is it true?' rasped Gertrude.

'It is, Gertrude. As far as I'm concerned I don't give a damn what the press write. But this has to be the most ghastly shock for Annabel. She had no idea that I was her mother, that Susan and Richard were not her real parents. I *must* go to England, Gertrude, immediately. Can you shoot around me? Please. It's urgent.'

'Darling.' Gertrude's voice was cool. 'You *know* we can't. We're coming to the end of the season, you're in *everything*. This has to be the best cliff-hanger ever, because "America" is starting up against us next season. Can't it wait?'

'No!' Chloe was desperate. 'No, it can't. It's my daughter's *life*, Gertrude. Isn't that more important than the show, for heaven's sake?'

'Frankly, honey, it isn't. I have every sympathy for you, I promise we'll get the publicity people to do the best they can to help you out of this mess, but we simply *cannot* and *will not* cater to the whim of an actress in this way.'

'Whim!' Chloe almost wept. 'Gertrude, this is the most important thing in my life!' She started to tell her the real story, but Gertrude cut her off.

'I'm in the middle of a dinner party, honey – now don't you worry,' Gertrude tried to soothe her. 'I don't think bad publicity will harm you. After all, you *are* a bitch.'

'I'm not!' Chloe screamed. 'I'm an actress and a good one too, which is why they all think I'm a bitch. Please let me go, Gertrude, please, just for the weekend. I must sort it out. Annabel needs me – I have to explain everything to her myself. I can't do it on the phone.'

'I'll have to speak to Abby,' Gertrude said crisply. 'I'll see what I can do. I've got to run now, my guests are waiting.' She hung up.

'*Damn* you!' yelled Chloe, tears welling up. 'Damn you all! I'm bloody going anyway.' Lifting the receiver, she called Vanessa. 'Get me on tomorrow night's British Airways flight to London, Van, and call a meeting here tonight with Christopher. I've got to face the music.'

'I'm going, Abby,' she said calmly the next morning, as she sat across from the huge man in his immense office.

He had been more sympathetic to her than Gertrude. 'We're going to let you go so that you can sort this unfortunate story out,' he said. 'It makes you look bad in the public's eye. If you just ignore it, the public will think you're a bitch. So although there really isn't a stigma about the illegitimate aspect, I think the public have got to know the truth, so you owe it to them, if not to the girl.' He chewed on his cigar and surveyed her kindly. When the chips were down, Abby usually came through for his stars. He liked Chloe and he knew she was nothing like the hardhearted vixen she portrayed.

'Go, sweetheart. Give a press conference in London for the media, that's important, but more important is the kid – how's she taking it?'

'I don't know,' said Chloe, fighting back the tears. 'I can't get through – they've taken the phone off the hook, and I can't reach her at college. It's really hard, Abby. This girl is the most important person in my life.' Tears started to flow down her cheeks. Abby, a sentimental man in spite of his hard exterior, felt his throat tighten and hastily passed her his handkerchief before he started to bawl too.

'Now, now, sweetheart,' he said gruffly. 'No tears, please, you'll only hold up production while they fix your makeup. Go back to the set, we'll release you by four-thirty so you can catch the flight to London and sort things out.'

Before the story broke, Annabel had been a well-adjusted young woman at college. She had been outgoing and happy, as well, in her home life in a secure family atmosphere. This did not stop the Fleet Street vipers, who fell upon the scandal like vultures. Anything about Chloe was news. This was huge, and they would play it up to the hilt. The glaring headlines shrieked their news daily.

'CHLOE ABANDONS LOVE CHILD', screeched the *Sun*.

'SELFISH SOAP QUEEN GIVES BABY AWAY', the *Star* squawked.

'Oh, Chloe, Chloe, how could you be so heartless? Where is your sense of moral virtue, your motherly instincts? Foolish woman. Do diamonds, furs, Hollywood mansions, and swimming pools make up for a child's life? For a baby you bore, and then gave away to your relatives while you pursued your career, chasing shallow fame and the frivolous good life and leaving your own flesh and blood to be brought up living a lie. . . ?' Every tabloid drooled on. It was a hot story and they milked it for everything it had. It was nauseating, thought Chloe.

She read the articles on the plane to London, more horrified at each one as she wondered how Annabel would take all of this. Vanessa was with her, excited about going back to London. Some of Chloe's fame had rubbed off on her and she had become something of a celebrity in Petticoat Lane, where her family still lived. Philippe was there too, sitting next to Chloe, asleep and snoring. He had been supportive of her when the news broke, and had insisted on coming along.

'What does it matter, sweetheart, what they say about

269

you?' he had asked. 'They all think you're a bitch anyway.'
He had infuriated her with his French pragmatism, which
had ended in a tearful argument.

The press were out in force at Heathrow – dozens of them
including TV cameras and news. As soon as she stepped off
the ramp, they were all over her, pushing, yelling and
snapping her as she strode down the drafty Heathrow
corridor, head held high. She wore a simple tan cashmere
overcoat belted snugly against the London chill. A smooth-
tongued BBC reporter thrust his microphone into her face,
demanding a statement. The woman from ITV insisted on a
quote too. NBC and ABC were there, as well as her parent
network BCC, and news crews from Europe and Australia.

'Wait a minute. *Wait a minute* everybody!' Christopher,
Saga's diminutive press agent, was flushed scarlet with the
effort of trying to control the excited crowd and the press.
'Miss Carriere is *not* going to make any statement at this
moment. As you all know, we have called a press conference
at the Ritz Hotel at four o'clock. Miss Carriere will then talk
to all of you in detail about – recent events.'

Chloe smiled through clenched teeth as three policemen,
two officials from the airline, Vanessa, Philippe and
Christopher tried to force a way through the throng of
photographers, journalists and rubberneckers.

This was going to be tougher than she had expected. They
had stayed up late the previous night planning their strategy.
Make it work, please God, breathed Chloe. Make it work.

23

Annabel's protected private world had suddenly become a public nightmare. Her face was splashed over the front pages of the tabloids. Her fellow students gossiped about her at college. Why hadn't Auntie Chloe – no, it was Mummie Chloe now, wasn't it? – told her the truth.

The gutter press started bombarding the neat terraced house in Barnes with phone calls, and Annabel's family went into shock. It became unbearable. When they were 'door-stepped' by dozens of journalists and photographers from all over the world, they turned the house into a fortress. They took the phone off the hook, kindly neighbours brought in food, and the family waited and prayed it would all be over soon and that the media circus outside would go away.

But it wouldn't. The reporters dug themselves in, waiting for action, and soon it arrived in the person of Chloe as they knew it would. When she arrived at the house she was inundated by a thousand intrusively crude, curious questions. Flashbulbs popped so rapidly in the afternoon gloom that she was almost blinded. Christopher, his diminutive height no barrier to his strength as he manoeuvred her through the jabbering throng, was red-faced by the time the door was opened by a pale, worried-looking Susan, who hurriedly ushered them into the narrow hall.

She, Richard and Chloe exchanged affectionate greetings and muffled words of encouragement, then Susan took Chloe aside, motioning towards the closed door of the living room. 'She's in there,' she whispered, as Richard took Christopher through to the kitchen.

'She's taking it very hard, Chloe. I've tried to tell her it wasn't your fault, that it was the way the world *was* then and that you did your best, but it seems that the more I say, the more upset she gets.'

'Thanks, Susie.' Chloe smiled at her sister-in-law and squeezed her arm appreciatively, remembering those long-ago days when they were schoolgirls, remembering the whispering, the giggling, the sharing of such delicious secrets when they were twelve and 'best friends' forever. And now here they were whispering secrets again. 'I told her you were coming,' said Susie, 'but she didn't say anything.'

'It's all right, Susie. I have to talk to her, I know how difficult it must be for her.' Chloe pushed the door open.

Annabel sat in the living room slumped on a flowered chintz sofa. Mother and daughter looked at each other. This was the moment Chloe had been dreading. Her throat was so tight she had difficulty swallowing, and she had developed a nervous tic in one eye, probably because she had not had a wink of sleep in the barely three days since the story about Annabel had broken. She looked at her daughter with love, but Annabel's eyes were cold, flat and detached.

A fire crackled in the grate. It was a cold March afternoon, and although only four o'clock, it was almost dark outside. The green velveteen curtains were drawn and the windows tightly closed, but even so, the hubbub and chatter of the press outside could still be heard.

Chloe had come straight from Heathrow, and as she stood in her tan suede boots and matching cashmere overcoat, she felt horribly Hollywoodish and overdressed in this simple, cluttered living room. On the piano and mantelpiece were photos of her and the family. In one corner sat a ficus plant Chloe had sent Richard for his birthday, in another, a plastic trolley held bottles of whiskey, gin, vodka and liqueurs. How she would love a drink, she thought fervently, but this was not the time.

Her daughter, her beautiful, joyous daughter, had turned away from her, her eyes hard.

'I suppose you expect me to fall into your arms and all will be forgiven,' Annabel said sarcastically in her clear young voice.

'No, of course I don't, Annabel, I would never expect that of you. You deserve an explanation, and I'm going to do the best I can to explain everything.'

Chloe took off her coat, tossing it onto an armchair opposite the sofa on which her daughter was curled up, her normally cheerful expression a hard mask. Her curly dark hair was caught up with a bright yellow plastic comb, which matched the yellow sweater she wore over blue jeans torn at the knees and cowboy boots. She was truly a lovely young girl who looked so uncannily like the young Chloe that an outsider seeing them together would have known instantly they were mother and daughter.

Susan had left a tray of tea and shortbread biscuits on the walnut table in front of the fire. There were two cups and an earthenware vase with a few early daffodils from the garden. The silence seemed endless. Annabel glanced at Chloe, then turned away again, drawing deeply on her cigarette and gazing into the fire.

Chloe tried to swallow. She knew she couldn't speak, say any of the thousand and one things she needed, wanted, to say until she had a sip of tea. Her throat was so dry it hurt. 'Would you like a cup of tea, darling?' Her voice sounded too bright, theatrical, her newly acquired transatlantic accent all wrong in the calm Englishness of this room.

'No, I wouldn't,' the girl's voice was low. 'What I *would* like is an explanation, *Auntie. Now.*' Sarcasm didn't become her.

She was unused to problems; hers had been a happy life, full of laughter and fun.

'I know, darling, I know and I – I want to explain. I really do. But I'm a bit dry from the plane.' Chloe managed a wan smile as she poured the tea with a shaking hand.

'Go ahead,' Annabel said coldly as she looked away from Chloe again and into the fire.

Chloe sipped the scalding liquid gratefully. 'Annabel, you must realize this is not easy for either of us.'

'You bet it isn't. God, how I despise liars.' She looked at Chloe defiantly. 'I hate the fact that you *all* lied to me all my life – every one of you lied. Mum lied, Dad lied, *you* lied. Why couldn't you have told me the *truth*, for God's sake, or at least told me I was illegitimate when I was old enough to understand what that meant?' she said bitterly. Chloe noticed that her nails were bitten to the quick, and she was clenching and unclenching her hands as she twisted a damp handkerchief in her palms.

'I want to know, *why* didn't you tell me? *Why*?' Her voice was accusing.

'I'm going to be honest with you,' Chloe said with a calmness she did not feel. 'But the events I must tell you about belong to a different era almost, a totally different morality, a period of time I know may be hard for you to comprehend, darling, but please try.'

The girl looked challengingly at Chloe. 'I'm *all* ears – ' that sarcasm again. Her hostility was a barrier, she prickled with rage. This was harder than Chloe had thought it would be.

'I was twenty-one years old, about the age you are now, so I'm sure you can understand maybe a tiny bit what that was like,' Chloe began slowly.

'Of *course*,' Annabel said coolly.

'I fell in love for the first time in my life,' Chloe continued. 'He was married, but I didn't care. I was completely infatuated with him – totally besotted. I couldn't think about anything or anyone else. He became an obsession.' Chloe stopped, lit a cigarette, her hand shaking.

'*Please* don't smoke. Mummy hates people to smoke in the house.' Annabel's voice was icy, and now her face seemed even more full of hatred for her mother. Chloe started to protest that Annabel had just extinguished a cigarette, but decided that was not the issue here. She swallowed. Her foot started to twitch; seemingly it had a life of its own. The tic in her eye flickered madly. She had to tell her everything. Annabel was her child. Even if it meant the end of the relationship they had had up to now, she would tell her every detail, all the reasons. Painstakingly, haltingly, Chloe described her bittersweet affair with Matt. Her hurt feelings when he had suggested an abortion. Her pain when he rejected her. 'I couldn't destroy that part of us that we created together. I simply couldn't, it was too precious. If ever there was a true "love child", it was you, darling.' Annabel didn't answer, but at least her attention had turned away from the flickering fire and to Chloe.

'It was a different time then. The world had just come out of the moralistic fifties,' said Chloe. 'Women were still second-class citizens; it's hard to believe, I know, but it was years before the sexual revolution. Before the sexual equality we have now. It was a time when nice girls didn't have sex, didn't take lovers. I was in show business, which had a different morality to most people's, so those attitudes never really applied to us. But Matt told me he wanted nothing more to do with me when I became pregnant, and I simply didn't know what to do. I was at my wit's end. The only way I knew to earn my living was to sing. I had to support myself because my father was dead and my mother made very little money working in a shop.'

'I see.' Annabel leaned forward, her eyes still cold, and took a sip for the first time at the tea that Chloe had poured for her. 'Go on.'

'I wanted to have you, Annabel. I wanted to have my baby so much. I couldn't do what some of my girl friends did when they became pregnant, go to some butcher on a back street, get it cut out, destroyed. I simply couldn't. I wanted you, Annabel. Can you understand that, darling?'

Annabel didn't answer and Chloe continued, trying to be as factual as possible. Trying not to get too emotional, trying to hold back her tears, both for the memories and for the hostility emanating from the girl she loved so much.

'There was no doubt in my mind, Annabel, that I couldn't destroy that life. Your life. My agony was knowing that an illegitimate child in 1964 would have ruined what little chance of a career I had, and that the child would grow up living with the stigma of "illegitimate". And it was an enormous stigma then – it really was.

'It would have been a nightmare trying to bring you up properly. It was difficult enough being a young single girl on the provincial nightclub circuit in England, what with one-night stands, bus and truck tours, standing in railway stations for hours in the middle of the night waiting for milk trains to take you to Wigan or Sunderland or Skegness. Having a baby along to look after would have been absolutely impossible. Singing was my only way of making a living, and if I'd kept you I would have had to give that up. Can you understand that?'

Chloe's eyes were blurred with tears, but Annabel's expression did not soften.

'Whatever your cheap, self-serving excuse, Mummie *dearest*, nothing can change the fact that you *didn't want me*, you didn't have a place for me in your life. You abandoned me. You simply didn't care, and you didn't have the guts to tell me before, when you could have. You had to wait until some rotten newspaper spilled the beans. Don't give me all that crap about loving me. You never loved me – you never cared at all. All that mattered was your bloody *career*. The limelight – the bright lights.' She looked as if she was going to cry; all the pent-up hostility and anger of the past three days came bursting out as she let loose a tirade of fury at her mother.

'What kind of a woman *are* you?' she screamed. 'Selfish, thoughtless – you never gave a thought to what might happen when you went jumping around in bed – a married man's bed,' she said in disgust. 'While his wife was away. I think that's nauseating.

'Oh, I *know* all about the sexual revolution of the sixties, women thinking they could fuck around like men. We're not like that today,' she said accusingly. 'Young women today think a bit more before we jump into bed, we *try* to be responsible, we take precautions, we have a bit of a social conscience. We are not promiscuous bitches in heat.' Her voice was rising now in evangelical fury. She was the new generation of sexually educated young women – the AIDS generation. Look before you leap, and don't leap unless you're very sure it's safe.

'Annabel, I was *not* promiscuous, so stop it, stop it *now*.' Suddenly Chloe was very angry. 'I've had enough of this.'

Annabel looked up, startled at the change in her mother's attitude.

'Stop being so judgmental. It's no good you going on at me, telling me what a terrible, lousy person I was. It's too late for that now, Annabel. We have to understand each other and to accept the past – make the best of it.'

She lit a cigarette in spite of Susan's 'no smoking' ban and continued, calmer now.

'I'm not going to excuse my behaviour in "abandoning" you, as you say, to be brought up by my brother and Susan. It's a fact that I *cannot* and *will not* apologize for any more. I did what I had to do. I still believe that it was the best thing for you too whether or not you think so now. You have had a very happy life. They adore you like one of their own. They think of you as their child – can't you realize that?'

Annabel looked at Chloe, her green eyes unfathomable, but Chloe thought she saw a spark of understanding.

'I've come six thousand miles today, Annabel, to tell you the truth. Yes, it's painful. Yes, it's horrible. Yes, it's unfair. I know these last days have been difficult for you; they've been no picnic for me either. But think about this' – She put both hands on her child's shoulders and she could feel her

277

trembling under the thin yellow sweater – 'I *could* have aborted you.'

Annabel shuddered and moved angrily away from her mother. 'Thanks for that,' she said flatly. 'I suppose I should be thankful, but knowing you now, you were probably too much of a coward to do it.'

'Damn it, Annabel, don't *be* like this,' Chloe exploded. 'I love you, I have *always* loved you and I have never gone to sleep at night without thinking of you – but I needed to make a success of my career. I *wanted* to be a singer. It was my life. If I had acknowledged you, I would have had to live with the scandal of having given birth to an illegitimate child. That would have meant *no career*. I would have been finished. I would have had you, yes, but I would have had to give up my dreams, my life.'

'I understand dreams,' said Annabel quietly – no trace of sarcasm now. 'They make life worth living.'

'I want you to remember, I *chose* to have you.' Chloe was calmer now. 'Susan and Richard were wonderful parents to their children and they welcomed you as one of them. I knew you would be in a loving home with a devoted family, brothers and sisters, that you would have a stable, happy life. So I made that decision – a decision I've thought about every single day of my life since.'

She paused. The memories were so painful: Matt's rejection of her and their baby, the agonizing sleepless nights when she found out she was pregnant, the frenzied discussions with Susan and Richard, the constant tears, trying to contact Matt, hearing his voice telling her he wouldn't see her again, he didn't want any 'aggro'. She was a big girl who knew what she had been doing. It was her problem. Hers alone. Yes, it *definitely* had been; he had done nothing. He considered it had nothing to do with him, so Chloe had dealt with it alone.

Annabel leaned her dark curly head on the back of the green sofa and bit into a shortbread biscuit as she looked at Chloe. She still felt angry, but her rage and turmoil were softening with comprehension.

'What are you thinking, Annabel?' Chloe asked, trying not to sound too eager.

'Oh, just a saying the kids are using at college.' A faint smile illuminated her sweet face briefly. ' "Life's a bitch – and then you die." ' Chloe smiled tentatively. Oh, how she wanted Annabel to understand and accept what had happened. She wanted to comfort her, wipe the unshed tears that must be shed from those clouded eyes. She remembered holding her at the hospital when the nurse first put her in her arms. Remembered the funny wrinkled little face, the warmth of that tiny body close to hers. Remembered how with a fierce primeval urge she had wanted to keep this infant with her forever. She remembered cuddling her daughter for hours in that stark hospital room with its acid-green, peeling paint. Annabel had rarely cried. Sometimes when she awoke and gazed up at Chloe with wise infant eyes, Chloe had felt the purest love she had ever felt for another human being.

Now Chloe looked into Annabel's eyes, so troubled now, and longed to hold her again, to stroke her hair, to tell her how much she loved her. But this was not the time. Not yet. Maybe tomorrow. Maybe next week. Maybe, God forbid, it would never happen; maybe Annabel would never forgive her, never accept what she had done. Chloe had said what she had to say, done what she had to do. Now it was up to her daughter.

'Ladies and Gentlemen – ' Chloe cleared her throat. This was *terrifying*, probably the most difficult audience she had ever had to face. No, she thought, telling Annabel had been worse. A battery of microphones and cameras was massed in front of the podium where she stood, palms damp, sweat rolling down her back, drenching her simple beige crepe de chine blouse. A sea of hostile faces confronted her. God, there must be at least one hundred of them! She panicked. Could she pull this off? A great deal depended on it. Most important were her daughter's feelings, but the public's opinion of her concerned her too. She was sick of their thinking of her as an inhuman bitch goddess.

Out of the corner of her eye, she observed Annabel giving her a tremulous smile and a 'thumbs up' sign. She began:

'Twenty-one years ago . . .' then – Oh, my *God*, who was that? In that sea of journalists, she recognized a face. It couldn't be – it couldn't! She took a deep breath and looked at him. He was staring at her with a vestige of that sexy smile she had found so irresistible so many years ago.

Matt Sullivan! Her selfish, sexy, self-absorbed lover, Annabel's father. Her first real love. Chloe was shocked, mesmerized into immobility. His black eyes, still remarkably sparkling, gazed mockingly into hers, as though the people around them didn't exist. He still exuded sexual confidence, amazing in a man of his age; he must be over sixty, she thought. He had lost most of his hair, but there was an animation about him that made him still attractive. A cigarette clung to his lower lip, as it always had – and what was that in his hand? A notebook! How could he? He was taking notes – he was obviously still a reporter. Apparently he didn't have what it took to become the editor of one of those sleazebag rags. At his age he was still just a hack, competing with twenty-five-year-olds. She felt sorry for him. For what gutter tabloid did he work now? Chloe tried desperately to pull her thoughts together and continue her speech. He must *know* that Annabel was his baby. Their love child. This was sick. The last time they had met, twenty-one years ago, he had told her to get lost. How could he be here now?

She swallowed, directing her attention to another part of the room and the other journalists.

'Twenty-one years ago, I was very naïve,' she began tentatively. 'I was starting a career as a singer, and singing was my life. At least I thought it was.' She glanced momentarily at Matt, who was looking at Annabel with an unfathomable expression.

'One day I fell in love, for the first time.' The press scribbled wildly – oh, the headlines tomorrow!

'He was a married man, much older than I. I know it was terrible to have an affair with a married man, but I fell in love – very much in love.' The truth was the only thing that could save her. This was tough, but she couldn't stop now. 'Don't let the bastards get you down, dear,' Vanessa had warned her before she had walked to the microphones.

Chloe told them the full story. How she hadn't been able to bring herself to have an abortion – to kill a life born of love. How her brother and sister-in-law, a secure and lovely family unit, had agreed to take the baby and bring her up with their own. How her career had meant so much to her and how, in 1964, giving birth to an illegitimate child could have wrecked her career and hurt the child irreparably.

Chloe realized she had their rapt attention now. Some of the more emotional sob sisters of Fleet Street were almost teary-eyed as Chloe finished her speech. She noticed Jean Rook giving her an encouraging smile.

'I know that many of you believe I have sinned, but my transgression was one of innocence and ignorance and love for my unborn child. Later I realized it would be terribly upsetting for my daughter to find out that her parents were not who she thought they were. I didn't want to upset her. She had a stable family, she was adored by her parents and her brothers and sisters. I kept the secret for the sake of my daughter's happiness, not for mine, and I sincerely hope you will believe me.'

They all seemed to. But first they had to ask their nosy Fleet Street questions. How did she feel when she found out she was pregnant? Did she feel guilt about having an affair with a married man? And, finally, who was he? Who was the man whom Chloe had been so passionate about? What was his name? Where is he now? They were really curious about this – desperate to know. She told her only untruth then, but she knew that if she did not tell a lie the investigative reporters would go to work. It wouldn't be too difficult to find some bartender, one of her musician friends, somebody who had seen her and Matt together in Liverpool, Manchester or

Newcastle back then. So she lied. 'He died,' she said simply, 'in a car crash in Marbella, just before the baby was born.' They seemed satisfied with that, although Annabel looked sad. 'And now, ladies and gentlemen,' she said, her voice tight with emotion, 'I would like you to meet my daughter.' Annabel joined her mother on the podium, the press went wild. Annabel's resemblance to Chloe was unmistakable. The same walk, the same cheekbones, the same eyes, the same dark curls. They posed for the cameras for five minutes until Christopher had to beg them to stop. Later, Chloe, answering questions, surrounded by a group of female writers from the more conservative women's weeklies, suddenly felt a tap on her shoulder. 'Good girl, I'm proud of you, Chlo.' Matt spoke to her as if they had last met yesterday, instead of twenty-one years ago.

She looked at him long and hard. Strange – even though he was almost old now, the feelings he had created in her could still flicker faintly. 'Thanks, Matt,' she whispered. Memories, came flooding back.

'She's a beauty – just like her ma.' He gave her a wink, then drew her aside, brushed his lips against her cheek and whispered, 'I loved you, Chlo. I didn't realize it then. Too young, too ambitious – too selfish, I suppose.'

Too drunk, too often, Chloe thought without malice. 'I don't think you loved me, Matt. You never told me you did. Please – don't say it now. I know it's not true,' she said

'I, well – you were just a kid, I was married. Still am.' He was rueful now. 'I'm a fucking grandfather. Can you believe it, Chloe? A grandfather!'

She could believe it. He was old enough. Still, her heart wondered, 'Why did he desert me when I loved him so much?' For years she had thought about him. His memory had never been fully erased – not until she met Josh.

'I'd like to see you again, Chlo.' His whisper was urgent. 'I'd like to get to know her, too. Spend some time together.'

'No, Matt. No.' This time it was Chloe's turn to reject him. She remembered the endless phone calls to his office, a secretary telling her he was out to lunch, off, away, not in, not available – all of the stock secretary's lines.

Not that revenge was sweet – that had never been Chloe's way – but seeing him again had closed their chapter forever. 'Goodbye, Matt,' she whispered, brushing his old man's cheek with her well-preserved one. 'Take care.'

'Goodbye, darlin', and good luck. You did it, Chlo! You made the buggers do you right this time!'

She watched him go, and to her surprise saw that he was crying.

Within a month the whole incident was forgotten when Prince Charles and Princess Diana announced that she was expecting again.

Emerald had tested well, she decided. Banishing her usual glamour, she had thought of herself as just a working actress, and got on with it. The crew applauded when she finished. Afterwards she went straight home to her penthouse in Century City, took off her makeup, told the answering service to ring through only if Eddie Barker called, and went on a bender.

For three days she lay on her bed drinking straight vodka. If she didn't get this role, she was determined to drink herself to death. What would be the use of going on? It was difficult enough to survive in this business. She couldn't *not* continue to enjoy her lavish lifestyle. She had sold all of her jewels that were worth anything, except one necklace. This she wore, with a tattered white terry-cloth robe, for the three days she lay in bed mindlessly switching TV channels and drinking vodka from the bottle.

She didn't talk, she didn't cry, she didn't think about anything. She was in limbo, waiting to be put out of her misery forever – or to rise to new heights.

The call came on Wednesday morning. 'Eddie Barker on the line,' said the voice of Gloria at her service.

'Hi, Ed. What's up?' The actress in her managed to banish

any hint of drunkenness from her speech. She didn't even slur her words.

'You've got it, kiddo,' he said excitedly. 'God knows, Emerald, you're a lucky woman, after the fool you made of yourself. Jail and all. But Hogarth loves you. He's had to practically suck cock at the network to get you for this.'

'Why?' she demanded. 'I'm still a big star.'

'Christ, Emerald, the truth, kiddo, *is* you've been in the game too long. The network knows it, the studio knows it, even the great unwashed public knows it.'

'I'm big – *huge* in Europe,' Emerald said proudly. 'I get mobbed when I walk down the Via Condotti.'

'So does Pia Zadora, dear. So what? Listen, Emerald, Europe is a *very* small piece of the action, and frankly, I don't see Zeffirelli banging on your door – even if you are big on the Via Condotti.'

'He couldn't,' she giggled. 'He doesn't like girls.'

'You are not a *girl* any more, kid. Face it, Emerald, however many studs you take into your bed, you are a middle-aged woman who is rapidly losing her pulling power – on *and* off the screen.'

'You don't have to rub it in, Eddie,' she moaned. 'I can still look good, though, and you know it.' She understood he was being harsh to her as a warning. This was her last chance.

'They want you in wardrobe next Tuesday. Eleven o'clock. Be punctual, toots – for a change. And they start shooting in a week. You're a lucky woman, Emerald,' he added gently. 'Don't screw it up.'

She knew he was right. In the intervening five days, she stopped drinking, cold turkey, lost eight pounds, spent two hours at the gym every day, bleached her grey roots back to their golden glory, and arrived in wardrobe punctually on Tuesday morning, almost as good as new.

Nobody else, she told herself, could have done it.

Part Six

JOSH

24

Josh yawned, stretched, and threw out his arms.

''Ere, watch it,' the little redhead with the thin frizzled hair groaned sleepily.

Not again. Self-disgust flooded him at the memory of last night's performances, on and off the stage. The opening night. The party. The people.

The Manchester Hippodrome was a far cry from Broadway and Las Vegas, where he had once done sellout business.

Show business was brutal, as all who chose it as their profession knew. Ultimately no one gave a shit. Every cliché was true: dog eat dog; jealousy thrives; adulation on the way up, indifference on the way down. Josh was on the way down, and he knew it. Self-pity and nausea attacked him simultaneously, and he groped for the paraphernalia to prepare his first fix of the day.

He lit the match under the spoon and watched the white powder dissolve into brownish syrup. After it hit him he turned to inspect the tiny girl by his side. Christ, this one was *really* young stuff. He lifted the sheets up. No more than fourteen or fifteen by the look of her. Even for him, this was younger than usual. He liked them in full bloom, just past puberty, in their first flush of womanhood – sixteen or seventeen was usually the age he preferred. Once he had been lucky enough to find sixteen-year-old twins. They couldn't do enough for him, unlike this little creature, who had lain back uncomplaining while he tried to whip up a fever for both of them. He had failed miserably. Maybe he was getting too old. But the forties weren't old these days. Tom Jones was still around, so was Julio Iglesias, and Jagger – Mick, the idol of all of them – was creeping up the old 4–0 ladder. Not to mention McCartney, Rod Stewart and David Bowie. Forty wasn't fatal – or was it?

''Ello,' the little thing said. God, she was *tiny*. Maybe she was even younger than fourteen. Innocent grey eyes gave him a tentative smile. She hurriedly skipped out of bed, hoping he wouldn't try and do again what he'd done so boringly last night.

Why did I do it? she wondered. He's old enough to be me dad. No, on second thoughts, he was possibly old enough to be her grandad. Her dad was thirty-two – Josh must be at least fifty. She dressed quickly, rehearsing tales with which to regale friends at school. Joshua Brown, big stud, big star. Her mum's favourite crooner. She had grown up to the sounds of his plaintive ballads on her mum's stereo. Her mum had had a real thing for Josh. Used to talk about him for hours. Boring old fart, she thought. Couldn't fuck his way out of a paper bag. Had a hard time even getting it up. Uncle Fred was much better. She struggled into black lace tights, green Lurex socks and, mumbling something about being late for school, skipped away.

Josh was relieved. Now he must get it together. Meet the press, then face the cast at rehearsal, discuss the reviews. Oh, God, the reviews. He was in no hurry to do so. During his final ballad last night, he had observed a steady trickle of customers edging out of the exit doors. The applause had been meagre at the final curtain. The stage manager had been hard-pushed to milk two curtain calls.

After the show last night, a supercilious, pockmarked

journalist from a down-market tabloid had cornered him at the party. Josh, conscious of the power of the press, was always ready to fraternize with them. He needed them now, if this show was to succeed, but basically he loathed their guts. Maybe this reptile could serve a purpose, though. Josh bandied wisecracks and charm for four full minutes before the reptile asked him the oh so familiar question he dreaded. 'So what's Chloe *really* like?' Josh played dumb. The hack plodded on. 'You were married to her for over ten years – is she *really* like Miranda?'

Chloe. That woman was ruining his life with her god-damn TV series and her 'over forty' fame. Some kind of fucking Joan of Arc for the blue-rinse brigade. She thought she was hot stuff now. Showing off her body in those magazines, bragging about how women over forty were just as sexy as twenty-year-olds. Balls. How could she know? She wasn't a man. Young, firm flesh was what most men were interested in. They were wrong, these feminists with their 'Look at us, we're over forty and aren't we wonderful' crap. Didn't they *know*, didn't Chloe realize, for Christ's sake, forty was *past* it?

It was pathetic. It was O.K. for him to be over forty – he was a man. But everywhere these days were these ball-breaking broads with their diets and exercise books, their hit records and their box-office pulling power. Tina fucking Turner, Jane fucking Fonda. And now Chloe.

To add insult to injury, only yesterday she had been on the front page of the *Daily Mirror* with Macho Man Luis Mendoza. 'SOAP'S HOTTEST LOVERS' screamed the headline, and the story chronicled how Chloe and Luis were making the screen ignite with their passionate love scenes and volatile chemistry.

'Not since Petruchio tamed Katharine the shrew have a pair of lovers excited audiences so much,' drooled the article.

'Luis Mendoza is the sexiest, most electrifying leading man to hit the TV screen since Tom Selleck. Already movie companies are standing in line to offer him contracts. All

America is at his feet, thanks to "Saga" and the combustibility of Luis and Chloe Carriere.'

Josh smiled bitterly, trying to hide his jealousy from the reptile. 'Oh, Chloe . . . Yeah . . . Great . . . She's a great girl. Deserves her success. Yeah, really. I'm happy for her.' Bullshit. The words, uttered for the umpteenth time, stuck in his throat, and he had to excuse himself to go to the men's room for a snort.

Sally had looked after him worriedly. He was too pale. The show had not been good. She had seen the audience's glazed faces as the subtlety of *The Private Lives of Napoleon and Josephine* went over their heads.

Poor old Dad. She had tried to cheer him up in the way she knew he loved – had looked around and seen the tiny redheaded teenager gazing admiringly into the space her father had recently vacated. She wandered over to her. 'How'd you like to meet him?' she offered casually. 'Ooh, not 'alf,' squealed the girl. It was easy for Sally to succeed in anticipating her father's wants and needs – though 'thanks' was not a word that was featured in his vocabulary these days. But Josh should certainly realize that Sally cared very much for him.

Josh, relieved that the girl was gone and feeling better as the cocaine took effect, dressed and left for a press luncheon at the Metropole Hotel.

A Fleet Street hag, invisible venom dripping from her ball point pen, pretended to give Josh her rapt attention. She was asking the inevitable questions again about Chloe. The practised answers flowed easily from Josh's lips as he tried to hide his chagrin. Would they never stop interrogating him about her?

'Phone, Dad,' Sally was at his elbow, steering him away. The hag seemed satisfied. She had her story. She would make up the rest. She always made it up. That was why she was called 'The Barracuda of Fleet Street'.

She had already written the story before meeting Josh today. It was titled 'The Fallen Star'.

'He was once a superstar in America and all over the world. Now he ekes out a meagre living playing suburban theatres in Britain. Joshua Brown, once the idol of millions, is now a broken man – a broken man full of broken dreams. His beautiful ex-wife, Chloe Carriere, has become a mega-soap star on American TV while Josh barely makes ends meet touring in mediocre musicals.' The article continued in this vein. This was tremendous stuff. The public would eat it up. They adored a rags-to-riches story, but when it was rags to riches and back to rags again, they loved it even more. And Josh was a natural with his bouts with drugs and alcohol, jail sentences, drunken rages, affairs with young girls – they all made great copy. The public longed to see him fall on his face.

The female barracuda had the perfect set of photos to accompany the story. Josh in 1965, all white teeth, tumbling black locks and shiny satin trousers, holding the mike as if it were his cock, and giving the camera his wildest, sexiest look. Then a recent photo of Josh hunched up in an overcoat and scarf, pale face, greying hair, spectacles, glancing suspiciously over his shoulder, surprised by the camera's flash and, hanging on his arm adoringly, a girl easily young enough to be his daughter. Before and after. How the mighty have fallen. Eat it up, all you readers! Two nice photos of Chloe. Chloe in 1962 – wide-eyed innocence, black hair and a neat fringe, a chaste miniskirt and knee socks. And there was Chloe now – sheathed in Rudolpho bugle beads, white fox and diamonds, lying seductively on a satin chaise, with a knowing and successful look on her painted face. Perfect. The hag cackled. She had never liked Josh anyway. Too big-headed by far. He had reaped what he had sown.

Chloe read the piece on Josh a week later. In spite of herself she felt sad for him. Why had he allowed himself to fall so far? He had had it all. If he found himself a decent agent, went to a psychiatrist, gave up drugs and bimbos and really concentrated on his work, on his music, he could have it all again. Maybe. Maybe not. Nothing in this business was easy.

She sighed and looked at Philippe, who lay next to her in

their huge bed with the art deco-padded satin headboard and lilac silk sheets. He was watching MTV, his favourite station.

Chloe thought it odd that a man of forty could become so hooked on the gyrations of Madonna and Michael Jackson. But he watched Music Television all day long when he wasn't working on her accounts or writing articles for *Paris Match*.

Philippe was always in the house. He was on a marriage kick again after seeing the article about Josh in the British tabloid.

'When are you going to get the final papers signed, *chérie?*' he asked, massaging her shoulders in the seductive way she loved. 'Why don't you get them? Then we can be married. Get rid of Josh, *chérie*, it's time.'

Oh, no, here he goes again, thought Chloe. Not wedding talk again. They had been living together for a year, but he kept going on about marriage. It was unusual for a man. Much as she adored him, she didn't feel like making a lifelong commitment. Josh was always at the back of her mind.

As tactfully as possible, Chloe gave him once again her anti-marriage speech. It didn't placate him and he sulked for the rest of the day to the sound of MTV turned up full blast.

Chloe left for the studio attempting to forget Josh's predicament and Philippe's sulks. She called Jasper from her car phone. 'What is the decision?' she asked. 'Has the network come up with the raise for next season, Jasper? We're on our last episode of the season. We've only got another five days to shoot.'

Jasper had met with Abby in the big man's sumptuous office at the beginning of the season. Abby's reputation as a producer who couldn't tolerate insubordination in actors and others who worked for him was legendary. To the world he played Mr Always Understanding, but in reality he was ruthless if anyone dared step out of line. Several members of the company had been fired for demanding more money.

Jasper had transmitted Chloe's discontent with the fact that after four years on 'Saga', contributing to its success in the ratings, and having become one of the most copied, admired and hated women on TV, she was still receiving far less salary than Sam and Sissy. Abby would not hear of an increase for Chloe. Through gritted teeth he spelled it out. 'Tell her if she wants to continue working in this town she'd better not make waves. If she doesn't conform, if she gives us any trouble, she'll be out. We'll kill her off; write her out. We won't be blackmailed, Jasper, not by her nor any of them. She's making forty thousand a week – that should be enough for an ex-nightingale from provincial Britain.'

He added with a shark's smile: 'Tell Chloe I'll expect her at my "Man of the Year Award" dinner at the Beverly Hilton next Tuesday, Jasper. She's seated at my table. She'd better be there.'

A command from the emperor. Abby wore his power easily. It confirmed his self-worth. God knows his wife, Maud, didn't care about it, unless it was his *net* worth. Abby was not going to let any actor, producer or director get the better of him, and he was not above deliberately humiliating any of them. Chloe would never forget what he had done to Pandora King last season.

Pandora had been late on the set too many times, made fun of 'Saga' too often on talk shows, and complained and moaned on the set about the poor dialogue she was getting and how her costumes were not as expensive as Chloe's and Sissy's. Abby and Gertrude were becoming thoroughly sick of her.

Pandora, along with the rest of the cast and crew, had attended the wrap party at the Beverly Hills Hotel for 'Saga' to celebrate the end of shooting. Everyone was in an 'up' mood, and it should have been a joyful occasion. Nine months of hard work were over. A three-month hiatus lay ahead of them. They could all do what they wanted. For the crew, this usually meant getting another job as quickly as possible, since they couldn't afford to be out of work for that long. For the three best-paid actors, Sam, Sissy and Chloe, it meant they could choose from the fat pile of scripts that their agents had waiting on their desks or go on an extended vacation. The rest of the cast were at the mercy of whichever producer or network chose to give them a job.

After dinner and the gag reel – a twenty-minute compilation of actors and crew doing inadvertently funny things, breaking up, tripping, choking, giggling or generally making fools of themselves – Gertrude and Abby went to the podium and introduced all the cast, each of whom was invited to the stand and to say a few words.

First Sam, as the most senior member of the cast, made his usual charming speech. He sounded good, even though he was beginning to look old without his thick orange makeup.

Vanessa whispered to Chloe, 'He's lost so much weight, his teeth seem to be getting too big for his mouth!'

Sissy flounced on, thin as bone, brittle as glass, wearing a grey taffeta strapless dress that made her shoulder blades look like chicken wings.

Then came Chloe, looking strained after another petty row with Philippe. He had refused to come to the wrap party, so she had to ask Ostie, her dialogue coach, to escort her.

Abby then called upon Pandora:

'And now we are going to hear from a lovely lady and a talented actress, who, regretfully, will not be back with us next season. Please all give a great round of applause to Miss Pandora King.'

Pandora's blood froze. *Not be back next season?* They couldn't. They wouldn't. Not after she had just turned down a firm offer from Disney for a half-hour sitcom. She had suspected for some months that her days on 'Saga' were numbered. That was the way the cookie crumbled in TV Land. Her fan mail had been getting sparser, and it seemed that the fewer letters she received, the fewer lines she had to learn. She was a realist and had been excited about the Disney series, looking forward to the challenge of a new project. However, after speaking to Abby, her agent had told her that she would definitely be back on 'Saga' next season with a hefty raise. Abby had assured him they all adored her. She shouldn't have believed a word of it. Now the sitcom at Disney had gone to another actress, and the bastard was firing her in front of the entire cast and crew. She swallowed her pride, aware that her face was aflame, and went up to the podium to say the few words she had carefully prepared but which now seemed horribly inappropriate.

After her speech, Chloe squeezed her arm sympathetically as they stood next to each other on the podium. It could have happened to any of them. In their hearts, all of the cast breathed a sigh of relief that this season, at least, they had escaped the hangman's noose. During the shooting of thirty episodes of the third season Chloe had tried to remain calm and not get upset when highly paid guest stars were brought in for seven or eight episodes to 'bolster the ratings' – which were already high. Neither the network nor Abby nor Gertrude had any qualms about paying these often fading stars twice the amount they paid Chloe.

'It's my fault for coming in so cheap at the beginning,' Chloe told Vanessa bitterly, having just played a scene with a 'famous name' who had blown his lines fifteen times in a row and who was getting sixty thousand dollars an episode.

Two days before shooting ended, Chloe received Jasper's news that her raise had once again been denied. Backed by Philippe, she grimly decided she had to take a stand before the next season began. Since she had not received the twenty thousand-a-week increase she felt she warranted, she informed Jasper that she would quit the show.

'I mean it, Jasper,' she said. 'I'm off to the south of France and I'm not coming back unless you can get them to change their minds.'

They didn't.

Although the network wanted Chloe to remain on the show, Abby and Gertrude were adamant. No raise. In their eyes, Chloe had committed the cardinal sin. Self-righteously they announced that Chloe had attempted to blackmail them. People who would cut each other's throats for a project, who

295

lied, cheated, schemed and manipulated, were up in arms over Chloe's deed. During the hiatus, which had been shortened from the usual three months to six weeks by the network's desire to have 'Saga' back on the air in late October, Jasper tried to negotiate a compromise with Abby, Gertrude and the network executives. To no avail.

They dropped her. They wrote her out of the first episode, giving her dialogue to other actors, and they sent her the news by cable.

Cold rage gripped Chloe when the cable arrived. 'The producers of "Saga" MCPC, and the BCC Network hereby inform Chloe Carriere that, effective today her services as a performer in the television series "Saga" are no longer required.' It was signed 'Abby Arafat, President of MCPC'.

She had been lying by the pool, basking in the warm Mediterranean sunshine, when Philippe handed her the cable.

'How *can* they even consider doing this to "Saga" even if they don't care about me?' said Chloe, amazed at how they would cut off their nose to spite their face.

'It's suicidal,' Philippe agreed. 'Everyone knows how popular Miranda and you are. You're the only reason anyone watches the damned trash in the first place.' It was four o'clock on the Côte d'Azure. It would be 7 a.m. in L.A., Chloe thought. The cast would be rushing to finish their makeup and hair to be on the set for rehearsal. Sissy would be putting her wig on while gulping down her vitamin pills and protein drink for the gruelling day ahead. Sam would be resting. The younger actors would be gossiping in the hair and makeup rooms.

Chloe felt a touch of melancholy. The view of the Mediterranean from the house was more beautiful than any in Beverly Hills or Malibu, but the thought that she might have blown her hard-won career made her even more melancholy.

'Drink?' Philippe asked. She nodded and he went to the bamboo bar, poured cassis and Dom Perignon over ice into a tall glass and brought it to her.

She drank it gratefully. 'All I did was ask for what I deserve, Philippe. No more, no less.'

'I know, *chérie*.'

'They all think I'm really a bitch,' she said bitterly, a sliver of self-pity in her voice. She gazed at the turquoise waves, oblivious to the semi-naked flesh that paraded unselfconsciously up and down the *plage*. Young and old, perfect and not so perfect, downright ugly – it was of no importance on the French Riviera. They all showed it off. 'Don't brood, *chérie*,' he said, leaving her to go surfing.

Her eyes scanned the bay. White yachts rocked gently on their moorings as their owners sat sipping cool drinks and watching speedboats piloted by tanned young men and barebreasted girls dart between them. Floating on the waves like multicoloured butterflies were the gaily-hued striped sails of the wind-surfers. It was a view Chloe never ceased to admire as she lounged in her beach chair luxuriating in the laziness of watching other people hard at play.

The telephone rang.

'Chloe, my dear, you *must* be back for the second episode or you will never work in television or movies again.' Jasper's long-distance voice was faint. 'They mean business, Chloe. You cannot fight them. I have done everything I can, dear, *everything*, but I must tell you that I have never seen Abby so resistant. He's very angry with you.'

'I thought he loved me,' sighed Chloe. 'He told me so often enough.'

'He does, in his way, he does. But I think it's more than resistance to you and the raise. It's Sissy's influence. I think if you come back, though, you just may get your raise, my darling.'

'What do you mean?' Chloe was puzzled.

'I found out that Sam has points in the show. It's supposed to be a deep, dark secret, but I found out. He originally signed only a two-year contract, and when it was up, the only way he'd agree to stay was if he got a financial interest in the show.'

'Ah!' cried Chloe. 'All is clear. It *is* Sissy, then.'

'Right, darling, Queen Bitch herself. She *will not*, as part owner of the show, allow you to have a raise, and she will rip Sam's balls off if he agrees to give you so much as one cent more.'

'Damn her,' said Chloe sadly. 'Why does she hate me so much?'

'Jealousy, my pet. You get more fan mail, more attention. You're more popular, your role is more exciting *and*, of course, you're better-looking. Don't fight it, toots, jealousy is a fact of life in this town. And don't take it personally, either. If it wasn't you playing Miranda, Sissy would loathe whomever it was. She's that kind of woman.'

Chloe sighed. 'I know, I've worked with her for all these years. She's not a lot of laughs, believe me.'

Jasper continued, 'The network told me in deepest confidence that if you come back, *they* will give you the twenty thousand out of their own pockets. But Sissy and Sam must never know.... Ignore the cable, Chloe dear. Come back Tuesday. I promise you within two months you will have your raise.'

'All right, all right, Jasper – I'll come back. Just as you knew I would, darling.'

Jasper was pleased. He liked Chloe. The fact that she hadn't saddled herself with the usual slew of personal managers, business advisers and tax-shelter specialists meant she had probably saved more of her earnings than most actresses in her position. Clever girl. Not only that, but she steered clear of booze, dope and the swingers scene. By Hollywood standards she was almost square.

Chloe hung up, her feelings still unsettled. She felt ill-used. The tone of the cable, the way she had been so swiftly written out of the premiere episode, gave her a sense of mortality that made her uneasy. I'm dispensable like Kleenex, she thought.

She watched Philippe on his wind-surfer as he manoeuvred the small craft across the waves. Brown curls clinging to his head. His body was tanned, lean and athletic, although he did little exercise. Emotionally he had been a rock, a difficult rock sometimes, but a rock nonetheless that she could lean on. In return he handled her finances and her business affairs, and most of the time she was content with him, although he could be stubborn, and he had incredible mood swings which turned him from Prince Charming into male chauvinist pig. His conversation was quite limited, though. She sighed. The more she knew Philippe, the less substance there seemed to be in him. But the more the fabric of their psychological relationship weakened, the stronger the physical side became.

She shivered in spite of the Mediterranean sun. He pushed her so often for marriage. *Why?* She was extremely wary. The pain Josh had inflicted on her had not gone away completely.

Josh. Poor Josh. Brilliant, funny, self-destructive, complex Josh. Where was he now? And what was he doing?

25

Emerald was the first big name to be cast in 'America'. She would play Evelyn Alexander McFadden, the female lead. The lusty, beautiful proprietress of a hotel saloon in the little Midwestern border town. But Burt Hogarth was having trouble casting the male lead. He had approached some of the most prestigious actors in England for 'America' with no success.

The network was anxious to start production by early July. They wanted the series ready to start airing in October of 1986. They had decided to programme 'America' opposite the so far invincible 'Saga', which had been the ratings winner practically every week for the past four years.

It was generally agreed by the producers of 'America' that the competition between Emerald Barrymore and Chloe Carriere would excite the viewers' interest. And they had shrewdly cast Pandora King, recently dumped by 'Saga', to play the second female lead.

The only problem that remained was finding a strong English leading man to play opposite Emerald – a man who would not be overshadowed by her star power. Sir Geoffrey Fennel had bowed out in favour of doing Mercutio at the

National. They approached Pierce Brosnan, Roger Moore and Michael Caine. All turned it down. The part of Malcolm McFadden called for a forty-to-fiftyish actor to be the heroic, tough and sardonic husband of Evelyn/Emerald. He had to be strong, sexy, masculine, have a sense of humour, ride a horse, fence, and be in peak physical condition.

Ten days before shooting commenced, the producers having interviewed and tested dozens of actors and watched hundreds of miles of videotape were still no closer to finding their male lead. Shooting was set to start the day after Independence Day. July Fourth was 'America' Day, but no suitable leading man had been found.

Josh lay in bed sweating. Pulses he never knew he possessed hammered in his skull and his tongue was a slab of decaying meat. The phone wouldn't stop. It kept on interrupting his dream – or was it a nightmare?

He and Chloe – young again. In love again. Kids, in the 1960s walking down King's Road laughing like teenagers. He never failed to have her in gales of laughter. She laughed a lot, and he wondered if she still did. He wondered if Philippe made her happy.

In his dream, he was hugging her so tightly he could feel his hardness against her thigh. Then people started to tug at him, pulling her away, as her expression of joy turned to fear. 'Chloe, Chloe – ' he tried to call her name, but the words wouldn't form. 'Josh,' she screamed, as hands, eager, excited hands, grabbed at her body and hair, tearing at her clothes. Then hysterical voices started yelling her name. 'Chloe! Chloe! Miranda! Miranda! We love you! We love you!' Faceless fans pushed Josh away. He staggered and fell to the pavement watching as they overwhelmed Chloe, pulling at her clothes, pulling them off, grabbing chunks of her hair and her flesh, tearing at her with their fingernails and teeth, huddling over her now as she lay bleeding on the pavement. She was screaming for help, but Josh couldn't move.

As the dream continued, he saw her body supine on the

ground. Fans crawled over her like ants: kissing, biting, ripping her flesh, sucking her everywhere as she screamed with horror. He couldn't stop them. 'Fuck off, Grandad,' yelled a punk with green hair who was about to plunge himself into Chloe. 'Fuck off or I'll ram this up yer arse.' He shoved Josh viciously and he fell against the wall watching helplessly as the fans ravaged his Chloe.

He woke up screaming her name. Finally he heard the sound of the ringing phone echoing Chloe's cries.

'What? Who is it?' he yelled hoarsely, needing liquid, anything to ease his throat. The voice on the phone was friendly.

'Josh, dear boy, it's Jasper Swanson. How are you, old boy?'

'Fine, fine, just great, Jasper. How's yourself?' He tipped a half-empty wineglass to his cracked lips and felt the sour liquid moisten his parched tongue. 'What's up, Jasper?'

'Well, dear boy, I don't know whether you'll be interested or not because I know the tour is going so well. . . .'

Fucking liar, thought Josh. The fucking *world* knows it's a flop. What's the old fart going on about? 'Not that well, Jasper.' He might as well be honest. 'I mean, if another gig came along I could be tempted.'

'Naturally, dear boy, naturally, which is why I'm calling you at this unearthly hour. You've heard of the book, *America: The Early Years*?'

'Yeah, of course, who hasn't?' He sat up, dying for a smoke. The ashtray was full of butts, the pack empty.

'Well, it's going to be a very important series. I think I have convinced them that you would be perfect for the part of Malcolm McFadden – the lead opposite Emerald Barrymore. Would that interest you, old man?'

There was silence as Josh digested this.

'Hello, hello, Josh? Are you there?' Jasper's time was money, and he was always impatient. He was a great agent, and he knew it. Some said he could sell the Vatican to the Pope, so good was he at his job.

302

'Yeah, yeah, I'm here.' Josh lit one of the butts. The smoke seemed to clear his fuddled brain. 'It's a soap opera, isn't it?'

'Well, I suppose you could call it that, but it's a very prestigious series. Burt Hogarth is the producer, and he is one of the most important men in Hollywood, let's face it, and of course Emerald Barrymore is still a major star.'

'She hasn't worked for a while, has she?'

'Neither have you, dear boy.' Frost crept into Jasper's voice. 'I think you should face the fact, *young man*,' he said with a hint of sarcasm, 'that Hollywood is not clamouring for the services of fifty-year-old English ex-pop singers.'

'Hold on, old boy, I'm nowhere near fifty,' said Josh, 'and I was *never* a pop singer.'

'This role could make you an important star again, Josh. Everyone knows you have talent, but we all know your – well – your problems. I've had a damn difficult job convincing the network that you don't drink now, and are certainly *not* doing drugs.' Disdain coloured his tone. Jasper despised both drug addicts and alcoholics. 'They have bought my idea of Joshua Brown as Malcolm. It's a hell of a role old boy, and a stupendous break for you. They will pay twelve thousand an episode this year, and twenty-five thousand next season. They will supply you with two first-class tickets from London to L.A., and first-star billing after Emerald. And they want you in Hollywood for costume and camera tests the day after tomorrow. We'll go through all the other details then.'

Josh's mind reeled. 'My musical – what about the show? We've got another week here, then Leeds and Manchester, all the provinces.'

'Your show is a flop. You know it. I know it. Even the British public knows it. The network is prepared to discuss a payoff with the theatre owners. They will spring you, in fact. What do you say, Josh? This could be a major comeback for you, something you cannot turn your back on.'

'Of course I'll do it,' said Josh excitedly. 'I have to – you know it. Book me into my old penthouse at the Wilshire. Can you get three plane tickets, first class?'

'No.' Jasper was cool. Starting his demands already, was he? 'If you need to bring two other people we can exchange the two first-class into three club. Remember, Josh, you are not a star in Hollywood. You cannot make demands – yet.'

'Yeah, well, O.K. Change the tickets. It's just that I need to bring Sally, and Perry, my valet.'

'Done, dear boy, done. Now, congratulations. I know you are not going to regret this. I'll be in touch tomorrow.'

Josh lay back on the bed feeling euphoric. Hollywood! A major TV series with a major star! Emerald Barrymore. Publicity. The studio machine in action for him. The big time – it could be the big time for him again. It could be. It *would* be.

He leapt out of bed, energized with excitement, not needing the fix he'd been subconsciously thinking about.

'Look out, Chloe, babe, here I come!' he yelled.

Chloe went back at work on 'Saga' for the fourth season. Due to pressure from the network, Abby and Gertrude had relented. They had wanted to make an example of Chloe, show the rest of the cast and actors in their other shows what would happen to a star who demanded more money. Although they had bragged that they could do without Chloe's contribution to 'Saga', they hadn't considered the network's reaction.

'Get her back on this show,' Irving Schwarzman, president of the network, told Abby. 'Give her the fucking raise – she deserves it, for Christ's sake. *Get her back.*' Despite Abby and Gertrude's protestations that the inmates would end up running the asylum, they were overruled. Chloe came back twenty thousand dollars a week richer.

But her life with Philippe was becoming somewhat confusing. He had often been loving and affectionate; at the same time he was constantly arguing with her about getting married. His own bourgeois ideas and his even more bourgeoise French mother were pushing him. His mother thought that at forty he was too young to be living with a forty-three-year-old woman. She wanted grandchildren. He was her only child and she was nearly eighty.

Philippe hoped he could persuade Chloe to get married and then persuade her it was still possible for her to have a child. Now that he had seen her with Annabel, he realized how maternal Chloe could be and was determined to have a baby with her.

That was his plan, but it clearly wasn't Chloe's. Marriage to Philippe and babies at her age – ridiculous.

'Ursula Andress did it,' he sulked. 'She had a child at forty-four. Many women do; it's possible, you know, *chérie*, and you would be a wonderful mother.'

'Why, Philippe? *Why* do we need marriage and a baby? We're happy the way we are – why spoil it?'

'You treat me like a stud,' he replied sulkily. 'You use me like men used to use a woman. You pick my brains and use my cock. You're just a user, Chloe.'

'That's not true and you know it,' she said angrily. 'Look, we're together, we live together. I love you. Please, darling, don't make me get married. I've done it once. It doesn't work for me.'

Annabel was living with them for the summer in the guest house. Both women were happy with each other. Their relationship was excellent and they spent hours together in deep conversation. Philippe felt annoyed and left out, and was sulking more than ever. Annabel swam in the pool, tended the rose garden, and scattered the pillows she beautifully embroidered all over the house. Making them was her hobby, that and playing her guitar.

Having Annabel around was good, the show was doing well, but Chloe often awoke in the night with nightmares. Sometimes in her nightmare she would see the face of the man with the knife whom the police said had wanted to harm her that night in Las Vegas. She wished they had never shown her his picture, that blank, emotionless face. When she awoke in the middle of the night, Philippe's strong arms and calming voice enfolded her, helped her go back to sleep.

Only eight more months left. Eight months before he was out of this fucking hellhole. He had made no friends. No one in jail wanted to be friendly except when they abused him sexually.

In his cell each night, Calvin took out the magazines he'd accumulated. *Penthouse. Playboy.*

He looked at them, gloating with excitement. In these magazines, the full-bosomed girls in their black lace underwear, with their open legs, all had one face. Emerald Barrymore's. Calvin had cut pictures of his idol from other publications and carefully pasted her head onto the bodies of the lush young creatures in his magazines. His Emerald. His queen.

He had been upset when he had seen the photographs of her in the tabloids emerging from jail. What infuriated him even more was the piece written in the *American Informer.*

'If the part of Miranda Hamilton in prime time's hit series "Saga" had gone to Emerald Barrymore, who lost the role to British singer Chloe Carriere, would Emerald have come to this pathetic end, living like a down-and-out and with no trace of her former beauty left?'

Calvin had scrunched the paper up into a tight ball, and thrown it into a corner of his cell. It was all *her* fault, that black-haired witch, that no-talent nonentity. It was because of Chloe Carriere that his Emerald was in this state. All because of her. She would suffer for it. When he got out of here she would really suffer for her sins.

There was no question Sam was not feeling up to par. He had lost an alarming amount of weight and couldn't seem to force himself to eat anything. During the day's filming he often became exhausted and had to lie down to rest. He first noticed the ugly red patch when he felt an itching on his chest. Forcing himself to look in the mirror, he saw with a sinking dread what he had feared, what he had tried never to allow to enter his conscious thoughts – a red patch, scabby, and swollen, the size of a quarter.

306

Bile rose in his throat. It couldn't be. It *couldn't*. Since the wild days of his youth, he had indulged in very few homo-sexual affairs. He had been more-or-less faithful to Freddy. Good old dependable Freddy. They were almost like a married couple – except a married couple who only do it occasionally have a tendency to do it with other people. He remembered Nick. He groaned. What about Freddy? Had he been with anyone else?

While the cat's away, the mice go down to the nearest gay bar. Did Freddy do that still? With AIDS the latest scourge? A rapping on the door announced that Sam was needed on the set in four minutes. He went back to the set, convincing himself it was all in his imagination, but he told his secretary to make a doctor's appointment as soon as possible.

He sat opposite Dr John Willows, who looked grave.

'I'm sorry to have to tell you this, Sam.' The doctor coughed. He was embarrassed. He'd known Sam for thirty-five years, but his homosexuality was a topic they had never discussed.

'What? What? Tell me for Christ's sake, John. Is it AIDS?'

The physician nodded. 'I'm . . . I'm afraid so, Sam. We tested your blood twice to make sure there was no mistake. I'm very sorry.' The doctor looked down at his mahogany desk, at the framed photograph of his wife, his grown-up children and his grandchildren. He thanked God he had always been faithful to her – for more than thirty years now. Thank God he hadn't given in to the temptations that had occasionally crossed his path. But what could he tell this ageing TV superstar whose gaunt, lined face suddenly looked much older than fifty-five? How to help him?

'I'm afraid there's no cure just yet, as you know.' He twiddled with the pencils on his immaculate desk. 'We can, of course, treat the carcinoma with ointments and antibiotics but eventually the patches will get worse, I'm afraid.'

Sam felt the room swimming before him. His career was in

ruins. He had caught the plague – some likened it to the bubonic plague – the Black Death. And as with the plague there was no cure for this scourge of the eighties.

'How long.' He gulped for air. 'How long do you think I have before it'll be obvious?'

'Hard to say – months, maybe years. I'm not an expert, Sam. You know we've only been really aware of this disease for a few years, but it's spreading. My God, it's spreading.'

'Will people have to know from you? Do you have to tell them?'

'Of course not, of course not.' The doctor's voice had a heartiness he didn't feel. God, Sam was the seventh person he'd seen this month who had contracted the virus. It was terrifying.

'Listen, sport, if you need counselling about this, there are experts who know how to deal with the problem.'

'Christ, no!' Sam was shocked. 'I can deal with it myself. My career will be shot if a word of this gets out. You do understand that, don't you, John?'

'Of course, of course I do. Don't worry, Sam. No one will know, but . . .' The doctor looked at his watch. He had a waiting room full of patients. 'You better check your contacts, your recent ones, that is.'

'Damn it, John, I've only had one contact.'

'Yes, yes, of course. Well listen, sport, come in next Tuesday and we'll get you set up with all the right stuff.' He was desperate to end this. Nothing he could do. He was just a doctor seeing these pathetic men, trying to help them. He managed a sympathetic smile as he walked Sam to the door.

Luis Mendoza's sudden fame astounded even himself. After appearing on the TV screen in 'Saga' only twice, he had received tons of fan mail. Women found his macho, slightly cocky good looks a total turn-on. He was suddenly the flavour of the month throughout the whole United States. Editors besieged Christopher McCarthy, the PR man for 'Saga', with requests for cover stories, photo sessions, interviews, anything and everything to do with Luis.

Before he knew what had hit him, Luis was on the cover of *US*, *People*, *USA Today*, *GQ*, the *American Informer*, the *National Enquirer*, the *Star*, the *Globe* and even the corner cover of *Newsweek*. It was heady stuff. Intoxicating. Luis had never been modest, and his Latin pride swelled even more at the sudden attention and admiration he was receiving.

Sabrina didn't like it. It wasn't that she was jealous. With her wholesome all-American beauty, she was in demand herself, building a solid foundation for a film career that she hoped would flourish for years. But she didn't like Luis's preening himself all day long, constantly combing his shiny black hair, working on his rippling muscles and admiring them from all angles in the three-way mirror in *her* dressing room. This was when he wasn't lying by the pool obsessively working on an already perfect tan, a sun reflector handy to catch every last ray. Their love life was still good, but there was something missing in their relationship now, and she didn't know what it was.

Sam stalked into Freddy's workroom and went directly to the bar. Satin and lace, half-finished beaded frocks for fashionable starlets littered the sofa and table. Fashion magazines from Italy, France and England were piled on the floor. An orange cat lay on the windowsill basking in the hot Santa Monica sunshine. Outside, Sam could see suntanned teenagers oiling themselves, surfing, eating hot dogs and laughing. Laughing. Ha! Would he ever laugh again? Could he?

'Who've you been fucking, you lousy little faggot?' he demanded, as he knocked back a whiskey and poured another.

'No one, no one, I *swear*. My love – I've been faithful.'

'Tell me the *truth*,' Sam screamed. 'Who? *Who?!* I know you did, I know it. I've got fucking AIDS, for Christ's sake, and you've given it to me, you bastard.'

'Oh, God, no, no, you can't – oh, my good Lord. How could it happen?' Freddy threw himself onto the pile of fabric on the couch and burst into tears.

'Don't fucking give me the fucking tears routine you mother-fucking queer.' Sam could not contain his rage. The cat looked up, decided this was the wrong place to be and padded to the kitchen with dignity.

'Only once,' Freddy sobbed. 'Only once, darling.'

'Don't call me darling.' Sam's voice was hoarse. 'Where, when, who with?'

'Oh, God, Sam, I love you, you know I do. Oh, my God, I don't know why, I swear I don't know how but . . .'

'Yes, go on.' Sam's lip tightened into a thin line. There was so much anger in him he thought he would explode. His face was crimson and his heart was beating so fast he thought he might have a heart attack.

'It was two years ago.' Freddy wiped his bloodshot blue eyes with a scrap of one-hundred-dollar-a-yard Fortuny silk. 'At the bathhouse.'

'The fucking bathhouse! Shit! Go on, who with?'

'I don't remember,' whined Freddy.

'Remember!' Sam grabbed him by his mauve cashmere sweater and leaned his face close to Freddy's. 'Fucking *remember*, or I'll fucking kill you.'

'Oh, Sam . . . Sam. It was awful, awful. I couldn't help it. I was drugged. God knows why I did it. It's you I love. You know I do.'

'Shut up, shmuck. I want *details*. All the details.'

Gulping back his tears, Freddy tried to explain.

His friend from the airlines had arrived one night from Acapulco. He had brought a new kind of dope with him.

'Acapulco gold is a Marlboro compared to this,' Hugh had told him, grinning from ear to ear.

They had smoked two joints, becoming so high that they didn't know what day it was – which was when Hugh suggested they visit the bathhouse. Since Sam had become

Freddy's lover, bathhouses were strictly off-limits. But the dope had taken effect – Freddy no longer cared.

The place was jumping with the usual Saturday night insanity. The two men had showered and gone into the sauna room. Freddy, a handsome short blond man of thirty-nine, was usually highly sought after. Although he had saved himself exclusively for Sam for the past few years – except for a very occasional and discreet fling, that is – the dope had made him feel not only high but also extremely sexy. He was approached by the three gorgeous young studs he had observed oiling themselves on the beach this morning. He lay back as the boys attended to him expertly. It was mind-blowing. Ecstasy. Three or four other men stood around watching.

'Don't stop,' begged Freddy. 'I want more.' By this time the other men were excited too. The first one rolled off Freddy and another took his place. Then the next, then the next. Freddy couldn't get enough of this incredible feeling. He felt like a satyr. The dope had made him insatiable.

'More,' he begged, and they were only too eager to oblige.

Freddy's joy continued into the morning hours. But his shame lasted considerably longer.

'So that's it, my love. That's what happened. I couldn't help it. I'm sorry. It won't ever happen again, I promise you.'

'Too fucking late.' Sam was weary now. Disgusted with Freddy's story. 'I've got AIDS. And you've probably got it. We're both going to *die*, Freddy, you know that, don't you?'

'Oh, God, what can we do?'

'Nothing.' Sam sat heavily on the sofa, his anger spent. 'There's nothing we can do now, Freddy, except wait.'

Sam lost more weight each week. He cleansed his system as much as possible, cutting out red meat, sugar, alcohol, salt and preservatives. He lived on the healthiest possible diet, slept ten hours a night, exercised, prayed, thought positively – and was terrified.

The hideous red scabs were gradually spreading all over his body until he could no longer bear to look at his flesh. He refused to allow his 'Saga' dresser to help him when he changed. He lived in constant fear of being found out. He couldn't even confide the dreaded secret to Sissy. He didn't trust her – he didn't trust anyone.

His private line rang one lunch hour when he was restlessly trying to nap in his trailer.

'Sam, how are you? It's John Willows.'

'Oh, hi, John. I'm . . . I'm fine.' He tried to muster a cheerfulness in his tone.

'Well, Sam, I've got some good news and some bad,' the doctor said, trying to sound heartier than he felt. 'Which do you want first, old man?'

'The good,' said Sam.

'Well, old man, it looks like we've arrested the virus – in your case. I wouldn't say you were in remission exactly, but the tests we did on you last week showed a slight but definite improvement. I think this new experimental drug from France could be working.'

'Great, great, that's wonderful news, old boy. Wonderful!' He felt instantly better. Arrested the virus! That meant he could maybe last for years, decades even. He smiled a genuinely happy smile for the first time in months.

There was a pause as John Willows cleared his throat – an embarrassed silence.

'And so what's the bad news, old man? Nothing could be *that* bad after what you've just told me.'

'Well, old boy, I've just had a call from the clinic.'

'What clinic?' asked Sam.

'The clinic where we sent your blood to be tested,' said Dr Willows, treading carefully.

'So – so what, what's so bad about that?' barked Sam.

'I have to level with you, Sam, this is terrible for you, I know, but when we sent your blood in to be tested, I told my assistant to put a phony name on it.'

'Yes! Yes!' Sam sat bolt upright, almost screaming now. 'So what happened?'

Silence.

'She did it, didn't she?' His voice rose to such a crescendo that Sissy, trying to nap in the trailer next door with earplugs in and eye mask on, sent her maid over to tell him to shut up.

'Fuck off!' Sam screamed at the woman as she knocked tentatively on his trailer door.

'I'm sorry, Sam,' continued the doctor. 'She didn't. She goofed. She's new, it was her first week here, fresh out of med school. Your name was on the blood sample we sent to the clinic. And there's a problem now. The problem is – '

'*Whaaat* – tell me what the fuck the problem is. I'm making a fucking series here, I can't shilly-shally around listening to you all day. *Tell me!!*'

'O.K., O.K., calm down, please. This is pretty embarrassing for me.'

'Embarrassing?' Sam shrieked, out of control.

'I'm very sorry to tell you, Sam, that the clinic's confidential log book containing the names of all the individuals carrying the virus has been stolen.'

'Stolen. *Stolen.* Who the hell would want to steal it?' Suddenly Sam thought he might black out. He groped for one of the cigars he hadn't touched in three months and tipped a bottle of Evian water to his lips.

'They think it's been stolen by blackmailers,' the doctor said quietly.

'*Blackmailers!*' Now he knew he was going to faint.

'In fact, the police are pretty sure of it.'

'Oh, my God, I'm ruined. I'm fucking ruined!'

'Well, if it's any consolation to you, old man, there are hundreds of others on that list who could possibly be ruined too. Prominent lawyers, politicians, doctors and actors. You're not the only actor in town who has AIDS, you know. It's rampant here. In San Francisco it's a nightmare. It's bankrupting the city.'

'Jesus Christ, Jesus Christ, Jesus H. Christ,' Sam kept repeating.

'I'm sorry, Sam. Look, I'll talk to you tomorrow. I – I have a few more calls I must make. You do understand?'

313

'Sure, John, sure, sure.' Sam hung up and, head in hands, sat stonily until Sissy walked in.

'What is it, darling? You look positively *vile*. And why have you started that filthy habit again?'

Sam didn't answer. Sissy was wearing a fawn 1930s fitted suit, with a beige fox collar and muff, and a ridiculous Cossack hat. Her blonde hair, teased to within an inch of its life, fuzzed out around the hat. Her eyes were shadowed by eyelashes like awnings, her lips a thin crimson slash.

'Sam. Answer me, Sam,' she snapped, used to his jumping to attention when she spoke.

He looked at her – at her angular hard body, her bony sparrow's face.

'Get out of here, Sissy, right now,' he growled.

'Sam – I – '

'Get out, you cunt,' he screamed. 'Out, *out*, out of here. I don't want to see your bloody face again. Get out of my dressing room.' The uproar caused two assistant directors and a couple of stand-ins to come over and gape at the normally charming, even-tempered star.

'Mr Sharp, Mr Sharp, calm down, *please*.' Debbie Drake shooed the others, including a furious Sissy, out of the trailer and slammed the door behind her.

'I'm sorry, sir. Is there anything I can do for you?'

'Nothing, dear, nothing. I'm sorry. Give me half an hour, Debbie, and I'll be back on the set. Tell Chelsea to shoot Sissy's close-up first. I just need a little time to myself, dear.'

'Of course, sir, of course. We will give you as long as you need,' she said, and tactfully left him, closing the trailer door quietly.

26

Horace Reid, editor of the *American Informer*, flipped through the pages of the thin book with mounting excitement. What a coup! This list was dynamite. It was mind-blowing. And to top it all it had come into his hands anonymously. He hadn't had to pay a brass farthing for this unbelievable and incriminating item. It would have cost at least thirty thousand dollars if he had had to buy it.

'Six actors, three of them household names, four politicians, two writers. It's *dynamite*. The hottest thing we've ever had. We'll have the sellout issue of all time when we print this list. We're gonna take TV ads, the works.' The ugly little man smirked with glee at his assistant, as he wondered fleetingly who hated someone on the list enough to do this.

'We'll leak it a little bit at a time, I think,' said Horace, picking his teeth with a paper clip. On the walls behind his desk were framed some of the more memorable best-selling front-page stories of the past decade:

'MARILYN MONROE A LESBIAN'. That had sold over eight million copies.

'I WAS ELVIS'S LOVE CHILD'. Close to eight and a half million there.

'PRESIDENT KENNEDY'S ASSASSINATION: MASTERMINDED BY HIS OWN FAMILY'. Another biggie.

Since leaving Australia and becoming editor of the *Informer* ten years ago, Horace Reid had turned the tabloid into a gold mine. He left no stone unturned to obtain the most intimate, degrading and damaging stories on celebrities: stars, politicians, British royalty. His assistant shook his head. 'It's definitely an original. If anyone else does have it, we go to press first, don't we?' He smiled, revealing jagged yellow teeth.

'Look at these names,' Horace said gleefully. 'Look at 'em. It's a dream come true! I don't even know which name we should devote the bulk of the story to.'

'I think it's obvious, don't you?' the other man said crisply. 'Sam Sharp's the one. I mean . . . "STAR OF 'SAGA' HAS AIDS". What a story! We'll sell ten million.'

'You bet your bollocks, sport,' chortled Horace Reid in his thick Australian accent. 'That poor old poofter is finally going to pay for his sins, and we're going to have our best-selling issue ever. Whoopee!'

'Saga's' diminutive P.R. man, Christopher McCarthy called Sam to his trailer a few days later.

'Sam, I'm a little worried.'

'Why, what's up now?' Sam replied irritably. He was like a cat on hot bricks these days, even taking to snorting a touch of cocaine each morning to get him out of his terrible black depressions.

'I've heard a rumour,' began Christopher tentatively. 'I know it's ridiculous, it couldn't *possibly* be true – and you can sue the arse off them, of course, but I've heard that the *Informer*'s cover story for next week is the most disgraceful they've ever had. And I'm afraid it's about you.'

'Me? About me?' Sam's words were a whisper. This couldn't possibly be true. So *soon*? It was impossible. 'What about me?' He sat down. He felt nauseous.

'Well . . .' Christopher was embarrassed, but he was a good

press agent so he had to get it out. It was his job. 'They say you've got AIDS. I *know* it's ridiculous, Sam.'

'It *is* ridiculous, it's disgraceful. Outrageous.' Sam summed up all his theatrical talent to make his outrage believable.

'It's disgusting,' sighed Christopher. 'They're unscrupulous bastards, those supermarket rags, absolute scum. Nevertheless we've got to fight this all the way, Sam. I think we should set up some interviews immediately: Oprah Winfrey, Carson and the morning news programmes. Then *People*, I'm sure, will do a cover story. I'll call Suzy, Liz Smith and the trades. We'll kill this whole thing. De-fuse the story right away. Show them how great you look. This is a vicious smear campaign and we *cannot* let those fuckers get away with it, right, Sam?'

'Right,' Sam said wearily. He had slumped onto the couch, shakily trying to pour whiskey into a tumbler, but his hand was trembling so much that he dropped it.

'Are you *sure* about this story, Christopher? Are they *really* going ahead?'

'I'm afraid so. In fact, I'm positive,' said Christopher grimly. 'It's unfair, Sam. It's the pits. I'll keep you posted. Don't worry about anything. I'll set up the interviews, and prepare a statement for the press to go on the wire service immediately.'

'Do that, Chris,' said Sam softly. 'Do that. I'd appreciate it.'

Chloe and Sissy were having a heated argument on the set with Luis Mendoza. He stood arrogantly, arms crossed, in his black silk shirt and white linen trousers, gold chain adorning his neck, challenging the two divas of soap. It was rare for Sissy and Chloe to agree about anything, but in this case they had no choice. Luis was becoming a conceited oaf. His astonishing success had swelled his head and ego to such an extent that few people could handle him any longer.

This argument, about Luis's motivation in the scene, raged while the crew stood around watching. When the shot rang out, everyone thought it was from the cop series on the next sound stage. It was only when Debbie Drake, calling Sam's trailer, didn't get an answer, and went to investigate, that they discovered what had happened. The hero of the United States, the actor who had so brilliantly portrayed Lincoln, Eisenhower and FDR – America's 'real man' – had killed himself.

Calvin was glued to the television set in the prison common room. A second celebrity funeral in four years, and he was missing it. Soon there would be a third and he'd be there that time. His lips parted in an animal snarl as he saw Chloe, escorted by Philippe, descend from a black Mercedes, dressed in dark grey and looking sad.

You're next, *madam*! he said to himself. Trumped-up bitch. She deserved to die.

'It's a nightmare, a fucking *nightmare*,' ranted Abby, stomping up and down the Aubusson carpet in his football stadium of an office. 'What the *hell* are we going to do?'

Gertrude's cuticles were picked to the quick. Her normally well-groomed frizzy hair hadn't been combed for twenty-four hours, and the network was in a furor. Sam's suicide was tragedy enough; but when the *American Informer* came out with its AIDS cover story on him, it was crisis time.

Hate mail for Sam started pouring into the offices of the producers, and especially to Sissy.

The grief-stricken widow had retired to the seclusion of her Holmby Hills mansion for ten days, emerging only for the funeral, a fragile ninety-five-pound figure sheathed entirely in Oscar de Renta black, wearing a veil as thick as a bee-keeper's.

She had cried herself to sleep for ten straight nights. She missed Sam more than she had ever thought she could. But there was something else. So little was known about AIDS – could he somehow, even though they had not had sex together for years, have given it to her?

To those privileged to see the early rushes, 'America: The Early Years' looked as if it was going to become a gigantic hit. The chemistry between Emerald and Josh was electrifying. Both were vibrant, dynamic and attractive. Sparks sizzled in their scenes together.

Emerald became seriously attracted to Josh, completely infatuated with his intelligence, his masculinity, his sensitivity and his fabulous sense of humour, listening to his anecdotes and jokes for hours. Josh loved having such an appreciative audience, but unfortunately he did not feel the slightest desire for her. He liked her – she was a competent actress and still a looker. Yes, she was in peak condition, all traces of the blowzy hag leaving jail just a few months before obliterated by a strict regime of early nights, no dope, no alcohol and lots of exercise. But she was not his type, and he was going through a period of celibacy.

Emerald was happy in her work. She enjoyed 'America', enjoyed being Queen Bee again, but she needed, wanted a man, and her luminous green eyes were firmly focused on Josh Brown. They spent a great deal of time together both during and after work, but however much Emerald practised her feminine wiles on him, Josh was simply not biting. He did not want to become involved with her. She was a man-eater, an extremely demanding female in her relationships with men. He liked her but was not prepared to be her next man. He didn't want or need that. What he *did* need was to concentrate on his career, on keeping fit, steering clear of booze, broads and drugs, and making this the best damn show on prime time. In everyone's mind was the desire to beat 'Saga' in the ratings. The network, the actors and the producers were all doing their utmost to make their show the best. And it was.

Long before the first episode of 'America' aired, those who had seen some of the rushes were raving about the quality of the production and the performances of the cast, particularly Emerald and Josh. Emmy talk was bandied about. Eventually Chloe heard about it.

On Chloe's instructions, Vanessa had visited the set of 'America' to check out the rumours and see what was going on. Vanessa had made a lunch date with Pandora King. Standing on the sidelines, watching Burt Hogarth direct, Vanessa realized this wasn't the usual hurried TV direction – this was feature time.

Each episode of 'America' cost twice as much as 'Saga'. The network executives were tearing their hair out, but Hogarth had been given carte blanche on this production, and only if he failed to deliver in the ratings could they change anything. Until then, they realized they had a gem on their hands even if it cost a fortune. They could not rock Burt Hogarth's boat. 'America' had more class than 'Saga'. It was masterly, artistic, stylish yet with a rugged outdoor realism depicting pioneer America. They were banking on the fickleness of the viewing public to switch gradually from 'Saga' and on to 'America'.

Vanessa stood quietly in a dim corner of the set watching Emerald and Josh rehearse. The rumours of their magnetism together were obviously true. Not only did Josh look more attractive than ever, but Emerald was as ravishing as she had been at thirty-five. It was astonishing, since she was fifteen years older than that, give or take. Granted, face-lifts, plastic surgery and platinum hair can do a lot for a woman, but Emerald had an undeniable glow about her, particularly when she was close to Josh and looked at him with the eyes of a woman in love. As a screen pair they sizzled.

Vanessa knew that she would have to report this news to Chloe, who still cared for her ex-husband in spite of their separations. The rumours that Emerald and Josh were having a passionate affair and were crazy for each other were upsetting her in spite of herself. Neither Emerald, Josh nor the network publicists denied the story. It was great publicity for the show. From the look of the two of them together on the set, Vanessa was pretty sure the rumours were true.

Poor Chloe. Vanessa sighed. She disliked Philippe and Vanessa knew that Chloe was becoming bored with him, despite her assurances that their love life was as good as ever.

Wait until Chloe sees the 'new' Josh, thought Vanessa. He was a changed man: more at ease, more in control, more manly and wittier than she remembered. He really was quite wonderful. His potential had come to fruition. Mmm, thought Vanessa. If I still liked men, I might even go for him myself.

There was no point in telling Chloe she had any chance of getting him back. He was obviously as crazy about Emerald as she was about him. Vanessa watched them as, arm in arm, they strolled towards the coffee machine, deep in conversation.

Chloe listened to Vanessa and died a little. So it was true. Oh, well, she thought regretfully, how could Josh help but fancy Emerald? According to Jasper, she was as beautiful and desirable as she'd ever been. Josh knew that Chloe was living with Philippe. She hadn't even called him in the six months he'd been back in California.

Stop thinking about Josh, she chided herself. Think about *Emerald*. If her looks and acting are as stunning as Vanessa, Jasper and half the town says they are, and the series is as brilliant as people think, 'Saga' could be in serious trouble, and Chloe's reign as Queen of Prime Time could soon be over.

'Saga's' ratings started to slip badly three episodes into the new season. It was as though the public's love affair with the show had ended with Sam's death. As 'Saga's' ratings dropped, 'America: The Early Years', which had come into the Nielsen poll with a 20 share in the first week, started to accelerate. As each week it picked up one or two more rating points, 'Saga' dropped a couple. 'America' was on the way up as 'Saga' was on the way down.

At a meeting in the offices of Gertrude and Abby, the creative forces of 'Saga' had come together to try and devise some new angles and clever story lines *fast*.

'Who got the most fan mail last month?' barked Abby to Bill Herbert.

'Chloe,' replied Bill, consulting his notes. 'Between ten and twelve thousand a month. That's more than any other series star, and she's been holding that average for over four years now.'

'Who's next?' Abby was impatient. He already knew Chloe got the most.

'Well, it used to be Sissy, but since Sam . . . er . . . left us, it's dropped considerably. Actually, Luis Mendoza's mail has increased tremendously, especially after his first love scene with Chloe.'

'We should definitely feature him more,' murmured Gertrude.

'Make him more important. Now we've lost Sam, we need a strong male character. You know it was Sissy and Sam who stopped Luis from getting a meatier story line. So let's build him up, make him our main male focus.'

'He's strong all right,' Bill grinned. 'I've never seen so much erotic fan mail from women. You can't believe the things they say they'd like to do to him.'

'Give him more screen time,' said Abby curtly. 'More scenes, strong emotional scenes with Chloe.'

'Make him the male lead,' said Bill.

'Exactly,' Abby replied. 'Build him up. We've got to regain our ratings from "America". They're fucking destroying us. The network is pissed. They want to see some action.' He turned to the show's three scriptwriters. 'Now get to work, boys, write some juicy scenes, for Christ's sake. Otherwise we'll *all* be out of a job by the end of the season.'

Josh looked at the magazine Perry had brought him. 'FROM HAS-BEEN TO TV STARDOM'. The 'shout-line' on the cover of *People* magazine heralded the favourable article inside.

Josh's smiling face was on the cover. It was the face of a handsome, sexy, confident man in his forties. His hair, showing few traces of grey, was pushed casually forward to disguise the fact that his hairline had receded slightly. His tanned face had a few lines around the eyes, and wrinkles here and there, but they suited him. They were the lines that appeared on a face that laughed a lot. It was the face of a man at peace with himself, who accepted his age, was comfortable in his own skin.

Josh had gone through many changes since his latest comeback. He had learned from his past mistakes. In addition to giving up drugs completely, he had cut his drinking to a minimum and no longer chased young girls. With a newfound success in middle age, he lost the need to prove himself between the sheets with women young enough to be his daughters. A psychiatrist had helped, too.

He had the occasional girlfriend – usually a woman over thirty, but lovemaking now was secondary to what he wanted from a woman. Conversation, wit and humour, shared values, friendships were his requirements now. He looked for these in the women he dated, but although they had some of the qualities he admired, none had them all – he realized he had found them all together only in Chloe. Often he dreamed about her – about their life together before his career had started to go foul, before little dollybirds had loomed too large in his life.

In sessions with Dr Donaldson, he realized what a shit he had been to her, how wonderful she had been to him.

Why, why did I screw it up? he often asked himself. The best goddamn woman I ever had and I fucking ruined it. Shit!

He sometimes fantasized that he and Chloe had reconciled, were together again as they once had been. He had never met a woman with whom he had enjoyed life so much, whose humour was on his own wavelength, who so completely understood him. God, what he'd put her through. How many reconciliations had they had? He couldn't remember. He'd been too heavily into nose candy and nymphets at the time. Trying to bolster his flagging career. Sticking his prick into whoever asked for it, and some who didn't.

And Chloe had known. But she had been there for him until it had become unbearable for her.

He heard she was happy with Philippe. He was glad for her, although it gave him a pang every time he saw pictures of them together. Occasionally they bumped into each other at a social or industry function – the People's Choice Awards, the Emmys, or a Beverly Hills screening room. She was always on Philippe's arm, smiling and friendly. Chloe was not one to bear a grudge, and she was genuinely happy for Josh's success.

If it was a scientific principle that no two objects can share the same space at the same time, then Chloe knew there was not enough room for Philippe in her life. She still thought subconsciously about life with Josh, although conscious thoughts of him were banished from her mind with military precision. But her dreams were peopled with images of their life as it had once been. Her weekdays were filled with 'Saga' work, 'Saga' minutiae, time-consuming problems with script revisions, dialogue changes, costuming, set politics. The public could never imagine what a hard, unglamorous drudge grinding out a prime time TV series could be. Her weekends were spent in a mindless daze drifting about the house without makeup, in a track suit, lazing, with Philippe ever attentive nearby.

Philippe's idea of a fun-filled evening was to watch three videos back to back, make love a couple of times and dine on takeout pizza in bed. Chloe, exhausted from her unrelenting pressure of work, enjoyed this at the beginning of the relationship, but she soon began to realize that culturally and conversationally Philippe was dull. True, he filled the present need in her for companionship without effort, intimacy without commitment, closeness without true emotional involvement – and she was fond of him. He demanded little of her except her presence, and since she was usually so exhausted after work, for a while this was welcome.

But on the rare occasions when they made the social rounds of the Bel Air circuit, he often succeeded in embarrassing her by his lack of depth and obvious disinterest in anyone other than himself or Chloe. It was, nevertheless, flattering to be so adored, thought Chloe as she observed Philippe lolling sleepily on a Regency satin couch at one of Daphne's star-studded soirées. Around him thronged two dozen of Hollywood's most famous and scintillating individuals, the women resplendent in designer dresses, designer jewellery and designer cosmetic surgery, the men all distinguished, whether they were six feet four and hirsute or five feet two and bald.

Chloe's friends had all made genuine efforts to conduct a civilized conversation with Philippe during the eighteen months that he and Chloe had lived together. All had eventually decided that it was a waste of time. He had little to say, no opinions to speak of, and other than his obsession with Chloe and his dashing good looks, none of them saw what she could find remotely interesting about him. Chloe found herself thinking the same thing as she touched up her makeup in Daphne's powder room. They had often quarrelled about his lack of enthusiasm and his disinterest in her friends, but he refused to compromise, making no attempt to ingratiate himself, leaving Chloe embarrassed by his dullness, and her women friends changing place cards in desperation at dinner parties so as not to sit next to him.

Chloe sighed as she adjusted the sleek lines of her black silk Donna Karan dress. The thought of sitting on the sofa attempting to talk to Philippe, who would try to make an early get away so that he could watch another video and try and jump on her for the third time that Saturday, was not enthralling. The man was insatiable, and she was weary of his incessant sexual demands and lack of communicativeness and empathy.

'Bored, let's face it, duckie, you're *bored stiff* with him, aren't you?' Daphne interrupted Chloe's reverie, red curls springing animatedly around her chubby Cupid's face, as she entered the room with her usual gusto.

'I mean, he really *is* dull as dishwater, dear. Good looking or not, I know you can do so much better. Don't you think it's time to dump him? I know this *divine* Italian marquis who is coming to town next week. Dying to meet you, duckie. If not you, then Linda Gray is his second choice. What do you think?'

325

She plucked off a few loose beads on the bodice of her old, but still serviceable, Norman Hartnell frock, and squinted at her abundant curves with satisfaction. At well over sixty-five, she was still a good-looking, sexy woman. She knew it and it had been proven many times throughout the past four decades by the number of stars who had shared her bed.

The walls of her tiny guest loo were decorated from floor to paisley-tented ceiling with photographs of Daphne in the company of many of Hollywood's and Europe's most famous celebrities. There were over one hundred framed pictures dating back to the late 1940s when Daphne and Jasper Swanson had descended to the shores of Malibu and the hills of Beverly fresh from their respective successes in England – his at Gainsborough Studios where he had starred in a dozen swash-buckling adventure films, and hers initially through a contract with Sir Alexander Korda, who had tried unsuccessfully to turn her into a clone of either Vivien Leigh or Merle Oberon. When the realization hit Sir Alex that bright curls, a perky smile and a thirty-nine-inch bust cannot compete with alabaster skin, smouldering black hair and a sylphlike body, he sold her contract to Ealing Studios, where she did rather better in black-and-white comedies with Alec Guinness and Jack Warner.

Chloe looked at the attractively saturnine face of thirty-six-year-old Jasper and vibrant thirty-year-old Daphne laughing arm in arm with the Oliviers and Sir Ralph Richardson on the lawn of Highgrove one long-ago summer afternoon. In another photo, Daphne gazed fondly into the faces of a handsomely togaed Richard Burton and a Grecian-draped Jean Simmons on the set of *The Robe*, a Cinema-Scope epic in which Daphne had played a small part. Daphne was smiling and laughing in many other photos in the company of what were, the gossips said, some of her many lovers. Errol Flynn, Gary Cooper, David Niven, William Powell – Daphne had been rumoured to have bedded them all, but would neither confirm nor deny to even her closest chums which, if any, of those illustrious lads she had tumbled with.

326

'Let's just say all my lovers have been well-endowed,' she would laughingly reply to anyone inquisitive enough to ask. 'Both *above* and *below* the belt, I require the utmost stimulation. Big cocks are not enough. I need big brains too.

'Take a look at him, duckie.' Daphne pointed with a long vermilion fingernail at a photo of herself with a young, very handsome blond boy taken on a film set in about 1950.

'That's the sort of man you should meet, dear heart,' she sighed. 'Dusty Lupino. He was a big star and one of the best lovers I ever had. I taught him a great deal too – even though he was eighteen and I was – ah – eh – over thirty. He's rich as Croesus now, duckie, and *still* only fifty-six. His business manager got him out of the movie business and into real estate when you could still buy half of Rodeo Drive for under a million. He's never looked back, and still looks divine even if he is a bit of a recluse.'

'Darling, darling! *Stop*. I *know*, what you're saying. Philippe is not right for me. I'm aware of that. I'm not as much of a fool as everyone thinks, Daphne darling. Yes, we squabble. Yes, he's not very stimulating or entertaining. But for *now*, Daphne, dear, I'm living with him, and when we end it, which, as you say, and as I *know*, is inevitable, I shall then cast my eyes further afield, but *not yet*, my dear.' She bent and kissed Daphne's Coty-perfumed cheek. 'Not yet. I can only handle one man at a time.'

'What a quaint, old-fashioned girl you are,' sighed Daphne in mock exasperation as they went back to the party. 'But remember, dear, when you *are* ready to dump him, all your friends will be rooting for you.'

'O.K., creep, time to get the fuck out of here.' The guard picked at a boil on his chin. 'Better not try anything again, creep. You'll be in a lot of trouble if you do. Now git!'

Calvin ignored the man. He was free. Free at last to go where he wanted – do what he wanted. He had to find her now. Track her down. Make her suffer as he had suffered over the years.

Although he had read in the tabloids that Emerald had the lead in the new series, 'America: The Early Years', it continued to infuriate him that Chloe Carriere was such a huge star in 'Saga', which was still a phenomenal success. He couldn't stand Chloe. He loathed her arrogance in that part. He detested her trumped-up English accent. He despised everything about her. Most of all he hated her because she was the reason his beloved Emerald had hit rock bottom. She had to be punished.

27

'And now, ladies and gentlemen, it's *America's Favourites*!' The crowd applauded frantically. Whistles and shrieks of appreciation greeting the master of ceremonies as he announced the nominees in each category.

Chloe and Philippe had arrived late. They smiled for the phalanx of fans and paparazzi who were gathered like a flock of sheep outside the Santa Monica Civic Auditorium. She held his tuxedoed arm, looked into his smiling face, smiled for the cameras – Mr and Mrs Togetherness, a portrait of bliss, even though they weren't wed.

Tonight was an important night. These January awards, both for films and TV, were considered the harbingers of the Emmys and the Oscars later that year.

Chloe wore a magnificent Christian Dior white taffeta dress, which cinched her waist and pushed up her bosom. Her black hair was piled high with diamanté combs, and around her neck was a beautiful Georgian rose diamond necklace that Vanessa had found for her.

As she and Philippe settled themselves, with whispered apologies, at the 'Saga' table, where Sissy, Luis, Sabrina and Bill Herbert were already seated, Chloe glanced around the auditorium. Josh was smiling at her. She smiled back. After all, he was her ex-husband. 'We must be polite, dear,' said Sissy snidely. She was dressed from shoulders to toes in yellow bugle beads that matched her hair. The six-month period of mourning was over and she was playing the merry widow with a good-looking young actor on her arm.

'Pour me some wine, darling, will you?' Chloe murmured to Philippe.

'You drink too much,' he whispered too loudly. Surreptitiously she looked over at Josh again. He was with Emerald, who looked dazzling in a mint-green silk jersey empire gown, the bodice embroidered in four-leaf clovers.

'How cute!' sneered Sissy. 'She needs all the luck she can get, Tyne Daly is the hot favourite tonight.'

It was a night of extreme competition. 'Saga' and 'America' were competing with 'Hill Street Blues', 'Dynasty' and 'Cagney and Lacey' for best dramatic TV series.

Chloe, Sissy, Emerald, Tyne Daly and Sharon Gless were up for best actress in a dramatic TV series. Josh and Luis, Daniel J. Travanti and Larry Hagman were nominated for best dramatic actor.

The tension was palpable as one by one glittering stars of screen and TV paraded their finery onto the stage either to present an award or accept one.

Chloe, having won the past two years, was less concerned than the others about the coveted crystal statuettes. She felt that Tyne or Sharon Gless definitely deserved one for their consistently fine work in 'Cagney and Lacey'.

Emerald was desperate for the award. 'America: The Early Years' was only in its first season, but it was a huge success – now neck and neck with 'Saga'. Winning would be a major step for her and complete her comeback.

Josh didn't really care. He had quickly joined the rarefied ranks of mature TV leading men and it would not mean anything to his career one way or another. What *did* mean something to him, although he was reluctant to admit it, was

330

the beautiful black-haired woman in the white gown sitting two tables away.

Godamn it, Josh, he said to himself for the hundredth time, why did you mess up that relationship? How the hell could you have let that woman go? You loved her, she adored you. . . .

Emerald pulled at his sleeve and whispered animatedly into his ear, but he hardly listened. He was watching Chloe out of the corner of his eye, across a room filled with some of the most beautiful women in the world. His Chloe. His forever lover, gone now forever. He watched her bend her dark head to Philippe's brown one, smile at something the Frenchman said, and put her pale hand on his arm in the loving gesture he remembered only too well. She raised her hand to Philippe's hair and ruffled it. She used to do that to me, thought Josh fiercely. They certainly looked happy, gazing into each other's eyes, fingertips touching. There was something about the tall Frenchman that Josh didn't like. He envied his relationship with Chloe, but there was something else that he couldn't quite put his finger on. It was a quality many people felt about Philippe. He made them uneasy.

Josh came out of his reverie to hear the nominations for best actress being announced.

Emerald had a hand on his knee, which became more vicelike as each name was called. She was about to cut off his circulation. He could see her moist cyclamen lips parted in anticipation, longing. She was lusting for this award, this accolade to symbolize her return to the top of the heap.

He glanced at Chloe, who looked cool, calm and collected. Sissy's face wore a fixed smile. She too was dying for this award. She had won it the same year she won the Oscar. It was time again. She deserved it. Hers was a performance – an acting tour de force. She was a wonderful actress; everyone knew it. Certainly for someone of her rancorous nature to bring such believability to the cloying role she played proved she indeed had considerable talent.

The 'Cagney and Lacey' actresses looked self-possessed.

331

Their show was a hit too. This award wouldn't affect it – or them – much. It would just be icing.

'The envelope, please.' Don Johnson was presenting this award. 'And the winner is . . .' He paused, looking mischievously at the audience, milking the moment.

'Once again, Miss Chloe Carriere!' A shriek of delight came from the fans and audience high in the gallery of the auditorium. Almost as loud was the cry from Chloe, who threw her arms around Philippe in a bear hug that almost strangled him, blew kisses to everyone at her table and, in a flurry of white taffeta, ascended the stage to make her acceptance speech.

In the gallery, Calvin's fury turned his face scarlet. It was Emerald, the Goddess, who deserved this honour. She truly deserved it. Not this second-rate British bitch. How *dare* she take Emerald's award?

His binoculars focused on Chloe's slim figure as she addressed the audience and the millions of TV fans. She expressed her happiness, thanked the cast, the crew, Jasper, blew a kiss, wept a little and was escorted triumphantly off the stage by Don Johnson, holding the statuette high above her head.

Calvin turned his binoculars on Emerald. She removed a tiny lace hanky from her rhinestone Judith Leiber purse and was blowing her nose. *She was crying!* Chloe Carriere had made his darling weep! Bitch!

Josh was trying to comfort Emerald when the award for best actor was announced. 'And the winner is Joshua Brown for "America: The Early Years",' Angie Dickinson announced with a big smile. Calvin ignored Josh's hasty departure to collect his award and continued to focus his attention and his binoculars on his lovely Emerald. He hated to see her hurt like this. Chloe, done up like a dog's dinner in virgin white, would pay for this. The time was coming for Miss Carriere. Oh, the time was coming *soon*.

*   *   *

In the eighth week of the autumn season, 'Saga' was rated the number two show and 'America' number one. One week later the ratings were reversed: 'America' was number two, 'Saga' number one. The following week, 'America' held its lead but 'Saga' lost a couple more ratings points, dropping to number six.

Panic reigned at MCPC. Advertisers started to cancel the time slots on 'Saga', which they now thought were overpriced. They preferred to sell their products on the rival network where, with more viewers tuned to 'America', their goods would sell better. The network was giving Abby and Gertrude a hard time. They must make the shows more exciting, more dramatic, meatier, so that they could regain their lost audiences. Gertrude and Abby screamed at the line producer Bill Herbert, they screamed at the writers, they screamed at the actors and crew. An emergency conference was called with Sissy, Luis and Chloe, to pick their brains for fresh story ideas. Everyone seemed to be becoming desperate to get back their place in the sun.

Chloe was not too concerned. She had always realized that the flavour of the month had to change. She still felt loyal to the show and enjoyed it, but she was looking forward to accepting other offers of miniseries and movies, singing again, making a video for MTV.

Luis hoped 'Saga' would be cancelled. He was hot for movies now. Jasper had three sizzling offers for him in the spring. In one he could even star with Sabrina. He felt he had done enough TV, although he had been in 'Saga' liitle over a year. He wanted to move on, become a real movie star.

Sissy, perennially discontented, wanted to stay with 'Saga'. Since she now owned her own *and* Sam's points in the show, she was making a fortune. She would make even more when it went into syndication.

After losing the America's Favourites Award to Chloe, Emerald had gone on another bender. Increasingly frustrated and upset by Josh's lack of interest in her as a woman, she had again sought solace in liquor. Try as she might, she could not get him to play her game. He had told her frankly, 'Look, Emerald, I think you're great. You're a terrific woman, beautiful, fun to be with. I just don't think of you that way.' Emerald bit her lip until it almost bled. Rejection from a man was hard for her – it had happened so rarely. Was this a portent of her future?

They were in Josh's car outside her house, having just returned from a screening and dinner at Corinna and Freddie Fields's house. Emerald had had many glasses of champagne and, feeling frisky, she tried to embrace Josh, but he had drawn away from her.

'Please, Emerald. I want to be your friend, I've told you that so many times. It's better that way.'

'Why?' Emerald almost yelled. 'Why just *friends*?' She spat the words. 'We've got so *much* going for us, Josh. I don't have anyone in my life right now and I don't think you do . . . do you?'

Josh didn't answer. He lit a Marlboro and stared out at the starless sky.

'Do you, Josh? If you do, tell me and I'll . . . oh, hell, I'll get over it.' A tear slid down her matt-complexioned cheek and dripped onto her green satin Enrico Coveri lounging pyjamas. He remained silent, smoking, his strong profile etched against the door of his Porsche.

'Are you in love with someone?' she asked again, so persistently that he turned to her and said quietly, 'Yes, Emerald, I suppose I am. I am "in love", as you say, with someone else.'

'Who is it?' He was silent. She *had* to know. 'It's Chloe, isn't it?' She felt bitterness. 'It's your ex-wife, isn't it?'

'She's *not* my ex-wife – not yet – and, yes, well, you're right. I haven't quite got over my feelings for her.'

'Oh, my God! Have you been seeing her?' Emerald took the cigarette from Josh's hands and took a deep drag.

'No, absolutely not. She's living with Philippe Archambaud. But I'd like to.'

'Damn, shit and hell,' cried the diva as she jumped out of his car and ran into her house in tears. *How could he reject her?* Emerald Barrymore. World-renowned beauty, idol of millions. Legendary sex goddess. How *could* he? She couldn't understand it. Not when she was looking so good and was so successful. She realized she was acting ridiculously but she couldn't help it. She loved him. Why couldn't he love her back?

Josh started his car and drove off. No point trying to calm her now. It was a difficult situation. He wanted to keep their working relationship a good one. It seemed that might be a little harder now. Oh, hell, he thought, I'd better send her flowers tomorrow.

His driving away infuriated Emerald even more. 'Damn you,' she muttered and climbed into her Cadillac to follow him down the canyon to the bright lights of Santa Monica Boulevard.

The police picked her up four hours later hopelessly drunk, without a driving licence, and weaving her car in and out of the Sunset Boulevard traffic. It took four cops to subdue her enough to get her into the police car, and a passing Japanese tourist with a camera made a fortune from the photographs he took of her and sold to the *American Informer* for a cover story.

Her second sojourn in a jail cell garnered even more publicity than the first. Out-of-control drunken TV actors were not what viewers wanted. Drunken actresses were even more of a turnoff. When the torrent of unfavourable press came out, turn off they did.

The ugly front-page photograph of Emerald fighting the police who arrested her harmed 'America's' ratings enormously. Public sympathy turned against her. The ratings started to plummet and soon 'Saga' rose like a phoenix from the ashes back to the number two spot again.

Calvin reread the article in *Daily Variety*. ' "Saga" boffo in ratings war once more gains five points.' His lips clenched in fury. He had just returned from another fruitless attempt to find out Chloe's new address, having failed to gain entrance to the 'Saga' studio where he knew she would be. He had bought a map to the movie stars' homes from a crone sitting under a faded umbrella in the boiling sun on Sunset Boulevard and staked out the vine-covered house on Blue Jay Road identified as hers for two weeks. But he never saw Chloe either coming or going. Three times the police had moved him on. Then, not wanting to arouse more suspicions, he had kept away for a few days. Eventually he struck up a conversation with the young housekeeper after bumping into her 'accidentally' at Hughes supermarket one morning. She was pretty, with long blonde hair and a cute Scandinavian accent. Casually he had asked what it was like working for Chloe Carriere, the famous TV star.

The girl had laughed at him as she threw packages of frozen peas into her basket. 'I vork for Dr Sidney, the famous plastic surgeon.' She giggled. 'I don't think he even knows Chloe Carriere, unless he did her face. He bought the house from her two years ago, I think.'

Calvin went back to the map-selling hag and screamed at her for selling false information.

She shrugged. 'Listen, fella, half the names on that list are dead. The other half has moved. I don't print it, I just sell it. So fuck off, fella, otherwise I'll stick this to ya.' She revealed a switchblade gleaming under her torn dress. Calvin backed away from the old witch. He had other fish to fry. He had to find Chloe's address.

On Hollywood's biggest night, Academy Award night, Mary and Irving Lazar threw their celebrated annual Award party in Spago. Every major name from movies and TV attended. The women wore their most elegant gowns and the men were equally well dressed.

Irving Lazar – 'Swifty' to his friends and foes – circulated through the well-dressed throng, dodging TV cameras and paparazzi and having a word and a joke with everyone.

Chloe sat at a corner table with Philippe and Annabel. She was glad Irving had invited Annabel to attend as it was a very insular Hollywood party – superstars and megacelebrities only. Annabel was again visiting from London. She and Chloe had developed a very close relationship.

Philippe didn't say much. Chloe sighed. When you ran out of things to say to each other, it was a sure sign of serious trouble in a relationship. She knew the relationship was more than just sour, yet she didn't have the heart to end it.

Across the room a battery of flashbulbs popped as Emerald and Josh entered Spago. Emerald looked radiant again in a jade-green velvet gown with deep décolletage. All traces of the drunken harridan of last month were erased. She certainly can pull herself together in a hurry, thought Chloe. Emerald was smiling glowingly as she gazed at Josh, who returned her look affectionately.

Chloe turned away. They seemed in love, so happy. She glanced at Philippe, who was eyeing a new redheaded vamp at a nearby table, brought in to boost 'America's' ratings.

Emerald and Josh were being seated at a table in the centre of the room. Oh, Lord, thought Chloe, Josh is right in my eyeline. He was indeed positioned in such a way that when she turned her head to the left she was directly facing him.

He came over to the table as soon as he saw her, gave Philippe a manly handshake, Annabel a hug and Chloe a kiss on the cheek. She shivered when she looked into his green eyes. He was, if anything, more attractive than ever; there was a quality of tenderness and compassion about him now that he had never possessed before.

Soon it was time for everyone in the room to become absorbed in the large TV screens which had been set up at strategic points throughout the restaurant. Chloe could not concentrate on who was winning, on the delicious pizzas with smoked salmon and caviar, on the vintage champagne. She kept sneaking glances at Josh.

This is idiotic, she said to herself. Stupid. A grown woman, a *middle-aged* woman at that, mooning like a schoolgirl.

During one of the commercial breaks as she and Annabel were in the powder room, Emerald swept in.

The two women eyed each other. Although they had attended a number of Hollywood parties, it was the first time they had been alone since 'America' had begun. The only other person in the room was Annabel, who was now in the cubicle.

'Hello, Emerald.' Chloe smiled, extending her hand.

Emerald didn't take the proffered hand. She simply stared, stunned with jealous anger as she realized that the sensational diamond and emerald bracelets encircling Chloe's wrist were *her* bracelets. Her favourite jewels, the last to be sold to Vanessa to keep the wolf from her door. Bitch! Chloe now possessed her bracelets *and* her man. It was just as many people said of her in this town – Chloe was a nouveau riche conniving bitch, and Emerald detested her.

Suddenly she leaned against the door facing Chloe with a strange expression.

Chloe realized she was more than a little drunk. Fishing scent from her purse, she turned to the mirror.

'So now I know,' said Emerald, her speech slurred. 'Now I *really* know.'

'Know what?' Chloe applied Obsession rapidly behind her ears, wishing Annabel would exit the loo so they could leave.

'What he sees in you, of course,' Emerald hissed.

'Who is *he*?' Chloe said, her voice betraying little of the emotion she felt.

'Josh, of course.' Emerald gave a brittle laugh. 'He loves you, don't you know that? He's never *stopped* loving you. Aren't *you* the lucky girl?' She staggered to the mirror pretending to be busy combing her hair but Chloe saw her eyes were blurred with tears.

'How do you know that?' In spite of herself she had to ask. Was it true? Could Josh still care as much as she did? Nonsense. It was nonsense, Emerald was stoned out of her skull.

'He told me.' Emerald looked at Chloe's reflection in the

mirror. 'He told me he loves you. Always has. Big deal. Who cares. *I* certainly don't. We're just friends – good friends – and that's how it's gonna be.' She turned away to inspect her painted face, dimissing Chloe with a shrug of jade velvet Giorgio di Sant'Angelo shoulder pads.

Annabel came out and Chloe grabbed her arm, as they quickly left the ladies room.

'I *heard*, Chloe. I heard it all,' said her daughter. 'Do you think it's true? Do you think Josh is still in love with you?'

'I don't know, darling. I really don't. She's drunk.'

'Well I hope he is,' said the girl, affectionately squeezing her arm. 'You know how I feel about Philippe.'

The two went back to the festivities. For the rest of the evening, Chloe tried to avoid Josh's eyes, but as winner after winner appeared on the TV screen and made their speeches, she heard none of them. All she could think of were Emerald's words.

'Give that bouquet of flowers the archer.' Chelsea Deane was peering through the viewfinder on the set of Chloe/Miranda's boudoir.

'The what? What is he talking about?' prop man number one asked prop man number two.

'Beats me, Stu, ask him. These limeys sure have a strange way of talking.'

'Sorry, Chelsea, what d'you mean?'

'*Archer*, that's slang for get rid of it,' Chelsea yelled with exasperation.

'What the hell's an archer?' yelled the prop man.

'Oh, Gawd, sorry, thought I was at Pinewood for a sec!' Chelsea smiled his captivating cockney grin. 'Spanish Archer – *El-bow*, get it?' The two prop men scratched their heads.

'*Elbow* the flowers – get rid of 'em,' Chelsea said with an up-and-down movement of his elbow, irritated by the men's obtuseness. Chloe gave him a sympathetic glance from where she sat with Vanessa and a coterie of makeup, hair and wardrobe assistants. She was trying to run through her lines with her dialogue coach, while the girls gossiped around her.

'O.K. first team, ready for you,' called Ned.

'Second team can relax.'

The couple who had been standing in the middle of the set for the past fifteen minutes while the crew set up the camera and lights went off to the coffee stand. Chloe and Luis took their places. They walked through the scene for marks only. After every move, the camera assistant used his tape measure to judge the distance from their faces to the camera.

God forbid it should be a millimetre out of focus in dailies tomorrow. Gertrude and Abby would scream blue murder, and if it happened more than twice, heads would roll, in particular, the camera assistant's – so he was a careful fellow.

It was freezing cold on the set today. As usual, the heating had gone on the blink. The studio was over fifty years old, freezing in the winter and boiling in the summer.

'That's when they put the bleedin' 'eating an' air conditionin' in,' said Chelsea acidly. 'Fifty bleedin' years ago.'

The crew all wore sweaters, parkas and scarves, but Chloe had on a low-cut black chiffon dress. The only thing she had to keep her warm was four hundred dollars' worth of Kenny Lane rhinestones around her neck.

They shot the master. They had to do it four times because once an aeroplane could be heard on the sound track, the second time a visitor coughed in the middle of Luis's impassioned 'I love you, Miranda', and in the third Chloe caught her heel in the carpet.

Eventually Chelsea printed the fourth take. 'All right. That's a print. Let's go in for coverage. We'll do Luis's close-up first, Chlo, you can relax, darlin'.'

Brad, from Abby and Gertrude's office, came on the set and handed around a piece of paper with last night's ratings score on it.

Chloe was glad to see that last night they had taken their time slot by a good margin and had got a thirty-one share that would definitely put 'Saga' among the top ten prime shows this week.

'How did "America" do last night?' she inquired.

'They're doing *very* well,' enthused Brad, even though they were on the rival network. 'Very well indeed. They're a big hit. Of course, Josh winning the award helped. The public have certainly taken to your ex, haven't they?'

Chloe was glad for Josh. She had sent him a cymbidium plant and a congratulatory note after he won. She wondered how he was. She hoped he was happy. She wished *she* were happier and wished she could do something about the information Emerald had drunkenly given her. Trouble with Philippe again. Another ridiculous row over nothing. Why was he so spiteful? Recently he had started to ridicule her. He called her 'Diva' and 'Megastar'. What was wrong with him?

'Darling, you'll never *guess* who I saw today!' Red hair hidden by pink rollers, Daphne sat next to Chloe under the dryer at the Bill Palmer salon, ready for a good gossip.

Chloe put down her magazine and smiled at her friend. She never failed to be amused by Daphne, whom she basically thought kind and funny, although a bit of a chatterbox.

'Joshua Brown, darling – looking, I *must* say, very, very fanciable indeed.' Chloe's heart skipped. Jungle drums started beating whenever she heard his name.

'Where?' She casually lit a cigarette. 'Where did you see him?'

'At his new house at the beach, darling. I interviewed him for *TV Faces*.'

'How was it? I mean, how was he?' Chloe was interested, intrigued. Damn it, she thought, I wish I weren't.

'Wonderful,' gushed Daphne. 'Darling, he is *so* divine, full of the old S.A. What a man! I mean, my knees were so all of a tremble I could barely balance my pad on my lap.'

'You don't use a tape recorder?'

'Of course I do, dearie. The pad is for background, you can't record *that*. Colour of sofa, what he was wearing, that sort of thing.'

'What *was* he wearing?' Chloe was curious in spite of herself.

'Blue shirt,' Daphne said breathlessly. 'Open, very simple. Very sexy. He's got a wonderful body, Chloe.'

'I know, dear. I was married to him, remember?'

'How could I forget?' Daphne laughed. 'Anyway, darling, we had this terrific *in depth* conversation. He told me *all* about his drinking and drugging – how it destroyed him.'

'Did he tell you all about his schoolgirls?' Chloe asked sarcastically.

'I'll get to that,' Daphne said crossly. 'Don't interrupt, dear. Anyway he told me that *he* was the one who ruined your marriage because of his drug taking. He said what a wonderful woman you are – the best ever.' Daphne smiled as she saw Chloe blush slightly.

'Anyway he was going on about you when his valet or whoever came in with a *terribly* important call from South America – something to do with a film he's going to do out there next year, so he excused himself and went and took the call.'

'And?' Chloe was more than interested.

'Well, darling, he'd left the door to his inner sanctum open. I absolutely couldn't resist – I peeped in, and *what* do you think I saw?'

'What?' Chloe smiled. She liked this.

'One whole wall, darling, is covered, I mean literally *covered*, with photos of you.'

'Come on – you're joking.'

'No, darling. I mean it. There must be twenty pictures of you. You alone, you with him, you and Annabel – even your wedding photo.' She leaned forward to give Chloe a conspiratorial nudge. 'I think he still loves you, dear, I really do. This is obviously his most private room. Oh, and there was also one of your records on the stereo – your last one, the love ballad.' She leaned back triumphantly under the dryer as she waited for Chloe's reaction.

'Well, Daphne, what a regular little Sherlock Holmes you are. That *is* interesting, darling, but I'm not interested in him. What's over is over.'

342

'Nonsense,' said Daphne. 'You never got him out of your system. If you had, you would have signed your final divorce papers *and* you would have married Philippe by now.'

'I'm allergic to marriage,' said Chloe sincerely. 'I'm not good at it.'

'You were *very* good at it, dearie, for all the years you were married to Josh. You looked the other way when he was unfaithful. You ignored his drug problems. You put up with a lot of naughtiness from him. You were too easy with him and too forgiving, dear. Treat 'em mean, keep 'em keen!'

'I know, I know. Look, Daphne, don't go on. I told you, it's over, I'm happy with Philippe,' she said crossing her fingers. She hated to lie.

Daphne's dryer buzzed. 'I must dash now, darling, I'm doing a cover story for *US* on Sabrina Jones.'

'Come to dinner next Saturday. Philippe's barbecuing,' called Chloe.

'Love to, duckie,' said Daphne, aware that she had stirred certain unexpressed feelings in Chloe.

Alone for a moment, Chloe sat very still, one thought continuously turning over and over in her mind. Emerald had told her the truth.

Calvin had finally managed to find a way to get onto the set. He had struck up a friendship with Debbie Drake, the second assistant director. He had observed her every day after work, going into the bar across from the studio. She usually sat and drank a few beers with the crew before getting into her little red Mustang and driving home to Westlake. He spent several days sitting at the bar observing her. She was a friendly soul, and it was not difficult to become acquainted with her. He cultivated their camaraderie over the weeks, although it made him feel disloyal to Emerald. Her hair was long and pretty and she had a nice smile and a pleasant personality, but Calvin didn't care about the girl one bit. All he wanted was to win her confidence and friendship enough to gain access to the 'Saga' set.

One day he casually mentioned that he would like to visit the set as he was a great admirer of Sissy Sharp. Debbie, ever anxious to please, arranged a visitor's pass for him.

One fine spring afternoon, when the temperature hovered in the nineties, Calvin Foster finally entered the 'Saga' set for the first time.

28

Philippe, his face flushed, stood before Chloe. His cream crocodile shoes contrasted with his immaculately creased dark-brown
trousers. He was impeccably turned out, as usual, even though it
was seven in the morning and the temperature was stifling.

Chloe, with a slight hangover from the previous night, was
attempting to get ready in her dressing room. She was already
half an hour late. It was unprofessional to be late, and it threw
the assistant director into a flap.

'*Chérie*, we have *got* to talk about this video offer. I thought
you *wanted* to get back into singing again.' He kept waving the
contract in front of her as she zoomed around the room trying
to dress, clean her teeth and brush her tangled curls.

'Look, Philippe, I *can't*, I simply *cannot* discuss it now. I'm
terribly late, can't you see?'

'We must agree on this deal, *chérie*. You're *always* too busy
these days – putting things off, procrastinating. Now, sweetheart – *calm* down – sit down and let's read the contract
together for a minute.'

'Philippe, listen to me, damn it!' Her rage, the rage she was
saving for Miranda's scenes with Sirope today, had built up so
much she could no longer control it.

'*I have to leave now!* I have a hangover. I've had four hours' sleep. *Please*, Philippe, let me go to work.' Her face was flaming, the heat and anger making her heart skip several beats. Could women in their forties have heart attacks? she wondered fleetingly. 'We'll have to talk later, Philippe. Tonight, I promise you.'

'O.K., O.K. You never listen to me, I'm just a dog. Forget the video deal – we'll just forget it, see if I care. I was doing it for you, but you never appreciate my efforts, Miss Diva.'

She felt she couldn't bear another day of his sulking. 'Darling, look, I know the video deal is important. I don't want to forget it, let's discuss it at the studio after work, before we go to Jasper's dinner, O.K.?' She gave him a fleeting kiss and as much of a smile as she could muster.

'O.K., O.K., we always have to fit in with your plans,' he grumbled, semi-placated by Chloe's affectionate gesture.

'Well, I *am* the one who has to be a "Saga" slave,' she said, throwing on a scarf and sunglasses and noticing in her full-length mirror that she needed to lose three pounds again. 'Come to the studio about sevenish, darling. It will be quiet then, we can go over the contract thoroughly without being bothered. Bye now, darling, I *must* go.'

Shooting went slowly. The sudden heat wave had affected cast and crew alike, and, as usual, the air conditioner was not working properly. It seemed to Chloe that the temperature in southern California was never temperate. It was always either too hot or too cold, and at the ancient studio the heating and air-conditioning units were as usual inoperative.

Tempers were frayed. Chloe had even had a tiff with Chelsea Deane, whom she adored. Sissy was more vicious and back-biting than usual, and the crew was glum. But when Bill Herbert brought the overnight ratings to the set, everyone brightened up – they had gained three places in last week's ratings, and now were one place above 'America'.

Wearily, Chloe sat in front of the portable makeup table and powdered her face for the twentieth time. She looked and felt exhausted, and there were dark circles under her eyes that even the thick TV makeup couldn't hide.

Calvin had been lingering on the periphery of the studio floor all day. A shadowy figure in his reddish wig, baseball cap and sunglasses, he had been observing Chloe's movements intently from the moment she had arrived. He noted how nasty she was when she walked off the set after a row with the nice little English director, phony tears running down her face.

He watched her pack of sycophantic bitches – Vanessa, Trixie, De-De – go to her trailer to placate her, listen to her demands, bring her tea, aspirin, cigarettes. Cater to the slut.

He overheard Sissy tell her girl Friday, Doris, what a selfish arrogant cow Chloe was. How she couldn't act her way out of a paper bag, how she only got her role because she had slept with Abby Arafat.

'Ugh, Abby is so gross, can you *imagine* four hundred pounds of heaving flab on your bones,' they giggled together in mock horror.

Calvin picked up a discarded copy of the *American Informer* and read that Chloe had simultaneously just been voted by their readers:

A. One of the most admired women in America.

B. One of the most hated.

There was no doubt how Calvin would have voted. Those who voted as he would have would thank him when he finally disposed of her.

He had failed before in Las Vegas, but this time nearly five years later he knew he was going to succeed. He felt it in his bones. His hands tightened over the handle of the seven-inch switchblade in his pocket. He had experimented on a couple of stray dogs. It had slit their throats extremely efficiently.

This was the third day he had hung around the set waiting for her. He hoped to get her that night in the parking lot. She had given up being driven by a studio driver since she had bought that flashy red Ferrari. He would wait for her in the

347

back seat of her car. She never bothered to lock it. Stupid bitch.

'O.K., it's a wrap,' called Ned. 'Same time tomorrow everyone. Goodnight.' Gratefully, the crew started packing up their equipment. It was 6.45 p.m. and already dark outside. It was not a late day, as TV shooting went, but most of the crew would still have to be back at six the following morning.

Chloe flopped onto the chintz couch of her tiny trailer on the sound stage. Wearily she removed her earrings and necklace. 'I'm too tired to dress,' she said to Trixie, and sat in her silk robe while Trixie put away her Miranda clothes and Vanessa poured her a much-needed glass of wine.

'Do you want me to stay with you, love?' asked Vanessa protectively.

'Not tonight, darling, Philippe's coming over with a contract to look over. I'll see you tomorrow.' She managed a wan smile.

'Bright and early!' chirped Vanessa, who never seemed to get tired. 'Don't forget to bring your blue Saint Laurent blouse.'

Outside, on the dark sound stage, Calvin waited. He was hidden behind a flat with 'Miranda's Bedroom' stencilled on it. He saw the two women leave the bitch's trailer, saw the last of the crew members trundle away their equipment. It was quiet now on the set except for a hint of thunder in the stale air. Stealthily he crept to the window of the trailer and looked in.

She was sitting at the dressing table in a red dressing gown, leafing through some papers. She was sipping wine and smoking. What a whore! He crept to the door. Pushed. It was unlocked. Careless slut.

With a gasp, Chloe turned to confront the intruder. Who was he? He smiled, a horrible grin. 'Good evening, Miss Carriere.'

'Who are you? Get the hell out of my dressing room before I call security.' She felt fear immobilize her.

'Don't you remember me, Miss Carriere?' He mocked as he took off his sunglasses and baseball cap, then slowly peeled off the red nylon wig.

Oh, my God! Chloe almost fainted. It was he, dear God. The man the police said had tried to kill her in Las Vegas. They had let him out. Why?

'What are you doing in my dressing room? What do you want?' Her voice exuded a confidence she didn't feel. Although she was petrified her hand went to the phone, but he grabbed it first.

'I want to talk to you, Miss Carriere. You remember me now, don't you?'

She didn't answer.

He put his face close to hers. *'Don't* you remember me, bitch?'

'Yes,' her voice was a whisper. 'I do.'

Close your eyes and he will go away. It's a dream, a nightmare. It isn't happening. Where is Philippe? He's supposed to be here at seven. Oh, God, where is he? Why isn't he here?

'We are going to talk now. I want to talk to you, Miss Chloe *Mega*star *bitch*, but first I've got a little *present* for you.'

He unzipped his jeans and revealed an angry red, rigid penis, which he held with filthy calloused fingers. In his other hand was a knife, its blade glimmering in the bright lights of her dressing room mirror.

He was inches from her, that revolting thing in one hand, the knife in the other. She picked up the glass of wine and in a desperate move threw it in his face. He gave a hoarse shout, blinded momentarily by the wine. His hands went to his face and he dropped the knife. In that split second, Chloe darted between him and the bunk bed in the tiny trailer and escaped onto the sound stage.

It was dark, except for the glimmer of a dim work light high above on the gantry, but she knew this stage like the back of her hand. Knew the location of the four exits. She had to get to one of them, find a guard. She realized it was futile to call

349

out. No one would hear her on this sound-proofed stage. Her high heels smashed into the pitted bare floor as she tripped over a cable and fell to the ground. She turned, sobbing, and saw the man silhouetted against the light of her trailer. Animal sounds issued from his throat. She could see the knife and his flaccid penis hanging outside his jeans.

She tried to stand up and, with a sob, realized she had wrenched her ankle. Gasping with pain and fear, she limped across the network of cables across to the library set of 'Saga', trying to reach the Exit sign.

'Bitch. Whore. I'm gonna get you, you fucking *bitch*!' She heard him crashing through the cables behind her as her bare feet felt the soft Persian carpet of the library. Only fifty more yards. The green Exit sign was like a beacon. She hobbled past arc lamps lined up like sentries, past the coffee wagon. Where was the guard? Where was Philippe? She was weeping with fear, unable to move any faster.

Suddenly she felt Calvin's hands clawing at her back. She tried to throw him off, but he had her. She smelled his sweat as he threw her onto the brown leather couch in the library and straddled her.

It was hard again, that revolting red thing. Her silk robe had fallen open and she was naked underneath, except for sheer black tights. He sat across her thighs, his erect penis pressing into her stomach, the knife at her throat.

'This is it, Miss Carriere. This is the end of the line for you. You *slut*!' He spat at her as he took his knife and slowly slit her tights from waist to pubis. Terror engulfed her as she struggled, but his knife was digging into her chin, drawing blood.

'*Don't!* Don't move, bitch. If you want to enjoy this – and you *will* enjoy it, won't you, don't you dare move, you ugly slut. I've read about how you enjoy doing it with everyone – everything – men – dogs – horses – right, bitch! Right? I heard all the filthy stories about you in prison, you whore.' He slapped her face repeatedly as he tried to force himself inside her.

Death was preferable to this, thought Chloe. Instant death was infinitely preferable to being raped by a homicidal maniac. With superhuman strength, screaming for help, she threw Calvin off her body kicking out at his groin as hard as she could. On her knees she started to crawl towards the door.

Outside the stage, Philippe thought he heard muffled cries as he slammed his car door shut. It was almost impossible to hear anything coming from the sound-proofed stage, but he sensed danger.

He pushed open the heavy doors and stopped in his tracks as he saw the horrific tableau before him. A nude Chloe huddled on the carpet, her face a mask of mute terror. Inches from her stood a man, his upraised hand holding a knife poised to strike.

Calvin looked up at Philippe, startled. For a second the tableau was frozen, then Calvin's hand sliced through the air, and the blade tore through Philippe's shirt.

Chloe's ears were ringing with screams, but she could no longer tell whether they were hers, Philippe's or the madman's.

They always watched the early-morning news on the tiny portable TV in the makeup room.

Emerald sat in one chair, her lovely new face having a delicate layer of Max Factor base applied to it. She looked at herself in the mirror, seeing again, with eyes that had with the passing years lost some of their clarity, the face of a beautiful thirty-five-year-old.

Josh leaned back in his leather-and-chrome makeup chair, eyes closed, thinking about the next scene while his face 'had the polyfilla applied', as he joked to the makeup man.

The TV announcement of the attempted murder of Chloe, and Philippe's death, jolted them out of their respective reveries.

'Christ! I must call her,' he cried out, springing out of the chair and into his dressing room. Chloe's phone number, the one he had obtained from Daphne but had never used, was busy – constantly busy. In frustration, he dialled and redialled.

'You are needed on the set.' Emerald came in without knocking. 'I wouldn't call her if I were you,' she said jealously. 'The woman has just lost the man she loved. The last person she wants to hear from is her lovesick ex-husband.'

Josh put the phone down. He asked Perry to send Chloe a basket of white roses and tulips, and wrote a note of condolence. The next day he left with the unit for a week of location shooting in the San Gabriel mountains.

Emerald travelled in the limo with him. She looked at him coldly as he sat, shoulders hunched in his woollen sweater, deep in thought, ignoring her. She bit her lip and settled back angrily into the fake leather upholstery.

She would try to get him out of her system. She would. She must. She had just met a new man, a stockbroker from Houston. He was rich, twice divorced, grey-haired but still reasonably attractive. Maybe he was finally the one. The one she had been searching for all her life yet could never find – would never find. She opened her compact to gaze at her face again. Yes, it was still gorgeous. It had not changed in the half hour since she had last looked. She still had 'it'. Beauty, charisma, fame, power. She was a superstar again. She had the world in the palm of her hand. Didn't she?

The radio was playing soft, romantic music. 'The greatest thing you'll ever learn is just to love and to be loved in return,' crooned Nat King Cole.

Josh listened to the words. That had been one of the songs he and Chloe had sung together in Vegas in the seventies. It had brought the house down.

He remembered her turquoise eyes, how they had glowed when they looked into his, as they harmonized those words, oblivious to everyone and everything in the smoky saloon except each other.

29

Philippe's funeral made front pages all over the world, getting almost as much coverage as those of Rozalinde and Sam. 'Saga' was hotter than ever, even if tragedy was the reason. Abby and Gertrude were ecstatic. They were now consistently ahead of 'America' in the ratings.

But Chloe was melancholy and depressed. She lived because Philippe had died. She mourned for him, for the love they had shared. She forgot his sulks, his stubbornness. She chose to only remember the happy times.

It was a hot Saturday afternoon in June 1987. Chloe walked slowly along the beach at Malibu, her little terrier dog panting at her heels. In two weeks, the fifth season of 'Saga' would end. What then? What would she do with her life in the three-month hiatus that stretched ahead of her? Should she accept one of the movie offers she had received? Or should she take a trip round the world with Annabel, who had been such a comfort since Philippe's death? Annabel had flown in from London to be with her mother as soon as she had heard the news, and she had not left her since. She was in the beach house now preparing Chloe's favourite dinner.

Chloe kicked a stone along the water's edge as she contemplated her future; the little terrier bounded joyfully after it.

'Good afternoon, Chlo. What a day, huh? Makes you glad to be a Brit in California.' The familiar voice interrupted her thoughts.

'Josh – what are you doing in this part of Malibu? I thought you lived in town.' She was thrilled to see him.

The reflection of the sun sparkled in his eyes. His black hair, flecked with grey, was tousled, a little too long, a little untidy. She had always loved it like that. Her eyes sparkled back at him, drank him in.

'I took a house just down there,' he gestured past where toddlers were playing and teenagers were now throwing a ball to Chloe's dog, pointing to a small redwood shingle house. The house had a little chimney from which smoke was rising. It looked cosy, faintly English, and had hollyhocks growing outside.

'What a sweet house,' said Chloe.

What a sweet face, he thought as he looked into her turquoise eyes, at the tan freckles dusting her upturned nose. She was wearing jeans and a plain white T-shirt. Her hair was tied in a ponytail and she wore no lipstick on her pale, full lips. He wanted to hold her in his arms, to kiss away the pain that he saw in the depths of those eyes.

'I got your flowers and note,' she said softly. 'Thanks, Josh.' He squeezed her arm gently. There was no need to say more. The sun was shining, the waves were lapping at their bare feet, and she was here.

'How about a cuppa?' he asked.

'English tea? I'd love some. I hope you have Earl Grey?'

''Course I do, luv – you don't think I'd drink *American* tea, do you, in *bags* with string hanging out of it? It's revolting. I've even got a new china teapot from Harrods, and scones and cream.'

'Biscuits?' Chloe smiled as they slowly sauntered across the sand to the little grey house. 'Do you have any English bickies?'

'Do I have bickies? – I most certainly do.' He looked at her with raised brows and a mischievous smile. 'Name your brand, luv, and I've got 'em. McVities chocolate digestive. Cadbury's custard creams. Scottish shortbread from Fortnum's. And brown bread and butter, with the crusts cut off. All your favourites, Chloe, all the ones you've always loved, darlin'.'

'What about sugar?' She liked this. She liked him. She more than liked him, she loved him – she'd never stopped. She knew it. The flame flickered stronger. 'I hope you've got proper sugar.'

'You bet I have, darlin', none of that saccharin sweetener stuff or brown crystals – turns the tea a funny colour. Proper sugar. Lumps, of course. White. Even if it is bad for you, I don't care. I'm English – I like my tea how it's meant to be.' They looked at each other for a very long moment, then walked slowly along the wet sand. The tide lapped their bare feet, and they laughed as they rolled up their jeans. A phalanx of seagulls swooped in the distance in perfect formation. The little dog chased them, wagging his tail, frolicking in and out of the waves. The Malibu ocean was flat, like deep blue velvet brushed the wrong way. The late afternoon sun burnished the gentle swell with golden reflections.

'And is there honey still for tea?' she murmured softly.

Josh's arm encircled Chloe's waist, her head folded into his shoulders and her hand found his and held it tightly.

Love and Desire and Hate

LOVE AND DESIRE
AND HATE

To Robin
For all his patience, love
and support

They are not long, the weeping and the laughter,
Love and desire and hate:
I think they have no portion in us after
We pass the gate.

Ernest Dowson *Vitae Suma Brevis*

PROLOGUE

Acapulco 1955

The Chief Inspector of the local police didn't like movie people at all. He disliked them disrupting his town when they were shooting, and he hated it even more when one of them died.

There was only one thing worse than a death on location and that was two deaths; now there were three.

This last tragedy appeared to have been an accident. An old wooden cable car carrying the unfortunate man had crashed down to the rocky beach, killing him instantly. For the third time in as many months Chief Inspector Gomez had been awoken from an untroubled sleep to attend the needs of this ill-assorted group of actors, producers and technicians.

They stood ashen-faced on the beach by the light of a sickly moon, the light Pacific breeze ruffling the chiffon and silk of the women's dresses.

He began by asking them some well-chosen questions.

The young *wunderkind* director, the first to have reached the body, told Gomez that without exception every member of the cast and crew had loathed the dead man.

The legendary leading lady protested that he had been a truly gentle man beneath his ruthless exterior.

The distinguished English character actor with the plummy voice announced that in his opinion the contraption had always been a death trap.

The under-aged, highly sexed ingénue kept repeating over and over, 'Death comes in threes', in her whispery French accent.

Her spinster chaperone wept, feverishly wringing her hands.

The award-winning screenwriter blew her nose and latched on to the comforting arm of a young policeman, explaining to him exactly what she thought had happened.

I

The dashingly handsome star said nothing, but wondered where his mysterious fiancée had disappeared to.

Just as Gomez was deciding to send everyone back to the set, a young police officer ran up and urgently whispered in his ear.

'One moment,' the Chief Inspector called out. 'One moment, please.' Then he proceeded to speak quickly in a low voice.

He told his shocked and attentive audience that a preliminary examination of the cable car wreckage indicated that it had been no accident.

'It is murder,' he said.

But of course one of them already knew that, because one of them had an excellent reason to kill.

As they stared at each other in shocked silence, no one noticed as the last of the amber beads which had been clutched in the dead man's hand rolled slowly into the warm sea.

PART ONE

I

Paris 1943

Inès awoke in the Ritz Hotel beside a snoring Italian officer, with waves of pain shooting through her body. Outside the windows of the sumptuously decorated Louis XIV bedroom she could see the chestnut trees which were just beginning to blossom, and felt the cool spring breeze on her aching body. Inès adored Paris with a passion which could not be extinguished by the multiplying throng of Nazi uniforms continually parading up and down the streets, the constant ache in her belly from lack of food, or the brutal men she had to serve.

She turned to look at the sleeping man next to her. By the skin on his body he appeared to be quite young, but his face, even in sleep, was cruel and insensitive, and his short bloated body bordered on the grotesque. *Merde* – what this monster had done to her last night. She shivered with revulsion, remembering his so-called lovemaking last night with horror.

She had met General Scrofo two days before in the Café Flore on the Left Bank, when she went there to observe *la vie de bohème* which appeared on the surface to continue much the same as usual. Artists, writers and students still sat sipping drinks on spindly iron chairs outside the bustling cafés. There was always good conversation, laughter, and gentle plumes of cigarette smoke. Only the men in grey and green uniform who sat there sharing the lazy friendly ambience indicated that Paris was an occupied city.

As Inès sipped her coffee, the hazy afternoon sunlight glinted on her golden hair, dappling her cheeks, emphasizing the bloom of her youth. Pablo Picasso was sitting at a nearby table surrounded by his usual group of sycophants and beautiful models.

His mesmerizing black eyes stared with interest in Inès' direction

5

as he puffed on his yellow Gauloise while luxuriating in the adulation of his admirers. Inès felt she could understand the fascination which this short, middle-aged, balding man held for the young women – were it not for the more pressing attentions of the Italian at the next table, she would have answered the artist's silent black-eyed call and joined his table. But General Scrofo advanced on her in his heavily flirtatious manner, an appointment was made and the die cast.

The following evening she walked to her rendezvous with the General, from the Boulevard Malesherbes, past the Place de Wagram and across the river Seine. The Boulevard Malesherbes, one of the longest streets in Paris, wound past the *marché* at the Porte de Champerette, which sold the few remaining scraps of food and clothing available.

Inès stopped for a sip of water from one of the bronze drinking fountains, the legacy of the English nobleman Sir Richard Wallace. Many Parisian streets boasted these charming yet functional sculptures. In the early 1870s, at the end of the Franco-Prussian War, Wallace had given them to the city which he loved so dearly, a token of his admiration for the bravery of its citizens in surviving the siege of the Prussian army. Inès hoped that in the 1940s the citizens of Paris would manage to survive the invasion of the Germans and Italians with equal courage.

Inès had been grateful for the water last night; the air was humid and dusty, and she was not looking forward to what awaited her. But it was her job – just a job, she must think of it only as that – Yves always told her so. There were few pedestrians on the boulevard and Inès passed only a dozen or so cyclists. There were no cars for private citizens in Paris now. Only the sinister black Mercedes of the Gestapo and the SS sped by, their darkened windows hiding the evil that lurked within.

Inès slowed her pace, thinking of all the enemy officers she and her friends had entertained at the Ritz and other Parisian hotels. Inès and Jeanette had often shared tricks together, joking hollowly about their profession, which was simply one of necessity, for if they did not sell themselves, they had no other skills with which to survive. Yves told Inès he was unable to support her now. She felt

trapped in this life but made the best of it, hoping it would not last for
ever.

One day Yves informed her that Jeanette's body had been pulled
from the Seine, horribly beaten and bruised. Inès thought how lucky
she was to escape the same fate, always aware that this could happen
to her, too. The Nazis – and their allies, the Italians – were cruel,
vicious men to whom whores were just toys to be used for whatever
perversions they desired.

Although Yves had forbidden it, Inès had gone to see Jeanette's
body in the morgue, staring horrified at the once-pretty young girl,
at the bruises that covered her bloated, water-laden body, the welts
and deep cuts across her breasts and belly. Inès' heart beat faster
with fear.

The night she died Jeanette had left the night club L'Éléphant
Rose with a group of drunken Italians. Jeanette had wanted Inès to
come with them, but Yves had a better trick for her that night and
Inès always obeyed Yves. Even though he was a pimp, he was a kind
man, considerate, knowledgeable, with a wicked sense of humour,
and she paid him the respect he deserved. Lucky for him that she
did, otherwise it could have been her broken body lying in the
morgue. It was Russian roulette with these enemy monsters. The
girls had to be nice to them, do whatever they desired, never sure
when they would turn into sadistic beasts.

But Inès was determined to survive this war, survive the Germans,
the Italians, the rationing, the privations and, most of all, survive the
indignities she suffered. She was going to make something of herself
one day: what, though, she did not yet know.

As she entered the most beautiful of all Parisian squares she
paused to admire the perfection of the octagonal Place Vendôme.
Honey-coloured stone buildings were perfectly enhanced by the
black and gilded enrichments of their balustrades and the grey-
green of their sloping roofs. The dozens of stone gargoyles above the
doorways of some of the buildings seemed to be jeering at her with
their lolling tongues so she did not linger long. Running lightly up
the red-carpeted steps of the Ritz, she was directed to General
Umberto Scrofo's suite by a contemptuous middle-aged concierge.

Although he had to serve Nazi generals, SS militia, Gestapo

officers, majors, captains and generals of Hitler's and Mussolini's armies with smiling servility, the concierge despised them all. Disapproval of Frenchwomen who fraternized with the enemy was all too visible on his craggy face as he watched the young prostitute going into the lift to the second floor and God only knows what degradation from General Scrofo. She was little more than a child. The concierge shrugged. It was none of his affair – he too knew the meaning of survival. These days it was every man, woman and child for themselves.

She was by no means the first under-age girl whom he'd directed to Scrofo's quarters in the past two years. The thirty-year-old General liked nubile, Nordic-looking blondes, and this girl looked a suitable partner for tonight's revels.

'Come in, *cara*,' said the General, surveying her with a cold smile. 'And close the door.' He was standing behind a marble-topped table and pouring pale amber liquid into a delicately fluted, gold-rimmed glass which, he had been assured by the most important *antiquaire* on the Faubourg St-Honoré, was from a set of glasses owned by Talleyrand himself. Inès noticed that many of the decanters on the table glittered in the soft peach lights, as only very expensive objects do, and her eyes opened wide with wonder as she took in the expensively furnished lavish room.

'Have some champagne,' he commanded, taking in her slim figure, blue eyes and golden hair. Yes, she was as freshly beautiful and young as he remembered from their brief meeting in the café. Her face was devoid of makeup and she looked virginally innocent. He ran a thick tongue across his sweating upper lip and, putting his hand casually in his pocket, felt himself hardening.

She would do. She would do very nicely indeed. He had chosen well. Now he would play with her, taunt her, in the piquant way he liked best.

'What is you name, *cara*?' he asked in a reassuring tone, watching her look of appreciation as she sipped the vintage champagne.

'Inès Dessault, sir,' she said, looking admiringly at an eighteenth-century ormolu and bronze clock on the ornately carved marble chimneypiece as it struck nine times.

'Inès, a pretty name for a pretty girl. Come here, Inès, take off

8

your coat, I won't bite you.' He laughed softly. He loved to tell them that he wouldn't harm them. A trusting look would come over their silly little faces and he could see their bodies visibly relax. No matter that they knew that he and his allies – Hitler's Master Race – had seized their country, pillaging it for every piece of treasure which France possessed. No matter that they all knew of someone, somewhere, who had been taken away in the middle of the night to some unspeakable place. A sliver of kindness from the enemy, a flicker of feigned affection, and the idiots smirked like gullible puppets. Stupid. They were all stupid, the French. Men and women. They thought their culture was without equal, that their pictures, their sculptures, their boulevards, their architecture, were supreme. Arrogance was inbred in them. Herr Blondell, who each day supervised the collection and shipping of dozens of works of art to Germany, said that soon all the Gallic fools would have left of their beloved culture would be their boulevards, their parks and their chestnut trees. All their priceless treasures – the furniture, the greatest artistry which the sixteenth, seventeenth and eighteenth centuries had to offer – the paintings, sculptures and objects d'art from Versailles, the Louvre and the Jeu de Paume, the accumulation of hundreds of years of collective genius, all would be gone. These riches would be secured in the Fatherland, owned by the Master Race – with the exception of a select little hoard which Umberto Scrofo was cunningly keeping for his own future, safely hidden in a cellar in the Rue Flambeau.

Inès slipped her thin coat off thinner shoulders. The red silk dress was new, Yves had given it to her only last week. She didn't ask where he had found it, it had obviously been stolen, but it was of beautiful quality and she recognized the couturier's label – Worth.

'Sit down, Inès Dessault,' Scrofo instructed, gesturing towards a crystal bowl filled with a gritty-looking black substance unfamiliar to her. 'Have some caviar.'

Caviar! Inès had heard of it, but this was the first time she had ever seen it. The taste was strangely salty but not unpleasant, and she was always hungry these days. She wondered if she might be appearing too greedy, but the General didn't seem to care. She sat on the edge of a blue moiré bergère, eating hungrily. He certainly was a strange-looking creature, this officer. No more than five foot three, he had a wide squat body and an enormous almost bald head which seemed out of all proportion. His uniform was thickly encrusted with medals and insignia, and he wore several rings on his stubby hands, which Inès did not think was quite correct for an officer. She saw the General's hand making circular motions in his pocket and smiled to herself. She knew that like so many enemy officers, he probably had a sexual problem. With the unforgettable atrocities which they witnessed at the front, the men often needed outlandish tricks to arouse them. A flash of thigh or breast was not enough. They needed titillation, stimulation, something to goad them to excitement. Yves had taught her how to do that, often practising with her in his big soft bed. Yves . . . whenever she thought of him, she was filled with love.

All her friends told her how lucky she was to have a pimp like Yves Moray – a man who loved her, even though he took her money. A man who never beat her, or abused her as so many of the other *maquereaux* did to their *poules de luxes*. A man whose warm kisses and caresses made up for the heartless and cold-blooded screwing which she endured from her clients. A man who made her laugh with his magic tricks both in and out of bed.

Deliberately, with ingenuous practised ease, Inès sat balanced on the edge of the bergère, her slender legs parted just enough to let the General see where her silk stocking tops ended and her slim white thighs began. She wore no panties and her stockings were secured with a pair of red satin garters, a flea-market bargain from last week.

She saw the General's eyes search for a more erotic sight, and she reached for the caviar, dipping her finger in it and sucking it slowly, her eyes never leaving his. Slowly she allowed her red silk skirt to slide up past her thighs so that Scrofo could see part of her golden mound. Nonchalantly, Inès dropped her other hand to the blonde fuzz, touching herself gently, and saw the small bulge in his trousers become more pronounced. This was going to be a piece of cake. With luck she would be out of here in half an hour, off to L'Éléphant Rose, leaving this lout satiated and snoring happily. There she would be reunited with Yves and they would sit together giggling at poor old Gabrielle when she sang her latest songs to the idiotic Germans who drank each night until they were sick.

She moved her index finger rhythmically, becoming aroused in spite of her lack of interest in the officer. Good. That would make it so much better with Yves tonight. She would tell him everything. Describe the reactions of the General staring in fascination at her sex under the red dress, laugh about the small bulge throbbing in his trousers like a little mouse. She would tell him what it felt like when the General took her, and how she felt with him inside her. Yves would get tremendously aroused and he would possess her so violently, yet so passionately, that they would come together in a burst of rapture. She shuddered with expectation, feeling herself moisten with desire. Well, so much easier for this great brute to shove it in. Why doesn't he hurry up?

She smiled up at him as Yves had taught her, then put a triangle of toast covered with caviar in her mouth, sucking it with relish while keeping her other hand busy.

He was ready now. She could tell. His breath was coming in shallow gasps, one hand fumbled with the buttons on his trousers; the other brought the glass to his lips, draining the last few drops.

'Go in there,' he ordered huskily, gesturing towards the bedroom. 'Get undressed, but leave your stockings and shoes on. Do you understand?'

Inès obeyed, feeling lighthearted. Soon it would be over. She had him now.

She lay back on the cool linen sheets of the four-poster bed, admiring the blue and gold ceiling. A magnificent chandelier hung in the centre, the cut crystals tinkling faintly in the breeze from the open windows. Her hands sensuously cupped her breasts as she continued to stimulate herself. It was, she had to admit, always rather exciting, making love with the enemy. It was something that she would never admit to Yves, but when one of the more handsome officers took her, if he was gentle, she would find herself responding to his moans of delight, and several times her orgasms had been quite genuine. But not tonight. Tonight she was saving her genuine passion for Yves. This Italian was a grotesque pig-faced creature. She must use her erotic expertise to finish him off quickly. But not too quickly, otherwise he might feel cheated and make her wait for an hour or two until he felt ready to do it again.

Umberto entered the room, still wearing his uniform. His hands were behind his back, but his rigid penis was sticking out of his unbuttoned fly. He looked utterly ridiculous, and Inès had to stifle a giggle. Most men looked ridiculous with their cocks stuck straight out in that silly way. But he looked even more so because his organ was small, about the size of a ten-year-old boy's. This didn't seem to bother him though as he strutted into the bedroom, the cigar in his mouth almost twice the length of the thing sticking out of his trousers. He removed his trousers and shirt swiftly, then leaning against the Louis XIV commode next to the bed he gestured to Inès to start on him. She concentrated on Scrofo's small, stiff penis, imagining it to be Yves'. Her soft fingers stroked the stretched skin seductively, and she started to caress his wide white thighs.

The slashing pain as Umberto suddenly brought a whip down with stunning force on to her naked back was completely unexpected.

'Whore! French whore!' He laughed harshly as he cracked the whip against her shoulders with all his force, and Inès screamed in agony.

'Yell all you want, Mademoiselle. These walls are completely soundproofed, and no one would come to rescue you even if they heard you. Suck me, bitch!' he commanded, his face a mask of sadistic pleasure as he slashed her again. Inès tried to obey, moving as best she could while he rained blows down on her, screaming obscenities.

'Sir, please *don't*,' she begged, trying to move away from him. 'You're hurting me.'

'That's the idea,' he leered. 'I love hurting whores, especially French whores.'

He grasped a fistful of Inès' long blonde hair, and dragging her up with it, held her face close to his. 'What are you?' he asked hoarsely, his eyes slits of brownish-black ice.

'Inès Dessault, sir,' she whimpered softly.

'*What* are you, I said,' he roared. 'You know what you are, don't you, Inès?'

'Yes, sir.'

'Then tell me, slut. Go on, tell me what a whore you are.'

'I'm a whore,' she whispered as tears coursed down her cheeks. 'I'm a–a–whore . . .' She hated herself, hated him, but was thankful because the beating had stopped.

'Of course you are, Inès. You're a disgusting little slut – a horrible rotten woman, and this is what a whore like you deserves.' He threw her roughly on to her stomach, forcing himself into her from behind with a moan of pleasure, his hands pulling her hair back so brutally she felt her neck would break.

Inès screamed as fresh pain engulfed her.

'Tell me again, slut.' His breath was coming faster now as he held her around the neck by her hair. 'Tell me what you are.'

'I'm a whore,' she whispered weakly, her tears raining on the pillow.

'Again,' he demanded harshly, the stubble on his chin scraping her back. 'Say it *again*, Inès. Tell me what you are, I like to hear you say it.'

'A whore. I'm a whore,' she wept.

'And a stupid one too,' he sneered. Suddenly he stopped and she collapsed on to the soft mattress, sobbing with relief. She heard him opening a drawer, and raising her head from the pillow saw that he had removed a terrifying object from it.

'Roll over,' he commanded harshly. 'On your back, whore, and open up those legs.'

Eyes wide with fear, Inès obeyed, staring in horror as he strapped to himself a rubber contraption like a giant penis.

'No,' she screamed. 'Oh no, no – please don't – you can't.' She tried to roll away but he grabbed her hair and in spite of her struggle started to force the hideous object inside her. She screamed but he clapped his hand over her mouth, hissing.

'If you don't shut up I'll ram this down your throat, and then you'll be a dead whore as well as a stupid one.'

Pain came and went in great waves as she closed her eyes, praying for this excruciating suffering to end. She had never felt such agony, such degradation.

At last his moans were becoming faster and Inès knew it must be ending. His hot breath scalded her shoulders and his saliva dripped on to her face.

'Yes, yes, you *whore*! You filthy French *cunt* – you disgusting bitch. This is for *you*!' he cried with a scream of satisfaction. He gave a final vicious thrust, at the same time punching her in the face until she lost consciousness.

He was born in Calabria, the toe of Italy, of a mother drunken and negligent and a father ignorant and weak, in the year before the outbreak of the First World War. It was a bitter winter's night when Umberto Scrofo was pulled into the world. His mother had suffered in agonizing labour for more than forty-eight hours before she was finally delivered of a child with a head out of all proportion to its tiny writhing body. The horrific ordeal and massive loss of blood left her only half alive.

Carlotta was barely twenty-three and the youngest of six children, all of them married and all with two or three children of their own. The already large family was growing fast, with many mouths to feed and precious little income with which to do it. The pitifully small amount of land which her father cultivated for vegetables had not only to feed his brood, but also to produce enough to sell at the market for necessities.

Carlotta never cared about her only child. Although it was hardly any fault of his, he had injured her so badly during his birth that intercourse was painfully uncomfortable for her afterwards. Umberto's father loved his son, but as soon as the boy grew old enough to know which of the men on the farm was his father, Alberto was conscripted into the Italian army and the family saw nothing of him for more than three years.

Carlotta called Umberto her little pig, her runt, and mocked him constantly. Full of resentment, she never forgave him for the pain he'd caused her, and for the loss of her sex life. She began to drink great quantities of rough wine all day long, and being an aggressive and strong young woman, would often pick fights with other members of the family.

Sofia, Umberto's grandmother, also had little time to spare for the ugly short boy with the huge head, and his cousins soon followed the example of their elders. By the time he was six Umberto was treated virtually as an outcast by the family, and was the butt of all their jokes.

At the age of seven, left in charge of his aunt's new baby girl, he decided to amuse himself one afternoon. He started sticking pins into the baby's bare bottom, never quite enough to draw blood, but enough to make the infant scream long and satisfyingly. This amused Umberto enormously, and he found that tormenting creatures smaller and weaker than himself gave him real pleasure. He once put a stray cat that he'd caught into a pot of water on the stove, watching it scream in agony as he boiled it to death. But he was discovered doing this, and Alberto pulled down his pants and thrashed him so soundly in front of the whole family that in future he became more careful. Umberto was so humiliated by the incident that he allowed his sadistic impulses to lie dormant for several years. Meanwhile he tried to find somebody to love him.

At the age of twelve, whilst peeing with three of his male cousins in a field, the eldest, Pino, a strapping lad of seventeen, pointed to Umberto's penis and with peals of laughter screamed, '*Guarda* the little acorn! Cousin, your little *cazzo* hasn't grown a millimetre since you were seven. Hey, look at Benno here.' He pointed to seven-year-old Benno, whose little penis pointed bravely into the ditch as he aimed his stream.

'*Guarda, guarda!*' Pino screamed with laughter, 'Umberto's got the tiny little dick of a seven-year-old!'

The other boys crowded around eagerly to peer at it, all of them proudly fingering their penises, which seemed to Umberto's eyes to be exceptionally long and thick. He cringed, and his cock cringed with him. It was indeed small, very small indeed, but he hadn't really taken much notice of it. Now it had become a thing of scorn, a freakish object for others to mock.

The boys soon told all the male members of the family of their discovery (the women would never have tolerated such vulgarity) and the news spread fast among the rest of the village men. Umberto Scrofo had a tiny penis the size of a bambino's and they never let him forget it. The ignominy and shame remained with him always.

Its size had never increased. He tried excessive masturbation, as one of his kinder cousins helpfully suggested that this practice might help it grow, but that only made Umberto interested in girls and sex, and he became even more frustrated.

At sixteen he attempted to make love to the plain young daughter of a neighbouring farmer. She was known to be easy and to 'put out', but when she saw his childish equipment she started to rock with laughter, saying, 'That's the most ridiculous excuse for a cock I've ever seen – it's no bigger than a thimble. I wouldn't even feel it inside me – take the pathetic little thing away, it's no good to any woman.'

Poor Umberto. It wasn't until he was drafted into the Italian army in the spring of the following year that he began to come into his own. From then on – as promotion followed promotion – he never looked back, knowing that in time he would find a solution for his humiliating inadequacy.

2

Yves Moray had found Inès when she was a weeping ten-year-old waif. Thumb in mouth, dressed almost in rags, she was standing outside a shabby block of flats where her prostitute mother had broken her neck by falling drunkenly down the stairs.

Yves the Magician, as he was called, had known the mother, Marie, but only slightly, since she was far too old to be one of his *poules de luxe*. A fleshy blonde, she was only thirty when she died, but already well past her prime. The frightened girl, her mother's sole mourner at the burial, was another story. She would be a rare beauty. Yves could see the potential in her tangled honey-coloured hair and in her innocent yet somehow carnal slanting blue eyes. But her personality was cold, frightened, uncommunicative. Little wonder. Marie had been short on maternal instincts, and Inès had been left to fend for herself since she was a toddler. Yves took the frightened girl under his protective wing since there was no one else who could do so, or would want to. He saw in her a kindred spirit for he too had been orphaned as a child.

But in the first weeks that she lived in the sanctuary of his house she never smiled. Yves opened up his sorcerer's basket for Inès, fascinating her by his sleight of hand with cards, his hocus-pocus with coloured scarves, his skill with the juggling of oranges. But the little girl would just sit there watching him wide-eyed and mesmerized, sucking her thumb with a sad solemn expression.

One day Yves was smoking a cigarette and found the child's eyes fixed upon him as usual. 'How about this one, Inès?' he said, and popping the lit cigarette inside his mouth with his tongue, he stared at her bug-eyed until two long streams of smoke issued from both ears.

At that Inès let out a shriek of pure laughter, and didn't stop until tears ran down her face. Yves picked her up, hugged her tightly and from then on the ice was broken. Inès had smiled, and whenever her beloved Yves was near her she smiled a lot.

Yves was gentle and kind with Inès, sending her to school, giving her warm clothes and enough food to eat. He loved bringing happIness to her sad little face when he did his magic act. Within a year she was wildly infatuated with him, following him around whenever he was home like a puppy, but he realized that Inès was really frightened of men. The only men she had ever known were the coarse oafs who had paid churlish court to her mother. Louts from back streets, they bought Marie's body for a few francs, and often abused her too. Many was the morning when Inès awoke to the sound of her mother's whimpers as she examined the black eye or swollen lips that one of her 'gentlemen' had given her. Eschewing Inès' timid offers of assistance, Marie would usually give the girl a cuff for her consideration, then send her off to school.

Sometimes Marie would be lucky enough to land herself a 'Mic', but usually he would be some heartless pimp from the alleys of Montmartre who would take all of Marie's earnings, spending it on whisky, other women and scented hair pomade in exchange for the loveless lovemaking that he would provide for her.

As she got older each of Marie's successive pimps seemed to become more avaricious, odious and unkind. Marie seemed to attract men who treated her badly and beat her, and often when they had drunk enough absinthe they liked to beat Inès too. The child grew to hate her mother and the vile men who punished them both, but there was little she could do about it.

At the time her mother died, Inès had never known a kind word from a man. She knew well what a pimp was and what he did. She saw how harshly they treated their women, and she knew in her childish heart that none of them was worth a sou. But Yves Moray proved a different customer altogether. Younger than the usual '*macrous*' that Marie had suffered, he had a roguish smiling face made even more appealing by a nose that turned up into a pair of curved nostrils which seemed to flare like a horse's whenever he laughed. His hair was pale brown, soft and curly, and when it was wet it clung to his head in tight Grecian curls. His eyes were a merry hazel, full of life and amusement, and when he laughed, which was often, they crinkled enchantingly. Inès used to stare at him covertly as she studied at the kitchen table at night. Some of his select stable of girls would sit adoringly at his feet while he regaled them with magic tricks, stroked them fondly like kittens and made them feel special and cherished. All of the girls worshipped Yves, not only for his kindness, amiable winning nature and impish smile, but for his fascinating conjuring act. He could juggle six oranges at a time without dropping one, as the girls whooped him on with cries of glee. He could do magical card tricks, making the ace of spades or the king of hearts disappear into thin air, and then 'discovering' it under one of the girls' skirts. This would cause such shrieks of laughter that Inès would look up crossly from her homework, wishing that she was part of the enchanted circle at Yves' feet. He had all manner of bewitching tricks to enthral his whores. For it was important to Yves to enthral. Since the age of ten his childhood and early youth had been spent on the streets of Montmartre performing the conjuring tricks and magic he had learned at his father's knee. By the time he was seventeen girls flocked around him, mesmerized by his cheeky charm. It wasn't long before he gave up his life of street busking and let the girls take care of him. With Yves the Magician there was never a dull moment.

Soon he had cast a spell over the child Inès, and in her pre-adolescent way she tried to attract him. She wanted him to love her. Craved his affection. He was the father she had never known, the benign kindly laughing uncle she had always wanted, the lover she needed to captivate and make her own. But although Yves found her appealing she was too young, so he made her wait for him for more than three years. Made her wait until she thought she would die for want of him. Made her wait as she sat sulkily in the front parlour of his house in the respectable Parisian suburb of Neuilly, listening while he made love to Francine or Olivia or Anna, or to any of the others. Sometimes she would eavesdrop on the sounds of his lovemaking, her ear against a thick tumbler pressed to the wall between their two bedrooms. Weeping bitterly, she listened to the sounds of the man she worshipped as he made love to other women, and sometimes she touched herself clumsily, finding a kind of relief.

Inès was precocious in both face and body. On her fourteenth birthday, standing before him rose coloured and golden, she kissed his lips to thank him for the many small presents which he had bought for her.

She particularly loved a slender bracelet of amber and silver beads which he had found in an antique shop off the Rue Jacob. As he fastened the filigree clasp around her slender wrist, he could almost smell the scent of musk emanating from her as she breathed, 'Oh thank you, Yves.' The smile of an innocent Venus made her look even more seductive. 'It is the most beautiful bracelet I have ever seen – I will never take it off. *Never.*'

She was wearing her simple school uniform, a white blouse with a wide collar, a dark blue serge tunic, mid-calf and pleated, sturdy shoes and long woollen socks. Her hair fell halfway down her back, curling in delicate tendrils around her oval face. With her clear blue eyes and golden skin, she looked like one of Botticelli's angels. Yves was a man who truly appreciated women, even though he exploited them. He examined her: the seductive, knowing look on her face that predicted delights in store for him; her budding breasts, whose rose-tipped nipples were hardening under the blouse. The parted pale lips seemed aching to be kissed. His eyes narrowed as they met the bold gaze that told him what she desired. She was ripe, she was ready, it was time. Finally Yves the Magician allowed the teenage seductress to conquer him.

They made love for hours in the warm, soft darkness of his bed. She knew how it was done – she had been in the room often enough when her mother had been at work.

Ever since Inès had reached the age of awareness – five or six – she had watched what Marie had done with her men. Some of them liked her mother's style so much that they came back week after week, for months, even years. So although Inès was technically a virgin, she had in her mother an excellent teacher of the erotic arts. With a natural instinct as well as lessons learned from hours of observation, she gave Yves the most enthusiastic lovemaking that he had ever had. From that time on Inès had shared Yves' bed nightly; he soon found himself entranced by this child with the gorgeous face, magical body and sexual tricks of an experienced courtesan, and he managed to teach her even more.

Six months later, with the advent of war, pandemonium ruled France and several of Yves' regular girls fled Paris. He had little choice but to put Inès to work, starting her off at a night club owned by Gabrielle Printemps, L'Éléphant Rose.

As the daughter of a whore, Inès wasn't really too upset. Yves loved her, she worshipped him and she didn't care much about anything else. Being a professional prostitute was only a job. She didn't like it, she didn't dislike it. It was just the obvious and inevitable way of her life.

The men she slept with meant nothing; her mind was far away when they possessed her body. She knew they could never possess her heart because that belonged totally to Yves, her wonderful magic Yves. She was his completely, and whatever other men did with her could make no difference to her devotion to Yves.

Their mutual passion was pure and strong, symbolized, Inès thought, by the shimmering amber and silver bracelet strands which encircled her wrist and represented the eternity of their love.

3

As the morning light began to flood into the bedroom Inès regained consciousness and looked around. Her head throbbed painfully. The linen sheets were encrusted with blood, her blood, and the pain all over her body was so intense that she wanted to weep. She had to escape from this loathsome creature who snored next to her, she had to get away immediately – but he had not paid her yet. No matter, she would take the money herself, God knows she'd earned it.

Please let him stay asleep, she thought as she crept from the bed, wincing in agony. His trousers lay on the floor where he had thrown them, next to the discarded whip and the disgusting false penis. She could still feel the numbing pain from it. Quickly she searched through his pockets but there was no money in them, only a grubby handkerchief. Glancing at the sleeping man, she tiptoed into the marble bathroom, where, in the full-length mirror, she saw her bruised and tear-stained face, her shoulders and breasts covered with welts and cuts, the dried blood on her thighs. She squatted over the bidet, washing herself with scented soap. Flinching in pain, it was then that she noticed the thick wad of francs lying by the side of the marble wash basin, next to his razor and toothbrush. There were a lot of notes, more than she usually made in a week. Should she take just what she was usually paid or all the money to make up for the horrible things Scrofo had done to her? 'Take them all,' she whispered to the reflection of the pale wounded girl who looked out sorrowfully from the mirror. 'You deserve them, Inès.'

Hastily she seized the banknotes, just as the Italian lurched into the room. When he saw what she was doing, he grabbed her by the hair and smashed her head against the marble wall with all his strength.

'A whore *and* a thief, huh?' he sneered. 'There's only one way to treat scum like you – give you more of what you had last night.' She

23

saw with dread that he held that disgusting rubber object in his hand and that he was erect again. He forced her over to the wash basin, all the time mouthing his litany of filth. Oh my God, he was going to do it again. He couldn't, he simply couldn't. It was unbearable, her body couldn't stand any more.

'Please don't,' she sobbed. 'Please, please stop – you can't do this again. Please, you can't. I promise I'll come back when I'm better. I am in so much pain – such pain, look, I'm still bleeding.'

'Good.' His grin revealed sharp yellow teeth and she could smell the reek of garlic and stale champagne, see that his eyes were bloodshot and wild. 'The way *you* want it, I only do with *proper* women,' he gloated. 'Italian women, *good* girls, ladies, not French harlots like you. I only do it like *this* with *scum*.' He bent her over the basin, and his small penis, red and throbbing, stabbed into her with the dull pain of a blunt knife. 'We will do it like *this* – and then we will do it again with *this*,' and he brandished the rubber plaything in front of her. 'My little rubber friend. You like him, Inès, don't you? I know you liked him last night.'

'No!' screamed Inès. 'No! Please!'

As if in a dream, her eyes suddenly focused on the old-fashioned cut-throat razor which was lying open on the marble counter. Without thinking, the terror and pain so excruciating, she picked up the razor and lashed out blindly behind her. She heard him scream in anguish and then a great crash as he fell. Inès gasped when she turned and saw what she had done. The blade had sliced across his throat as cleanly as a seamstress cuts into a length of cloth. Blood bubbled from the wound and his eyes rolled back in his head. There was no doubt that he was dying. Ghastly rasping sounds isued from his throat but his tiny penis still stood lewdly erect, like some defiant flagpole. As she watched, stricken into immobility, his huge bald head, spattered with the blood that pumped from his throat, lolled sideways on to the floor. Inès gazed at the dead man, panic-stricken. She had killed an Italian officer of the occupation. What on earth was she going to do?

Frozen with fear, Inès didn't know how long she stood staring at Scrofo as blood ran from his neck and mouth on to the shining black and white marble tiles. She glanced at her reflection in the mirror, seeing a terrified girl whose hair hung over her face in matted snarls, whose eyes were wild and who had blood on her hands. She had to get out.

It was seven o'clock. How long before one of the General's aides would call for him? He was bound to have army matters, manoeuvres, something to do, he was an important part of the war machine. He had told her that at the café. Her mind raced with every kind of possibility. She could just leave, after she dressed in the red frock and shabby coat which she had worn the previous night. The concierge had barely looked at her when she arrived. He wouldn't remember her – would he?

Her fingers rubbed her chafed wrists, raw from Scrofo's brutal treatment, and she ran them under the warm tap water. Then with a shock she realized that her lucky bracelet was missing. Fear made her limbs tremble uncontrollably as she rushed into the bedroom, throwing back the bloodied sheets, searching desperately for her precious beads. The bracelet – her talisman – anyone who knew her would instantly recognize the fine string of amber and silver beads which she always wore. If they found the bracelet, it would only be a question of how long before they found her. In a frenzy she dropped to the floor, crawling about on her hands and knees, but the bracelet wasn't there. Tears rolled down her face, stinging her cut lips, her bruised cheeks. Then she remembered: she hadn't been wearing it last night! The clasp was loose and Yves had promised to take it to be mended. Thank God, oh, thank God.

Back in the bathroom she grabbed the wad of notes – they were well paid, these Italians – then ran back to the bedroom and flung on her clothes. She found everything except one red garter. So what? Every whore in Paris wore red garters. They couldn't possibly trace her with that – could they?

She shoved the other garter and her stockings into a pocket and cautiously opened the suite door, looking down the long, deserted corridor. Her heart beating painfully, she tiptoed down the passage towards the back stairs, hoping to find the staff entrance. As she crept down she heard laughter and a door opening, and hid herself around a bend in the stairway as several chambermaids came chattering down the hall to begin their shifts. Entering a changing room in shabby dresses, they emerged in starched blue and white uniforms, and sped off to begin their work.

Inès' heartbeat was so loud that she imagined the chattering girls might hear it. She wondered what sort of security the hotel would have at the back entrance. Would they, like many hotels, have guards who must check the staff out for possible theft after every shift? Would the employees have to carry identity cards which proved they worked there? It was almost more of a risk than to leave by the front entrance – nevertheless it was a decision she must make.

She looked at her wristwatch, another present from Yves – nearly seven thirty. Over half an hour since she had sliced the razor across the General's throat. She shuddered at the thought of how the authorities would punish her if they ever caught her. Execution would be the least painful death she could expect for someone of her age and looks. They would no doubt inflict on her the most sophisticated tortures, after the inevitable multiple rapes. Death would be a blessing. No, she was determined that this would not be her fate, this was not the way she had envisaged her life. In spite of her past, in spite of the ignominy of her profession, Inès possessed innate pride and a strong belief in herself. She was determined to escape. The stream of arriving girls had now slowed to a trickle. Two more exhausted, gamine-faced young women little more than children arrived, then there was a lull; it was now or never.

Mustering all her courage, she strode purposefully into the small room in which the maids changed. None of the girls even looked at her, so busy were they dressing and gossiping. Keeping her head down, Inès moved along to the last shabby overcoat hanging on the row of hooks. Below each hook was a locked wood and wire netting cage in which the girls kept their handbags and walking shoes. Their identity cards would, no doubt, be in those handbags.

Inès put on the tattered overcoat, which was too long for her. There was a flimsy scarf in the pocket and thankfully she tied it around her matted hair. All she needed now was another girl's identity papers. Stealthily she pulled at several of the little hatches on the wire cages, but they were all securely locked. Never mind, she had her coat and scarf, and most important of all, she had great courage. Tightening the belt on the overcoat, she followed two gossiping chambermaids who were going off shift. They clattered down granite steps to a small foyer inside the door leading to the Rue Cambon. A Ritz security guard sat at his desk, cigarette drooping from a tired mouth. Behind him stood a Nazi officer staring at the wall with a look of deep melancholy.

Hans Meyer was usually one of the most zealous and thorough of guards. This morning, however, his mind was elsewhere. The previous night he had received a letter from his fiancée in the Fatherland: she had fallen in love with his own father – a widower for many years – and they would be married by the time Hans received the letter. She was very sorry, of course, wartime stress and all that, but *c'est la vie*, and she hoped Hans would try to understand. He had been so full of rage that he had drunk himself into a stupor and was now suffering the worst hangover of his life. He took no notice of the prattling maids who were emptying their handbags on to the trestle table for the guard to examine. His father! His beautiful twenty-two-year-old flaxen-haired Fräulein was going to marry his bald-headed sixty-year-old father. Between bouts of nausea, he plotted his revenge, totally ignoring the guard's cursory examination of the girls' belongings.

Inès emptied her handbag on to the table and the guard halfheartedly flicked through its meagre contents. Lipstick, mirror, comb, a door key, a few francs. The wad of two thousand francs was well hidden in her shoe.

'Okay, you can go,' said the guard. 'Next.'

Praying the soldier would not question her lopsided walk, Inès bundled her possessions back into her bag and strode out into the rich golden Parisian sunshine.

Free! She was free. But how long would it last?

4

That spring of 1943 the Gestapo seemed to be everywhere in Paris, and they were a sinister sight. They lurked in black Mercedes, wearing black leather overcoats, with the dreaded black swastika emblazoned on their sleeves. They smoked harsh cigarettes and looked with cold dead eyes at everyone who passed.

They always pounced at night. Small groups of men, their hard faces insensitive to any human suffering, sometimes accompanied by ferocious Alsatian dogs straining at their leashes, would come to their victims' homes without warning. The dogs could root out 'enemies of the Reich' hidden anywhere – in cellars, cupboards, even concealed behind walls.

Every night the Gestapo discovered groups of hidden Jews, herding them into trucks to be sent to God knows where. All French Jews had to wear badges, on which JUIF was printed in large yellow letters, and none of them ever knew when they could expect to hear the dreaded sound of barking Alsatians, the staccato rap of the SS at their front doors. Every Jew lived in fear, but all of them did their best to disguise it.

Polished leather jackboots glistening, grey uniforms bristling with insignia, the long, dark shadow of the Third Reich fell across the entire Jewish population of France that spring. But although every patriotic citizen detested the sight of the enemy soldiers, with true French spirit they tried to live as normally as possible. The Nazi soldiers, their coarse faces framed by ugly helmets, leather straps tight under their chins, were ruthless, completely without mercy. They had been trained a long time in Germany for this moment and they treated the French nation with undisguised contempt.

Agathe Guinzberg had spent the last of her teenage years hiding in a basement in Montparnasse. The house was owned by Gabrielle Printemps of L'Éléphant Rose, the club next door, a favourite haunt of enemy officers and their floozies.

Gabrielle lived with her grandfather, mother and crippled eighteen-year-old brother, Gilbert. By chance, that particular evening when the Gestapo arrived to arrest the Jewish family, Agathe was at the Printemps' house, reading to Gilbert. When the Printemps family saw what was happening across the street, they made Agathe hide down in their basement. Peeping through lace curtains, Gabrielle saw Agathe's family pushed unceremoniously into the back of a truck. There were three little girls under twelve, boys of about fifteen and sixteen, and their mother and father. The commandant didn't seem to realize that he should be taking a family of eight *Juden* off to await deportation to the camps. He was weary. This was the fourteenth family they had 'collected' that night. He knew that there should be several children, and indeed there were, so that was that, he had filled his quota for the night, now he could go off and enjoy himself.

The truck took the Guinzbergs, with all the other Jewish families from the street, to a makeshift camp outside Paris. There they joined several hundred other families and were soon put on a train to Buchenwald, from where none would ever be heard of again.

Hidden in the Printemps cellar, eighteen-year-old Agathe slowly learned to adapt to living alone among the spiders and the cockroaches; with the mildew and the stench of drains; with the rats, the mice and the unspeakable horrors of her fertile imagination. She had been given a supply of candles but was told to use them sparingly. Her only substantial meal was delivered by Gabrielle in the morning, when the last drunken footsteps of the enemy echoed down the cobblestone streets. Only then did Agathe allow herself to light a candle, eat her food and spend the next few precious hours reading in the recesses of her tomb. Occasionally a brief note from Gabrielle accompanied the food – the latest news of the war, good or bad, or perhaps a concerned query about her welfare. Gabrielle was terrified to the point of paranoia about talking to Agathe. She believed that walls – even floors – had ears, and consequently kept conversation to a minimum. Agathe was able to wash only once a week, when Gabrielle would send down a basin of lukewarm water, and soon her clothes hung on her sparse body in filthy tatters. Whenever her head itched so much that she could hardly stand it,

30

she would pick the lice from her scalp, cracking their bodies between her thumbnails like peanuts.

Agathe's mind began to inhabit a world of its own as each day drifted into endless night. There was darkness all the time except for the blessed candles; it was bitterly cold and damp; but she had the most comforting thing of all – the books.

If her body suffered from lack of nourishment, her mind did not. Gabrielle's grandfather had been a bookseller who specialized in rare books, and the cellar was crammed with leather-bound volumes of Balzac, Molière, Racine and the great Victor Hugo; poems by Byron, Shelley, Voltaire, Baudelaire and Robert Browning; and escapist adventure stories by Dumas and Rider Haggard – all piled high in the damp cellar. Better mildew on the precious volumes, Grandfather had said, than for them to fall into the hands of the Germans. Throughout her numberless lonely months, Agathe read hundreds of books as she prayed for the occupation to end.

Agathe had studied ballet since she was a child – her ambition was to be a prima ballerina. To retain her sanity, she would often practise, whirling and bending frenziedly in the darkness, humming the music of *Swan Lake* and *Giselle*, her mind full of the glory that could be hers when she was released from captivity. Unable to count the days to her freedom for she had no idea when it would be, she was a prisoner without parole – a jailbird with no end to her sentence.

Gabrielle had given Agathe her own rosary and crucifix when she first went into the cellar. Despite being Jewish, Agathe took comfort in the amber beads, constantly caressing them, praying for her deliverance.

Sometimes she scribbled plaintive notes to Gabrielle: 'How much longer will the war last?' The reply would always be the same: 'Not much longer, child, I hope. Have faith, we are all praying for it to end soon.'

Every night Agathe heard the raucous laughter of German and Italian officers who patronized the night club next door, the shrill, high-pitched shrieks of their young whores, and Gabrielle's husky voice singing to them. As rats and cockroaches scurried around her feet, and her body shook with the cold, she began to learn the meaning of hatred.

31

Early one evening before the club had opened, the Gestapo came to the house for a routine search. While Gabrielle and her family were being questioned, two Alsatians sniffed around the bedrooms, the front parlour and the kitchen. Agathe could hear the boots clattering above her, and froze. The cellar opening was covered by a sheet of metal set into the floor of the scullery, camouflaged by cracked linoleum. Agathe trembled on her filthy bedding in the blackness beneath them, but remained undiscovered because the dogs were far more interested in the appetizing scent of meat in the larder, and barked enthusiastically.

Whenever Gabrielle passed a platoon of soldiers in the street she shuddered and looked away. Each time she took a plate of food down to Agathe, she wondered fearfully how long it would be before the girl was discovered and Gabrielle's own family were persecuted for hiding her. But as the months and then the years passed she began to realize that Agathe had been forgotten by the Nazis, she no longer existed.

As the Jewish population continued to be systematically exterminated, as the hunger pangs of France grew more severe, the Resistance worked on.

Maurice Grimaud was the best forger in France, the unrivalled expert in counterfeiting identity papers and passports. A highly valued member of the Resistance, he fraternized at L'Éléphant Rose several times a week, playing the jovial drunk, the buffoon, making the hated enemy laugh. The Germans enjoyed his idiotic antics, encouraging him to sit at their tables to joke with them. Since liquor loosened tongues, he picked up an enormous amount of information which was invaluable to the Resistance.

Maurice was a man of so many faces who had so many hiding places that the Gestapo were never able to track him down because they had no idea who he really was. He was a master of disguise, an expert in calligraphy and counterfeiting, and his efforts on behalf of the French Underground were legendary. He had nine lives and had not yet lost one.

He was a generous old friend of Gabrielle, who was becoming extremely worried about Agathe. She decided to talk to Maurice about the girl. The last time Gabrielle had shone a torch on Agathe's face, she could hardly believe what she saw. Agathe was wasting away to nothing, her hair had turned white, her face was so thin that her cheekbones stuck out like pieces of jagged glass, and the deep hollows around her eyes were those of a forty-five-year-old woman. Her appearance had changed so radically that Gabrielle decided that, with new identity papers, she could be released from the cellar. No one would ever recognize her. Gabrielle also thought that if the girl died – and with Agathe looking so frail and ill this was not a remote possibility – getting rid of the body would be a great problem. Besides which, Gabrielle needed someone to work behind the cash desk at her club. Agathe could work for what she ate, and sleep on a cot in the parlour.

Thanks to Maurice, Agathe soon possessed an authentic-looking set of identity papers, passport, birth certificate and even a complete set of school reports going right back to kindergarten. They were masterpieces of his art and Maurice was proud of them.

When Agathe was finally helped out of the cellar and took a few faltering steps into the back yard, the faint autumnal sun was such a shock to her system that she fainted. She weighed barely ninety pounds. Her skin was as pale as mountain snow and her black hair had turned silvery white. She looked completely different from the plump, laughing teenager who had disappeared nearly two years ago, and the neighbours who had known her before gave her no glance of recognition.

In the following months Agathe sat silently behind the cash register at L'Éléphant Rose, watching the Germans and the Italians fraternize, observing how they used and abused the young French whores. Her hatred for every one of them grew like a cancer in her weakened body.

Traitors. Those girls, so young and pretty, were despicable traitors who betrayed their country and their people by consorting with the enemy. She hated all the Frenchwomen who hung over the soldiers and officers, laughing with them, fondling their bodies, kissing their cruel lips. No one ever gave *her* a second glance and Agathe realized bitterly that her prettiness was gone for ever. Although she was just twenty she looked close to fifty, and though she ate heartily her body remained almost skeletal. Silently each night she sat in the tiny glass-walled booth at the back of the night club, to all intents and purposes immersed in the accounts. Her silver hair and pale skin glowed spectrally in the dim lighting and she constantly fingered her rosary as she simmered with a quiet but consuming rage and a desperate desire for revenge.

5

'You did *what?*' Yves' eyes narrowed and the colour drained from his face.

'*Chérie*, it is *not* possible. Why did you have to *kill him?* What he did couldn't have been *that* terrible, surely?'

'It was, Yves, it was torture. You have no idea of the pain and the horrible things he did.' Inès tried to control her hysteria, sipping at the whisky which a rabbit-faced waitress at L'Éléphant Rose had brought her. 'I *had* to do it, Yves – I had to, he would have killed me if I hadn't, he threatened to kill me. I know he would have done – I know.' Tears streamed down her cheeks.

Gabrielle, with a murmur of sympathy, passed her a handkerchief. *Merde*, what slime these men are, she thought. She had seen the bruises and cuts on Inès' body and looked pityingly at the girl who, in her grief, looked little more than a child.

They were sitting in a dimly lit back booth. Although it was eight thirty in the morning, the club had only just closed. Yves' brain raced with the problems they all now faced. Whatever Inès had done, no accusing finger must ever be allowed to point at L'Éléphant Rose. The club was much too valuable to them all and too many lives would be put at risk. Even though most of its habitués were the enemy, the club was one of the most important cores of the Resistance in Paris. The enemy must never know that the killer of an Italian officer had in any way been assisted by the Resistance.

'Thank God you met him in that café and not here,' Yves said. 'Did anyone see you with him? Anyone at all?'

'No, no, I don't think so – he was sitting at a table alone – it all happened quite quickly. He knew very well what I was when he picked me up. I was wearing that low-cut green dress. We only spoke for a moment or two before he propositioned me. And told me to meet him last night at the Ritz.' She started to cry again and

35

Gabrielle poured her another shot of whisky. 'I should've gone and sat with Picasso,' sobbed Inès. 'He smiled at me too.'

'Shut up, Inès,' snapped Yves. 'The concierge last night – do you think he saw you?'

'I can't remember.' Inès did her best to recall the events of twelve hours ago, which already seemed like an eternity. 'I don't think he looked up at me when I asked for Scrofo's room number – but you never know with concierges, do you?' More tears ran down her face and her shoulders heaved with sobs. Gabrielle squeezed her hand sympathetically.

'No, I suppose you never do.' Yves' voice was grim. 'But since you *did* speak to the concierge, the Gestapo are sure to question him. There are probably no more than two or three hundred blonde teenaged prostitutes in Paris. It's only a matter of time before they trace you, line you up for the concierge to identify – and then accuse you. Don't forget, they will find fingerprints.'

'Yes – yes, of course,' Inès groaned. *Why* hadn't she thought to clean the marble surfaces of the bathroom, the handle of the razor, the champagne glass? It was too much to think about. She felt dizzy and nauseous. All she wanted was to sleep in the safety of Yves' arms. She wanted him to stroke her hair, comfort her, tell her that everything was going to be all right, promise that he would take care of her, as he always had done.

'Come. We must go to see Maurice right away,' Yves said decisively. 'We have no time to lose.'

After four days the scandal and gossip about the murderous attack on the Italian General began to die down. No suspect had been found, and the concierge at the hotel had a conveniently patriotic memory block about the prostitute whom he had seen going up to Scrofo's room. No one else had seen Inès at the Ritz that night, and there were simply no clues as to the identity of who had slashed the General's throat.

While Yves and Maurice decided what to do with her Inès was hidden in the same cellar where Agathe had lived for so long. When Gabrielle came down to cut and dye her long blonde hair, she told Inès that plans and arrangements were under way to smuggle her over to England.

'He was a complete bastard, that Italian General. I heard all about him,' Gabrielle said as she fluffed up Inès' newly dyed shoulder-length dark hair.

'You would not *believe* the disgusting things he did with some of the girls.' Her voice was full of bitterness. 'They say that *he* was the one who killed Jeanette. Everyone who knew him, even his so-called friends in the army, seems happy that he's gone. I think you did us all a big favour, *chérie.*'

'When will Yves get me out of here, Gabrielle?' Inès said plaintively. 'I'm so lonely and frightened. There are hundreds of spiders and rats and cockroaches. I have the most terrible night-mares – I keep on seeing Scrofo's face – I just can't sleep. I'm scared.' Inès began to cry but Gabrielle grabbed her hair, bringing the girl's face close to hers.

'Listen, little girl,' she whispered fiercely, 'you are very very lucky. *Whatever* that swine did to you, you *are* a whore, and it's your *profession* to serve and satisfy men, even pigs like him.'

Inès winced as Gabrielle continued: 'We are all risking our lives every day for you, you ungrateful selfish child. And as for being frightened, we had to keep Agathe down here for nearly two years, and she never complained. You're lucky to have a man like Yves who loves you – even if he is only a pimp,' Gabrielle told her. 'Not many little whores are so lucky. And to let you know how *really* lucky you are, my friend Maurice has been working day and night for you on your identity papers. Tonight' – she leaned forward – 'tonight, you have a nice surprise coming, and you don't deserve it.'

'Hmm, good. Excellent. Very convincing.'

Yves admired the worn French passport, the set of bound school reports dating back over ten years and the ragged identity card with Inès' photograph. They were all made out in the name of Inès Juillard, and they appeared completely authentic.

'From now on, that will be your name,' Yves told her. 'You must forget that Inès Dessault ever existed. She is gone for ever.'

They had been cycling through the leafy country lanes of Normandy towards the coast at Calais, where they were to meet their contact. Now they were lying under a huge chestnut tree and the afternoon sun dappled Inès' dark brown hair with highlights of burnished gold. They felt almost safe while they ate their frugal sandwiches and drank from a bottle of rough red wine. They could see some farmers toiling in the fields, and it seemed country life was going on much as usual.

Inès leaned forward to kiss Yves. He wore scruffy peasant clothes, with his hair cropped and a three-day stubble on his cheeks, but his sexual magnetism stirred her more than ever.

'Yves,' she whispered, her tongue softly tracing his lips, 'oh, Yves darling, I love you so much.' Her hands caressed him inside the coarse cloth of his shirt as his lips hungrily responded to her delicate kisses. She stretched out like a cat on the soft, sweet grasses, surrendering herself to his touch and his mouth.

Danger made their coupling sweeter. The smell of crushed grass mixed in her nostrils with the scent of Yves, the warm familiar smell which Inès loved beyond all others.

Their bodies fused, fuelling each other's fire. Inès loved this man so intensely; he was the only person in the world whom she had ever truly loved, and she knew she could never love another.

Too soon he looked at his watch, saying briskly, 'It's three o'clock, *chérie* – we must go or we will never be in Calais by eleven.'

He spoke almost lovingly to Inès, although he knew he had never really loved anyone in his life. But he had decided that it was necessary that he accompany her to England. If the Italians ever discovered who had murdered Umberto Scrofo, life for those who had anything to do with Inès would become very unpleasant indeed. Like the Gestapo, they were not particular about whom they tortured, or how they did it, and a murderess' pimp could expect no mercy from Mussolini's men.

An old blue and white rowing boat was waiting for them in a small cove down the coast from Calais, exactly where the Resistance had said it would be. In it were three men who were also, for one reason or another, being smuggled out of France by the partisans.

As Inès sat hunched in the tiny craft, watching the French coast recede, she breathed the fresh sea air gratefully, feeling more free than she had for days. The four men rowed vigorously. It was a fine, spring night with little wind and few cross-currents, so they made the crossing in good time. Four hours later Inès blinked in wonder as she saw the magnificent chalk cliffs of Dover appear, dimly lit by weak moonlight.

As soon as the boat beached, the men hauled it quickly up on to the pebbles, covering it with fishing nets and clumps of seaweed. They waited for their contact to arrive. As they had been told to expect, a man cautiously approached them through the darkness, mumbling a few words of welcome. The contact handed them a brown paper parcel which contained five English ration books made out in fictitious names, identity cards and some crumpled pound notes. There was also a timetable for the local trains, and four different addresses in England.

Inès and Yves eagerly peered at their own particular address:

Madame Josette Pichon
17 Shepherd Market
London W1

'Shepherd Market.' Inès rolled the name on her tongue, savouring the Englishness of it. 'How pretty it sounds. Oh Yves, do you think there will be lambs and chickens and a maypole with ribbons on it in the middle of the village square?'

'Hardly, *chérie*,' Yves chuckled at Inès' naivety. 'England is suffering in this war almost as badly as France. Night after night German planes bomb London to hell and back. From what I've heard, Shepherd Market is right in the centre of everything. We'd probably have been safer in Paris.'

'I don't care where I am, *chéri*,' Inès sparkled, 'as long as I'm with you.'

6

London 1943

'Oh, dammit, not again,' Phoebe mumbled to herself. She had just crawled into bed, shattered after another long night of toil at the Windmill Theatre, where 'We never close' was the famous motto. 'Not another bloody air raid. Will it *never* end?'

Half asleep, she pulled on her warm dressing gown and sheepskin slippers. Carrying a Thermos of hot tea and a bag which contained her worldly essentials and went everywhere with her, she staggerd down seven flights of stairs into the scant comfort of the crowded air-raid shelter.

Along with the other occupants of her block of flats she tried in vain to doze while the sound of exploding bombs echoed through the darkened and shuddering shelter, babies cried and children whimpered with fear. As soon as the all clear had sounded the weary group picked up the bits and pieces of their lives and ventured shakily back to their flats . . . until the next time.

Phoebe sighed with exhausted relief as she let herself in, and throwing herself on to the bed she slept the dreamless sleep of the innocent. She had survived yet another night of Luftwaffe air raids, yet another night of earth-shattering, deafening noises as the anti-aircraft guns blazed and the German bombs blitzed the city to hell.

In the morning she listened to the BBC as the solemn tones of Alvar Lidell broadcast the extent of the damage to the city. Over seventy buildings had been partially or completely destroyed, fifty-two civilians killed and more than twice that number injured. His voice was grave as he recited the death toll and Phoebe switched off the wireless. She couldn't bear to hear such bad, sad news.

After patiently queuing in her local tea shop for a cup of strong tea and a sticky bun with a few raisins on it, she picked her way fastidiously down Great Portland Street towards the West End. The streets were covered with shrapnel and debris, but none of the buildings that she passed had collapsed. Most of the bombing had been concentrated near the river, from where she could see a tall grey pall of smoke rising above the chimney pots of Oxford Circus.

Phoebe's natural exuberance managed to flourish even in war-torn London. At twenty-three she had the robust curves, creamy skin and wilful red hair inherited from her forebears – stalwart country men and women from the north of England, not afraid of hard work and deprivation. Hardy British stock, they had all been survivors, and she was going to survive this bloody war, even make the best of it. She wasn't going to allow herself to get depressed. She had a job to do at the Windmill Theatre: to entertain the boys – the boys in blue, the boys in khaki, the boys in green, even the boys in white. They were all on leave, all with weary, jaundiced eyes that spoke of dreadful war experiences – which their raucous laughter belied. The showgirls would give seven performances today, as they did every day. They would change their costumes no less than forty-nine times – seven changes in each show – and some of them would even bare their breasts for the soldiers to gawp at.

Phoebe's thick cuban heels clacked down Regent Street, daintily avoiding the street cleaners who were trying to sweep up 'Jerry's garbage'. In spite of the nightly air raids, Piccadilly Circus was always a hive of festive activity. The statue of Eros, God of Love, had been removed from the centre of Piccadilly to a safe haven. Allied military men of every nationality milled about in a maelstrom of colour and movement, and dozens of young women mingled on the pavement, chatting to them animatedly. There was a carnival atmosphere in Piccadilly Circus, a desperate gaiety on the faces of the crowds as if to say that the war could not affect them.

No matter that for many servicemen leave was over tomorrow, and they were off to fight in North Africa or Burma or Salerno. It was party time all the time in London, especially in the West End and particularly at the Windmill Theatre.

Phoebe walked past Lyons Corner House, where two long queues stood waiting patiently for it to open, and hurried up Shaftesbury Avenue.

Entering the stage door, she stopped as she beheld one of the best-looking young men that she had ever laid eyes on, talking animatedly to the stage doorkeeper. Thick, dark brown hair in unruly waves, jet black curved eyebrows, a handsome, slightly saturnine face, and she thought his nose and cheekbones were almost like a living replica of Antinous, the youth so beloved of the Emperor Hadrian. Navy blue eyes met hers briefly, then turned away without the remotest flicker of interest as he continued chatting to the old man.

The stranger was dressed in a grey Prince of Wales check three-piece suit, pale blue shirt and extravagant tie. A light grey homburg was tipped rakishly over his eyes as he leaned forward to talk to the doorman, charm oozing from every pore.

'But look here, old chap, just tell the boss that I've had *years* of experience in variety. Manchester Hippodrome, Gaiety Theatre, Liverpool, the Alhambra in Brighton. I've topped the bill at all of them. And,' he whispered conspiratorially, 'I've got the best repertoire of blue jokes this side of Blackpool Pier – I've had them rolling in the aisles, old chap, everywhere. Here.' He handed the uninterested man a typewritten résumé glued to the back of an eight-by-ten smiling photograph of himself. 'What's your name, old chap, by the way?'

'Fred,' said the doorman unsmilingly.

'Julian Brooks is my name – comedy's my game.' Julian gave Fred the benefit of a smashing smile with a perfect set of even teeth, framed by a small, beautifully trimmed Ronald Colman moustache.

'Why aren't you in the army then?' asked Fred, looking suspiciously at the photograph which the young man was waving at him.

'Flat feet, old boy. Not very honourable, but there we are.' Phoebe felt a tingle of excitement as her eyes connected again with his for a fraction of a second.

'That's why I'm so anxious to do my bit for the boys, old chap. I've got comedy routines that will have them splitting their sides. They'll go back to fighting Jerry with a big smile on their faces – and so full of piss and vinegar, the Hun will run like rabbits.' He smiled engagingly, but all to no avail. His charm fell on stony ground with the doorkeeper.

'Nah, sorry, mate.' Fred pushed the photograph back at him. 'We're not 'irin' anyone, guvnor's orders, and even if we wus – I ain't the one wot does it, so piss off – and go peddle yourself somewhere else.' He picked up the *Daily Mirror*, immersing himself in Jane's cartoon exploits, leaving Julian standing there in disappointed frustration.

Phoebe stepped forward. Mustn't let this one get away – handsome, still young, obviously not about to be posted to foreign parts, to become cannon fodder like some of her ex-lovers.

'Hello, I'm Phoebe Bryer,' she gushed, holding out a well-manicured hand. 'I work here. May I help you?'

'You most certainly may.' Julian looked at her tumbling Titian curls, fresh complexion, sparkling eyes and luscious curves. What a cutie this one was, he thought, a delectable dish indeed. Sending out availability signals, too. Perfect.

'I think you just might be able to help me, Miss Bryer,' he said, his Royal Academy of Dramatic Arts accent smooth as silk and twice as seductive. 'Perhaps you would you allow me the honour of buying you a delicious cup of tea and a sticky bun at that little coffee shop on Shaftesbury Avenue?' He looked her up and down with the requisite amount of lust and Phoebe felt herself starting to tingle.

'It would have to be after the next show,' she said excitedly. Not again, Phoebe, said her warning conscience. It's much too soon after Jamie – whoa, my dear, slow down. She gave Julian a sweet but saucy smile. 'We break at noon, but only for half an hour, I'm afraid, so you'd better be on time.'

'Wonderful, I'll meet you here on the dot. Okay?' He smiled again.

'Okay,' said Phoebe with a maidenly blush.

Fred put down his newspaper and, with a meaningful look at the clock, announced, 'Curtain's up in fifteen minutes, duckie, and from the look of yer, you'll need all that time to put yer slap on.' He then gave Julian a baleful glare and snorted, 'Time to move orf the premises, laddie, let the little lady get to work,' and he buried his face in his tabloid again.

'Noon, then, it's a date.' Julian winked at Phoebe and, tipping his hat rakishly, left her with a waft of Brylcreem in her nostrils and romance in her heart.

7

Julian Brooks had been packed off to a prep school on the south coast at the age of eight. He had been short for his age, and, being an only child, was shy and nervous around other children.

Amid the hustle and bustle of Victoria station he clutched his much-loved teddy bear tightly, weeping quietly as his mother, fair and pretty under her aigrette-feathered hat, bestowed a dry peck on his wet cheek, and bade him a fond farewell for the duration of the three-month autumn term.

In the railway carriage with five other sniffling eight-year-olds all trying to control their misery, an equally sad Julian gazed unseeingly at the damp Sussex countryside while the train sped on.

With the exception of his austere mother, women were rather a mystery to Julian. His father had been killed at Arles in 1917, two months before Julian was born, and his mother and nanny had taken sole charge of him since his birth. He had been deprived of the companionship of an adult male and was terrified at the idea of living with over a hundred other boys. He wanted to be with his mother and his beloved nanny; he had dreaded going away to boarding school.

But school turned out to be much better than he'd expected. He found he could head off the teasing the boys gave him because of his lack of stature by making jokes about his height, sometimes even drawing attention to his shortness before they did and sending himself up about it. Soon he progressed to imitations – Charlie Chaplin, W. C. Fields, Buster Keaton, Harold Lloyd – regaling the dormitory each night with his impressions of these and other favourite stars, making his classmates laugh so loudly that Matron would bang on the door, issuing fierce threats.

When he was thirteen he was sent off to Eton College, where much against his will he developed a mad passion for Wilson Minor, who occupied the room next to his. Because of his strikingly beautiful face Julian was soon nicknamed Looks Brooks by the older prefects, a nickname which would stay with him for the rest of his life. He became much in demand as a 'fag', running errands, picking up jars of Marmite or honey from the village stores and delivering notes from the prefects to boys in other houses. Some of these boys of seventeen or eighteen made no secret of their desire to have Looks Brooks for themselves, but Julian always deflected their passes with a quip or a one-liner. He was popular in the rooms of the older boys at night, where he would happily perform turns from the cinema and music hall, and regale them with his vast repertoire of filthy jokes.

One hot day in June, Simon Gray, a tall, eighteen-year-old senior boy in Julian's house, who had been making unsuccessful passes at Julian for some time, sent him off to deliver a note to his current lover.

The boy's house was over two miles away, an exhausting run on a boiling hot afternoon. On the way, Julian sat down for a rest in the shade of a great Dutch elm, fanning himself with the envelope which soon came unstuck in the heat. Curiosity never having really killed the cat, he opened it, reading, to his horror: 'Darling boy, isn't Looks Brooks *divine*! And I've been having him regularly for the past six months! Maybe when we meet next Tuesday, we can both have him *together* . . . Eternally mad for you, Simon.'

Julian's heart jumped and he could feel a deep flush spreading over his face and neck. That he could be discussed like a cheap tart or a piece of meat came as an ugly shock. He and Wilson Minor always referred disparagingly to boys who 'did it' with each other as poofs or queers. That he should be thought of as 'one of those' was infuriating. Julian started worrying about his feelings towards his best friend. Although not exactly platonic, they never spoke of their mutual attraction or their love for each other; it was a 'manly relationship', but one that now, obviously, had to end or Julian would be thought of as a poof. He couldn't bear that, not to mention the fact that the shame would probably kill his mother.

Wilson was as blond, blue-eyed and delicately skinned as Julian was dark, heavy-lidded and exotic-looking. They had, of course, experimented sexually with each other, as most boys had at English public schools. The odd, unspoken fumble or mutual masturbation when too much beer or Pimm's had been drunk was never to be discussed by the light of day. But a poof? Him? Julian Looks Brooks – never in a million years! He would rather die than have people think that of him.

Twenty minutes later, as Simon's lover read his note, Julian saw a look of sly interest creep across his face. Licking his lips, the prefect examined the boy from head to toe with lascivious eyes, which made Julian's face blush the colour of poppies. Sauntering to his desk, the prefect penned a quick reply to his paramour. Julian naturally read it on the way home: 'He is certainly divine, darling, but I'd much rather have you. Next Tuesday *comme toujours* – eternally yours.'

From then on, Julian became the most sports-mad boy at school and even more of a clown. Although he adored his best friend Wilson, he felt somehow that these feelings were wrong, so he ended the relationship abruptly, much to Wilson's stunned unhappiness. Every holiday he arranged to spend with boys whom he knew had sisters and female cousins, and at fourteen he started on his magical primrose path of the seduction of the fairer sex. Since he suddenly grew several inches in height between the ages of fourteen and fifteen, he had little difficulty in persuading even the most virginal and blushing of damsels to allow him at least a discreet kiss. From then on, such was his sex appeal that it was usually easy to persuade them to go even further.

When he was twenty he had the distinction of being not only the most handsome boy at the Royal Academy of Dramatic Art, but also the finest actor, easily the most popular student, and the man who had the most success with women.

At twenty-one he went into a repertory company where he deliberately and systematically seduced every female in the company whether she was young or old, pretty or pretty ugly.

He loved sex. He liked to prove himself, adored feeling his masculinity conquering the weaker sex. He learned everything he possibly could about women. Seducing them was too easy. His looks were so arresting that with just a little smooth chat any chickie could be cajoled into the feathers before she even knew what was

47

happening. Julian excelled at the superfuck. He flew his conquests to the moon and back again on a surging sea of sexual rapture which none of them had ever experienced before. He was a true Don Juan, the peerless romantic Romeo, Casanova in corduroy trousers. Irresistible to women, he would go to any lengths to ignite them, to make them his for ever.

Phoebe had little difficulty in arranging an audition for Julian. After all, her uncle was one of the Vivienne Van Damm's major shareholders. (Indeed, this was how she had obtained her own job, despite having limited experience in singing or dancing.) The Windmill Theatre was short on smart young comics with a clever patter and genuinely good jokes. The servicemen, who all loved to watch the long-legged, full-bosomed Windmill Girls dance, preen and posture, also wanted to hear raunchy, dirty, close to the knuckle humour, delivered by someone who wasn't their fathers' age.

Julian was very funny. His repertoire of jokes ranged from droll, dry, almost too subtle humour to those which were so incredibly and disgustingly filthy that some of the younger soldiers were quite shocked.

Julian and Phoebe lost no time in slipping between the sheets together. Phoebe was considered fast. At twenty-three she had enjoyed at least a dozen affairs and she was uninhibited and natural in her lovemaking. Men were to be toyed with, to be enjoyed, and Phoebe enjoyed them well and often.

As for Julian, he soon realized he had fallen into a pot of honey. Although his chosen profession was acting, he had not had a legitimate theatre role since leaving Maidstone Rep. Despite this he was convinced, as indeed was Phoebe, that his day as a leading man would eventually dawn. Until then he was happy to be the resident comedian at the Windmill all day and to share Phoebe's cosy bed all night. He allowed her to think that he had fallen in love with her. He knew that was what all girls wanted to believe, although he himself had never managed to fall in love with anyone for longer than a week. He had happily fucked his way through RADA and rep and although now apparently settled, he still managed discreetly to seduce almost all the girls at the Windmill whilst still living with Phoebe. This was further tribute to his palpable sex appeal, spellbinding charm and expert manipulation of the female sex.

Everyone thought Phoebe was the perfect mate for Julian. They shared a similar sense of humour, and possessed ambition. When Phoebe suspected Julian of bedding her friends and co-workers, she wasn't prone to bouts of jealous nagging like all his previous girlfriends. She just looked the other way, pretending not to see. Her mother had given her that piece of valuable advice. Their love-making was a source of delight and, despite the war, they enjoyed their life together immensely.

Yes, they were a good couple, well suited. Everyone said so. Perhaps Julian should marry her.

8

Hydra, Greece 1944

He was hungry, terribly hungry, but Nikolas couldn't remember when he hadn't been hungry. His body was pitifully thin, the flesh drawn tightly across his olive-skinned cheekbones, his stomach was concave and his ribs showed through his only shirt.

He was standing on a parched grassy hill high up on the island of Hydra while the black-robed priest droned on and on. The sea was a dark blue mirror, and the Peleponnese Mountains of the Greek mainland just a smoky haze in the distance. The body of the last of his sisters was being laid to rest in her pathetic grave. His mother leaned heavily on him, her thin frame draped in black, her eyes reddened by endless tears.

But Nikolas Stanopolis would not cry. At sixteen he was the head of the family. It had been less than a year since his father had been executed along with eight other Greek fishermen who had been accused of aiding and abetting the partisans in the mountains. Nikolas would never forget that terrible day.

Down in the port where a few fishing boats bobbed lazily, pulling gently at their moorings, he had watched a group of men in the centre of the square being savagely beaten with rifle butts until their faces became pulp. The entire population of Hydra had been forced to watch them beaten and then shot. What made the event even more horrible was that the Italian soldiers who had carried out this atrocity and many others seemed to derive brutal satisfaction from seeing these wretched men die. The soldiers joked with each other, cheered and laughed as their prisoners screamed in agony.

Silently, in a ragged circle, the population of Hydra had stood watching. There were three hundred or so black-shawled women, the young almost indistinguishable from the old, so wizened and

51

weak were they from lack of food and the cruel deprivations of the island's occupation. A few puny children scampered about, even the horrors of war powerless to suppress their antics. A dozen adolescents stood transfixed with horror, and a handful of toothless old people shook their wrinkled heads as they watched yet another execution with a stoicism born of longevity and passive resistance.

Nikolas had clasped his arms around his mother, trying to give her support and comfort as she leaned against him, burdened with grief. His mother was thirty-four but looked more like sixty – worn out with fear and the torment of watching her children suffer and die. At her breast was the youngest of her brood, a little girl who weighed no more than twelve pounds though she was nearly a year old. The nourishment she received from Melina's shrivelled breasts would not be enough to sustain her for much longer.

There was hardly any food left in the village. No goats, no pigs, not even any donkeys – the villagers survived only on what they were allowed to forage from the sea.

Within a year, Nikolas' last brother and sister would die slowly and painfully, along with almost a third of the island's children.

The Hydriots were a simple but proud race, used to hard work, and their island had given them a good living for several hundred years. Such was the determination and resilience of its inhabitants that Hydra was the only Greek island which had never before fallen to an enemy. Even the Turks had found it impossible to conquer a hundred years earlier.

The Germans had stolen all the available food to feed their armies fighting in the Afrika Korps. Crops were seized, sheep and goats slaughtered, olive groves and orchards laid waste. The Nazis had battles to fight, and little or no feeling for starving women and children.

When the Germans left in 1941 the Italian army came to garrison Hydra. As it was considered a backwater post – it was eleven miles long and sparsely populated – the dregs of the Italian army were sent. Louts from Calabria, Sicily and Naples who could barely read before the war issued orders, made rules and used their tyrannical power to instil more terror in the islanders than the Germans had ever done.

Benito Mussolini was their revered leader and their idol. No matter that he was so self-conscious of his puny height that he insisted in all official photographs that he be photographed from below, every halfwit in the Italian army blindly worshipped Il Duce.

Nikolas' thoughts of his father's terrible death were interrupted by a chilling shriek from his mother. Her baby's pathetic little coffin was placed in the grave and she slid to the ground in a spasm of grief. Melina's worry beads slipped from her feeble grasp as the priest gravely offered her a shovel to sprinkle the first spadeful of dry earth on to the tiny driftwood box.

Wailing in sympathy, three women helped the weeping Melina back to her feet. The priest's voice droned on, ignoring the women's sobs. He had become so conditioned to grief that he was almost immune to the agony of his starving villagers. He couldn't count the number of children he had buried in the past two years. The poor Stanopolis woman had lost four as well as her husband. But at least she still had the boy, and at sixteen, although painfully thin, he was tall and had the resilience of youth. At least Melina had someone to depend on: recognizing the look of defiance in his face, the priest felt instinctively that the boy would survive. He brought the simple service to a close, and watched as his congregation shuffled away.

Almost doubled up with grief, Melina, escorted by the three women and Nikolas, slowly made her way to the sanctuary of the cool stone walls of her little hilltop house. The small group of mourners climbed the steep cobblestone steps of the narrow winding street, and one by one entered the shuttered darkness of the Stanopolis house. The women fussed over Melina while Nikolas went to his room, his eyes prickling with the stinging tears he had tried so desperately not to allow his mother to see.

Opening up the chipped blue shutters, oblivious to the beauty of the olive and almond trees which grew outside his window, he thought of vengeance. Vengeance on the Germans, vengeance on the Italians. But most of all, vengeance on the commanding officer of the Italian garrison, the fat pig who now ruled Hydra without justice and without mercy, and whom the locals called 'Gourouni'.

Nikolas fidgeted fiercely with his mother's translucent yellow worry beads which he'd picked up at the graveside, passing them back and forth between his fingers. He leaned out to gaze at the highest point of the island, where all the glorious eighteenth-century mansions stood, built by rich ship-owners. Gourouni had chosen the most beautiful and imposing of them to be his official residence.

He was the undoubted cause of the recent crop of executions, the cause of the deaths of Nikolas' father, his brothers and sisters. Nikolas thought him filthy, depraved, corrupt scum, a travesty of Mussolini. All of the villagers silently mocked the squat fat figure as he preened and postured in his ludicrous musical-comedy uniforms thickly encrusted with gold braid, glinting with stolen medals.

In his exquisite neoclassical villa, set in lush gardens of grape, olive and pine trees, was the plunder from a dozen of the wealthiest Hydriot mansions, and from the fabled temples of the surrounding islands of Spetsai and Aegina. Rare paintings, tapestries, sculptures and eighteenth-century furniture which would hardly have been out of place in Versailles filled the villa which he proudly believed to be the finest in all Greece. Some of the luckiest villagers were employed as gardeners, cooks and housemaids.

Elektra Makopolis was one of the latter. Exactly the same age as Nikolas, she had lived next door to him all their lives. Occasionally she managed to smuggle a loaf of bread or some fruit or cooked meat out of the Commander's fortress. She would share anything she pilfered with the Stanopolis family, as there was no one left of her own. Her father had been deported to a labour camp by the Germans, and soon afterwards her mother had starved to death. A young Italian lieutenant with a grain of sympathy in his heart heard about the wretched girl's predicament and found her a job in 'the Palace' where she worked hard polishing marble, cleaning furniture and scrubbing floors. Everything Elektra knew about the Palace she had described to Nikolas in minute detail. Every atrocity which she saw committed by Gourouni she reported to him . . .

There was a faint tap at his bedroom door and Elektra appeared.

'Nikolas,' she whispered, 'I've brought you some cake and coffee.'

Coffee! How had she managed to find coffee? Nikolas didn't want to ask. She had stolen it from Gourouni's villa, knowing full well the penalty if she were ever found out. He swallowed the bitter liquid and wolfed down the delicious honey cake greedily.

The two of them leaned out of the window and Elektra ran a hand through Nikolas' untidy curls. He tried to muster a smile. He loved her and she loved him. It was all very simple. Both their families had known for years that one day they would be united by the marriage of Nikolas and Elektra, and now it was inevitable.

'He showed a movie last night,' whispered Elektra. 'Some of us sneaked into the projection booth to watch it. Oh, Nikolas!' Her lovely young face glowed with excitement. 'It was so wonderful – you cannot believe what an exciting film it was. American, of course, with a wonderful little girl with ringlets who sang and danced. She was tiny, maybe six or seven years old – but so clever, and so pretty. I wish you could have seen it, Nikolas, you would have loved it – I know how much you love movies.'

Nikolas was passionate about films. Before the war, he had gone to the open-air cinema to watch his idols. He was mesmerized by the brilliance of film directors like Alfred Hitchcock and John Ford, and he studied their techniques, returning time after time to see their work.

But there were no longer any film performances for the villagers. Now the only place movies were shown was up at the Palace where Gourouni somehow always managed to procure the latest offerings from Hollywood.

Elektra looked at Nikolas. His eyes were riveted on the Commander's citadel: it seemed to glow with a fiery light as the late-afternoon sun reddened its white marble walls to the colour of blood, and the hated Italian flag flapped gently in the faint breeze.

They both thought of the toad-like creature who now inhabited the house. A sadist who regularly sent innocents to their deaths, who tortured men for pleasure, all the while accumulating the spoils of war.

'He's probably busy stuffing his ugly face.' Nikolas' voice was full of hatred. 'Guzzling meat and wine, thinking about which movie he'll show tonight. He's a murdering monster. He shouldn't be allowed to live.'

'Nikolas, guess who made the film?' Elektra tried to change the subject. When Nikolas started talking about Gourouni, it was difficult to get him to stop. He seemed to have an obsession about the man. 'My American uncle, you remember him? The one who went to America years ago, before we were born – the one who has done so well.' Her face beamed with pride. In the past, her mother had often talked of her eldest brother, the brash young man who was always so ambitious, so determined to leave Greece, to succeed in the new country, and who had finally triumphed there.

'Spyros!' she said proudly. 'Spyros Makopolis. I recognized his name at the beginning of the film. It was in *huge* letters – "Produced by Spyros Makopolis". Isn't that wonderful?' Her smile was radiant. 'He's from Hydra, Nikolas, and he produces films in Hollywood.' She leaned towards him, fingers gently stroking his face. 'If he can do it, Nikolas – so can you.'

'One day – if ever this war is over – we will both go to Hollywood and I will make such wonderful films that the whole world will want to see them,' said Nikolas bitterly. 'But not before that sadistic pig is dead.' His voice rose in passionate rage and he looked again towards the mansion and thought of the destruction of Gourouni, and how only fools underestimate the pride of the Greeks.

It had been a convivial evening. The film, the latest offering from the MCCP studio, was excellent, and the female star was a ravishing creature, blonde and ripe, who looked no more than eighteen. Both the Commander and his aide de camp, Major Volpi, found her so appealing that thoughts of her juicy charms lingered pleasurably.

The wine had been excellent. A Château Lafitte 29, two cases of which had been discovered last week in the cellar of one of the Hydriot mansions.

The Commander stretched and yawned as he unbuttoned the gold buttons of his skin-tight blue uniform. He admired his reflection in the narrow eighteenth-century gilded mirror which was hung on his dressing room wall in the most flattering light. He was a *bella figura*, no doubt about that. His resemblance to his idol Mussolini seemed to be increasing, particularly now that he had completely shaved his head and always copied Il Duce's latest uniforms in the most painstaking detail. The one he now wore was impressive, of the finest gaberdine, one of many made for him by a good Greek tailor on the island.

Never mind that the uniform he should be wearing as Commander of Hydra was a drab grey. The stupid villagers knew no better, and as for his soldiers, with the exception of Volpi whose palms were more than well greased with silver, they were a bunch of dolts.

The Commander undid the heavy gold buckle of his wide leather belt, then took off his jacket and shirt and tossed them on to a brocade-covered Jacobean bergère.

The dim peach lamp on the armoire illuminated his face and torso with a soft flattering glow. He smiled at his reflection admiringly, his small eyes almost disappearing into the pads of fat surrounding them. The bald bullet head, sensual lips and strong chin were pleasing to him, as were the hirsute barrel chest and thickly muscled forearms.

The only thing about his physical appearance that didn't please him was the thick keloid scar that traversed the base of his adam's apple in a clean three-inch line. He always attempted to conceal it with his high-necked uniforms. The rumour on Hydra was that someone had tried to kill him, that he had hovered between life and death in some Paris hospital for several weeks, and only the attentions of the finest throat specialist in France had saved his life and his larynx. Now he could talk only in a harsh, rasping whisper, which further added to his terrifying demeanour.

He fingered the scar gingerly. They had never found the girl who had slashed his throat with his own razor and left him for dead on the cold marble floor of his bathroom.

He had survived that bitch's murderous attempt only by his overwhelming physical strength and will to live. But even though the throat surgeon had done a brilliant job in saving both his life and his voice, Umberto Scrofo would never be satisfied until he found the girl who had almost killed him, and paid her back for her crime.

9

Nikolas leaned his head against the whitewashed stone wall of the tiny balcony and sobbed. His beloved mother, the last family link he had left, was dying, withered by starvation, her heart broken.

Melina lay on her bed, weakly fingering her rosary, mumbling over and over again the names of her dead husband and children. She had simply lost the will to live. The light had gone out of her warm brown eyes, leaving them expressionless and dead, and she weighed less than ninety pounds. Two of the village women attended her, their faces stoic masks of suffering. She had even refused to eat the small fish which Nikolas had managed to catch by spending some fourteen soul-destroying hours in his boat.

Nikolas was in total despair, his mind numbed by misery and privation. All he could do was fish, and pray that his mother wouldn't die. He went back into his room and opened the drawer next to his bed. From beneath a meagre pile of shirts and socks, he took out his knife. It was in a brown leather sheath, shiny and new. He had found it yesterday as he was cleaning his nets on the beach. One of the soldiers had obviously dropped it and Nick had quickly put it in his pocket, hoping he was unobserved.

Now he slowly pulled the shining blade out of the holder and watched the dying moon's reflection shimmer on the polished steel. He ran a thumb gingerly down the cutting edge, feeling the sharpness of it. How he would love to plunge this blade into Gourouni's fat stomach and wrench it until his entrails spilled on to the ground like a gutted fish's.

Nikolas knew he would take great satisfaction in watching that sadistic swine wriggle in his death agonies. He imagined the Italian's face contorted in agony, pleading for help, but he was interrupted in his fantasy by the sound of his mother weakly calling his name. Quickly replacing the knife in its hiding place he ran downstairs to kiss her and to bid her a tender goodbye. It was time to fish now, to catch the only sustenance left for them.

He strode purposefully down to the harbour, his thoughts still full of Gourouni.

Although it was not yet five in the morning there was a bustle of activity in the tiny fishing port. Nine or ten fishermen, all either under sixteen or over sixty-five, were carefully arranging their yellow and cream nets in the bows of their boats, preparing their lines for today's catch. The bare bulbs in Dmitri's beach bar glowed yellow, giving a jaundiced look to the hard faces of the Italian guards who lounged about, paying no attention to the fishermen, thinking only of when their watches would end. Some looked so drunk that there was little chance of their protecting anything should the Allies have picked that moment to invade Hydra. But there was no likelihood of that. The Allies had no strategic interest at all in the remote little island. Dmitri gave Nikolas a friendly '*Yassou*' as he poured him a small cup of thick, sweet coffee and pushed a tiny piece of honeyed baklava across the counter. The boy drank and ate gratefully, pleased that Dmitri always managed to have coffee and cake in his bar. In return, he hoped to bring Dmitri some *pompano*, red mullet or sea bass, although the fish had not been jumping recently. Even at the nearby islands of Mykonos, Spetsai and Poros, it was as if all sea life knew there was a war on and wanted no part of it.

Dmitri leaned conspiratorially towards Nikolas, with a glance at one of the snoring Italians.

'I listened to the wireless last night,' he whispered, making a great show of wiping some glasses with a grubby rag. 'It's going to all be over soon, Nikolas, very, very soon.'

One of the sleeping soldiers gave a loud snore which made Nikolas jump nervously.

'They say it's only a matter of weeks before the war is over. And they say that the Allies will win for sure. They've really got the Boche going now.'

The boy drained the dregs of his coffee. 'It's incredible news, Dmitri, I hope it's true.'

'It's true,' whispered Dmitri excitedly. 'Believe me, Nikolas, it's true. The Allies have got these pigs on the run. Keep your fingers crossed, Nikolas – maybe this time next week we'll be free, we'll have our island back again.'

Nikolas nodded his thanks to Dmitri with an excited conspiratorial smile, and set off to fish, feeling more lighthearted than he had for months. Soon the war would be over and the Hydriots would be rid of their murdering oppressors. It would be time for the villagers to forget. But Nikolas knew he could never forget his hatred for the Commander.

Umberto Scrofo read the terse orders on an official paper which had arrived during the night by messenger from his commanding officer.

Propped up in his heavily carved venetian bed between the finest linen sheets to be found in all Greece, he was surrounded by old master paintings of erotic scenes. A richly coloured tapestry had been draped carelessly over an elaborate Henri Jacob daybed against one wall, and a set of four magnificent sculptures – which might have been by the hand of Michelangelo himself – lurked in the shadows of the four corners of the room.

But this particular morning Scrofo derived none of his usual pleasure from any of them.

As soon as he read the message he leaped furiously from his bed on to the pale aubusson carpet, mouthing profanities at the hapless officer who had brought him both the message and his chamber pot. He aimed into the delicately painted receptacle, held in the trembling hands of the young lieutenant, while launching into another wildly vituperative verbal attack. The scar on his neck throbbed as it always did whenever he was angry. He bounced around in his short silk nightshirt so much that the unfortunate youth could barely manage to keep the pot under the General's Lilliputian organ.

Barking out orders in his rasping voice, Scrofo darted about his bedroom, flinging objects into gaping leather bags which had miraculously appeared, wrapping precious artefacts and bronzes in thick velvet cloths, helped by a handful of clumsy grey-uniformed soldiers.

The message received that morning had galvanized him into a

vindictive rampage. So he was supposed to evacuate the island immediately, was he? And leave behind all the priceless booty which he had so painstakingly collected? He would see about that! He wasn't going to leave any of his treasures on this pitiful excuse of an island.

Squeezing into a black uniform which had grown too tight with the many months of excess, and pinning on as many medals as time permitted, he clattered down the marble staircase.

'I want every last one of the islanders here at once,' he barked in his strange croaking voice to Major Volpi. 'Go into the village and round them all up now. Every man, woman and child.'

'Very well, sir,' said Volpi, saluting smartly while privately thinking what an oaf this general was. But who was he to cast stones? Before the war he had been in prison for murder, now he was a favoured citizen.

'The sick ones too?' he inquired.

'Every one of them,' snarled Scrofo. 'Every single one of the inhabitants.'

He paced feverishly around the magnificent villa admiring and appraising the pictures, statues and furniture which filled the place, taking mental stock. It seemed to him that his plunder was smiling at him in a most pleasing way, bathed as it was in the gentle morning sunshine. Peerless treasures of only the highest quality – all his, all stolen. His dream had been eventually to take his treasures back to Italy, and once ensconced there he would become a respectable *antiquaire*, selling beautiful things to collectors and competing with the best art dealers of London, New York and Paris. That dream would now be shattered unless he could get everything packed, crated and transported down the three hundred or so cobbled steps to the harbour at once. His plan was to load them on to a hidden pleasure yacht, sail over to Albania, and from there, on to Italy. He would take only four trusted accomplices with him whose pockets had already been well lined with gold bullion. And he was well prepared. Up from the cellar came wooden crates, cartons and great quantities of packing materials. At once his troops set to work, wrapping and crating the pictures and sculptures as fast as they could.

Soon the villagers arrived. Small children, old men and frail women were divided into makeshift working groups to pack up Gourouni's loot.

Melina had been pulled from her sickbed by a posse of soldiers. Now, almost too weak to walk, helped by the devoted Elektra, she was commanded by Volpi to wrap a collection of exquisite enamel and gold Fabergé eggs. Even in their weakened and dazed state, the women were stunned by the beauty of the jewelled snuff boxes, the richly gilded and inlaid furniture, the brilliant colours of the eighteenth-century paintings and the golden flesh tones of the Rembrandts.

Melina's eyes were so clouded that she could hardly see. Her hands were trembling so badly that it was practically impossible for her to hold on to anything. The soldiers moved among the women, yelling at them, giving them a sharp punch if they didn't seem to be working fast enough. The frightened children had been given the task of crating up Scrofo's collection of extremely rare first editions of Dante, Goethe, Shakespeare, Schiller and Tolstoy, and the little ones stumbled about with frightened eyes as they tried to handle the volumes without damaging them.

Suddenly with a startled cry, Melina let slip a crystal egg encrusted with seed pearls and precious stones. With a noise like a gunshot the priceless treasure shattered on the marble floor.

Everyone stopped what they were doing, to stare at the wretched woman. Melina's eyes were so glazed with despair and fever that she felt no fear as the dreaded Gourouni approached her.

'Do you see what you've done, you stupid idiot!' he rasped, his face scarlet with fury. 'Idiot. *Idiot! IDIOT!*' He cracked his pistol down on to her skull with the full force of his rage. She felt no pain as blood coursed down her waxen face. She felt nothing as she lay in a crumpled heap and the enraged Scrofo rained down blow after blow on her face and head.

'Back to work,' Scrofo grated as terrified children ran crying to hide under their mothers' skirts. 'Back to work or you'll suffer the same fate. And no one had better break anything else.'

Some of the villagers crossed themselves while several people moaned quietly or openly wept. Quietly Elektra asked permission to remove Melina's body and Volpi nodded a curt affirmative. She wrapped the pititful, wasted shape in her long black shawl and two other women helped her to take Melina out into the bright sunshine, where with tear-stained faces they laid her gently down in the cobbled courtyard.

When Nikolas returned to the harbour at sundown he was pleased with his catch. It was the best for a long time – almost half a kilo of whitebait, several red mullet and a couple of plump *pompano*. They would have a feast tonight. Dmitri was sure to give him some olive oil and some potatoes and tomatoes, maybe even a small bottle of wine in exchange for a few fish. He, Elektra and his mother could then celebrate the imminent end of their island's occupation.

As he hauled his boat up the pebbled beach, a weeping black-shawled Elektra, her long hair ruffled by the breeze, ran to him and threw herself into his arms.

'Nikolas, oh, Nikolas, I'm so sorry.'

'Sorry – for what? What is it, Elektra?' He was suddenly apprehensive. Elektra was usually such a strong, resilient girl. Toughened by the harsh life of the island, she retained an innate gentleness which inspired devotion in all who knew her.

Sobbing quietly into Nikolas' shoulder, she told him of his mother's death.

Nikolas' face hardened. He had known his mother could not survive much longer, but the war was nearly over – surely then she would have recovered? He tried hard not to weep. He would never forgive Gourouni for this – never.

'Where are all the soldiers now?' he asked harshly.

'Gone. Every last one of them. They sailed this afternoon. We burned their flag when they left,' she told him. 'All of their flags.'

'Did the bastards murder anyone else before they left?' Nikolas asked as Dmitri came out of his bar bringing him a glass of brandy.

Dmitri put his arms around Nikolas, trying to comfort the boy whom he loved like a son.

'No,' Elektra said gently, her hand stroking Nikolas' cheek. 'No one else.'

Nikolas drained his brandy, the unfamiliar burning sensation fuelling him with unaccustomed power. Seeing the forlorn faces of his friends, he was filled with such anger that his skin became suffused with a red glow. The fury that he felt almost had a life of its own. He needed to kill. He wanted to plunge his knife into the Italian pigs, killing them all, but especially he wanted to put his hands around the throat of that diabolical Commander and squeeze the life out of him. He wanted to watch him die before his eyes. Wanted to hear his fat lips beg for mercy. As he felt the knife in his pocket, Nikolas knew he had the power of death in his fingers and knew too that his hatred would eventually give him strength to do what he had to do.

'One day – one day – one day,' he muttered harshly, fingering at his mother's worry beads furiously as though they were the tendons of his enemy's neck. 'I'll kill him if it's the last thing I do in my life. I shall find that murdering bastard and make him suffer more than he ever dreamed possible. By the time I have finished with Commander Umberto Scrofo, he'll be begging me to kill him, I swear it.'

London 1944

Inès was perfectly content living in London, although she missed her beloved Paris. The tiny flat in Shepherd Market on the top floor of an old Georgian house was cosy, and its leaded glass windows trapped every ray of the pale London sunshine. Often she sat on the window seat, looking out over the tops of the plane trees in Green Park, her mind far away, thinking about Paris. Were the Gestapo still searching for her? The nightmares about the dead Italian General still disturbed her sleep, but Yves' arms were always there in the night to soothe her fears when she would wake screaming and drenched in sweat, and in the morning he would make her laugh again with some of his magic.

Yves kept up with news of the French occupation through the newspapers and wireless while Inès devoted herself to mastering the English language and keeping house for him. She would spend her mornings trying to buy food with ration books which allowed them only the barest essentials. Casseroles were hard to make with four ounces of meat, and it was impossible even for a French girl to make an omelette for two with just one egg.

Yves had contacted some of the names he'd been given, intent on building himself a new life in London. He was often out all day, while Inès listened to the wireless and sang as she cleaned and dusted the flat, relishing her new domestic role. For the first time in her life, she was living a normal existence and she worshipped Yves more than ever.

She struck up a friendship with Stella Bates, a redheaded girl who lived on the floor below. Often they would shop together, carrying their string bags in search of groceries, sugar, butter or jam – all commodities in short supply and for which coupons from their ration books were necessary. Stella regaled Inès with amusing stories of her life. She was a successful prostitute, with few qualms about her profession. A couple of years older than Inès, she had an attractive body and a flaming halo of red hair which ensured that she rarely spent her evenings alone. She was also very funny and even Yves was amused by her cockney repartee.

He had recently brought up the matter of Inès' returning to 'work', a subject she hated to discuss. She didn't want to be a prostitute any more. Her intense love for Yves made the thought of being with another man an anathema, and the experience in Paris was still far too vivid. But Yves was becoming more insistent. Money was always short, they had rent to pay. He couldn't make enough on the black market to keep them both, and he wasn't qualified for anything but menial work or his clever tricks.

'I'm not good enough for the music halls, *chérie*,' he laughed. 'It's up to you to start making some money for us.' But Inès resisted for as long as possible, hoping against hope that Yves would get some sort of job, maybe even marry her, so that they could continue this proper life that she was enjoying so much.

Eventually Yves convinced her that she must become the breadwinner so she confided most of her life story to Stella, without mentioning that she had killed a man. Stella gave her good advice.

'It's time to stop trollin' the streets, darlin', you're much too classy for that. I've got a really nice, exclusive clientele now, duckie – references only – so, just give me the word and I'll fix you up with one of my classy titled gents. No kinky stuff, I promise you.'

Inès grimaced, but Yves was hungry and demanding. She had no choice but to become a whore again. But at least this time it would be with 'gentlemen', not enemy louts.

London was swarming with servicemen of all nationalities and a party mood prevailed. Even though the Blitz continued as the German bombs hit their targets with monotonous regularity, London's night clubs still had a carnival atmosphere which made people forget that a war was going on. The favourite haunt of the party-goers, the Café de Paris, had sustained a direct hit the previous year, killing at least forty revellers, but the wartime festivities continued unabated.

The following night Stella invited Inès to a night club with her. 'I've got a date with a very nice gent an' a couple of friends of 'is, and they're anxious to make whoopee, luv – so come with us, we'll have a lovely time, I promise.'

Inès reluctantly told Yves who insisted that she go.

'You must start working, *chérie*,' he said heatedly. 'We need the money.'

'I know,' said Inès gloomily. 'Oh Yves, how much longer will I have to do this? I hate it.'

'Not much longer, *chérie*,' smiled Yves, stroking her luxuriant hair and nuzzling into her neck in the way that always gave her excited shivers. 'When the war is over we will be able to go back to Paris, I will get a job there, I promise you. Now be a good girl and get some good clients tonight.'

After dressing carefully in her one good black dress, ruffled off-the-shoulder and with a wide belt which accentuated her narrow waist, Inès stood balanced on the tiny kitchen table while Stella first painted her bare legs with dark pancake and then carefully drew a line down the back of her calves with a stub of eyebrow pencil.

'There,' chuckled the redhead when she'd finished, pleased with her handiwork. 'Now duckie, if you can get a hold of one of these Yanks you won't 'ave to do this any more – it'll be nylons, nylons, nylons all over the bleedin' place, not to mention chockies and cigarettes and all sorts of lovely goodies. But tonight we concentrate on the toffs.'

'OK,' said Inès gloomily. 'You're the boss, Stella.'

The Bagatelle was in a gala mood, packed with revellers. As Inès followed Stella she admired the baroque decor of the fashionable night club.

A wide red-carpeted staircase swept grandly into the bar, the walls of which were covered in great golden mirrors. On scarlet velvet chairs dozens of well-dressed vivacious young women sat engrossed in conversation and flirtation with a variety of men, many in uniform, some in black tie. Paul Adams' band was playing the catchy current hit tune, 'I Left my Heart at the Stage Door Canteen', and Inès felt her pulse beat faster to the rhythm of the music. She was suddenly quite excited to be on the town again. Her months in London had given her a passable command of English, which she was eager to practise, and in spite of her trepidation about the evening the animated atmosphere started to whet her appetite for a good time.

Stella's date was an educated, jovial titled man in his thirties, up from Shropshire and determined to paint the town red. Champagne flowed, and so did his jokes, which Inès found mostly incomprehensible but which had Stella bent double with hilarity. The club was dark and smoky and the tiny lights with their pink pleated shades on each table cast a flattering glow on everyone's face.

Stella was in top form, her cockney humour fired by the atmosphere, trading wisecracks with Lord Worthington, whispering to Inès that he was a real live lord. ''E's in some top position at the Foreign Office, a real toff,' she said when he went to greet some friends who had just arrived.

'And bloody generous 'e is, too, luv – gave me a tenner extra last night, and sent me over a pound of bacon and a pair of nylons this morning – look!'

Proudly she extended her slender legs for Inès to admire the new nylon stockings.

'Ssh, 'ere 'e comes,' warned Stella as Lord Worthington returned with two younger men in tow.

'I've brought over a couple of chums, my dear. I hope you don't mind if they join us – Charlie and Benjie. Introduce your friend, will you, old girl? I'm off for a pee.'

Charlie, who was short and plump, turned out to be the Honourable Charles Brougham, and Benjie, who was tall and skinny, was Viscount Benjamin Spencer-Monckton. The two young men ensconced themselves on either side of Inès, both seemingly spellbound by her cleavage.

'What a splendid accent you have,' murmured Charles, his hand brushing against her knee, his eyes on her chest.

'Yes, it's absolutely spiffing. French, are you?' said Benjie.

'Yes.' Inès smiled demurely, not altogether displeased by the young men's interest in her. Lord Worthington had now returned and was howling with laughter at another of Stella's bawdy jokes. Inès thought her two titled admirers were not bad-looking in a bland

English way, attentive and well mannered, even though both were quite drunk. They were infinitely preferable to the portly pomposity of Lord Worthington.

'Would you care to dance?' Benjie asked as the band began 'Moonlight Becomes You'.

'I'd love to,' smiled Inès. 'I haven't danced in a very long time.'

As they wended their way through the throng of swaying bodies Inès suddenly stopped dead in her tracks, an all too familiar fear gripping her. She shook her head as if to dismiss the hallucination. Surely it couldn't be? It simply couldn't. Benjie was pushing her politely to move on, and she edged past the man's table with mounting dread.

Cold black eyes met hers for an instant, and she froze again. How could he be here in the Bagatelle in London when almost a year ago in Paris she had killed him? What was Umberto Scrofo doing in London? An Italian General from Mussolini's army sitting at a ringside table as bold as brass, with a bottle of champagne in front of him and flanked by two young blonde hookers. It was impossible.

But there was no mistaking the tiny vicious eyes, that huge bald head, the cruel mouth. Mesmerized, she stood before his table unable to move a muscle. The man's eyes caressed her body for a second, then swivelled back to the two blondes, and Inès was swept into the middle of the packed dance floor, trembling violently as Benjie took her in his arms.

'Are you all right, old thing?' he asked solicitously. 'You're shaking like a leaf. You look like you've just seen a ghost.'

'I think I have,' Inès whispered, holding on to him tightly, willing her heart to stop beating so wildly. She looked over again at the table where she thought she'd spotted Scrofo. A fat, bald man was sitting there, shoulder to shoulder with two buxom blondes, but it certainly wasn't Umberto Scrofo, of that she was now absolutely positive. She laughed out loud, a great burst of hysterical relieved laughter. How stupid she was, what a silly fool, with her fertile imagination. Of course it couldn't have been Scrofo – he was dead. But in those horrific dreams which haunted her subconscious so many nights, he was very much alive. She could still clearly recall every last detail of the grotesque Italian, and just glimpsing a man with similar features or a similar shape was enough to plunge her into a turmoil of fear and anxiety. Inès knew very well that her imagination had always been too vivid for her own good and she breathed a great sigh of relief that it had been no more than her fancy which had conjured him up. Scrofo was dead and gone – for ever – and that was that.

As the waves of panic subsided and the orchestra started to play the romantic 'Bewitched, Bothered and Bewildered', she decided to concentrate her attentions on Benjie's erect penis which was begging for notice as it prodded insistently against her thigh. She smiled up at him, slyly acknowledging it, and his pale, almost transparent grey eyes, fringed with sandy lashes, looked away from her shyly as he blushed.

Poor bashful man, she thought sympathetically. He was obviously unused to being in such close proximity to a woman. To make him feel more at ease she rested her head lightly on his shoulder and placed her hand gently on the back of his neck as the romantic music washed over them. She started singing, 'I'm wild again – beguiled again, a simpering, whimpering child again – bewitched, bothered and bewildered by you'.

Benjie's breathing became more erratic and as the dance ended, he bent his sandy head to hers, whispering self-consciously, 'May I see you again, Inès? I know it's a bit of an imposition because you've probably got a boyfriend and all that, but I do find you terribly attractive.'

Inès smiled. He was titled and rich, personable, from a good family. Yves had been telling her for weeks that she had to work again. This young man seemed kind, and cultured. If she had to continue her career as a prostitute, she could do a great deal worse than become the mistress of Viscount Benjamin Spencer-Monckton. After all, there was a war on.

Even though the war was at its harshest peak and nightly Blitzes were devastating London, Benjie took Inès on a social whirl such as she had never known before. Although he must have known she was a professional, he treated her like a girlfriend whom he wanted to woo. His manners were impeccable and Inès became caught up in the time of her life.

The night after they met he took her to a film at the Odeon
Leicester Square and then next door to his favourite night club, the
400, where he seemed to know everyone, and everyone knew him.
The intimate private club was jammed with young aristocrats and
society figures. Some of the men were in uniform, some in black tie,
a few of the more conservative even wore white tie. They were a
high-spirited, jolly crowd bent on merry-making, and Benjie and
Inès moved from group to group as he introduced her to his friends.
They were so young, these men, Inès thought. Babies, some of
them. No one could see there was any fear or trepidation in the
men's hearts by their behaviour. The abandoned pleasure-seeking
and frantic revelry made each night like a New Year's Eve spree.
Many of the young people at the 400 seemed madly in love, and
there was a great deal of petting and smooching on the congested
dance floor.

'More people get engaged here than anywhere else in London',
Benjie shouted to Inès, a twinkle in his pale eyes, as they danced to
the music from the new Broadway musical *Carousel*.

Benjie's elusive hardness started to poke again at Inès' thigh, and
she smiled up at him as she sang seductively, 'If I loved you, words
wouldn't come in an easy way'.

'Lovely,' breathed Benjie, holding her so close that his pro-
tuberance almost made her wince. 'You have a lovely voice, Inès, in
fact everything about you is lovely.'

'Thank you,' she smiled. 'You are very sweet, Benjie.'

The following night he took her to dinner at the Gay Hussar in
Greek Street, then to the Berkeley where they danced the night
away to Ian Stevens and his peppy music. As usual the place was
swarming with pleasure-seekers of every nationality. The band
played all of Inès' favourite tunes, and she hummed and sang some
of them to an enraptured Benjie. He particularly liked her version of
'This is a Lovely Way to Spend an Evening', and insisted that the
band play it several times.

Afterwards they walked home through Berkeley Square as the
birds were singing their morning song and the soft fingers of dawn
were creeping across the plane trees.

'Tomorrow?' he asked softly as they arrived at Shepherd Market.

'Yes,' she whispered, wondering when and if he was ever going to kiss her.

'We'll go to the Savoy with Charles and his girlfriend, Henrietta,' said Benjie. 'Black tie, I'll pick you up at eight.' With a dry kiss on her cheek he tipped his hat and walked away off towards Curzon Street.

'Well,' asked Yves sleepily from the bed as she came into his room. 'Has it happened yet?'

'Not yet,' sighed Inès, flopping on to the bed and into her lover's warm arms. 'Not yet, *chéri*. He's English, this may take a little more time than usual. I think he needs to get to know me first.'

'Hmph,' snorted Yves. 'He better hurry up. It's all right for you being wined and dined every night, but this poor Frenchman is starving to death. 'Oh *mon Dieu*, I would *kill* for a steaming cup of *café au lait* with three teaspoonfuls of sugar, and a hot croissant dripping with raspberry jam.'

'You'll just have to live on love,' teased Inès, kissing his lips. 'Until I break down Benjie's British reserve, love will have to do, my darling.'

Inès was running out of smart evening clothes. Indeed she was running out of any clothes at all. Her clothes cupboard, like their food cupboard, was practically bare, and she had so far worn the same second-hand black dress from Lanvin on every date with Benjie. In desperation she asked Stella if she could borrow something, and the girl threw open her wardrobe door for her friend.

'Whatever you like, luv – take anyfink.' She smiled generously. 'We're about the same size – 'cept I'm a few inches shorter an' a bit more flashy than you, luv.'

That was an understatement, thought Inès. Stella's wardrobe was crammed with brightly coloured frocks, decorated with all manner of sequins, buttons and bows.

'What about this?' Inès reached into the darker recesses of the cupboard and pulled out a pale grey crêpe dress, the bodice trimmed with gunmetal bugle beads.

'Ooh, that was me mum's!' shrilled Stella. ''Er only good frock it was, she got it from a lady she did a good turn for. It's a bit too drab

for me, dearie. It would look good on you though. So you can 'ave it –
it's a present.'

'Oh Stella, *thank* you,' cried Inès. 'You're the best friend I've ever
had in the whole world.'

Inès tried on the dress. It was the first full-length gown she had
ever worn, and it accentuated her height and slim curved hips. It was
bias-cut, with short puffed sleeves, and the skirt ended in a fan-
tailed pleat which Inès almost tripped over as she tried to walk across
the room.

'You'll 'ave to practise with that, luv,' laughed Stella. 'You'll look a
bit of a burk if you come a cropper on the dance floor in front of all
those la-di-das. You need some matching shoes too. C'mon, let's go
to Dolcis. For seventeen and six you can get a nice pair dyed to
match – it'll look such a lovely outfit then, an' I'll teach you how to
walk with the train.'

'But I haven't *got* seventeen and six,' wailed Inès. 'Stella, I don't
have more than a few shillings.'

'I'll treat you to the shoes,' grinned her friend. 'I've 'ad a very good
month, dear, thanks to the Hon. Charlie Boy – you can do the same
for me, dear, if I ever go through a dull period. Look out Oxford
Street – 'ere we come.'

Inès had enough clothes coupons in her ration book for the shoes
which Stella bought, and enough coupons left over for at least two
more dresses. She had only bought a few things since arriving in
England but although she had the precious coupons she had no
cash.

After their shopping trip Stella came to Inès' flat to inspect the
contents of her wardrobe.

'Oh dearie me, duckie, you'll never be successful on the game
wearin' that little lot,' she said disparagingly, flicking through Inès'
meagre supply of clothes. 'Tell you what, as soon as the Hon. Benjie
manages to get his noble pecker up, we'll go on a little shopping
spree, you and I – at least Yves can get you some clothing coupons on
the market, can't 'e?'

Inès nodded.

'Good,' said the redhead. 'Never forget, Inès my friend, money maketh the man, but clothes, my dear, most definitely maketh the girl.'

They dined at the Savoy Grill amid soft lights and the soothing melodic sounds of Carrol Gibbons' Orchestra. Like everywhere in London it was packed with eager diners and even more eager dancers. The five-course menu was delicious and Inès wished she could smuggle some leftovers to take to Yves.

'Damn good spread for five bob, don't you think, Charlie?' asked Benjie.

'Absolutely spiffing, old boy. Soup – fish – meat – sweet – savoury, excellent, just as it should be. Let's order a bottle of claret, shall we?'

Inès looked around. She felt ill at ease with Henrietta, a debutante from a titled family who had merely sniffed when introduced to Inès, looking her up and down rudely before turning her head dismissively. Inès had blushed. She wondered if Charlie had told Henrietta that she was a tart. She hoped not, but Henrietta seemed to avoid any kind of conversation with her, hanging on the two men's every word.

They were on the fish course when the air-raid siren went. Its harsh, familiar sound caused a sudden silence in the room. Almost at once their waiter was at the table.

'Won't you please follow me, ladies and gentlemen,' he said in a smoothly assured voice. 'Your dinner will not be interrupted, I promise you.'

Bemused, Inès followed the waiter down several flights of stairs. The entire roomful of people trooped in an orderly manner to the basement, where almost a facsimile of the Grill Room met their eyes. Dozens of tables were laid with sparkling white cloths and highly polished knives and forks. They were ushered to their table where their dinner and the dancing continued as if nothing had happened, until the all clear sounded and everyone went back upstairs to the Grill.

'Is this normal?' Inès asked Benjie.

'Oh yes, my dear,' he said airily. 'The Savoy is completely organized so that if the bloody Blitz interrupts their sacred dinner time, they have everything prepared to continue busIness as usual in the basement. Good idea, what?'

'Absolutely spiffing,' smiled Inès.

The next week went by in a haze of night clubs, bars and restaurants. Inès was taken by Benjie to the Milroy Club in Mayfair where they listened to the melodic piano playing of Tim Clayton and the Orchid Room in Brook Street, where the maître d'hôtel, Jerry Marco, greeted Benjie like a long-lost brother. He insisted they try a new drink from New York called the Bronx. It was a potent mixture of gin, orange juice and curaçao and Inès drank so many of them that she found herself getting almost too forward with Benjie. He drew away from her swiftly and she realized he needed to make the first move.

'I think I'll stick to champagne or white ladies in future,' she groaned to an impatient Yves the next morning.

'I don't care what you drink, *chérie*, as long as you make some money soon,' he sighed. 'This poor *macrou* has an ache in his belly that only a good meal will dispel.'

'I'm trying,' said Inès. 'I'm really trying, Yves.'

A few nights later Benjie took her back to the Bagatelle again with Charlie and Stella. Edmundo Ros was playing torrid Latin American music and the sexy beat excited both girls.

'C'mon, let's do the conga,' yelled Stella excitedly, grabbing Charlie's hand and leading him on to the packed dance floor.

'Come on, Benjie, let's do it too,' said Inès, trying to pull the young viscount up.

But Benjie was too embarrassed and inhibited to attempt the conga, even though several of his friends were part of the long line that wound through the club whooping and shrieking. He was drinking pink gins dripping with angostura and occasionally he would put a match to the mixture, watching with childlike glee as it ignited.

'Whew, that was a good one,' exclaimed Stella, out of breath and laughing as she came back to the table, her red hair in disarray and her lips bare of their usual scarlet slash. She leaned towards Inès conspiratorially as she reapplied her lipstick with a heavy hand.

'It's a whoopsee-do and up to the chandelier with *that* one, dearie!' She gestured towards Charlie, who had a satisfied expression on his face as he adjusted his trousers.

'What do you mean?' asked Inès.

'I mean, dear, 'es like the bleedin' Eiffel Tower in 'is private parts. Ready, steady, AND GO – whoa – whoa – I won't 'ave to work too 'ard tonight, luv, I guarantee – it'll be an easy bit of goosey-gander. 'Ow're you doing with yours, ducks? 'As 'e 'ad the 'orn yet?'

Inès shook her head regretfully and looked at Benjie. Was he ever going to make a move? A week had gone by without any sort of pass. It was definitely time for her to try to seduce him before Yves wasted away to nothing. If Benjie wasn't going to play, maybe she should look around for someone else. There were plenty of available-looking men around, a lot of cute young Americans too. It shouldn't be too difficult to find one who wanted her, they all seemed to give her the eye and wolf whistles whenever she walked by. Yes, maybe she should go off with one these good-looking Yanks. At least she'd get paid and probably even get some nylon stockings, and tins of fruit too, if she picked a generous one. But she decided to give Benjie one more chance.

After they left the Bagatelle she realized that Benjie was quite drunk. Hailing a taxi, she bundled him into it.

'Shepherd Market,' she told the driver. 'And quickly, please.'

In her flat, in the bedroom next to the one she and Yves usually shared, she threw herself on to him with excited cries and appropriate moans, and eventually succeeded in getting his clothes off him, and into bed. Once there, however, she immediately realized that he might have a few sexual problems. He seemed not able to rise to the occasion.

'Oh, dear, naughty thing – where's he gone?' giggled Benjie, pink with embarrassment. 'He was certainly there on the dance floor the other night. Why is Willie being such a bad boy?'

'Don't worry,' soothed Inès, applying expert pressure to the limpness lying crumpled forlornly against his thigh. 'Willie will be back, I guarantee you.'

'I say, that's wonderful,' said Benjie a few moments later, a twitch betraying the return of his amorous appetite. 'I rather like that!'

'Thank you, *Monsieur*,' Inès smiled, working diligently with delicate expertise. 'We aim to please.'

'Go on,' whispered Benjie hoarsely, 'don't stop, Inès – it's awfully good.' But unfortunately, with the exception of that one tiny initial spasm, the viscount's noble cock remained sadly flaccid.

'Don't worry, *chéri*.' Inès was all sweetness and understanding. 'I will take care of it – just relax. Don't do anything, Benjie, just enjoy this.' Yves had shown her how to turn clients on when this happened – as it so often did.

There were several traditional methods of arousing a limp cock, and Inès decided she would try them all. After all, if Viscount Spencer-Monckton was to be an important client she had to please him. Enough to get a good remuneration. Maybe if she was really good she'd get a tenner. First she attempted the ice in the mouth then hot-water method. This succeeded only in making Benjie squirm and giggle like a ten-year-old, and diminished his manhood even more. She then gave him the ever popular ice-cream-cone treat. Although genuine ice cream was a rare commodity in wartime London, Inès improvised with a few ounces of her precious jam ration. But it was all to no avail. Benjie's cock was so soft, so shrivelled with terror that it seemed to want to go to ground in his scrotum.

'He's a naughty little fellow,' sighed Benjie, mortified. 'Maybe you should smack his bottie.'

Ah, a clue at last, Inès thought, and leaping into action she commanded in a menacing tone, 'Turn over, Benjie.'

He eagerly obeyed and his pink skin started to redden as Inès began smacking his small, tight buttocks.

He murmured into the pillow, his cultured voice sounding as high-pitched as a five-year-old's, 'I've been *so, so* naughty, Nanny, *such a bad boy*.'

'Then the naughty boy must be spanked,' Inès said sternly, biting her lip to stop her giggles.

'Ooh no, Nanny,' cried Benjie, 'you can't spank me – it'll hurt.'

'Oh but I can,' said Inès gruffly. 'Like this, you bad boy. You naughty, naughty little boy.'

Harder and harder she pummelled him, his moans of delight

muffled by the pillow, his writhing bottom proof of his growing excitement.

'You are a wicked, terrible creature,' she admonished, slapping away at his skinny shanks. 'Nasty little boys must be punished.' Slap – slap – slap. 'They must be beaten until they beg for mercy.'

'Punish me – oh – PLEASE, Nanny,' Benjie groaned in ecstasy. 'Oh, Nursie, tell me what a bad boy Benjie has been.'

'Bad boy – bad *méchant, petit garçon*.'

Inès' palms stung, and her breath came in gasps. She was desperately trying to stop laughing. But then she started to become strangely excited herself. She had rarely inflicted pain on a client before, and suddenly she was finding it quite exhilarating. She picked up Yves' ivory shoehorn from the bedside table, and rained a series of sharp blows with it on Benjie's now scarlet bottom.

'Ooh, ooh, Nanny, you punish me so well,' groaned the naughty boy. 'But now I'm going to punish *you* with my big nasty sticking-out stick, Nanny dear, so turn over, it's Benjie's turn now.' With that he rolled over, confronting Inès with an enormous smile and a matching penis.

'Lie down now, Nanny, quietly,' Benjie whispered authoritatively. 'Don't let Mummy her what I'm doing – you must keep quiet. You've been such a naughty Nanny that now Benjie must punish you with this.'

With that he thrust into Inès, riding her with joyful, throaty cries while his pale patrician face with its refined features contorted in ecstasy.

'That's right, Nanny, you deserve this. Benjie's got you where he wants you now, and you – you – you better not tell – Mummy or Daddy, oooh – ahhh!'

Half an hour later, after a glass of vintage port and some digestive biscuits which Yves had managed to find, the viscount was ready again. This time Inès improved her dialogue, finding acting talents which she never thought she possessed as she embellished the bad-little-boy/naughty-nanny scenario. Benjie was in seventh heaven, and Inès found herself feeling curiously maternal towards him, even somewhat protective. When he left at dawn he put a pile of crisp white five-pound notes on the dresser and Inès was delighted.

After stocking up on essentials to feed the hungry Yves, she and Stella took Oxford Street by storm. She had twenty pounds and enough clothing coupons for four new dresses.

'Gor blimey, luv, he's bleedin' generous for a 'onourable,' said Stella enviously. 'Twenty-five quid 'e gave you?'

Inès nodded.

'Your you-know-what-twat must be lined with gold, duckie, that's all I can say,' snickered Stella as they admired the dresses in the windows of Bourne & Hollingsworth. 'Lord Worthington only gives me a tenner, and the Hon. Charlie the same. Whatever did you do to get twenty-five quid?'

Inès said nothing, changing the subject as she spotted a dress she liked in the window. 'Ooh look, Stella – it's lovely is it not?' She was admiring a dark brown satin frock with a sweetheart neckline edged with pink silk. It had a large pink bow at the daring décolletage, three-quarter-length sleeves with a little bow at each elbow, and an intricately draped skirt.

'Mmm,' Stella sniffed disparagingly at it. 'It's a bit drab for my taste, ducks, but I s'pose it would look good with your hair.'

'What's the price?' Inès peered at the tag.

'Thirty-seven and ninepence,' said Stella. 'That's a bit of all right – it won't break our little bank. C'mon, ducks, let's get you glamorous.'

After they had bought the brown dress, and then a black one, and another pair of shoes, and some new earrings, Inès started to feel frugal, but Stella was insistent. She liked Inès and enjoyed helping her.

'We've got to do somefink about yer boat-race,' she said, dragging a reluctant Inès down Regent Street towards Swan & Edgar in Piccadilly Circus.

'My what?' asked Inès, almost colliding with a handsome City gentleman who tipped his hat, smiling at her charming figure laden with packages.

'Yer boat race, dearie – yer face.'

'What's wrong with my face?' asked Inès defensively.

'Look, duckie, I always call a spade a spade – well almost always,' said Stella. 'Frankly, ducks, you're gettin' a bit too long in the tooth to go around with the scrubbed virgin look.'

'I'm just eighteen,' said Inès indignantly.

'I know, I know, and I'm King George's auntie,' said Stella. 'It don't matter 'ow old you are, dear – the bloom's startin' to go orf – you know what I mean? You've been on the game for four years now since you was fourteen, so it's time to tart yourself up – get a nice sparkling new look. 'Ere, now get a load of that – ain't they pretty.'

They stopped at the cosmetic counter in Swan & Edgar, one of the few places that still sold bits of makeup in London. A long queue of eager young women craned their necks to look at the desirable, hard-to-obtain articles, and Inès looked into the glass showcase full of lipsticks and rouge pots with excitement.

'Do you think it will suit me?' she asked anxiously after she had parted with a precious half crown for one scarlet lipstick which smelled of candle wax, and a small pot of brick-coloured rouge. The makeup was rationed, one to each customer, but some of the girls after making their purchases quickly slipped to the back of the queue again to buy some more.

'You'll look the Queen of bleedin' Sheba by the time I've shown you what to do,' smiled Stella. 'We need one more thing now.'

'What's that?' asked Inès as Stella hustled her down Piccadilly towards St James's Street.

''Ere we are,' Stella said proudly, as they arrived at the exclusive gentlemen's bootmaker Lobb. 'By appointment to 'Is bleedin' Majesty 'imself – come on, Inès.'

Inside the shop she pointed to a tin of black boot polish displayed discreetly on the polished oak counter.

'We'll 'ave one of those,' she told the salesman. He looked them up and down disdainfully. Two obvious tarts if he ever saw one, although the dark one was sexy in a foreign sort of way.

Inès gave the man sevenpence for the boot polish, and the two young women rushed home giggling like schoolgirls. Stella was going to give Inès a lesson in makeup.

'Now you're the dark and sultry sort,' Stella told her. 'Me, I'm the outdoor type, with a talent for indoor games!' She opened the tin of shoe polish and began to paint it around Inès' pale blue eyes with a little brush. 'Now no peeking.' She doused Inès' face with white powder, dabbed a generous amount of lipstick on to the girl's full lips, and stroked her cheekbones lightly with rouge. She fiddled with her long hair with curling irons for half an hour, and then allowed Inès to look.

'An' *voilà*, *chérie*, or whatever you say in Froggie land,' exclaimed Stella triumphantly. '*La grande transformation* – Cinderella into Hedy Lamarr.'

Inès looked at herself in amazement. The woman who stared back at her in the cracked dressing table mirror looked like a Hollywood vamp. Dark red lips in a pale almost translucent skin contrasted brilliantly with her light blue eyes. They glowed with a sultry sparkle, the heavy shadowing of black boot polish exaggerating their lustre and depth to great effect. Her dark hair was parted in the middle and hung each side of her face in asymmetrical waves and curls.

'*Mon Dieu*, is that me?' breathed Inès.

'You bet it is, dearie,' chuckled Stella. 'And I'll tell you somefink for nuffink. When the Hon. Viscount Benjie sees you tonight, dearie, 'is little wee willie winkie is going to get as 'ard as a bit of Brighton rock. He'll be N-S-I-T tonight, I betcha.'

'What does that mean?'

'Not Safe In Taxis, dearie,' sniggered Stella. 'Now throw some of this over yourself tonight, luvvie.' She handed Inès a small bottle of perfume in a distinctive geometrical bottle.

'Chanel Number Five,' whispered Inès reverently. 'Where did you get this, Stella?'

'Never you mind, luv, never you mind,' said Stella mysteriously. 'All I know, duckie, is that once old Viscount Benjie-poo gets a whiff of this, 'is dickery-dickery will be up 'igher than a bleedin' barrage balloon.'

'His what?' laughed Inès.

'Dickery *dock*, dearie,' said Stella in mock exasperation. 'It's rhymin' slang, see. Don'cha know what dickery dickery dock means?'

'Oh yes, I get it,' smiled Inès. 'OK, Stella, I think I'm ready to go to the rub-a-dub-dub tonight.'

'You're learnin', girl, you're learnin'.'

Soon Inès had Benjie and several of his society friends totally under

83

her spell, and her career as one of London's most beautiful and successful courtesans was well and truly launched.

Inès entertained her viscount three times a week. He preferred to visit her in the evening after dining at his club.

She hardly saw Yves except at weekends when her bluebloods returned to their country estates from London. Yves was pleased with the money she was now making, and she saved up her own sexual thrills, or at least most of them, for weekends with him. Although she did occasionally become aroused by some of her clients, Yves was her man, their sex life was as torrid as ever, and he still made her laugh like no one else could.

Inès was happy. The money rolled in, enabling them to afford more luxuries from the black market. Her clients occasionally brought her expensive presents and always treated her like a lady when they were not treating her like a nanny. She loved Yves and he seemed to love her. Everything was almost too good to be true.

Since clothes coupons were hard to come by and Yves had found several bolts of beautiful pre-war fabric, Inès decided to learn to sew. Yves bought her a second-hand sewing machine and she quickly learned to love dressmaking. Although fashion magazines were hard to come by Inès went to the cinema often, and she would copy the gorgeous clothes the Hollywood glamour queens wore. She particularly liked the gowns Esther Williams wore in *A Guy Named Joe* and Lana Turner's in *Slightly Dangerous*. She gave the first dress she made – a floral print in shades of cyclamen and dark blue – to Stella.

'You're a real chum, you know that, duckie,' the redhead said, her eyes shining gratefully. 'No one's ever given me anything before, unless I've 'ad to give out to get it – if you know what I mean. Thanks, Inès, I really appreciate it.'

Inès smiled. Stella was the first real girlfriend she had ever had, and she valued the friendship tremendously.

'Oh by the way, duckie, I've been meaning to ask you this.' Stella was admiring her reflection in the new dress. 'You are taking care of yourself, aren't you?'

'What do you mean?'

'Against the old you-know-what. Against falling in the family way – you're doing something, aren't you?'

'Well, not really.' Inès started to blush. 'Yves always has said I'm too young to get pregnant so I just cross my fingers –'

'You little fool.' Stella was cross now. 'Yves is even more of a bloody burk than I thought. Right, my girl, I'm making an appointment with Dr Wright in Weymouth Street first thing tomorrow. We're getting you fitted with a good old Dutch cap.'

When one or other of them was not entertaining clients, Stella and Inès were inseparable.

Inès taught the redhead how to sew on her old Singer machine, and the two women spent many afternoons devouring fashion magazines, searching for new styles to copy.

Under Stella's tutelage Inès learned the intricacies of cosmetic witchery. How to put up her hair with three pins and a lick of glue, and where to find the precious dye to keep her blonde hair the dark brunette that she now preferred. She learned jokes and songs, for Stella was a cheery soul who liked a sing-along with the wireless. Stella knew all the popular songs of the day, and taught Inès the lyrics to most of them. She also taught her how to do the conga, the rhumba, the jitterbug and even the lambeth walk, and they practised them together to Stella's old gramophone with girlish squeals of laughter.

The two of them often went to the cinemas in Leicester Square to see the Hollywood musicals that were being churned out of the studios to fulfil the needs of a public which craved light entertainment.

Sometimes they window shopped together in Oxford Street and Bond Street, admiring the expensive things that were far beyond their means.

Inès was thrilled to have a female companion in London. Since Jeanette had been murdered she had had no one with whom to share confidences and dreams. She simply adored having a best friend. Stella was like a kind older sister to her and made life much more fun.

But after a time, Inès' close and sisterly relationship with Stella seemed to cool. Suddenly Stella never had time any more for their shopping trips or for the intimate chats on personal philosophy and life which had become so important to Inès.

85

Stella had told Inès that she was terribly busy with her afternoon clients, and since Inès' clients visited mostly at night, they gradually just drifted apart.

'Yves, Yves, darling,' Inès called excitedly as she opened the front door of their flat. 'I'm home.'

She was happy. A naughty weekend at the viscount's country house with plenty of giggles and spanking had ended abruptly when a telegram arrived, announcing that his dragon of a mother was returning home a day early from a trip to their Scottish estate. It had thrown him into a complete tizzy. Frantically, Benjie bundled Inès into his Bentley, drove her to Godalming station and put her on the London train with a cursory peck on the cheek and a thick wad of clean white fivers in her bag.

She hummed to herself as she walked into the hall of the flat. It was only two o'clock on a Sunday, and the beautiful summer afternoon stretched ahead for her and her lover.

'*Chéri!*' she cried, dropping her suitcase and running through the small drawing room towards his bedroom. 'I'm home. Get up, lazybones. I've had a reprieve from his lordship, isn't that a –' Her voice trailed off as she opened the bedroom door, to see the two of them curled up together, asleep like kittens in a basket.

She couldn't see the girl's face, only the long, carrot-red hair which fanned out over Inès' favourite antique linen pillowcase; that pale freckled arm thrown possessively across the muscular shoulders of her man. Inès' stomach churned and her legs started to buckle.

Her loud intake of breath stirred them into sleepy wakefulness.

'Oh my Gawd,' Stella muttered glumly, picking up a transparent black chiffon robe. 'Christ all bloody mighty. Sorry, luv, you know 'ow it is, I'm reelly sorry.' She disappeared into the bathroom and Inès heard the sound of water running. She felt as if a fist had thudded against her heart, smashing it to pieces.

Yves lit a cigarette with a great show of indifference. It dangled from his lips as he stared at Inès dispassionately, both arms behind his head, the smoke rising into his curly brown hair. His hazel eyes were narrowed, giving her no clue to his feelings as he said, 'Why didn't you tell me you were coming home?'

'I thought you loved me, Yves,' she said, her voice choked with tears. 'How could you do this? And with Stella – my best friend – how *could* you?'

'*Chérie*, I did love you – I did. I *do* love you.' He dragged at his cigarette, searching for words. 'I love you like a – friend – like a sister . . . like my own daughter.'

'What are you saying?' Inès was stunned. 'What we do together, Yves, is hardly what a brother usually does with his sister.'

'I know. I know. Look, Inès, I have to be honest. I know you'll understand, but things happen. *C'est la vie*, I suppose.' His voice was low and sincere. He evinced no sign of guilt, no pang of remorse; he seemed quite cool, very collected.

Inès sank slowly into the armchair at the foot of their bed, staring into the face of the only man she had ever loved, her broken heart fluttering wildly. She felt sickened.

'I know this is hard for you, Inès, but four years is a very long time for a man like me to be with one woman. I think I've taught you a lot, and I love you, *chérie*, but I must admit my love has been more . . . more – well, paternal, lately.'

'No!' cried Inès. 'No. Yves, it's not true – what are you saying?'

'I'm leaving you,' he said flatly. 'I must. I was going to tell you next week – I'm going back to Paris. I want to go back.' He paused, taking a deep drag on his Gauloise. 'And I'm taking Stella.'

'Stella? You're going with *Stella?*' Inès could barely speak from the shock and pain. '*Why?* Why with her? Do you love her?'

'No,' he admitted, frowning. 'Not at all – it is hard for me really to love, Inès. You know that. But certainly it is – well – more than brotherly love at the moment. I think Stella will do quite well in Paris now that the occupation is over, there will be a lot of work for her. And you are doing fine now, you have good clients – plenty of them – you will become more successful, make more money. You don't really need me any more.'

'I do,' she sobbed. 'I need you – there's never been anyone for me like you; there never will be.'

'You'll find someone,' he said coolly. 'A girl like you – you'll find a new man.'

'You bastard, you two-timing *macrou*. I loved you. How could you do this to me with that ... that *creature?*' She was becoming hysterical now. The thought of losing Yves was insupportable. It couldn't happen, he was her life.

The sound of running water ceased abruptly. Inès knew that Stella was probably listening at the bathroom door. Stella – her best friend. She was filled with pain and rage and grief. Suddenly memories of the Italian she had murdered came flooding back. She almost wished that she could find that same razor, slice it into Yves and Stella, kill them both, the ache in her heart was so palpable.

'Yves – oh God, Yves,' she cried despairingly. 'You've broken my heart today, just as if you'd smashed it into the ground. You've destroyed me, Yves – completely destroyed me.' Fresh tears filled her eyes but he stopped her.

'Listen to me, Inès ... I always thought you should make something of yourself. But I'm not the man to be with for that. You'll be better off without me, *chérie*, I know you will. You're young, beautiful – too beautiful to be a *poule de luxe* for ever. You'll make a life. Find a good man – not a pimp, a *macrou*. Someone to really love you, because I know for damn sure I'm not the one for you.'

Inès stared at him. 'You are,' she sobbed. 'You are, Yves, you're all I've got, all I've ever had. All I want.'

'Stop it, Inès – stop it please, *chérie*. It's over, can't you see that? Where's your pride? It's over between us; you must understand that now.'

'I'm going for a walk,' Inès said in desperation, running her fingers wildly through her hair. 'When I come back, I hope you and that – that – red-haired *whore*' – she spat the word, even though her voice was almost cracking with the effort of holding back her tears – 'will be gone.'

'*Chérie*, I'm sorry ...'

'Goodbye, Yves,' Inès said in a tiny broken voice. 'And good luck in Paris – *au revoir*.'

She strode from the room, her head held high, clutching desperately to what remained of her pride, her throat aching with unshed tears. She was eighteen years old and she was completely alone in the world once again.

*

After Yves and Stella left for Paris, Inès wept bitterly for days, pounding her pillow in frustrated anguish, crying Yves' name throughout the long wakeful nights. But she was young and resilient, and after a period both of intense rage and grief-stricken mourning, she slowly began to entertain her clients again. It was, after all, her only livelihood, and to live in war-time London was expensive. She frequented night clubs, jazz clubs, bars and restaurants, hoping to meet a man for whom she could feel something – anything. She wanted to find love – she desperately wanted to stop her life of whoring before it was too late.

She had been a prostitute since the age of fourteen, and though it had meant little to her then, lately she had begun to feel more and more contempt for men's lust; disgust as their sweat dripped on to her; loathing as she mechanically pleasured them with her mouth. She was so erotically expert in what she did that all her clients were completely enthralled by her. But she hated it, and she started to hate them too.

She wanted a real boyfriend, someone with whom she could build a proper life, marry. She wanted to raise a family who would receive all the love and attention from her that she had never had from her mother. She wanted to become a normal woman.

As the weeks and months passed, as Inès searched for the elusive commodity called love, she realized that to find the type of man she sought she must become worthy of him.

She began an extensive course of self-improvement of both her mind and body. Every morning she exercised vigorously, the window open to all the sights and smells of Shepherd Market. Then she meditated, as she had learned to do from an ancient book written by an Indian seer. She tried to cleanse her thoughts of her clients, their depravity and kinkiness, to fill her mind with purity. She started going to church, praying for her soul and the souls of the men who used her. She found an inner peace in the teachings of Christ and in the Desiderata. She was convinced that she would one day shed the decaying skin of prostitution and become a member of the human race again. She knew she had to.

With mind and body purified, she spent almost all her afternoons at libraries and museums, letting great works of art fill her with wonder. She read voraciously – philosophy, religion and art history; she went to the theatre, to concerts and to the opera. She studied the newspapers, becoming well informed about current affairs and world events and then she started debating with some of her clients. Much to their amazement and delight, they soon found that the mind of this beautiful whore was almost as fascinating as her face, her body and her incredible sexual skills.

Sometimes, so involved would both become in a discussion of Buddhism or poetry or the work of some new artist that a client would forget the original intention of his visit, and sipping dry sherry, they would argue fiercely and debate long into the night.

Inès was pleased with her progress. The frightened whore-child, ignorant of everything but men's desires, was gone for ever. Instead, a woman of intelligence, beauty and knowledge was emerging, a woman of whom a man could be truly proud.

London 1945

It was finally over. Six long and bloody years of hell ended on a warm May night, and all London seemed to be in Trafalgar Square celebrating the German surrender.

No one was in a more joyous mood than Phoebe and Julian, for it was a double celebration. They had finally been married in Caxton Hall Registry Office the previous weekend. Julian had been reluctant, but Phoebe was pregnant. Ever the gentleman, Julian 'did the right thing'.

Now, along with thousands of other revellers, they danced, laughed, cried with joy around the fountains in the square. The sky was illuminated by a dazzling fireworks display, and everyone was singing 'Rule Britannia', 'God Save the King' and other patriotic songs in drunken, tuneless delight. Groups of French sailors with their pom-pommed berets tipped over their eyes, drunkenly chanted the 'Marseillaise' as they tried in vain to stay on their feet.

In the grand houses of England the armistice was being welcomed with lavish parties. Rare vintage wines and spirits were uncorked. Exotic tinned fruits, hams, cheeses, quail eggs, pheasant, sides of beef and delicacies not tasted since the outbreak of war adorned the groaning tables. Even the most stingy of the aristocracy had on this occasion given in to the black marketeers, and were sparing no expense for this glorious celebration.

The ordinary citizens, the common people – the backbone of Great Britain – had taken to the streets to celebrate together. Thousands of them had gone to stand outside Buckingham Palace and cheer the King and Queen as they waved from the balcony. The crowds stretched down the Mall to Trafalgar Square, where servicemen in uniform frolicked in the shallow, cold water of the fountains alongside boys and girls, middle-aged mums and dads with their floral skirts or flannel trousers hitched uninhibitedly over their knees.

A few brave souls tore off their clothes in a frenzy of exhibitionism, posturing before the cheering crowds. Some of the younger people were so carried away with excitement that they openly made love on the backs of Landseer's colossal lions, guardians of Nelson's Column. Dozens of church bells rang out as the crowd formed circles, dancing the knees up, the conga, the rhumba, even the highland fling.

Bottles of champagne and beer were tipped to laughing lips as groups of giggling young girls ran around hugging and kissing anyone who took their fancy, sometimes even those who didn't. Every car had its headlights on and its horns blaring, and every municipal and government building was brilliantly lit. It was the bacchanal to end them all, the party of the century. But in all the crowd's jollity there was a frenetic desperation, for many had lost loved ones or possessions and homes during the war.

'I love you, Mr Brooks,' Phoebe yelled above the din.

'I love you too, Mrs Brooks.' Julian laughingly kissed his wife's full lips, then was unceremoniously pulled away from her by a teenage soldier.

''Ere, give us a kiss too, lovey,' said the boy with a cheeky smile, and Phoebe obliged him with a smacker.

'Strumpet.' Julian looked at the vermilion lipstick smeared across Phoebe's laughing face.

'Scoundrel!' she giggled. 'And, speaking of which, look at that!' They observed a naked young woman being powerfully serviced by a French soldier whose trousers were around his ankles, while another young soldier hung on to his arm and vomited into the fountain.

'Charming! What a delightful sight. I think I've had just about enough of this party, old girl. Let's go home and celebrate being married in a rather more traditional way.' Julian slid his hand over her full bosom.

'Naughty boy – people looking.' Phoebe slapped his hand away coyly.

'Who cares?' laughed Julian. 'The war's over, darling – it's finally over.'

'OK, let's go home to make love, celebrate our new baby, celebrate *life*, my gorgeous husband. That's the only proper way to end a war.'

'There's a bloke 'ere to see yer – says 'e's from a film studio or somefink.' The stage doorkeeper poked a grizzled head around the door of Julian's minuscule dressing room, where the young comedian was taking a catnap between shows. It was tough work performing seven times a day and night. All right for Phoebe and the showgirls. They just had to wander across the stage, tits up, feathers erect, perform a little bit of a song and dance, and look sexy and pretty.

Julian had to think up amusing, hilarious and original monologues night after night, day after day – and after eighteen months it was becoming more and more difficult.

Before he could say anything the door was pushed open by a man in his late forties wearing a double-breasted black cashmere overcoat, a black homburg and grey suede gloves. He walked into the room and removed his hat. His nose was full and fleshy, and his lips were those of a gourmet – a man who appreciated only the finest in food, wine and, no doubt, women. His eyes were masked by thick-rimmed, dark-lensed black spectacles, and his skin was deeply tanned. He exuded an aura of supreme self-confidence, that of a man used to giving orders which would be instantly obeyed, of making decisions that would always be right, and of always having the very best of everything which life had to offer.

'Good evening. My name is Didier Armande.'

Julian stood up immediately, impressed and excited. Didier Armande – *the* Didier Armande. Probably the most important and influential film producer in Britain. Julian knew it was he who had produced the unforgetable *Romeo and Juliet*, the extraordinary *Woman of Baghdad* and the revolutionary epic, *The Life and Times of Louis XIV*. It was he who had discovered not only the legendary Elaine Roche, the gorgeous Maxine Von Pallach and dashing Jasper Swanson, but had helped his own sister – the sultry and mysterious

Ramona Armande – to reach the heights of international and Hollywood stardom, in his avant-garde production of *Mata Hari*. What on earth was Didier Armande doing here in this tatty dressing room? And what could he possibly want with Julian Brooks?

'May I sit down?' The older man's faint accent gave the impression of culture and education.

'Of course, of course.' Hastily Julian brushed a pile of his discarded clothes from a small chair.

Mr Armande sat down, his silver-topped ebony cane resting lightly between his knees. Taking a leather case from the pocket of his overcoat, he proffered what was surely the first Havana cigar Julian had seen since before the war.

Havana cigars! Where the hell had he managed to find such a luxury? It was hard enough in austere Britain to find a packet of Woodbines, let alone a cigar. Julian accepted one, and Didier coolly lit both cigars with a heavy-looking gold lighter, into which the initials D.A. had been set in small diamonds.

'I know you don't have much time,' he said, glancing at his slim platinum wristwatch, whose shape and design were of faultless taste, 'but I have watched you perform for the last few days and I wanted to express to you my most sincere congratulations.'

'Congratulations? Whatever for?' Julian was mystified. All that he'd done recently was to trot out some old gags, fumbling in his memory for a bit of business or some material that he could remember from other comedians' acts – anything with which to raise a laugh from that sea of servicemen who sat enthralled each night by the tawdry glamour of the Windmill.

'You are indeed a comedian *par excellence.*' The man inhaled deeply on his cigar, filling the tiny room with a haze of delicious blue smoke. 'You made me laugh even when I'd heard the same joke before.'

'Thank you.' Julian was pulling himself together, feeling more secure with the compliments. 'That's most kind of you to say so. I was always told that the hardest thing for any comic to do is to make the same audience laugh twice at identical material.'

'Exactly, my dear fellow. It is an art, a true art. However, I realize from watching you carefully that you possess much more that just a talent to amuse, as dear Noël is so fond of saying. You were an actor, were you not?'

'Yes, I was. Still am, really. Now that the war is over, I hope to go back into acting, but so many of the reps are still closed.'

'Perhaps you won't have to go back to repertory.' Didier Armande inspected the glowing tip of his cigar carefully. 'Have you ever thought of making films?'

'Films! Well, no, actually I haven't, I've always done theatre.'

'I'll get straight to the point.' Didier leaned forward, his hands resting casually on his cane, on which Julian could see an eagle, its wings spread, emblazoned with some kind of writing.

'My company, Goya Films, will shortly be making a film about Charles ii, and the fascinating relationship that he was reputed to have with one of his illegitimate daughters.'

Julian leaned forward, almost tipping his chair into Armande's.

'You bear a most striking resemblance to some of the portraits of Charles ii,' Armande said. 'Similar colouring, even bone structure. It is uncanny, actually, quite amazing.'

'Oh,' said Julian feeling at a loss as Sammy, the call boy, poked a cheery carrot head around the door.

'Five minutes, matey,' he chirped.

Didier Armande handed Julian a white card engraved with his name, that of Goya Pictures, an address and a telephone number. 'If you would be interested in screen-testing for the role of King Charles, please have your agent call my office within the next two days. You may want some time to think it over.'

'Oh – no. No, I don't need any time, I'll do it – I mean, I'll test. I'd love to test, absolutely love to!'

'Très bien, Mr Brooks, good news indeed. I shall have my people call your agent.'

'Great, great, that's wonderful. Oh, God, I'm sorry, but I don't have an agent.' Julian felt embarrassed.

'You have no agent?' Didier raised black brows eloquently – an actor without an agent? How odd. Even if agents didn't seem to do much, they were a necessity when things got rough.

'Well, no – you know how it it at the Windmill – nonstop work, nose to the grindstone all the time, never even have time to write a letter. Actually I was really waiting until the war ended to get an agent, and I just don't seem to have got around to it yet.'

'Very well. That is of course no problem. If you will be so kind as to give me your telephone number at home, my people will contact you in order to make the necessary arrangements.'

Didier Armande rose, pulling tight suede gloves over his muscular hands, which were the only thing about him that seemed less than elegant.

'*Au revoir*, Mr Brooks, until we meet again at Pinewood Studios, I hope.' He extended his hand to Julian, who clasped it firmly.

'May I inquire what the film is to be called, sir?'

'It's called *The Merry Monarch*. The script was written by the Academy Award-winning writer, Irving Frankovitch, and it'll be directed by Francis Lawford who I'm sure you must know. We fully expect the actor who plays the King to be nominated for the Oscar next year. It's a hell of a role, Mr Brooks, a hell of a role, and one for which you were born.'

Julian Brooks and his career were both thriving. He looked wonderful as Charles II. His own hair was covered by a shoulder-length wig of lustrous tumbling black ringlets, and a delicate moustache enhanced his gorgeous face. He swashbuckled his way through the film: fighting, romancing, duelling, perfectly cast as the suave, vain, highly sexed and romantic King. The story was based less on historical accuracy than on the fertile imagination of the American writer Irving Frankovitch, but it was exactly the kind of romantic epic for which post-war film fans yearned, and Julian was the kind of romantic hero female fans lusted after.

Goya Pictures' publicity department moved in on Julian, type-writers and cameras clicking. When not wearing his seventeenth-century costume, Julian was dressed by the wardrobe department in a variety of well-cut threads so that Didier's number-one stills photographer, Curly, could snap to his heart's content.

Bronzed by the wizardry of the makeup department, Julian posed for hours, self-conscious in the freezing stills studio, wearing bathing trunks or rolled-up blue jeans, tennis shorts or sometimes only his Restoration doublet and hose from *The Merry Monarch* and a bare chest. And the chest had better be bare. Modesty, also known as the Production Code Administration, or the Hays Office, regarded a hairy chest as a major cause of moral corruption. Therefore, on the morning of every stills session, Julian's pectorals would be painstakingly shaved by the makeup man and covered with deep bronze makeup which was then topped off with a thin sheen of oil. This made his chest glisten like polished mahogany, and many a maidenly heart beat faster when she saw her favourite in all his masculine glory smiling out from the magazines. Beefcake was big business, and Julian epitomized it totally.

Before *The Merry Monarch* was even released, publications all over the world were clamouring for more and more photographs of Looks Brooks. The less clothes he wore, the more his fans seemed to like it. It did not matter that as yet none of these fans had even seen him on the silver screen – he was a world-famous star before his first film had been released. He bared almost his all whether he liked it or not: on a beach, tossing a medicine ball, swinging an axe with convincing dexterity, pulling a rope, flying a plane, riding a horse, always dressed in appropriate gear. Once the crafty Curly even had him wrestling with a giant rubber alligator. Julian found this endless posing and shaving of his chest tedious, to say the least, but Phoebe, ever the pragmatist, and a teeny bit envious of all the attention he was receiving, encouraged him to do anything and everything which the studio asked.

'You want to be a star – well, this is how it's done,' she told him bluntly.

After having miscarried their baby, Phoebe had made Julian's career ever more her concern. Not satisfied with the simple domestic life of their new flat in Cadogan Square, she appeared constantly on the set, watching over him jealously from the sidelines as he played love scenes with a succession of glamorous actresses. She inwardly seethed when he embraced them, her innate common sense beginning to founder in a sea of envy. Phoebe was not as pretty as she had been. Lines of discontent had started to form on her face, and her voluptuous body was becoming soft and flabby.

Superficially she revelled in her husband's success, but she began to have acting ambitions herself. These had lain dormant until Julian started riding the crest of success, and now she too wanted to bask in the spotlight of fame. Several times she subtly suggested to Didier Armande that she would be right to perform opposite Julian or even play a second lead, but Didier diplomatically laughed off her aspirations, pretending that he didn't really understand.

'One star in the family is enough, my dear,' he would say, patting her plump, powdered cheek. 'Our boy needs to be taken care of, Phoebe, and you do that so beautifully it would be a great pity to do anything to prevent the golden goose from laying his lovely valuable eggs.'

Phoebe bit her lip and kept quiet, but the more famous he became, the more the long green fingers of jealousy gripped her heart.

And Julian just went on posing. When he wasn't acting he gave interviews. He confided his life story to *Picturegoer* and *Picture Show*, *Illustrated*, *Photoplay* and *Look* magazine. He laughed and joked with the cameramen and crew as he stood beside boats, planes and cars with the all-important macho stare. He chatted long distance to the twin witches of Hollywood, Hedda and Louella. He was becoming the most popular actor in England but he still considered movies as just a means to an end. His ultimate ambition was to do classical stage roles, with aspirations to the crown of Olivier himself.

'There's no doubt about it, no doubt at all – the man's got star quality,' Didier muttered to his assistant, delighted with his personal choice of a leading man after seeing the first rushes of *The Merry Monarch*. Didier stared at the last frame of Julian's beautifully lit, handsome face gazing into the camera with tears in his velvet eyes, the black poodle curls and rakish feathered hat accentuating both his innate masculinity and a brooding sensitivity.

'Run them again, Johnnie,' Didier commanded, slipping back in the grey plush chair, eyes half closed to bask again in Julian's aura. 'Run them again.'

'Star quality,' he murmured softly to himself. 'If you've got it, you don't need anything else – except perhaps a little bit of luck.'

Hydra 1945

Nikolas Stanopolis stared at the thick blue envelope in astonishment. It carried a US airmail stamp, and in the top left-hand corner
was printed importantly:

MCCP Studios
7700 Melrose Avenue
Los Angeles, California

On the back of the envelope was a name that made Nikolas' heart
leap with excitement. SPYROS MAKOPOLIS, PRESIDENT. With
trembling hands he handed the letter to his wife, Elektra. It was
addressed to her, but she smilingly handed it back to him.

'No, no, Nikolai, *you* open it.'

He ripped open the letter, reading it with mounting elation:

MY DEAR NIECE ELEKTRA,

I was happy to receive news of Hydra, but so sorry to hear about
your dear departed mother. My heart is very heavy at her passing,
but I shall think of the good days when we played together as
children in that sunlit paradise of a village.

My congratulations on your marriage to Nikolas Stanopolis.
He sounds like a fine young man, and his interest in the business
of film making is most interesting.

If you are able to make your way one day to Los Angeles, I
would be happy to see Nikolas as you have suggested, and perhaps
give him an opportunity to work at this studio if he seems suitable.

Please remember me to Dmitri Andros at the old bar in the port
– I am happy to know the old man survived the war and remains in
good health.

I am enclosing a little gift which may help you if you decide to come to America.

Be happy, my dear young niece,

Cordially,
Your Uncle Spyros

'Oh, my God – Elektra, this is fantastic, wonderful news – America! He wants us to come to Los Angeles! Hollywood! Elektra, do you know what this means?'

'Yes, yes, Nikolai my love, I do.' Elektra's face shone with joy as she looked up lovingly at her husband. 'And look, Nikolai – look at this.' Triumphantly she waved the cheque at him. 'He's sent us money. My uncle is a truly wonderful gentleman.'

'Money?' Nikolas grabbed it. 'How much?' He looked at the unfamiliar writing on the cheque.

'*Five hundred dollars!*' Elektra gasped. '*Five hundred dollars*. That is a *fortune*, Nikolai. Now we can go to America, my darling, we can both go to Hollywood.'

But the passage to America was not as easy to negotiate as Nikolas and Elektra had hoped. A few days later, having changed the five-hundred-dollar cheque into drachma, Nikolas took the weekly ferry from Hydra to Athens to make preparations for their trip. His first disappointment was finding out that it was extremely difficult for a Greek national to visit America, and it involved a considerable amount of red tape. Then, in the offices of the new Olympic Airlines, he discovered that two airline fares to Los Angeles cost more than twice the amount that Mr Makopolis had sent, and with a heavy heart Nikolas returned to Hydra to break the news to his wife.

'Never mind, Nikolai. You must go first to America, make Uncle Spyros give you a job, then in a few months I can follow you there.'

'But I need you with me,' said Nikolas sulkily, 'I won't go without you, Elektra.'

'No, Nikolai. No. You must go,' the girl said firmly, pouring out two glasses of wine. 'It will be too difficult for us if we both go now. You will be worried about me – about where we shall live – about too many things. First you must go and make money, then I will follow. Now eat your supper before it gets cold.'

Nikolas marvelled at his young wife's understanding, as she raised her wine glass in a shy toast. 'To America, Nikolai, and to us.'

Nikolas Stanopolis arrived at Los Angeles airport on a cold November night in 1945. Shivering in his thin cotton jacket, he stood outside the busy terminal, wondering what he should do. Why was it so cold? He had been told that California weather was warm, sunny, like the weather of the Greek islands. Well, they'd been wrong, those fools who had told him this. It was freezing; a light rain was falling, and a foggy, choking, dark mist wafted in from the Pacific.

Everyone seemed to be busy rushing somewhere, as if they had a purpose, knew exactly what they were doing, where they were going. Nikolas waited forlornly outside the terminal where the giant four-engine plane had brought him from New York. He felt lost and homesick as he thought of his beautiful Elektra, of his beloved Hydra, thankfully now slowly recovering from the war and the atrocities committed by Umberto Scrofo.

Scrofo – whenever he thought of that odious Italian, he felt blinding rage. One day he would find him and make him suffer as his mother, father, brothers, sisters and so many others on Hydra had. The desire for revenge consumed him almost as much as his desire to succeed in the film business. He had no clue as to where the Italian was living now: whether in fact he was still alive, but that did nothing to assuage his two burning ambitions.

Nikolas' English was limited, picked up mostly from an old man on Hydra who had once worked in London and from the movies, but he spoke enough to communicate his predicament to a porter. The man wore a red cap and a blue shirt and he had the black, shiny hair and olive skin of a fellow Greek; but he was Spanish, having himself only recently arrived from Barcelona. He took pity on Nikolas, escorting him two blocks to the sign DOWNTOWN BUS and chatting to him in a mixture of Spanish and English.

Nikolas stood shivering behind two round, gossiping women, not unlike the women of Hydra. When the bus arrived he gave the conductor five dollars, but became confused when asked for his destination. 'Downtown,' he said in heavily accented English. 'Downtown LA, please, sir.'

The man shrugged, giving him a handful of change. 'Downtown's a big place, kid,' he said. 'Whereabouts downtown?'

Nikolas had been given the name of a hotel by one of the Greek officials in New York. So he said proudly, 'I'm going to Roosevelt Hotel, Hollywood Boulevard, in Hollywood, sir.'

He was on his way.

The following morning Nikolas Stanopolis presented himself in a state of high excitement at the imposing entrance of MCCP Studios.

There was a flurry of activity around the high wrought-iron gates, but the uniformed guard told him bluntly, 'Get lost, buddy, you're too early – no one's in the administration offices yet.'

Nikolas pleadingly brandished his letter with the offer of employment written by Spyros but the gum-chewing guard barely raised his eyes from his copy of *Variety*. He barked something unintelligible in a harsh voice, but the body language was clear. Nikolas would not be able to get in, nor could he hang around the gates.

'I said, get lost buddy,' snarled the cop. 'Git outta sight. Now.'

In desperation, Nikolas crossed the road to sit on a bench plastered with advertising signs. Here at least he had a front-row view of the studio, and could see a good deal of what went on behind the iron gates. For several hours he sat completely fascinated, watching all manner of people come and go.

The costumes of the extras particularly enthralled him. Cowboys and Indians, peasants and soldiers, cops and robbers all milled about, fraternizing with one another. At eleven o'clock a group of beautiful showgirls, their long California legs encased in flesh-coloured fishnet tights, trooped out from a huge building marked Stage Three.

Nikolas sat up, his eyes widening. These were women such as he had never seen before. The women in Greece wore modest, all-enveloping clothes – even Elektra covered herself from neck to calf. The thought of her body started to excite him as he looked longingly at the showgirls.

These women were crimson-lipped, their hair was marcelled yellow, flame red or jet black. Hips swaying provocatively, they sashayed around the courtyard, laughing, smoking cigarettes, drinking Coca-Colas straight from the bottle. He saw the studio employees, men in work shirts and denim trousers, eyeing the girls lecherously as they passed, some of them making, he was sure, suggestive or lewd remarks at which the girls just laughed. Nikolas was shocked. Although he had seen women like this in movies, he was amazed that they could prance about half naked in public so brazenly, placidly ignoring the men who flirted with them.

One particular girl caught his eye. She was lissome, with luxuriant black hair tumbling halfway down her back, where it was caught up with scarlet feathers. Although slightly shorter than the other girls, she possessed the most magnificent breasts he'd ever seen, which were more than half exposed in their gold lamé bra.

Nikolas felt dry-mouthed with desire. How he missed Elektra. It had been more than a week since he'd last seen her, she who gave her body to him joyously yet modestly every night, every morning, and sometimes even in the afternoon. This buxom girl in red feathers reminded him slightly of Elektra, and shaking his head he walked down the boulevard, trying to rid himself of carnal thoughts, concentrating again on the problem of how to pass through the hallowed studio gates.

Spotting a telephone booth, he scanned his dog-eared letter to read the number, but unfamiliar with even a Greek telephone, it took him ten minutes and as many nickels and dimes before the number rang and a cheerful-sounding voice chirped, 'MCCP Studios, good morning'.

'Spyros Makopolis, please,' said Nikolas, his Greek accent making his words practically incomprehensible to the telephone operator.

'Who?' she squawked.

'Spyros Makopolis.' He enunciated each syllable carefully, as beads of sweat trickled down his forehead. The noon sun was at full blast and the kiosk felt like a furnace.

'Hold on a minute,' the voice snapped.

'Mr Makopolis' office.' Another female voice, this one mellow and cool, was on the line. Gratefully Nikolas spoke in Greek, hoping that the voice would understand him. Several times he repeated his name, and the halting English words, 'My wife's uncle. I am nephew of him.'

Finally the woman seemed to understand, but after her crisp 'Just a moment, I'll see if Mr Makopolis is available' the line went silent again.

For several more minutes Nikolas stood sweating in the cramped booth as occasionally voices came on the line instructing him to insert 'Five cents, please'. He was praying for Mr Makopolis to answer before he gave up the last of his coins.

Suddenly the cool female voice was on the line again. Nikolas couldn't understand her, but he hoped salvation was at hand as she said, 'I'm putting you through to Mr Makopolis now, sir.'

Then a deep friendly Greek voice came on the line: 'Nikolas, Nikolas my dear boy, where are you?' Spyros spoke in Greek, his voice warm and welcoming. When Nikolas told him he was only across the street the old man said happily, 'Come, I must see you now, Nikolas – I will leave a pass for you – come to see me right now.' With enormous relief Nikolas knew then that everything was going to be all right.

However, things did not go as smoothly as Nikolas had expected. Instead of immediately giving him a job on a film set, as he'd hoped, Spyros Makopolis was blunt with him.

'There is no way that you could work on a film now, Nikolas.'

'Why not, Uncle? You said you could give me a job.'

'Well for one thing, you speak hardly any English, which, of course, will eventually be remedied,' said Spyros. 'For another, our unions are tighter than a rat's ass and newcomers to technical jobs are unwelcome, to say the least.' Nikolas looked confused. 'Listen, son – listen to me,' said the old man. 'The war has just ended. Young servicemen are pouring back to the States from Okinawa, Bataan and Anzio. A lot of these soldiers, sailors and marines worked at the studios before the war, now they find their jobs going to younger men, or sometimes to even older ones, who don't want to give them up.' Spyros sighed. 'And they're all having tricky times. All the studio heads are trying to repatriate and reinstate the men who fought for us. There's hardly any room for new blood, Nick.'

Nick looked crestfallen and Spyros patted him comfortingly on the shoulder.

'Another major problem all the studios are facing is that they aren't sure what the public now wants to see at the movies.'

Nick's face was puzzled. 'Movies – they just love any movies, Uncle.'

'No, my boy. Post-war audiences are tougher, much more discriminating than they were. The harsh realities of daily life are difficult. Appetites have become cloyed by the bland diet of musicals, comedies and lightweight films; audiences are demanding more robust fare. It's a problem, Nick – a big fat problem, my friend.'

The old man was right. Escapist movies had been churned out by every studio to boost the morale not only of the armed forces, but also of those who by reason of sex, physical disability or age had stayed at home to keep things running. 'Serious pictures' were in vogue now. Some were blatant copies of Roberto Rossellini's *Open City*, a harshly neorealistic film about Rome during the war. Films about GIs returning to civilian life were extremely popular. *The Clock* with Robert Walker and Judy Garland, *Hail the Conquering Hero* with Eddie Bracken and *I'll Be Seeing You* with Joseph Cotton and Ginger Rogers had all done well at the box office.

'Now MCCP is making its own neorealistic pictures, of course,' said Spyros proudly. 'We're on that bandwagon. And we're also making Westerns, gangster movies and musicals. We hope to entice whole new audiences into the cinemas, Nick, after all the studio is humming with activity. We've got eighteen pictures shooting, twenty-two in post-production, and at least eighty in the development stage.'

'That's wonderful, Uncle,' said Nick, relieved. 'Then you must have a job for me?'

The old man sighed and fidgeted with some scripts on his cluttered desk.

'I'm gonna do my best, m'boy,' he boomed. 'But you're gonna start at the bottom, son – just like I did.'

To Nikolas' disappointment the only position which Spyros Makopolis could find for his nephew-in-law was one of the lowliest jobs on the lot – in the mail room. But at least it was a job, a well-paid job, and Nick was going to take the opportunities he was given and run with them. He was ambitious, not only for himself and Elektra but also for his secret plan. The foul cloud of hatred that hovered in his subconscious had to be expunged and there was only one way to do it.

13

London 1945

The end of the war meant little to Inès. It would hardly change her life at all.

Every evening, and many afternoons, she received one of her gentlemen callers. She now had an elite clientele, consisting of several of the most illustrious men in Great Britain. Unconcerned that by being a prostitute she was breaking the law, she was dedicated to self-improvement and to money. The money was her key to escaping from this life, and she saved every penny she could in her goal to live normally one day. She loved to hear the rustle of the crisp five-pound notes which men gave her. She squirrelled them away in a copy of Stendhal's *Love*, thinking the title ironically apt. She had painstakingly cut out a square centre section of the book, into the hollow of which she fitted her takings. *Love*, she thought with a wry smile, was only to be found in her bookcase, along with *Who's Who*, *Burke's Peerage*, *The Diaries of Samuel Pepys* and dozens of richly illustrated books on art, British history, the great houses and collections of England, and biographies of influential men and women.

Every Friday at lunchtime, elegantly dressed in one of the outfits she had made herself, she would take her thick wad of notes to Coutts Bank in the Strand, ceremoniously handing it over to the clerk, who would credit it to her ever-growing bank account. It had been Yves who had opened an account for her at the prestigious bank whose customers numbered not only members of the Royal Family but some of Inès' own clients. How Yves had managed this was still a mystery to her, since a client's breeding was often as important to Coutts as his wealth.

It gave her enormous pleasure, when shopping in the exclusive

Burlington Arcade or in Bond Street shops, to pay for her purchases with a Coutts check. Certainly none of the salespeople would ever have imagined that this poised young beauty was a common prostitute. She looked, dressed and behaved like a lady. Although only nineteen, Inès possessed the manners and sophistication of a woman far older; she now prided herself on a quiet elegance which spoke of breeding and old money. It was one of the attributes which most intrigued her clients when they took her to dine at the 400, the Caprice or the Coq d'Or. In her perfectly cut chic clothes she seemed to belong in these places far more than many of the English matrons in their frumpish pre-war dresses. As she snuggled into the womblike comfort of these establishments jealous glances were often thrown her way. Inès had the Frenchwoman's innate understanding of clothes, and was always beautifully and stylishly dressed in outfits mostly created by herself. During the day she lived the life of a woman of leisure. Sometimes she strolled up Shaftesbury Avenue on her way to the Queens Theatre or the Globe to see the latest play by Terence Rattigan, Noël Coward or Emlyn Williams, passing the Windmill Theatre, where she would glance at the front-of-house photographs of the semi-nude showgirls and the leering comics.

Now she never thought of herself as a whore, but as a courtesan, and had improved herself to suit her new role. She had decided to keep her once-blonde hair dark. It framed her pale, high-cheekboned face with its slanting blue cat's eyes and sculpted chin. She had grown taller in London, her body svelte and toned, her legs those of a thoroughbred, her breasts magnificent. Underneath all her elegance, her mound of golden pubic hair was trimmed to a heart shape, which further fascinated her devoted clients.

Courtesan. She liked that word. A courtesan was a woman who shared the fantasies of a man's secret life, who knew everything about his occupation and all that it entailed. She knew about his wife, what that particular woman liked in bed, and what she didn't; she knew which schools his children attended, and even what they wanted to be when they grew up. She knew what wInès he preferred, how dry he liked his martinis, how strong his whisky and soda. She knew his favourite foods and sometimes, for a special client, she would prepare them for him perfectly. She knew which books he read, which plays he'd seen, in which sports he participated, what politics he favoured, but most important of all, she knew what excited him in bed.

Inès was quick to discover what a man liked sexually. Most of the time it wasn't anything that he couldn't get from his wife, except that from what she'd discovered, most English wives were not keen on oral sex. Thanks to Yves this was one of Inès' specialities. Most women wanted to please their husbands but often didn't have the time, energy or knowledge.

A sexually inept female is a turn-off to most men, and Inès became accustomed to hearing many clients complain that their wives just 'lay there like stone and never responded'. She could bring a man to orgasm within minutes. When men kissed her breasts, or her mound of Venus, running their fingers and tongues into her most intimate places, arousing her, they made her body shake with lust, for Inès had become an accomplished actress. She made sure her clients thought that they were exciting her, and that excited them more than anything else. They kept returning to her, often referring their friends to her. But Inès was careful about whom she entertained. She had never forgotten the perversions of the Italian General, and in her cosy, well-decorated flat she interviewed prospective clients carefully, questioning them as strictly as a duchess employing a chambermaid.

Politicians, members of Parliament, aristocrats, industrialists, men of finance, power and position, these were the men she entertained. Credentials were essential. Most of them became entranced with her, more than one proposing matrimony, but although Inès was ready for that she knew she had to fall in love. Visions of true love haunted her. She still thought about Yves, dreamed about him, his laughter, his magic, his crinkly eyes and his soft hair. And she also dreamed too often of the Italian whom she had killed that April morning, awakening with a scream on her lips, vividly reliving the horror. She never allowed a man to spend the night with her during the week, and only for her most special clients would she consent to spend a weekend away. In her search for love she found all men lacking, and the more she saw of their weaknesses and foibles the less she felt she would ever meet the right one for her.

Armistice night she spent alone, in front of her sewing machine, working on a velvet Maggy Rouff suit which she was copying from *Vogue*. Inès felt more truly alone than she ever had before. All her clients were with their families and friends, and she had no one with whom to share this momentous night. Not a man, not a woman friend, not even a pet. From her windows she could hear the boisterous sound of revellers outside singing, laughing, hooting with joy.

On the wireless the excitement in the voice of the normally severe BBC commentator was contagious. The BBC was broadcasting from every European capital, so that their listeners could hear how the rest of the free world was celebrating victory.

She sat quietly working, listening to a French-accented voice describing the frenzy of the Parisian crowds. When the announcer started to describe with poetic reverence the beauty of Notre-Dame Cathedral completely lit up, glowing like an exquisite gothic fairy-tale castle, and surrounded by French patriots singing the 'Marseillaise' at the top of their lungs, tears ran down her face for the very first time since Yves had left.

'Paris,' she whispered, as her fingers deftly cut cotton and threaded her needle. 'Paris. I wonder if I will ever see you again. I wonder if there's anything left for me there any more.'

14

Calabria 1945

Umberto Scrofo returned to his native village in Calabria a very rich man. With his spoils of war he was able to purchase the land to build an enormous house on the highest part of the mountainous region. The terrain was harsh, rocky, difficult to farm, but since the whole region was so desperately poor and even more so as a result of the war, Umberto found no shortage of peasant labour to cultivate his unproductive land.

Because of his now enormous assets and possessions, he was able to wield great power in Calabria. Not, however, as great as the power of the Cosa Nostra; they still ruled the lives and destinies of those around them with total and unquestionable authority. But Scrofo had more than enough power to guarantee him the serenity he longed for.

Inside his new fortress he had built a screening room where he revelled in his passion for the latest Hollywood movies. Most nights he sat alone in the velvet-tented room watching carefully, admiring the beauty of the young blonde actresses he desired: young virginal types like Bonita Granville, June Haver, Mary Beth Hughes were his great favourites. Girls who gave the illusion of being fresh from puberty. Often, as he watched them, his Lilliputian penis would stiffen and he would pleasure himself.

Since his 'accident' with the French whore in Paris, he had rarely indulged in sex. He had found the olive-skinned, black-haired women of Hydra unappealing, preferring his own secret fantasies to coupling with them.

In addition to the Hollywood films, he possessed a large collection of blue movies imported from Scandinavia. The cool Nordic beauties who frolicked naked in sauna baths and pastoral streams could always arouse him.

As he rested his overstuffed body on an overstuffed couch one afternoon, he looked up from the Christie's catalogue he was flicking through and saw, tending his flowerbeds, a young blonde of exquisite beauty. She looked up, caught his eye, then blushed and looked away. Scrofo found her beauty and innocence exciting. It was the first time in years that he had felt such a strong desire for a woman, and it stimulated him into action.

On making inquiries he discovered that she was the niece of his gardener. Her parents had been killed in a road accident and she had been adopted by the gardener and his wife. Her name was Silvana, and she was seventeen years old.

Umberto insisted that the girl be given a job inside the house as parlour maid. It would be her job to dust and clean some of the treasured objects d'art that glittered on the tables and in the display cabinets of his villa.

Every day Silvana performed her tasks happily, humming quietly, a smile playing around her gently curved, soft pink lips, blushing whenever she caught Umberto's intense stare.

Soon he became obsessed by the girl, his thoughts full of her breasts, her innocent grey eyes, the way her body undulated underneath the plain blue calico house dress. He ordered another uniform to be made for her by one of the village women – the costume of a French maid, just as he had seen in so many movies. Silvana was embarrassed to be seen in it, but Signor Scrofo insisted, and, after all, he was her respected employer.

One afternoon Silvana shyly entered Umberto's drawing room with a timid knock on the door. She was wearing sheer black hose, a short frilly black skirt, a white organdy apron and, perched on her abundant yellow curls, a little mobcap such as might be worn by an eighteenth-century maiden in a picture by Boucher. As she knelt to dust the legs of a console table, Umberto could see her lacy panties, and he caught a tantalizing glimpse of succulent white thighs above black stockings.

He strode to the double doors, quietly closing and locking them. Silvana was busy cleaning round the gilded crevices, and cried out in fright when Umberto crept up behind her, grabbing her breasts through the flimsy silk of her blouse.

'No, please no, Signor,' she whimpered, her frightened eyes exciting him so much that he thought his tiny cock would burst through his trousers.

'Yes, yes, my dear, yes, *now*,' he rasped, his harsh wheezing voice thick as he ripped open her blouse, exposing her mouth-watering, rose-tipped breasts. 'I must have you *now*, Silvana – I must. Be a good girl now – I won't hurt you.'

Her terrified cries continued to inflame him as he wrestled her down on to the flowered aubusson carpet. The heavy velvet curtains were drawn against the strong afternoon sun, and the thick stone walls were as good as soundproof.

Umberto's gross body pinioned her to the floor and no one heard Silvana scream as he raped and sodomized her throughout the afternoon. Blood ran down her face and back as he beat her, and after a while she mercifully lost consciousness. She reminded him of that French tart in Paris and this drove him to hurt her more.

'Whore,' he said viciously, slapping the girl's unconscious face. 'Cheap whore, you deserve this.'

At last he was finished. Silvana lay slumped in front of the fireplace, her uniform in tatters, her face bruised and puffed from weeping and his beatings, her body covered in blood. Umberto looked at her coldly as he zipped up his trousers. Her eyes opened, looking at him pleadingly. She was disgusting to him now. No longer desirable – a discarded toy.

'*Signor* – help me, please,' she said, crawling across the carpet, her words muffled by her swollen lips.

'Get out,' Umberto said curtly, mopping his sweating head with a silk handkerchief and rearranging his clothes.

'Out – now.' He turned away from her, pouring himself a brandy with a gratified smile. 'I've finished with you, little slut.'

So – he gloated to himself. He could still perform, and very well too. This was the first time for over two years that he had done something like this with a woman. Ever since that creature in Paris had robbed him of most of his sexual desire with her vicious attempt on his life. But that little whore hadn't succeeded. He was still a man, a stallion, a stud, in spite of the tiny penis which had caused so much mirth in the girls he had attempted to make love to when he was young.

And he was still young, was he not? He preened in the mirror, his eyes not seeing the bloated features, the thick lips, the short, scarred neck. All he saw was a facsimile of Benito Mussolini – a soldier, a patriot, a man of power, irresistible to women. Alas now dead, hanged by his own people in disgrace. But Umberto was too pleased with himself to dwell on Mussolini's untimely death. He felt his sexual vigour to be in full and potent flower again. He was ready to take other women now. Many others. He didn't give a thought to Silvana; she meant less than nothing now that he had had her. But perhaps she had a nice friend, a sister, or a cousin? He would find out.

The following night as Umberto lay asleep in the canopied Empire bed which was reputed to have once belonged to Napoleon, the locked doors burst open, and four men, hats pulled low over their eyes, surrounded him. They said nothing as they pulled him roughly out of bed, nothing as he called out hoarsely for his servants. Where were they, why didn't they answer him? Where were all his bodyguards? His entourage of lackeys? But no one answered his screams for mercy, and the house was dark and silent as a tomb as the men bustled him roughly down the marble staircase, out across his manicured lawns, ghostly green in the moonlight, down to the rough pebbled beach.

Whimpering with terror, the scar on his neck throbbing, the soles of his feet bleeding from the jagged rocks, Umberto was experiencing a fear unknown to him ever before.

His hands and feet were tied tightly with rope and he was tossed roughly into a small fishing boat resting on the shoreline. The four men climbed into another boat and began towing Umberto's tiny craft out to sea, into the notoriously dangerous currents which swept down the coast. They grinned in the reflected moonlight, but their eyes were dead.

'What are you doing to me?' Umberto choked, feeling his throat constrict. 'Where are you taking me?'

'We're sending you to die, scum,' the leader snarled. 'Die, pig, alone and scared. If you live to come back to this place ever again, we'll find you and we'll kill you in a way that will make you wish you had never entered this world – you have our word on that.'

One of the men then unhooked the tow rope and the swift current started to carry Umberto further and further out to sea. 'Why? Why are you doing this?' he bleated. 'What you I done?'

'This is for Silvana,' the tallest man shouted harshly. 'We are her blood brothers. If you return to Calabria we will cut off your balls, stuff them in your mouth, and then kill you – and you'll be begging us to do that by the time we're finished. Antonio Rostranni has given us his blessing to do so, and he wants to watch.' The men all laughed coarse, loutish laughter, and Umberto froze. Rostranni, the most feared name in the whole of southern Italy. The Padrino himself; the Mafia chief whose word became unquestioned law. If the girl Silvana was indeed related to someone in the Cosa Nostra, he could consider himself extremely lucky that they hadn't slit his throat while he slept.

The boat was swept further out to sea and the four men sat motionless, staring after it. Umberto then noticed the oars, an earthenware jug of water and some dry biscuits, provisions for an existence of a few days, if that, and only if he could find a way to remove the ropes which tied his wrists so tightly that his arms were starting to go dead.

'Where am I to go?' he whispered. 'I can't survive in this boat. How can I save myself? Where do you want me to go?'

'Go to Hell,' the leader jeered as the two boats drifted further and further apart. 'You belong with the perverts there, with the other scum, go to Hell, pig.'

There was much rejoicing in the small Calabrian village when the hated Umberto Scrofo suddenly disappeared. Although foul play was suspected not a single one of Umberto's numerous servants had either seen or heard anything the night that he had mysteriously disappeared. In spite of extensive police investigations no trace of him could be found. Several months later the remains of a small fishing boat were found washed up on the northern shore of an Italian beach. It was smashed to pieces and contained only a few tattered scraps of what the police identified as Scrofo's clothes. With that evidence, Umberto Scrofo was then declared officially dead.

His palatial mansion was sold, and his magnificent possessions were divided between the remaining members of his family in Calabria. The cousins, aunts and uncles who had mocked and despised him as a child found themselves the heirs to the glorious pictures and booty which he had scavenged from Paris and Hydra.

A funeral of sorts was held, which the family attended, but no one could have been said to mourn him. Very soon he was completely forgotten by everyone in the world except for Ines Juillard and Nikolas Stanopolis. Neither of them could ever forget him.

PART II

I

Elektra knew that life wasn't going to be easy for her in America. Nikolas had sent for her about three months after he'd arrived and now she was almost beside herself with excitement as she caught a glimpse of his tall wiry body leaning against a pillar inside the arrivals hall at LA airport.

'Nikolai, oh my darling Nikolai – I can't believe it's really you –' she said ecstatically as she threw herself into her husband's open arms, which were not as warmly welcoming as she'd expected them to be.

'What's the matter, Nikolai?' she asked tentatively as he pulled away from her embrace with apparent embarrassment.

'Elektra, I'd like to you meet Errol,' he said in Greek, gesturing towards an enormous black man wearing a burgundy uniform, trimmed with an excessive amount of gold braid.

'Welcome to LA, Missus Nicky,' beamed the man as he stood to attention. 'Sure are glad to have you here – our Mr Nick he's bin pinin' away, he never stops talkin' about you.'

'This is Errol – Uncle Spyros' chauffeur. Uncle Spyros has lent us his personal car today. He wanted you to have a special welcome to this wonderful country.'

Elektra nodded in silence, wishing that Nikolas had come to meet her alone. The chauffeur seemed pleasantly friendly but Elektra was shy, and she had wanted to be reunited with her husband in private.

A cheerful porter carried her only shabby piece of luggage through the jostling crowds as they all walked out to the pavement, where Elektra's mouth opened wide with amazement. Waiting at the kerb was the longest black car she had ever seen. There were no vehicles of any kind on Hydra, and she had hardly seen any cars before except on occasional trips to Athens. She looked fearfully at the busy street where cars, buses and taxis sped by at terrifying speeds, and laughing pedestrians seemed to defy death as they dashed between them.

'Come on, Elektra.' She thought that Nick's voice seemed to have a more authoritative edge to it than before. 'Hurry up, stop gawking, we must get to the house before dark. Aunt Olympia has prepared a Greek feast to welcome you.'

Clumsily Elektra climbed into the cavernous back seat of the Cadillac, conscious that her skirt had bunched itself up well above her knees. Blushing furiously, she pulled it down and huddled in a corner, looking anxiously out of the rear window to see if the porter had brought her suitcase.

Nick jumped in effortlessly, and gave her a brief hug. He held her hand, talking to her excitedly in their own language for a few minutes, but then he became involved in a long conversation with Errol in English. The men were laughing loudly as Errol seemed to be telling some kind of amusing story. Elektra leaned her head back on to the lush leather upholstery, closing weary eyes. She hadn't slept for days. It had been a long and exhausting trip to California, but she was here at last on the other side of the world. She hoped it wouldn't take long to become as settled and Americanized as the loving husband who had left her only three months ago.

Olympia Makopolis was a warm, motherly, comforting woman so like the women of Hydra that Elektra felt immediately at home with her. In spite of her husband's enormous wealth and position in Hollywood, Mrs Makopolis still insisted on cooking and preparing everything herself, and her vast dining table was laden with familiar dishes from their homeland. Great plates of taramasalata, dishes of baby shrimp, squid and *pompano*, *tzadziki*, vine leaves stuffed with meat and rice, succulent baby lamb with aubergine, crisp lettuce tossed with diced pieces of goat's cheese, *bourekia* wrapped in pastry, and freshly baked bread, mixed with the powerful aroma of freshly chopped garlic in the *skordalia* sauce – a sauce so overpoweringly pungent that it was considered bad manners to eat it before a social event unless everyone was having it. Jugs of cooled white wine had just been put on the table when Olympia heard the crunch of the limousine on the gravelled driveway.

'Welcome, my dear Elektra, I'm *so* happy to see my cousin's daughter at last,' said Olympia, embracing Elektra warmly and feeling an immediate rush of affection for the shy girl.

'Come, come – we eat right away – you must be starving.' She looked approvingly at Elektra's full-bosomed and rounded figure, in such contrast to the greyhound-sleek body of her very pretty niece Vicky Zolotos who was Americanized to within an inch of her life.

'Vicky, this is Elektra, my wife,' said Nikolas proudly.

'I'm thrilled to meet you, honey, Nicky has talked about you *so* much,' gushed Vicky, her long shiny blonde pageboy, tightly belted green gaberdine suit, and tiny matching hat tipped over one ravishing turquoise eye making her appear to Elektra like a fashion plate straight from the pages of *Vogue*.

Elektra cringed. She couldn't understand a single word the girl said, even though Nicky, who seemed to possess such new-found confidence, quickly translated.

'Vicky also works in the mail room at the studio,' he said rapidly. 'Her father is one of Uncle Spyros' board members – she's just out of university – her mother is Greek and she's a cousin of Uncle Spyros. She's been helping me learn English, and we're both slaves of the studio system, aren't we, Vicky?' He flashed a confident grin at the beautiful girl who made Elektra feel hopelessly drab, dowdy and old-fashioned. Elektra's long serge skirt, sensible brogues and heavy lisle stockings were hardly a match for this American beauty's slim nylon-clad legs, sculpted bosom and perfectly made up face. Although she thought that they must be about the same age, Elektra felt hideous and inadequate beside her.

Olympia had lived in California for nearly thirty years, but she was still a simple Greek woman at heart. Seeing Elektra, so small, frightened and awed by the sumptuousness of these alien surroundings, reminded her of herself three decades ago, and Olympia made up her mind to help this girl to make the difficult adjustment to the American way of life.

Later that night, as Nikolas gently undressed his wife, whispering passionate endearments to her in the language she understood, Elektra felt herself beginning to relax at last. The tension in her knotted muscles began to ebb away as her husband's sensual fingers slowly caressed her. Gently his hands encircled her breasts and his fingers as gentle as butterfly wings touched her nipples, causing gasps of joy to spring from her throat. Nikolai, her husband, the only man she had ever been with – the only man she could ever love – was still hers. He loved her. Now she knew that she had nothing to fear in America.

Nikolas Stanopolis, with his natural aptitude for languages, had learned English surprisingly fast. Now not only could he read and write with few mistakes, but he had become a master of American slang, almost a necessity in the movie business.

But for Elektra adjusting to American life was a struggle. Everything confused her. The language, the hectic pace of LA, the motor cars, and the planes which shattered the afternoon peace of her siestas. The gadgets in her kitchen might as well have come from another planet, and the fast streamlined supermarkets all made her feel a hopeless wreck. She felt stupid, dumb, completely alien to this modern world.

In spite of Olympia's patient coaching, and in spite of the beautiful, bright and breezy Vicky coming to dinner several times a week to help her with her English, Elektra couldn't manage to grasp more than a few words. Desperately she studied phrase books and dictionaries, read magazines and newspapers, but her brain, already befuddled with trying to cope with electric cookers, washing machines and refrigerators, and trying to cook with tinned and frozen ingredients foreign to her, simply couldn't cope. Nikolas, Vicky and Olympia insisted that she listen to the news programmes, plays and variety shows on the wireless, but the foreign language was still a foreign language to her. She tried gallantly to make herself understood at the enormous Food Giant supermarket on Canon Drive where Olympia had insisted she shop. Numbly, pushing her shopping cart around the endless aisles stacked high with colourful products, none of which she'd ever heard of, she was jostled by confident wholesome women in crisp shirtwaist dresses, their faces made up, their hair coiffed into soft curls or covered by a becoming hat. Elektra couldn't even begin to think of shopping for new clothes even though Nick asked her when she was going to get rid of her dowdy dresses.

'Why don't you buy some new gear, honey?' he asked her one night, grimacing as he saw the overcooked meatballs and aubergine croquettes which she'd done her best to prepare on the incomprehensible modern cooker. 'We can afford it; I'm making good money now.'

They were sitting at a shiny yellow Bakelite kitchen table in one of many little bungalows Spyros reserved for his nearest and dearest. There was a tight enclave of Makopolis relations living on the land which bordered his estate. Vicky Zolotos lived in one with a female cousin, Olympia's three sisters lived in another, and Spyros' uncle and aunt lived next door to them. Unfortunately for Elektra, all of these Greek immigrants seemed to have had no difficulty at all in learning English. They chattered away effortlessly, switching back and forth between English and Greek with the practised ease of people who had totally adjusted to both cultures.

Nikolas was glued to Jack Benny on the wireless, laughing at his jokes until tears ran down his face while Elektra silently ladled the hardened, lumpy meatballs on to his plate.

'You used to cook these so well in Hydra,' he said during the commercial break. 'What happened?'

'I'm sorry,' mumbled Elektra, close to tears. 'I just can't get this cooker to work.'

Nikolas took another bite, and made a face. 'You've got to adjust to the modern world, Elektra, this is 1946, the war's over now, the men are all back, everyone is competing in America for jobs – position – everything. You've got to compete too, Elektra – you must – you've got to try.'

'I can't.' She slumped down at the table with her head in her hands, starting to weep. 'I just *can't* learn English – I can't cook with this stove – I don't fit in here, Nikolas. I don't belong in America. I want to go home – back to Hydra. That's where I really belong.'

Nikolas stroked her long dark hair sympathetically. He loved her very much, but he couldn't help but compare her simple rounded peasant looks to the glamorous women he came into contact with daily at the studio. Vicky was always flirting with him, joking in that sassy cute way so many American girls seemed to have. He liked it. He liked Vicky too, and why shouldn't he? After all, she was his distant cousin, albeit a couple of dozen or so times removed.

'Try, Elektra – please try – for my sake,' he said, tuning back into another wisecrack from Jack Benny and Rochester.

'I'll *try*, Niko,' sobbed Elektra despairingly, 'I will, but I don't think I'll ever succeed. I don't have the ear.'

'You must be patient, and try harder,' said Nick firmly. 'You *must*, Elektra – for us – for our family. Our future is here, Elektra – in America, in Hollywood – with these people. I'm going to become a director one day – Spyros has promised, I'm going to be a great director. This is our life here now, Elektra, and we're never going back to live in Greece. Never!'

Elektra nodded, trying to control her welling tears. 'I know,' she said sadly, thinking of the mountains, the sea, the beauty of her island. She felt a great lump in her throat and her heart was heavy as she realized that they might well never see Hydra again. 'I will try,' she whispered. 'I'll really try, Nikolai.'

And she did. She studied for hours each day. Olympia became a mother hen to her, and Vicky, if not quite like an older sister, at least helped her with her wardrobe.

'You've gotta get out of those dowdy duds, kiddo,' she insisted. 'You look like a total frump – it's time for you to get hip.' She dragged Elektra off to Saks to sharpen her image in spite of Elektra's protestations that they simply couldn't afford to buy such expensive new clothes. But Vicky took no notice at all and they returned from their shopping trip laden with boxes and bags full of pretty cotton shirtwaist dresses, slim capri pants, frilly blouses and shorts, most of which Elektra vowed that she'd be too embarrassed to wear.

Vicky laughingly contradicted her. 'Honey, when the hot weather gets here you're gonna *live* in those shorts, and you'll wonder how you could ever have put on those old fuddy-duddy long black skirts.'

After a very long time Elektra finally managed to learn to speak English, albeit falteringly, but she never felt completely comfortable with it. She still read, with pangs of homesickness, the Greek newspapers and magazines which were sent regularly to Olympia

Makopolis. She never really found any American friends, preferring the company of Olympia and her three sisters to the wives and girlfriends of Nikolas' co-workers. But she both worshipped and respected her husband, and to her he was king.

As for the luscious Vicky, she still terrified Elektra with her stylish clothes, glossy pageboy and fast talk. Elektra suspected that she would never feel at ease with her. She still felt left out when Nikolas and Vicky chattered together for hours about the film business, sharing industry gossip and jokes together in the American slang with which they both seemed so comfortable.

Elektra's happiness only flowered completely the year after her arrival in Los Angeles when the first of her beautiful babies was born. Then she was in her element, taking care of little Alexis totally, eschewing the nannies and nurses which Vicky and Olympia recommended. To Vicky's shocked amazement, Elektra breast fed the baby until he was more than a year old and she was already pregnant with her second.

I will never become Americanized, particularly now with my baby boy and girl to look after, thought Elektra, looking at her bonny plump reflection in her dressing table mirror. She didn't have time for sessions at the hairdresser or for afternoons browsing at Saks or Magnins. She was perfectly happy in their little bungalow with her lively children and her beloved husband, who alas, wasn't there as much as she would have liked. He was becoming more and more involved with his work at the studio, and although he was a good husband and a loving father to the babies, Elektra knew that work was fast becoming the most important thing in his life.

Elektra woke up gasping and choking, unable to breathe. It was pitch dark in the bedroom and strong hands were clamped around her neck trying to squeeze the life from her. The figure was on top of her, the wiry fingers so tight around her throat that had she not awakened she knew it would have been only a matter of seconds before she was asphyxiated by this maniac. She tried to scream for help but no sounds would come. Where was Nikolas? Where was he? And how had this intruder got into their bedroom?

Elekra fought for her life, hearing nothing but the harsh breathing of her assailant. She knew she had to attack his eyes before she lost consciousness but his body was strong and pinned her to the bed. She struck out blindly with the remains of her strength where she thought his eyes were and to her horror heard the man exclaim as her fingernails raked his flesh:

'You bastard. You fucking scumbag – this is it, pig. I've got you now and I'm going to kill you.'

In panic Elektra heard her husband's voice screaming this litany of hatred at her. Nikolas trying to kill her. O dear God, thought Elektra as unconsciousness threatened to engulf her. God no. How could he do this? Her gentle, kind Nikolas. Was he mad? Weakly she tried to cry out, but realized that she was completely powerless. She was going to die. She was going to die at the hands of her husband –the man she loved. She could feel the last thread of consciousness breaking . . .

'Mama – Papa – what are you doing?'

The bedroom light suddenly illuminated little Alexis standing at the door in his pyjamas, his eyes wide with fear as he saw his father straddling his mother, hands gripping her throat.

'No, Papa, no,' the boy screamed, running to the bed and tugging at his father.

As if from some great distance Nikolas heard his son's voice and opened his eyes which had been tightly closed in rage. When he saw what he had been doing to his wife he stopped with a scream of terror.

'My God, Elektra, oh Jesus, Jesus, what have I done?'

The baby girl now toddled into the bedroom holding her teddy bear and crying, wakened by the noise.

Elektra moaned and drew deep, gasping breaths into her aching lungs.

'God, Elektra! Oh God, are you all right?' cried Nikolas. He was weeping now with the horror of what he had done. The two children were crying and his beloved wife was groaning in agony.

'I – I'm all right, Nikolas,' Elektra managed to say as she tried to sit up.

He pressed a glass of water to her white lips.

'God, I almost killed you.' Nikolas looked like a man possessed. His hair was dishevelled and his whole body was shaking.

'Go back to bed, children, Mama is all right,' Elektra managed to croak. 'Everything's going to be all right now.'

'It was a nightmare,' cried Nikolas after he had tucked the children safely back in bed and sought the sanctuary of Elektra's arms. 'I thought you were Scrofo,' he wept. 'It was a nightmare, Elektra, I didn't mean it. You know that, don't you?'

'Of course,' she soothed. 'Of course I do, Nikolas.'

'I thought about Mama's death,' he said softly, 'then I saw him and I tried to kill him, but it was *you*! Oh God, Elektra, can you ever forgive me, can you?'

'Of course I can – of course,' she soothed again.

'The dream was so vivid,' he murmured, his body still shaking and sweating. 'Where do you think he is now?'

'You mean Scrofo?' she said gently, holding him safely.

'Yeah, Gourouni – the bastard. Commander Umberto Scrofo.'

Nick's eyes began to gleam with rage again in the dim light from the bedside lamp.

Elektra was surprised that he was still so obsessed with Scrofo. They had been in America for nearly four years. Surely his anger must be waning by now?

'Don't think about him, Nikolai,' she murmured. 'That's all over now – it's all in the past.'

'Mother of God, Elektra – here we are in America, in this nice house with my good job – the American Dream.' His face was contorted with fury. 'And that fucking piece of scum is probably still alive somewhere.' He pounded the pillow with all the force of his frustrated anger. 'The murdering bastard is still alive, do you realize that? Do you?'

Elektra tried to calm him down again but he was like a wild man.

'Sshh, you'll wake the babies again,' she admonished. 'Stop thinking about Scrofo, Nikolai – you must stop – you'll make yourself ill.'

'Elektra.' He turned to face her, his eyes wide and full of passion. 'I said it that day on Hydra, but I *know* it now – one day I'm going to find that bastard – and I'm going to kill him with my bare hands.'

'Sshh – no, Nikolai, no.' She tried to hold him but he leapt out of bed and stood before her – a naked avenging angel.

'I swear it – I swear it on the lives of our children – on the memory of my mother – I'm going to find Umberto Scrofo and I'm going to kill him if it's the last thing on earth I do.'

Ever the nepotist, Spyros Makopolis had taken Nikolas and Elektra to his bosom. He often invited them to join his family at their table, which was always groaning with Greek delicacies. At work he pushed Nikolas for promotion after promotion. From the mail room he went on to become a gofer in the publicity department; from there he became assistant to the assistant editor in the cutting rooms. He stayed there for nearly four years until he understood everything there was to know about editing, splicing, dubbing and the entire technical process of film making. Finally he graduated to the floor itself. Third assistant director, second assistant director, first assistant director, location manager, production manager, and finally, joy of joys, Spyros called him into his office one day to announce the promotion he ached for more than any other: director.

Spyros sat behind a desk covered with scripts, puffing on his ever-present Havana.

'Take a look at *that*, kid,' he beamed, throwing a bound blue script at him. 'Something special, something real cute and zany.'

Eagerly Nick caught it, but his face dropped as he saw the title. '*Bobby Soxers in Space?*' Nick looked astonished. 'What's this, Uncle – do you want me to give you a budget breakdown on it?'

'No! No!' the old man boomed out. 'No, my boy, I want you to *direct* it.'

'Direct *Bobby Soxers in Space*? My God! You've gotta be kidding, Uncle.' Nick didn't know whether to laugh or cry. For years he had been yearning to direct a feature film – any feature – but *Bobby Soxers in Space*? Even he had his pride. The title was a complete joke, and the content probably much worse.

'My boy, I won't lie to you,' Spyros said with a sigh. 'Not to put too fine a point on it, our studio is in deep and rising shit.'

'How can it be? According to the trades, our last five movies grossed millions. Is that a lie?'

Spyros nodded sadly. 'Alas, my boy – the publicity department did a sterling job in telling the world that our last five films did well. I must admit, however, it's not true. In fact it's a fucking lie.'

He paused, dabbing his florid face with an enormous silk handkerchief, choosing his next words with care. 'Understand, my boy, that after the war, MCCP could do no wrong – no wrong at all.

'Spyros Makopolis could do no wrong, either,' he continued. 'As the major stockholder, president and chief executive in charge of production, I was the golden boy to all the bankers and brokers.'

Nick listened, aware that his uncle was under intense strain. This was obvious from the puffy liverish bags under his eyes and in the way he leaned heavily on the vast desk to relight his cigar.

'What happened, Uncle?'

'Television happened,' Spyros spat out bitterly. 'Tee bloody Vee is *destroying* the film business, Nick, *ruining* it. Do you realize that after the war, *ninety* million people a *week* went to the cinema? You know how many go now?' he asked accusingly. 'Three years ago, in 1950, only *sixty million* people a week. Down to only sixty million. It's terrible, Nick, just terrible, and it's getting worse all the time.'

'But it's not just our studio – it's all of them, surely?' asked Nick.

'Yeah, yeah – Zanuck, Warner, Cohn – we're all in the same kind of shit. Our jobs are hanging by a thread, Nick. If this decline in movie-going continues, by the end of this decade movie studios as we now know them will be practically extinct.'

'But I don't understand. Surely this space movie is just another piece of shit,' Nick said. 'Who the hell is going to see something like that?'

'It's something *different*!' cried Spyros excitedly, getting up from behind the desk to throw a beefy arm around his nephew's shoulders. 'Something new, something zany, crazy – a novelty for the kids that adults will love, too. They'll love it, Niko, I know it. Now look, I know it's low budget, but if you can bring this picture in for one hundred fifty thousand, kid, I guarantee it will gross at least ten times that. We'll bring it out for Easter vacation – the college students will love it. You'll be a hero, my boy, a hero.' He patted Nick benevolently and smiled broadly at him. 'Especially to me.'

'But, Uncle, why do you want *me* to direct it when I've never directed before? I mean, I'm honoured, sure, but what about Weston or Ratoff, surely they'd be better?'

'I have to be honest with you, Niko – none of them will touch it with my left testicle,' Spyros admitted. 'Only a newcomer can do this movie, Niko. Someone fresh, young, with new ideas. Someone who understands the youth market. It's a break for you, kid, a big break.'

No one would touch it? This was bad, very bad. Nick had expected to start by directing low-budget films, yes, but hopefully more of the quality of *The Window* or *Laura*. With *Bobby Soxers in Space*, he could quickly become the laughing stock of the business, then he'd never be able to get a decent movie to direct. Hollywood was a tough, snobbish town where you were only as good as your last film. If that film was a turkey, or, even worse, a lemon, no one was likely to take another chance on using you again.

'Do I have to do it, Uncle?'

'Yes, yes, you can *make* something of this, boy – I know you can,' growled the old man. 'This is your big break, Nick. I could give it to one of the young contract directors but I'm giving it to *you*. It's not a bad script, it's cute. You can shoot it in Death Valley with a non union crew and some of our contract players – it'll only take four weeks. If you do well, there'll be other scripts – I promise you, Niko. For the sake of the old country, for your mama, for all of us Greeks who must stick together – you direct this picture and there'll be plenty more, I promise you. Plenty. You've got the talent, boy. Just do this for me, and for the studio.'

That night, with a heavy heart, Nick began to read the ridiculous script. Hidden beneath the tired old clichés, the heavy-handed humour and the worn-out gags, there were grains of originality – a modern twist which might well be hilarious. If he could get a decent rewrite from one of the contract hacks who wasn't a lush, use some of his own ideas – and he was never short of those – and get a couple of halfway decent actors, maybe *Bobby Soxers in Space* could turn out to be the sow's ear which became the silk purse.

2

For seven consecutive years Julian Brooks had been one of Britain's top box-office stars, each film propelling him to even greater cinematic glory. The fans simply could not get enough of him. His films were nearly all in the romantic adventure genre, and men and women alike doted on them.

His first film, *The Merry Monarch*, had been the precursor of his swashbuckling roles, and he'd continued to play a succession of brave adventurers and heroes on locations as far away as the Sahara Desert, the Amazon and the South China Seas. Didier Armande had signed him to a vice-like contract, and in spite of the fact that almost every major studio in Hollywood wanted him loaned to them Didier simply would not let Julian Brooks go. He was unquestionably England's number one male star, he was Didier's discovery and the shrewd producer was going to get his pound of flesh each and every year from the water-tight seven-year contract. Not only that but Phoebe wasn't at all keen on going to Hollywood.

'Better a big fish in a small pond than vice versa,' she snapped whenever the subject came up. 'Here you're a star, there you'll just be one of the players on C. Aubrey Smith's cricket team.'

Julian was in his element for the first two years of his contract. Mr Christian – Beau Geste – Chopin – Sir Walter Raleigh – he played many of the great romantic leading men and he also starred opposite some of the world's most desirable actresses. For even if Didier was not keen to lend them his most important star, American studios were more than happy to allow their beautiful contract actresses to cross the Atlantic to star opposite Julian Brooks. Soon there were few leading actresses whom Julian had not played opposite, and not only played opposite on screen, but off screen too.

He seemed irresistible to practically all women. For Julian, making love to each new leading lady was as easy as tying his Charvet tie. The actresses were all more than willing, and he was more than eager to please, as long as there was always complete discretion. That was the only proviso in Julian's liaisons. He insisted that no breath of scandal should leak out to the gossip columns or magazines. He always made it quite clear before an affair began that he was happily married, and not prepared to either hurt his wife or damage his marriage. Many was the Hollywood siren who, having sampled the delights of Looks Brooks' lovemaking techniques, was loath to let him go when their director had called the final 'cut'.

'Not since Gary Cooper,' one actress told her friend who was off to London to play Roxanne to his Cyrano, 'not since Coop has *any* guy made me come so many times and *so* deliciously.' She shivered with pleasure at the memory.

'That good, huh?'

'Yeah – better than Sinatra – much better than Flynn.'

'What does the wife think about all these shenanigans?' inquired the friend – Candida Willow, one of MCCP's most promising young stars.

The redhead tossed her Titian pageboy. 'Oh, she doesn't care. He doesn't flaunt it – he lets you know it's just a fling – but oh boy, what a fling! Honey, you're in for some treat, I'm telling you.'

'You mean his wife doesn't *know*? She doesn't even suspect?' asked Candida, big blue eyes wide with disbelief.

'Sure she knows. But she's so busy huntin' at Harrods 'n' Hartnells 'n' hobnobbing with the gentry, that she turns the other cheek – know what I mean?' The redhead winked and Candida giggled.

'Well, I'm certainly looking forward to getting to know this Mr Brooks,' said Candida. 'But I won't sleep with him, because I *don't* have affairs with married men – besides, you know I'm in love with Gerry.'

'Just wait 'til Looks turns on the charm,' laughed the redhead. 'You won't be able to resist those navy blue eyes, honey. Take it from me.'

'Well, maybe *he'll* fall in love with *me*,' smiled Candida, confident in her twenty-two-year-old glory. 'Then the shoe will be on the other foot.'

'Forget it, honey – everyone's tried – Ava – Lana – Liz – they all got nowhere with our Mr Brooks. Wham, bam and thank you so *terribly terribly* much, ma'am – that was absolutely delightful – I'll see you on the next picture.'

'We'll see,' laughed Candida. 'I'll send you a postcard from Jolly Olde England and let you know what happens – you know I love nothing better than a challenge.'

While Julian pursued his career and his leading ladies, money continued to roll in and Phoebe became no slouch at spending it. Aware of Julian's little flings, she was equally aware that he would never leave her, and she proceeded to spend, spend, spend with zest.

As Julian's fame grew, so did their accommodation. By 1953 they had moved seven times, and now lived in a beautiful Queen Anne house in Connaught Square just behind Hyde Park. But Phoebe was already preparing to upgrade again, and had her eye on a large country mansion only a few miles away from Sir Laurence and Lady Olivier. The Brooks now numbered among their intimate friends the Oliviers, Ralph Richardson, John Gielgud, Noël Coward, Gertrude Lawrence, and practically every other major film and theatrical name in England, not to mention many choice members of the aristocracy and a couple of minor royals.

In spite of Julian's looks, sex appeal and fame he was so funny and self-deprecating, so down to earth and nice that all the men liked and admired him, whilst their wives simply adored him. Some of them lusted after him fiercely, often making it quite apparent, but Julian would never have an affair with the wife of a friend. Only actresses and single women not in his set were his province. Consequently he continued to enjoy the reputation of the man's man that he'd always had, while remaining supremely attractive to all women.

When two years of his seven-year contract with Didier had expired, he agreed to sign for two more, but only if he were allowed to appear in a West End play every eighteen months. This gave Phoebe the chance she had been waiting for and she cajoled and persuaded her husband to finally cast her opposite him in some of the classics in which he performed.

She was hardly a staggering actress, her only previous experience on the stage having been in skits at the Windmill, but she tried hard and she still looked quite attractive. Buxom, creamy skinned, and with abundant red curls and a sparkling personality, she appeared reasonably successfully with him in *The Taming of the Shrew*, *Present Laughter* and *The Importance of Being Ernest*.

They had just finished a successful three-month limited run at the Aldwych. Julian was now preparing to go to Normandy to play the lead in a film of *Cyrano de Bergerac*, but this was going to be the first time that he had not played a romantic part. He was keenly anticipating the challenge of playing a character part, a character who, for once, does not get the girl.

He had decided to take his black Bentley across the English Channel to the Normandy location. He enjoyed long drives and was expecting Phoebe to fly over to join him the following weekend. They were dining together at the Caprice. It was a quiet Monday night and the softly lit peach walls of the elegant restaurant reflected the orange highlights in Phoebe's dyed hair as she nibbled and sucked noisily on a fat asparagus stalk.

'Darling, I've decided not to go with you to Normandy,' she said, her lips glistening with melted butter, a trickle of which was running down her chin. Julian leaned across and wiped it off with his damask napkin.

'Why not?' he asked, popping a piece of pâté de foie gras into his mouth while Phoebe repaired her lipstick.

'Darling, how can I *possibly* go to Normandy in the middle of the season?' She bared capped teeth in what she assumed to be an ingenuous girlish beam, but which at thirty-three was beginning to look a little frayed around the edges.

'I mean next week is the Derby, two days later the Cavendish wedding, then the Oliviers are having that big birthday party for Michael, and I promised that I'd help Vivien with the decorations.' She paused for a sip of wine as Julian looked across at her with raised eyebrows.

'Do I detect a mild dose of social climbing fever here, my dear? Nothing before has ever kept you from visiting me on location. How on earth will I manage without you?' he asked – his sarcasm totally missing its target.

'Oh darling – I *know*. Do understand, my pet – please.' She patted his hand with the absentminded gesture a nursemaid might make to her charge, and prepared to tackle the Beef Wellington with sauté potatoes which a waiter placed before her. 'It's just that it's a terribly bad time now, what with redecorating the house, all these parties, and then the charity. The actors' charity, you remember, darling, you're on the committee. Surely you're going to fly back for that, aren't you, pet?'

'Phoebe, how *can* I?' he asked exasperatedly. 'I know it's for a very good cause and so forth and I know we're both on the board but I'm in practically every damn shot of *Cyrano*. I can't *possibly* get away in the middle of the week, even for a charity.'

'Exactly,' crowed Phoebe triumphantly. 'So I'll have to be there to represent you – the Rahvis girls are making me the most divine gown – completely covered in beaded topaz flowers, darling – you'll love it, it matches the topaz necklace and bracelet you gave me for the opening night of *Shrew*.'

'Mmmm.' Julian was not listening. He picked at his roast chicken, his mind absorbed in his forthcoming characterization. He really didn't care whether Phoebe was with him or not on location. She was just a habit, always around like some annoying lucky mascot. He'd even become used to her complaints, which were becoming more frquent since she'd struck up an apparently close friendship with Vivien Leigh. Although Phoebe considered Vivien to be her best friend Julian knew that she was little more than another one of the actress's sycophants. Phoebe was neither intellectually stimulating nor amusing enough to be an intimate friend of the scintillating actress.

'So you won't be coming to Normandy at all then?' asked Julian, not really caring what his wife's answer would be.

'Well, I'll *try* and pop over for a few days, darling,' trilled Phoebe. 'But don't forget there's Ascot – we're expected every day in someone or other's box or in the Royal Enclosure. The Denhams are having that big lunch for the Aga Khan, then Lord Cheltenham and the Countess of Rathbone have taken a huge tent for Ladies' Day, and of course, Binkie's special outing – Noël and Gertie are *definitely* coming to that – I couldn't *possibly* not be there, darling.'

'To represent me, I suppose?' said Julian with even more sarcasm.

'Of course, darling,' she answered, yet again missing the barb as her mind whirled with the dozens of new outfits that were even now in the process of being created for her by Norman Hartnell, Rahvis and Jaques Fath.

'What I *will* do, darling, is when I have to go to Paris for my fittings, I'll pop up to Normandy and see you for a few days – how would that be, pet?'

'That would be just dandy, dear,' said Julian, signalling to the waiter and at the same time noticing that Phoebe had spilled gravy down her creamy lace cleavage. She was becoming quite sluttish recently, and many a couture gown had been spoiled by her greed and lack of dexterity at the dining table.

'Well, good. Then that's that, dear. You'll be fine without me, you'll have all your cronies with you, won't you?'

'Yes, of course,' he said, thinking fondly of his makeup man, his dresser and his stunt double who always accompanied him on every picture.

'Then I don't really have to worry too much about you, do I, darling?' smiled Phoebe, dabbing with a damp napkin at her Hartnell lace collar. 'You'll be quite all right then?'

'Don't give it another thought, my dear – I'll be perfectly all right,' smiled Julian, signing the bill with a flourish. 'I'll be perfectly fine.'

Indeed, as it turned out, Julian was more than perfectly fine. As soon as his navy blue eyes connected with the sexy yet innocent blue eyes of blonde Miss Candida Willow it was instant and spontaneous combustion.

Phoebe heard no rumour of the affair until three quarters of the way through the filming. She had been so heavily involved in her social whirl that she had been able to think of nothing but society balls, garden parties and weekends with the Oliviers. She did not bother to stop off in Normandy when in Paris for her fittings, as Paris suddenly had a little flurry of *petite saison* before the *haut monde* rushed off in opposite directions to Deauville and the Riviera. So Phoebe's Parisian friends stole the time that she had earmarked for her husband. Not that said husband minded one whit. He was quite content living with his entourage in a charming farmhouse far from the bright lights of Paris, London, and the Riviera. He was adoring playing Cyrano, the tragi-comic figure with the enormous nose who loves the gorgeous Roxanne in vain. And the gorgeous Roxanne herself, Miss Candida Willow, was so hopelessly in love with him and, in addition, such a sweetly adorable girl, that Julian's cup was, if not exactly running over, most definitely full to the brim.

It was one of those idyllic summer film locations, shot in the wilds of the French countryside in which everything went completely to plan from start to finish. The director was a poppet, the actor who played Christian was talented and affable, and Miss Willow was even more enchanting than her name, everything which a man could want in a temporary paramour.

The crew, many of whom had worked with Julian before, were as always well aware of what was going on, but such was their loyalty to Julian that no breath of scandal concerning the two lovebirds was allowed to leak into general circulation.

Phoebe breezed in and breezed out of the location one brief weekend between attending the Oaks at Epsom and the Henley Regatta. Julian dutifully performed his marital obligations with eyes closed, although for the past several years Phoebe had been a less than enthusiastic partner, but Julian persisted because he was still hoping that they would have a child. They had now been married for eight years, and except for being pregnant when they were married, Phoebe hadn't conceived since. Now at thirty-three her biological clock was rattling on very fast indeed, but Julian's sincere longing for a child far outstripped her own. Although she pretended to want a baby, and indeed did nothing to prevent its possible conception, she lost no sleep about her failure to conceive, having plenty to occupy her in other ways.

They were in his trailer and Phoebe was preparing to leave for the airport. 'Well, darling, I'll see you in London in a few weeks then,' she trilled, adjusting her new Dior cream straw hat which overflowed with silk strawberries and violet ribbons. Julian thought that it clashed rather alarmingly with her red hair, whose colour had become more pronounced with each passing year, but things of that nature never seemed to bother Phoebe. She loved vivid colours and strongly believed that they suited her vibrant personality.

'Yes, dear, enjoy Cowes, won't you – give my love to Larry and Viv and the gang,' he said, abstractedly examining his huge rubber nose in the mirror of his portable trailer. It was terribly hot today, and the rubber prosthesis applied so painstakingly this morning by Tim, the makeup man, was in grave danger of peeling off round the edges. Damn – he had a close-up to do after lunch and that would mean that Tim would have to come back again with his bottles of glue and his orange sticks and fiddle about for hours to attach it again properly. It was most important that this nose look perfectly authentic. The new film system – Cinemascope – showed up every tiny pore, each and every crow's foot. Every minute detail of a face was magnified a thousand or so times. Nothing would appear more ridiculous than for Cyrano's enormous snout to look like little more than something a circus clown might wear. It was desperately humid in the cramped little trailer, and with his heavy plum velvet tunic and breeches, yards of lace ruffles and two-pound wig, sweat was streaming down Julian's forehead, threatening to wash the nose away completely.

'Timmy,' he shouted, 'get in here right away and save this fucking nose. I think the bloody thing's about to slide off my damn face.'

'Well, I'm off then, pet,' said Phoebe, typically oblivious to his problems. 'The limousine has to get me to the airport by three – I suppose if we leave now, I'll have plenty of time to catch the plane?'

'Yes, yes, yes,' snapped Julian – why wouldn't the bloody woman leave and let him get on with his bloody job, for Christ's sake? This nose was killing him – it was made of solid rubber, smelled absolutely foul and seemed to weigh a ton. Now the tip was beginning to droop, making it look even more ridiculous.

'Bye, dear – bon voyage.' He blew her a vague kiss, as he yelled again, 'Tim, Tim – where the bloody hell are you?'

'Right here, guv – sorry, just finishing me dinner.' The makeup man rushed in, almost colliding with Phoebe who was floating out in her white silk frock like a ship in full sail. With a final wave to her husband she left, and Julian sighed with relief. Closing his eyes, he allowed Tim to probe about under his false nose with orange sticks covered in cotton wool and acetone.

'Hell, Tim, this elephant's trunk is bloody uncomfortable, you know. In this damn heat I feel about to explode.'

'Well, you know what me dear old mum always said, old sport,' grinned Tim, deftly picking tiny bits of rubber out of the gaping cavern of Julian's rubber nostrils.

'I can't say that I do, Tim,' groaned Julian, squinting at his grotesque reflection in the mirror. 'What did the dear old thing say?'

'You've got to suffer to be beautiful, duckie.'

That night in his cosy rented farmhouse, Julian slouched comfortably on the sofa, his arm around the delicate white shoulders of Candida Willow. Candida was gently nibbling at his ear while he leaned his head back and they listened to extracts of *La Bohème* on the old-fashioned radio gramophone.

He was exhausted from the long day's shooting, and also from a whole weekend with Phoebe, which had not been without its usual share of squabbling. Now he was looking forward to some languid stress-relieving lovemaking with his delectable co-star, and then a long restful sleep.

'Julian, let's get married,' the delectable star suddenly whispered, between licks, into his ear.

'What – what did you say, darling?' Julian sat suddenly bolt upright, all hopes of a relaxing evening dashed.

'I said I want to marry you, Julian – I love you – I've never loved anyone like this before. You love me too – don't you, darling? Let's do it – please, please.'

Huge pleading eyes turned to meet his, eyes which looked so radiant and gorgeous on the huge Cinemascope screen, but which now welled with huge Cinemascope tears.

Julian was dumbstruck. Surely she must know the way this game was played? He was a married man. This was just a location romance – he'd told her that when they'd begun their affair. Why on earth was she carrying on like this? Lovey dovey, getting all emotional – talking marriage babble? Oh hell. Women – women – women – damn the whole bloody lot of them, he thought, Henry Higgins was right. His mind desperately searched for a way to get himself out of this situation with his dignity and her pride intact.

'Darling heart, you *know* that's impossible,' he said sincerely, in spite of his growing exhaustion, making the effort to appear serious and lovingly understanding.

'Why – why? You don't love Phoebe. You can't. I saw her again today. She looks like a painted old tart,' spat Candida tearfully. 'I saw her with you all weekend – it almost *killed* me.' She burst into sobs, spattering them both with tears. 'The thought of you together – in bed – oh, oh, oh, it was terrible.'

'Were you spying on me, darling heart?' scolded Julian gently. 'That's very naughty, you know.'

'Yes – yes I was,' wept the girl, her tears flowing unabated. 'I looked through your bedroom window one night. I saw her in her nightdress – she's fat. How can you possibly prefer her to me?'

Julian maintained a dignified silence as his mind raced. Candida looking into the windows like some peeping tom. What sort of a woman was she?

'She's not *right* for you, Julian. I can tell. I watched you. You're like chalk and cheese together. You must know she's not the woman for you – you can't possibly love her. She's so old, how can you?' Fresh tears erupted and he automatically handed her his hand-kerchief.

He didn't answer her. The heartrending strains of the last act of *La Bohème* were moving on to their inevitably tragic end, the finale in another sense of an almost perfect evening which Candida was insisting on ruining. 'Look, my darling girl,' he said, gently wiping the tears from her cheeks, marvelling as if for the first time at how fresh and beautiful she was, 'I don't want to hurt you, dear, but I *cannot* and *will* not marry you – EVER. Do you understand that?'

'No,' said the girl churlishly, picking up her glass of wine and tipping the contents down her throat. 'I don't. You *told* me you loved me, Julian – you know you did – didn't you? Were you lying?'

It was Julian's turn to be churlish now, and he knocked back his brandy with frustration. Of course he'd told her he loved her; it was all part of the game, dammit – a game he'd been playing for years now. Didn't she know the rules? You always told them that you loved them when you were making love to them; it just wasn't gentlemanly behaviour not to – but one never ever spoke of love when out of bed. All his other mistresses had understood it perfectly well. Why didn't this little fool, for God's sake?

'The picture finishes next week.' Candida sounded desperate

now, tears still dripping from her eyes with a persistence which unnerved him. 'I can't live without you, Julian – I can't go back to America, my darling – I need you and I want you. I want to be with you always – always.' With that she threw herself on to his chest, her body shaking with sobs that were verging on hysteria. Julian heaved a long inward sigh.

Throughout the long and sleepless night Julian talked reassuringly to her, explaining patiently all the reasons why it was impossible for them to marry. He told her that she must be a big girl, a grown-up girl and that she had to accept that their relationship must end when filming stopped. By the time they attempted to sleep cuddled up together in the big four-poster bed, Julian thought that he'd successfully calmed her down, and had at last made her see reason. He was wrong.

When Julian woke up to Tim's knock and his cheerful 'Five thirty, Julian – time to open those baby blues, chum, coffee's on the way up' he found that the other side of the double bed was empty. He moved an exploratory foot over to the other side, finding it not only empty, but cold. Candida had obviously accepted what he'd said to her, and decided to make a dignified exit during the night. So much the better, he thought. He hated scenes and confrontations, and much as he had liked Candida and adored making love to her, he knew that she was just another one of his flings. She was a charming child, an adorable sex kitten, but if he were ever to leave Phoebe, a thought which had certainly crossed his mind from time to time, then the woman for whom he might consider sacrificing his marriage would have to have a great deal more character, intelligence and personality than some cute but limited California cupcake.

He swung his feet on to the cool wooden floor and padded into the bathroom. Nothing could have prepared him for the appalling sight which met his bleary eyes. Lying in the old-fashioned splay-legged bathtub, floating as prettily as Ophelia in the rushes, was Candida Willow. One slim arm was hanging over the rim of the tub and the dark red slash in her wrist was making a rich crimson pool on the floor. Her eyes were closed and her head submerged almost up to her nose.

'Christ Almighty – *Candida* – Oh my God – *Candida!*' He leaped towards the girl, sweeping her up into his arms, aware that the bathwater was tinted the colour of rosé wine. 'Tim – *Timmy!*' he called at the top of his lungs. '*Get in here, for God's sake!*'

Within seconds Tim, who was carrying a tray of coffee and croissants, rushed into the bathroom and dropped the whole thing as soon as he saw the ghastly tableau. 'Jesus Christ, guv – why the fuck's she done this?' he asked as they hastily carried the girl to the bed. Julian applied mouth to mouth resuscitation while Tim swiftly and efficiently shredded pieces of Julian's discarded white shirt into strips to stem the flow of blood from her wrists. Candida had slashed both of them with Julian's cut-throat razor which lay bloodied on the bathroom floor.

'Is she alive?' breathed Julian hoarsely.

Tim nodded. He had been in the ARP during the war and had had more than his fair share of dealing with serious injuries during the Blitz.

'Just about,' he said grimly. 'She's lost a lot of blood – we've got to get her to a hospital and pronto – otherwise she'll snuff it, guv, 'n' then the shit'll really hit the fan.'

'Oh my God,' whispered Julian. 'Oh God, the silly little girl – poor baby.'

'If I were you, guv, it's *me* that I'd feel sorry for,' said Tim bleakly. 'The girl'll probably recover, but if this gets around you'll be in deep deep shit. You won't be winnin' any popularity contests after this little lot, I'll bet my bottom dollar on that.'

Somehow they managed to keep it out of the newspapers. Candida was young and strong and by pure luck Julian had discovered her just in time. She would only have had two days' more shooting before her part was completed, and Didier Armande's imaginative publicity machine concocted a story about a sudden appendicitis attack which had made it necessary for her to be flown back to America immediately. Candida stayed in the local Normandy hospital for a few days and then her mother and father arrived with a lanky young lawyer from Pasadena called Gerry, who turned out to be Candida's fiancé.

'We're engaged,' he drawled, having managed to steal an hour away from his bedside vigil to watch the shooting.

'How long have you two been engaged?' Julian asked, as Tim raised an eyebrow at him.

'Oh, two years now. We've been going together since high school, but Candy – that's her real name, Candy Wilson – the studio thought Candida Willow suited her better – well, Candy wanted to wait to get married until she'd forged her career – made a success, you know?'

'I know,' said Julian, scratching his great itching nose, which was starting to droop again in the heat.

'Well, that's all changed now,' said Gerry brightly. 'She's decided, for the best, I think, to give up all this acting stuff and come back and live in Pasadena with me. We're gonna get married next spring.'

'Congratulations, mate,' said Tim, busy once again with his orange sticks in the crevices of Julian's nose. 'She's a nice little gal – we've enjoyed having her, 'aven't we, guv?' He winked at Julian cheekily, his face inches away.

'I hope you'll both be very happy,' said Julian sincerely, trying to ignore Tim. 'Candida is a lovely girl, very lovely indeed.'

'I know,' said the young man, 'I'm a real lucky guy.' And he looked over in surprise at Tim as the makeup man gave a great snort of suppressed laughter.

Although the general public was never allowed to hear about Candida Willow's suicide attempt, before long the entire show-business community from Paramount to Pinewood knew the whole story. Julian's charm and sex appeal were magnified tenfold, and he became almost a living legend. Nothing creates so much excitement as a woman trying to kill herself for the love of a man, and Julian found himself in even more demand both as an actor and as a lover.

He had felt guilty and responsible for Candida's suicide attempt, and had tried to visit her in the hospital, but was told that only her relations were allowed to see her. So he sent her a letter and three dozen white roses, and tried to put the incident out of his mind.

As she was young and healthy, Candida's recovery was swift. As soon as she was out of intensive care, and the doctors said she could travel, the studio rented a private plane and packed her, and her entourage, back to California.

Julian never did get the chance to talk to her, and his letters to her in California were always returned unopened. He decided to be a great deal more careful with his love affairs in the future. And he did try. But Julian Brooks found it hard to change. In a matter of weeks, he was continuing on his path of casual philandering once again, and Phoebe was continuing to squander even more of his money.

Although Julian never mentioned Candida's suicide attempt to Phoebe over the telephone from France, the West End jungle drums were not long in relaying the news to her. It was one of the two Hermiones who imparted this particularly succulent piece of gossip to her while the women were lunching together at the Savoy Grill. It was all Phoebe could do to hold down here *sole bonne-femme*, while Hermione rattled on about the wretched girl's suicide attempt.

'In Julian's bathroom, if you please! And I gather that the whole thing has been kept under wraps by Didier's film company. My dear, can you imagine what could happen if the story ever got out?'

'I certainly can,' said Phoebe grimly, pecking at a piece of melba toast in a vain attempt to diet. 'The papers would destroy Julian.'

'I know I shouldn't really be telling you all this, darling,' said Hermione. Her evident relish for relating the sorry tale to the injured party seemed to increase her already healthy appetite for plump roasted grouse, mounds of mashed potatoes and brussels sprouts, all of which were washed down with copious amounts of dry chardonnay. 'But although they say that the wife is always the *last* to find out, I think you *should* know, my dear. You deserve to hear the truth, don't you agree?'

'Absolutely,' croaked Phoebe, almost choking on a fish bone. 'Damn it, this thing is supposed to be filleted,' she snarled. 'Tell me everything, everything you know.'

'Well, we all *know* what Julian's always been like – don't we?' giggled Hermione coyly, intimating by a flicker of false lashes that she also might have been among the lucky ones to have partaken of Julian's charms.

Phoebe stared at her with exasperated sarcasm. '*What is* he like, Hermione, dear? Do tell me.'

'You're a woman of the world, Phoebe, so I'm sure that he's never managed to pull the wool completely over your eyes – not *quite*, has he, my dear?'

'Never,' snapped Phoebe, trying to pour some more chardonnay into her glass but spilling it on to the linen tablecloth. She felt a deep flush of humiliation creeping over the collar of her fuchsia silk dress – now almost a perfect match to the colour of her face. 'I'm not stupid, Hermione – I've always known he played around, of course, all men do – especially actors.'

'Of course you have, dear, we're women of the world, we've always known. Well, there's nothing you can do really, I suppose, except pretend that absolutely nothing has happened, put on a happy face as it were.'

'I always do that,' Phoebe said icily. 'Turn the other cheek, all that sort of stuff – what the eyes don't see . . .'

'The heart doesn't grieve over,' finished Hermione with a patronizing chuckle. 'Exactly, dear. My mother taught me that too. It gets you through life pretty well – especially with the way most men are.'

'What do you mean "most"?' said Phoebe viciously. 'They're all alike, Hermione, and you must know that better than anyone, surely?'

'Really? I don't quite see the point of that last remark, Phoebe.' Hermione raised a questioning and irritated pencilled brow. 'What exactly do you mean, dear?'

'Well I suppose it's bad enough that everyone knows that Julian has been pathologically unfaithful to me for years,' said Phoebe, lighting a cigarette, and allowing a cloud of smoke to drift across her luncheon companion's face. 'But at least he's unfaithful to me with women.'

'And just what are you implying?' asked Hermione, looking suddenly wary and defensive as she shifted in her chair and fanned at the cigarette smoke with a lace-bordered handkerchief.

'Really, Hermione, is it honestly necessary for you to be quite so naive?' Phoebe laughed lightly, enjoying the look of growing discomfort on Hermione's heavily powdered face, into which she blew another cloud of smoke.

'What I mean is that although *my* husband has been busy screwing lots of young girls, *yours*, my dear, has been equally busy with lots of young boys!'

'Absolute nonsense!' Crimson spots now appeared on each of Hermione's normally porcelain-white cheeks. 'That's utterly ridiculous – it's a slandereous lie, Phoebe, and you know it.'

'Oh do come off it, Hermione. You can dish it out but you obviously can't take it. Your precious Basil is as queer as a seven-pound note – you know it, I know it, everyone in the bloody business knows it – even the press knows it, for God's sake, so don't pretend to me that *you* don't know. You just make yourself look even more of a laughing stock.'

'Well, I don't believe it, and even if it were true – I – it doesn't matter. Basil loves me – he simply adores me,' stammered Hermione. 'He worships the ground I walk on.'

But Phoebe was too fast for her. Leaning forward she hissed with calculated vehemence into the other woman's face, 'Listen, Hermione, Julian may cheat on me, but he's a man – a real *man* – and although he fucks other women he *always* comes back to me – *me*, do you hear? He makes love to *me*, and I'll have you know he does it bloody well – now, duckie, can you say the same for your Basil?'

Hermione glared back at her, speechless. Some of the other people in the restaurant had turned in their direction now, watching with great interest the two well-known women in heated discussion.

'Well I was only trying to help,' said Hermione huffily, patting at the frizzy curls beneath her flowered hat. 'After all, that's what friends are for, isn't it? I was just trying to let you know, my dear, that you have many many friends who are fully behind you, while you're going through this perfectly horrible situation.'

'Thank you, Hermione.' Phoebe signalled for the bill. 'But probably not *nearly* as many as dear Basil has had behind *him*!' With a flourish she signed it, leaving an unnecessarily large tip, and brushing her friend's cheek with her own, said through clenched teeth, 'Thanks for all your interesting advice, dear ... I'll think about it, and I dare say I'll see you both at Binkie's on Sunday.'

By the time Phoebe got back to Connaught Square she had worked herself into a complete fury. Ignoring her butler who opened the front door, she raced up to the master bedroom and throwing her hat, gloves and handbag on to the bed, stood in the middle of her Colefax and Fowler chintz room seething and shaking with rage. That smug bitch. That vicious backbiting cow. How dare she give advice on how to handle Julian and his affairs when everyone knew that *her* husband was camper than a row of tents, and more than likely hadn't made love to her in years. How could he want to anyway, when he had to look at a face like hers. She paced up and down the room, puffing furiously on one cigarette after another. There was no way she could stop Julian's philandering, she knew that. She had allowed him to get away with it almost since the first day they'd met at the Windmill. He knew that and she knew that he knew that she knew. She could hardly make him stop now – it was far too much of a habit for him. But obviously his affairs were heating up, becoming more than just meaningless flings. This little harlot – starlet – trying to kill herself for love of him meant that Julian must have made romantic promises to her, maybe even heartfelt protestations of true love. She gritted her teeth. God, if he'd started to do *that* then her days as Mrs Julian Brooks could really be numbered. Before she even knew anything about it he could make some girl pregnant – become all broody, and ditch her to become the daddy he'd always wanted to be. Maybe she should really try to become pregnant. She pulled a face – the idea was utterly repugnant to her. Motherhood in any of its aspects definitely didn't appeal to her. But perhaps she should attempt that ultimate sacrifice. After all, she thought, Julian was getting to that vulnerable age for a man, when the right woman could steal him away from her if there wasn't a tiny little Brooks junior to cement their bond.

'Not while I'm still around and breathing,' muttered Phoebe, and with a great burst of energy she disappeared into his dressing room.

A week later Julian returned to London to find Phoebe not at home to greet him in her usual manner. Everything in the house seemed perfectly normal but when he went upstairs into his dressing room and opened the heavy mahogany doors of his wardrobe, he was greeted by a sight which, to a man who prided himself on his sartorial elegance, was one of ultimate horror. Three dozen or more Savile Row suits hung, perfectly separated by a precise three-inch space, dark to the left, lighter cloth to the right, but every last one of the jackets had been cleanly cut off at the elbow, and all his trouser legs had been chopped off at the knees. Julian let out a howl as he fumbled through the rest of his costly and extensive wardrobe, and found to his horror that his Turnbull & Asser shirts, his beloved Charvet ties, Huntsman cashmere and vicuna coats, and dinner jackets and tail coats from Kilgour, French & Stanbury, had all been systematically and very deliberately slashed to ribbons. Everything was completely ruined, nothing was salvageable, not even any of his dozens of silk boxer shorts. Phoebe had taken a vicious petty revenge, and Julian, realizing the penalty had now been paid in full for his potentially fatal indiscretion with Candida Willow, knew that he would have to try to toe the marital line – at least for the moment.

In its autumn issue, *Life* magazine named Julian Brooks as The Most Handsome Man in the World. They featured him on a full-colour cover in his costume from *The Devil is a Man*. He was standing at the tiller of a ship, wearing blue jeans, and a black shirt opened to the waist revealed the glistening muscles of his broad chest to their best effect. His head was thrown back, and he was laughing into the wind which was blowing his unruly hair back off his famous noble forehead. The article and accompanying photographs inside the periodical painted an idyllic portrait of Julian and Phoebe as happily married lovers living in intimate connubial bliss in Connaught Square, and sharing the theatrical limelight in the West End. They printed photographs of the two of them *seen enjoying a joke* at Ascot in the company of Noël Coward and Sir Crispin Peake, and they even printed a photograph of Phoebe in the kitchen of their house, wearing a simple dress and to many people's great amusement, a modest apron, as she stirred a steaming casserole at the stove. In the background Julian held one of their many Persian cats and smiled fondly at her. The text was syrupy. The female writer had evidently fallen heavily for Julian, and the article was a paean of praise to his charm, talent and physical beauty. Phoebe had dozens of copies of the magazine sent over from America, as it was hard to find in London, and sent them to all their friends. She even had one in an Asprey's silver frame on top of the grand piano.

Even though they were right in the middle of rehearsals for *Hamlet* Phoebe still found time to give an interview to one of the more sympathetic journalists from the *Daily Express*. She was delighted when she read the text of the article which appeared a month before they were due to open, and which helped make the box-office queues grow. It was headlined 'If he cheated on me – I'd kill him' and in it in no uncertain terms, Phoebe warned the women of the world to keep away from her man.

'I know very well that because Julian is regarded by many as the handsomest man in the world, women will always be chasing him,' gushed Phoebe in the article. 'But I also know that he's completely faithful to me, and to me alone. Oh yes, of course I've heard all those silly rumours about his flirtations with his co-stars when he's away on location, but Julian just can't help but be charming and helpful to everyone he works with. It doesn't really mean a thing. We've been married for over eight years and our marriage is as sound and loving today as it ever was. No woman could ever come between us, and if anyone did try to steal him from me – I'd kill her.'

Several copies of the *Daily Express* were passed around in the dingy hall in Camberwell where *Hamlet* was in rehearsal, and the cast couldn't help giggling when they read about Phoebe's bravura performance in the paper.

'My dear, she acts so much better for the tabloids than she does on the stage,' exclaimed Sir Crispin Peake at the local pub during a lunchtime break in rehearsals.

'Frankly, if she carries on giving newspapers these perfectly wonderful pieces of fictionalized nonsense, she'll be able to make far more money writing penny-dreadfuls than Julian makes as a film star.'

3

St Tropez 1954

Often when the mistral whistled tirelessly through fragrant hills of cypress and pine, Agathe Guinzberg would bring out her scrapbook. Unlike the more docile winds of the sirocco, on whose hot breezes the scent of Africa wafted, the mistral was a demon wind. The shrill clattering of the rigging continued ceaselessly on the many vessels moored in the tiny harbour of St Tropez, and the larger boats heaved against each other with a sound like the groans of ravening beasts.

But Agathe could disregard it all as she slowly and deliberately turned the pages of her album to gaze at the face of the man she adored. If the mistral became fierce enough to whip the village women's long skirts above their knees, to whisk the kerchiefs from their heads, and force old men to chase through narrow lanes after their black berets, then the loudest church bell would toll three times. When Agathe heard the bell ring out from the old tower she felt relieved, as this was the signal that there would be no school today.

Then she would sigh with pleasure, snuggling back under her goose-feather quilt as she leafed through her scrapbook and imagined herself with the man who so enriched her life. Julian Brooks and Agathe were dancing together, in glorious Technicolor, their bodies melting into one, as the orchestra of the Paris Opera played Tchaikovsky's *Romeo and Juliet*.

Agathe had thrilled to Julian's romantic exploits and escapades in *The Merry Monarch* and the many other films which had made him the most glamorous leading man in England, and now she seemed to live only for those moments when she saw him on the screen.

There were dozens of photographs of him, cut from *Ciné Monde*,

Ciné Revue or *Jours de France*, which she had pasted into her thick scrapbook. Although he was England's biggest star, the French still preferred their actors home-grown, so Gerard Philippe, Jean Gabin and Fernandel were the masculine faces most frequently featured in French magazines. But nevertheless Agathe still managed to find quite a few pictures of her idol. Here was Julian clipped from the cover of *Paris Match* wearing a blue turtleneck sweater, tweed jacket and, his trademark, a fedora tilted at that rakish angle she adored. He was leaning against an oak tree, an ironic smile on his face, his thick dark hair tumbling wildly over his forehead as he gazed into the camera with the tantalizing expression which Agathe and millions of other female filmgoers worshipped. She knew it was ridiculous for a woman of thirty-one to have such a passion for a film star, but she didn't care. To her he epitomized all that was romantic, gallant, quixotic and mysterious – he was her life.

Reverently she turned to another page where Julian, suavely dressed in white tie and tails with his hair slicked back, clasped the eighteen-inch waist of some ravishing actress. They gazed into each other's eyes, appearing deeply in love, while a remarkably authentic studio moon shone down brightly on their enraptured faces. Agathe sighed. She really didn't like looking at photographs of Julian with other women. She preferred to look at h'm alone, bounding out of the waves on to some beach, his chest bronzed, wet and glistening, wearing a pair of tight-fitting white shorts. That kind of picture always gave her a strangely thrilling feeling in her loins that she knew was wrong.

At thirty-one Agathe was still a virgin, who had never been involved with a man romantically. Sometimes at night as she looked at Julian's photographs an overwhelming heat would make her thighs and groin tingle so much that she would touch herself there guiltily as she had done in the cellar years before. But her sense of relief was always followed by such feelings of shame and self-disgust that she would feverishly turn the amber beads of her rosary, begging forgiveness from the Virgin Mother. Those beads and her prayers had been her comfort and salvation when she had been hidden beneath Gabrielle's house for eighteen months, and Jewish or not, she still treasured them.

The shutters outside her window banged loudly and monotonously against the ivy-clad, pink-painted granite of the little house. The terrible force of the wind was tearing the jasmine and mimosa, so carefully nurtured by Aunt Brigitte, from the lattice-covered wall. Even the Nazi occupation hadn't been able to make her aunt's mimosa perish, but now the pale blossoms were falling to the ground like confetti.

'Agathe!' Aunt Brigitte's cross voice interrupted Agathe's reverie, and with a sigh she slid the album under the safety of her mattress.

'Close those shutters, Agathe,' her aunt shouted, her voice sounding feeble against the howling of the wind. 'Now!'

Agathe opened her window to reach the shutters, and the wind caught her long white hair, whipping it around her face in a blinding swirl. She gripped the heavy shutters, pulling and locking them firmly with the rusty catch.

Her aunt peered into the bedroom with a suspicious expression on her lined face, then went off muttering under her breath. Aunt Brigitte was a faded woman of sixty-four. Her thinning hair was almost white and her face mirrored all the suffering and loss of the war years, including the death of a much-loved husband. Now all she had left in the world was this strange niece whom she'd inherited when the war had finally ended, and with whom she had nothing in common.

When the repatriation of families decimated by the Nazis began, Agathe had been reunited with the last surviving member of her family. Aunt Brigitte had escaped Paris just in time and had fled to the south of France and relative safety. She had insisted that Agathe come to live with her, securing a job for her at the local school, where she was able to use her ballet training to teach the young girls.

Aunt Brigitte always looked as if the troubles of the whole world rested on her thin shoulders, and Agathe often wondered if her grim-faced aunt had ever been carefree and happy even as a girl. She sometimes studied the yellowing black and white photographs on her aunt's dressing table, pictures of the extensive family which no longer existed. How many of them there once were, and how pitifully short their lives had been. Agathe particularly loved one picture of the father she had known for barely eighteen years. How handsome Papa was, with his tanned, intelligent face and his thick black curls. His arms were holding the beautiful young girl who had been her mother, whose eyes were laughing and filled with joy. They had obviously been madly in love. Agathe sighed. Would she ever fall madly in love? Or was she destined to spend the rest of her life as a childless spinster, a ballet teacher, whose only joy was collecting photographs of a man she would never meet?

Well, there would be no school today, the mistral had conveniently seen to that. The whole day now stretched ahead of her – hours of emptiness which somehow had to be filled.

She decided to take a walk into the village – maybe the new edition of *Ciné Monde* was out, perhaps even with a photograph of Julian which she hadn't yet seen.

In her favourite café on the quay, the locals sat about glumly sipping their glasses of rough Provençal wine or cognac, staring out at the churning grey sea with grim resignation. Each day of mistral was a day of work lost, so the fishermen's families would eat little tonight. In spite of the wind, the blazing sun glittered on the rolling mass like shattered diamonds, and the air was fresh and cool.

Agathe yearned to leave St Tropez, to go somewhere, anywhere, away from the stern prying eyes of her aunt.

In the distance she could see boats bobbing even more furiously in the waters of the normally protected port. The Mediterranean had whipped itself into a foaming frenzy, and now golden sand swirled like clouds of smoke through the narrow streets. It seeped through even the most tightly closed doors and windows, while the wind screeched incessantly.

Agathe sipped her coffee, gloomily thinking that judges in the south of France tended to be lenient in their sentencing if a crime, even murder, was committed during the mistral. They blamed it on 'mistral madness', because the unrelenting winds had often been known to drive people quite literally mad. Mad, maybe that was why she had no friends. Everyone in St Tropez thought she was slightly mad, she herself thought it a miracle that she wasn't, in fact, insane. If only everyone knew what she had been through during the war, perhaps they would be more friendly towards her. She had no friends of her own age, nor indeed of any age; and men friends, as

Aunt Brigitte said, were all a waste of time, 'All that giggling and gossiping, going to cafés and dances. You have responsibilities, *chérie* – no time for such nonsense.'

As she stared out to sea Agathe began to daydream. Visions of a soft meadow came to mind, where wild flowers grew in great tangles and a gurgling brook ran nearby; there she wandered hand in hand with a friend, a lover perhaps, sharing hopes and dreams and confidences. Not that Agathe liked men, they frightened her. Only with Julian did she feel she could come into her own. The unattainable Looks Brooks. Unattainable, like all her dreams.

4

'Dominique. Dominique! *Regarde ici.*' The girl, pigtails flying, raced along the cobbled back street of St Tropez, excitedly waving a piece of paper. 'Dominique. Stop – *please*, you must see this,' she called breathlessly to her friend, who stubbornly strode on ahead, a large knapsack full of books resting easily on her sturdy young shoulders.

'Not now, Genevieve,' Dominique said impatiently. 'You know I'm late for class and Madame will give me hell again. *Merde*, that's the second time this week M'sieur has kept me late for talking in his science lesson. I think he must hate me.' She increased her pace as Genevieve, two months younger than the sixteen-year-old, and a few inches shorter, hurried to keep up with her.

'Look, Dominique. Look at this, please, you are *such* a stubborn idiot,' the girl said firmly, thrusting her prized piece of paper in front of Dominique's enormous green eyes. 'They have been giving these away outside the school, at the patisserie and the butcher's shop and all over the village. Some Americans have come down from Paris and they are looking for someone –' she said secretively, her freckled face attempting a look of mystery '– someone like you.'

'Oh, Genevieve, you're *so* naive.' Dominique broke into a run as she heard the church clock strike three and realized she should already be in her leotard, ballet shoes and tights. Madame Agathe would even now be flouncing into the chilly practice room, dispensing sarcastic comments to the disgruntled group of twelve schoolgirls who all strived for the perfection which, alas, Madame Agathe had never achieved herself. But Agathe thought Dominique showed some promise and she encouraged her constantly, helped her, grilled her, instructed her, perhaps seeing in her the young ballerina she herself might have been if it hadn't been for the war.

'If you won't look at it yourself then I'll read it to you,' squealed

Genevieve, keeping up with her taller friend's long strides with difficulty.

'OK, OK, I'm listening,' said Dominique, 'but read it fast, Genevieve. Between Madame Agathe and M'sieur Millet, they'll finish me off – *les salopes*.'

'Listen.' Genevieve blushed at Dominique's language, although she had heard it often enough before.

'"Wanted to audition for American film: classical ballet and jazz-trained girls aged between fifteen and twenty. Must have some acting experience and be willing and able to travel to the United States to work in a Hollywood film. Bring dance clothes, sheet music of one classical and one modern dance piece. Ten a.m., Saturday, March fifth. Théâtre de Comédie, Boulevard des Anglais, Nice."'

'*Tiens!*' Dominique stopped dead in her tracks and, snatching the piece of paper from her friend, stared at it in wonder. 'Do you think this is some sort of joke, Genevieve? Maybe the boys from the parish school have printed this up to make us look like fools. We all turn up in our tutus full of great expectations, and that bunch of spotty creeps will be waiting there to giggle at us.' Most of the young girls who lived in St Tropez hated boys, or at least pretended they did. Refined young ladies had nothing in common with uncouth teenage louts, avoiding them as much as possible. Boys seemed interested only in *boules*, darts, football and wrestling with each other in the meadows of the surrounding Provençal countryside. Girls were a total mystery to them – just boring and fragile creatures to be teased mercilessly.

'I don't really think it is a joke,' Genevieve insisted. 'Dominique, you simply *must* go!'

'Genevieve!' gasped Dominique. Her eyes were sparkling, her long hair, tied into a ponytail, glistened like black swansdown in the fading afternoon sun, her sensual gamine face radiated excitement. 'This is *fantastic – amazing!* An *audition* – right here in the south of France.'

'Well, not exactly right here,' Genevieve pointed out pragmatically, peering again at the paper. 'To get to Nice will take the best part of four hours on the bus. I suppose you could take the train, but Papa says it was only Hitler who managed to get the trains running on time, and that now they're even *more* hopeless than they were.'

'Never mind, never mind, never mind,' cried Dominique, breaking into a run. 'Even if I have to leave at *five* in the morning, I *must* go to this audition. Genevieve, *quelle chance*! I could meet Gene Kelly or Fred Astaire! I could even become a *Star*. Well, maybe,' she said as her friend giggled. 'Look, I must run now, I'm so late – but thank you, Genevieve. Thanks!'

In the cloakroom Dominique quickly changed. Hearing Agathe already instructing the dance class, she burst in flushed and rosy, her heart pounding with excitement at the prospect of her audition, and was immediately scolded for her lateness. She tried to execute the complicated pirouettes and *jetés* that Madame Agathe was now showing her pupils, but she couldn't keep her mind focused. It kept returning again and again to the audition. A Hollywood movie! Hollywood! America! Dominique had so often fantasized about becoming a Hollywood star. No matter that she was French: so were Leslie Caron and Zizi Jeanmaire!

Sweat trickled down the neck of her tight cotton leotard, and her legs felt hot and sticky in their thick lisle tights.

'Pay attention, Dominique,' Madame Agathe snapped, banging her slender silver-topped cane down hard on the parquet floor. She always carried this cane when she led the class; it gave the impression of authority which she needed to control this group of overexcitable adolescent girls.

Most of the girls made fun of Agathe behind her back – of her white face and hair, her gaunt body in its shapeless clothes, her eyes which possessed such a fierce flame of discipline that they seemed to burn right into anyone who made a mistake.

'Those who can, *do*. Those who can't, teach,' Genevieve had once told Dominique, another of her father's observations. Dominique now stood, head bent, chastened because Madame Agathe was giving her a tongue-lashing for the lack of spontaneity in her solo.

'I'm sorry, Madame,' Dominique said, close to tears. Madame could be very cruel when she wanted to be, her criticisms always hitting the mark with brutal accuracy. 'I'm very sorry.'

'I want you to stay behind after class, Dominique,' Madame said brusquely. 'We will go over this *again* – the solo you were *supposed* to have practised this weekend. Obviously your ballet homework has not been done, so you will have to do it *now*.'

'Yes, Madame,' Dominique mumbled, exchanging a quick look with another girl, who shrugged sympathetically.

Sometimes Madame's tongue was so biting and razor sharp that the girls joked that if she swallowed it she'd slit her own throat. There was no doubt that Madame could be quite a tartar. Her quiet, inhibited exterior concealed a savage temper and a great fury with life which lurked just beneath the surface.

At last the class was over and the other girls filed out. Dominique stood alone, and silent, while Agathe lectured her and then went on to demonstrate some of the steps for her. Agathe now showed an infinite patience; kindness radiated from her eyes which were no longer burning points of suppressed rage, but warm and understanding.

Dominique felt a wave of pity mingled with affection for this woman whom the village children all rudely called 'the mad old maid'. Suddenly she decided to confide her plans for Saturday's audition. Excitedly she told Agathe about it and how badly she wanted to go.

'*Chérie*, this is very, very exciting,' Agathe breathed, a faint pink flush colouring her pale cheeks. 'Certainly it is a very important opportunity. You must be good. You must be more than good. Dominique, you must be the absolute best.'

'Yes, Madame.' The girl nodded, her eyes bright, her legs suddenly no longer tired. 'Will you help me?' she blurted out. 'I need to practise much more, I know I do. Oh, Madame' – she looked at Agathe, her young face flushed and joyful – 'Oh, Madame, I want this – I want so much to go to Hollywood – can you imagine?'

'Yes, yes, I will help you,' Agathe said simply. 'I will rehearse you now and for the next three days before the audition, and you must practise at home too,' she said sternly. 'It will take much hard work, but you, more than all the others in class, have the talent, the potential to succeed.'

'Thank you, Madame, oh, thank you,' Dominique breathed, thrilled by her teacher's rare praise. 'I will kill myself working, I promise you.'

'And I will take you to the audition myself,' Agathe said, looking fondly at her lovely young pupil. 'We will work very hard now, *chérie*, and on Saturday morning you will be prepared, and . . .' She paused, her dark eyes twinkling now with an unaccustomed pleasure. 'And you will be the best, Dominique. You will be given the part, you will go to Hollywood – and who knows, perhaps I will even go with you.'

Dominique was so hot and overexcited after her afternoon of intensive rehearsal and about the upcoming audition, that after an early supper with her parents and three young brothers, she took her bicycle and rode into the centre of St Tropez.

The sign Gaston's Glaces emblazoned in purple on a small yellow wagon looked so inviting that she propped her bicycle carelessly against a tree in the Place des Lices, and sauntered over to investigate.

'I'll have a *framboise*,' she said, fishing for change in the pocket of her shorts. 'Double, please.'

'It's on the house,' Gaston said, not only giving her an extra scoop of ice cream, but also the benefit of perfect white teeth in a beautifully tanned face.

She smiled back. 'Merci, *M'sieur.*'

He admired her beautiful gamine face, sparkling green eyes and long tanned legs. She had an aristocratic accent, but her attitude was modern and free – not like the snobbish young tourists from England and Scandinavia who usually bought ice creams from him.

Gaston instantly decided that she was a prize not to be missed and that there was no time to lose. He quickly locked the wagon and matched her stride as she wandered into the tiny square.

'I'm Gaston Girandot,' he volunteered. 'I own the joint.'

'So I gathered – I'm Dominique du Frey,' she said, licking at the melting pink ice cream.

'Daughter of the banker?'

'Yes,' she said.

She watched him slyly out of the corners of her slanting eyes. *Tiens*, but he was very good-looking, she thought, better-looking than any of the boys at school.

'My parents have a patisserie on the Avenue Bazoche,' he volunteered.

'I think our cook buys from them sometimes,' said Dominique, looking up at him through her thick black lashes with an expression which was both challenging and shyly sensual.

'Would you like a cup of coffee?' He felt gauche for the first time in his nineteen years. Because of his good looks, girls usually made advances to him, but it was different with this one. She was cool and, although very young, seemed quite sure of herself.

'Yes,' smiled Dominique, 'I'd love one.'

In the outdoor café, drinking espresso and smoking Gauloises, they talked until nearly ten o'clock, when Dominique, noticing the time, jumped up. 'Ooh, I must go, I have to practise my ballet tonight. Madame wants me to practise three times a day. She says practice makes perfect.'

She smiled her kitten smile at him and he stammered, 'Will I see you again?'

'Of course,' said Dominique, suddenly wise beyond her years. 'You know you will, but probably after my audition. I must work like a dog now.' She extended a slim, soft hand. '*Au revoir*, Gaston Girandot.'

He kissed her hand solemnly, gazing into her face as if he had just discovered a priceless treasure.

'Tomorrow – Tango Beach, eleven o'clock?'

She nodded shyly. 'Maybe, Gaston – maybe.' Then with a smile that took his breath away, she climbed on to her bike and pedalled off into the darkness, leaving him with stars in his eyes and a thumping heart.

That night, lying in her bed, Dominique thought about the beautiful boy and about the power she felt she had had over him during their brief meeting. Power. Power over men. It was an exhilarating sensation that she was experiencing for the first time. She didn't particularly like the local boys but this one was slightly older than the others and was so good-looking, with his dazzling white smile, tanned face and tight black curls that she thought she might make him the exception.

The following day, after a hot morning of vigorous ballet practice with Madame Agathe, she decided to go down to Pampellone for lunch, a swim and some sunbathing. She pedalled fast over the two miles of hilly road outside central St Tropez, arriving in good time at the beach. She wondered if Gaston would be there, as there seemed to be only a few people on Tango Beach. The pale yellow sand was clean, and several sailboats and motorboats zoomed about on the sea which was calm and invitingly deep blue. About a dozen empty wooden sunbeds covered by yellow and white striped mattresses were lined up on the beach waiting hopefully for occupants. She paid the mahogany-skinned beach boy a few francs, and he settled her up near the sea, stuck a parasol in the sand, and brought her a small slatted wooden table on which he set a glass of Coca-Cola. She took off the short cotton sundress which she was wearing over her bikini and lay back on the mattress, letting the glorious rays fall on her body. Closing her eyes behind her sunglasses she was almost asleep when she felt a gentle touch on her shoulder.

'*Bonjour*,' said Gaston Girandot, squatting down on the sand beside her, his brown muscular body gleaming with Ambre Solaire, a shy grin on his face.

'*Bonjour*, Gaston,' she smiled up at him through her glasses.

'What a perfect day,' he said.

'Yes, it was so lovely after my practice I decided I needed a swim.'

'So what are you waiting for?' said the boy. 'Come on, Lazy Bones – get up, let's hit the water. I'll race you.'

Laughing and protesting, Dominique allowed Gaston to pull her up, and the two teenagers dashed into the warm inviting Mediterranean.

By three o'clock they were both starving. They strolled up to the tiny thatched outdoor restaurant where bamboo tables with yellow checked cloths were laid for lunch. The sun filtered through the bamboo blinds which protected the diners from its fiercest rays, throwing striped shadows across Dominique's and Gaston's smiling faces. They ate salad niçoise, provençal chicken with fried potatoes, and *tarte tatin*, washed down with a robust beaujolais nouvelle. They talked and giggled all through lunch, watched over benignly by the portly proprietor who had known them both since they'd been children.

'Why have we never met before?' asked Dominique, feeling completely satiated by the delicious lunch, and exhilarated by Gaston's company.

'I've been at college in Aix-en-Provence for the last three years,' he said. 'Before that we probably saw each other here – at the beach.' He bent his head until it almost touched hers. 'I didn't notice you then, nor you me – but if you'd looked the way you do now I certainly would have done.'

Dominique blushed and lowered her eyes. She was experiencing all sorts of new exciting feelings with this boy, and later when he brought his mattress next to hers on the beach and they were lying next to each other half asleep, their bare shoulders almost touching, Dominique knew that she would like to see much more of Gaston Girandot – much much more.

In her chaste narrow bed Agathe was unable to sleep. She was too excited by Dominique's news. She had herself read one of the notices which had been distributed in the village and had experienced her own quiet thrill. When Dominique had spoken to her after class, she had felt that the forthcoming audition might be the key to an escape from her dull schoolmistress's life.

If the girl won the audition, if she were given the part in a Hollywood film, *she*, Agathe, could go with her. Why not? Dominique's parents had heavy responsibilities. Her father was a locally important banker. Her mother was tied down by three young sons, and visibly pregnant again. If . . . *if* . . . if . . .

She was too agitated to sleep, the possibilities of the future too exciting. She turned on her light and took out her scrapbook again to gaze lovingly at the handsome face of Julian Brooks. Would she meet him if they went to Hollywood? Maybe not; he was a British star, who worked in England. She knew he had never been to America. But the joy, the freedom to leave her bourgeois and claustrophobic life in St Tropez, to go out into the real world, to go to America! Everyone wanted to go to America. The golden land of opportunity, where all men – and women – were equal. Agathe would find friends there, a new life – she knew she would.

She had never thought she would care again about the future of a young, pretty girl. The past years had not been kind to Agathe. Nothing in her life of freedom could ever minimize the damage of her time in that cellar, and after that her years in L'Éléphant Rose. Watching the traitorous whores fraternizing with the monsters who had destroyed her family, her life, her future, had been purgatory. But worst of all was her deep sense of self-loathing.

She felt that she was hideously ugly. Whenever she looked into a mirror and saw the gaunt white spectre reflected there, she remembered how she had been as a young girl. Almost as pretty as Dominique. Well made, a little plump, with dark sparkling eyes and blue-black glossy hair. Pretty and far more talented. She had never been vivacious, but her quiet charm had its own appeal.

It was gone now for ever. All of it – her talent, her looks, her appeal. She had heard the whispered taunts of the village children: 'Old Maid'. 'Ugly witch'. She saw her aunt's disapproval of her. Brigitte's pursed lips and lack of communication with Agathe revealed clearly enough what her aunt thought of her. But Agathe had no money. What else could she do? Where could she go? Only into her imagination, where she walked in fragrant meadows, hand in hand with laughing friends, or Julian Brooks – only there was she always happy.

Unless Dominique du Frey could win that audition . . . and perhaps give her the key to a new life in America.

5

Inès had returned to visit Paris nearly two years after the end of the war, and found sadly that she cared little any more for the beloved city of her birth. She thought her fellow countrymen brusque and humourless, although she had to admit they had reason to be. So many of them seemed bitter and resentful about the long Nazi occupation, and now they faced a relentless day-to-day struggle to rebuild their broken lives. Everyone seemed involved only with themselves and their families. Food, a national obsession, was still in very short supply, although the grand hotels and better shops were well stocked and open for business as usual.

After her years in London, Inès felt as if she didn't really belong in Paris. She missed the English sense of humour, missed her pretty flat in Mayfair. She revisited a few familiar haunts to look for old friends, but her only real friends had been Yves, Gabrielle and the rest of her 'family' from L'Éléphant Rose. When she went to the old familiar club in Pigalle she found the building shuttered and locked with an *A Vendre* sign on it.

She made inquiries of the neighbours and learned, to her horror, that Gabrielle and many of the girls who had worked at the club had been condemned as traitors and collaborators when Paris was liberated. They had been publicly humiliated in a nearby square by having their heads shaved, spat at and abused by the local patriots, and then ostracized. All seemed to have vanished without trace, and Inès' efforts to track them down were all to no avail.

Why didn't the neighbours and Free French defend them and put the record straight? Tell them of the sacrifices these women had made during the war? It was too unfair. They had all done so much for the Resistance from the headquarters at L'Éléphant Rose, and to be punished in such a brutal way was hideously unjust.

But Paris still held so many memories for Inès, both good and bad, that she found it difficult to tear herself away. Just wandering through Montmartre, Pigalle and the glorious narrow streets of the Rive Gauche brought a rush of nostalgia. She knew that there was nothing left for her here any more, but she felt she couldn't leave just yet.

One day she sat at one of the rickety iron tables outside the café Deux Magots, which was packed to capacity. Tourists, laughing students and a sprinkling of old men wearing the shabby black berets indigenous to France, and who could nurse a cup of coffee or a glass of red wine for hours, all sat watching the comings and goings of the Boulevard Saint-Germain. Inès sipped at a glass of cognac, remembering that day when she'd sat almost at this very same table and been propositioned by the odious Italian General Umberto Scrofo. What would have been her fate if she had not kept that fateful appointment which had ended in his death?

Would she have simply remained in Paris working as one of Yves' girls? Or would she have been condemned as a traitor and sent away in disgrace? Yves. At the thought of him her heart lurched in spite of herself. Did one ever get over those infatuations of youth? It had been nearly three years now since he'd left her, but whenever she thought of him it was still with warmth.

She stared out into the busy street, her eyes suddenly focusing on a thin man with a grubby beret perched sloppily on his untidy brown curls, a cigarette hanging from his lips, who was walking slowly down the Boulevard Saint-Germain. It couldn't be, it couldn't.

'Yves! *Mon Dieu*, Yves!' Inès jumped up, the people around looking at her irritably as she stumbled through the tables and chairs to the street and grabbed his arm. It was almost as if she'd willed him to appear.

'Yves – it's you – it's really you!' Inès' eyes shone, her face was flushed and glowing as the man swung around and turned to face her.

'My God – Inès!' Yves smiled slowly and she noticed that his teeth had become yellowed from too much smoking, and there were deep lines around his eyes. 'What the hell are you doing in Paris?'

'I came to see the sights,' said Inès breathlessly, 'visit old friends – except that there don't seem to be any old friends around any more.

But now I've found you.' She saw that his cheeks were gaunt and unshaven, and that the collar of his blue shirt was grubby. 'D'you have time for a cup of coffee with me?' she asked eagerly. 'I'd love to talk to you.'

'Of course,' he said. 'I don't have anything else to do. I have all the time in the world, *chérie*.'

They weaved their way back to her table, and he ordered coffee and armagnac for both of them.

'But you'll have to pay for it.' He winked at her wryly. 'I'm a little short today.'

'Of course,' Inès said brightly. 'So tell me about yourself, Yves. 'What are you doing? – are you still with Stella?'

He shook his head, lighting another cigarette from the stub of the old one. His hands were shaking, his fingernails dark with dirt, and the index finger of his right hand was deep yellow with nicotine stains. Yves had always been quite a dandy – extremely fastidious – and Inès was startled by his transformation.

'Stella – poof – she's gone.'

'Oh.' Inès didn't know whether or not to feel a frisson of triumph over an old rival. Certainly this Yves, this man in the shabby overcoat with a three-day growth of stubble, was by no means the handsome lover she'd always remembered him to be. 'Why did she go?' she asked.

'A better offer.' He laughed bitterly. 'A better *macrou*. Someone who gave her more thrills in bed.'

In spite of herself Inès felt herself blushing. Yves had always been a superb lover if nothing else.

'That's ridiculous – you were wonderful in bed – why should she leave for that?'

'*Merci, chérie*, but *malheureusement* a little problem arose when our great country was liberated.' There was no mistaking the bitterness in his voice now, and she saw sadness in his eyes as he threw back his brandy and signalled to the white-aproned waiter for another.

'Do you really want to know what happened to me, Inès?'

'Yes,' she whispered, 'I do – tell me – please.'

'You won't like it,' he said bluntly.

'I don't care – tell me – tell me everything.'

'When Stella and I came back here from London in 1944 the war was not yet over, you remember – although Paris had been liberated by de Gaulle. We found a flat, near here actually, and Stella went back to work. She was a good worker but times were bad, food was short.' He paused and Inès leaned forward to hear his voice, which had become quieter. 'I got involved in the black market. I was doing it in London you remember, and I still had many contacts here.'

'Yes, I know.' Inès took a sip of brandy, listening intently, watching Yves' dead eyes growing more impassioned as he continued his story.

'One night a truckload of champagne was coming into Paris from Epernay. I'd arranged with my contacts to buy it – ten million francs, almost all the money I had, but New Year's Eve was on the way and there was a growing demand for all the best champagnes and wines; everyone wanted to celebrate. Don't forget that even though people had suffered during the war, many of them made a great deal of money from it.'

'Yes, I know that. Go on, Yves,' she coaxed. He'd stopped, the pallor had returned to his face and his hands were now shaking badly. She pushed her glass across the table to him, watching as he drained it immediately.

'I was supposed to meet Gino, you remember Gino? He was one of my most trusted boys, at eleven o'clock on the Quai d'Orsay. He was driving the truck, I had the money. I gave him the cash then I drove the truck on to my warehouse – I distributed the cases to the clubs and restaurants through my boys – and then I went home –'

He stopped again and Inès saw how difficult it was becoming for him to continue.

'Then what happened?' she coaxed, but he didn't answer, lighting another cigarette, his hands as frail and shaking as an old man's. Both of their glasses were empty and she motioned to the waiter to bring more brandy.

'I don't know why I'm telling you all this.' He gripped her hand suddenly, his bloodshot eyes those of a frightened animal. 'You won't like it.'

'I don't care, Yves – please – please tell me – you must – maybe I can help you.'

'Help me – ha! – that's rich – that's very funny indeed.' The waiter brought the brandies and Yves knocked his back in one gulp. His hands stopped shaking and he continued. 'Three nights later, while Stella and I were asleep, they came for me.'

'Who – who came for you?' whispered Inès.

He shrugged. 'Them – the boys – the Mob – who knows? It was a set-up, and I was the patsy. They dragged me off in the middle of the night.' His voice dropped to a whisper and tears began to roll down his face. 'They took me to a warehouse – somewhere near Les Halles I think it was, I could smell the stink of the fish.' He stopped, the muscles in his neck quivering.

'And then,' Inès prompted quickly.

'The bastards accused me of watering down the fucking champagne. They accused me of fixing it to make a bigger profit. Do you know what, Inès? It wasn't champagne at all in those bottles, it was some kind of cheap coloured fizzy water. Someone – and to this day I don't know who – palmed me off with three hundred cases of fake champagne and they blamed me – the scum blamed *me*, Inès.'

He was sobbing quietly, unashamedly now.

'So what did they do to you?' Inès almost didn't want to hear the answer.

'Guess?' He looked up at her with a cynical smile. 'What's the worst thing you could possibly do to a pimp?'

'I – I don't know,' said Inès, feeling faint but mesmerized by this pathetic wreck of a man whom she'd once loved so desperately.

'They castrated me, *chérie*.' He put his face very close to hers and grinned horribly. 'They made me into a eunuch.'

'Oh my God, Yves – no, it's not possible.' Inès felt sick as Yves' calloused hands clutched hers tightly on the iron table.

'They cut off my balls and they told me that was the *lightest* penalty that they usually gave to someone who tried to doublecross them. Emasculate them, turn them into a *nothing*.'

Inès' head was swimming. This couldn't be – this couldn't have happened to Yves. Her Yves who had lived for making love, who had taught her everything she knew about it.

'*Mon pauvre* – Yves, I don't know what to say – I'm so sorry, so terribly sorry.' She was crying now, and took out her handkerchief to

171

wipe her eyes, oblivious to the curious stares of people at other tables.

'Don't be sorry, *chérie*. I hadn't exactly been Prince Charming all my life, I probably deserved it.'

'*No! No! No one* could deserve that,' said Inès in horror. 'It's barbaric – did you go to the police?'

'Police?' He laughed bitterly. 'You must be joking, *chérie*, they knew what my game was. They despise black marketeers. I got as much sympathy from them as Adolf Hitler would have got if he'd been bleeding to death in a concentration camp. They took me to the hospital, of course, sewed me up. It's not serious, you know – being a eunuch. It doesn't endanger your life or anything, but it sure as hell fucks up your sex life.' He laughed again, a hollow dead sound, and lit another Gauloise. 'A dead cock. A neuter. It makes you a laughing stock, but people pity you too.'

'So what did you do? What do you do now? How do you live?' Inès stammered, her face flushed and hot.

'I have a few friends left,' he said. 'I do odd jobs, this and that, betting on the horses, fencing a few bits and pieces, nothing too expensive of course. I'm OK. I'm fine.' He smiled, trying to reassure her, and Inès could see that the armagnac had done its work in making him stronger. He had obviously become completely dependent on alcohol. Now he sat straight, his hands no longer trembling, his gaze direct. 'Stella left, of course, like a poxy rat deserting a ship – I can't say I blamed her. She liked a good fuck, did Stella, and she couldn't get it from me. Well, *chérie* – that was more than two years ago – I suppose we all have to play the cards that fate deals us – that was a shitty hand for a *mic* to get but I've coped with it. I've tried. What about you, have the gods been good to you?'

'Oh – I'm – well, I'm fine actually,' mumbled Inès, her mind still reeling from his revelations. 'Pretty good really.'

'Got any good clients?' he asked. 'Rich mugs?'

'Yes, oh, yes – very good – I mean – yes, they're all right.' Inès felt stifled, even though it was cool outside the café.

'I bet none of them can do this,' exclaimed Yves and he flicked his tongue into his mouth with the burning cigarette on it, closed his lips and stared at Inès with the wide-eyed comical look that had so entranced her when she was a little girl. As she watched in dismay, two long puffs of smoke came out of Yves' ears.

Inès felt she had to escape. She wanted to run – run like the wind. She wanted to go back to her hotel and weep bitter tears for her erstwhile lover, who smiled, pleased with himself as he stubbed out the damp cigarette and looked to her for approval. She smiled weakly and he smiled back.

'Good, *chérie*, that's good. You always were a clever little *poule de luxe*, Inès, one of the best, you deserve to do well.'

Suddenly Inès wanted to leave Paris right now. She felt sick, dirty, sullied. She wanted to cry for this sad little man she had loved so much, for the friends she had lost. As if reading her thoughts Yves leaned towards her, brushing her cheek briefly with dry lips.

'*Au revoir, chérie*,' he said briskly, arranging the beret on his greying curls. 'I have to go now. Thanks for the drink.' He stood up, the sun shining on his lined face, and Inès could see clearly how much he'd changed, how the years had taken their toll. 'Good luck, Inès.'

'*Au revoir*, Yves,' she whispered. 'Goodbye.'

He tipped his beret and as he walked off down the Boulevard Saint-Germain, his shabby overcoat flapping around his thin body, Inès silently thanked God that her heart was no longer in Paris, that her life was in England now.

The next day Inès stood outside the Ritz Hotel in the Place Vendôme, staring up for one last time at the window of the room where she had killed Umberto Scrofo. She was on her way to the airport back to London, and she knew now that Paris held nothing for her but sad, bad memories.

During the next few years in London Inès became more and more disenchanted with her life of prostitution, even though her clients were all rich and reasonably attractive. The frightened, ignorant teenager had matured into a sophisticated, chic woman of the world who suspected that true love existed only in novels and women's magazines. The pain of Yves' betrayal had never really healed. She had not been able to find a man to inspire feelings of truly belonging to someone body and soul.

As the years passed and her savings grew, Inès gradually eliminated most of her clients, keeping only a few of her most powerful and influential customers. Apart from Viscount Benjie, for whom she had a special affection, a series of mentors had kept her – in particular three rich, middle-aged Englishmen. One was an aristocrat who had come out of what he called a 'good war' with a chestful of medals to prove it; the other two were more bourgeois men of the City, securely married industrialists who between them appeared to own half the home counties.

They had given Inès money – though not an enormous amount, since 'old' English money is never thrown around by those who possess it. But what they had given her that was infinitely more precious than cash, expensive trinkets, or the occasional visit to Deauville, Cannes or New York, was knowledge. An understanding of politics, of stocks, bonds, equities and market prices – they had imparted secret share tips to her, and insider advice on futures. An overheard phrase in a business telephone conversation at her flat, an artfully veiled question or two from her, and she would call her stockbroker to buy coffee beans, nickel, tin, gold or silver. Knowledge is power, and Inès learned fast. Her portfolio grew, as with a shrewd Frenchwoman's understanding of financial matters she made it her business to protect her future.

But Inès became resigned to never finding her own man, to never falling in love. She supposed it was her fate never to settle down in security with a safe husband and two-point-three children. One day soon, however, she would have enough money to stop working and to retire. What would she do with herself then? It was a thought she did not like to dwell on. Her flat was filled with expensive beautiful objects, and revealed no clue to her profession. But there was no one to admire her pretty things. No one to share her life when she would finally end her 'career'.

Inès had felt little emotion for any man since Yves – only a vague fondness for them, an almost niece-like attitude. To her, men were all the same: mostly selfish, sexual animals. The more they used her for their pleasure, the less she felt for them. Week after week, month after month, year after year as she plied her sexual trade, she yearned for a romantic love which, in her heart, she believed did not exist.

She had met many eligible men – young men, handsome men, clever and ambitious men, some with great futures. None of them had moved her one iota. She tried desperately to fall in love, to feel some small part of the passion, ecstasy and joy which she'd known with Yves, but she felt nothing. Sometimes she wondered cynically if it was Yves' magic tricks which had so entranced her and that at heart she was still ten years old.

Then one afternoon she went to a matinée of *Pygmalion* at the Aldwych Theatre. There on the stage was a tall handsome actor with curved black eyebrows. His dark hair was severely brushed back, tortoiseshell spectacles were perched on his aristocratic nose, and a deerstalker hat sat on his head at a jaunty angle.

His name was Julian Brooks, Looks Brooks, the Idol of the Odeons as he was known in the tabloid press, and not since Yves had Inès seen a man who so captured her heart and her imagination. Julian entranced her with his charisma and waspish sexy charm. When he was on stage her eyes never left him for a second. She perceived in him a quality of warmth and fun that she knew was the real person and not just the actor. Inès knew that she had to meet this man, even though she was not alone in her adoration. From her seat in the stalls, surrounded by the rustle of chocolate wrappings and the excited murmur of the matinée matrons, she could sense his innate sensitivity spiced with roguish masculinity and humour.

Inès did not miss a single matinée performance of *Pygmalion* for the remainder of its run, and she made it her business to find out every scrap of information she could about the man who had started to inhabit all her waking thoughts.

6

London

As Julian became a bigger and more glittering star, Phoebe had gradually changed into that kind of dreadful snob which only a middle-class Englishwoman can be. She loved two things beyond all else: money and social position. Her main interest in Julian's career, other than landing herself a plum part, was the position in society and the wealth which it could bring them. She rarely spoke to any of the cast or crew with whom Julian worked, choosing only to speak to stars and important directors. The artistic side was of no interest to her; she couldn't have cared less whether he was starring as Othello or Charley's Aunt. She loved being Mrs Julian Brooks, close friend of the Oliviers and the Redgraves. She loved the life of a star's wife: the society rounds of Royal Ascot, Wimbledon, the fourth of June at Eton, Cowes, Henley; charity balls and weekends at country houses with the aristocratic and the famous, as well as gleaming black limousines and accounts with all the best couturiers and shops. Fuelled by Julian's success, her acting ambitions came into full flower when she had forced him to cast her in his plays. She would have made his life quite intolerable had he not given in to her. Appearing on stage with Julian gave her even more cachet with her friends and naturally she always insisted on having above-the-title billing: not just a star's wife, but a star in her own right.

But at this moment she was absolutely furious with Julian. She had been furious ever since he'd categorically refused to allow her to play Eliza Doolittle in *Pygmalion*.

At thirty-five, she looked at least a dozen years too old to play the part of the waiflike cockney flower girl, not to mention the indeterminate number of excess pounds which gave her the look of a well-to-do matron.

'I'm perfect for the part, *perfect*, you always *said* I was,' she yapped. There was lipstick smeared on her front teeth, and her heavy makeup did nothing more than to bring the deepening lines of discontent on her face into sharper focus. The henna which she used so liberally to brighten her fading hair glowed garishly in the thin afternoon light which filtered into Julian's dressing room at Pinewood Studios. He was in the last stages of shooting *The Buccaneer*, another swashbuckler for Didier Armande, and in the middle of intense casting and pre-production sessions for *Pygmalion*. Exhausted after two long months on such a physically demanding movie, he had been trying in vain to take a nap on the daybed in his dressing room when Phoebe burst in, dismissing his dresser with a typically waspish 'Get out. I don't *care* if he is asleep – I'm his bloody wife!' She stood angrily before him, hands on hips.

'Phoebe, for God's sake,' Julian pleaded, looking up bleary-eyed at his once desirable wife, now an outraged, overweight virago.

'How *could* you have cast that *slut* Louise James as Eliza?' she said, spitting venom. 'She's *hideous*. She can't act and she's *far* too old!'

'She's twenty,' Julian said simply. 'She won a Tony award on Broadway last year, she's been acting since she was eleven and, what's more, she happens to be very pretty.'

'*Pretty?*' Phoebe screeched. 'You call that baggage pretty? She's got a face like a . . . like a cheap china doll. *I'm* your wife. How about some loyalty to me, *me!*'

'Phoebe, please. Please do be reasonable.' Julian was trying hard not to lose his composure, not to say his temper. He had an important emotional scene to play this afternoon, and Phoebe's rages were far from helpful. 'You're just too old for Eliza, can't you see that, dear?'

'No, I bloody can't.' She started to cry the crocodile tears which Julian had grown to know so well. 'I'm the same age as Vivien. She plays young girls.'

'Look in the damned *mirror*, Phoebe. It doesn't *lie*, you know. You're almost thirty-six. You *can't* play an eighteen-year-old, Phoebe, you just can't, and that's that.'

'I *can*,' she wept. 'Oh, Julian, *please please* let me. I'll lose some weight, I'll be so good . . . Look at my reviews for *Present Laughter* – they said I was enchantingly young and vibrant.'

'That was several years ago, old thing.' Julian knew he had to remain adamant; Phoebe was doing everything she could to manipulate him and he couldn't allow the balance of power in their marriage to shift in her direction. God knows she tried all the time. It was always an uphill struggle, but he had to remain in control. He believed in the dominance of the male, and just as importantly, the strong professional standards he wanted maintained.

'Years ago, Phoebe,' he went on, 'and the role of Joanna was of a woman of the world. Eliza's almost a *child*. I'm sorry, but it's done now. I've cast Louise, and the announcements go out to the press tomorrow.'

Phoebe stopped crying and looked at him warily. 'I see,' she sighed, wiping her smudged eyes with a mascara-stained handkerchief. 'Just like that – humped and dumped. Thanks a bunch.'

'Don't be so bloody ridiculous, Phoebe. You've got a damned good life. I try to give you *everything* you want. You've been in practically every one of my plays, but you're just not going to be in this one. So let's finish this stupid argument, and for God's sake let me get some sleep.'

Phoebe thoughtfully fingered her huge Kashmiri sapphire and diamond ring from Garrard's, then adjusted her gold and pavé diamond choker from Van Cleef & Arpels and toyed with the buttons of her beige cashmere Jacques Fath couture suit. These were all too familiar signs to Julian that she was plotting something. He threw himself back on the couch with a sigh, his body craving rest. He'd been up since five that morning. Phoebe had insisted that they go to the opening of *Ring Around the Moon* the night before, and afterwards to yet another of Binkie Beaumont's lavish parties. He had slept for only three hours and was shatteringly exhausted.

'I'm so tired, Phoebe,' he said simply. 'Would you mind leaving me now? I need a bit of a doze – got an important scene this afternoon.'

'Oh, yes, I'll leave. I'll leave, all right,' she hissed frostily, pulling on her beige suede gauntlet gloves trimmed with mink and shrugging her new sable jacket from Bergdorf Goodman's of New York City on to her hefty shoulders.

'I'm not exactly happy with you these days, Julian. I don't think I'm going to enjoy being around London while you're rehearsing with that talentless trollop.'

Julian sighed again. What now? Which threatening ploy did she have in mind this time? Was this bitch never satisfied?

'Last night at the party Hermione was telling me that she wants to take a little trip,' she went on. 'I think I'll join her. I'm sure we'll have a lot of fun together; Hermione's so amusing.'

'Wonderful, dear,' Julian sighed, closing his eyes, praying that she would now leave. He heard the assistant director knocking at his leading lady's dressing room next door.

'Where will you and Hermione go?' he asked, more out of a sense of politeness than interest.

'Around the world,' Phoebe snapped, striding to the door. 'It's expensive, of course,' she added with smug satisfaction. 'About ten thousand pounds for the best hotels, restaurants and so on. But since I'll be bored being around here with you and that James girl, probably fucking like rabbits, I know you won't mind too much forking out. Oh, by the way' – she stopped at the opened door – 'don't forget – you've promised me Ophelia. *That* I will never give up. *Never.*' She sailed out, slamming the door just as Julian's dresser appeared carrying his usual wake-up cup of espresso.

'Everything okay, guv?' he asked sympathetically, seeing the evident strain on Julian's face.

'Fine, Freddie, fine. Thanks, old boy. Tell Tim in makeup I'll be over in five minutes.'

Ophelia my arse! he thought as he knocked back the bitter but reviving espresso, then pulled on his black leather boots. The way she looked now she'd be a more likely contender for Gertrude. Maybe even Gertrude's mother if there was such a part. He was in a black mood when he stomped into the makeup room, only to be greeted by a warm smile from his current leading lady.

That evening after shooting had finally ended, Julian was a most welcome visitor in the dressing room of his gorgeous, pouting co-star, Rebecca Chamberlane. There he released all his anger and pent-up frustration, leaving them both so delightfully sated and fulfilled that their liaison continued right up until the movie was finished.

7

Nice

'Jesus, what a bunch of *dogs*.' Bluey Regan leaned back in his seat in the darkened auditorium of the old theatre in Nice. He studied the line-up of forty-seven nervous teenage girls who huddled together on the stage in their skimpy black leotards, mended tights and shabby ballet shoes.

'Not a decent body among them,' he muttered to Nicholas Stone, the hot young director who was leaning forward in the seat next to him, staring intently at the girls. He was whispering something rapidly to his secretary, who was writing as fast as her limited shorthand would allow her.

'They've got no *tits*, Nick,' complained Bluey. 'Not one of 'em has anything more than a thirty-two A-cup. *That's* going to look *real* great in an off-the-shoulder period gown, in glorious Technicolor, up there with Julian Brooks trying to act as if he wants to screw her brains out.'

'Shut up, Bluey,' Nick snapped. 'Haven't you heard? We're doing the sixteenth, not the eighteenth century. She's supposed to be a princess and she'll be dressed in something loose. Just *forget* tits for a minute, if that's remotely possible for you. Just look for the raw talent, the photogenic faces, the quality of these girls. And if you don't want to watch, go for a walk, go get laid, go get lost! I'll weed 'em out myself.'

'Yeah, well, remember, you're the charlie who's gonna be directing her.'

'I know, and I know what I'm doing,' said Nick implacably. 'If you stay, keep your moth *shut*, Bluey. When I want your advice I'll ask for it, and tits are no big deal in this case.'

'OK, OK,' Bluey said, slumping back in his seat. He looked again at the group of terrified girls, muttering one last disparaging remark loudly enough for Nick's French secretary to hear.

'Please do not forget, *Meestair* Regan, that we have only come out of a war – an occupation – less than nine years ago,' the woman said frostily. 'These young girls 'ad very leetle to *eat* when they were babies and that is why they are so small – the *contraire* of your well-fed *American* girls.'

'Well, I guess a few good American steaks, fries and chocolate malts would fatten 'em up. Get 'em lookin' as good as Marilyn Monroe and Jane Russell quicker than you can say Metro fuckin' Goldwyn Mayer, right?' Bluey smiled lazily, offering the woman some chewing gum.

'Quite,' said the Frenchwoman, refusing. 'But I don't think any of these girls are quite that type of *mademoiselle*. They are all French – *typiquement française* – and you will find, very proud of it, *Monsieur*!' She turned away from him, unable to disguise her extreme dislike for Nick's leathery assistant.

A frail redhead in a burgundy leotard and tights which did nothing for her colouring stepped forward on stage, shyly handing her sheet music to the pianist. She performed the dance of the dying swan from *Swan Lake*; it was technically perfect, but had no passion at all. Shaking his head, Nick Stone whispered to his secretary to dismiss her. She was the fifteenth applicant they had seen so far. This was going to be much harder than he'd anticipated.

An hour later, Bluey was snoring loudly when Nick nudged him excitedly. 'Take a look at this one,' he whispered. 'Now *she* is much more the type I had in mind for Isabella. What do you think?'

Bluey sat up, watching with a critical eye as Dominique danced a fandango from *Carmen* with such style and barely suppressed sensuality that both men found themselves aroused and intrigued.

'Hot damn, she's *good*,' breathed Bluey. 'Fucking good, eh, Nick? And getta load of those legs. Looks like the kid's got star quality if ever I saw it.'

'Yeah, she sure does,' Nick agreed, scribbling notes and tossing them into a folder. 'She's sure one helluva dancer, helluva looker too. Maybe she's the one, Bluey.'

'About time too,' said Bluey. 'At least this hasn't been a complete waste of time.'

At the back of the auditorium, Agathe clasped her hands joyfully as she saw how well her pupil was performing. All of her extra rehearsals had paid off. If there was any justice in the world, Dominique must get the part, be off to Hollywood, away from this Provençal backwater. And with a little luck, Agathe would be going with her.

'Well, what d'you know.' Bluey stared with mounting admiration at Dominique as she finished her second audition piece, a perfectly executed version of Eleanor Powell's tap dance from *Broadway Melody*.

She had thrown a short skirt round her black cotton leotard which accentuated her tiny waist and small, firm breasts. Her long hair was loosened and it seemed to float in the air like soft black tendrils around her flushed face.

All but five of the girls had been dismissed. They sat cross-legged in the wings, cardigans and shawls draped over their shoulders, grudgingly admitting to each other that Dominique was very good, far better than any of them. She was more than good. She had a magical presence, a powerful charisma, a sweet gamine quality which could change like quicksilver into smouldering sensuality.

Dominique had now finished, and stood pink and shaking with nerves in the centre of the vast stage. She waited, trembling, as the two men approached her.

'Very nice – *very* nice indeed,' Nick said. Since his recent success he'd become partial to the suave Fred Astaire school of dressing. He wore cream gaberdine slacks with an open-necked pink shirt and a navy blue polka-dot cravat. Even with his black curly hair greased down, it still looked wild, accentuating his boyish good looks. At twenty-seven he now had two major hits under his belt in less than a year and he was considered one of the hottest of Hollywood's new generation of directors.

Bobby Soxers in Space had been the teenage cult movie of 1953, grossing over twenty million dollars at the box office, and giving Nick his first taste of the critical acclaim which he'd so longed for. His second movie, a screwball comedy, had done equally well with critics and audiences alike, although the original script had been fairly mediocre. But Nick had a magic touch with film. He understood and respected it, he revered it, he could see the whole film in his mind's eye before he even shot it. He was sizzling in Hollywood, MCCP's golden boy, Spyros Makopolis' favourite, and now for his third film they had given him the prize plum of the year to direct - *The Legend of Cortez*.

After shaking Dominique's hand, Nick handed her a stiff white card with his name engraved in bold black letters.

'Come and see me this afternoon at three o'clock at the Carlton Hotel in Cannes. Can you get there all right, honey?'

Dominique almost fainted. She only managed a nod, and a whispered, '*Oui, Monsieur*, I can. May I bring my chaperone?' She nodded towards the dim figure of Agathe shrouded in gloom, far beyond the footlights.

'Of course.' Nick smiled at her. She was adorable, sexy, fresh and sweet. 'Bring your mother and father, your grandmother and all your aunts and uncles too, if you want. We are going to talk business, young lady, and I think you're going to like what I have to say.'

Dominique shook back her waist-length hair. Jet black and fluffy, it framed the perfect oval of her face as she shyly looked up at Nick with green lynx eyes through her forest of lashes.

'*Merci*, M'sieur Stone,' she whispered in a girlishly sexy voice which both men immediately realized would be another major asset to her. But those eyes. Nick found himself entranced by them, and Bluey's experienced gaze roamed over her young body like a gourmet before a feast. Gorgeous – yes, she was gorgeous all right. A tasty young dish to set before a king – or in this case an explorer.

In the darkness of the auditorium Agathe smiled to herself. She sensed the reaction of the two men to her pupil but clenched her fists in spite of her pleasure in Dominique's performance. It was always the same with men. Show them a young, pretty girl and they turned to putty. Once a woman was no longer young, no longer pretty, no one would bother to give her a second glance. In spite of her good wishes for her young pupil, Agathe felt a twinge of jealousy. If it hadn't been for the war, that could have been her up there.

8

Rome

In the spring of 1954 an American film company came to Rome to shoot a frothy escapist movie featuring two famous stars of the thirties. Ramona Armande and Gregory Mendelson were playing a middle-aged couple who find both adventure and autumnal love in Rome, amidst its romantic beauty and its broken stones.

The film company had been setting up lights and equipment in a small piazza for a scene between Ramona and Gregory. It was unusually hot and the stifling room above the café, which had been provided for Ramona's relaxation, was becoming uncomfortably warm.

She decided to walk a little, to explore the endlessly fascinating side streets of Rome, where each shop seemed to hold even more eye-catching exquisite treasures than the last. Ramona adored collecting, and the more bizarre the objects the better they could be shown to advantage in her exotic house in Acapulco. She looked the height of chic in a beautifully tailored cream linen belted suit from Balenciaga, and a large beige straw hat, laden with silk lilies of the valley, perched on her shining black hair. Dark sunglasses covered her famous amber eyes, but even with them the sun was so blindingly strong in the piazza that she squinted against its brightness.

'*Principessa*, where are you going?' asked Tinto, the first assistant director, with a concerned expression on his permanently anxious face as he hurried after her.

'Don't worry, Tinto my dear,' smiled Ramona in the charming manner with which she always managed to endear herself to the crew. 'I'm just going for a little stroll down the shaded side of the Via Babuino. I shan't be gone for more than half an hour and by that time you should have finished lighting the set, *si*?'

'*Si, Principessa,*' smiled Tinto, admiring the slim straight-backed figure as she wandered off up the cobbled and sun-dappled street. She was still a beautiful woman, even though there was no question that she would ever see fifty again.

Ramona strolled slowly along the hot dusty street enjoying the faint breeze which gently ruffled her hair. Each little shop was a treasure trove of beautiful things, and she lingered in several of them, admiring an eighteenth-century painted lace fan with an ornate silver-gilt handle, then a pair of 1920s emerald and diamond ear clips, and finally a beautifully sculpted bronze figure of a muscular youth throwing a discus. But it wasn't until she found herself outside the last shop in the street that she caught her breath. The ivory and ruby bracelet which lay on a black velvet cushion in the window was truly breathtaking. To her experienced eye it was of museum quality, with its sugar-loaf cabochon rubies surrounded by brilliant-cut diamonds all set into a wide cuff of creamy ivory. Immediately intrigued, Ramona opened the door and stepped into the cool, darkened interior. An extremely ugly fat man who reminded her of a toad sat behind the glass counter examining a diamond bracelet through a loupe. He looked up at her, and as the bright sunlight from the street only illuminated her as a silhouette he did not immediately recognize her.

'May I help you?' he inquired, his voice sounding harsh and uncultured. Ramona thought she detected the southern accent of a Neapolitan or a Sicilian, certainly not the refined tones of a Roman gentleman.

'Yes – the ivory bracelet in the window – I'd like to see it, please.'

'*Prego* – sit down, *Signora.*' The man gestured to a carved eighteenth-century bergère, which she noticed, like everything else in the shop, was of superb quality.

Ramona looked around her admiringly at all the shelves and cabinets which were full of jewels, small enamel and gold boxes, carved figures and other objects d'art. Obviously he was a man of taste in spite of his grotesque and off-putting appearance and that curious rasping voice.

'There – it is ravishing, is it not?' He placed the cuff gently on a velvet pad, watching her carefully as Ramona reverently picked it up.

'Beautiful – it's absolutely stunning,' she breathed, removing a glove and admiring the bracelet on her slim wrist. 'Such quality. How much?'

'Ah . . . for you, *Signora*, a very special price indeed,' beamed the *antiquaire*, having recognized her when switching on the desk light. 'Only ten million lire to you, *Signora*.'

'It's superb,' breathed Ramona, 'truly beautiful – ten million you say?'

He nodded encouragingly. His tiny eyes were slits, his hands clasped across his imposing stomach. But Ramona noticed how the excellent quality and cut of his suit managed cleverly to disguise so much of his bulk, and that his watch and cuff links were from Cartier.

'I have an idea,' she said as she leaned forward, removing her sunglasses to give him the full benefit of the amber lynx-eyes which had captivated so many audiences for more than three decades. Their magic obviously still worked, for she saw him swallow, and a faint pink tinge begin to suffuse his sallow complexion.

'This bracelet looks wonderful with this dress, don't you think?'

He nodded, quite captivated by the extraordinary glamour and mystery of the woman.

'We're in the middle of shooting a movie down in the Piazza Barbarini –' Ramona clasped his arm with her delicate scarlet-tipped fingers like an excited child. 'Let me wear it in the next scene. The production manager will be there to see to the insurance and all of that sort of thing – and' – she positively glowed as she continued – 'when we've finished filming this afternoon, *Oggi* are shooting a photo layout of me all around Rome. You know the sort of thing, throwing coins into the Fontana di Trevi, wandering around the Forum and the Piazza di Spagna. If I was wearing this bracelet, I should *insist* that the magazine give your shop a credit for it in the article – then perhaps the price might be a little less?' She smiled ingenuously, pleased with her little plan, and he couldn't help but smile back. She was certainly an enchanting woman. A woman of the world – no doubt at all about that – but with a childlike charm which he found quite irresistible.

He pretended to heave a great sigh and then shook his shiny bald head from side to side. 'The Signora drives a hard bargain,' he smiled. 'But as it is you, Madame Armande, such a great, great star' – he gave a little bow in her direction and Ramona acknowledged it by inclining her head regally – 'I can see no way in which I could refuse you – with one proviso, of course.'

'Which is?' asked Ramona, unable to tear her eyes away from the glorious cuff and the diamonds which glittered brilliantly on it in the dim light.

'That I might be allowed to accompany the Signora on her trip around Rome this afternoon, perhaps even to show her some sights that she has not yet seen – then perhaps – if she would permit – to have the honour of escorting her to dinner tonight at Taverna Livia?'

Ramona studied him. He would certainly be an unprepossessing escort – short, fat and ugly. But she found that he had a certain kind of charm, and obviously from the exquisite contents of his shop, he had an enormous knowledge of art and a great eye for beautiful things.

She was becoming bored by the fawning Italian gigolos who had found their way to her suite in the Grand Hotel. Bored too by the laboured huffing and puffing of her co-star Gregory Mendelson during their occasional bouts of lovemaking. They had indulged in a torrid affair some years ago, when he had been a desirable stud and the idol of millions, but unfortunately time had been unforgiving, not only to his hair and waistline, but also to his sex drive. Although he'd made a valiant effort to satisfy Ramona in bed for old times' sake, their perfunctory couplings had become less than gratifying for them both.

'Very well.' She inclined her head to him again. 'I should be happy for you to accompany me – and delighted to accept your invitation to dinner.' She glanced at her wristwatch. 'Oh dear, now I must go – it's time for the filming to start, I mustn't be late. Won't you join me, *Signor?*'

Pulling a bunch of keys from his pocket and carefully locking the door of his little shop behind them, the jeweller followed Ramona out into the blistering Roman sunshine.

He picked her up at the Grand Hotel at nine o'clock. His car was an open black Lancia, and his portliness was again adroitly disguised in a midnight blue shantung suit from Caraceni. He was wearing a white silk shirt from the Burlington Arcade, and a fairly garish crimson tie. If it weren't for the ugliness of his face and body and the cloying cologne which he seemed to have bathed in, he would indeed have cut quite a *bella figura*. As it was, he complemented Ramona who was elegance personified in a champagne lace cocktail dress which nipped her tiny waist into a handspan, and gave her a cleavage that Miss Marilyn Monroe would envy. Around her neck was a simple diamond necklace from Fulco of Rome, and on her wrist she wore the beautiful ivory and diamond bracelet. They made an arresting couple as they walked through the lobby of the hotel and several people turned to stare in genuine admiration at Ramona's style and presence.

He couldn't help feeling pleased with himself. He had never gone out with a woman as ravishing and as famous as Ramona, in fact no beautiful or even pretty girls would even give him a second glance unless plenty of lire changed hands. But Ramona seemed not to care about his lack of height or looks. She seemed more interested in his knowledge of jewellery and pictures. As they drove in his open car through the streets towards the quieter outskirts of Rome, she covered her hair with a chiffon scarf and listened carefully to the replies he gave to her many questions.

Ramona was an excellent listener, a natural expert in finding out every detail about a person's past. With a subtle and well-chosen question or two, she tried hard to piece together her escort's life story. As they sat at a table outside the elegant restaurant in the balmy night air, sipping champagne from heavy Venetian glasses, Umberto Scrofo told Ramona everything that he thought she should know about his past life.

Umberto had been an extremely lucky man. When the Mafia thugs had left him to fend for himself in the tiny rowing boat off the coast of Calabria, it had been a moonlit night and the sea was flat and calm. Without the aid of a compass, and with more luck than skill, he had managed to drift around the cape of Calabria, the southernmost part of the Italian mainland, and through the Straits of Messina.

There he had been found floating by a fisherman out in his boat who had rescued him and taken him, half dead, to his home in a tiny Sicilian village. When Umberto had recovered, he contacted a distant cousin, not a member of the Cosa Nostra, who had, with the help of a few gold coins, taken him to Rome.

Always prepared for any eventuality, Umberto had made it his habit to sleep with a money belt round his waist, in which he kept some ancient gold coins and a small fortune in loose diamonds, emeralds and rubies. The Mafia gang had luckily neglected to give him a full body search when they broke into his room, so he was a rich man when he arrived in Rome to begin yet another new life.

After a few months he opened an antique shop on the Via Babuino with many of the precious things that he had stolen from the French and the Greeks, and had shipped to Italy for storage during the war. Because so many of his pieces were from lesser-known museums and the great houses of France he soon owned one of the most beautifully stocked antique shops in Rome.

He shrewdly released only a few selected items from his looted plunder on to the market each year, being extremely careful not to attract the attentions of Interpol, who were still on the lookout for the thousands of works of art that had been stolen during the war.

The gold rings and bracelets of all the unfortunates who had been tortured and sent to their deaths during his regime had provided an excellent income for him. He still had many of the silver and gold icons, enamel vases, alabaster figures and candlesticks pilfered from the Greeks, and from France he still had what he referred to as 'my pictures'. Among these were masterpieces by Manet, Van Gogh, Renoir, Cézanne, and three large and highly important cubist canvases by Picasso. These were all kept secured in an underground vault in his new house close to the Piazza di Spagna, waiting for the rainy day when he might need to sell them.

Umberto was a rich man, but a bored one. The pleasures of the flesh no longer titillated him much unless they were of a truly bizarre nature, and it was becoming tedious sitting in his shop day after day. He certainly didn't need the money. What he really needed was something to stimulate him, but apart from sex, he could not think of anything.

But when he stepped into the Piazza Barbarini that sunny day, and saw the huge arc lights glittering down from the iron girders, saw the hustle and bustle of the film company, the glamour and enthusiasm which everyone seemed to have, he realized at once that at last he had found the answer to his long days of ennui.

It was during the making of *One Sunday in Rome* that Umberto and Ramona became firm friends. Umberto, who had always been intrigued by Hollywood, began to be even more interested by the fascinating business of film making, and became a regular fixture on the set. He met the producer, Henry Hornblower, an over-the-hill grizzled Hollywood legend, almost ready to be put out to pasture, but still full of gutsy anecdotes and stories about the days before talkies were invented. He met the director, a brash young whizz kid well on his way up the ladder, ambitious as hell and absolutely sure both of himself and of his talent; and he met the money men, the mysterious financiers who had managed to raise the money for the movie like conjurors. He expertly picked all their respective brains, convinced that he too could find the money to both finance and produce a film in Italy. And why not? It was now an open city for film making, the very hub of the movie industry in Europe.

All roads truly led to Rome in the early 1950s. The Via Veneto was a constant hive of activity, as busy as the terrace of the Carlton at the Cannes Film Festival. Every table at Doney's and the other cafés was packed with producers, financiers, writers and entrepreneurs, as well as a heavy sprinkling of Italian and American movie stars. The Via Veneto was the place to be seen, to be noticed, to clinch a deal.

It was hard to tell the difference between the aspiring starlets who table-hopped from group to group with calculated charm, and the prostitutes who plied their timeless trade up and down the Veneto. Both groups were equally attractive in their tight low-cut dresses, bouffant hair and made-up faces.

Everyone seemed to have a movie which they wanted to make or were about to shoot, and everyone had a deal or a contract ready to be signed. Rome was Little Hollywood on the Tiber, and movie people from around the world were flocking in hordes to the Eternal City.

When Umberto confided his plans to Ramona one evening as they were sitting at the Café Doney, sipping *crème de menthe frappé* through long pink straws, she turned to him in surprise and exclaimed, 'Why Umberto, I never knew you were interested in this crazy business. When did all this happen?'

'Well, a long time ago, I suppose,' he laughed, eyeing a sloe-eyed blonde slowly cruising the street looking for some action. 'During the war we used to see many American movies – some with you in, my dear.' He kissed her hand gallantly, his downcast eyes in fact following the progress of the young blonde's swaying buttocks up the pavement. 'Those were always my particular favourites.'

'How sweet of you, my dear Umberto, how very very kind you are.'

'Not at all, my dear. But you are so much more beautiful in life than you ever were on the screen.'

She laughed girlishly. 'Now Umberto, don't go too far, my dear, after all I am nearly forty, you know.' She lied with a smile, as he smiled back, playing along with the joke.

'Forty or not you are lovelier than *any* of these girls walking here tonight.'

Another tall slender blonde, wearing a figure-hugging red sheath dress which was cut completely down to the vee of her bottom, tossed her hair and winked at Scrofo as she swayed past their table. He feigned indifference, but remembered her well from the week before. She'd been very hot indeed. He still had her number somewhere. Tonight he would call her – later. Much as he liked and admired Ramona he did not find her sexually attractive at all, and he was only too aware that the feeling was mutual. So much the better. Business and lust never made good bedfellows.

Ramona was well aware of his eyes on the red-sheathed blonde, but pretended not to notice. Removing a black Sobranie from her platinum Boucheron cigarette case, she carefully placed it between her vermilion lips and waited for him to light it, which he did immediately with a heavy gold lighter.

'Umberto, I have a little proposition for you,' she said, leaning forward confidentially, allowing him to peek down her white chiffon décolletage – if he felt so inclined.

'What is it, *cara*?' He smiled at her, aware that at the surrounding tables everyone was whispering about her. He was pleased when a couple of papparazzi snapped photographs of them deep in discussion, and he posed casually, without looking at the cameras. There had already been several photographs of the two of them together in the Italian magazines, and she had also been snapped in his shop for the *Oggi* layout. The gorgeous bracelet on her wrist had created so much publicity for his business that he now had to have an assistant working in the shop.

'What is your proposition, *cara?*' he asked after the papparazzi had moved off in search of fresh prey.

'I have a wonderful script that was written for me last year. It's an art film of a kind, but it also has so much scope for action and spectacle,' she said excitedly. Umberto's face was impassive as he sipped at the sticky *crème de menthe*. 'My brother Didier in London has some backers who could put up more than half the money and we're looking for the rest, and also for someone to produce the film. That someone could be you, Umberto,' she said, her voice rising so that an American posse of journalists at the next table stared at them curiously. 'Would you be interested?'

'I could be – in fact I could be very interested indeed, my dear.' Umberto tapped his cigar into the ashtray, his heart beating fast with unexpected excitement. But he did not want Ramona to know how truly he wanted to grasp this key that she was offering him.

'Tell me something of the story – what's it all about?'

'It's called *La Città Perduta – The Lost City,*' she told him excitedly, 'and it's wonderful, Umberto, just wonderful – it'll probably win every award at all the festivals next year – it's tough – gritty – and very modern.'

'And I'm sure there's a great part in it for you,' he smiled, his mind racing.

'Naturally.' She smiled archly, puffing on her cigarette. 'I would play a grandmother. A young one, of course, darling,' she giggled, 'poor, destitute, hungry, who has a teenage daughter with an illegitimate baby all living together in Rome. It's the story of her courageous struggle to build a life for them all after the war.'

'It sounds promising,' he said, chewing on his cigar.

'It certainly does. I'm not a complete fool, Umberto – I know that there are younger, prettier, more bankable actresses than me out there today. They're the ones who are getting the pick of the roles, girls like Grace Kelly, Ava Gardner, Marilyn Monroe. I'm no longer among the top box-office stars any more, I'd be the first to admit it, but I still do love to work.'

He patted her beautifully manicured hand, adorned as it was with the staggering forty-carat diamond which he knew was a present from her husband, the mysterious Prince Kasinov, and told her, 'You're *Numera Una* with me, *carissima*, and if this movie is half as good as you say it is – I would like very much to become involved with it.'

Ramona beamed at him. 'Wonderful, Umberto, wonderful. I have a copy of the script back at the hotel – I'll give it to you to read tonight.'

'One thing,' he asked, 'how much money did your brother say that you're looking for from the other side?'

'Oh, peanuts, darling, only peanuts,' trilled Ramona. 'I will work for virtually nothing, of course, just a percentage of the profits. We will cast an unknown girl for the daughter, and this new young director on *Sunday in Rome* is very talented; I'm sure we could get him for a song. So the above-the-line is minimal. I would say about four hundred thousand dollars –'

'Excuse my ignorance, *Principessa*, but what does "above-the-line" mean?'

Ramona laughed lightly and said, 'That is the salaries for the stars and the director, Umberto. I suppose we would need about one million dollars total financing, certainly not much more.' She looked at him, batting sooty eyelashes. 'A million dollars isn't really too high a price to pay to get into the movie business, is it Umberto, darling?'

'Not if it means working with you, *carissima*,' said Umberto, a sudden burst of adrenaline making his heart pound. The movies! At last. Umberto Scrofo, a film producer – no longer an obscure antique dealer, but someone truly to be reckoned with again. A wheeler-dealer. A force. A *bella figura*. 'What about the film's promotion and distribution – all of those kind of things?' he asked. 'I know absolutely nothing about all that, you know.'

'Oh, Didier will take care of that – I'm sure. He's the expert of the family. He wants to do everything to help me, and I know he'll want to help you too.' She smiled dazzlingly, raising her glass to him, her face looking amazingly young and joyous in the light of the Via Veneto street lamps. 'To *La Città Perduta*,' she breathed, 'and to a long, happy and profitable association with you, Umberto.'

And Umberto Scrofo clinked glasses with the beautiful star and smiled triumphantly.

9

St Tropez

Even though Dominique had many things to do before she left for America she found her mind whirling with thoughts of Gaston Girandot. After she had given the thrilling news that she was going to Hollywood to star in a film to Maman, Papa, Genevieve and all her relations and friends, she felt she must tell him too.

It was a humid evening when she pedalled her bicycle once again to the Place des Lices and saw with a lurch of pleasure the little van with its gaily painted slogan, Gaston's Glaces.

Leaning out of the hatch on to the ledge where he was serving a couple of lanky teenage boys was Gaston Girandot, more handsome than ever, and Dominique was thrilled to see him.

'*Bonsoir*, Gaston.' She smiled innocently as she slid five francs across the shallow wooden counter. 'I would like a double *framboise*, please.'

'Dominique, *quel surprise!*' His white smile and brown-tanned face made him look more than ever like James Dean, screen idol of all the girls and boys in France. 'I haven't seen you for ages – I expected by now you would be flying off to Hollywood, giving Leslie Caron a run for her money.' He winked at her and slid the coin back. 'This is on the house.'

'*Merci*,' smiled Dominique, licking her ice cream with a pert pink tongue as her eyes searched the boy's face for signs that he was still interested. They were certainly still all there, and his eyes burned into hers so steadily that she felt a hot blush start under the bodice of her blouse and spread to her cheeks.

She turned away and started to walk across the little square to where the old men were smoking Gitanes and playing *boules* outside the Café des Lices.

'Where are you going?' He was beside her, slowing his stride to match hers. 'Would you like to go for a ride on my new motorcycle?'

'Oh, Maman would *murder* me if she knew I went on a motorcycle,' squealed Dominique, the forbidden thought of it nevertheless filling her with excited anticipation.

Gaston sensed it. 'Come – come with me,' he said in a suddenly proprietorial manner, and taking her arm, steered her out of the square and down one of the narrow cobbled streets. 'There,' he said, proudly gesturing to a shining green machine parked boldly next to the gendarmerie. 'Isn't she a beauty?'

'Beautiful,' breathed Dominique, hearing her mother's voice instructing her that she must *never* accept rides with any men. Especially on scooters. 'Absolutely *ravissante*.'

'We can go for a little ride now, come –' he said, quickly jumping astride the black leather seat and patting the space behind him invitingly.

'Oh no – I *can't*.' Dominique was in two minds now. He looked even more like James Dean as he sat astride the machine, smoke from the cigarette in his mouth making his eyes half close in a sexy way that she found extremely tempting, his blue jeans tight across his muscled thighs.

'Come on,' he said insistently, 'don't be scared, it won't bite you – neither will I.'

'Oh all right,' said Dominique tentatively, sliding on to the pillion. 'But only for a little while, Gaston. I *must* be home by ten thirty, promise?'

'Right,' said the boy as the motor sprang to life, and she clutched him around his waist with both hands as he guided the motorcycle carefully down the stony streets. 'We'll go to Tango Beach,' he said, 'it's not too far.'

The beach was dark and deserted and only a sliver of pale moon illuminated the black sand.

'Goodness it's so dark,' shivered Dominique who, instead of feeling nervous, was experiencing thrilling new sensations in the pit of her stomach. The ten-minute ride with her arms and head nuzzled into Gaston's cotton shirt had excited her, her mouth was dry with anticipation of an unknown which she felt sure she was going to like.

He turned off the engine and they sat for several minutes listening to the almost-silence. Dominique was sure that he could hear the thumping of her heart mixed with the faint lapping of the waves. A soft breeze ruffled her long black hair and all was very still.

Without words Gaston took her hand and they walked across the sand to the water's edge. Simultaneously they flopped on to the sand, still slightly warm from the afternoon sun, and for a long moment sat staring up into the star-littered sky.

'It's beautiful, St Tropez, isn't it?' breathed Dominique, conscious of Gaston's muscular arm resting lightly on her shoulder.

'Beautiful,' he said softly, 'but not nearly as beautiful as you, *chérie.*' His head turned to her and she saw the pupils of his eyes were so dilated they almost hid his irises. '*Mais tu es belle, Dominique,*' he whispered. '*Trop belle – trop, trop belle.*'

His lips were on her hair now, searching for the softness of her neck.

'No, Gaston, no.' Dominique heard her faint yet unresisting voice as his soft lips gently bit her neck. 'No.'

'Yes,' he said insistently. 'Yes, Dominique, yes yes.' He bent her body back slowly on to the warm sand, and she could feel the cool water of the sea lapping at her feet as his mouth traced a pattern of exquisite pleasure around her lips. His tongue was delicate, probing, sensitive. It seemed to know where she wanted it to go. Her mouth opened to his kisses and she felt the heat of desire starting to burn through the thin cotton of her skirt. She shivered as waves surged over her feet, and she felt his hands move to the buttons of her blouse.

'No – Gaston, not here,' Dominique said, almost starting to giggle with nerves. 'We're right in the middle of the beach, what if someone comes along?'

'No one is going to come here at night, little goose,' he said. 'But I suppose you're right. Let's go up to the restaurant – we'll be safe there – come.' He helped her to her feet and they ran towards the dark outline of the beach bar.

It was pitch dark in the interior and smelled of cooked garlic and herbs, a warm comforting smell. Gaston held Dominique's hand tightly as they fumbled their way through the stacked tables and chairs to the back of the bar. Piled against the wall were dozens of the striped mattresses that were used for sunbathing during the day.

'Here,' said Gaston as he helped her clamber up on to the top one. 'Up here, Dominique – it's nice here.'

'I feel like the princess and the pea in that fairy tale,' giggled Dominique, feeling incredibly grown up, nervous and excited at the same time. 'Lying on top of so many mattresses – ooh, Gaston, I hope we don't fall off.'

'I won't let you,' mumbled the boy, his hands busy with the tiny buttons of her blouse. 'Don't worry, Dominique, my darling, I will protect you. I promise.'

With the scent of Ambre Solaire filling her nostrils and the gentle sound of the sea in the background, Dominique abandoned herself with a sigh of pleasure to the fervent kisses and caresses of the young ice-cream vendor.

From then on they met several times each week, and Gaston taught Dominique many new delights. Their silent private world at the back of the beach hut was a haven of pleasure where Dominique amazed Gaston by her sexual ardour and enthusiasm. She had no prudery or false modesty. Her only fear was that she might become pregnant, but he protected her from that. She was a willing, wanton partner, and as he often told her, 'made for love'.

When the crisp telegram finally arrived from MCCP studios informing Dominique that it was time for her to leave for Hollywood to prepare for the filming of *The Legend of Cortez*, the young lovers wept copiously.

'I won't forget you, I promise,' cried Dominique, clinging to Gaston in the comforting darkness of their love nest. 'I'll write every day – every single day.'

'I will too, my darling,' said the boy, desperately trying not to weep. 'I will not stop loving you, Dominique, and I will be waiting for you when you come back from America.'

A few days later Gaston Girandot stood on the upper level of the white concrete terminal at Nice Airport, watching Dominique and Agathe board the huge Air France four-engine airliner which was taking them to New York. Dominique was dressed formally in a new black and white checked suit with black shiny buttons on the jacket and a tight black belt. The skirt was full and mid-calf length, and she wore a small felt hat on the back of her flowing hair which was tied with black grosgrain ribbon. Around her neck was a white Peter Pan collar trimmed with a small black bow, and in her white-gloved hands she carried a black patent boxy handbag which matched her high-heeled shoes. She looked grown up and sophisticated as she posed prettily at the bottom of the aeroplane's steps for a lone photographer from *Nice Matin*.

In the background Agathe, the chaperone, smiled proudly at her young charge. At last they were off. After months of waiting and delays they were being summoned to the magic land of Hollywood. In little more than twenty-four hours they would be there, and maybe some of Agathe's dreams would finally come true.

London

The applause was deafening. Even by Julian's standards, it was an unusually enthusiastic and tumultuous first-night ovation, and he revelled in it. Handsome and romantic in black cotton tights and a loose white linen shirt, he held hands with the woman beside him, smiling at her with well-concealed fury, bowing yet again to the thunderous applause. The bloody bitch had been upstaging him all evening. Each time he had turned to her on stage, Phoebe had managed to remain two or three steps behind him, thus enabling the audience to see all of her, but only three quarters of him. He was the star, after all – Julian Brooks *was* Hamlet. Ophelia was just a supporting role, and the redheaded witch was trying to muscle in on his territory to beef up her role.

But what was even more galling was that he knew that the Oliviers and Johnny Gielgud were in front, watching what Phoebe was doing. No doubt they were having a good laugh at his expense. 'Ophelia upstaging Hamlet – what *is* the theatre coming to?' they would be saying. 'Julian must be going mad.'

True, he had promised his wife some seven years ago that if he ever played Hamlet, she would be his Ophelia, but she'd been more than two stone lighter in those days. He had finally given in wearily after her vastly expensive trip of revenge with Hermione. To play Ophelia she had lost fifteen pounds, and with a three-foot-long, curly auburn wig and brilliantly cantilevered costumes, she wasn't altogether terrible. Certainly not Vivien Leigh, but not Sophie Tucker either. Julian had naively thought that by letting Phoebe share some of his glory, it might help their marriage. But on the contrary, it only served to show her up as the mediocre actress she undoubtedly was, and make him look a complete fool for having cast her. To top it all their marriage was now practically in name only.

He was reminded of the story about the flamboyant actor-manager Sir Donald Wolfit who, on a tour of the English provinces, stepped towards the footlights after his curtain call, announcing to the audience in stentorian tones, 'Thank you, dear people, for your most kind reception tonight given to our play. Next week we shall be presenting here at the Alhambra Theatre, Shakespeare's *Othello*. I myself shall be playing the stately Moor, and my lady wife shall give her Desdemona.'

A voice from the gallery called out, 'Your wife's an old ratbag.'

There was a very long pause. 'Nevertheless,' continued Sir Donald, 'she shall *still* be playing Desdemona.'

That was him and Phoebe, thought Julian, knotting his dressing gown cord savagely. He was the star and she the ratbag, and an upstaging ratbag to boot.

Even though there were eleven curtain calls, he was still seething in the dressing room.

'Now look here, Phoebe, I've had just about enough of your continual upstaging. Dammit, how many times have I told you that in my "Get thee to a nunnery" speech, you *must* stay downstage. Are you *deaf* or something?'

'Oh, I *know* you did, dear,' fluttered Phoebe, as helpless as a leopard in a jungle. She sneered at him in the fly-specked mirror, rubbing a touch of the powder and paint from her cheeks and removing a smidgin of eye shadow with the corner of a turkish towel. After all, there was no point in wasting perfectly good cold cream to take this lot off, when she would only have to put it all back on again for the party. Besides, she was too lazy. Excited by the first-night fever, she ignored Julian's exasperated tirade as she primped and fussed with her carroty curls in preparation for the tidal wave of backstage visitors. Even now, she could hear them coming down the draughty stone corridors of the Haymarket Theatre. They'll put a stop to Julian's nagging, she thought.

Vivien and Larry, Johnny and Ralphie, Noël and Sir Crispin, and the two Hermiones all burst into the dressing room together in a rush of excited praise. 'Darling, you were *divine* – simply *marvellous*,' gushed one of the Hermiones to Julian, who stood in the middle of the cramped dressing room in his navy blue and crimson Charvet dressing gown, modestly accepting the sincere compliments of his peers, along with a glass of champagne from his dresser.

'Best Hamlet I've seen in *years*, old boy,' said Larry, patting him on the shoulder. 'Really bloody good.' Then he bent down, whispering conspiratorially, 'Better than Alec's last year – much better.'

'Not really, Larry.' Julian smiled broadly, luxuriating in the praise from the supreme actor's actor. 'But thank you very much.'

'Dear boy, you were good; very, very good indeed,' said Noël, a twinkle in his Chinese eyes, an ivory cigarette holder clenched between his teeth. 'I've never seen you better – you must do more of the Bard, dear boy, although I hear Hollywood's crooked little bejewelled finger has been beckoning you – right, dear boy?'

How did he know that? Julian wasn't really surprised. Noël knew everything that went on – not only in the West End, but on Broadway and even in Hollywood. He was a walking cornucopia of fascinating theatrical gossip.

Another call from Julian's Hollywood agent had, in fact, come only yesterday. His agent was insistent that Julian make a film in America. He had missed the boat twice before and it was high time he didn't miss this one. Selznick had wanted him to play Rochester opposite Joan Fontaine in *Jane Eyre* but Didier had dithered for so long that the part had gone to Orson Welles. Three years ago they had wanted him again, this time to play opposite Joan's sister, Olivia de Havilland, in *My Cousin Rachel*, but he had been in the middle of a Restoration epic with Margaret Lockwood, so the role had gone to Richard Burton. Now Hollywood was beckoning again – with a juicy contract and Didier's blessing, lots of lovely dollars and a peach of a part: the title role in *The Legend of Cortez*. It was a difficult decision and Julian felt torn. Although *Hamlet* was only playing for a limited run, Phoebe was pregnant for the second time. He was delighted, but she wasn't happy about it at all – not that she was ever happy about much unless it involved spending money or hobnobbing with high society. It was almost an immaculate conception, as Julian had hardly gone near her at all since *Pygmalion*, but for Phoebe it was a trump card. Rumblings of incipient miscarriages and morning sickness kept him in line. She was hardly two months into her pregnancy, but she was more difficult, tetchy and discontented than ever.

'*Hollywood!* Over my dead body,' she had hissed at him that morning as she lay in bed in a maribou bedjacket, which always made her sneeze, while she cooed and caressed one of their five cats. 'We can't leave the cats, and I *hate* Americans and their perfectly dreadful food – hamburgers and chilli dogs – ugh, it makes me retch to think of it.'

'Phoebe, what bloody difference does it make?' Julian roared, standing before her in his striped pyjama bottoms, his face covered with shaving cream. 'What the blazes – we'll import a bloody cook from England. We'll have fucking bangers and mash, boiled beef and carrots – whatever you want, Phoebe, but for Christ's sake, don't make me give up this big chance, *my* big chance, just because you don't like bloody Yankee food.' Phoebe started to splutter, but he shut her up.

'If we go to Hollywood, I'll do this three-picture deal for Spyros and then we'll come back to London, I promise you. Then we'll buy that fucking house in Sussex, if that's what you want.'

'The one near the Oliviers?' Phoebe asked eagerly.

'The one near the Oliviers,' said Julian resignedly.

'I'll think about it,' Phoebe pouted, pulling the green and pink chintz-covered eiderdown up to her chins. 'I'll let you know after the opening tomorrow. I must rest now. Doctor's orders. Please leave me alone.' She closed her eyes dismissively as Julian Brooks, matinée idol and leading male star of the British screen, stood helplessly in yet another fury of frustration.

Now, surrounded as he was by the *crème de la crème* of the theatrical profession, Julian tried once again to control his anger towards his tiresome wife. Tonight, he was a great success, that was all that mattered at the moment.

'Darling heart, *go* to California, you simply *must*,' said Vivien, her beautiful cat's eyes alight in her perfect face. 'But *do* come to Notley Abbey next weekend before you go.'

'I could think of nothing I'd rather do more,' Julian said with a big smile. That should placate Phoebe. She wouldn't have too much morning sickness down there, he was sure of that. Not with Larry and Viv and Johnny G., and Noël and Binkie Beaumont for company. She'd do her best to be the life and soul of the party, and she could be if she felt like it.

'Hollywood can be *the* most ghastly bore, of course, but the *money*, darling – you can't, you simply *can't* turn it down,' said Sir Crispin Peake, ever the pragmatist. 'Take it and run, my dear. I've just bought an enormous house near Windsor and the most ravishing little Renoir you've ever seen, and both with my last pay cheque. You must come down and stay, if you ever manage to tear yourself away from Notley Abbey!' He winked as he was sucked into the crush of wellwishers.

'The British invasion, darling, that's what they call it,' croaked Hermione One. 'Hollywood simply adores the Brits, dear – they all play cricket at dear Aubrey's every Sunday in white flannels, and eat cucumber sandwiches at every opportunity.'

'It's nothing to be ashamed of – we've *all* done it,' said Vivien, looking over at her husband. 'Even Larry, and he fought against it like a *dervish*, darling – didn't want to go at all, did you, pet?'

'No – but once we went we had a glorious time. The weather is divine, the work conditions excellent, and the natives are really quite amusing - aren't they, darling?' said Sir Laurence, smiling fondly at his wife. 'And the women are terribly pretty.'

'So are the men.' She smiled back at him slyly.

'Go, dear boy, go, you simply simply must,' said Noël. 'Let's face it, England is just a backwater these days, and who can ignore all that lovely green lolly?'

'Certainly not Phoebe,' answered Hermione Two impishly as Phoebe glared at her, and Sir Crispin stifled a snigger. 'She loves a buck, don't you, dearie? Cannot say no to ye olde filthy lucre, never could, even when she was a Windmill cutie.'

'Well, now I think it's time for us all to go to the Ivy,' announced Noël, sensing a sudden chill in the atmosphere. 'Let the revels begin, my children, it's fiesta time. Let us eat, drink and become very, very merry indeed, and toast dear Julian's grand success.'

*

The first-night party in the Edwardian back dining room of the Ivy bubbled with the aristocracy of film and theatre. Conversation was brittle and brilliant. The expensive smell of cigar smoke wafted through the air, mingling with the dozens of scents worn by the glittering women, and Julian modestly accepted congratulations and praise from friend and foe alike.

Everyone was exquisitely dressed. In the theatrical world of the 1950s, actresses were not afraid to look the part of the glamorous stars that many of them were. The rainbow colours of their taffeta, satin and velvet gowns were perfectly complimented by all the elegant men in their black dinner jackets and crisp white shirts.

Television was not taken at all seriously by anyone in the profession. Even actors who appeared in films were looked upon with a certain disdain by their more respected thespian brothers and sisters, which was part of the reason why Julian had decided to play *Hamlet*. He wanted the respect of his peers, which he knew he would never earn by toiling in his romantic potboilers for the screen. But he equally wanted, and Phoebe needed, the large sums of money which he made from his screen career.

Phoebe's outgoing personality was spilling over, as were her enormous breasts, which bounced like two pale sponge cakes, half in and half out of her Norman Hartnell ice-blue dress. She circulated tirelessly, passing on snippets of theatrical gossip and naughty jokes with gusto. She was totally without diplomacy as she told vicious and hurtful stories about everyone. Many disliked her for it, but Julian was so popular that they put up with Phoebe's bitchiness and backbiting for his sake.

As the clock struck midnight the star of the evening suddenly found himself alone at the bar, with only a glass of Dom Perignon for company. He lit a cigar with his gold lighter – a present from Phoebe when he had played Othello at the Old Vic, opposite her far too curvacious Desdemona. Slowly he became aware of a subtle scent and a pair of magnetic eyes staring at him.

He turned to meet the cool gaze of a tall young woman who was leaning elegantly against the bar, staring at him with barely disguised interest. She was beautiful, in a sultry way, but there was an aura about her which spoke of much more than beauty. There was danger in her eyes, a look that signalled trouble for any man who got too close. She looked to be in her mid-twenties, with shoulder-length dark brown hair, and a thick fringe which seemed deliberately to draw attention to electric-blue eyes. They were boldly outlined in kohl and drawn in that doe-eyed slant which Audrey Hepburn had made so fashionable. Her lips, curved, full and sensual, were painted a deep glossy scarlet; she now parted them, placed a cigarette between them and waited with a faint, expectant smile. All the while her eyes never left his.

Like all good actors, Julian always picked up his cue. In an instant he was at her side, gold lighter at the ready.

'*Merci.*' Her voice was low, husky, evocative of endless evenings in smoky clubs and long nights of love. He was instantly captivated. 'You were excellent tonight,' she smiled. 'The best Hamlet I've ever seen. Better than Guinness. Maybe even better than Olivier.'

'Thank you, *Mademoiselle*, you are really too kind. But I'm afraid you have the advantage of knowing who I am, while I don't know you.'

'Inès,' she replied softly. 'Inès Juillard.'

'A beautiful name for a beautiful woman.' Julian couldn't help the cliché. He felt himself blush and noticed the girl's faint smile, but there was warmth there, and a sexual interest he could feel. Usually when he felt mutual attraction this strongly he went after it immediately. Having had many affairs during his marriage, he fully intended to have as many more as he wanted. No matter that Phoebe was finally pregnant, that was not going to stop him, particularly with this gorgeous creature who was oozing sexuality and fascination.

Suddenly he wanted Inès Juillard very much. He wanted to touch and caress her long, slim curves, wanted to feel those elegant hands with their short, unpainted nails rake his back, wanted to strip that severely chic clinging black dress from her body, feel her breasts against his chest. All those thoughts passed rapidly through his mind in the time it took for him to inhale his cigar, and for her to brush the ash from her cigarette.

Inès, of course, read them all instantly. She had been around men long enough to understand them completely, and since she had been intrigued by and attracted to Julian ever since she had seen him in

Pygmalion, she was thankful that he obviously found her desirable. But she needed to be clever here. Very clever indeed. He was devastatingly good-looking, charming, famous, fascinating – and married. Looks Brooks - the most handsome man in the world. Every woman must be after him – some, so they said, had tried to kill themselves for love of him. She must make herself extra special, more than special to him.

'When can I see you?' Julian whispered urgently, as he saw out of the corner of his eye a particularly vicious gossip columnist who was bearing down on him. 'I want to see you soon, Inès – as soon as possible. Please.'

'Grosvenor 1734,' she whispered, wafting away like some beautiful black wraith in a fragrant cloud of scent. 'Call me during the day, any time. *J'attends*, Julian, *j'attends*.'

Julian could hardly wait. He had to see Inès Juillard. He rang the next morning, she gave him her address in Shepherd Market, and he was out of the Connaught Square house and into a black cab before Phoebe had even opened an eye from her hangover slumbers. He knew that she'd have a fit when she saw her notices, he definitely didn't want to be around when she read them. The critics had not been kind to her, and although they praised Julian's Hamlet, they castigated him as producer for casting his wife in such an unsuitable role.

He was perfectly turned out in a camel cashmere belted overcoat and with his caramel-coloured fedora worn at its usual angle, so it was not surprising that the cabbie recogized him.

''Ello, Mr Brooks.' He smiled genially. 'Good reviews, guv. Didja see 'em? Even James Agate liked it.' London cab drivers loved celebrities, often letting them travel for nothing in exchange for an autograph.

Julian smiled his thanks dismissively. He didn't want to talk to the cabbie. He only wanted to think about Inès. For the first time in years his interest in someone else overshadowed his interest in his reviews. His anticipation was electric. He felt like a small boy on Christmas Eve. He had not been able to put her out of his mind since last night. The cabbie took the hint, allowing Julian to be alone with his thoughts until they arrived at Shepherd Market.

Inès opened the door wearing a black poloneck sweater and a full black and white checked skirt which was cinched with a wide patent leather belt into her tiny waist. She was ravishing, yet with a sweet vulnerability that he found incredibly refreshing. Her skin was devoid of any makeup, but her face glowed serenely, her complexion fresh and clear.

Julian noticed that on the walls of her flat hung exquisitely framed neoclassical drawings by Delacroix, Ingres and David. He thought he also recognized some early drawings by Boucher and Fragonard. The furniture was good, some of it very good, and there were spring flowers everywhere in blue and white pots. This was obviously a woman of considerable taste and style as well as great beauty.

Inès was playing him as gently and carefully as a fisherman landing a prize salmon on a slender trout rod. Finally he was in her flat. Julian Looks Brooks. The Idol of the Odeons in person sitting on her sofa, sipping espresso from one of her Sèvres cups, his eyes looking at her with steady desire.

She gave him no clue to her profession, gave him none of herself either – not that day, nor the next, nor even the following week. For more than a month she refused to even let him kiss her. It wasn't until he'd convinced her that he was mad with love for her that she finally allowed him to possess her. And, of course, she made him think it had all been his idea, that he had talked her into it.

He had suggested that after his Saturday performance they drive to a tiny cottage in the country. Phoebe had bought it in an uncharacteristic flash of country life fever but had visited it only once, preferring the streets of St James's and Piccadilly to the muddy lanes of Gloucestershire.

Once there Inès concocted a gourmet feast on the old-fashioned cooker, produced a bottle of distinctive claret, and cuddled up to Julian after dinner in front of the roaring log fire.

She knew the time was ripe for him to seduce her, and she made him try extremely hard until she succumbed to his ardent kisses. But once they were ensconced in the downy soft feather bed, Inès took the initiative, amazing Julian by her athletic ardour.

They made love all night long and it exceeded his every expectation. It was an experience beyond his wildest fantasies.

Although Julian had had dozens of affairs, they had been mostly with English or American women, usually actresses, none of whom could exactly have been called passion flowers. They had moaned, groaned, writhed and performed with all the appropriate wiggles, thrusts and the 'Oh my *God*, darling, it's so good', but he had always felt that there was something important missing in his lovemaking with all of them. They gave their bodies enthusiastically enough, but he knew that their hearts were seldom truly in it.

With Inès it was totally different. The white heat of her passion seemed almost to scorch him and he never wanted to stop. He knew it was real, he could feel it was not a performance, that it was just for him. Her skin drove him wild. It was the colour of crushed pearls, and smelled like jasmine. When she wrapped her amazingly long slim legs around him, whispering eroticisms in that husky French voice of hers, he would become like a man possessed. He'd never been with a woman like her before. Few had specialized in the sexual arts and crafts which Inès had been perfecting since her early teens. She was a walking mantrap, desire and lust incarnate. A wonderful wanton with such incredible sexual skills that even the sophisticated and worldly Julian was dazzled by them. That long weekend in the cottage as he tried to doze after yet another blissful session of lovemaking, she would take his sleeping cock in her mouth as gently and delicately as a snake would swallow a small mouse. She was insatiable and tireless, her tongue an instrument of pure pleasure, a lethal weapon, as were her mouth and lips which she used to take him to the highest stratosphere of pleasure, from where he never wanted to return.

More than anything, Julian felt that her passion truly matched his. Her lust and physical need for his body were as strong as his for her own. After their affair started it was nothing for them to spend the entire morning together, and then the whole afternoon in her soft bed, until it was time for him to go to the theatre. They made love at least three times a day and at nearly thirty-seven, Julian became possessed with the sexual energy of a seventeen-year-old. He sometimes had odd pangs of fear that expending so much of his precious essence might somehow interfere with his performance on the stage, but in fact it seemed to do just the opposite. His Hamlet soared to new heights each night, and audiences cheered and applauded him until the rafters of the Haymarket Theatre seemed to shake. He often told her that, like Cleopatra, she never made his appetites for her cloy, but instead made hungry where most she satisfied.

Of course Phoebe soon suspected that another affair had begun. She had miscarried their baby again and, although secretly relieved, was making an enormous show of her misery. When Julian made a halfhearted attempt to make love to her one night, simply because he thought he should, Phoebe rejected him huffily.

'Don't point that tired old thing *near* me,' she hissed. 'You must wait at least three months. The doctor says I mustn't have sex until then, so just go and jerk off in the bathroom, like a good boy, or whatever else you've been doing.' She bit viciously into another chocolate biscuit.

His wife's attitude suited Julian perfectly. He was totally consumed by thoughts of Inès, his angel, his gorgeous French beauty, his *grande passion*. He was her slave, completely besotted, and not only sexually. He had never felt such pure joy in a relationship with a woman, and soon realized that he could no longer imagine his life without her.

Inès had still given Julian no hint of her true profession. At twenty-nine she knew that her years of successful and financially rewarding whoring were coming to an end. Julian was handsome, rich, successful, and a wonderful lover. She knew that he was the man for her, but she also knew that he lived by the usual convenient double standard, like so many Englishmen. He had been a philanderer and womanizer most of his adult life, which she was able to accept. However, she soon found out that her own past life needed to be practically perfect to please his curiously exacting moral values – he would never be able to accept the fact that she had been a whore. That was the one thing she would never be able to tell him. However much in love he was, she was sure that should he find out, their relationship would be destroyed.

Inès was in a difficult position. The chances of Julian's discovering the truth about her past were fairly slim, since most of her clients would be terrified of exposure themselves. She had stopped seeing all of them as soon as the romance with Julian began, telling them she was going away for a long time. She had concocted a thin web of lies about her life which Julian unquestioningly believed, and she prayed that he would never discover the truth.

She had told him that her parents had been killed in a car crash in Paris when she was very young. She had been brought up by a maiden aunt in Yorkshire who had died when Inès was twenty, leaving her this flat, some pretty and valuable bits and pieces, and enough money to live well on. He had believed her. In spite of his own promiscuity, Julian was extremely old-fashioned. He couldn't even think of Inès with another man. She had admitted to having had three boyfriends, but had refused to go into details about any relationships, saying that he just couldn't be jealous of past loves.

Having completely sexually and emotionally enslaved him, and tangled him up in her beauty's web, prying him away from his wife was her next problem. And it was a major problem. Phoebe would not let Julian go without a fight. Even though she was no longer in love with him and the marriage was little more than a sham, she loved her life as Mrs Julian Brooks and all that went with it. Phoebe was a tough, single-minded woman, both shrewd and clever. But perhaps not quite as shrewd and clever as her rival.

Inès had hinted at marriage but Julian had not been enthusiastic – why should he? Phoebe always turned a blind eye to his affairs, realizing that they would all eventually come to an end and he would return to the marital fold.

And she was right, of course. Inès knew that there was a certain time between a man and a woman when the desire for each other was so strong that marriage was inevitable. If it didn't happen at that time, then it never would.

Julian seemed to be completely hooked now, and Inès knew the time was propitious to give him her ultimatum.

'Marriage, Julian darling,' she said calmly as they sat by candlelight at her lace-draped dining table eating *coq au vin* from Spode plates. 'We must get married.'

'Darling girl – my angel, it's impossible, I've told you,' Julian demurred. 'Phoebe will never let me go, we both know that. Angel, can't we just stay the way we are? I'm so happy like this, Inès.'

'No, Julian,' said Inès firmly, aware that she was treading the trickiest of ground, but shrewdly knowing she had to do it. 'In that case I can't continue seeing you.'

'Of course you can, my angel,' said Julian confidently. 'We love each other, Inès, how could we bear to be apart from each other?'

At that moment Inès knew this was going to be much tougher than she had expected. She worshipped Julian, wanted desperately to marry him, to be with him for ever. There was only one way to get him now – she had to play a brilliant game, and for high stakes. Julian was a rare prize.

The following day Inès withdrew from Julian's life completely. She packed a small suitcase and disappeared for a week without telling him. Then she sent a brief note to the theatre telling him she was in the country and only giving him her telephone number.

Instantly he was on the telephone, begging to see her.

'No, Julian, no. I cannot see you again,' Inès said firmly, her heart pounding with longing for him. 'I love you too much to go on like this without marriage. We must forget each other, *chéri*.'

'No!' roared Julian, beside himself at the thought of losing her. 'You can't do this, Inès, you simply can't. What's your address? I'll come and see you, angel.'

'No,' said Inès softly. 'No, Julian. It's marriage or it's over between us. We have been together now for seven months. If we don't marry I must get on with my life. If it has to be without you – so be it.'

She hung up, leaving Julian staring blankly at the telephone. He knew she was right, of course, his marriage with Phoebe was a farce. Divorce. He would divorce Phoebe and marry Inès. That was the inevitable way it must be.

It had been a tough ultimatum for Inès. Please God, let it work, she prayed. She wanted to be with Julian for ever.

When Julian finally confessed his passionate affair to Phoebe, and his desire for a divorce so that he could marry Inès, Phoebe went berserk. Ranting and raving, she threw all her valuable painstakingly collected Chelsea and Bow porcelain at her husband, in a furious barrage that lasted half an hour. She threatened Julian with the most dire consequences if he left her.

'I'll create a scandal that will *ruin* you. That Candida *bitch* trying to commit suicide will be nothing compared to this,' she screamed, her face ugly and puffy, her bloodshot eyes swollen with tears. 'You'll *never* be Sir Julian Brooks now. Not with a divorce behind you.'

'My dear girl,' Julian said, trying to remain calm as he brushed bits of broken china off his sleeve, 'I don't give a damn what you do. And I don't give a damn about becoming a knight. I'm an actor and that's all I bloody well care about.'

'You're not an *actor*,' Phoebe spat out contemptuously. 'You're just a joke. When you first came on the screen as Charles II with that dead poodle on your head, everyone screamed with laughter. Everyone says you can't bloody act to save your bloody life.'

'Thank you, Phoebe,' Julian said quietly, 'for those few kind words. Your undying loyalty is most touching.'

'That French *whore* – I suppose *she's* loyal.'

'Yes,' he sighed. 'She is.'

'Does she know you're a pansy?'

Julian paled. Since his passing attachment to Wilson at school, he'd gone out of his way never to do, say or appear as anything other than the most masculine of men. But he had once in the early days of their marriage confessed to Phoebe his fondness for the boy. Like the elephant, she never forgot.

'And what's that supposed to mean?' he asked coldly.

'Nothing.' She shrugged, realizing her barb had found its mark. 'Nothing at all, Julian.'

Phoebe had never suspected it herself, but maybe this man with whom she'd lived for nearly eleven years did have some homosexual tendencies. She always thought that Julian flirted with Sir Crispin Peake when they laughed and teased each other. Unfortunately, she had no proof. Pity – that would have been the perfect stick with which to beat him. He couldn't have put up with the stigma of being thought of as queer.

Julian's seemingly genuine love for this other woman enraged Phoebe. Whatever was wrong with their marriage, it was no worse than that of many other theatrical couples. Phoebe had always assumed that like other couples they knew, she and Julian would last for ever, conveniently if not romantically. Now he'd turned her whole world upside down all for the sake of love. *Love!* What a joke, she thought viciously. There was no such thing.

Julian tried to pacify Phoebe with offers of lump sums of money. He offered her the house, the furniture, the paintings, all of the possessions which they had carefully collected during their years together. He would give her everything in exchange for his freedom to marry Inès. But Phoebe refused.

It was Inès who at last found the answer. She came to the conclusion that Phoebe would give Julian his freedom only in exchange for a cut of his future earnings – for life. She suggested he offer Phoebe ten per cent. After mulling it over for twenty-four hours, Julian confronted his wife with the more than generous proposition.

'Twenty per cent,' Phoebe fired back.

'Fifteen,' said Julian wearily.

'Oh all right, you mean son of a bitch,' sniffed Phoebe. 'Fifteen it is, then – for life dear, don't forget. Till death us do part, *lovey*.'

'Done,' said Julian, feeling as if some intolerable weight had been lifted from his shoulders. He was free at last. Free of Phoebe. Free to be with Inès for ever and free to fly to Hollywood.

I I

Rome

Umberto Scrofo strutted on to the sound stage at Cincitta Studios, his cigar jutting from fleshy lips, his step self-assured. He was overseeing the final days of shooting of his film *La Città Perduta*. The word was out on the streets of Rome, on the Via Veneto, on the beaches of Ostia and Fregene where the film people gathered, even in the cutting rooms of the rival Scalera Studios, that Umberto Scrofo, this newcomer to their ranks, had a hit on his hands – and it was all his own work. Well, not quite all his own – after all, the script had been written by Irving Frankovitch, and Didier Armande had helped raise most of the money, but it was Umberto's name on the film, and everyone knew it.

He smiled with smug satisfaction as he stood watching carefully from outside the enchanted circle of arc lights, inside which his actors were performing. He had a proprietorial feeling towards his actors. It was as if they belonged exclusively to him. Not that they did, they had all in fact cost a fortune. Even Ramona had eventually demanded a salary, albeit small. It hadn't been easy. Whoever told him that to break into the Italian film business was a breeze was a fool. He'd had to fight hard to get this script off the ground. Ponti, De Sica, Fellini and Visconti seemed to have rented all the studio space and hired every decent technician and piece of film equipment in Italy. He'd fought the American film companies as well. They had come to Italy in droves after the war, with fading stars of the 1930s and 1940s, ploughing millions of dollars into crap, pure crap, and getting a guaranteed release, just because some faded Hollywood has-been's name was above the title and it was an American picture. Umberto had watched the Italian film industry thrive since the war, and with it the fortunes of the film makers, and he wanted to thrive too. Oh, how he longed to succeed, how he yearned for Hollywood to beckon to him, and one day soon it would, of that he was certain.

12

Los Angeles

Dominique loved Hollywood and Hollywood loved Dominique. Each morning on her way to the studios, she gazed with childlike excitement through the windows of her chauffeur-driven limousine, wondering what joys the day would bring. She adored California. She thought that hot dogs, hamburgers, drive-in movies, Hula-Hoops, the Santa Monica beaches and the California sun, which always seemed to be shining, were the best things ever. She especially like the camaraderie with the other actors and dancers at the rehearsal studio. She laughed at their quick repartee even though she didn't quite understand it, as she studied hard, learning English, and the sensual dance she would perform in *The Legend of Cortez*. She loved the exciting bustle of MCCP's commissary, watching the comings and goings of the stars, but best of all she liked television. Her favourites were *The Jackie Gleason Show*, *Cavalcade of Stars* and *The Milton Berle Show*. There had been no television in St Tropez, no hot dogs, no film studio commissary, no excitement at all – except for Gaston. Now she never wanted to go back there; California life was nothing less than terrific. She belonged here.

Gaston had written her several impassioned letters and she had sent both him and her family pages and pages of exciting news, but as each day passed, St Tropez, her family and Gaston Girandot seemed further and further away. Soon she had almost forgotten what he looked like.

Only the memory of those nights on Tango Beach brought his image back to her. She imagined them lying together on the striped beach mattresses with the smell of Ambre Solaire in her nostrils, remembered how thrilling it had been. But it was all work work work now, no time for romance – which was just fine with Dominique.

The studio wanted to make her into a star and she was more than willing to help.

The only fly in her ointment was her chaperone. With her eerie, bleached-looking skin, silver hair, those burning black, sad eyes in her haunted face, Agathe made most people uncomfortable. There was so much suffering in her face, such sorrow in her eyes, no joy in her life. Her clothes were old-fashioned, dark, dowdy – and far too heavy for California. Her manner was quiet and almost lethargic. What Dominique and others didn't realize was how thrilled Agathe was to be in Los Angeles; she was simply incapable of showing it.

Dominique, on the other hand, was bursting with vitality. In Levis and plaid shirt, with her long hair in a ponytail, she had become hooked on the American way of life, their fashions and customs. She was almost beside herself with anticipation on this steamy November afternoon as they headed towards the studio for her first costume fitting.

'Oh, Agathe, I'm *so* excited I can hardly breathe! My first fitting – what do you think it'll be like?'

Agathe made no reply as the car pulled into the studio lot. She was, as always, mesmerized by the extras walking about. Today they were dressed in *fin-de-siècle* winter costumes, incongruous in the heat and humidity.

They drove down several winding streets, each of which had a completely different character, towards the wardrobe department. Here was a New York nineteenth-century tenement which connected to an exact facsimile of a part of London's Eaton Square, complete with perfect replicas of Regency houses, plane trees and laburnum shrubs. Here a cobblestoned French medieval village, the narrow houses with strings of washing hanging between them looking so authentic that both women suddenly felt a pang of homesickness for St Tropez. This led to the wardrobe department, which was simply an unpretentious clapboard building with brown paint peeling from its drab exterior.

While Dominique was being fitted, Agathe explored the department, awed by the multitude of costumes housed there on endless racks, ranging from Roman togas to thousand-dollar beaded evening gowns. After the fitting Agathe suggested an uplifting visit to the Los Angeles Museum of Art, but Dominique had other plans. One of the dancers had told her about a new night club on Sunset Boulevard where all the young actors and dancers hung out. It was the ultimate in cool, she'd been reliably informed, and she was dying to go there to jive the night away.

'I'm exhausted.' She smiled at Agathe, feigning a yawn. 'I want to sleep for fifteen hours. Drop me at the hotel, then you take the car on to the museum. But I must sleep, Agathe, *ça va?*'

'All right,' muttered Agathe, thinking how sophisticated Dominique had become after only a few weeks in Hollywood. The typically French schoolgirl seemed to have blossomed overnight into a genuine American teenager, complete with a mouthful of chewing gum, and all the right slang. Why was the girl so at ease while Agathe herself felt like an awkward fish out of water?

'Now don't you worry, Agathe,' Dominique said as the car pulled up outside the Château Marmont. 'I'm going straight to sleep with a glass of hot milk, and I'll see you in the morning bright and early.' Blowing a kiss to Agathe she ran lightly up the steps of the hotel, giggling to herself. Poor old Agathe, it wasn't too difficult to pull the wool over *her* eyes.

Agathe stared unseeingly ahead of her as the driver edged into the heavy Sunset Boulevard traffic. She felt a terrible envy of her charge boiling up inside her, an envy which spread like some fast-acting drug through her veins, and she hated herself for it. Maybe it was because Dominique was so young – almost the same age as Agathe had been when she was banished to that cellar; or maybe it was because Dominique had her whole life before her, a joyful, exciting life filled with promise. At thirty-one Agathe felt that her own life was as good as over except for one thing. The prospect of meeting the star of *The Legend of Cortez*, Julian Brooks. When she had heard that he was to play the lead, Agathe had almost swooned. The prospect of finally seeing her idol in the flesh was so overwhelming that she had to lie down to stop the terrible dizziness. Now she waited each day, hungry with anticipation until the moment when she would finally meet the one man in the world that she knew was her destiny.

*

Dominique dressed carefully in the height of hip teenage fashion: a black sleeveless sweater, pencil-tight blue jeans, a wide black patent belt clinching her waist into an impossibly small eighteen inches, and flat ballet pumps. She outlined her eyes with a heavy black pencil and carefully arranged her bed with pillows and towels to appear as if she were sleeping in it if Agathe came snooping around. She crept down the back stairs to walk the eight blocks to the Rock 'n' Roll Club.

Although it was only nine o'clock, the small, smoky dive was already crammed with people, all young, all out for a good time.

As she waited for her friends to arrive Dominique stood at the bar sipping Coke, and surveying the dancers bopping and jiving beneath the flashing coloured lights. A good-looking black boy whose muscles bulged out of his short-sleeved yellow shirt, and glistened under the prisms of light, swaggered up to her.

'Wanna dance?' he asked in a bored cool voice, extending a calloused brown hand without even looking at her. Dominique was thrilled. She'd never danced with a black boy before; indeed, until only recently she'd hardly ever danced anywhere but at dancing school. This kind of dancing – close, grinding, primitive – was all so new to her.

'Sure, love to,' she drawled, trying to sound cool and bored herself.

'How old are you, girl?' the boy asked as he threw her out on to the floor to the rhythm, catching her expertly and twirling her back to him.

'Sixteen,' Dominique answered, feeling excited. This boy smelled different from other boys. There was an aroma of musk and sweat about him. He smelled of the West Indies – as she imagined them to be.

'What's your name?' she asked.

'Cab. Yours?'

'Dominique.'

'Hi there, Dominique, I guess you're French, huh? And sixteen, huh?' He winked at her as he pulled her back to him. Then he started to hold her close and she suddenly felt something large and hard against her thigh. 'That's old enough then, ain't it?' he breathed, his lips close to her ear.

'For what?' Dominique asked, almost stumbling to the unaccustomed new slow beat.

'For a smoke, hon. Ya done it, ain't ya?'

'Oh sure,' drawled Dominique. 'I've done it loads of times.'

Dominique sensed danger, but was stimulated by it. The lights were flashing. The Dirty Dozen was playing a hot beat with pounding expertise, and the crowd seethed with sensuality and youth. The black boy – well, brown really – was deliciously different. Agathe would *kill* her if she knew what she was doing, and so would her mother.

'How old are you?' she yelled above the din.

'Twenty,' he said, flashing snow-white teeth. 'An' I've seen it all, hon. I want to show some of it to you, too – c'mon.' The band finished, and as the teenage audience whistled and clapped enthusiastically, Cab grabbed Dominique's hand and led her through the surging throng out through the kitchen to the back door.

In a narrow alley, Dominique leaned breathlessly against a brick wall, watching Cab remove a few things from his pocket. Tobacco, cigarette papers, matches. It was so dark that she couldn't really see what he was doing but when he lit up, inhaling deeply, she could smell a sweetish, pungent odour which make her think of an exotic jungle.

'Take a drag on this, kid – an' let the good times roll!'

He drew deeply again on the cigarette, and Dominique watched, fascinated by his glittering dark eyes with their thick black eyelashes, and by his fleshy pale mauve lips.

She was tingling with anticipation and her high was already halfway there before she even took her first puff of marijuana.

'*Ooh la la.*' She coughed as acrid smoke hit her lungs. 'What *is* this?'

'Jamaica Joy, babe,' Cab said, taking the joint from her fingers and passing her a flask which he'd taken from his back pocket. 'It's the best – it's crazy, man – real cool stuff. Now take a swig of this an' you'll feel better than you ever felt in ya whole life, girl.'

Dominique tipped the flask to her lips, almost gagging at the harsh taste.

'Wow, what's that?' she gasped.

'Gin of course, kid. Good old mother's ruin.' He looked at her with amusement. 'It won't hurt ya. You wanna feel real good, doncha, kid? Cool, crazy and real real good?'

'Mmm. You bet.' Dominique nodded. Suddenly she certainly was feeling good. She was feeling excellent. She was experiencing a great rush of love for the whole beautiful world, for California, and especially for this exotic dusky animal who stood before her puffing on his magic weed and looking at her with glittering black eyes full of some secret amusement.

He passed her the reefer again and she drew it down deeply into her lungs, feeling the drug explode in her head like a catherine wheel. It burned her throat with its bitter aftertaste, but it felt wonderful, delicious. Her head was as light as a puffball; it seemed to be stuffed with feathers, balloons, and those little globes of gossamer lightness which grow in summer meadows, carried by breezes to other pastures. It was as if her head were one of those puffballs, and if Cab's face came a millimetre nearer to her, his lips would blow it away, breaking her cottonwool skull into a million specks of dust. But she wasn't in a meadow. She was in the dank back alley of a club on Sunset Boulevard in Hollywood, surrounded by the putrid stench of dustbins and the raucous sounds of rock 'n' roll.

As if from a great distance, she saw Cab's enormous lips approaching her. Closer and closer they came, unattached to anything, like some figment of Alice's imagination in her Wonderland. He had no face, just those great mauve lips, coming towards her closer, closer – so close that her eyes crossed, trying to keep them in focus. The lips were moving, saying something, but she couldn't hear what it was.

They looked terribly funny, those enormous lips, suspended in space, in time, moving rapidly, yet with no sound coming from them.

Then suddenly, the lips were on hers, but they were not alone. A wet snakelike tongue darted from between them, entering her mouth like a reptile slithering into its lair. The slimy, slippery serpent filled her mouth with its mushy wetness as the enormous lips tried to suck her mouth into its cavern.

'No, no, *stop* – I can't breathe!' Dominique spluttered, the tongue still probing her mouth and the great lips continuing to scour her face like a wet mop over a kitchen floor.

'*Don't!*' She pushed him away hard, looking at him with distaste.

'What were you *doing?*' she gasped. 'That was horrible!' Despite her new and unaccustomed sense of power over men, Dominique was not experienced in repelling unwanted suitors. When Gaston had kissed her it was delicate, tender, his tongue exploring her mouth with gentle ardour. This boy was rough, pushy, crude. She hated what he was doing.

The lips opened, revealing teeth as big as tombstones. 'That's good, kid, that's really, really good.' The lips covered the teeth now, and the big black head bent closer to hers as two huge hands grabbed her shoulders.

'You're messin' around with things ya don't know nothin' about, little girl.' Her head lolled from side to side as he shook her shoulders roughly. 'I give ya a joint and whadda I get? Eh? Horrible – ya say – *I'm* horrible. That's great, isn't it, eh? I don't give 'em for nothin', ya know. Whadda I get then, what's *my* reward for givin' ya a good time? C'mon, tell me – what?' He started shaking her so hard that tears came to her eyes.

He tugged her head back by her hair, clapping a sweating palm over her mouth. 'Now you better keep away from me in future, girl,' he hissed in her ear. 'I know your kind of motherfucker. Pretend you've got the jungle fever, then ya chicken out.' He slammed her against the brick wall until she hardly had any breath left in her body. 'I'll have the word out on you, so don't be hangin' 'round here no more if ya know what's good for ya.' With a final vicious shove at her, he strutted splayfooted back to the club, muttering 'Cock-teaser' under his breath, loud blasts from the rock band escorting him down the alley.

A few minutes later, Dominique limped her way down Sunset Boulevard towards the hotel. The whole experience had been far from pleasant, but she had felt stimulated by the danger and the knowledge that the boy desired her. He had been vile, crude and offensive, but the delicious sensation she had felt when she smoked the reefer still lingered. She knew that Cab's warning or not, she would go back to the club again. But the next time she'd go with friends.

When she reached Agathe's room she heard the sounds of television so she crept silently into her own room to ruminate on this latest episode in her California adventure.

Agathe stared intently at the television screen. Wearing a highwayman's mask, a loden-green frock coat adorned with silver buttons and a black velvet tricorn hat pulled low over his forehead, astride a rearing black stallion with the muzzle of his flintlock pistol pointed at the beautiful, terrified face of Margaret Lockwood, was Julian Brooks. Agathe was riveted. She was watching one of a series of romatic swashbuckling films which Julian had made in England during the late forties, but it still held up. Agathe thought it was marvellous. How handsome he was, how dashing. She could barely breathe as Julian leaped down from his stallion, flung open the door of the carriage and pressed his lips to those of the frightened heroine.

'*Quelle merveille,*' breathed Agathe, her excitement mounting as their kisses intensified, and Miss Lockwood was swept with a passion which Agathe shared. How wonderful to have the lips of that man who looked like a Greek deity pressed against hers. She could almost feel the electricity between them, as her hand went to her mouth and her own lips opened to the barren dryness of her thumb. 'Julian,' she moaned softly, closing her eyes to everything but his television voice. 'Oh, Julian. *Je t'aime. Que je t'aime, mon amour.*'

13

In a huge mansion hidden high in the canyons of the Hollywood hills, the legendary Ramona Armande was preparing for an evening out. A battalion of maids, hairdressers and *visagistes* hovered in reverential silence around the ivory and silver Ruhlmann dressing table at which the great star now sat, fastening diamond and emerald pendant earrings to her plump earlobes.

She was a tiny, raven-haired woman who'd been a legend and a star for so long now that most of her early life was shrouded in mystery. Such was her exquisitely romantic past, which she'd read about in countless fan magazine interviews for some thirty years, that Ramona now believed each romantic word. The fact that she and Didier and their parents, Rachel and Eli Levinsky, had fled Hungary during the First World War, was not to be found in any of her biographies. The Levinsky family had been fortunate to find some relations in the East End of London, and Eli had continued as a fishmonger while she and Didier had been sent to the local school to learn English and the British way of life. Names were changed and both children's lives went on to great success.

Though small in stature, Ramona had a strong character. Woe betide the hapless menial who might misunderstand his mistress's commands at any time, but especially during her elaborate three-hour *grande levée*. Misunderstanding an order from the Princess would cause the unfortunate wretch to receive a withering look from her fabled amber eyes, fringed in lashes long and thick as spider legs, and a few well-chosen phrases from her were more than enough to terrify even the most insensitive.

In her vast bedchamber the lamps were kept dimmed to their lowest wattage to flatter her pale, fine skin which was always covered with a special foundation created especially for her by Mr Max Factor himself. It helped to camouflage the tiny wrinkles which, in spite of all the creams and potions which she applied every night, were multiplying over her precious face. What did it matter that her milky skin wasn't as perfect as it had been in the days of silent movies? She was still a star and one who had every intention of remaining in the firmament, and she expected to be treated like one. Ramona was a true child of Hollywood, who knew the tricky ropes as well as Mr Zanuck, Mr Warner and Mr Cohn. Tonight she was going to beat them at their own game.

'Bring me my diamonds, Maria,' she commanded in the distinctive voice which had been her salvation when talkies had arrived. When many of her compatriots were being laughed off the screen because of their unsuitable voices, Ramona's dulcet tones had, thanks largely to her English education, appealed to the public and her career had continued to flourish.

She thought about some of her contemporaries who had failed, as she studied her reflection in the three-way mirror. Poor old Jack Gilbert. Audiences had shrieked with laughter when they heard his voice. The great lover who had bedded so many stars of the silent screen and broken so many famous hearts, abandoning their beautiful owners to sob for him into their lace pillowcases, thought only of Greta Garbo, his one great passion. Garbo, Ramona thought, gritting her teeth – she'd certainly managed to pass the talkies test with flying colours. If it were possible the public's love affair with her had grown even stronger when they all heard her first husky utterance: 'Gimme a viskey, ginger ale on the side, and don't be stingy, baby.' Audiences all over America had screamed with excitement, and Garbo had become the greatest star of all time.

Ramona frowned as she thought of her former arch rival. Annoyingly, she was still continually in the American public's eye, as she slithered from yet another transcontinental train or transatlantic liner sheathed in a long coat, floppy felt hat, and always wearing those stupid sunglasses, stage-whispering, 'I vant to be alone'.

Ramona knew very well that this catchphrase was just another publicity ploy. She knew that Garbo really secretly loved the interest which her self-conscious mystery provoked. Garbo thrived on it. The more she 'vanted to be alone', the less, of course, she was allowed to be. It was irritating and infuriating to Ramona, but Garbo was still continually in the newspapers and magazines, despite not having made a single appearance on celluloid for more than ten years.

Plucking a Lalique scent bottle from the massed ranks of objects cluttering her dressing table, Ramona sprayed herself with an expensive cloud of Shalimar, while her maid attached a diamond and tortoiseshell comb to her sleek black chignon. Ramona clasped the magnificent emerald, natural pearl and European-cut diamond necklace around her withering throat and surveyed herself critically. 'Perfect,' she breathed to herself, 'perfect.' She was ready at last, as ravishing as she could possibly make herself.

Tonight was another Hollywood party, this time to welcome the distinguished English actor Julian Brooks into the enchanted circle of Beverly Hills. He would be with Inès Juillard, the woman for whom he had left his wife, the woman all Hollywood was eager to meet. Their romance had been conducted discreetly because of his impending divorce, and few, if any, photographs had as yet appeared of the loving couple. The party was to be at the house of Spyros Makopolis, president of MCCP and one of the most important men in town. Ramona was determined to look more beautiful than ever before, fresh from her recent success in her new Italian movie. Tonight she would show the elite of Beverly Hills that Ramona Armande was still a star of the greatest magnitude – still someone very much to be reckoned with.

In the aubusson-carpeted drawing room of her mansion, Ramona's escort for the evening and the producer of her new but as yet unreleased film, Umberto Scrofo, sat admiring her collection of Impressionists and sipping champagne while he waited patiently for her to finish dressing. This was his first trip to Hollywood and he was in a fever of anticipation about tonight's A-list party.

He couldn't wait to belong and to take charge once more.

'Spyros' house is lit up like a bloody Christmas tree!' Julian Brooks observed. It was true. Every window blazed with light, and the white, Palladian-style villa, set in manicured lawns among tall cypress trees, had been strung with thousands of coloured fairy lights, reflecting something which few Californians ever saw.

'Snow! *Mon Dieu!*' Inès exclaimed, leaning closer to the limousine window. 'For goodness' sake look, Julian – it's snow! How could we have snow here? It's been over seventy degrees today.'

Julian looked down at the thick sparkling expanse of virgin snow which carpeted either side of the long, winding driveway, and grinned at Inès who was staring at a gargantuan jade-green Christmas tree, some thirty feet high, which was completely covered with sparkling baubles of every imaginable colour.

The door to their limousine was flung open by a parking valet who was dressed, much to his own embarrassment, as one of Santa's elves. Most of these boys were out-of-work actors, so they managed to conceal their embarrassment fairly convincingly as they politely helped the glamorous guests from their cars with 'Good evening, ma'am, sir, and a very merry Christmas to you.'

Inès stifled a giggle at the sight of Spyros' impeccable English butler, Sanderson, now dressed in the unlikely costume of Santa Claus. His solemn face hardly matched the jolly seasonal red outfit and white beard. He had in fact refused point blank to wear the costume, even threatening to resign, but Mr Makopolis had finally persuaded him to don it in the way that he persuaded everyone to do anything: with money.

'This could never happen in England or France, could it, darling?' Julian whispered, squeezing Inès' hand as they exchanged amused glances. Inès was amazed. Ten years of associating with aristocrats and people of culture and breeding in London had given her a definite knowledge of what is done and what is not done. So far, what she had seen of the overdecorated Makopolis mansion had been frightful. A butler dressed as Père Noel? *Quelle horreur!*

'But, *chéri*.' Inès was still puzzled. 'Today I was sunbathing by the pool. How can it snow here at night?'

'Fake, my darling, fake,' Julian laughed. 'I'm quite sure that old Spyros had the prop department whip up this little concoction.'

'But how?' A sophisticated woman of the world as far as most things were concerned, Inès found the ways of Lotus Land a total mystery. 'You cannot make snow, Julian. How can you?'

'Crystals and cottonwool,' he explained. 'Must have cost the studio prop department a bloody fortune. Good old Spyros, he's an amazing old coot.'

'But why would he want to do that when it is so pretty here without it?'

'One-upmanship, my darling,' Julian said. 'Next year everyone in Hollywood will have their driveways and lawns covered with *faux neige* – and dear old Mr and Mrs Makopolis will be crowing to themselves because they were the first on the block to think of it.'

Julian took a slim flute of champagne from a footman, this one ludicrously dressed as Rudolph the Red-Nosed Reindeer, and winked at Inès. Already half the female guests were eyeing him covertly and looking enviously at her. Muted chatter without beginning or end flowed throughout the room as Spyros and Olympia Makopolis bore down on Julian and Inès with overflowing bonhomie. Taking them in tow, they introduced them to the rest of the famous guests, all of whom were dying to meet 'the new Olivier', as Julian had recently been dubbed by the MCCP publicity department, much to his embarrassment.

Ramona Armande stood to one side, talking to her brother and Umberto Scrofo. Didier was carefully eyeing his protégé while Umberto stared at the beautiful woman Julian was escorting. Ravishing, she was absolutely gorgeous. He couldn't see much of her face but her creamy décolletage was quite mouthwatering. Umberto appreciated rare beauty, and this woman was A first class. He hoped he'd get a chance to meet her later on. She was obviously cultured; they could talk about paintings.

Didier thought Julian had done well – extremely well – since the time of their first meeting in his dingy dressing room. Didier had always recognized those who possessed star quality, and those who did not. Julian Brooks had it in spades, and it had been polished and honed throughout the years until it radiated from him almost palpably.

In the years that Julian had been under contract to Didier's company, he had achieved precisely what had been planned for him. He had become unquestionably the biggest star in England. And this in spite of his bitch of a wife who, Didier thought, had always been an impediment to Julian. Phoebe and her social climbing, her pathetic attempts to become some kind of aristocrat, and all those damn cats of hers had not helped Julian's career. Happily, thanks to Inès, Phoebe was ancient history. All that the couple were waiting for now was the decree nisi. Once that obstacle had been cleared, they would be free to marry.

Inès observed the chattering throng in Spyros' vast drawing room, admiring so many faces which she'd seen in the movies since childhood. All the women were impossibly glamorous, groomed like prize fillies in the parade ring before a race. Their toffee-tanned, sleek bodies, even some of the plumper producers' wives, were corseted, girdled and brassiered to within an inch of their lives, and there seemed to be no such thing as a grey head of hair.

A sea of décolletage bobbed around. Breasts of all shapes, sizes and shades, many pushed up with underwiring and Merry Widow corsets, spilled seductively over the colourful satin, chiffon, làmé and lace gowns of Hollywood's most illustrious women. And their jewels! Inès had only seen jewels like this in the Tower of London or on the Queen of England.

But if Inès was fascinated by the women of Hollywood, the entire Hollywood community was more than curious to meet the woman for whom it was said Julian had given up everything but his talent. Despite the attempts of Julian and Didier to keep the terms of his divorce settlement quiet, the news had soon become common knowledge in the business. There were few secrets in the tight-knit community – none in fact – and everyone at the party knew every detail about Julian's divorce.

The women grudgingly agreed that Inès was very beautiful. The slim column of champagne silk worn with a simple string of pearls, the long, dark brown hair, unteased, unsprayed, uncurled, and the fine porcelain complexion with barely even a hint of cosmetic enhancement were in sharp contrast to the flashy looks of so many of them. Dark red lips and smoky kohl-shadowed eyes were her only makeup.

'She's so French,' breathed one buxom starlet to another as they teased, sprayed and painted in the green marble splendour of the Makopolis powder room.

'Yeah, she just oozes class, don't she?' said starlet number two, painting an already pouting lower lip into a cyclamen moue.

'I bet she's from a *real* top-drawer family,' breathed the first girl, inserting a hand deep into her cleavage to push up her breasts until her chin could almost have rested on them.

'Yeah – aristocratic all right. She sure didn't have to graft to make out like we've had to.'

'Yup,' said the first, spraying a generous amount of Evening in Paris into her ample cleavage. 'She's a real lucky dame. I bet it all came real easy to that one. Just as easy as pie.'

'Ah, there's Julian,' Shirley Frankovitch said as soon as she saw the English star. 'Damn, he's great-looking, isn't he, Irving? No wonder they call him the handsomest guy in the world.'

Her husband, a lugubrious man of nearly sixty, nodded. Early in his career he had written several fictional masterpieces and been hailed by the literati as the natural successor to Hemingway. Upon his meeting Shirley Horowitz, however, ten years his junior and ambition her middle name, his brilliant literary style had gradually been eroded by her demands and influence.

Ignoring the plays and novels of genius which were fermenting inside him and which his publishers begged him to write, he had become her mentor. He was in fact so besotted by her that it was her writing career which had become his obsession, while his own had taken a back seat.

In 1946 Shirley had had her first book published – a novel which had owed a great deal to Irving's literary talent and a certain amount to her own fertile sexual imagination. *Valentina*, the tale of a gorgeous courtesan in eighteenth-century France, had become an overnight bestseller all over the world. Soon Hollywood had beckoned, wanting Shirley to write the script for the movie. Shirley craved a Hollywood career, and who was Irving to argue?

They had taken the train to the West Coast from New York and installed themselves in the Garden of Allah. For six months they had partied with Hollywood's finest, between bouts of serious writing. The fruits of their labours – Shirley's *Valentina*, a dreadful yet successful movie, and Irving's infinitely better *Silence of the Damned* – both became box-office smashes.

Irving then went on to have enormous Broadway and London

successes with his two plays about distinguished political-historical figures, while Shirley then wrote *Valentina and the King* and two more smash-hit sequels to her carnal heroine's adventures.

With Shirley's bawdy portraits of seventeenth and eighteenth-century heroines, and Irving's critically acclaimed scripts, the Frankovitches soon earned a reputation for really knowing their onions when it came to historical melodrama. Who better than they to write the screenplay for *The Legend of Cortez* which was being heralded as the greatest historical epic since *The Ten Commandments*?

Shirley licked her lips in anticipation of meeting the star of their movie. Julian was catnip to women, a fact she appreciated only too well. After all, she had been quite a swinger herself for a while, although her own unspectacular looks had now turned to bloated flesh. But Shirley appreciated male beauty, aware, always, of the unlikelihood of her fantasies ever turning into reality. After all, a girl could dream, and it was Shirley's dreams which translated so convincingly on to the printed page.

There were so many people at the party that it was impossible for Julian and Inès to meet them all.

Every important star, director, producer and studio head had been invited, along with a spicy seasoning of contract starlets of both sexes. By nine o'clock there was such a heated crush in the three enormous reception rooms that Olympia Makopolis insisted that dinner be served at once.

Fifty tables covered in silver lâmé cloths and each laid for ten people had been set up inside a giant red and white striped tent in the sprawling back garden. The walls of the tent were draped in evergreens, ivy and red poinsettias, and hundreds of tiny lights twinkled down from the ceiling, interspersed with more than ten thousand red roses suspended in silver mesh baskets. A vast eighteenth-century rock-crystal chandelier, some five feet in diameter, blazed down on the guests from the centre, casting prisms of light on their expectant faces.

Spyros was known to give wonderful parties but this one was set to top them all, it seemed.

A groaning buffet table, covered in scarlet satin and decorated with holly and silver lâmé ribbons, held huge Baccarat crystal bowls of Beluga caviar, silver salvers of lobster, baby crayfish, *foie gras* with the finest black truffles, smoked salmon flown in from Scotland, quail eggs and a profusion of exotic salads. At the opposite end of the tent a twenty-piece band in red dinner jackets played Gershwin and Cole Porter, and over a hundred waiters and waitresses, all dressed as fairies or elves, took the guests' orders from individual menus, written in exquisite calligraphy, which rested in front of each place card. Money was no object at the Makopolis house; after all, the studio was paying, and they were in the black this year.

Inès was seated between Spyros and the scintillating Cary Grant. Across the table Julian had Olympia Makopolis on his left – not much fun in the witty repartee stakes – but to his relief vivacious Rosalind Russell had been placed on his right and she kept Julian amused with a stream of fascinating and hilarious anecdotes.

In the centre of each table an enormous cornucopia overflowing with Christmas goodies – tiny wheelbarrows filled with miniature Santa Clauses, jack-in-the-boxes, Raggedy Ann dolls, gift boxes, fairies, pixies and candy canes – spilled over in elegant yet ordered disarray on to the silver lâmé tablecloths. In front of each guest was a present, a hallmarked silver Tiffany frame, wrapped in sky-blue paper and tied with silver ribbons and sprigs of holly. In the frame was a photograph of the smiling and paternal-looking Sypros Makopolis, Mrs Makopolis, and their five children, all looking stiffly self-conscious.

'Hollywood, darling,' mouthed Julian with a wink across the table to Inès as she opened her package. 'Take it as it comes.'

Inès sipped her heavily scented wine and smiled inwardly. So this was what it was really like. This was the Hollywood that the fans revered and the movie magazines gushed about; the magic place which intrigued everyone who went to the cinema. She would have to learn to like it, in spite of the incredible excesses of vulgarity she'd seen tonight, but she knew she could like anything as long as Julian was by her side. As long as she could be Mrs Julian Brooks. How long – oh, Lord, how long would it be before his final decree was granted in London?

Across the sea of faces and noise, seated at a table of less important guests, the other newcomer to Hollywood gazed around in impressed delight. Umberto Scrofo fingered the scar beneath his tight collar uncomfortably. As usual, when he was excited or ill at ease, it itched and burned like the devil. He fought the strong desire to rip open his collar and scratch it fiercely. Tonight he must behave like a gentleman even though he felt out of place. He'd felt like a country bumpkin when introduced to Grace Kelly, Marilyn Monroe and so many other stars. He was so overawed that his conversation dried up and he knew he was making a *bruta figura*. He was angry with Ramona Armande who seemed to have deliberately ignored him from the moment they arrived. She flitted from group to group, laughing her affected laugh, stopping often to huddle with her brother. The two were known to be inseparable when Didier was in town, inspiring the nickname the Magyar Mafia. He noticed angrily that Didier had been seated at the top table with Julian Brooks, while Ramona was at an adjacent table far away from Umberto. Insulting bitch.

One of these days, I *will* belong there, at the number one table, he thought, manoeuvring a dollop of caviar into his mouth. When these Hollywood people see *my* finished masterpiece, I'll be courted and admired the way Julian Brooks is with that woman who isn't even his wife.

He had caught another glimpse of Inès' profile earlier as her dark hair swung around her shoulders and she smiled at Julian. There was definitely something familiar about her – something which struck a strangely responsive chord in him. He'd wanted to get a closer look but she and Julian were surrounded by Gary Cooper, Errol Flynn and Clark Gable, all laughing, sharing secrets that men who looked as they did always seemed to share, so he couldn't get near them.

Umberto exchanged a few remarks across the table with Irving Frankovitch who had written his superb script for *La Città Perduta*, then tried to listen to the boring babble of the woman next to him, a fat, overdressed monstrosity in a purple satin tent covered with flowered sequins. She had obviously tried hard, but failed miserably to pull herself together for tonight. Face powder in an unsuitable shade of orange caked the pores of her sweaty face, and her grey hair was frizzed and sprayed into an unfashionable style. But his jeweller's eye noticed that she was wearing a magnificent parure of diamonds and sapphires, obviously of extremely high quality, so she must be someone. Everyone here seemed to be someone.

He was becoming bored by her chatter, as he disliked ugly women, and it was only when Irving Frankovitch spoke to her that he realized she was Frankovitch's wife. While Irving was in Rome writing, Shirley had stayed in New York so Umberto had never met her. Ah, this was much better. Shirley Frankovitch was a force to be reckoned with. A brilliant writer, an important woman in this town. He decided to cultivate her. She could help him with his plans of glory.

Shirley had been drinking steadily. Four or more glasses of Krug before dinner, and three glasses of Stolichnaya with her Beluga had been knocked back faster than a sailor on shore leave. She had signalled to her waiter, good-looking even though he was dressed as an elf, to keep her wine glass topped up. By the time Spyros was making his introductory toasts, she was feeling no pain. Irving had tried to stop her drinking but she reprimanded him sharply. She felt good – she liked the way she felt when she'd really blasted a few.

Shirley hadn't been a heavy drinker when she was a teenager, but as she grew older and Mr Right hadn't crossed her path, drinking had somehow become second nature to her. She had less than fond memories, in the days when she'd been a struggling writer in New York, of getting drunk night after night – always in the company of men, none of whom could ever have been remotely considered the answer to a maiden's prayer. Shirley had been so shy, insecure and intimidated by almost everything and everyone that she tried to lose herself in the romantic worlds which she created in her writing. But in sober reality, constant rejection was more the order of the day. Rejection from the publishers, rejection from the men. Only a diet of pink ladies, dry martinis and champagne cocktails could instil in her the illusion that she really mattered. Through her haze of alcohol she was able to amuse some of her male drinking partners enough to end up in bed with one of them occasionally. But the following morning she would always wake with a throbbing hangover. Sometimes she would find herself slumped across crumpled linen sheets in a shiny penthouse in uptown Manhattan, but more often than not her puffy eyes opened to a peeling fly-specked ceiling in some dingy mid-town bedroom. There the object of last night's lust, typically some bleary-eyed blue-jawed brute, would avoid looking at her, which made her feel even cheaper.

It would have been stretching it to have called Shirley attractive, but she was eager to please, longed to be loved, and had good legs and big breasts. When the lights burned low and the hour was late, many men would lose their former powers of discrimination through drink, and slake their lust with Shirley. She always knew that she was never the first, second or even the third choice of her passing parade of paramours, but she never let her bitterness show. Instead she made every effort to become the life and soul of whatever party, club or bar she happened to find herself in. As she knocked back cocktail after cocktail, the skirts of her evening dresses hitched steadily higher as the evening progressed, revealing a tantalizing glimpse of suspender belt and white thighs to entice the boys.

Occasionally, one of the boys would prove to be more than just a one-night stand, his attentions lingering towards her for a week or two, even for a month, but these liaisons always seemed to wane rapidly, and the shapely legs, the thirty-eight-inch bust and the increasingly bawdy repartee were never enough to sustain any permanent interest.

By the time Shirley Horowitz met Irving Frankovitch, she was pushing thirty-five and filled with an inner discontent and anger with a life which she felt had dealt her a rotten hand. Irving, however, the unassuming, unattractive, but brilliant writer from Hoboken, fell heavily and totally under her spell. He thought Shirley was the wittiest, funniest and sexiest woman in the world. The fact that his experience of women was severely limited, due largely to his shyness and unassuming looks, did not brother Shirley at all. Finally she had hooked herself a man.

Both sets of parents in Brooklyn and Hoboken breathed a communal sigh of relief when their respective only children were finally married in a burst of post-austerity glory. At the strictly Jewish wedding where the guests tucked into mountains of smoked salmon and sturgeon, potato *latkes*, wedding cake and expensively imported French red wine and champagne, Shirley became very drunk indeed. When Irving had finished his wedding speech, she rose, her veiled headdress of orange blossoms askew on her mouse-coloured hair, and drawled triumphantly to the assembled throng,

'I know that all of you probably think that Irving doesn't look like much, but at least he's all mine, so hands off, girls, I've staked my claim.'

Some of her girlfriends giggled, but a disapproving murmur echoed from the older members of the Frankovitch clan, and Shirley's mother raised a warning eyebrow at her daughter. But the bride, taking another few sips of champagne, would not be halted. Swaying from side to side, her massive bosoms pushed up so high by her underwired bra that they seemed on the point of an escape attempt, she hiccuped loudly several times, then said, 'Yeah, I know he's got a body like a shrunken little runt, but he's a real tiger between the sheets, girls – real hot stuff.' The younger members of both families screamed with laughter, as the parents, uncles, older cousins and aunts sat rigid with disapproval, and Irving's normally sallow face flushed deeply as he lowered his head in embarrassment. Clutching her new husband's hand, fuelled by the laughter and the sea of upturned smiling faces around her, Shirley couldn't stop herself. Grabbing Irving's glass of wine she downed it in one gulp and screeched,

'You may all think he's got a face like a big rabbit too what with those big ears and that funny twitchy pink nose of his, but let me tell you, girls' – her voice dropped to a conspiratorial stage whisper – 'I'm happy to tell you he sure as hell fucks like one!'

Shirley let out a screech of delight as she threw back another glass and almost everyone, except Irving's parents, screamed with laughter. The new bride could feel great waves of love washing over her, as the laughing faces looked up at her with admiration. She revelled in it. Taking no notice at all of Irving's pained discomfort, ignoring the furious stares of his parents, Shirley threw her enraptured audience a final outrageous tidbit:

'Confidentially, girls . . .' She steadied herself with her hands on the table, whispering in such a way that the hundred guests had to lean forward to catch her every word. 'Between you 'n' me – he's the greatest little sex machine I've ever known, and believe me I've known more than my fair share, much *much* more. He can go *all* night 'n' every morning and although his little *schlong* may not be up to very much in the size department, what he lacks in inches he sure makes up for in staying power, he can *schtup* the night away, girls, and the afternoons too.'

Her audience was in the palm of her hand now and Shirley had never had such a good time. Heedless of the disapproving maiden aunts shepherding the juvenile members of the party out of the room, oblivious to the guffawing waiters, some of whom had rushed from other parts of the hotel to hear her, she turned to her flushed and shell-shocked bridegroom and planted an enormous open-mouthed kiss on his gaping lips. 'This little *putz* is the greatest *schtupper* I've ever known, and I've known 'em all!'

The whole room burst into applause, except for Irving's horrified father who was fanning Irving's deeply-shocked mother with his fringed *tallith*. They were unable to comprehend why their precious only son had married such a vulgar drunken slut. A small gaggle of wide-eyed nephews and nieces stood snickering at the door, not understanding what Aunt Shirley had said, but knowing from the reaction of their elders that, whatever it meant, it sure was hot stuff.

That night, in the privacy of the honeymoon suite, Irving gave vent to his anger, and burst his bride's balloon of happiness.

'You behaved like a cheap tart, Shirley,' he told her, a pulse beating in his neck, the only physical sign of his shame and rage. 'Worse than a street-corner tramp. I know that isn't the *real* you, which is why I forgive you, but I beg you, *please* honey, you must stop drinking – it doesn't suit you, Shirley, and it's so undignified.'

'Why should I?' snapped Shirley, tossing her orange-blossom headdress to the floor and gratefully unfastening the tight ankle-strap sandals which had been pinching her feet for hours. Irving was a spoilsport. He was bringing her down from an all-time high. Why was he trying to ruin everything now when everyone had adored her this afternoon?

'It's degrading,' he said mildly. 'It makes you look foolish, Shirley.'

'Foolish, shmoolish, what the fuck – who *gives* a damn – they *loved* me – all of those people – all our relatives, and friends – even Mom and Dad. They never gave a shit about me before but they were laughing their heads off – did you see 'em laugh? Didja?'

'Yes, I did, Shirley,' said Irving patiently, noticing that Shirley was calming down, becoming her old self again as the effects of the lethal mixture of wine, champagne and brandy alexanders started to wear off. 'I did see them laugh, but they were laughing *at* you, honey, not *with* you. There's a difference – don't you see that, honey?'

'No I don't. I had a great time, Irv, and you're bringing me down now.'

Shirley flounced into the bathroom, her eyes bright with hot tears, and slammed the door. Then Irving heard her violently throwing up, and shrugged. He was a kind and patient man, who loved this woman, his new wife, recognizing many of her fears and insecurities. But the Beaujolais Belligerence she evinced when drunk would have to go. He would see to it that she stopped drinking. He felt sure he would be able to handle her now that they were married.

Irving glanced over at Shirley as Spyros started talking. No doubt about it – she'd had much more than a snootful. From the way she was glaring at everyone, she looked about to explode at any moment. He sighed, mentally fastening his seatbelt for the bumpy ride which looked now to be inevitable.

Spyros introduced Julian, who rose with a modest bow to enthusiastic applause from the guests. How Hollywood loved a true thespian from the British theatre. The *crème de la crème* of the cinema always felt inferior, somehow insignificant beside an actor who regularly performed the classics on stage. With all their fame, looks and wealth, many of these stars were desperately insecure about their abilities and envied Julian his impeccable theatrical reputation.

Many also respected his brave stand against Phoebe. Few of them would have given up a perpetual slice of their earnings, a house and all its contents, just for the love of a woman. Consequently Inès was the object of enormous conjecture and gossip, most of which she passed with flying colours. Her beauty and style couldn't be faulted on any level. Those who talked to her found her charming, witty and cultured, not bitchy in the slightest.

Julian started to speak now, his melodic baritone entrancing the guests with a particularly amusing and self-deprecating joke at which the crowd roared its approval. Inès looked at him, admiring his poise and his velvet voice.

Shirley glanced around the room irritably. Every eye seemed riveted on Julian or on the woman across from him. No one was looking in her direction. Why not? *She* too was a Star. A star writer and a star novelist who had written the script that had enticed Julian to America. *She* had single-handedly kept MCCP afloat through the lean, tough times after the war when audiences didn't know what the hell they wanted to see. But they'd all gone to see the movies she'd written, hadn't they. Especially the *Valentina* series. If it weren't for writers, *nothing* would ever happen in this town. No one seemed to appreciate how important they were to the movie product. No one.

'He's a lucky guy to have a woman like that,' Irving said admiringly.

'And what's so great about her?' Shirley slurred belligerently. 'She looks like a cold fish to me.'

Irving ignored her as Julian told another joke and the rapt faces laughed again.

God damn it – Shirley realized furiously that she wasn't even at the top table. Shit, shit, shit. What a bummer. Okay, so she was seated with Zanuck and Orson Welles – neither of them exactly *schleppers* in the business, but she still took it as a personal insult. After all she'd done for Spyros, this was his appreciation. Voices inside her seemed to be having a furious argument as they battled for supremacy. Good little Shirley was telling off bad little Shirley, but bad little Shirley seemed to be winning. Shirley knew she was losing control. Her head felt stuffed with cottonwool, her mouth dry. She quickly slugged back another glass of champagne, looking around the room with a challenging expression.

Irving's eyes were glued to Julian. Or was it Julian's French mistress he was staring at? Shirley squinted, trying to figure out *who* held her husband's attention. Yes, she was right, bad Shirley thought triumphantly. He was staring at the stuck-up Frenchwoman who looked as if butter wouldn't melt in her cocksucking mouth. Irving should be looking at her – her, *her!!!* He was *her* husband, for Christ's sake. If he loved *her*, he should be paying attention to *her*.

Angrily, Shirley stuck a Lucky Strike in her mouth, turning to Irving for a light. He ignored her. He's ignoring you, Shirley, said the bad voice. As if you were nothing, no one, a fucking stranger!

'Gimme a light, Irving,' she snapped, so loudly that Julian paused momentarily in his speech to look over at her.

Irving gestured that he had no matches, ignoring her again as his attention returned to Julian. In a fury, Shirley scrabbled through the cornucopia in front of her for matches. Some of the guests began to notice the disturbance and to make shushing noises. There were no matches in Santa's goodie box, and no one was smoking at Shirley's table.

'Fuck, fuck, *fuck!* Where are the motherfucking matches?' she screamed.

Julian stopped speaking as every head turned towards her and collectively Hollywood tut-tutted its silent disapproval of the bleary-eyed writer. Empty glass in hand, unlit cigarette dangling from slack lips, she was obviously completely, unbecomingly smashed.

Julian resumed his speech as Shirley's cute-looking waiter-elf dashed forward and struck a match for her. Inhaling deeply, she watched the sycophantic faces as they turned again in unison to listen to the actor's speech. What bullshit, she thought. They're all full of shit, every single one of the motherfuckers.

No longer giving a damn what anyone thought, Shirley suddenly stood up and said in a sarcastic, belligerent voice, 'Everything that you say is absolute bullshit, your lordship. Everything in this room is bullshit – everyone in Hollywood is just a piece of *crap!*' She belched loudly, weaving violently as Irving grabbed her and pulled her into her seat.

'What the *hell* are you doing?' he whispered furiously. 'For God's sake, behave yourself, Shirley. You're way out of line and making a complete fool of yourself again.'

Everyone was looking at her now, some even standing up to get a better view. The whole damned tent – five hundred pairs of curious eyes were staring at her in shock, yet with the secret pleasure that tomorrow they'd all have something really juicy to gossip about.

That's the way it ought to be, Shirley thought, pleased with herself as she greedily downed another glass of champage. They *should* be talking about her. Then she hiccuped so violently that the glass of champagne she was drinking spilled all over the front of her sequined tent. When the cute waiter rushed forward to try and help her, he tripped over a piece of loose grass-green carpet and landed head first in Shirley's ample cleavage to shrieks of shocked laughter from the guests. Then to Irving's intense embarrassment, Shirley's humiliation and the rest of the guests' hilarity, the two of them plummeted in slow motion to the floor, the tiny waiter in his elf's costume almost disappearing into the massive folds of Shirley's caftan.

Hollywood, of course, hushed up the story and closed ranks, as Hollywood always attempted to hush up the scandals and peccadillos of its darlings to the outside world. Nothing at all appeared in the press. But telephone wires hummed the next day throughout the Hills of Holmby and Beverly as chattering tongues broadcast the delicious news of Shirley's scandalous behaviour to friends and acquaintances who'd neither had the luck nor the clout to have been invited to what must have been the party of the season.

Exaggerations abounded. By the end of the week, the story had been completely blown out of proportion. Not only had Shirley Frankovitch been utterly legless, but she'd ripped off her dress, danced half naked on the table, then pulled the waiter under the table, where she'd tried to give him a blow job. Olympia had become hysterical and had to be given a sedative by Dr Zolotos. And Spyros had threatened Shirley that he would never use her again on a movie and fired both her and Irving from *Cortez*. Tittle-tattle and scandal. How the town loved it – revelled in it. Gossip, power and the movie business, these were the three ingredients which made its world turn and its inhabitants thrive.

*

On the way home from the party Inès couldn't stop talking and laughing about the party and the excesses of vulgarity she'd seen.

'Don't worry, darling,' smiled Julian, 'it's not always quite as tawdry as that – actually, many people who live here do have the most wonderful taste. Some of the most knowledgeable private art collectors in America live here. Many of them are even actors, believe it or not.'

'Who?' inquired Inès. 'I would like to meet them, Julian. Some of the pictures I saw on Mr Makopolis' walls were absolute fakes. Anyone could see that. The original of the Renoir above the fireplace in the library is in the Louvre! How can Mr Makopolis be so gullible?'

'Good old Spyros. He knows everything about the movies but not much about the art world. Tell you what, darling. Next week we'll go and see Eddie G. Robinson or Vincent Price, they're both extremely knowledgeable about pictures and have marvellous collections.'

'Mmm, I'd love to.' Inès rested her head on Julian's shoulder as he drove them through the darkened empty streets of Beverly Hills towards their hotel.

'But all I want to do now, my love, is to go home and make love with you.'

'You've got yourself a deal, *Mademoiselle*,' said Julian gravely. 'And you are not allowed to go back on your word.'

14

Even though it was December it was a boiling hot day. Dominique was playing volleyball on the Santa Monica sands with a group of shrieking teenagers, mostly boys, leaving Agathe with little to do but lie in the sun – something which she hated – or to eat lunch, which she'd already done. She decided to go for a walk. She wandered down the asphalt pavement which bordered the beach, thinking, thinking, thinking, oblivious to the cars speeding past, to the high, bright sun, indeed to anything at all except the vision of Julian Brooks which now filled her thoughts constantly.

They had met at last. Well, not exactly met. She had been having lunch in the MCCP commissary with Dominique and Kittens, the costume designer, when he'd come over to introduce himself. Agathe felt a deep flush suffuse her entire body as he stood chatting charmingly at their table. The flush seemed to rise from her between her legs and engulf her until she felt that her face was a scarlet mirror in which he could read all her most secret thoughts.

She hardly dared to meet his eyes; she just listened to his melodious voice as he spoke and laughed with Dominique and Kittens. The easy camaraderie the three of them seemed to share goaded Agathe into a silent jealous frenzy. Julian stood so tall and easy, one hand casually resting on the back of Dominique's chair, while the girl giggled up at him, chattering nineteen to the dozen. Agathe had frozen. She had been unable to meet his eye even for a second or two, conscious of the sweat which trickled down her back, the flush on her face and the horrible, embarrassing tingling in her groin. He could sense it – of course he could sense it. That was why he was ignoring her, wasn't it? Julian tipped his hat to the women as he left, and Agathe felt herself relax. Dominique's face was flushed and happy as she bit into her hamburger.

'Golly, he sure is cute for an old man, don't you think, Agathe?'

Kittens nodded in agreement.

'I'm sure I don't know what you mean,' said Agathe stiffly.

'He's terribly good-looking,' sighed Dominique, then leaning towards her chaperone, she whispered, 'I hear that practically every actress he's ever worked with has fallen for him!'

'Don't say things like that, it isn't right for young girls like you to have thoughts like that,' snapped Agathe. 'Eat your lunch.'

Dominique grinned to herself. If Agathe only knew what thoughts she did have, the poor old thing would probably have a nervous breakdown.

Inès woke up to the Beverly Hills sunshine, which streamed into the hotel room through the cloudy muslin curtains. She was nauseous and her head felt fuzzy. Strange, as she usually was able to handle champagne. Julian had left early for the studio's Malibu ranch for the first of his stunt-riding lessons. It was essential to be an expert horseman, and the eight-weeks instruction period would hopefully guarantee by the end of it that Julian would be able to deal with a horse better than the grizzled handlers at the ranch.

The telephone rang, the shrill sound making her head throb. It was Julian calling from the ranch.

'Darling.' His voice was warm. 'How are you feeling?'

She lied and assured him she was feeling fine.

'Good, good. Darling, I've just bumped into Flynn down here at the ranch. He's asked us to dinner tonight at Romanoff's – will you be up to it, angel?'

'Of course, *chéri*. I liked him so much when we met last night. And I've always wanted to go to Romanoff's.'

'Good. OK, I've got to run, my love. God, my arse is so sore from that damn horse. They must have been supermen to ride without saddles.'

'I'll kiss it better when you come home,' Inès murmured, laughing.

'Can't wait, darling. See you later – dinner's at eight. We'll meet him there.'

After a lazy, relaxing day, Inès dressed carefully for dinner, in a black *peau de soie* cocktail dress with a full mid-calf skirt. Her only jewellery was Julian's simple diamond engagement ring, small diamond stud earrings and her lucky bracelet, but she looked ravishing and Julian couldn't stop telling her so.

Romanoff's was on Rodeo Drive. One of the most famous restaurants in the world, it was owned and run by Prince Michael Romanoff, a self-styled exiled Russian prince with impeccable manners and immense charm. Because there were no top tables at Romanoff's – hence no Siberia – he managed to have half of Hollywood dining there regularly without ever offending any of their fragile egos. Stars always sat where Prince Michael put them and never complained.

He now stepped suavely forward to greet Julian and Inès as they came through the thick glass doors into the foyer. Every table was in full view and most of the diners looked up as they entered. Though small in stature, Prince Michael was big on personality. Inès could feel the power behind his twinkling brown eyes as he charmingly kissed her hand, murmuring to Julian, 'Looks, m'boy, you've done it again as usual – what a ravishing gel – French too – excellent. I'm very happy for you, m'boy – come, Errol's waiting.'

He led the way down the carpeted stairway while everyone in the room stared at Inès and Julian. It was as if the restaurant had been designed for people-watchers. None of the booths was high-backed, so one group could easily chat to another at the tables on either side and behind, and could see everything else that was going on.

Julian nodded hellos to Cary Grant and Darryl Zanuck as they wended their way to the table where Errol Flynn sat beside a pretty girl who looked young enough to be his daughter.

Prince Michael took their drinks orders in his clipped English accent then, clamping his cigarette holder firmly between his teeth, left them to greet the ravishing Grace Kelly, who was standing at the top of the stairs with a handsome escort.

The room buzzed and then went silent as every detail of Grace's hair, makeup and outfit was analysed by the women, while every man marvelled at her beauty. Inès thought she was breathtaking. She deserved her title of Hollywood's reigning princess. She was flawless, besides being a highly talented actress.

It was an exhilarating dinner, and Errol was in top form, although drinking heavily. His young companion spoke little, content to giggle shyly at his jokes, most of which she didn't really understand, and to eat everything put before her. Errol embroidered on the fracas created by Shirley Frankovitch at Spyros' party the other night, and had everyone in stitches.

Several studio executives stopped by the table, ostensibly to pay their respects to Errol, but after a perfunctory greeting to him, they seemed far more interested in Julian. By the end of the evening his pocket contained half a dozen cards from some of the most influential men in town, with instructions to call them as soon as possible.

Flynn was not given even one card. Although only in his mid forties he was almost finished in Hollywood. He had been a great star, but he was now considered box-office poison, having outraged moral Middle America with his amorous antics, his philandering with under-age girls, his drunken brawls, and his 'I don't give a damn' attitude. Studio publicists had been unable to hold down the lid on his scandalous behaviour, and he'd become Hollywood's whipping boy – almost a pariah. But he was wonderfully charming, Inès thought, full of humour, and a truly great raconteur. He must have been glorious-looking once, she decided.

When Inès went to the powder room, the peach-mirrored haven was empty but for one girl whose enormous overly tanned cleavage swelled out of an unfashionably short tight white lace dress which cupped her too-plump derriere in a most unflattering way. Her big lips were painted with thick pink gloss, and her mane of platinum hair heavily teased. Inès realized that the girl had gone to enormous trouble to try to look as much as possible like Jayne Mansfield, one of the town's leading sex symbols. The starlet was a true Hollywood cupcake, and eyed Inès' simple black Balenciaga dress admiringly while she applied yet more hair spray to her platinum helmet.

'I saw you the other night at the Makopolis party,' she confided in a friendly way, removing another cosmetic necessity from her pink plastic and rhinestone bag, bending over so far that Inès could see her nipples. 'I just *love* the way you dress. It's so chic – so French!' she gushed.

Inès murmured a thankyou. What a pitiful girl – professional, obviously; Inès could always recognize one of her own. And this one was on the brink of losing her looks. Poor thing, she hoped she'd been clever enough to put some money away. She wondered who'd had the bad taste to bring such an obvious tart to Romanoff's.

Outside the powder room a tall, thin man stood waiting. He turned to Inès, and with a shock which electrified every nerve in her body she recognized him immediately. She tried to move away, but it was too late, he had seen her, and he pounced.

'Inès! Hello. Well, goodness gracious me. What the blazes are *you* doing here, old girl?'

'Benjie.' Inès' voice was a hoarse whisper. 'What a surprise. Oh, dear, I'm terribly sorry, Benjie, but you must excuse me – I have to go back to my table – they all want to leave.' She moved away, but Benjie grabbed her arm, and with growing horror she saw that they were now in the foyer of the restaurant, in full view of the whole room. What was Benjie doing here? He never left London except to go to the country or Monte Carlo. Beverly Hills was unquestionably non-U to his set.

'Oh, no you don't – I'm not letting you get away again. I've *missed* you, Nanny.' He bent his head closer as she tried to edge away. She could smell the gin on his breath which had always made him desperate to play his kinky sex games.

'Benjie's missed Nanny, vewy vewy much.' He was lapsing into baby talk now, much to Inès' discomfort . . . 'Benjie's been bad, a vewy *naughty* boy – needs Nanny to spank him *hard,*' he whispered, looking pleadingly at her, his long, bony fingers still holding tightly on to her arm. She could hardly put up a struggle in front of Hollywood's elite. He would never dare behave like this in London at the 400, the Café de Paris or any of the haunts that he and his friends frequented. Benjie had always behaved with the most impeccable manners everywhere in London, the perfect English gentleman. Only when he'd been in bed or drinking heavily, which was obviously what he'd been doing tonight, did his aristocratic demeanour lapse.

The door to the powder room opened and the Barbie Doll minced over, patting her hair. Benjie loosened his grip on Inès' arm as he greeted his platinum-haired companion.

'Well, it's been very, very nice to see you again, Inès,' he said with a sly smile, taking the blonde's arm in a proprietary way. Inès was even more amazed. In London he would never have allowed himself to associate publicly with such an obvious tart.

'We must get together, I'm here until Sunday – where are you staying?' he asked.

'Oh – er – with friends,' Inès said. 'They're waiting for me. I must go – goodbye, Benjie.'

At that moment Prince Michael came over to escort the couple to their table, but before he walked away, Benjie, sotto voce and with a wink, said, 'Do give my very best regards to *Nanny*!'

Inès felt her face flame, truly shaken by this unexpected encounter. Her past seemed to be catching up with her already. Benjie had recognized her instantly, of course. With her pale matt face, red lips, kohl-rimmed eyes and distinctive long, dark bob, she would always stand out in a crowd. Most women today wore their hair in a curly, short poodle style, or in a gamine cut. Inès had not changed her look for nearly ten years.

She walked unsteadily back to her table, and Julian watched her curiously. She seemed flustered, and Inès was a woman who was rarely flustered.

'Wasn't that old Benjie Spencer-Monckton you were talking to?' he asked. 'I remember meeting him once or twice at White's in London.'

'Yes it was,' she said, taking a long cooling sip of ice water as she saw, to her dismay, that Benjie and the starlet-tart were being seated in a booth almost opposite theirs.

'You've never mentioned him,' Julian persisted. 'How do you know him?'

'I don't,' Inès lied. 'I mean, not really. We met at a weekend house party in the country once. I'm surprised he even remembered me.' She laughed, the sound ringing tinnily in her ears, her eyes scanning Julian's face for any sign that he might not believe her. But he'd obviously accepted what she'd said. This time.

The blonde looked over at Inès, smiling amiably, through lipstick-smudged lips. No doubt she was questioning Benjie about Inès, just as Julian was questioning her about Benjie. Would Benjie tell her the truth? He wouldn't dare – surely? They had been too fond of each other. But if he did tell this hooker that Inès had also been a whore; if he told her of the perverse games that they had played together, the occasional *ménage à trois* they'd had with some of his friends; if these stories began to circulate in Hollywood and Julian heard of them, her life with him would be finished. Inès couldn't bear to think about it. She didn't know what Benjie was doing in Hollywood nor what he was now whispering to the giggling girl. All she felt at that moment was the imminent danger that she might lose everything. She felt sick.

Inès' premonition proved horribly accurate. Later that evening, after having said goodnight to Errol and his girlfriend, who had decided to join another table of friends, she and Julian were standing outside the restaurant, waiting for their car to arrive. Suddenly Inès became rigid with fear. This was too much, much too much. It simply couldn't be true, it just wasn't possible.

Escorting a sable-clad Ramona Armande from Romanoff's was a short, bald paunchy man. Even though she only glimpsed his profile, Inès recognized, to her unspeakable horror, the loathsome face which had haunted her dreams for so many years. That squat body, the thick neck, that bullet head – she could never forget him. Eleven years had gone by, along with most of his hair. He was much fatter now, deep lInès had etched themselves into his forehead and between his nose and mouth. His fleshy lips were thinner and pulled into a grimace which he no doubt thought was a charming social smile, as he leaned towards Ramona to whisper in her ear.

But he was dead. She'd killed him, hadn't she? She had washed his life blood from her hands with the perfumed soap at the Ritz. Wiped it on the soft white towels. But there was absolutely no doubt about it at all. It was the face she knew from her most terrifying nightmares. It was undeniably Umberto Scrofo. The man she thought she'd murdered in the Ritz. The man who had worn the uniform, bristling with medals, of an Italian general. The man who'd forced her to have brutal, sadistic sex, who'd degraded and beaten her so violently that the thought of his repeating those vile acts had made her kill him.

She had always believed that she had killed him. But if he were dead, how could he possibly be here, standing outside Romanoff's on Rodeo Drive in Beverly Hills? Was she going mad? Was this another nightmare? Some horrible, sickening hallucination? Or was this reality?

Inès felt about to faint. Her palms were soaking wet and her heart pounded like a piston. Her sense of panic was so suffocating that she could hardly breathe. Umberto Scrofo, here, alive, in the all-too-gross flesh.

She turned her back, facing Julian so that the man couldn't see her features. Would he recognize her? She prayed he wouldn't. Surely she'd altered physically a great deal since Paris in 1943 – but had she changed enough?

'I want to look like this.' Inès handed the hairdresser a photograph of Grace Kelly that she'd cut out of *Look* magazine, and watched him expectantly.

'But you look so great the way you are,' the hairdresser said in amazement. 'Why d'you wanna change, honey?'

'Please, just do it,' said Inès simply. 'I want to, that's all.'

The hairdresser shrugged indifferently. He would never understand dames as long as he lived. Here was an original beauty, distinctive, classy, a real elegant European lady, who wanted to change herself into another Kelly clone. Well, he thought, at least she didn't want to look like Marilyn Monroe, the other great flavour of the 1950s. So what, he'd do it, he was getting paid to do hair not to be a psychiatrist.

Inès buried herself in a book while he mixed his colours, and she didn't watch as he cut and coloured her long dark hair. Only when the hairdresser had finished his work did she look at herself critically in the mirror. It was uncanny – the transformation from a dark-haired, sultry, European-looking sophisticate to a distinctly American-looking rose was extraordinary. She was almost unrecognizable but, happy to see, still beautiful. Her hair was cut into a soft bob which skimmed her earlobes, with a low parting and soft waves around her forehead. The new colour was masterful. A pale ash gold, almost the colour of champagne, not the bright yellow gold of her teenage years, but a subtle, classic colour with delicate bronze highlights. The style and shade were different enough to separate her from her past and anyone who had known her then.

Inès spent the rest of the afternoon at the Elizabeth Arden Salon, completing her transformation. She invested in a complete new range of cosmetics, powder blue eyeshadow, light lipstick, pale rouge, and a new wardrobe for the upcoming Acapulco location. Pastels, frothy chiffon and light cotton gowns in pink, powder blue, lemon yellow. She would no longer wear those favourite severe blacks and whites of past years. She would be transformed. A new life. A new image. A new Inès.

Inès Juillard the courtesan was now dead. She was going to be Mrs Julian Brooks in only a few weeks. No one from her past would ever be able to recognize her now, nor could they ever hurt her again, of that she felt sure.

15

Umberto Scrofo sat glumly in his Hilton suite waiting for the telephone to ring. He had called every single studio head since he had been in California, trying to arrange a meeting or a screening for his film. Not one of them would even take his calls. He was always sloughed off to one of their assistants who, with smoothly insincere voices, gave Umberto a dozen excuses as to why their bosses were too busy to see him.

'So what if the picture stars Ramona Armande?' Spyros Makopolis had growled to his second-in-command. 'Who cares? She's an old has-been. She's been around longer than Garbo, for Christ's sake – and no one's interested in some goddam Italian art film, even if it is supposed to be better than Rossellini's.'

'Mr Makopolis will let you know,' the silken-voiced secretary had informed Umberto. And so indeed would Mr Zanuck, Mr Warner, Mr Cohn and Mr Schary. All had given him the cold shoulder, the frozen mitt. He was feeling unspeakably frustrated.

Didier Armande, who had been responsible for most of the financing, had seen a rough cut of *La Città Perduta* and had thought it a minor masterpiece. But although he was a powerful film producer in England, Didier didn't have the same clout in Hollywood, and even he couldn't persuade the tycoon moguls to attend a screening.

Umberto scratched furiously at the thick keloid scar on his throat until it was almost raw. Even the under-age prostitute whom a bellboy had procured for him the night before hadn't managed to alleviate his rage. He had pummelled into her pale quivering body until she had cried out with pain, and he had to slap her across her snivelling face until she was silent. But he had never tried to do again what he had done with that little blonde whore at the Ritz all those years ago, or in Calabria with Silvana. The revenge that had been meted out to him had been too terrible. How he had survived either attempt to destroy him had been a miracle. Whenever his secret erotic senses told him what he wanted, where he was headed, he always managed to stop in time. Thoughts of parched and starving days adrift in a fishing boat filled him with dread, and the memory of the blonde tart's terror-stricken face as she slashed his razor across his throat would haunt him for ever. The authorities had never found her. Was she still alive? Probably, but if she was she would now be some broken-down old strumpet selling her poxy, raddled body in the back alleys of Montmartre for a few sous. It must be eleven years ago now, but he had not forgotten. He would never forget, he thought as he once again scratched at his constant reminder of her.

He looked out at the fine blue December sky, but couldn't see too much of it. All his attempts to get one of the best suites at the Beverly Hills Hotel, the Beverly Wilshire or the Bel Air had failed miserably. Money didn't talk in Hollywood. Power and fame did. Umberto had a great deal of money, but no one here knew or seemed to care who he was. He had only managed to get this suite at the Hilton which had no view at all, and was decorated in a revolting shade of orange, by heavily bribing the man at the front desk.

He decided to go for a walk down Wilshire Boulevard to take some air. He had loved walking in Rome recently. There he was somebody. People stopped him in the cafés, glad to see him. '*Ciao, Umberto, come sta?*' they asked, eager voices showing their respect and admiration. On the Via Veneto he was the new King of the movies, ever since the word had spread about *La Città Perduta*. Here he was treated like a piece of shit. He put on a green mohair cardigan, similar to one he had seen Dean Martin wearing at a golf tournament. Tying a poison-green paisley scarf around his throat to hide his scar, he put on large dark sunglasses and a pristine panama hat, so new that it shrieked vulgarity.

He sauntered down Wilshire Boulevard towards the Beverly Wilshire Hotel, smiling at the few pedestrians. He passed the shining red-lacquer door of the Elizabeth Arden Beauty salon, and idly looked into the windows at the displays of delicate lingerie, casual sportswear and cosmetics.

When the red door opened and a waft of subtle perfume caught him, he turned to see a delicate profile, a waterfall of shining champagne hair and a tall, lithe body dressed in powder blue. The woman walked briskly, disappearing in the direction of I. Magnin. Puzzled, he stared after her. He knew that woman, he was sure of it. There was something terribly familiar about her. He had thought he'd recognized someone at the Makopolis party too – but that girl had been a brunette. This one was a classic blonde. But she struck a definite chord. Now where had he seen her before? He shrugged. It wasn't important. What was important, all he cared about now, was getting Zanuck, Makopolis or Jack Warner to see his movie. If they didn't he might as well get out of this ghastly place and go back to Rome.

PART III

I

Acapulco 1955

The above-the-line cast and technicians began dribbling into Acapulco early in January. Set designers, architects, carpenters, painters, plasterers and prop men had already been there for four months creating the grand and elaborate sets needed for *The Legend of Cortez*. The film's plot, which didn't even pretend to be historically accurate, given that this was a Cinemascope epic, was fairly thin. In 1518 Hernando Cortez and his fellow adventurer Francisco Pisarro were sent by Charles v on a mission to find gold. Their expedition landed in Mexico with only six hundred men. At first Cortez was received by Montezuma – who was to be the last Aztec emperor – like a god, but Cortez repaid this honour by imprisoning him and, later, by conquering his entire empire.

When Cortez' men attempted to leave Montezuma's capital, then called Tenochtitlan, the Aztecs finally rose up against him. They unsuccessfully fought Cortez and his troops in a pitched battle, largely because so many of Montezuma's men deserted and went over to the side of the Spanish invaders.

The Aztec emperor died in prison, leaving Cortez to win the heart of his fiery, beautiful daughter, and they supposedly lived happily after.

But Spyros Makopolis needed a much stronger plot than that. Historical epics were in vogue, the bigger the better. Chariots, togas and ruins were fascinating audiences everywhere, as long as the historical facts were beefed up, and Irving and Shirley Frankovitch had been hired to try to glamorize the life of Señor Cortez. They had started diligently searching and writing early in 1953, spurred on by Makopolis' offer of an unprecedented hundred thousand dollar advance plus seven per cent of the gross profits. The following year, the studio sent teams of scouts all over the world to find the most suitable yet cheapest locations for this four-million-dollar Technicolor Cinemascope extravaganza. MCCP had high hopes for a box-office bonanza and were sparing no expense to achieve it.

Location scouts had returned from months of all-expense-paid trips to dozens of exotic places to inform the studio that, with its thirty-eight lush beaches, dozens of gorgeous tropical bays and lagoons, clear, calm water and incomparable sunsets, Acapulco was the most perfect location for the movie.

After Irving and Shirley had written their first two drafts in New York and their third in Los Angeles, they arrived in Acapulco to give it the final polish. The couple now sat on the vine-covered balcony of their Villa Vera suite, sipping *piña-coladas* in the humid dusk and waiting for the new arrivals.

'Here comes Julian with his fiancée.' The perpetually inquisitive Shirley was able to get a good close-up view of the couple with the help of a strong pair of binoculars.

It was obvious, from the proud looks she gave him, and by the way in which she held his arm, that Inès Juillard, svelte in champagne linen, was utterly devoted to Julian Brooks. He looked a little overheated for such a handsome star, Shirley thought. Under his cream panama hat beads of sweat shone on his matinée-idol brow, and his usually crisp moustache appeared to be wilting.

Inès spotted the glint of the binoculars in the reflected sunlight, looked up and then smiled at Julian. She wondered who could be watching them. No, not them, *him*, Julian; he was the star, the one the world was interested in. She knew that the studio and the Frankovitches had gone to considerable lengths to make the part of the buccaneer-adventurer Cortez to fit Julian, who at thirty-eight was now at the height of his masculine beauty.

Although the split from Phoebe had taken its toll on him financially, in the time Inès had been living with Julian she believed that he had found true contentment. He really loved her. More than he had ever loved anyone before. But he was, after all, an actor, so if he ever did stray a little, she knew that she would have to turn a blind eye. Her years as a courtesan had taught her that so many men were just like little boys. Sex was a sport, a hunt and a challenge to them.

Even when they loved their wives madly, the best of men thought little of sexual infidelity. Unfaithfulness had been accepted in Europe as a fact of life for centuries, and intelligent wives had always ignored it. Inès had played brilliant sexual games, intrigued Julian with her quick mind, her knowledge of art, politics, music and finance. She had woven a bond of magic that made him feel as he never had with any other woman before.

Now, with the new year Inès would soon start a whole new life as Mrs Julian Brooks. She was now nearly thirty years old. Beautiful, intelligent and desirable. To make her situation complete, she suspected that she might be pregnant. Julian had often spoken of his desire for a child, and although they were not yet married she felt confident that he would be thrilled if her Los Angeles doctor confirmed her suspicions.

Julian smiled at his bride-to-be. She was the perfect woman for him in every way.

It never ceased to amaze him that after he'd had a grinding fourteen-hour day at the studio or on a location, fencing, riding or performing his own difficult stunts, she could make his homecoming an event. An ice-cold martini would be waiting, made just as she heard his car coming up the winding driveway of their house. Exquisitely dressed in the latest fashions from Paris, coolly elegant, she always managed to reveal a glimpse of something which would be guaranteed to arouse him. Perhaps the curve of a perfect breast through some transparent chiffon, or a creamy shoulder emerging from the depths of velvet, or her gorgeous legs through a split satin skirt. She would rub the back of his neck to relieve his tension, her cool fingers caressing his tired muscles. From this massage, Inès could always gauge his mood. She could tell if he'd be receptive to lovemaking or not; he almost always was. They would bathe together in the cool marble bathroom, in the shower which had powerful yet soothing jets positioned in strategic places, where she would wash his tired body with scented Guerlain soap.

As she kneaded his cock gently and lovingly with the soap, the tips of her nipples would brush lightly against his chest and he would harden; then her tongue would make its way into his mouth, as the strong jets burst into power, and she would position his body where the water would touch him most pleasurably.

She never seemed to mind that her makeup and hair were ruined by these few blissful moments. The only thing which truly mattered to her was giving pleasure to her man. Sometimes she left him, still tumescent after the soaping and the kissing, to withdraw to her bedroom to anoint herself with various oils and moisturizers. Usually he would come and take her as she stood in her curtained dressing room, possessing her fiercely, with stallion speed. But often they would linger in the shower. Before it was over, and when he was almost bursting with pleasure, she would take him to one of the many places that she'd designed for love. She knew all the answers to a man's tired libido and used them cunningly. Afterwards, she washed him gently, leaving him to doze on cool linen sheets while she prepared dinner, which she would take to him on a tray. While he ate she would watch him. If he wanted to talk, she chatted away. If he craved silence, she would be quiet as a mouse; if he wanted to study his dialogue, she would read a book. She was the perfect woman who wanted to be the perfect wife: a tigress in the bedroom, a sophisticated lady everywhere else. The only thing about her which displeased him was the new colour of her hair. He had adored her long thick dark brown hair, loved twining it around his hands like silken ropes. This new style, although soft and becoming, made Inès somehow lose her aura of strength and individuality.

Never mind, it was probably only temporary. Her short Grace Kelly style would be nothing more than a passing phase, and before long she would once again return to being his ravishing brunette. But whatever colour Inès' hair might be it didn't ever seem to stop men staring at her admiringly wherever she went.

Many men coveted Inès, sensing her almost palpable sexuality. But she belonged to him. Whatever relationships she had had in the past, they were now meaningless. She had told him about her only three lovers, refusing to go into any detail at all in spite of his pressing insistence. She was a clever woman. Julian knew that the more she told him the more he would jealously want to hear about her past. For Looks Brooks, Inès had no past. Her life had only begun when he met her.

2

Umberto Scrofo sat in his drawing room in Rome, surrounded by some of his favourite furniture, pictures and sculptures; he was picking his teeth with a paper clip and reading an airmailed copy of *Weekly Variety.*

La Città Perduta – The Lost City in English – was a massive success. He had been right to insist on a European publicity tour with Ramona and the rest of the cast. *La Città Perduta* had received a phenomenal boost, and despite the actors demanding perks like grand hotel suites and limousines, it had all paid off handsomely. The picture was a smash hit in Europe. It was his first taste of cinematic success, and he was immensely pleased with himself.

His young housekeeper entered the semi-dark room which was shuttered against the afternoon sun, her manner subservient.

'May I get you something, Signor Scrofo?'

'Yes,' Umberto snapped in his croaking voice, wondering why she always sounded so fucking apologetic. 'Iced coffee with plenty of sugar, and don't spill it on the tray like you did last time.'

'Yes, *Signor*,' bobbed the girl, and hurriedly disappeared. Signor Scrofo terrified her, but she wanted to keep this job, it paid well and her large family needed the money.

Umberto sighed. He was bored, and Umberto disliked being bored. It was about time for another visit to Signora Albertoni's apartment in the Via Sistina. *She* never bored him. Not when she stood tall and Aryan in long black boots and black silk stockings, a lacy suspender belt cutting into the flesh of her strong thighs, her blonde hair flying around her flushed face, as she let him whip her with any one of the assorted implements which she kept for her clients' pleasure.

Five minutes later the housekeeper fluttered in nervously. 'It's the telephone for you; I think it's America.' When she smiled her face looked almost pretty. America. He knew how she'd love to go to America. So would he. He yearned for it. Maybe he would, now that the picture was a success.

When he'd been in LA, Umberto had signed with the William Morris Agency, unconcerned that they represented almost three hundred producers worldwide. His ego was big enough to stand the competition because he knew he had produced a great picture. Everyone in Rome had said so. Umberto was a man who had never lacked a highly developed sense of his own worth. Even though he was ugly, he thought himself irresistible, witty and cultured. It was everyone else's stupidity that they couldn't seem to see it.

He opened one of the shutters and glanced outside at all the tourists milling about the Spanish Steps, cursing to himself that they were ruining his beautiful neighbourhood with their loud voices and their cameras.

Gia brought him the telephone and he heard the crackle of the long-distance line as Abe, his agent, came on the line.

'Hi, Umberto, how ya doing?'

'I'm doing fine, Abe, just fine. What's the latest news on the movie?'

'Picture's doing great business in Europe as you know, Hubie baby. I'm sure you've seen *Variety*. We've had some interest in you here too,' he said.

'Really?' Umberto lit his cigar, his fat face beaming. 'Any of the majors?'

'Well, not exactly the majors, but there's been some independent interest – Roger Corman, for instance.'

'Roger Corman!' Umberto spluttered. 'He makes horror films, for Christ's sake – I'm beyond that now. I told you, Abe, that after *La Città Perduta* I want to produce something in Hollywood – haven't you been trying?'

'We're trying, we're trying,' said Abe in the Hollywood agent's usual semi-placatory tone which they used on actors and producers alike. It didn't really matter a fig to Abe whether Umberto Scrofo made a film in America or not. Producers grew on palm trees in Hollywood; they hardly needed to import them from Europe.

Umberto's film was a success in Europe, but it had caused little excitement in America. It couldn't even get distribution. Abe, overworked and underpaid, was not about to go out of his way to push Scrofo. He was just one of thousands of William Morris clients, and this was simply a bread-and-butter call.

'If you read the European grosses in *Variety*,' Umberto asked, 'why don't you tell everyone about them, for fuck's sake?'

'Yeah, yeah, we told 'em it's a great picture, real great. We're tryin' to get it to Cannes for the festival, you know. I just want you to understand that we're working hard on a whole lot of things, Umberto,' the agent said easily. 'A whole bunch of things. Something could happen very soon, believe me. Just keep the faith, sweetheart, keep the faith.'

'I am a good producer, Abe, maybe even a *great* producer,' Umberto said coldly. 'Not only *Oggi* but *Gente* and *Tempo* said I am the new De Laurentiis – and those putzes in Hollywood – Makopolis, Cohn, Zanuck – they wouldn't even go to *see* my movie.'

'I know, I know, Umberto baby,' said Abe soothingly. 'Just be patient, something'll come up – something big – so hold on for a little longer, be patient, we'll get a picture for you soon. Listen, I gotta go now. We'll keep in touch. *Ciao* for now, baby.'

'*Ciao*, Abe,' said Umberto crossly as he banged down the receiver. He swallowed his iced cappuccino with a scowl. If this picture was so big in Europe, why wasn't America interested? It had become his obsession to make an American film, to be an important man in Hollywood. To be up for an Oscar, to go to parties at Jack Warner's, Ray Stark's and Charlie Feldman's. He had adored the Makopolis Christmas bash. It was a stinging blow to his ego that the excellent reviews for *La Città Perduta* hadn't led to anything in the States. But he wasn't going to sit around and feel sorry for himself. He had three European projects on the boards, and he was dedicating himself passionately to them.

'Fuck America,' he said to himself, rubbing the itching scar on his neck. 'Who needs them? I'll stay here.' Better a big fish in a small pond . . .

He gazed now at a beautifully lit Manet which hung on the pale gold damask-covered wall. This picture always gave him enormous pleasure, although the blonde girl in it vaguely reminded him of that whore who'd tried to kill him at the Ritz. Maybe he'd find her one day. Then he would exact the revenge he'd dreamed of so often. Meanwhile, he had motion pictures to make.

3

'I could live like this for ever,' chuckled Bluey Regan. 'Who needs the movie business when you've got a boat?'

The Irish-American, Bluey Regan, had been an assistant director since the talkies began. As he would constantly remind people, there was nothing he didn't know about the picture business. Full of life, always cheerful, he was a director's dream, and Nick Stone valued him immensely as his right-hand-man; what Nick didn't know, Bluey would.

Nick agreed with Bluey. It was perfect. Nothing was more exhilarating than the camaraderie between men on a boat.

It had been thirty-six hours since they'd left Los Angeles marina on a cold, misty morning. The seas were a sulking, churning mass in which a hundred-foot ketch had great difficulty manoeuvring just to get out of the port. The *Jezebel* with its crew of five had travelled some fifteen hundred miles in this bad weather. In spite of Nick's Greek boyhood as a fisherman and a love for the sea which matched Bluey's, he had succumbed to bouts of *mal de mer*. But this was all behind them now; the icy grey Californian Pacific had gradually turned blue as they sailed closer to the tropics. Both men were bronzed, fit and muscled as they stood at the helm taking turns to steer, caught up in an easy flow of jokes and conversation.

Bluey was forty-eight, with hair bleached yellow-white by the sun and wrinkled skin sunburned to the colour of caramel. His blue eyes danced with humour; he was never happier than when sailing on a trip like this. He was in a state of total relaxation, tinged faintly with the anticipation of the work ahead.

Nick was less sanguine. Against his will, he'd been persuaded by Bluey to make the trip down to Acapulco by boat. Much as he adored the sea, his first instincts had been to fly down, as he had much to do and many decisions to make before shooting started.

But his first assistant had been adamant. 'Heck, Niko, it takes almost as long to fly to the damned place as sail. First, you've gotta drive to Tijuana on that shit road that takes at *least* six or seven hours. Then you grab a broken-down, two-engine plane left over from *Wings* – Richard Arlen's probably still the pilot. When you finally get to Mexico City, ya gotta stay overnight, and there's so much crazy fuckin' night life there you'll end up with a hangover the next day that'll make your teeth fall out, which is when you'll have to take Aero Nervoso de Mexico, or whatever the fuck it's called, and boy, oh boy, will you be needing a handful of their sick bags then, kid.'

Nick could feel himself smiling as Bluey went on.

'I'll tell you the truth, Nick, you won't get me on *any* plane that hasn't got a good ole American pilot in the cockpit with at least five years' service in the US of A Air Force.' He smiled beguilingly. Nick was laughing now.

'Come with me on the *Jezebel*, kiddo – you'll have four days to relax, work on the script, you'll arrive in *great* shape, and I promise I won't keep you up drinking all night.'

The crew, all Bluey's buddies, doubled as bodyguards, companions or valets when they weren't being stewards or cooks. Bluey's 'boys' had been together for years so the atmosphere was one of a close fraternity, in which practical jokes and laughter were the order of the day.

Nick was worried about his line producer, Zachary Domino, who hadn't been well recently. Zack was sixty-eight and tired. With more than fifty years' experience, starting as a runner on some early Chaplin films, graduating to camera assistant on Mary Pickford features, then assistant director in the twenties with Clara Bow in *Red Hair* for First National Pictures, he was an excellent, knowledgeable and tough producer. He understood every aspect of the movie business and Nick was looking forward to learning a great deal from him. In fact he needed him badly. This was Nick's first major block-buster movie, and everyone, not only in the studio but in Hollywood, would be carefully watching the results of this one. If it was a flop, he would be back to directing *Bobby Soxers in Space*, and then only if he was lucky. If MCCP lost its bets on *Cortez* he would probably never work again.

So Nick was understandably edgy about *Cortez*. He knew many people at the studio didn't want him to direct it, considering him more of a boy-wonder cult director, in spite of the fact that the two pictures he'd directed had been box-office successes. There were so many other directors they preferred. George Cukor had been first choice, followed by David Lean and Fred Zinnemann. But dear old Uncle Spyros, waving his nepotism like a tattered flag, had insisted on using Nick, and since he was the ultimate arbitrator, the studio had had to capitulate – for the moment.

MCCP's administrators couldn't believe that Nick was capable of handling this huge assignment. He was only twenty-seven. This picture needed a man of immense experience, a director used to dealing with thousands of extras, handling fragile star temperaments, coping with the thousand decisions which needed to be made daily on a picture this size. They didn't believe that Nick could do it, and they were waiting to be proved right. But Sypros had great faith that Nick would do an excellent job on this film, particularly with Zachary Domino as line producer to help him. Good old Uncle Spyros – he'd come through at last.

Bluey threw an affectionate arm around his friend's shoulder as he expertly handled the tiller with the other.

'What's the matter, Niko?'

'I just hope Zack holds up,' Nick replied quietly. 'I read the doctor's insurance report, Bluey. He smokes sixty a day, drinks like a fish, and he's had a heart murmur for years. But he's still one helluva great producer and we need him with us on this.'

'Don't worry, kid, Zack's a *fighter* – tougher than an army boot with rusty nails in it. He'll have whipped everyone in shape, kicked their fat asses, and got all the wheels in motion on location by the time we arrive. Stop worrying, Nick – everything's gonna be okay.'

On the flights all the way from Los Angeles, Dominique had kept up a nonstop stream of excited chatter. Her girlish enthusiasm increased the closer they came to Acapulco. The trip had taken almost two days and Agathe felt that she would scream if Dominique didn't stop babbling. The girl had bought every single movie magazine at the airport, and had scanned them all intently for any photographs of the stars who might be in *Cortez* or vacationing in Acapulco while they were making the movie there.

Agathe's head was splitting with one of the migraine headaches which were becoming more prevalent lately, but despite her telling Dominique that she was feeling terrible and needed to be quiet, the girl didn't stop to draw breath.

The noise of the plane's engines exacerbated Agathe's headache and she had absolutely no interest in looking at the celebrity photographs which Dominique insisted on pointing out to her.

'Look – *voilà* – Julian Brooks. Ooh, wow, Agathe, he is *magnifique*, *n'est-ce pas?* A really cool guy.'

Agathe snatched the magazine out of Dominique's lap. Magnificent was an understatement, she thought. He was a god; a giant among men, a true living Adonis. The pit of her stomach churned as she feasted her eyes on his glorious dark perfection. His arm was around some woman, probably his latest leading lady.

'The fiancée,' Dominique said, jabbing the photograph with her finger. 'He's now engaged. She's beautiful, too, don't you think?'

Fingers of ice curled around Agathe's heart. Fiancée? Julian was engaged? Who was she? Agathe stared at the woman, who was in profile, her long dark hair almost obscuring her face, but from the way Julian was looking at her they were obviously mad about each other.

Viciously, Agathe threw the magazine back to Dominique. '*Tais-toi*, Dominique,' she snapped. 'I'm not interested at all in these movie stars. Rest now and stop this chattering, you've got important days ahead of you.'

She closed her eyes and tried to sleep, but a jealous disappointment gripped her whenever she thought of Julian and the woman, robbing her of rest. How *could* he? How could Julian be marrying someone else *now*, now that Agathe was so close to being with him at last? How could he be doing this to her?

4

As soon as they arrived at the Villa Vera, Nick called Elektra, who was thrilled to hear his voice. Then he unpacked, showered, changed and within twenty minutes was sitting in one of the suites which had been turned into a production room. His production staff were assembled around a long table – art directors, set designers, costumiers, assistant directors, stunt coordinators, editors, the writers – that baleful-looking New York couple, the Frankovitches –and most important of all, Zachary Domino. Zack's eyes were weary, his shoulders stooped, and he chain-smoked Camels with nicotine-stained fingers.

'How are you feeling, *amigo?*' Nick asked.

'Not so hot today.' Zack's smile was half-hearted. 'But don't worry, I think it's just a touch of Montezuma's famous revenge. He's probably mad at us for doing his life story.'

The crew all chuckled, except for the costume designer, Kittens, who looked anxious.

'Montezuma's revenge doesn't last for three weeks, Zack,' she said, then aside to Nick, 'He's been feeling bad for a while, Nicky. We've been worried.'

Nick clenched his fists. Jesus, he'd only been in the place for an hour and already everyone was concerned about the main cog in his wheel.

'I *told* him to take Pepto-Bismol and to eat less meat,' said Shirley Frankovitch impatiently, as though it was all his own fault. 'But he wouldn't listen, would he, Irving?'

'No, dear,' said Irving. 'He wouldn't.' Irving spoke little, his mind spinning constantly with new and different ideas for characters and situations in *Cortez*. Half the time he didn't listen to Shirley at all. Her embarrassing scene at the party had caused him to become more aware than ever of what a vulgarian his wife was. He didn't like to think about it.

Irving glanced out of the window of the second-floor suite. The sky was the softest blue, tinged apricot by a sun which was beginning to sink behind one of the curving hills. Irving sipped his drink, imagining what the effect of coconut milk on the taste buds of his hero would have been when he first reached La Roqueta island. He looked at the palm trees, their branches a vivid green and swaying softly in the gentle breeze. Abundant and luscious foliage grew in the hotel courtyard. Acapulco was a green, tropical paradise and the variety and beauty of its plant life were a continual source of wonder to Irving. He wasn't really listening to Zack, who had been talking about some of the many technical problems which they'd discovered in transporting their cameras and equipment on to La Roqueta.

But Irving was brought back to reality when Zack announced that the studio wanted the scene in which Cortez first makes love to the beautiful princess to be much more erotic – but within the bounds of censorship. The MCCP top brass insisted on sex, lust, sensual romance. Barrages of telephone calls and cables were constantly arriving from Hollywood. They wanted perfection, and it was up to Irving and Shirley to make the script the best goddam script of the decade. As writers, they could only do so much – because once the script fell into the hands of the actors and director, God only knew what damage could be done to 'great' dialogue. The Frankovitches were old campaigners on the Hollywood trail. Irving had seen two of his scripts destroyed by the studio and several others badly butchered, so he and Shirley intended to be around all the time, even though a writer on a shooting set was about as welcome as a nun in a whorehouse.

The heat in the production office became more oppressive as the sun sank lower. The room was stifling, and even the large white ceiling fan made little difference. The men were all shirtsleeved, sweat glistening on their faces; Shirley wore a muumuu, one of many which she had bought at the local market. Shirley adored a bargain, and clothes here cost a fraction of what they would in New York or Beverly Hills. The muumuu was the perfect solution for her, as her weight had ballooned still further in the past months.

She glanced at Zachary Domino and wondered how on earth he was going to survive eighteen weeks of tough location work around beaches, mosquito-ridden swamps, forests and rivers.

Zack lit another Camel in spite of doctor's orders. In Los Angeles he had visited his doctor for the usual studio check-up. Dr Zolotos had assured him that he was in fairly good health for his age. 'Just remember to take a salt pill every morning, never drink the water – in spite of what the Mexican government may say, it's poison! Stay away from raw fruit and vegetables, especially lettuce, don't exert yourself too much, and stop *smoking*!'

Easier said than done. When you were line producing one of the major motion pictures of the decade – quite impossible. He was practically living on cigarettes and coffee. Zack sipped some salty-tasting mineral water. Everyone was smoking, no one apparently giving a thought to what they were doing to their lungs or heart. Zachary inhaled deeply, trying to contribute to the discussions, although he was stifling.

Across the table, Shirely glared at him with her cunning, laser-beam eyes. There was no love lost between the two. He thought her a pushy shrew who constantly and irritatingly interfered during production meetings. She was also a lush, and Nick had told him what a fool she'd made of herself at Spyros' party. Zack tried to explain to the Frankovitches that their latest rewrites would be much too expensive to shoot.

'Money, money, money – that's all you ever fucking *think* about, Zack,' Shirley suddenly yelled at him. 'This is *art*, you fucking moron. *Art!*'

'You don't *need* two hundred and fifty extras watching Cortez and Princess Isabella strolling along the seashore.' Zack tried to remain calm. 'It's supposed to be lyrical, romantic. We don't need a bunch of fucking voyeurs standing around them just staring.' He raised his voice, his efforts to stay calm failing miserably. 'I'm taking them *out* – do you understand, *out*. *No* extras. And that's that – *finito*.' He hated shouting matches, but knew he had to win this point, otherwise the Frankovitches would walk all over him.

Nick nodded his approval. 'I agree. I'm sorry, Shirley. Zack's right, we don't need 'em, so that's that.'

Shirley was absolutely furious. She wasn't about to give up her two hundred and fifty extras without a fight. *No one* messed with Shirley Frankovitch. She was a star writer. She looked over to Irving for support, but he just shrugged. Although Irving possessed infinitely more talent than she, he'd subjugated it much too often to her pleading banshee wails, her sly feminine wiles, her insidious whining.

It meant a great deal to Shirley to win. She wanted *her* script to be the one that was shot. She wanted the studio to know that *they*, the fabulous team of Shirley and Irving Frankovitch, were the most brilliant writers on the Hollywood scene. But it was evident that at this lengthy production meeting they weren't winning. As the meeting continued many of their most original, daring and innovative ideas were shot down – by both Nick and Zack. The meeting, like the room, was becoming increasingly heated. Expletives were bandied about and the air hung heavy with the smell of hostility, sweat and cigarette smoke.

Irving raised a laconic eyebrow in Shirley's direction. They would thrash this out later, privately. He sighed, remembering fondly his rapport with Umberto Scrofo during the shooting of *La Città* in Rome a year ago. Irving had praised Umberto to Shirley highly – he had been sympathetic to everything that Frankovitch had wanted – and Umberto Scrofo had been more than eager to cultivate the most important screenwriter in Hollywood.

Even though Shirley had made a complete fool of herself at the Makopolis party, it hadn't stopped Scrofo from wining and dining the Frankovitches during his Los Angeles trip. She found Scrofo amusing, liked his acerbic wit and bitter comments which perfectly matched her own cynical attitude to the world. She thought that his *La Città Perduta* was excellent and had invited Spyros Makopolis to a screening of it, but at the last moment the old Greek had cancelled and she had been unable to get him to reschedule.

Scrofo agreed with Shirley that writing was absolutely the most important ingredient in film making and that everything and everyone else was secondary. It didn't matter if the movie had the most shimmering stars or the most elaborate sets, if it wasn't on the page the public wasn't going to see it on the screen.

Nicholas Stone shifted uneasily in his chair. His instincts were turning out to be right. Shirley Frankovitch was a meddling bitch, and her husband was a pathetic, pitiable excuse for a man. He thought their script was good in parts, but much too overwritten, too flowery, too excessive for what he wanted. He envisioned a simple tale of adventure and discovery, of the battle of wills between Cortez and Montezuma. He wanted a simple sensual love story between Cortez and Princess Isabella. He wanted to show the untouched beauty of the Mexican country, the incomparable lagoons, the ravishing sunsets. He wanted to reveal real people with real emotions, ambitions, passions. The Frankovitches didn't seem to want this at all. Their script was one gargantuan battle after another, an endless array of wounded, bleeding men being dispatched by the point of the hero's sword; scenes of sticky passion so trite that they'd be out of place in a shopgirl's weekly. And now, the sight of Zachary, his most important support, obviously unwell, was not a promising omen.

Suddenly Zack called a halt. The production office had become so unbearably hot that tempers were frayed to the boiling point.

'Let's sleep on everything, boys and girls,' he said quietly. 'We've still got a few days before shooting starts to sort out our problems. Tomorrow, ten A.M. sharp, we'll have a read-through with some of the cast. Until then, let's get some rest.'

Inès was suffering a mixture of jet lag and morning sickness which seemed to continue well into the afternoon and early evening. She was sleeping so soundly that Julian decided to accept Nick's invitation to dinner on the terrace of a restaurant away from the Villa Vera. They wanted to escape from the prying eyes, the clacking tongues and the electric tensions which always fill the air before a movie begins. The cool verandah looked down to the curve of Acapulco Bay where the ink-black water seemed striped with thin slivers of luminous silver and a faint breeze blew in from the sea.

They dined on *ceviche* – raw fish marinated with onions, lemon and avocado – giant prawns, charcoal-grilled, and a great deal of tequila and beer. They chain-smoked as Nick shared his problems with Julian, who listened attentively, becoming increasingly aware that Nick was facing some serious hurdles.

'If Zachary is totally on your side,' he said, 'then what's the difficulty? You're the director – he's the producer – you've both got the final say, after all. Tell the Frankovitches to get stuffed.'

Nick stared at him with a worried frown. 'I don't know,' he said. 'I just can't figure it out. I don't think Zack's up to par, and that bitch Shirley is out to have his balls for *huevos rancheros* on her breakfast tray. I want to make this film as realistic and as modern as possible. I want the audience to *identify* with Cortez. Oh I know he's a sixteenth-century man but I want him to be a man of the moment – a today kinda guy. I know that's what audiences are looking for now. They've had too much escapist crap, musicals, biblical epics. They've gotta believe this man is made of the same flesh and blood as them. I just hope the studio isn't going to try and sabotage it. I think the Frankovitches have got enormous pull with Spyros in spite of the bitch getting plastered at his party. Jesus, Julian, some of their new dialogue is unspeakable – and a couple of the scenes! Straight out of Grand Guignol.'

Julian nodded. 'I don't believe they're as bad as you think, Nick. I got the rewrites earlier this evening, but I'll look them over again tonight. So what are you going to do about all of this?'

'Tonight, my friend, I'm going to get very drunk.' Nick drained his tequila with a wicked smile. 'Then tomorrow, like Scarlett O'Hara, I'm gonna think about all of this, and work my ass off to get it right. Maybe it's just my old Greek instincts working, pal, but I'm worried.'

5

Dominique arrived late next afternoon. She looked around her luxurious hotel room and giggled, 'What a dump,' giving her imitation of Bette Davis in *Petrified Forest*. She pranced to the window and gasped at the view. Thick pink-flowered bougainvillea curled around the stone terrace, the ocean glittered invitingly and the brilliant cobalt sky, which shaded to a bluish grey as it met the curving hills surrounding Acapulco Bay, made the alluring picture complete.

Dominique's portable record player was in her luggage, along with her much treasured box of records. She flipped through them, finally choosing one of her favourites, Edith Piaf singing 'La Vie en Rose', then lay back on the sofa feeling gloriously grown-up and romantic as she thought about Gaston's latest love letter and the naughty things it said.

Feeling a sudden surge of energy, she got up to look through her suitcases for something to wear to the pool. The studio had provided her with plenty of clothes for the many photographic layouts they expected of her. Dozens of coordinated summer costumes had been carefully packed in layers of tissue paper by the wardrobe department and she riffled through them, humming happily.

Putting on a tiny pink gingham bikini with a matching short skirt, she grabbed a straw hat and her script, and skipped down the cool stone steps towards the inviting azure swimming pool. Thankfully, Agathe was sound asleep. The tropics didn't agree with her and she was exhausted after the long flights from Los Angeles and Mexico City. But Dominique loved being on her own, particularly when she had new pages of her script to study. It was just after two o'clock, and most of the Villa Vera residents were at lunch. There was nobody at the swimming pool except for a lackadaisical Mexican boy who was removing crumpled, damp towels from the deckchairs.

Placing her towel on a white-painted chaise longue, Dominique put on her sunglasses, perched her straw hat on top of her head and gazed contentedly around. Gorgeous, there was no question of that. The pool was edged with tiny blue and white square tiles and looked truly inviting. It was set into reddish-pink, rough hewn stone, and surrounded by huge white pots of flaming bougainvillea, their colour dazzling – lilac, mauve, fuchsia, cyclamen, shocking pink – a riot of reds and purples. Beyond the pool lay a garden dominated by tall palm trees, whose thick leaves gave shelter to a wide grassy lawn and tropical flowerbeds. Floating on the pool were dozens of white, red and yellow hibiscus blossoms. A tulip tree, its flaming red torchwood branches standing like bayonets, shaded most of the far end of the pool. Further away were sharp spires of banana trees, hibiscus bushes, frangipani and an occasional banyan tree with its huge, ancient twisted roots, an ideal shelter for the tropical birds that flew about happily in the jasmine-scented air.

In spite of the heat, Dominique could feel a slight breeze as she lay under a blue and white striped umbrella. A smiling waiter appeared, asking in Spanish if she wanted a drink, Latin eyes drinking in her lissome body. A flash of lust crossed his adolescent features. Dominique was getting very used to men responding to her youthful sex appeal. She asked for a Coke and lay back comfortably, the *Cortez* script in front of her. The only sound was the splashing of water into a small stone pool around which enormous velvet-winged butterflies hovered and danced. The sound was soporific and soothing.

Suddenly, from down on the beach, came the music of a mariachi, the gay chants of a Mexican band which had struck up. She'd heard that Acapulco nightlife was exciting, although nothing compared to that of Hollywood. She knew that Lana Turner, Ty Power and Errol Flynn were all staunch aficionados of Acapulco, coming here regularly. Perhaps she might even meet them.

From his secluded terrace Julian Brooks was able to look down at Dominique as she buried her glossy head in the script.

In the time he had been with Inès he'd been as dutiful and loving as a man could be, never tempted once by the many offers to which his striking looks and fame made him prone. Inès was attentive, beautiful, kind – what more could he want? What more indeed, he thought, except now the sight of Dominique's ravishing face, waist-length black hair and honey-coloured limbs was suddenly a powerful stimulant. Most intriguing of all was her resemblance to Inès. She seemed like a younger version, with the same appealing mixture of sensuality and innocence. Odd, perhaps, but this similarity made Dominique an object of great interest to Julian.

He pulled his panama hat down further over his eyes, watching intently as she stood up and peeled off her tiny skirt, revealing a bottom so round and peachlike in her bikini that he caught his breath.

Stretching unselfconsciously, unaware of her admirer up on his terrace, she ran her fingers through her long black hair, removed her sunglasses and dipped her feet in the pool. The sun, filtering through the leaves of an old palm tree, dappled her shoulders. Thinking about the bathtub scene she would have to film next week, and not wanting to have any white marks on her shoulders, she slipped off the straps of her bikini top. She then looked around to make sure no one was lurking and undid the hooks, tossing it to the edge of the pool, then she slid slowly into the water until it just barely covered her breasts.

Julian's mouth was dry. This was one of the most erotic little scenes he'd witnessed for a long time. He was, after all, only a man – a fact which the discomfort inside his immaculately cut linen trousers confirmed. He thought he'd seen few more glorious sights. This golden-skinned goddess, almost naked in a swimming pool, wet black hair flowing around her shoulders, was all too deliciously and enchantingly exciting . . .

Up to her waist in the pool, out of the corner of her eye Dominique had become aware that she was being observed. She lazily splashed water over her shoulders, enjoying the coolness on her hot skin. A smile crossed her face as she realized that it was Looks Brooks who was watching her beneath his panama hat, and she started to sing 'La Vie en Rose' in her best Edith Piaf voice.

6

Agathe was unable to sleep. A full moon shone through the bamboo window slats, and the ceiling fan did little but churn the sluggish air. She was roasting, her cotton nightgown soaked with sweat, her mouth like dry cardboard. The plastic carafe next to the bed was dry as a bone. She got up to get some water from the bathroom tap, then remembered all the dire warnings she'd been given: *Do not drink the water.* Searching through her valise, she found nothing to drink except for a bottle of cough medicine.

Slipping off her nightgown, she threw on some cotton shorts, a short-sleeved shirt and rope-soled espadrilles. Grabbing the room key and a handful of pesos, she glanced at the seductive moon suspended over the black sand, closed the door quietly and ran down to the lobby. It was empty except for a fat concierge in a white singlet dozing over a copy of *Hola*. She asked him in French and English where she might find something to drink, but he understood nothing until she spoke the magic words Coca-Cola. His greasy face, slippery with sweat, perked up as he jabbered away in Spanish, pointing across the road to the beach.

There was little traffic on the dark road. She heard the occasional *fut-fut* of a motorcycle, and in the distance mariachis playing. From some nearby houses came exciting-sounding Spanish love songs which made her senses quicken. How she'd love to dance to that music. How she would whirl and twirl – if only Julian could be with her too. She could show him how well she danced. He must be here in Acapulco by now.

The beach was deserted, the sand pockmarked with thousands of footprints. There were a few thatched-roof beach huts on the sand, around which abandoned white-painted chairs and tables were clustered. A few yards away, a larger thatched hut boasted a flickering neon sign saying something incomprehensible in Spanish.

She would surely find a drink there, she thought, as she made for the light.

Four tough-looking Mexican men sat at a cigarette-scorched table, playing cards. Behind them were four tired hookers, their black hair and exotic Spanish dresses only emphasizing their state of fragile weariness. At the bar stood several equally truculent-looking men, most of them drunk. Agathe blushed, wishing she'd worn a bra and panties underneath her skimpy clothes. The barman looked less ferocious than the others.

'Coca-cola *por favor,*' she said quietly.

He unsmilingly passed her the bottle and a damp, chipped glass. She drank greedily, eyes downcast, and asked for another, while hostile eyes continued to stare at her.

She asked the barman if she could take the bottle with her, then, throwing some coins on to the zinc-topped bar, casually walked out, pretending not to hear remarks in Spanish from which she could make out the words *guapa* and *linda.* In spite of herself she felt flattered that the men had noticed her.

Once more enveloped by the sultry night, her thirst satisfied, a chilled drink in her hand and her adrenaline pumping, Agathe didn't feel like going back to the hotel yet. It was barely midnight. She would take a stroll along the beach.

In the distance she could see the lights of the town, and some brightly lit boats. She walked slowly along the shoreline, enjoying the sensation of the cool waves lapping at her feet, catching the scent of jasmine and the salty tang of the sea. She thought about the upcoming film with excitement. As Dominique's chaperone she knew that she was only a tiny cog in the wheel of *Cortez,* but still, she was important. Everyone was important, because she'd been told that filming was a group effort. But the most thrilling thing of all was that she would be near her Julian Brooks. She wondered if she would see him soon, if they would talk of mutual interests – of art, philosophy, religion. She knew that he must be a man of superior intellect to match those superior looks of his. She fingered the small crucifix which she always wore around her neck. The tiny amber beads on the fine silver chain were her talisman – her luck. Superstitiously she believed that if she didn't wear it, something unspeakable would happen to her.

Lost in reverie, she did not hear the muffled footsteps approaching behind her. Coarse hands grabbed her from behind and another pair clamped themselves over her mouth. There were two men – or three? – she couldn't tell. Their arms seemed to be everywhere. As wiry as her body was, there was no way she could overcome the combined strength of three men, try as she might. She heard hoarse drunken voices mocking her and, with a surge of fury, brought the bottle in her hand up behind her with all her strength. She heard a satisfying crack as it connected with a nose, and with a yelp, one was out of the fray, blood pumping from his nostrils. But there were still two holding her. One of them yanked at her blouse viciously as the other tried to pull off her shorts. They had loosened their grip on her mouth and she screamed desperately. 'Help . . . *à moi* . . . please help me.'

She could see the sharp stubble on their chins, their bloodshot eyes; smell their unwashed bodies, the beer on their breath. There was no doubt at all what they were trying to do. They threw her on to the sand, tearing off her shorts and shirt. She tried to crawl away, seeing in the moonlight that they were now unzipping their trousers. She was a thirty-one-year-old virgin, this couldn't be happening to her. Not after everything she'd been through in her life.

'No, *mon Dieu, no*,' she sobbed as one of the men tried to force his sweating hulk on top of her. With a dancer's dexterity she twisted her naked body away, scrabbling sideways over the sand like a demented crab. With trousers around their ankles, both men were at a momentary loss, which gave her the edge. Crying, shouting for help, she ran as fast as she could, hearing their heavy footsteps coming closer, closer, closer, gaining on her. However fast she ran, they were stronger and quicker. She knew she couldn't outrun them, it was a losing battle. She heard them cursing harshly, yelling with drunken rage as they were in danger of losing their prey – she could almost feel their blood lust. Where was everyone? Oh, sweet Jesus – was no one going to help her?

Three or four hundred yards away the pleasure boats were bobbing gently in the bay. She saw their lights, heard faint music, the gentle laughter of women. Some kind of civilization, but still so far away. She must get to the boats before these animals caught her –

she had to. She felt a hand grab her nude back, but slick with sweat, she twisted free. The thundering feet ran faster, she could smell the sour, garlicky stink of their last meal.

Julian was the first to hear the faint feminine cries. He'd spent the evening with Nick and Bluey on the *Jezebel*, discussing yet more problems: Zack's health, Shirley's subversive bitchery and various studio vendettas. Inès had decided to give Julian an evening out with the boys, and now he was eager to get back to her. Straining his eyes across the darkness he thought he saw a naked girl being chased by two ruffians.

'Good God,' he whistled, running down the clattering gangplank, calling out for Nick and Bluey. 'Damsel in distress, boys. Let's go.'

As he got closer, Julian saw it was that weird Agathe woman, Dominique's chaperone. What the blazes was she doing on the beach at this hour? Time to ask questions later.

With Nick and Bluey hot on his heels, Julian launched himself at the nearest would-be rapist. The trio made short work of Agathe's attackers with a few well-placed kicks and punches. It was all over in a matter of seconds, and the Mexicans ran off shouting empty threats.

Agathe sank to the sand, trembling with fear and shame, trying in vain to cover her naked body. Tears were streaming down her face, and she was covered with painful cuts and bruises.

'Here.' Julian took of his shirt and handed it to her. 'Put this on. We'll go back to the boat. You need a drink, my dear.'

She put it on quickly, thankful that it was long enough to cover her thighs. Nick went off to retrieve her clothes as Julian helped her down the beach. She looked at her watch. It was only five past twelve. Everything had happened so terrifyingly fast. What would those men have done to her if Julian had not saved her? She couldn't bear to think of it, or of what he must think of her. He must think her insane.

'You must be insane,' he said with a gentle smile, putting his arm around her trembling back. 'What on earth were you doing strolling on the beach at night? Don't you know how dangerous it is?'

'I was thirsty,' she said in a small voice, realizing how ridiculous it sounded.

'Well' – he smiled – 'that doesn't exactly explain a helluva lot, but come on board. You need a good stiff drink.'

He helped Agathe on to the deck of the *Jezebel*. She seemed so frail and vulnerable with that ice-white hair and skin; she obviously needed protection. Any woman who was stupid enough to wander alone at night on a Mexican beach could hardly be called mature. Old-fashioned feelings of responsibility stirred in him as he ushered her into the main cabin. She collapsed on to the sofa, tring to get her breath, and Julian strode over to the bar on which stood a vast array of bottles. He poured her a large drink which she sipped gratefully, the amber fluid warming her comfortingly. He smiled. She smiled shyly back, a frightened waif, dirty and bruised. What would Dominique say if she heard about her midnight stroll? She'd surely think she was no longer either fit or responsible enough to be a chaperone.

'Why don't you take a shower? – clean up, I'm sure you'll feel a lot better,' said Bluey. 'C'mon, I'll show you where the head is.'

'Thank you,' said Agathe, blushing as Julian's eyes smiled sympathetically into hers again.

Warm, invigorating needles of water tingled on her sore and aching body and she scrubbed away until she felt completely clean. Bluey's towels were rough and smelled strongly of camphor but they felt good; she was relieved to rid herself of the sand, the sweat and the touch of those rough, filthy, grasping hands. She pulled on her shorts, managing to just barely secure them with the loose top button, and Julian's shirt, tossing the remains of her own into the waste basket. There was a brush on the dressing table, and she tried to tame her tangled wet hair. She looked at herself in the mirror. Better. Although still frightened, at least she was no longer such a total wreck. She padded back into the salon, where Bluey, Nick and Julian were sitting with large drinks at a table strewn with yachting magazines and books. Julian stood up with a benevolent smile.

'Come and sit down, Agathe,' he said. 'You look done in, poor dear. Drink up.'

Agathe took another sip of her soothing drink, grimacing at the strength of it.

'Bluey's special remedy.' Bluey winked at her. 'Good for what ails you, sweetheart – seasickness, tummy upsets, first-day nerves on the set, whatever it is, the Bluey Special will cure it.'

'What is it?' she asked tentatively, liking the taste though she rarely drank anything alcoholic except for an occasional glass of wine.

'Ah-ha, that's a secret,' Julian said, smiling at her. She was such a strange, quiet girl, but she seemed sweet and terribly innocent, with her soulful eyes and tragic face. Certainly not his type, though he realized from the way she was looking at him that she could probably fall for him all too easily. Agathe seemed so demure – she even wore a little crucifix around her neck. But he could sense that there was something lurking beneath the surface, something strange about her – what was it? Oh, Lord, he could almost see the look of love growing in her eyes. It made him nervous. He'd never been in the business of hurting women nor of encouraging them in their fantasies. That he saved for the screen.

'Drink up,' he said looking at his watch. 'It's nearly one o'clock. We've all got to get up early for the reading tomorrow. And we don't want anyone to find out about what happened tonight, do we?' He winked conspiratorially at her. She smiled nervously but with a little more confidence.

'Oh, no, they would think I was such a fool – everyone warned me about going out alone. Please promise you won't tell anyone.'

'I promise, Agathe, so do the boys,' Julian said, his smile so gentle it seemed to her almost like a caress. 'It's our little secret, Agathe.' And she felt herself flush with pure happiness.

Agathe was too excited to sleep. In her humid room she hugged her pillow to her aching body and, closing her eyes in a kind of ecstasy, relived the enchanted hour that she'd spent with Julian. It had almost been worth being attacked, she mused, to have had her idol's attentions so intently focused on her. Her pulse fluttered as she remembered how his firm brown hand had gently stroked her hair away from her forehead. His shirt. She still wore the blue cotton shirt which he'd so gallantly taken off and given her. It smelled of him – of his Turkish cigarettes, the faint and far from unpleasant smell of his sweat mingled with a subtle trace of his aftershave.

She rubbed the loose shirt up and down her body, between her legs and across her breasts. She began to feel feverish as his face filled her imagination; in her mind, his eyes gazed into hers with tenderness and love. His bare chest streaked with rivulets of sweat was next to hers now . . . his muscular arms encircled her shoulders, his lips kissing her hair. She felt herself rising to peaks of pleasure which she'd never known before. Rocking from side to side, eyes tightly closed, with Julian's shirt squeezed between her legs, her body stiffened into a series of shuddering and glorious spasms of release as she breathed his name over and over again in the darkness.

7

Zachary Domino had achieved something which Hollywood believed to be impossible. He had a secret mistress.

He and Ramona Armande had enjoyed their on-again-off-again clandestine affair for more than five years. It suited them both. He was single, and even though Ramona was married, her husband was absent so much that few people had ever seen him in the flesh. Hollywood had always been intrigued by Ramona in all of her thirty years on the scene, but no real gossip had surfaced about her. No one really knew exactly how old she was, but she was certainly well into her fifties. Her face was almost unlined, however, her body lithe, and her sexual vigour that of someone half her age.

She and Zack were in her extraordinary villa on a hill above Acapulco Bay, their privacy guaranteed by a highly efficient security system of guards with German Shepherd dogs.

She had cooked dinner for him herself: chicken enchiladas, and his favourite – refried beans with tortillas, which she believed had aphrodisiacal qualities. She had given him a good claret to drink and a fat Havana cigar to smoke after dinner. Now they were discussing the film and especially her part in it. She was unhappy with her role and had accepted it only because parts for women her age were rather thin on the ground. Playing Dominique's mother deeply rankled her.

'I've been a star,' she complained. 'Such a big, big star, it's a *scandal* that all I play now is a supporting role.' She spat the 'supporting' from between her lips as if it were a piece of tobacco from the end of an untipped cigarette. 'I had a wonderful part in my Italian film – wonderful. I don't expect to play leads any more, but I wish I had more to do in this one.'

Zachary gently stroked her arm, looking hopefully towards the bedroom. He wanted to change the subject as quickly as possible.

He wanted to get laid, then go home to his own bed and study the script again. He wanted to get his rocks off and not listen to all her woes and complaints. Staying overnight with Ramona was taboo, on the off-chance that her husband might appear unexpectedly. Zack didn't feel like getting into yet another discussion about Ramona's career. He had had a bitch of a day. Between the appalling Shirley Frankovitch's continuous whining over the script, Irving supporting her with threats of returning to New York, Sir Crispin, who was playing King Montezuma, having a tantrum over his wig, the studio screaming about overheads, and the postponing of the first day's shooting until the script problems could be worked out, he'd had a real bellyful.

'Hell, let 'em go,' he'd insisted wearily to Nick earlier when both Frankovitches had flounced out of the room, slamming the door. 'We've got a halfway decent shooting script, we'll bring in someone else from Hollywood to rewrite certain scenes if it's necessary. We don't need 'em. Fuck the Frankovitches. They're more trouble than they're worth.' Nick had agreed with him; the two men were formidably strong allies.

Now Zack sighed. He desperately needed to forget all his problems in the arms of his sultry mistress. As if anticipating his needs she looked at him with a seductive simper and glided gracefully into her vast white marble bedroom. He quickly followed her.

After they finished making love, Ramona rose immediately from her bed and padded across rose-coloured rugs to her bathroom. There she deftly massaged Zachary's semen into the skin of her face and neck, an invaluable beauty tip which her friend Mae West had taught her years ago.

'Forget all those expensive face creams and fancy lotions, hon,' Mae had drawled. 'If guys are good for only one thing, it's that essence they produce. Don't forget, honey, they use us, we can use them – *I've* been doin' it for years!'

Ramona smiled as she thought of raunchy old Mae while Zack lay on the bed smoking his usual après-sex Camel, watching the tropical fish darting about in the aquarium which almost filled one entire wall of the bedroom. Idly Zack wondered about the whereabouts of

Ramona's husband, the White Russian Prince Ivor Kasinov who was even more mysterious than his wife. Why was he always so often away on business? No one had any idea what business the Prince was involved in, but he seemed to be colossally rich in cash and other assets – one of which was this magnificent mansion and its precious contents. Sheherazade was a palace in the tropical jungle. Made of onyx, marble, glass and stone, all supported by marble Corinthian columns brought from Italian quarries at phenomenal expense, the villa was like a Visconti film set.

Ramona had been married to Prince Kasinov for more than a decade. She had returned to Hollywood from making a movie in Vienna after the war with the diminutive Prince in tow. Hollywood bowed and scraped, impressed with Ramona's pedigree prize, and she had queened it in Beverly Hills for several years until the Prince had decided to move to Mexico for certain unexplained reasons. She then became the most celebrated society hostess in Mexico, an invitation to one of her parties much lusted after. She was throwing a gala next week – to launch *Cortez*. Dozens of Hollywood celebrities would be flying in, as well as the society and showbusiness press of the world.

Other than her intimates – of whom there were few – everyone who knew Ramona never called her anything but Princess. Unless she was working on a film – then she became more democratic. In some small way this compensated her for the decline in her movie career, as did her glittering parties and, of course, her lavish photo-layouts in *House and Garden* and *Vogue*. She was determined that this party would be the most dazzling to date.

Looking at the Cartier clock on the bedside table, Zack saw it was time for him to leave.

The key technical crew and main actors were congregated in one of the assembly rooms of the Villa Vera for the ten o'clock read-through. All were punctual, but Zack had not yet appeared – unusual, as he was always the first to arrive. The room was dominated by a huge oak table around which everyone could sit comfortably. A silver urn dispensed coffee, and there were bottles of mineral water on the table. Nick glanced at his watch nervously; it was nearly a quarter past ten. He wanted to give a short motivating rah-rah speech to everyone, but he needed Zack's support. Where was he?

'I think I'll call him,' Nick said to Bluey. 'He's *never* late.'

There was no answer from Zack's room and Nick looked over at Bluey with concern.

'I don't understand this at all,' he muttered.

'Hang up. Let's start anyway,' Shirley's nagging voice rasped. 'We don't need to wait for him. C'mon, Irving and I have written a coupla new scenes – we want to read them to you.'

'No, we can't do that, we must have him here, we need him. It's just not right,' Nick replied.

He looked over at Shirley, whose face was puffy and already shiny with perspiration. God, she was a malevolent bitch, and a drunkard into the bargain – a lethal combination.

Julian was chatting with Agathe whose eager black eyes never once left his face; although she was blushing she still managed to retain a pinched, white look.

Then Dominique sidled up to Julian, green eyes sparkling, perfectly shaped breasts pointing at his chest. 'Did you sleep well, Julian?' she asked with a sly smile, wondering if he had dreamed of her.

'Like a log.' He smiled, aware more than ever of her fresh young beauty. Her resemblance to the young Inès was truly striking. They were the same height, had the same delicious oval face, small nose, sensual lips – but this little girl was years younger. Jail bait. 'Don't even *think* about it, Julian,' said his conscience. 'It could never be worth it.'

'I'm *so* excited,' she sighed. 'This is going to be a *thrilling* film, *n'est-ce pas*? And I'm so honoured to be playing opposite you, Julian.' She was giving him the sexual come-on. He had never been wrong about female vibrations before, but this one was only a teenager! But what a teenager. He remembered the sight of her luscious body in the swimming pool and his eyes flitted appreciatively over her breasts, barely covered by a flimsy pink and white blouse. 'Yes, it certainly is going to be exciting,' he said. He felt that disturbing stirring again, and moved away from her to the coffee urn.

'Yes – well, I'm looking forward to working with you too, Dominique my dear,' he said as he poured himself a cup of coffee while the girl smiled secretly and Agathe glared at her jealously.

'I'm going to Zack's room – find out what's going on.' Nick banged down the phone. 'I'll be right back,' he said, and strode out.

The cast and crew started to gossip and chatter. Dominique monopolized Julian's attention again on the pretext of discussing the script, completely cutting Agathe off from the possibility of any further conversation with him. She went to the window to stare sulkily at the view and to relive last night with Julian on the boat. Suddenly the telephone rang harshly. Bluey answered it.

'Oh, my God, Jesus Christ – no, I don't believe it.' Bluey's face hardened and he leaned against the wall for support. The room became hushed. 'I'll be right there. Have you called the doctor?'

'What on earth's the matter?' Julian asked.

'It's Zacharay, he's – er – not well, it seems.' The normally unflappable assistant director was trying not to sound flustered. 'I'm going up to see if I can help.'

'What do you mean, "not well"?' Julian insisted. 'What's wrong with him?'

'I don't know, I'll go and see. Don't worry, I'll be right back,' he added as he raced out.

The group began muttering. This sounded ominous. A film crew has a sixth sense about one of their own, and they realized something must have happened to Zachary. Something which could affect the movie.

His face the colour of chalk, his eyes open, blank and staring, Zachary was lying on the bed. He had obviously tried to get up because of the strange angle of his body, but hadn't been able to make it.

'He's dead,' said Nick numbly. 'Oh Christ.'

'Jesus,' Bluey gasped. 'How the hell did it happen?'

'I don't know,' sighed Nick. 'I suppose it must have been his heart.'

He felt for Zachary's pulse but there was nothing, the body was cold. He'd obviously been dead for some time – maybe several hours.

Julian came in, immediately followed by the frantic hotel manager, who crossed himself, raising his eyes to heaven when he saw the corpse. Death was terrible for business in the hotel trade. He wondered if they might be able to hush it up. They wouldn't be able to rent this room for a while, that was for sure.

'Oh, God,' Julian groaned when he saw Zack's body. 'Poor old chap.'

Nick nodded slowly, staring at Zachary, his eyes brimming with tears. He had seen his mother, father, baby brothers and sisters, almost all of his family, in death and he had always tried not to weep, but somehow the sight of this stalwart old man, who had meant so much to him, who had helped him and guided him, touched Nick deeply. Tears ran down his cheeks as he heard Bluey's shocked voice saying, 'Well, Jesus H. Christ! Who the hell is going to produce this fucking movie now?'

Shirley Frankovitch was rapidly on the telephone to Spyros Makopolis, but he had already heard the news half an hour earlier and had called an emergency meeting of the MCCP board.

'I know we need a new line producer down here right away,' she said in her gravelly voice. 'I've just had a *great* idea, Spyros, it's simply *great*.'

'And what's that?' Spyros asked. He'd always had a soft spot for Shirley. Her films had made the studio pots of money. She was smart, despite being a woman, an ugly one at that and a bit of a drunk, but he admired her talent, especially her undoubted ability to make the coffers of the box office rattle.

'Umberto Scrofo,' Shirley said triumphantly. 'He produced *La Città Perduta*, the film Irving wrote in Rome last year. He really is a *wonderful* producer, Spyros darling, very talented. Irving can't speak highly enough about him. You met him at your party, remember? He came with Ramona. He's intelligent, cultured; he has innovative brilliant ideas. He's great with budgets, understands cast and crew, and I think you can get him cheap.'

'Well, I was thinking of Gregory Ratoff,' Spyros said after a slight pause. 'But I'm told he's shooting in Egypt. We've already contacted the agents for Spears Farnsworth and Jack Hall, but they're both probably booked. We can't afford to waste any more time, Shirley. It's already costing us more than ten thousand dollars a day just to keep everyone in Acapulco. Our studio has no acceptable producers available at the moment.'

Shirley shot back with a triumphant 'Well, use Scrofo – take a chance on someone new for a change – someone who isn't part of your family.' She bit her lip after she'd said that, realizing she had probably gone too far, but Spyros answered as if he hadn't really been listening.

'How do you know if this Scrofo guy is free?' he asked.

'I spoke to him last week in Rome,' Shirley lied. 'He's a good friend of ours, Spyros, he's available, and I *know* he's ready to do an important American movie. You saw *La Città*, didn't you, darling?' she asked, knowing he hadn't.

'Sure, it was great.' It was his turn to lie and, covering the receiver, he hissed at his assistant to find a print of *La Città* right away.

'And he brought it in for under a million,' Shirley persisted. 'With that amazing cast – Mendelson, even Ramona.' A slightly sarcastic tone entered her voice. She was not enamoured of Ramona Armande; indeed, she did not like actors in general, considering them all shallow, vain creatures whose only interest was getting as many close-ups of themselves as possible. Her only exception was Julian Brooks who, in spite of herself, she admired.

'Give this guy a call,' Spyros conceded. 'If he's available, have him telephone me at my office immediately. We've got to get moving on this, Shirley, this delay is gonna cost us thousands.'

'Right away, Spyros my darling,' crowed Shirley. 'I'm on the blower now.'

Shirley hung up, a victorious smile splitting her pumpkin face. This is it, she said to herself. Signor Scrofo, you better be good to us. This is a gift I've given you – a fucking *gift*. And picking up the telephone, she instructed the operator to place a call to Rome immediately.

It was six o'clock in Rome. The vast apartment was chilly and Umberto Scrofo was freezing. His southern Calabrian blood never seemed to have adjusted to the cold of these Roman winters. He picked up the telephone after only two rings.

'*Pronto*,' he snapped. He'd been receiving a good many unpleasant calls recently, perhaps because of the excessive nudity in his movie which had caused some offence to the Catholic community. The shrill tones of Shirley Frankovitch crackled down the transatlantic line.

'Umberto, it's me, Shirley, Shirley Frankovitch. Do you remember me?'

'Of course,' he said gallantly.

'I have some *great* news for you, Umberto. Tell me, are you working on anything right now?'

'Well, there are a few things in the pipeline, Shirley my dear, many things actually,' Umberto hedged, glancing at the small pile of dreadful scripts on his desk. 'But I must confess, nothing definite – nothing I'm really excited about.'

'How about coming to Acapulco and taking up the reins of our movie *Cortez*?' Shirley asked excitedly. There was a pause as Scrofo digested this.

'Hello – Hello Umberto, can you hear me?'

'*Cortez*? The Makopolis film with Julian Brooks? Of course I've heard about it, but I thought Zachary Domino was producing?'

'He's dead,' Shirley stated triumphantly. 'He died this morning. Heart attack, they think. I've spoken to Spyros about you coming down here to produce, Umberto, and he seems keen. Are you free? Can you do it?'

'Well, yes, yes, I am free actually, I certainly am.' Umberto couldn't keep the eagerness out of his voice. 'Er, how sad about Zachary, he was a fine producer.' The realization of what this could mean to his career was hitting Scrofo like the rush of cocaine.

'Then call Spyros Makopolis right away. Here's the number – Crestview 77933. Get your ass on the first plane out of that Eternal fucking City,' cackled Shirley, 'and fly on down to Acapulco. We've got work to do, Umberto. Lots and lots of work.'

'*Ciao*, Shirley – and thank you, *cara*,' shouted Umberto. As he replaced the receiver his heart was beating so erratically that he thought it might stop altogether, then all his dreams would be ended before he even clambered on the first rung of his stairway to Hollywood success. Quickly he dialled the international operator but was frustrated to find all circuits to the US were busy.

He took his solid-gold pen, an 'end of picture' gift from Ramona, and started to doodle on a pad. PRODUCED BY UMBERTO SCROFO. Somehow that didn't look right now. Not that there was anything wrong with Italian names. On movie credits they hadn't hurt Carlo Ponti or Federico Fellini, but there was something . . . well . . . unpleasant about *his* name. Scrofo – in English it sounded like 'scruffy' or 'scrofulous', a bad connotation. No, it wasn't right for an above-the-title important Hollywood producer, he needed something better.

He doodled some more, leaving out the S. CROFA. CROFF. CROFT. Croft – now that was a good surname. It sounded vaguely Scottish to him. Croft. It reminded him of a charming cottage in the Scottish Highlands that he'd visited once. Umberto, of course, he would change to Hubert. Hubert Croft. Excellent. One thing was missing, though. He thought of the producers who were his idols: David O. Selznick. Jack L. Warner. Darryl F. Zanuck. A middle initial – that's what he needed. He would take the S from Scrofo. Hubert S. Croft. Now that was a fine name for a fine Hollywood producer.

He was on his way.

8

As the day of her party dawned, Ramona woke up in her shimmering white bedroom with an appalling headache. Zack's tragic death was still fresh in her mind. Her maid brought her breakfast in bed, with a copy of the *Acapulcan News*. It was crammed with gossipy details of tonight's lavish party for *Cortez*. According to the society reporter, this would be the most spectacular society event here of the whole year. Lana Turner and Linda Christian were flying in from Hollywood, with Errol Flynn, Ava Gardner and Gilbert Roland. Miguel Aleman, until recently the President of Mexico, had also promised to attend. The festivities would begin at sunset because Acapulcan sunsets were of such particular and extraordinary beauty, and probably not end till dawn.

Ramona had hired two bands to play: one from Mexico City, and a strolling group of mariachi players called Los Paraguayos who would play Mexican folk songs.

Ramona regularly made the 'ten best hostesses in the world' list in the glossy magazines, and for this occasion she would live up to her reputation. A small army of servants had been up since dawn, scrubbing, scouring, polishing, and sweeping the vast areas of marble, glass and stone. The two swimming pools were to be covered with a floating veil of flowers. Tonight hundreds of imported white roses, costing thousands of dollars and so much more unusual than jasmine or hibiscus, would float in her brilliantly lit pools.

The fiesta was going to cost a minor fortune, but Ramona wouldn't be footing the bill. Although the Prince indulged her every financial whim, her childhood in Hungary had left her with a solid respect for the value of money. Didier, who had himself started at the bottom of the film ladder before finally becoming the most powerful producer in England, had taught her all she'd needed to know. His advice was: Never pay for anything yourself if you can get someone else to pay for it. Didier had scolded her when he'd discovered that she'd been buying her own stockings and gloves for a movie in which she'd only had a small role. 'Always charge *everything* you can to the production – that should be your credo.' Ramona had learned well from her brother, so when Zack had approached her to give the *Cortez* launch party, she'd agreed, provided, of course, that MCCP would be footing the bill.

Pragmatic and unsentimental, Ramona wasn't going to allow Zachary's death to spoil her day. To her, there was no point in mourning too long after the departed had been sent off in a civilized manner. It had been three days since Zack's furneral. That was long enough; the show must go on.

She dressed quickly in a cream cotton caftan. Catching her long hair with a tortoiseshell comb and leaving her skin bare of cosmetics, she began her long list of household checks.

Everything must be perfection tonight, not only to impress the glamorous guests, but because she was looking forward to again seeing her friend Umberto Scrofo, Zachary's replacement as producer. Irving Frankovitch had let slip last night that it was to be him, but that he had wanted to change his name. Not only had she enjoyed working with Umberto in Rome last year, but he'd also been an interesting and knowledgeable escort. She had played one of the starring roles then. Now she hoped that Umberto might be persuaded to build up her role in *Cortez*, something Zachary hadn't been prepared to do in spite of their relationship.

Scheherazade was a vast, multi-level mansion modelled after an Arabian mosque. From the top level, which was some ten stories high, an old white wooden cable car with creaky metal gear teeth and thin wire pulleys ran down the side of the house to Ramona's private beach. Although antiquated, the cable car always had regular safety checks, and all visitors to Scheherazade used it to take them down to the secluded beach.

This top level was a huge open terrace paved with diamond-shaped mosaic tiles. A fountain gushed in the centre and palm trees and tropical plants grew in luscious profusion. There was an enormous white marble bar, and here and there, as if resting at some oasis, stood a dozen or more white stone camels.

On the second level were six bedroom suites, nestled together in an intimate group around their own swimming pool.

Down winding steps lined on each side by jungle foliage, through sparkling white arches so bright that they dazzled the eye, was the unbelievable vista of the main salon. From here there was a panoramic view of the Pacific revealed in all its glittering glory, for where the south wall should have been was only the peerless beauty of the sea. Around the salon snaked the main swimming pool, its very edge the horizon. Were it not for the marble figures at the edge of the pool, pool and sea would appear as one.

A large golden snail with *trompe l'oeil* butterflies painted on its shell guarded the entrance to the grotto where revellers were often serenaded long into the night.

Set into the wall was a huge shell of shimmering pearl big enough for a small woman to sit in. Ramona had done that herself once for Zack, wearing just a pair of golden stockings and a smile. He'd been quite insatiable that night. Poor Zack.

At the bottom of more steps was her own private beach – the only private beach in Acapulco – and Ramona used it with pleasure and great pride.

It had taken Ramona and her Prince five years to construct Scheherazade – five arduous years in which the the most brilliant architects and designers from Mexico, New York and Paris had created this fantasy masterpiece. Now the perfectionist Princess Ramona reigned supreme, secure that it was the grandest house in Mexico.

Nicholas Stone shaved with his customary speed. He hated wasting time on shaving and showering and other mundane things. His mind constantly whirled with every tiny detail of the movie which would finally begin shooting on Monday morning. The jet-set party tonight held no interest for him. Parties of any description were just not his scene. He was a simple man and having to make small talk with the *beau monde* was not his idea of a good time. He had tried to telephone the new producer, Hubert S. Croft, the night before, but had been informed by the hotel operator that Mr Croft was sleeping off his arduous trip from Rome and was not to be disturbed under any circumstances.

He had, however, spoken to Elektra and his children, and in spite of a bad connection he could hear the warmth in their voices which always brought him such happiness. He knew it was time now to pick up Bluey at his boat and, grabbing his keys, he glanced briefly into the mirror and made a face.

In complete contrast to Nick the newly christened Hubert S. Croft spent a great deal of time on his toilette. Unfortunately, his beautifully cut cream-coloured suit from Caraceni of Milan did nothing to minimize his bulk, and his sallow complexion was not enhanced by a striped voile shirt with a tight white collar. He had hoped that the midnight blue silk tie would give him the look of respectability and authority that he craved. It was most important that he make the right impression tonight.

He knew how much was at stake. With a big Hollywood film to produce, he needed to earn the trust of the director, encourage the actors, ingratiate himself with the crew and show everyone that he knew exactly what he was doing. He'd succeeded in Rome; he would succeed in Hollywood at last and he had excellent ammunition in that he believed in himself. He also had strong allies already in the Frankovitch team and Ramona Armande. A good set of cards in his hands. Very good indeed.

He flicked back what little remained of his hair and doused himself with the pungent French cologne which he'd worn for so many years. Inserting a pair of gold links set with enormous sapphires into his cuffs, he wondered if his favourite sapphire stickpin might not be a little too fancy for the tropics. He was already sweating profusely, even in the relative cool of the hotel room. He hoped it would be cooler at Ramona's. He must make a *bella figura* tonight – he had to let the cast and crew know who was boss. And the first person he must convince of this would be the young hotshot director, Nicholas Stone.

Inès looked in the mirror and put the finishing touches to her makeup, liking what she saw. She was glowing. A one-shouldered sarong dress of pale green silk complemented her elegant figure. It was clasped at the shoulder with a jade and ivory brooch which

Julian had given her just this morning, on receiving a letter from Doctor Langley in LA, confirming her pregnancy. Tiny jade studs gleamed in her earlobes, and her hair was tied back with a simple emerald green ribbon. On her wrist she wore as usual the delicate amber and silver bracelet given to her by Yves. She never took it off, it was her lucky mascot. The only night she had not worn it was the night she had struck the Italian General down with his own razor. She shuddered. Forget about that night, she told herself. Why was it so hard to forget?

Julian, casually immaculate as ever, healthily tanned, magnificently handsome, looked at her approvingly.

'Darling, are you sure you're up to tonight?' he asked. 'I'm worried about you. You know how we both feel about the baby, I don't want you to risk overdoing it.'

'Don't worry, my love,' she said, coming close to him, touching his cheek with her gentle fingers. 'I feel fine – it's just a touch of morning sickness and Dr Langley told me that almost every woman suffers from it, particularly with the first baby.'

'I hope you don't get it with our next one,' said Julian sincerely, cupping her face in his hands and gazing lovingly into her eyes. 'And the ones after that. You know how much I love you – want you – want to be with you all my life, don't you, my angel?'

'I do, darling – I really do,' Inès whispered, her heart full of love for him.

'This is going to be a tough film for me, darling – I just need to know that you'll be as understanding as ever – and that you'll always, always be here with me.'

'You'd better believe it, Mister Brooks,' Inès replied with a big smile. 'Looks, honey, you ain't never gonna get rid of this particular woman.'

'And I never want to – ever,' he said, his expression so penetrating and sincere that Inès looked surprised.

'Julian – darling – what is it?' she asked. 'You seem so worried suddenly – why? What's the matter?'

'I don't really know,' said Julian, moving away and looking out of the window at the dark blue velvet of the sea.

'Everything's so perfect, Inès. Almost too good to be true.

Everything. You – the two of us together – the baby – I just couldn't bear anything to go wrong, ever.'

'Nothing's going to go wrong, silly,' said Inès lightly, thinking that it was so unlike Julian to voice this kind of thought. 'Phoebe has agreed to your terms, we can be married as soon as the decree comes through – the baby's fine, and Dr Langley says he sees no reason why I can't have *lots* more – so why are you so suddenly worried, darling?'

'I'm not – I'm not, forget it.' He scooped her up in his arms and kissed the soft fragrance of her neck. 'I'm just behaving like a stupid superstitious actor before the show starts. Come on, old girl, let's get off to this dreaded gala.'

She kissed his cheek, feeling the rush of pleasure from the knowledge that she was going to have his child.

He smiled back at her tenderly. She was the woman he wanted to be with for ever. He loved her so much – but how he wished that these new and alarming erotic images of Dominique would stop coming into his head whenever he made love to the woman who was not only carrying his child but who was soon to be his wife.

After Dominique had awakened from her afternoon siesta she stood under the shower, letting the tingling cold water revive her. She was looking forward tremendously to this evening. She loved parties, the new thrill of dressing up, painting her face, designing her hair in some daring new style. She loved to flirt – and now, she especially loved to flirt with Julian. Julian Brooks. So famous and charming – and the handsomest man in the world.

She knew she had his male libido in a spin. She smiled to herself as she sat at her dressing table fiddling with her lipstick. Although her face hardly needed any cosmetic assistance, playing with paints and brushes gave her more time to think. Looks Brooks liked her. She smiled like a cat while she applied Revlon's Fire and Ice to her full lips. He more than liked her – he desired her, too. She'd become aware of that when she'd spotted him watching her in the pool. On the few occasions that they had met since, it was increasingly obvious to her how he felt.

Dominique was beginning to understand how desirable she was, how much power her youthful beauty gave her. She loved it. So Looks Brooks wanted to play, did he? At sixteen she was hardly an expert in the game of love, but she was going to try and experiment. She'd enjoyed her affair with Gaston, in St Tropez, very much. But she'd had to come to America for this film just as she was really beginning to enjoy lovemaking. What would it be like to make love to Julian?

That Julian was both engaged and in the middle of a divorce didn't bother her at all. Love was all only a game, wasn't it, she thought as she clipped on a pair of big golden hoop earrings. After all, Inès was French too, and Frenchwomen understood about these things. So she wouldn't mind if Dominique flirted with her fiancé – it was all part of the game.

Dominique chose a short strapless dress from her wardrobe. The waist was tightly cinched and the hemline high, which drew attention to her endless legs. Her hair was dry now and she brushed it until it tumbled in luxuriant splendour down her bare back.

She knocked on the door of the room next to hers. 'Ready, Agathe?' she called out in her breathy little girl's voice with its newly acquired American accent. 'Let's hit the road, baby.'

Tonight she was determined to have a wonderful time and perhaps to captivate Julian Brooks even more.

Irving and Shirley put the finishing touches on their respective toilettes. He felt comfortable in a pair of loose cotton trousers and an old cotton shirt; he cared little or nothing about his appearance, his only concern was his work.

Shirley fussed miserably in front of the mirror. The new caftan she was wearing, in its bright shades of orange and yellow, did nothing to disguise her ballooning girth. She was allergic to the sun so her face was white, and her salt-and-pepper hair clung to her head in tight, old-fashioned curls, giving her an uncanny, but hardly becoming, resemblance to Harpo Marx. She had done her best with her makeup as she wanted to look as good as possible when she met Umberto Scrofo again. Or Hubert S. Croft – she didn't care what he wanted to be called. He'd rung the day before, informing the Frankovitches that now that he was making an American film, he wanted an American name. Since only Irving, Shirley and Ramona knew him as Umberto Scrofo, he would appreciate . . . must insist, actually . . . that they never refer to him as anything but Hubert S. Croft. Hell, she'd call him Donald Duck if it would help their cause. Croft was sure to be the Frankovitches' ally, the man to reinstate those violent battle scenes and those lyrical pages of prose to the shooting script. Zachary Domino and Nicholas Stone had callously sabotaged it; now Scrofo would be their saviour. He would be as strong and authoritative as he had been in Italy, even inspiring fear in some of the cast and crew. That was good. That was how a producer should be, respected. A hard task master. He would make this truly a Frankovitch film, not one for which the critics would praise only the director and the actors, leaving the writers un-appreciated as usual. Shirley smiled grimly as she pinned an emerald brooch to her broad chest. Oh yes, she'd call him anything he wanted as long as he helped the cast and crew of *Cortez* to realize the true worth of the Frankovitch team, and give them the respect and glory which they so richly deserved.

9

Ramona was a vision of composed loveliness as she waited for her guests in the centre of her marble entrance hall. Wearing a slim column of white silk crepe, her ebony hair caught up with a diamond comb from the estate of the Prince's family, enormous pear-shaped diamonds glittering on her ears, and several diamond bracelets on each wrist, she was coolly elegant, but exuding that charming effervescence which is the mark of every good hostess.

Agathe and Dominique were the first to arrive, Agathe in a long matronly floral dress in which she appeared to be rather uncomfortable. Her normally expressionless white face was awestruck. Not only was she a guest at one of the most talked-about houses in the world, but soon her idol would be here. He would smile at her. They would chat wittily. He would see how bright she was, how cultivated.

She accepted a glass of mineral water and was content just to sit on a divan watching the fabled sunset and waiting for Julian's arrival.

Dominique sashayed around, looking older tonight than her sixteen years. Tanned to a golden honey colour, she mixed gaily with the arriving guests, chatting and joking with genuine camaraderie and charm.

Agathe envied her. Where had she found that poise, that sophistication, her ease with people? Just a few months ago she was a French schoolgirl; now she was a woman of the world – glamorous and confident. She made Agathe feel even more like some insecure country bumpkin.

Soon the marble floors echoed to the chatter and laughter of the jet set, Hollywood stars, local celebrities and politicians. Bluey and Nick were both impressed by the sheer scale of the house.

'Jesus H. Christ,' whistled Bluey. 'I've seen some pads in my time, but this takes the cake, cherry, icing and all.'

Nick nodded. In spite of having lived in America for ten years, he was still unaccustomed to the palatial, often vulgar residences of the high-living Hollywood stars, directors and producers, but this extraordinary villa was more lavish than any he'd ever seen there. His director's eye was enthralled by the beauty of the landscaping, the exotic pictures, sculptures and other objects, the depth and dimensions of all the rooms. He set off on his own to examine them more closely.

Usually jaded photographers from *Life*, *Look*, *Vogue* and the movie magazines – *Photoplay*, *Modern Scene* and *Motion Picture* – were so excited that they jostled and pushed each other to take pictures. There were stars galore to fill both their columns and their lenses. Lana Turner, with her new husband, Lex Barker, had arrived; she with silver-blonde hair was more tanned than any Mexican, and he was as handsome as any film star had a right to be. Hedda Hopper and Louella Parsons had only sent their stringers, but influential fast talking Walter Winchell from New York and Harrison Carroll from the Los Angeles *Herald-Examiner* had arrived in person, and now mingled with the elegant crowd, whose voices competed with the music of the strolling mariachis.

As the sun dipped into the horizon, the guests gathered at the end of the huge white terrace to view its fading glory. Even the waiters stopped work to admire it, for to Mexicans the sun is the symbol of eternal life. There were appreciative gasps as the sun made a dramatically rapid exit to the west, casting a soft apricot glow over everyone and everything. It was such a magnificent sight that many broke into spontaneous applause. The mariachis now played more wildly and the margaritas began to stir everyone's blood with fiesta excitement.

No one noticed the entrance of Hubert S. Croft as he stood at the top of the tall marble staircase and watched the partygoers. They all seemed so childish as they oohed and aahed at the sunset. He gave a sneering smile.

Ramona was the first to see him; she hurried over to greet him effusively. 'Hubert, my dear Hubert, I'm *so* happy to see you again. You look very well.' She was careful to use the new name which he'd insisted on.

Hubert took her hand and with European gallantry bowed his

head over her fabled forty-carat diamond. 'Ramona my dear, you are more ravishing than ever – and what a superb house. Magnificent, my dear, magnificent.'

Ramona beamed as Hubert accepted a margarita from a passing waiter, then she whisked him off to be introduced to her other guests.

Across the sea of laughing faces, Inès froze in horror. No. Not again. Not here in Acapulco. Was this a dream or a ghost? Her eyes were riveted to the short, paunchy man who strutted around shaking hands and smiling and who in turn was being greeted with friendly smiles by everyone. But of course he must be some friend of Ramona's, she had seen them both outside Romanoff's last month. Why was he here?

As he came nearer to her she could see the unmistakable face and squat body which had haunted her dreams. His fleshy lips were at this moment pulled into an expression which he imagined to be a charming social smile, but which made him look like some grotesque gargoyle. But there was no doubt at all that this was the face from her past. She clung to Julian's arm; her heart was hammering as Umberto Scrofo advanced towards her with an ominous tread and with that ghastly smile plastered on his hideous face.

There was nowhere to hide.

'*Bon soir*, Julian,' Dominique said, licking pink glossy lips and smiling up at him seductively.

Julian beamed. 'Dear girl,' he said heartily, 'you look very pretty tonight, very grown up – doesn't she, Inès?'

'Thank you, Julian,' Dominique smiled, her attention focused totally on him. She completely ignored Inès even though she was arm in arm with her fiancé. 'And you look very – what is the word? – dashing. Yes, that's it, you look very dashing tonight, Julian.'

Julian laughed, again finding himself uncomfortably bewitched. Damn, damn. This child-woman was irresistible.

'Would you have a few minutes to discuss something with me, Julian?' Dominique went on, her eyes now downcast shyly. 'There's a scene that I didn't quite understand and I would so appreciate your advice about it.'

'Well, this *is* a party, my dear. Perhaps tomorrow –' demurred Julian.

'I don't think I could sleep tonight for worrying about this, Julian,' Dominique implored, looking up at him again beseechingly with her Circe-green eyes. 'It is so important to me, this film. And I am only a beginner, you can teach me so much, Julian.'

Julian shot a quick look at Inès, but she was staring out towards the main salon with a curious blank look on her face. Probably admiring the decorations, he thought.

'Excuse me, darling – I hope you don't mind. Dominique and I are just going over to the edge of the pool to discuss a scene.'

She nodded, not speaking, and Julian let go of Inès' arm and allowed Dominique to lead him into the shadows at the base of a nearby palm tree. By God, she was having an amazing effect on him. He was becoming aroused just by the soft touch of her fingers on his hand. What was wrong with him – was he mad?

'Now which scene is it, Dominique?' he asked sternly, annoyed with himself as he felt his cock starting to harden.

'This one,' she said simply, opening her pouting mouth on to his, running a tongue full of silent promises across his dry lips, and pressing her yielding body to his. Before he had a chance to respond, she pulled away, looking up at him with a kittenish smile. 'I thought that perhaps *this* should be how we did the first kiss after my dance, the firelight scene – what do you think, Julian?' She looked at him in mock innocence while she gently dabbed at her lips with her handkerchief, then wiped his with it.

Julian was dumbstruck. He had always thought that he understood the workings of the female mind, at least as well if not better than the next man. But Dominique was so much more unpredictable than any other woman he had known – even Inès. She was flaunting her sexuality tonight like bunting strung across a pleasure boat. She was a pubescent jade, a wanton child-woman – and God, he desired her.

As Julian stood there dumbstruck Dominique reapplied her lipstick, whispering conspiratorially, 'Think about it, Julian, *chéri*. It should be a tender moment, don't you agree? I mean, really sexy but sweet, like Liz and Monty in *A Place in the Sun. N'est-ce pas?*'

Before the spellbound actor could reply, the little minx disappeared into the shadows with a roguish smile, and an embarrassed and tumescent Julian stared after her, alarm bells ringing in his ears.

Inès prayed that Scrofo wouldn't remember her, or that her scarlet face would not betray her. She had tried to disappear into the crowd, but after Julian had finished his talk with Dominique he had found her in the marble bar and taken her over to meet the new producer, who was with Ramona.

'Inès my dear, I should like you to meet Hubert Croft – Hubert, this is Mademoiselle Inès Juillard, Julian's fiancée,' said Ramona.

'How do you do, Mademoiselle,' said Scrofo in a rasping harsh voice. '*Enchanté.*'

'Hubert is our new producer,' beamed Ramona. 'And we are very lucky to have him.'

Inès felt faint and put her trembling hand in Julian's for support.

Producer? Umberto Scrofo was Zachary's replacement? It simply wasn't possible.

'How do you do,' Inès mumbled. She knew she had to say something. She felt her knees begin to buckle and only Julian's steady arm prevented her from swooning.

In horrified fascination she stared at the rim of a pink puckered scar which was slightly concealed under his flashy expensive shirt. She had caused that scar. It was because of her that his voice was that grating whisper. So she hadn't killed him after all.

For eleven years she had believed that she had killed this man, who was here shaking her hand with a ghastly smile on his brutish face. This was certainly no ghost who held her gaze and rasped, 'You're a very lucky man indeed, Mr Brooks.'

He drank in her loveliness with no visible sign of recognition, although he'd held her gaze for perhaps a second longer than necessary. But that was something Inès was used to. Her beauty often caused men to react in strange ways. Croft shook hands with Julian, expressing his delight at being on the movie and his admiration for Julian's fine work in the past. Then his eyes began flitting back to Inès. Faintly she could smell the same sickly aftershave that he'd worn that night at the Ritz. She wanted to flee to the other side of the room, to escape his probing stare, but Julian held on to her hand tightly. Her heart thumped so hard she felt sure someone would notice. How in heaven's name had Umberto Scrofo ended up here? Why had he changed his name? How on earth could he possibly be producing Julian's movie? But most of all, why wasn't he dead?

As if reading her thoughts, Hubert turned to look at her again wtih a penetrating stare.

'You're a very beautiful woman, Mademoiselle Juillard.' He had barely a trace of an Italian accent. 'Very beautiful indeed.'

'Thank you,' she murmured, gulping at her margarita, the salt that encrusted the rim of the glass stinging her lips. She looked at Julian for help, but he was busy talking to Hedda Hopper's stringer, who was scribbling into a notebook.

'Have we not met somewhere before?' His beady black eyes roamed over the contours of her breasts.

'I don't think so,' Inès said quietly, trying to move away, 'I'm sure I would have remembered.' Hubert took a step closer and yet another wave of his familiar cologne hit her. She felt her stomach churn.

'I never forget a face. Never.' His eyes searched hers as he suddenly sensed her fear. Who was this woman? He felt sure he knew her from somewhere. But where? What was the story of this beautiful creature? He must find out. He would make it his business to find out. Hubert always needed to know every detail about everyone with whom he worked – knowledge gave him power.

'Where are you from?' he probed.

Inès felt as if she were going mad. She had murdered him, hadn't she? She remembered all too vividly the look on his face, the blood covering the bathroom floor, the hue and cry in Paris when they'd searched for his murderer. Her flight to England to escape certain death. Surely, though, there was no chance that he would recognize her today. She looked so very different from the skinny yellow-haired teenage prostitute of wartime Paris. She was now an elegant, chic woman of the world, in her prime. But she'd tried to kill him. No one could ever forget a face seen in those circumstances. Could they? But her face wasn't the same – or was it? The style and blondness of her hair were different, her cheekbones were more pronounced. She was *not* recognizable, she told herself.

But she knew she couldn't lie to him about her nationality. Everyone here knew where she was from.

'London,' she murmured. 'I'm from London.'

'London?' he said in surprise. 'But you cannot be, you are French are you not?'

'Yes,' said Inès quietly. 'I am French.'

'Inès has lived in London for twelve years,' smiled Julian, turning away from the reporter, his actor's instincts sensing tension. 'That's where we met, isn't it, darling?'

'Oh really,' smiled Umberto, still staring at Inès. 'Where were you born, Miss Juillard?'

'France,' she whispered.

'France?' he said, raising an eyebrow. 'France? France is a very big country. Which part of France, Miss Juillard?'

'I was born in Lyon,' she lied.

His eyes narrowed. 'Lyon, really?'

'Yes.' Then, more boldly, 'Lyon. Have you ever been there?' She could barely keep the loathing from her voice.

A crafty smirk crossed his slug-white face. She was *avverso* towards him, was she? He was used to that. It certainly wouldn't be the first time someone had disliked him on sight. He couldn't place her, but it seemed that she was most anxious to hide something from him. 'Lyon, hmm?' He looked carefully at her again. 'I was never in Lyon, but I know that I'll remember where it was that we met; it's sure to come back to me. As I say, I never, ever forget a face, or where I saw it.'

He smiled genially and strolled out on to the terrace to rejoin his hostess.

Inès felt as if she'd been kicked in the stomach. Julian had been right in thinking that everything was almost too perfect. She had to get away. Julian was holding court in one corner of the vast room. She needed to be alone, to have time to digest Scrofo's words, his presence here.

As soon as Scrofo left her, she ran down the stone steps which led to the beach, and stood on the toffee-coloured sand, staring out to sea with unseeing eyes. She was now sure that Scrofo would inevitably remember her as the whore who had slashed his throat. She shuddered at the word: *whore*. How would it affect Julian's career if the world found out that his fiancée had been a Parisian prostitute and an attempted murderess? A woman who had serviced the enemy during the war? She couldn't bear even to think about it, or what it would do to their relationship.

However much he professed to love her, Julian would dump her immediately – she knew that. Although she believed that he truly loved her, she knew that Julian Brooks simply couldn't handle the ramifications of marrying a woman with such a sordid, even criminal, past.

No, her life would be totally ruined if Julian were to discover any part of her past. Ruined. His divorce was supposed to be final in two months. They must marry soon, before her pregnancy became obvious; before he had time to learn the truth. If he did, it would be the end. He would leave her, she knew. Oh, he would be kind – he would give her money, which she did not need. She had invested wisely and could provide for herself. She would be left with nothing of his except his child. No one even knew that she was pregnant. If they found out, that would no doubt cause another scandal, but not nearly as ignominious as the one Scrofo could cause.

Inès sat down on a rock, her mind spinning. What could Scrofo possibly want from her? She was no threat to him. But if he recognized her he would want his revenge, naturally, and from the way he stared at her it was only a matter of time before he did.

She placed her hand comfortingly on her still-flat stomach. Sweat trickled down the inside of her thin silk dress. She took off her shoes, putting them on one of the rocks which lay around like beached sea monsters. Across the bay in the dusk she could see a speedboat weaving about, filled with laughing people. The sea was flat and oily, without the slight wind that usually came from the bay. A fisherman suddenly emerged from the water in the crepuscular light, a baby octopus impaled on his rusty spear, its saclike pink body hanging limply like the scrotum of an elderly man. Inès shuddered. She had seen too many of those. The thought of ever again having to make love to any man except Julian was anathema.

She paddled her feet listlessly in the tide in the hope of cooling down, but it was too warm, only making her feel stickier. She bent down to splash some water on her flushed face. Her mind was crowded with thoughts of the embarrassment, the humiliation, the indignity if her past were to be discovered. Julian would never be able to forgive her. He was the traditional public school English gentleman just as much as he was an important star. He'd sacrificed his marriage and a great deal of money for Inès, but she knew he wouldn't be willing to sacrifice his future. Her female instincts warned her that she was in grave danger. She had to do something drastic about Scrofo before he tried to ruined her life all over again.

Agathe had been looking forward with mixed feelings to the party. She usually felt out of place and ill at ease at social gatherings, but as Dominique's chaperone she had had to go. Still, there was the presence of Julian to look forward to.

She sensed his arrival at once, almost smelling him across the room, the same scent she cherished in the fabric of his blue cotton shirt. She had kept it hidden away under her mattress, and slept with it entwined around her body every night.

He was even more glamorously handsome than the last time she'd seen him, more sexually arousing to her just from across the room than during her fevered nights when her thoughts were constantly of his body curled around hers, their two mouths one. He was wearing a white shantung suit of exquisite cut, and the palest of blue silk shirts open at the neck to reveal the dark curly hair of his chest. His brown-black hair tumbled over his bronzed brow as he laughed into the face of the woman by his side. Laughing joyously, intimately with a slim ash-blonde woman in a green sarong, his hand casually resting on her one bare shoulder.

Agathe drew in her breath with a gasp. The hair was different. The style, the sophistication. But there was no one from those wartime days Agathe could *ever* forget. What was Julian doing with that tart?

How could he be with that slut-child who'd slept with half the Gestapo in Paris? Surely *she* wasn't his fiancée?

They were being greeted by everyone like an emperor and his

consort. Inès was no empress, Agathe thought. She was a cheap whore and a bitch, a traitor to her country. Why was Julian, who deserved only the pure and the good, engaged to this . . . this personification of evil? She must have put a spell on him, for it was impossible for a man so wonderful, so kind, so perfect in every way to want to take a murderess as his wife.

Agathe remembered the magazine photograph which Dominique had shown her on their flight to Acapulco. The woman with Julian had been in profile and had been dark haired so it was no wonder that she hadn't recognized her, but there was no mistaking the traitor now, even though she was blonde and innocent-looking.

The past came flooding back to her. This was the whore who'd killed an Italian officer. They had hidden her in the same cellar by L'Eléphant Rose where Agathe had been made to stay for so long. But Inès had spent only a few days there before becoming hysterical. She had no stamina; she was weak and bad. Of course they had all rallied around her. Her pimp Yves, old Gabrielle, all of them who hadn't raised a finger to help Agathe until she was almost *dead*. False passports, changing her name, colouring her hair, sending her off to the safety of England, spoiling the little bitch. Agathe had never heard anything about her again after that. But now, here, engaged to the man Agathe worshipped, was Inès Dessault, smiling at the world as if she owned it.

Bluey and Nick watched the sunset from the second level of Scheherazade, and Nick enthused, 'It's the most goddam beautiful thing I've ever seen in my whole life, far more beautiful than the sunsets in Hydra. I want to be able to have this sort of look in the last battle scenes, Bluey – it could symbolize the tragedy of Mexico – the dying sun, the sun that the Mexicans so revere – dead and dying soldiers lying in the sunset when the battle's over –' Nick rattled on excitedly about the pathos and symbolism of the sunset, but Bluey, having seen it far too many times to wax lyrical, only noticed his margarita was finished.

'C'mon, let's get a refilll, kiddo,' he said. 'There'll be plenty more sunsets.'

Nick looked back at the amber sky, ideas fermenting in his mind as he reluctantly returned to the party. He had to capture this on the screen, had to.

The mariachi music in the main salon was only slightly louder than the conversation and laughter, now that all the guests had become more relaxed with one another. Nick and Bluey strolled to the bar, and Ramona, like a sliver of moonlight, drifted over to them.

'Darlings, our new producer has arrived. I've been looking everywhere for you. You must come and meet him.'

'Of course, I've been waiting for this,' said Nick as Ramona led him through the jostling crowd.

In the middle of a small group consisting of Irving and Shirley Frankovitch, Dominique and Agathe, stood a short overweight man, his back turned, wearing an expensive-looking tailored suit.

'You haven't met Hubert, have you?' Ramona smiled.

The man turned around to face Nicholas, whose heart almost stopped as he stared into the stony black eyes of Umberto Scrofo, his nemesis: the man who had murdered his mother.

Nicholas stood transfixed while introductions were being made. As if by remote control, he shook the sweaty hand of Gourouni, the man who'd destroyed his entire family in Hydra more than a decade before. His mouth was so dry that to speak was out of the question. He knew that no sound would come out of his throat. He couldn't even hear what anyone was saying, so loud was the pounding in his ears. He could only see the toadlike face of the man he'd vowed to himself he would destroy one day. Granted, with the passing years, with the fading of excitable youth, his burning hatred and desperate desire for revenge had diminished. But now, face to face with Scrofo on this tropical night in Acapulco, it surfaced again with deadly vehemence. And it was all he could do to hold back from throwing himself at the fat swine screaming out that he was a murdering bastard. But he held his tongue and said nothing.

He knew that he must appear to be behaving stupidly. Ramona was looking at him quizzically, and Scrofo was eyeing him with a strangely patronizing expression. Through the fog in his brain, Nicholas heard the Italian say, 'I'm delighted to meet you, Nick, we will make a great picture here, I know it. I like most of the script and

325

we've got a terrific cast, haven't we? We need to meet before the others tomorrow morning so I can give you a few of my ideas.'

Nick knew a remark was expected of him, but he was unable to reply with even the simplest platitude. He nodded, muttering something unintelligible under his breath.

Hubert Croft scrutinized the young director coolly. His appearance had so often alienated him from people that over the years he'd found ways in which to camouflage the rejection, including doling out saccharine doses of charm and heavy-handed wit. But this Nick Stone, the *wunderkind* of the 1950s cinema, was behaving in a particularly strange manner. Was he drunk? Had tequila taken its inevitable toll so early in the evening? Hubert smiled and said, 'When I saw your first picture, Nick, I knew you had talent – anyone who could make something witty and fresh out of *Bobby Soxers in Space* must be a genius.'

'Mmm, thanks,' mumbled Nick – his throat so dry it was painful to speak.

'And your next movie was a work of art too – brilliant. I'm proud to be working with you, Nick – really thrilled.'

Nick's gut instinct was to take the fat Italian's neck between his hands and squeeze the life out of him. He felt that he was no longer in Acapulco, but back in war-torn Hydra. He was a sixteen-year-old boy whose brothers and sisters had died in starving misery, whose father had been bludgeoned to death in front of all the villagers by Scrofo's barbarous men, whose mother had died at Scrofo's very own hand, and whose friends and relations had been either starved or tortured to death.

Less than a minute had passed when Bluey pressed a fresh margarita into his hand. Nick drained the glass, his eyes never leaving the Italian. Bluey looked at him in mild surprise. Nick seemed in a trance, like a man lost in a dream. His face was drained of colour and he seemed to have lost both his tongue and his composure. Bluey cracked a joke as he was introduced to Hubert, who flashed him a beaming smile, glad to have his attention diverted from the dumb Greek director.

Mumbling some excuse about feeling ill, Nick desperately wanted to escape. This meeting was so unbelievable that he simply couldn't cope with it. He had to be alone. He had to have time to think. He must telephone Elektra. He was just about to leave when there was a sudden fanfare from the mariachi band and Ramona, grabbing him firmly by the arm, announced that dinner was served. Nick was trapped. The Princess's arm was like a handcuff as she led him down the winding onyx staircase to the main terrace.

The tables were set exquisitely. In the centre of each of the round tables of ten, all covered with gold lâmé tablecloths, a thick gold-painted palm frond stood proudly in a gold pyramid-shaped container embedded into what looked like fine golden sand. Circled around the sand were a dozen tiny. flickering lights which cast a flattering glow on the faces of the guests. On either side of the pyramid, two sleepy-eyed ceramic camels nestled each other. The knives and forks were of solid gold, as were the salt shakers and the pepper mills, also shaped like camels.

Ramona considered herself an expert at the tricky art of *placement*. The first three tables were the most important, and table one was naturally presided over by Ramona herself. She had placed Hubert on her right and, to his dismay, Nick on her left. Next to him was Shirley Frankovitch, which made Nick's spirits sink even lower. He actively disliked this pseudo-intellectual mean-spirited woman, who thought herself some kind of literary giant, but who owed most of her success to her husband.

'Good evening, Nicky,' she said to him sarcastically as he sat down. 'Gorgeous party, isn't it? Ramona's got so much class, doncha think?'

Nick ignored her, signalling to a waiter to fill his glass with wine. He needed to get drunk – very drunk indeed.

Next to Shirley sat Julian, who was also not overly fond of the blowsy writer, but as if to make up for this, Ramona had thoughtfully placed Dominique on his left. Between Dominique and Inès sat the American ambassador to Mexico, who drank much and talked little.

To her utter distress Inès found herself sitting only four places away from Umberto Scrofo's penetrating stare. The only guests between her and the vile Italian were Teddy Stauffer, owner of the Villa Vera, self-styled 'Mr Acapulco' and leader of local society, and the beautiful Gene Tierney, 'Laura' herself.

The celebrities, press, cast and crew at the other tables all seemed to be having a much better time than those at Ramona's. A movie company works and plays hard, and tonight was supposed to be playtime, but as an experienced hostess, Ramona wondered why on earth there was such a chilly atmosphere at her table. She chatted away animatedly with Hubert, who responded with his usual heavy-handed wit, but Nicholas Stone, she thought, was being little more than downright rude. His morose eyes never left his plate, and he knocked back the Château Lafitte 1929 as if it were lemonade.

'You are as ever looking glorious tonight, *Principessa*,' smiled Hubert, oilily raising his golden Venetian goblet in a toast to her. 'More ravishing than ever.'

'Why thank you, Hubert dear.' If Ramona could have managed a maidenly blush, she would have summoned one up, but her thespian gifts were not that munificent.

'Tell me, my dear, who is the woman who is engaged to Julian? I think I know her from somewhere.'

'Oh.' Ramona seemed disappointed that the conversation had so quickly turned away from her. 'Julian met her in London, Hubert. She's French, from quite a good family I understand – orphaned before the war and brought up by an aunt in Yorkshire.'

'Hmm.' Hubert sipped his wine, regarding Inès less covertly as she attempted conversation with the ambassador. 'Attractive woman, I'm sure I've met her before.'

Ramona gave no answer and Hubert realized that he had committed the cardinal sin of discussing another woman's merits too glowingly in front of his hostess. She was now attempting conversation with a sullen-looking Nick Stone. Croft leaned across Ramona to talk to him.

'I think one of the things we must do, Nick, is to build up the role of the Queen, don't you agree?'

Nick nodded, unable to speak, still convulsed with fury. The nerve of the slime. Script and character changes already and he'd only been on the picture ten minutes.

'Oh Hubert, do you really mean it?' glowed Ramona, her amber eyes glowing like a teenager's. 'I've got *so* many ideas about my character – do let me tell you some of them.'

'I'd love to hear them, my dear,' said Hubert. 'Tell me everything you would like us to do, I'm sure we can work it out to everyone's satisfaction.'

Across the table Inès picked at her food, trying not to watch as Umberto Scrofo stuffed his odious face, occasionally dropping bits of food down his tie. Every few minutes her eyes would catch his, which were observing her carefully, asking silent questions about her identity.

She was beautiful, Hubert thought, seemingly aristocratic and elegant – meeting her would surely have left an indelible impression on him. She looked about twenty-eight or thirty, which meant that if he'd known her in the past, it must have been about ten or twelve years ago when she was in her late teens. And since he had visited London briefly in 1946 – maybe he had met her there? Ten years ago he'd been on Hydra. She certainly hadn't been there. Twelve years ago, however, he had been in Paris. Could he have met her there? No, it was impossible, she would have been too young. He barely listened as Ramona prattled on, giving him ideas and suggestions about how the script could be vastly improved by making Princess Isabella's mother a more sympathetic and interesting character. He hardly heard her; he was concentrating on unearthing the mystery of the enigmatic beauty who sat opposite him, so pale and quiet.

Lyon – Lyon – Lyon? But he'd never been to Lyon in his life.

Julian was unaware of Inès' distress because Dominique had decided to play footsie with him. She had slipped off a shoe, and her bare foot caressed his ankle as she gazed into his eyes, finding his desire for her incredibly stimulating. Julian looked towards Inès, but she seemed so totally oblivious to everything going on around her that he decided he might as well play Dominique's little game with her. After all it meant nothing. She was just a young girl testing the waters of flirtation. He could easily handle her.

10

By the time they returned to their hotel, Inès was feeling like death. Throughout the evening the continual gaze of Umberto Scrofo had haunted her. After dinner, when the guests drifted down to the lower terrace to dance, she had wanted desperately to leave, but Julian was dancing with Dominique, deep in conversation, so she hadn't wanted to interrupt him. Inès understood that actors filming together needed to spend time getting to know each other. Since Dominique was so young and completely inexperienced in the world of movies, Inès was sure that, being the true professional, Julian would want to help her as much as possible.

She was just coming back from the powder room when a damp hand clutched at her bare shoulder.

'Why do you always seem in such a hurry to get away from me, dear lady?' Hubert said. 'Let us dance together.'

'I'm afraid I'm not feeling very well,' she said, pulling away from his grip. 'I don't want to dance.'

'Then let us sit this one out,' he said, firmly taking her arm and leading her to a carved ivory seat close to the dance floor. 'I want to talk to you.' Scrofo appeared to possess that formidable inner strength which came from being used to having his orders carried out without question.

'I remember you now,' he said suddenly, with a basilisk stare.

She looked back at him, struggling to keep her eyes expressionless. 'How could you? We've never met.'

'Oh, but we have, my dear young lady.' His voice was rancid oil. 'We most certainly have.' He paused, waiting for her to react, relighting his cigar, surveying her through narrowed eyes. She didn't flinch, willing him not to remember.

'Of course you look quite different now. Almost twelve years makes a great difference to a pretty young girl.' He smiled, still waiting for her reaction. She found it hard to stop her glass from shaking, and her stomach felt as if it had turned to stone.

'Well, if you won't remember, then I shall have to remind you,' he said ominously. 'I'm sure you recall a certain hotel room in Paris in 1943?'

Her expression was impassive. 'I'm afraid I don't. What are you trying to imply? This conversation is getting us nowhere – excuse me.'

She made a move to leave, but he was too quick for her and his hand shot out to her arm. She felt the unforgettable frisson of cruelty in his fleshy, vicelike fingers.

'I told you I never forget a face. I never forget a name, either. Foolish of you not to have changed it; Inès is an unusual name – so beautiful that you decided that you wouldn't change it when you gave up your occupation. *Whoring!*' His lips were close to her ear now as he spat out the word; she saw the undisguised hatred which had turned his sallow complexion florid.

'Mr Croft, I don't know what you're talking about. Please, let me go. My fiancé is waiting for me.'

But she was unable to extricate herself from his tight grip. As if in a dream, she saw the dancers whirling around the floor, the band playing, guests laughing. She heard the faint hum of the night-time insects, smelled the soft scent of jasmine – but all she could think of was the torture of this man's vicious attack on her, and how she had repaid him for it.

'Ah, yes, I can see you remember now, don't you?' His teeth split his face like a Halloween pumpkin. 'You don't need to answer, Inès. Your silence is enough; besides, as I told you, my memory never fails me. You were that little whore who came to service me at the Ritz Hotel, weren't you? And then you tried to kill me, didn't you?'

Inès felt she was in a nightmare from which she could never wake up. Less than twenty yards away, the man she loved so passionately was dancing with his leading lady. She wanted to be close to him, to hold him, to be Mrs Julian Brooks, as soon as possible. She wanted to go home. That was all she wanted – but this reptilian creature held her rigidly in his grip. To escape him she would have to create a scene.

332

'So, Miss Prim and Proper, Miss Fiancée of the Star, Miss *Murderess*.' He blew a cloud of blinding cigar smoke straight into her face. He obviously hadn't changed much in all these years. He was still a sadistic monster. 'So here we are – together again.'

'What is it you want from me?' she whispered.

'Nothing, my dear, absolutely *nothing* – yet. I just want you to be aware that I know who you are, Inès . . . whatever your name has become. I remember you very well. You were a young prostitute, obviously you'd been one for some time. You were good – very, very good.' He licked his lips in recollection. 'And then you tried to kill me, didn't you?' He bent his suet face to hers, so close that she could see the tiny broken veins on his nose and the stubble on his chins, smell that sickening cologne.

'You nearly succeeded, too – bitch!' His fingers held her upper arm so tightly she knew that by tomorrow their imprint would be there in blue bruises. 'I almost died because of you, you lousy whore. Look –' Quickly he loosened his tie, pulled open his shirt to reveal the thick scar at the base of his adam's apple. Inès gasped out loud. The wound was three or more inches long, white, shiny and raised.

'I was in that fucking military hospital for week after week after fucking week.' He pulled her nearer him, his saliva almost hitting her face, and Inès thought the whole room must be watching them now . Then he smiled – a rictus grin. 'I shall have my revenge for this,' he hissed ominously as he straightened his tie. 'I've waited a long time to find you, young lady, and you are going to curse the day you ever met me.'

Inès shuddered. 'I don't know what you're talking about, Mr Croft,' she said defiantly. 'Whatever happened to you was a long time ago, and it had nothing to do with me.'

He was even more loathsome than she'd remembered. With a wrench she managed to pull her arm away, just as the dance number was ending and Julian sauntered over, his arm casually around Dominique's waist.

'I'm so tired, darling,' Inès whispered, moving into the safety of her fiancé's arms. 'Can we go home now, please?'

'Of course, we'll go now, darling. Goodnight, Dominique.' His eyes held Dominique's for a fraction longer than necessary.

'Hubert, good to have met you, I expect we'll talk tomorrow.' Arm in arm he and Inès strolled away to say goodnight to their hostess.

Umberto Scrofo's eyes stared after them. However much she might deny it, he was positive that it was her. He knew it was. The whore from Paris.

So he'd finally found her. The girl who'd tried to kill him – the skinny slut he'd dreamed of meeting again – of doing the most unspeakable things to, of punishing her. Well, her punishment must wait – but only for now. Priorities. The *Cortez* film had to be number one on his list – and Mademoiselle Inès Juillard was going to be of great help to him in that particular direction, whether she liked it or not.

Inès slept fitfully, visions of the sadistic Scrofo tormenting her subconscious. She tossed and turned, thrashing in the humid darkness, crying out in her sleep. Julian held her close, whispering comforting endearments, feeling waves of love for her. He tried to make love to her during the night, to calm her from her unspoken fears, but for the first time in their relationship, Inès refused him. Julian was slightly piqued, and tried in vain not to let his thoughts and fantasies turn to Dominique.

'I'm sorry,' Inès said shakily. 'I'm really sorry, darling. I . . . I . . . don't feel well; I don't know what's wrong with me, Julian, but I just can't. Not now. Please understand, my darling.'

'Of course, darling,' said Julian soothingly as he held her closely. 'I understand.'

He drifted back into an untroubled sleep but she lay awake throughout the night, staring up at the ceiling, thinking only of her enemy.

The following morning Inès found patches of blood on the sheets. Horrified, she called her gynaecologist in Los Angeles, but it was Sunday; he was out playing golf. Inès crawled back to bed, suggesting to Julian that he go off for the day by himself.

'I'll be fine, darling,' she assured him. 'I just want to rest.'

She didn't tell him about the haemorrhaging. She hoped that if she rested, it would stop.

Again she didn't want to make love.

Julian was as edgy, restless and nervous as most actors were the day before production started. Inès' second rejection of him, this time giving him no reason other than saying that she felt unwell, made him even more restless and irritable. Julian was a highly sexed man, and he needed an outlet for the eve-of-picture tension which was building inside him.

He was quite nervous about this film. Even though he had made so many, this was his first American movie, and there was much at stake.

He looked down at Inès who lay white and drawn on the pillow, a faint sheen of sweat on her normally cool forehead. 'Are you sure you're all right, Inès?'

'Oh yes, fine, just fine, darling,' she murmured weakly. 'Just exhaustion from the party.'

'Well I think I'll do some water-skiing after the production meeting,' he said. 'Are you sure you don't mind being alone?'

'No, I'll be perfectly all right,' she said, not wanting him to leave at all, yet needing her solitude to think. 'Have a wonderful day, darling – don't fall off the slalom. I'll see you tonight.'

She blew him a kiss as he left the room but he didn't return it, and Inès slumped sadly back on to the crumpled pillow, thinking that Julian's strange premonition of last night was coming horribly true.

I I

Although it was barely eight o'clock, the secret breakfast meeting was in full swing. Irving and Shirley Frankovitch and Hubert Croft sat on the shaded balcony of Hubert's suite, the glass table in front of them piled high with scripts, revisions, budgets, coffee cups, tropical fruit, assorted muffins and breads, jams and preserves.

Hubert ate continuously as he talked. When he wanted to make a point, he would jab his finger in the air and gesticulate wildly. Whenever he did this, his resemblance to Mussolini was quite remarkable, thought Shirley, picking at another piece of fruit, Hubert's appetite inspiring her own.

'The main problem as I see it, is that Nicholas Stone appears to have drastically changed the original script as *you* have written it.' He glanced at Shirley. 'It was a brilliant script, Shirley my dear – you did your usual stunning job.'

'Every new suggestion we had – every idea – everything clever and innovative – Nick has shot down in flames,' Shirley said bitterly, pleased by Hubert's praise. 'It was a great script, wasn't it, Irving?'

'Bluey is Nick's main ally,' Irving chimed in. 'Between the two of them and Zack Domino, who had the total support of the studio, we were completely outflanked.'

'No longer.' Hubert smiled. 'No longer, my dear friends. I've read both scripts – the one you wrote, which Zachary Domino and Nick Stone tried to ruin, and the one of which Nick approves. There is no question in my mind as to the one which possesses the greatest merit.'

'Ours!' snapped Shirley, slipping another sliver of papaya between sausage lips.

'Yes, indeed. To that end, we now need to get the studio, the rest of the cast and some of the senior technicians on our side.'

'Of course,' Shirley and Irving both agreed.

337

'Ramona Armande is no problem,' Hubert said. 'She can, and will, be an excellent ally, as well as being an excellent actress.'

'But she hardly has a part.' Shirley frowned.

'I think we can possibly improve her role,' Hubert said smoothly, 'without damaging your script at all.' Shirley looked dubious, as Hubert continued.

'The little girl – Dominique – what has been her reaction to both scripts? I tried to speak to the young lady last evening, but she seemed to have other things on her mind.'

'You bet,' Shirley smirked. 'Looks Brooks' cock is on that young cookie's mind, and it'll be in certain other places besides her mind soon enough, I should think.'

Irving shot his wife a disapproving look. Sometimes her gutter Brooklyn manner was repellent.

'Really? Very interesting.' Hubert made some notes in his brown leather folder. 'Tell me more.'

Irving sighed. He didn't believe the Julian-Dominique gossip which was circulating already, but Shirley had been babbling on about seeing the actress draped all over him the night before. She rarely missed anything; and many of her observations gave her a kind of vicarious pleasure, as her sex life with Irving was negligible these days. He tried hard, but he basically wasn't interested any more.

'His fiancée is a very beautiful woman – why should he want to stray?' Hubert fingered his scar, images of Inès' elegant limbs flashing across his mind.

'He's an actor.' Shirley shrugged. 'You know actors – all cock and no confidence, most of 'em.' She again ignored Irving's disapproving look and pushed some more papaya into her mouth. 'He's famous for putting it into anything that's playing opposite him. Several of his co-stars have even tried to kill themselves over "the handsomest man in the world",' she sneered.

'I see. How do you find *his* allegiances then?' Hubert was still scribbling his notes. 'Whose side is he on?'

'Middle of the road,' said Irving. 'He likes some of our stuff and some of Nick's. He's difficult to sway because he goes for the scene that he feels will be of benefit to the film; he's not as much of an egomaniac as Shirley makes out, he's a team player.'

338

'Hmm.' Hubert prodded his teeth with a toothpick while he studied a yellow bird perched at the edge of his table, which was pecking happily at the remains of the food, but his thoughts were evidently elsewhere.

'Nick is on the phone *constantly* to the old man in Hollywood. He's some kind of relation, y'know, and being Greek, of course, they all stick together,' Shirley said sarcastically.

'Naturally.' Hubert was not surprised. He remembered the fierce family loyalty of the Greeks when he'd commanded Hydra.

'And Sir Crispin?' he asked, referring to the world-famous and much-loved English actor who was playing Emperor Montezuma. 'What about him?'

'Oh, just the usual full of shit, faggoty Old Vic actor-knight, who thinks he knows everything,' Shirley whined. 'Always sounds to me like he's got his mouth full of plums. So far, he's kept a low profile though. Too busy chatting up beach boys. I think he rather fancies our Mr Brooks too, so he'll probably agree with anything the great movie star wants.'

'We have to get *all* the actors on our side, then there will be no contest with the scripts,' said the Italian. 'The studio will have to go along with the majority, otherwise we will have unrest and trouble on the set. That costs money, and you know how the studio hate wasting money.'

'Right,' said the Frankovitches in unison.

'But how are you going to do that?' Shirley asked. 'There's a production meeting with Nick in two hours. He'll fight our script, he always does.'

'Leave it to me,' Hubert said, Inès' pale face flickering across his mind like some old black and white movie. 'Leave it to me, my friends – I'll find a way to shoot *our* script, believe me, that I guarantee.'

At the official production meeting Bluey fidgeted uncomfortably – he hated confrontations. The only scenes he enjoyed were the ones he viewed from behind the cameras. But Nick needed him. Nick looked odd today. His olive skin was a greenish white, and his normally smiling mouth was clamped tighter than a rat trap.

The oily Italian, whom Bluey had disliked on sight, sat flanked by the Frankovitch team on one side of the table. As a trio, they'd be hard to beat in an ugliness contest, he mused. A war of words was in progress which was becoming even more heated by the tropical sun beating through the windows.

Hubert Croft held two scripts before him, one red, one blue.

'I will make no bones about it, Nick,' he rasped in that gravelly wheeze Nick remembered so well. 'This script –' he held the blue one high above his head in a boxer's gesture of victory – '*this one* is magic, pure cinematic *magic*. I read it last night and I cried tears of happiness that I was *privileged* enough to be involved in a project that uses the talents of these two wonderful people who wrote these wonderful words.'

Irving and Shirley beamed and nodded like ventriloquists' dummies as Bluey gave an audible groan.

'It's really up to the studio which script we shoot, isn't it?' Nick kept his voice crisp and businesslike, belying his fermenting fury at this man's astonishing audacity. One Italian film unreleased in America was all he had under his tight belt – Nick had checked that out last night – and he was now giving orders like the Mussolini clone he'd always felt himself to be. The hairs on the back of Nick's neck rose and he thought of Scrofo on Hydra, remembering the squat body stuffed into the ridiculous medal-lioned musical-comedy uniforms, prancing and puffing his way around the island, creating havoc and hatred wherever he went. But he mustn't think about that now – he couldn't. He must get his film made the way he wanted it.

If this movie failed, *he* would be blamed. Not the loathsome trio of the Frankovitches and Scrofo, not even the stars. No, it was *his* ass, Nick Stone's, that was on the line, and all his years of yearning, struggling to be a decent film director, would end up on the scrap heap. God, *why* had Spryos agreed to send this toad, this scowl on legs, to Acapulco? He had telephoned the old man last night, and had been told to 'shut up and do your job – that's what you're being paid for'. So much for family loyalty. With a film as expensive as *Cortez*, someone would have to be the whipping boy if it failed, and he knew that it would be he alone up there on the sacrificial altar.

His script was gritty, historically accurate, with battle scenes which showed the true horror of war. His love scenes were sensually realistic, not the lovey-dovey treacle syrup of the Frankovitches. And his dialogue was pithy and modern, in contrast to theirs which was stilted and flowery.

Tomorrow they would shoot the first scene of the movie, where Cortez and his men greet Emperor Montezuma on the shore. Nick wanted Cortez and a small boatload of sailors arriving to greet the emperor, who would only have a handful of warriors with him. The Frankovitch script had six hundred extras with Cortez, and several hundred men on shore with Montezuma. It certainly wasn't going to be easy, but that scene was going to be shot *his* way, or not at all. Let them fire him, he'd go back to the mail room if he had to.

As soon as the production meeting was over Nick hurried back to his room to try again to telephone Elektra. She was his rock, his sanity, and she was wise, not so much in the ways of the modern world, but in the simple ways which really counted. Wise about life, about people, about relationships. Her brand of wisdom was the wisdom of centuries, handed down from generation to generation by the power of the family, by which the Greeks all still lived. All international lines had been down yesterday and he had spent a frustrated night, needing to speak to her.

'Elektra.' He was so delighted to hear her soft voice that he immediately started talking rapidly in Greek. She still preferred it, even after nearly a decade in America.

'What can I do, Elektra? They're all ganging up on me, I know it – I can't stand it, darling – I'm about ready to walk off this picture even if Uncle Spyros sends me back to work in the mail room.'

'No, Nikolai.' Elektra's voice was quiet but insistent. 'You cannot do that. You have worked too hard for this opportunity – you cannot let it go, Nikolai – and you mustn't.'

'But you don't understand, Elektra,' he said despairingly. 'You don't know who's producing this film.'

'Who?' she asked.

'Scrofo,' he said grimly. 'Umberto Scrofo.'

'*What?*' cried Elektra. 'No, Nikolai, don't be ridiculous. It's not

341

possible – he's dead – you remember we heard that he'd died in Italy years ago?'

'Well, he isn't,' said Nick bleakly. 'I'm afraid the bastard's very much alive. He's here, and he's about to make my life a complete fucking misery. I want to *kill* him, Elektra – every time I look at his monstrous face I think about what he did to my mother and I feel this urge to crush the life out of him.'

His face became contorted and he started to sob into the telephone as Elektra tried to soothe him.

'Now Nikolai, *stop it*, you cannot allow him to win. First of all you *must* go ahead with the film – you must, you have to – for us, for Uncle Spyros, for the children.' She paused as she heard her husband's voice down the long-distance wires, still quavering but more in control.

'I know, Elektra – I know I've got to do it – but how in the bloody *hell* can I possibly work hand in glove with that murdering thieving piece of scum? How can I?'

'I know it's going to be difficult,' she said softly. 'I know it will be hard for you to forgive him for what he did to your mother.'

'Forgive him – *forgive Gourouni!* That motherfucker! Forget it!' hissed Nick. 'I'll never forgive him – how can I? I thought that maybe my hatred had died, Elektra – I thought that now I'm older I could never have the same kind of thoughts I did about that bastard when we were on Hydra. But I was wrong, completely wrong – my hatred was only dormant. It never died.'

'How, Nikolai, what do you mean you were wrong?' she asked fearfully.

'I want to kill him.' His lips were very close to the receiver and she heard the intensity in his voice as he spat out the words. 'I want to kill him, Elektra, and I'm going to kill him.'

'No, Nikolai, don't talk like that.' Elektra was afraid as she remembered how he'd tried to strangle her in her own bed. Sometimes her husband's temper and hot blood got the better of him. 'You mustn't do anything foolish, Nikolai,' she pleaded. 'Please don't.'

Talking to his wife had made him feel suddenly better, more in control, stronger. 'Don't worry – don't worry about it now, Elektra.

I'm not going to do it at this moment. I'll make this damned movie, I'll eat crow – I'll even work side by side with that filthy maggot – but when it's *over* with – I swear to you Elektra, Umberto Scrofo will be a dead man.'

It was lunchtime and as Julian walked along the burning sands to Caleta Beach, where local water-skiing instructors were chattering like magpies beneath the cool thatched huts, he thanked God that the hot-blooded production meeting was finally over. Frankly, he didn't really care if Cortez had six men or six hundred with him when he arrived in Mexico. Characterization was the most important thing to him, and the Frankovitches, Croft and Nick had nothing to say about that.

He orderd a *cerveza*, a local beer, instructing Angelito, the boat boy, that he wanted to go skiing right away.

'Oh, *Señor*. I'm sorry,' said Angelito. 'The Señorita Dominique, she book me for this afternoon.'

'Well, what about you then? Are you free?' Julian asked another boy irritably.

'It's fine with me, *Señor*, fine,' smiled Miguel, the proud possessor of a perfect set of gold-capped teeth which must have cost him a year's pay. 'My boat ees good – we ski well together, *Señor*.'

Suddenly there was a ripple of excitement from all the beach boys as Dominique arrived. Seeing Julian, she gave a little squeal of joy and rushed over to kiss him, letting her firm breasts crush against his chest through her flimsy *pareo*.

'I'm *so* happy to see you, *chéri*,' she gushed. 'Why don't we ski together?'

'Well, I – I've just booked Miguel,' Julian actually heard himself stutter.

'Oh, don't be silly,' cooed the peach, flashing Julian an irresistible smile that would no doubt bewitch her film audiences as much as it bewitched him. 'We can ski together, we're both alone.' She grabbed him by the hand and led him down the hot golden sands.

'You can teach me how to para-ski – they say you're so good at it.' She winked mischievously. 'Come on, let's go.'

*

Inès' doctor called her back from LA after lunch, ordering complete bed rest.

'Complete, you understand? That means you do not *move*. You stay in bed. You get up to go to the bathroom, but that's *it*. *No* sex for a fortnight, no moving about at all for at least a week.'

'Oh, no.' Inès was dismayed. 'But the film starts tomorrow, and Julian wants me to be on the set all the time, or at least nearby, and well – you know Julian is a very sexy man,' she said, feeling rather embarrassed.

'Well, I'm afraid Julian has little choice,' said the doctor brusquely. 'He can have you, or he can have this baby, but certainly not both. I warn you, Inès, if you exert yourself in any way, you could lose this child. I told you it was going to be difficult for you to conceive, you're lucky that you did; if you want this baby, be a good girl, stay put.'

He prescribed pills through a local doctor and Inès asked the concierge to pick them up for her; then she lay back, trying to relax. She felt feverish, her head a furnace, her mouth parched, but the more she drank, the more thirsty she became. She tried to lie still, but her knees were trembling with fear as she felt warm blood trickling slowly from her – blood that she thought might be her baby.

She couldn't lose this baby conceived in love, which would be so adored and that Julian wanted so desperately, she just couldn't. She drifted into a light, feverish sleep from which the deafening jangle of the old-fashioned telephone next to the bed woke her.

She instantly recognized the chilling tones.

'Mademoiselle Juillard,' inquired the gravelly voice.

'Yes?'

'I know you're alone because I saw your husband on the beach this morning, going water-skiing with our beautiful young star.'

'So? What do you want, Mr Croft, I'm resting.' Inès' voice was frigid. She wouldn't let him intimidate her. She was a strong woman, a survivor. Her experiences with men, Scrofo in Paris, Yves' cavalier departure from her life, her perverse English aristocrats, had made her vow that she'd never allow any man to abuse her again. She was a woman of the world, engaged to a famous man, beautiful, secure, pregnant and happy. So she'd tried to kill an enemy officer years ago.

So what? What could Umberto Scrofo possibly do to her now that could affect her life? she reasoned.

If he let it be known to the cast and crew that she'd been a whore, and that he had been one of her clients, they would realize, if they didn't already suspect, that he'd been one of Mussolini's bloodiest generals. Many of the film crew had fought on the beaches of Anzio, Dunkirk and the Pacific, or in the deserts of North Africa or over the skies of Great Britain. The war had ended scarcely ten years ago, but many people still treated Germans, Japanese and Italians with antipathy, particularly if they thought that they had been actively involved. No, Signor Scrofo would make a bad mistake with everyone if it was discovered that he had been a high–ranking officer in occupied Paris. She held a winning hand of cards in her well-manicured fingers – she could bluff him out.

'Since you're alone,' continued the hateful voice, 'I must insist upon seeing you. It is for your own benefit, Miss Juillard.'

Inès sighed. 'Listen to me. I'm unwell. My doctor has told me I must rest, which is exactly what I'm trying to do. If you feel you have any business with me, please state it on the telephone.'

'Miss Juillard, right now I'm downstairs in the lobby of your hotel.' His voice held more than a hint of menace. 'I will take up no more than five minutes of your precious time, but I must see you.' The 'precious' held an insulting innuendo. 'There are several people standing around here, including some crew members of *Cortez*. I do not think, Miss Juillard, that you would want them to hear what I have to say to you, do you?'

'Very well,' said Inès with a deep sigh. 'Room seventeen, on the second floor.' And she banged down the receiver.

Julian and Dominique lay back comfortably on their brightly coloured towels as the tropical sun warmed their bodies. The boat was a relatively crude affair, but Angelito was expert at manoeuvring it. Acapulco Bay was peacefully calm, and Angelito made a smooth circuit before turning towards La Roqueta.

Julian found Dominique's proximity, as she snuggled next to him, unnervingly erotic. Her eyes had cast a spell on him again and her curved, honey-coloured body, in the tiniest bikini, was driving his cock mad. He usually made love to Inès at least once a day; being deprived yesterday and this morning had made him acutely aware that the damn thing had a mind of its own, especially when it was near Dominique. His erection was becoming so obvious that he edged away from her before he made a complete fool of himself.

'Angelito, I want to ski around the bay,' he ordered. The tiny craft slowed down and Julian leaped over the side into the sparkling water, thankfully feeling his erection subsiding.

Angelito threw him a ski and the rope. Julian signalled to the boy, with a jerk the ancient boat sputtered and accelerated, and Julian rose from the water on his slalom like an arrow. Dominique cheered, admiring his marvellous physique. She thought that Looks Brooks possessed a body and face which even a Greek god would envy. His week of resting, sunshine and rigorous morning workouts had brought him back to perfect shape. His hair was now slicked down flat to his head by the wind and water as he gestured to Angelito to go faster.

There were only a few luxury pleasure boats moored in the port and around the bay, but many speedboats and tiny sailing boats. Angelito steered the boat past the 'morning' beach, where laughing brown children played together in the waves while their weary fathers stared blankly out to sea. Mothers, aunts, sisters and grandmothers ceremoniously laid out the Sunday lunch on the beach for the one day the family all spent together. The children, many of them naked since bathing suits were a luxury few Mexican families could afford, waved excitedly at the passing speedboats.

They zoomed past the 'afternoon' beach, the more tourist-oriented area of Acapulco, where under straw hats overweight American vacationers from visiting cruise ships sampled the pleasures of this new resort. Sipping *piña-coladas*, they oiled themselves as the tropical sun turned their white bodies to various shades of scarlet. On the shore, Julian could see the skeleton of the new Hilton Hotel, its black iron girders an eyesore. If those hideous high-rise hotels start appearing all along this shore, it will be only a matter of time before this glorious place is ruined for ever, he thought. Salt water stung his face as he criss-crossed over the wake several times with professional panache, until he finally let go of the rope and waited for the boat to pick him up.

'Bravo,' cried Dominique. 'Oh, Julian, you're brilliant. Where did you learn to ski so divinely?'

She leaned over the bow of the boat, looking so sexy that it would have been hard for any man over the age of seven not to have been affected by her. Julian had noticed the bulge in Angelito's trunks when the boy helped Dominique into his boat, brushing his arm unnecessarily against her soft, lightly tanned shoulder. She was an incredibly sensual girl, a little French minx who had learned – too well – the art of driving men crazy.

Angelito looked questioningly towards an island of mustard-coloured rock shaped like a fat man sleeping after a good lunch. Julian nodded, and the boat sped across the bobbing waves.

One o'clock was early for lunch at La Roqueta, and few people were there yet. The jovial *patron* offered them the most secluded table in the restaurant, his eyes goggling at the sight of Dominique in her virtually transparent *pareo*. Angelito's brief words in Spanish gave him the lowdown on Julian, the big movie star.

'Let's have the biggest, strongest, most Mexicanish drink in the house,' Dominique said, a mischievous glint in her eyes.

'What a marvellous idea,' Julian laughed, already half drunk with her charms. 'Let's have two each.'

Soon they were sipping, through straws, from coconut shells in which pineapples, bananas, three kinds of rum, some tequila, brandy and fruit juice had been expertly blended.

'Mmm. Delicious.' Dominique smiled. 'Better than a chocolate malt any day.'

The tropical air on his skin, the sense of wellbeing and exhilaration from water-skiing and the sight of this delectable female all left Julian feeling incredibly alive, virile and young. Not even the most exotic lovemaking with Inès had ignited him in this way; he felt like a slow-burning coal which had either to be doused completely or be allowed to burst into leaping tongues of fire. He didn't understand himself at all. He didn't want to.

He downed both drinks fast, then blurted out, 'God, you're so beautiful. I know this sounds strange – and I know I shouldn't say this – but I want so much to kiss you, Dominique.' All inhibitions seemed to have flown and he watched the slow smile spread across her exquisite face.

'It's what I want too, Julian,' she whispered huskily.

Her total lack of pretence and archness was so unlike the ways of the women he usually met that Julian felt like a sixteen-year-old schoolboy again. That delicious innocence which hadn't yet learned to say *no* when desire was saying *yes*, made her sensuality more erotic than if she were lying naked in bed beside him.

After several more strong drinks and a lunch of plump grilled shrimps, lobster and rice, Julian and Dominique set off to explore the tiny, almost deserted island. Only the restaurant, now half filled with tourists, was evidence of any habitation. Julian felt as if he were going to burst. The touch of Dominique's hand on his arm was sending electric shocks of desire through his whole being, as they strolled around the rocks and out of sight of the few tourists.

Dominique felt a shiver of excitement and anticipation as they rounded the caramel sands where an ancient banana tree shaded a small beach.

Julian stopped, held Dominique's lovely face between his hands, and let his mouth gently explore hers. Her lips were petal-soft, more yielding than any he had ever kissed before. They were innocent, trusting, naive, the lips of a little girl – then as her tongue came to claim his, they became wantonly erotic. It was the mouth of a woman who knew exactly what she wanted and knew how to get it, and knew instinctively where all the pleasure sources lay. His hands dropped to the ribbons of her bikini top. How he had longed to hold these glorious breasts, to trace their contours, exploring with fingers and tongue, to watch her excitement increase. But Dominique was not quite ready to grant his wish yet.

Moving away from him, she took a bottle of suntan oil from her straw bag and, leaning against the trunk of the banana tree, started to rub it slowly into her shoulders and chest. With her head thrown back, her eyes closed, Julian watched, mesmerized, as her bikini top started inching down and her rosy nipples became visible. Her breathing accelerated as she started to massage them with the oil. They glistened and shone in the sunlight, her nipples now erect, like pink shells. Julian moved towards her, but she stopped him with a gesture, continuing her erotic caresses — the ones that Gaston had taught her that summer. Her top was off now; her fingers had

348

worked their way down to her flat stomach, to the band of her bikini bottom. Julian was now dizzy with desire as the vision shimmered before him in the heat. Soon she was completely naked, abandoned, leaning against the tree, her skin glistening, and her eyes signalled that now it was time.

Dominique's fingers entwined in Julian's thick brown hair as his tongue and lips pleasured her breasts and his own fingers encircled her soft but muscled rear. She gave little whimpers of ecstasy as she stripped him of his shorts, aggressively pulling him down on to the hot sand, oblivious to discomfort. She clumsily but enthusiastically took his cock into her mouth as Gaston had taught her, and he felt the eruption start to rise deep within him, an explosion which took every ounce of his concentration and willpower to control. Her catlike eyes smiled up at him as her lips anointed him and she slid his hard, bursting skin in and out of her warm mouth.

He had to take her now – he could wait no longer. He forgot Inès – forgot their love, their baby, their marriage. All he could think of was this enchantress. Gently he lifted her from him, moving until his body lay on top of hers for a magic second or two, then with a groan of pleasure he entered her. She was a more than willing partner, moistly receptive. Their sweat mingling, lips and tongues entwined, her eyes wide open, smiling, willing him on, he plunged into her, his face contorted in fierce ecstasy as he set the rhythm of their passion. She could feel an imminent and unfamiliar convulsion building inside her.

'I love you,' she whispered. 'I love you, Julian. I love you,' truly meaning it as she cried out his name in joy.

As the sound of speedboats hummed in the distance and as the waves lapped near their bucking bodies, the lovers orgasmed together with shouts which seemed to echo around the whole bay.

And from far away, the lone passenger in a small motorboat focused his telescopic lens and clicked the shutter of his camera again and again.

With her silk kimono sticking uncomfortably to her moist skin, Inès lay on her bed in agony listening to what the detestable Scrofo had come to say. 'Please, get to the point, Mr Croft,' she said weakly, lighting a cigarette. 'I must rest, it's my doctor's orders.

'Then you shouldn't smoke.' His tone was irritatingly patronizing. 'Especially since you are pregnant.'

'How do you know I'm pregnant? No one here knows. Besides, it's none of your business.'

His voice was steely. 'I know everything, I'm the producer of this film and I make it my business to know everything about everyone.' But he smiled inwardly. It had been an educated guess, but it had hit its mark. 'Don't forget that, ever – don't underestimate me either, Miss Juillard.'

'Well, what's your business with me? I have nothing to do with your precious film, so what do you want?'

'You have *everything* to do with the film. You're the fiancée of the star. It seems that the great star doesn't much like the excellent script which Mr and Mrs Frankovitch, writers of the highest proficiency and artistic merit, have written. He and Bluey Regan were quite difficult with me this morning.' His pig eyes drilled into hers. 'And the Greek, Nicholas Stone, the so-called *wunderkind* director who has directed only two films, he also does not like the script.'

'But what does all this have to do with me?' Inès cried, 'I hardly know Nick Stone or the Frankovitches.'

Scrofo's body oozed over the edge of the chair in which he sat while staring at her contemptuously. She felt a terrible stab of fear. How could this man not inspire fear with his evil smile, twisted mind and grotesque body in his vulgar and self-conscious clothes. He looked ridiculous in his powder blue safari suit, his gross hairy arms bulging out of the short sleeves, and the military style gold buttons which looked about to bust from their button holes as they strained across his great belly. In spite of herself a look of revulsion came into her face as she noticed the silk scarf knotted loosely around his neck, and the hideous scar for which she had herself been responsible. But he'd made her do it, there was nothing else she could have done. She shuddered at the memory of the agony and humiliation Scrofo had caused her, and a cold fury came over her as she pictured herself as that young girl in Paris. How could she ever forget the pain? Dr Langley's sinister words suddenly came back to her: 'You're a healthy woman, Inès, and there's no reason why you shouldn't have a beautiful baby, but you've obviously had a very bad time with someone. You have scar tissue, you must have been injured once.'

'Could it affect the baby?' Inès had asked tearfully.

'Not if you're careful. But you've suffered quite a bit of damage to your womb and cervix – and I'm not saying it necessarily will, but it *might* affect your pregnancy unless, as I say, unless you're very careful.'

Now as Inès stared back at Scrofo with undisguised loathing in her eyes, she suddenly understood. Of course, this man was the very reason why she was lying here in her bed of pain, bleeding, unable to move, all because of those monstrous and perverted acts which he'd inflicted on her years ago.

Scrofo moved from the wicker chair to stand at the end of Inès' bed, his brown boots clattering on the marble floor, his grey-white face covered with a thin film of sweat. Inès could hear luncheon being served and happy Mexican music from the patio below. She looked out at the beautiful day, at the sun-flecked cottonwool clouds. How she wanted to be outside, anywhere but here, alone with this horror.

'So,' he said, his voice now becoming venomous and threatening, 'I'll spell it out for you, *whore*, you murdering whore.' Involuntarily he fingered his scar, his lips twisting in that familiar and repulsive way she could never forget.

'Nobody knows anything of your past here, do they? Not even your precious fiancé?' He looked at her menacingly. 'Do they, Inès? Prostitute, whore, streetwalker – from what age? How old were you when I had you? Thirteen? Fourteen?'

Inès felt her brain fill with a kind of red mist. She was reliving the nightmare – she could almost feel the razor in her hand as she'd sliced it across his yielding throat. She felt her stomach contracting in intermittent spasms of pain. Warm blood had made her thighs feel slippery. She made an immense effort to calm herself.

'It's none of your business, Scrofo! Tell me what you want of me, for God's sake.' She stubbed out her cigarette, lighting another immediately. The bed was now wet with blood, but she couldn't move. There was a buzzing in her head. This spectre from her past was going to ruin her future, her perfect future.

'I'm not going to say anything more to upset you now.' He looked at her in mock pity. 'You're white as a sheet, you don't look at all well. You should get some rest, so I'll get to the point and then leave you in peace. I want to tell you just one thing. As I have told you, I have discovered that nobody either in America or on this film – and most certainly not Julian Brooks – is aware of your sordid past. I'm going to need your help at certain strategic times during the filming. I know you discuss the script with your fiancé, I know he depends very much on your advice. When I tell you' – he leaned towards her menacingly – 'I repeat, when I tell you that I want Julian to prefer scene A rather than scene B, I want you to coerce him, exert every particle of influence that you have on him to see that he accepts my choice. *Do you understand?* If you *don't* comply with my wishes, well, let's just say there'll be very serious consequences.'

She nodded silently. She would have agreed to anything just to get this creature out of her sight.

'All right, I will. I promise,' she whispered, holding back her tears.

'Good, then your secret, as they say, will be safe with me, Inès my dear.' He waddled over to the door. 'The first two scenes will be arriving this evening. Be sure you insist that Mr Brooks prefers the first one.' And with that he closed the door behind him.

With an animal sound, Inès staggered to the bathroom, seeing, to her horror, that her blood was streaking the marble tiles scarlet.

'Oh, no,' she cried. 'No, no. Oh please, God, no!'

After the incident with Croft, Inès had spent the rest of the afternoon trying to recover. When Julian returned from his afternoon with Dominique, she was able to greet him with a semblance of normality. Caught up in her own personal trauma, she failed to notice that Julian was somewhat distant, lacking his usual affectionate attentiveness.

But he was still extremely concerned about her condition, even though she assured him that Dr Langley had said that, as long as she was careful, all would be well. He was secretly relieved that lovemaking was forbidden for at least two weeks.

It would give him time to think, and to savour the enchanted afternoon he'd spent with Dominique, who had visited him in his dreams that night. He awoke, covered with sweat, and to feelings of guilt and horror, mumbling her name. But Inès was sleeping soundly, a pill helping her to expunge the memory of Scrofo's threats.

Julian was worried and ashamed of his behaviour with Dominique. He tried hard to analyse what spell she must have cast over him, but he couldn't. Their lovemaking that afternoon had been both wonderfully exhilarating and quite exceptional, but maybe it was because she was so young, just a schoolgirl really, and the added spice of being outdoors and the possibility of being discovered had made it all the more thrilling.

He sighed heavily, looking at his frowning face in the bathroom mirror. 'You're a rat, Julian Brooks,' he mouthed to himself. 'A dirty rotten rat. What the fuck are you doing?' He gazed at himself for a minute or two but his reflection gave him no answers. Throwing cold water on his face, he walked back into the bedroom and settled down to study his dialogue for tomorrow's scenes.

*

In the morning while they breakfasted on their terrace, Inès and Julian chatted desultorily. This was to be the first day of shooting, and he seemed preoccupied. There was a dull ache in the pit of Inès' stomach, whether from a possible miscarriage or the fear of Scrofo's threats, she didn't know. She only knew that for the first time since they'd met she was pleased that Julian was going out. The previous evening she'd done her utmost to persuade him that the scene in script A was so much better for him as an actor than the scene in script B. Appealing to his ego seemed to have succeeded and she thought she'd managed to convince him, even though he went off with both scripts in his haversack.

She was left alone with her thoughts, and with only the calls of seabirds for company.

Nick tried hard to overcome his first-day nerves as he stood in the sandy bay, starting to block the first scene of the morning when Cortez, Pisarro and their men arrive on the shores of Mexico for the first time. Cortez was to be greeted by Emperor Montezuma and his warriors, while his beautiful daughter, Princess Isabella, stayed modestly in the background.

Dominique had been enveloped by the wardrobe department in thick folds of embroidered linen. She had little to do in this scene but play the virgin maiden, eyes appropriately downcast as she sees bold Cortez for the first time.

She tried to catch Julian's eye as she was sitting on her canvas chair under a large umbrella planted in the sand. It was only eight in the morning but the heat was already overpowering, encased as she was in the yards of itchy fabric, with an enormous hank of false hair under her headdress, which weighed a ton. She cooled herself with a woven straw fan and sipped ice water as her makeup crew buzzed around her.

Suddenly an aide came running down the beach waving two telegrams – one for Nick and one for Croft. When Croft had read his, a triumphant look came into his face. He knew victory was his now.

Julian had called him late the night before, informing him that he preferred the first script. Croft had also had a short telephone conversation with Dominique, who'd been anxious to do whatever Julian wanted, and Sir Crispin too had agreed.

Now there would be more audience-pleasing spectacle, more pomp and circumstance, more crowd scenes, more battle scenes. Croft and the Frankovitches would make *Cortez* a much more important movie – a worthy successor to *The Robe*, *Quo Vadis* and the other epic blockbusters of the fifties. The actors would glitter and shine like thirty-carat diamonds in a Van Cleef & Arpels setting.

Nick stared in silence at his own telegram, which was also from his uncle. He'd lost.

Spyros Makopolis had made it abundantly clear. He and the vice-presidents of MCCP, having carefully reviewed the relative merits of the two scripts, had been unanimous in their verdict. The most bankable script was definitely the Frankovitch one. That was the one they wanted Nick to shoot, that was the one he was going to have to shoot.

They wanted pageantry, histrionics, lavish spectacle and violent bloody battles. The Mexican extras were paid so little that it wouldn't make much difference to the budget if the film company used sixty or six hundred of them. They were even now being outfitted in the uniforms of sixteenth-century sailors and warriors, while two hundred and fifty others, stripped to the waist, were having wads of black hair attached to their scalps and skimpy loincloths draped around their hips.

'You've won, you leprous bastard,' Nick hissed, grabbing the Italian's arm with furious strength as Scrofo's livid face stared back at him in triumph.

'You may have won this round, pigface, but don't you *dare* tell me where I should put the extras or the actors or any piece of fucking furniture in any scene. Don't you dare tell *me* how to direct my actors – they'll say the motherfucking lines *my* way, and if you put your gross face near any one of my crew, I'll slam it into that rock until it's nothing but mincemeat.'

Dominique pricked up her ears and watched with the rest of the cast and crew in amazement as Nick and Hubert Croft battled it out at the water's edge.

Next to her sat Sir Crispin Peake, his noble brow beaded with sweat which trickled out from under his large black wig. He now put aside his *Times* crossword to watch the argument between the two men. He never liked to miss anything, and he and Julian exchanged knowing glances.

Sir Crispin adored Julian, and they'd been in several West End plays together. He had agreed to appear in this film only for a substantial salary. Although his *King Lear* had been a great success with the London critics, the public, alas, had not flocked in any great numbers to see it. He'd accepted this job partly in order to save face but, as he was fond of remarking, also to 'keep Tony in gold taps'. Tony was his handsome young live-in companion, who was constantly redecorating their two enormous houses.

As befitted his position as one of Britain's theatrical knights, he'd been given his own personal dresser, the ubiquitous Alf, who busied himself bringing 'His Nibs' all that was required for his rarefied English blood to better withstand the tropical climate. Even now in the ninety-degree heat, Sir Crispin was sipping a hot cup of lapsang suchong tea from a delicate china cup, as he held a Friebourg Treyer cigarette between his elegant fingers. A Chinese paper fan was doing little to cool him and his patrician features were flushed.

Scrofo's much more plebeian features were also puce as he strode about on the sand, waving his arms and shouting at Nick in his throaty squawk, his blue voile shirt already wringing wet and his few remaining strands of hair stuck to his scarlet scalp. He was exhausted. Unable to sleep last night due to a combination of heat and excitement, he'd been up at dawn, awaiting confirmation from Spyros Makopolis that the studio would agree to shoot the Frankovitch script. And he had! Success was his.

Nick and Bluey now found themselves outflanked, outnumbered and outvoted.

Umberto started to speak but Nick's fingers, which were still holding on to his arm, dug tighter.

'You don't remember me, Gourouni, do you? But I remember you – I remember you very fucking well no matter what you call yourself now, I'd never forget you, never. I'll do this fucking script the way you and those two scumbags and the fucking studio want me to. I'll have the thousand fucking extras and the goddam battle scenes and the charge of the fucking Light Brigade.' The whole beach was now riveted by the screaming fury of the normally soft-spoken young director. He towered over the squat Italian, and even though the crew couldn't quite hear any of the words, the body language was unmistakable.

'But just watch it, you pasta-loving prickhead,' Nick spat out venomously. 'Watch your fat ass. I'll play *everything* by the rules, but it's gonna be *my* film, the way I want it, with or without a crowd of extras standing around scratching their balls.' With a snort of contempt he released Scrofo's arm and the Italian stumbled, almost falling over.

Taking his well-fingered Greek worry beads out of his pocket, Nick started turning them in his fingers rapidly while calling, 'Okay, Bluey, let's go. I want first team and all the extras for a line-up – *now!*'

As the Pacific ebbed around Umberto's handmade shoes, he was torn between elation and blinding rage. Yes, he'd won. He was going to produce a film with all the brilliance which he'd put into *La Città Perduta* but the angry young director had berated and humiliated him in front of the entire cast and crew, made him look idiotic – weak – foolish. And God how he hated to look a fool, for people to laugh at him.

Stone's hatred, Scrofo thought, was out of all proportion to their short working relationship. They'd known each other only for a few days. Since Nick was Greek, Umberto wondered if perhaps he'd lived on Hydra during the time of his command. So what? The Greeks were all so stupid. All those peasants had gone to their deaths without protest or resistance whether it was by starvation, torture or firing squad, like silent and obedient sheep. He had no respect for any of them. Reluctantly, however, Scrofo had to admit that this Greek had balls, even though he'd humiliated him.

'Well done,' Ramona said admiringly. 'Well done, Hubert my dear.' The sun was glittering on her heavily embroidered costume as she gushed, 'I'm *so* glad we're going to shoot the Frankovitch script, darling, I *much* prefer it.'

Umberto knew she preferred it only because she had a few extra scenes to play, but he smiled his thanks, even though he was seething, and conscious of the entire crew looking at him out of the corners of their eyes – probably laughing at him, he thought.

'Now Hubert, I have an idea.' Ramona linked a braceleted arm through his while they strolled across the beach towards the set-up. 'That wretched hotel where you're staying has no air conditioning and such terrible service, I'm sure you didn't sleep much last night. You didn't, did you?'

Umberto shook his head.

'I'm in that huge house all by my little self,' she said coquettishly. 'I have more guest rooms than I know what to do with. You'd be *far* more comfortable staying there with me. You can have the whole second level of rooms for your offices and secretary, and of course we're only five minutes from the Villa Vera. What d'you think, Hubert dear, would you like that?'

'I should like that very much indeed. Thank you, Ramona my dear,' he said, grinning. 'You're very thoughtful, as usual.'

'Wonderful,' Ramona beamed. 'I've also asked the little French girl, Dominique, and her guardian to stay.' She leaned confidentially towards him. 'It's not safe for young women to walk alone at night in Acapulco any more. I heard that the chaperone was attacked and almost raped on the beach only a few nights ago.'

'Really?' Umberto raised his eyebrows, looking towards the ghostly, waiflike figure of Agathe who was hovering near Dominique. Who could possibly want to rape *her*?

Since there were never any secrets on a location, the entire crew seemed to know the story of Agathe's narrow escape from the thugs in the bar. And some of the boys were already taking bets as to when Julian would pack Inès off to Europe so that Dominique could move in on him lock, stock and eyeliner. It seemed to be even money on that.

13

Sir Crispin was staring down the beach at Dominique's tanned dancer's body as she played around at the water's edge with several of the younger male crew members. They had been shooting for over a week now and she was friendly with all of them.

'Surely that child must be jail bait?' he asked Ramona, who sat sipping iced orange pekoe tea with him beneath the shade of an enormous striped umbrella.

'Of course she is,' smiled Ramona, who had become more than a little maternal towards Dominique. 'But I'm quite sure she's still an innocent, Crispin, after all she is only sixteen and she comes from a good family in France.'

Sir Crispin slowly nodded his head, which was weighed down with the coarse plaited hair of a dozen Chinese maidens.

'I wouldn't believe that for a second, my dear. And what's France got to do with it?' he asked, watching the squealing and giggling Dominique being chased into the waves by one of the better-looking stuntmen. 'She certainly has oomph, but she looks as if she likes to do a great deal more than just kiss and cuddle.'

Ramona took off her sunglasses in order to get a clearer view of the laughing nymph at the sea's edge.

'Nonsense, Crispin, Agathe guards that girl like a tigress. She couldn't *possibly* be anything but a virgin. There's no doubt she's destined for stardom, wouldn't you say? With that face and that unbelievable shape – how could she not be?'

'I wouldn't know, my dear, she's not really my type,' Sir Crispin replied with an ironic little smile. He looked quizzically into Ramona's painted face. She really was a creature of cosmetic myth.

'My dear, it was your star which surely shone the brightest when the Hollywood dream factory was at its zenith. Now, of course, the star system, as we both used to know it, is fast disintegrating,' he said.

'It most certainly is,' agreed Ramona. 'And the studios are signing fewer and fewer contract players each year; the big stars are now all trying desperately to be independent.'

'Out of the dozens that they do sign, how much longer after the initial burst of fame do you think their moment of celebrity will last?' Sir Crispin asked dryly.

Ramona made no reply, as she thought about her own long and eventful career, remembering herself at Dominique's age.

'What, I wonder, does *her* future hold,' the old knight speculated, almost to himself. 'Is she a Cinderella-girl, who will return to St Tropez in a few years to become just another *femme de ménage*? Or will she become an addict of all the hoopla and idolatry, and throw herself away on a succession of unworthy men?'

'She'll hardly do *that*, Crispin,' laughed Ramona. 'She's so ravishing that they'll be standing in line to escort her. She's not a girl to lose her head over a man.'

'Humph,' said Sir Crispin enigmatically as Julian joined them, hot and sweating from the scene he'd just been shooting.

'Jesus, it's a scorcher,' he gasped, ripping off his velvet doublet and pulling open his shirt to the waist. 'How you stand that bloody wig on your head all day old boy, I'll never know. Why on earth don't you take it off?'

'My dear fellow,' Sir Crispin answered drolly, 'this hideous object is attached to my poor scant-haired scalp by at least a pound of the most foul-smelling glue. I can assure you that its removal every evening is absolute torture, dear boy, worse than anything which could have been thought up by Torquemada and his frightful Spanish inquisition.'

Ramona and Julian both laughed, as Julian's dresser appeared bringing him a glass of cold beer, which he tipped to his lips, watching the object of his new passion who was still cavorting in the waves.

Sir Crispin turned his beady eyes towards Julian, paying particular attention to the hard muscles of his golden chest, which quivered deliciously as he swallowed his beer. Sir Crispin was always attracted to a magnificent male body, and few he'd ever seen were as magnificent as Looks Brooks'. Julian had always reminded him of a breathtaking Bernini sculpture of Apollo that he'd once seen in a museum in Rome.

'Dear boy, we were just talking about yon vestal virgin,' he said waggishly. 'I was saying to Ramona that I thought she was *no* stranger to the world of the championship blow-job. What do you think, Julian?'

Julian almost choked on his beer, and to his horror, he felt himself blushing.

'Now, now, Crispin, we'll have none of that,' he said with a splutter as his dresser sprang forward to mop his velvet breeches.

'God, Crispin, you're terrible,' chuckled Ramona. 'Dominique's just a baby. How can you say such things?'

'It seems to me that the younger they are, the more sex they always want,' said Sir Crispin authoritatively.

'Well, I suppose you should know, old chap, shouldn't you?' Julian winked, grinning at Ramona.

Suddenly Dominique let out an ear-piercing shriek as one of the men she'd been fooling around with jumped on top of her in the water.

'Our baby is growing up fast,' observed Sir Crispin, his liquid brown eyes glittering with amusement from behind his pebble glasses. 'And my dears, if *she's* a virgin then *I'm* Edith Evans.'

'Now you come to mention it, you've actually developed an uncanny resemblance to Edith recently,' Julian teased, trying his best to ignore Dominique, who was now completely soaked, her long black hair flying in the wind, as she was chased repeatedly across the waves by two large and excitable members of the camera crew.

'Yes, I think it must be the wig,' laughed Ramona.

'That mass of hair, old chap, is identical to the one Edith had to wear as Cleopatra,' Julian said with tears of laughter coming into his eyes.

'But I have bigger breasts than she has,' Sir Crispin said with a note of triumph, revelling in his audience's laughter. 'I remember going to see a matinée of Edith's Cleopatra,' he reminisced. 'My dear, the audience consisted of three old ladies and an afghan hound, and the afghan hound appeared to be having the most fun.'

They laughed again just as Dominique, like a giggling dervish, streaked towards them, hotly pursued by her group of admirers.

'Julian, oh Julian, help me please!' she squealed in mock terror as she threw herself down into his lap.

'Those men, they're teasing me so much,' she said, nestling her wet body on to his warm chest, feeling him stiffen beneath her. 'Please help me, Julian,' she said plaintively, peeking up at him through her wet sooty eyelashes which partially hid the secret message contained in her eyes. 'Please!'

As Julian felt an embarrassing erection stirring, he quickly but playfully tumbled her off his knees and on to the sand.

'What do you think you're doing, young lady?' he scolded. 'Nick told me the next scene is with you and all of us, and here you are messing about in the waves. You're a very naughty girl.'

Dominique pouted prettily up at him.

'Most unprofessional, dear girl,' said Sir Crispin, wagging an admonishing finger. 'Never keep them waiting, my dear – better you wait for them – as alas we've all being doing for *hours*.'

'OK, OK,' laughed Dominique, cheekily grabbing Julian's beer from him and taking a large sip. 'I'm going – I'll be ready in less than ten minutes, I promise, you know how fast I can be.'

'We'll take your word for it,' murmured Sir Crispin, noticing with a frisson of pleasure that Julian was rearranging the bulging crotch of his trousers. He congratulated himself for not having missed the stimulating sight of Julian's sudden and impressive erection. 'Oh well,' said Sir Crispin blithely, 'where there's youth, there's bound to be gaiety – isn't that true, Julian dear boy?'

'Absolutely,' Julian agreed, finishing his beer and casually picking up his script to cover his lap.

'She's certainly a bright and spirited young maiden, our little *mademoiselle*,' smiled Sir Crispin, 'I dare say she'll break many hearts before we're all much older.'

The small house party usually dined quietly each evening on the second terrace. Shooting finished at sundown, and after Umberto had attended a series of production meetings in his offices, spoken to Hollywood half a dozen times, and screamed at everyone who'd crossed him that day, a calm civilized dinner would be served.

Dominique adored living in Ramona's palatial mansion; it was as

362

if she'd found herself in some great big beautiful doll's house. Agathe was quietly impressed by some of the pictures and sculptures, and she lived in constant nervous anticipation that Julian might be invited to dinner.

When Ramona first extended a dinner invitation to Nick, the young Greek asked her bluntly, 'Will Croft be there?'

'Why yes – of course he will,' answered Ramona, somewhat flustered by Nick's burning brown eyes. 'He's one of my house guests.'

'Then thank you very much for the invitation, Princess,' he said, 'but I don't intend to spend any more time in the company of that grotesque creature than is absolutely necessary.'

'I see,' said Ramona, raising pencilled brows, not seeing at all. 'In that case perhaps it would be better if I didn't invite you again.'

She seemed so piqued that Nick, always trying to be the diplomat and also a genuine admirer of Ramona, said, 'Please don't take it personally, Princess. You know, as well as the whole crew does, that there's no love lost between Croft and me. In fact we loathe each other. Please try to understand, will you?'

'Of course,' said Ramona graciously. 'But I hope that one day you may change your mind.'

He smiled grimly. 'If the Toad is guaranteed not to be there then I'd be delighted to dine with you, Princess.'

'It's a date,' smiled Ramona, mentally removing Nick from the guest list which she kept permanently in her head.

Sir Crispin Peake, whose eccentric English humour livened up the sometimes sombre gatherings, was one of Ramona's favourite guests. Attractive young diplomats from the American embassy, visiting socialites, film stars and politicians would also often be asked. Ramona's table was famous, and invitations from her were much in demand, but to Agathe's disappointment Julian never came to dinner.

Inès had become virtually a prisoner in her hotel suite. Doctor Langley had insisted that she spend the next seven months in bed if she really wanted to have this baby.

'Just get up for the wedding day. And *no sex*. Not even necking,' he told her continually.

Although Julian had been extremely understanding about her condition, Inès knew there was a limit to a man's sexual altruism. She was torn between her love for him, and wanting to show it, and her longing to have his child. Every night they were together and he studied his script whilst she lay in bed trying not to feel sorry for herself, trying to make bright and interesting conversation. But it was difficult to make interesting conversation when she spent every day flat on her back staring at the ceiling. Although Inès tried hard, she had the ominous feeling that Julian was drifting away from her, his mind on other things. She knew that the movie was arduous and that there was a good deal of tension on the set. What Inès didn't know was that each lunch hour and practically every day after shooting, Looks Brooks and Dominique were making passionate love behind the locked doors and curtained windows of her trailer.

14

The studio was ecstatic about the first week's rushes. Nick was doing a masterful job of injecting an intimate, realistic style into the Frankovitches' overly melodramatic and flowery script. The result was a brilliant contrast with the sixteenth-century grandeur and pageantry. The studio believed it was going to create a new look in film, and they were eagerly planning other historical epics for Nick to direct.

Each day Agathe would sit on the set and quietly watch, saying little. The crew hardly ever spoke to her. With her strangely forbidding looks and manner, and her stiff and correct English, it was almost like trying to communicate with a wax mannequin. She tested Dominique on her lines and watched over her while she daydreamed constantly of Julian.

Since Agathe's experience on the beach she regarded all men, with the exception of Julian, with great suspicion, but she was totally blind to the smouldering affair which was going on between him and Dominique. To her, Dominique was nothing more than a school-girl. Granted she was an actress now and in a major motion picture, but she was still a child, a girl who knew nothing of life. Agathe's mind was a kaleidoscope of images of Julian. She couldn't keep her eyes off him when she sat on the sidelines at the beaches, lagoons and mountains, watching the shooting. Through her dark glasses and with a hat tipped over her forehead she would observe his every gesture, his every movement.

The fact that he was friendly, even flirtatious, with Dominique was attributed by Agathe to the natural closeness that all film people seemed to develop with one another. How she envied them that. The easy jokes, the sarcastic familiarity which bordered on a kind of rudeness, seemed to bind them all closely together.

The only person who spent any time with her, other than

Dominique, was Sir Crispin Peake. He often sat beside her underneath a big striped umbrella, regaling her with long-ago anecdotes and tales of the British stage. Agathe thought him tedious since she found it difficult to understand his theatrical humour, but she tried to sit near him because Julian adored him and would always come over to talk to him between set-ups. With his doublet off, his tanned chest gleaming with a faint sheen of perspiration, he would laugh his head off at the old knight's stories and captivate Agathe still more. After those days when she sat on the golden sands with Sir Crispin and Julian, Agathe's nights would be gloriously erotic and she would pleasure herself frantically.

One day, when no one was near, she had purloined another of Julian's shirts from his portable dressing room. It was of white cambric, one that he'd worn in a duelling scene. The wardrobe woman had several doubles of it, and this one had been ripped. As it couldn't be used again, Agathe didn't consider that she was stealing. She was just borrowing something of Julian's which would bring him even closer to her. She could almost feel his body next to her when she lay with it at night.

As for that prostitute fiancée of his, Inès, she never appeared, although rumours were rife around the unit that she was pregnant. Pregnant! Agathe didn't ask Julian if it was true, she hardly dared talk to him at all because she always blushed so furiously that she felt sure he could read her thoughts. But she was filled with bitter rage that this magnificent man could have sown his seed in the body of that traitorous whore.

15

Dominique now believed that she was madly in love with Julian. Two weeks of abandoned lovemaking made her want him all the more. When they were together on the set it was as if an electric current flowed and crackled between their bodies. Her eyes glowed like beacons whenever she was near him, and their sexual combustion on the screen was so visible that rapturous telegrams were sent from Hollywood to Nick congratulating him on creating and capturing such magical chemistry on film. The screen almost melted the first time Julian and Dominique kissed. Gasps of amazement rippled through the screening rooms, as many of the normally hard-bitten executives sighed with vicarious pleasure.

'More love scenes! These two are hotter than even Gable and Leigh, Clift and Taylor. Write more,' went the gist of the telegrams which were fired off to Nick and Hubert Croft.

'More love scenes!' cackled Shirley, crouching over her ancient typewriter, a cigarette dangling from between her lips. 'What a pity we can't shoot the hot ones going on in that hussy's trailer every lunchtime. I'll give 'em more love scenes – we'll scorch the screen with 'em.'

Irving didn't bother to answer. He ignored Shirley when she was bitchy. She was so obviously vicariously enjoying the steamy affair which was being played out right under everyone's noses that he thought he would give her the job of writing the new romantic scenes between Julian and Dominique that the studio craved. He was sitting at the other end of their Villa Vera sitting room with a yellow legal pad on his lap as he yet again re-wrote the ending of the film.

Nick had not given up. Even though MCCP were still insisting on shooting the original Frankovitch script, Nick was such a perfectionist that he was constantly harassing the Frankovitches into changing a line here – making a scene better there – polish, polish, polish. Irving admired and respected his persistence, and he'd had to grudgingly admit that Nick was almost always right. Croft and Shirley were usually unanimous in *their* criticism and denunciation of all Nick's ideas, and the battles between them still raged on, but now with Irving more often taking Nick's side of the argument.

Shirley rat-tat-tatted away on her typewriter, spinning out the erotic scene in which the young Princess Isabella has to perform a dance for Cortez before they make love. She wondered what she could possibly do to make it really hot – 'to melt their zippers' as she put it – to make it sexier than anything that had ever before been seen on the screen. She thought of some of the recent films: *The Robe* had been far too pure in its content, as had been *The Ten Commandments*, and even *Miss Sadie Thompson* with Rita Hayworth. Everyone in Hollywood had made such a big song and dance about her but the movie had turned out to be as tame as a pet parrot.

'*Gilda* – now that was a sexy film,' Shirley said out loud.

'What dear?' Irving asked.

'The dance Hayworth did in *Gilda* – you remember, "Put the blame on Mame, boys" – sexy, wasn't it?'

'Very,' he replied. 'But a little out of period for us, dear. We're trying to stay in the sixteenth century – *Gilda* was 1947.'

'Hmmm.' Shirley tapped at her teeth with a pencil. 'What about Ava in *Pandora and the Flying Dutchman?*' she yelled across the room to him. 'She sure lit up the screen in that scene where she swims out to the Dutchman's schooner in the nude.'

'That was a great scene,' recalled Irving, 'and it really was shot in the moonlight too – on actual locations in the Mediterranean, I believe.'

'Yeah, yeah, yeah – I'm gonna use it,' said Shirley, tapping excitedly on her machine. 'It'll be great, just great, Princess Isabella's gonna swim out to Cortez' boat in the nude,' she said gleefully. 'She's gonna climb on board, in the nude.' Now she was becoming even more gleeful. 'And *then* she's gonna do her hot little dance for Señor Cortez in the –'

'Don't be ridiculous, Shirley, you *can't*.' Irving was shocked and irritated at his wife's stupidity. 'The Hays Office will have all our asses. We can't have any nudity up there on the screen.'

'Oh yes we can.' Shirley picked up the telephone from her desk and barked at the hotel operator, 'Get me Hubert Croft.

'We can and we will, Irv,' she went on. 'The studio'll love it – we can shoot it two ways – with and without veils.' She cackled and shrieked into the phone, 'Hubert – Shirley – now listen, I've just had this great idea – can you come over and see us right away? Right – OK. You're just gonna *love* this scene, Hubert – yeah, I'm quite sure.'

Julian was in a stupor of erotic tension. He hardly knew what had hit him. He adored Inès, worshipped her. His divorce from Phoebe would be final in a month, and his marriage to Inès had been planned for the following week. This was what he still wanted in his heart. But he knew that he somehow had to get Dominique out of his system. To do this he had convinced himself that if he made love to her as much and as often as possible he would grow tired of her. But the more wildly they made love, the more he wanted her. He simply couldn't get enough of this teenage temptress who reminded him so much of a younger version of the woman he really loved.

For him, Inès' illness was a blessing in disguise, although he suffered pangs of desperate guilt which made him drink more than usual. But Dominique's glances full of promise, her creamy lusciousness, her sensual touch, caused him to think of nothing but his hunger for her. One morning during shooting she deliberately teased him by repeatedly moistening her lips with her little pink tongue. This caused him a painfully embarrassing erection which lasted until she allowed him to take her, in a blazing burst of passion, in her dressing room during the lunch hour. They'd both been in full costume, but he'd plunged into her in such a frenzy of abandonment that the thin plywood walls had begun to rock, and many of the crew grinned knowingly at each other.

'Location romance my foot,' said Tim. 'I ain't *never* seen the guvnor like this before – he's gorn, 'ook, line 'n' sinker.'

Dominique loved it. She had found her ultimate power in the discovery of sex. This famous and gorgeous star, engaged to another woman, was hers to twist around her finger as much and in as many

369

ways as her heart desired, and there was absolutely nothing he could do about it.

'It's quite impossible, Dominique. I could never allow you to do this scene – it's disgraceful, disgusting. Scandalous.' Two red dots burned on Agathe's pale cheeks as she confronted Dominique with the new blue pages of script which had been delivered that evening.

'Don't be such a square, Agathe,' yawned the girl. 'What's such a big deal about it? Why should I mind about a bit of nudity, it's perfectly natural – bodies are nothing to be ashamed of.'

'It's immoral,' spluttered Agathe. 'It's – it's – disgraceful – it's demeaning and cheap – swimming out stark naked to a man' – her voice rose almost an octave – 'then climbing on to the boat and dancing naked in front of Julian Brooks.' Her tone of voice had become so hysterical and outraged, and she was obviously under so much nervous tension, that Dominique looked up at her in astonishment.

'What do you care, Agathe – as long as I don't. I can't see what's the big deal – aren't you overreacting?'

'I'm your chaperone, young woman, in case it's slipped your mind,' huffed Agathe. 'I am supposed to look after your welfare, your morals, and help you sustain the values instilled in you by your parents.'

'Bull,' said Dominique rudely. 'My parents didn't instill any values in me.'

'That's a lie and you're a wicked, wicked girl to say so,' Agathe shrieked. 'I know your father. He's one of the most respected bankers in St Tropez – *mon Dieu*, what will he say when he sees you prancing about in the nude? *Quelle horreur.*' She crossed herself and rubbed the little crucifix she always wore.

'Stop being such an old fuddy-duddy, Agathe,' said Dominique. 'Look – just take a look at this girl – she's French too, and her parents are *petit-bourgeois* too, just like mine.' She threw over a copy of *Cinemonde*, the French movie magazine that she'd been reading earlier.

Agathe picked it up and gasped at the photograph. A beautiful young blonde lay on her stomach, her hair covering the curves of her breasts, but her bare buttocks were prominently exposed and she was staring into the camera with an alluring and provocative smile.

'*Mais c'est porno* – what is the world coming to?' gasped Agathe, shocked to her foundations.

Dominique shrugged. 'That's Brigitte Bardot,' she said as if that were enough. 'She's a couple of years older than me, maybe eighteen or nineteen, but that's what they're doing in France now – that kind of movie. They're shooting it now with a young new director called Roger Vadim. It's called *And God Created Woman*.'

'I don't care if it's called *And God Created Shit*,' hissed Agathe in an unusual burst of blasphemy. 'I'm going to see our producer right now and tell him I will never *allow* you to shoot this disgusting scene! *Never*, do you hear?'

Hubert Croft was trying unsuccessfully to take a nap when Agathe burst into his room unannounced and with only a perfunctory knock at the door. He'd taken off his shirt and trousers and was dressed only in his voluminous underpants and a somewhat soiled singlet when his visitor appeared.

'How *dare* you send Dominique this filth,' she yelled, brandishing the pages of the scene under his nose. 'I cannot permit my charge to perform this degrading act. She's my responsibility and I forbid it.'

'And what does your so-called charge have to say about it?' asked Hubert sarcastically, hastily shrugging his bulk into a towelling robe, complete with Ramona's royal crest embroidered in red and gold on the breast pocket. 'I'm sure she probably doesn't mind the idea in the least.'

'That's not the point – she's a child and she knows no better,' Agathe replied stiffly. 'I'm the adult who's responsible for her and I *will NOT*, indeed *cannot*, allow her to reveal herself in such a debasing and disgusting fashion. It's abominable. I'm calling her parents tomorrow to tell them what's happening. She's under age, you people shouldn't even suggest that she do it.'

'Sit down, *Mademoiselle*,' said Hubert calmly. He gestured to a turquoise suede armchair, and Agathe sank into its depths, quite out of breath and fanning herself with the offending pages.

Just the thought of Julian seeing Dominique totally naked filled her with such conflicting feelings that her whole body was tingling.

Her Julian – her love – watching Dominique perform this wanton dance wearing nothing but a smile. It was bad enough when she'd had to watch them making love for the screen. She had sat on the sidelines, out of sight, dry-mouthed with lust while the two of them kissed and caressed each other with such a passionate frenzy that she'd felt the moisture welling up in the most secret and private part of her body. It had almost been unbearable watching her Julian hold that immature child in his strong arms, seeing his full lips devour hers, her breasts pressed to his muscular chest, his arms holding her tightly. It had been a bitter-sweet sensation, particularly as Nick had insisted on shooting the love scenes from several different angles. She had suffered, oh how she had suffered the pangs of jealousy and desire. She'd been unable to control herself, and had crept away to Dominique's empty trailer to relieve herself in the only way she knew. Whispering Julian's name, biting her lips until they almost bled, rubbing herself ferociously with his scarf – another purloined object – she came to one torrential orgasm after another.

'Now, Mademoiselle Guinzberg,' said Hubert, lighting a cigar and closely observing her through his narrowed eyes, 'this is all a lot of nonsense. You know that, don't you?'

'I certainly don't,' she huffed peevishly. 'Dominique is only sixteen – I'm her guardian and –'

'Shut up, Mademoiselle Guinzberg,' snapped Hubert. 'Sit down and stop behaving like a two-faced bitch.'

'What – what did you call me?' His sudden orders stunned her and she felt confused and angry.

'I said you're behaving like a two-faced hypocrite,' he continued. 'Do you think I don't make it my business to know what's been going on?'

'I don't know what you're talking about,' gasped Agathe.

'Don't pretend to be as stupid as you look,' snapped Hubert. 'Listen to me for a minute before you start telephoning the girl's parents or the police or the fucking coast guards.' He sucked on his cigar and pinioned her to the chair with his look of contempt. She squirmed uncomfortably, feeling the power of his penetrating stare. God, he was ugly. The crew, who all seemed to dislike him, made jokes about him all the time, and had christened him the Toad. He looked like a great bulbous toad now as he sat hunched in the dark green robe, his bald head glistening with sweat, and stubble like black sandpaper covering his several chins.

'Don't for one minute think that I don't know *everything* that's going on in this film unit,' he said slowly. 'I mean *everything*.'

'And what's that supposed to mean?' Agathe tried to sound resolute, but there was no question that Croft not only repelled her but also terrified her. She disliked any kind of confrontation, and she was starting to wish that she'd never come.

'I know what you think, Mademoiselle Agathe Guinzberg.' He leaned forward, staring so intently into her eyes that she had to look away. 'I know your every thought when you're on the set watching Julian Brooks work.'

'What – what do you mean?'

'You love him, don't you, Agathe?' he leered. 'You're passionately in love with him, and you lust after his body.'

'No – No, I don't, it's a lie, a monstrous lie.'

'Nonsense, woman. I've *seen* you – I miss nothing, you know.' Hubert's cigar had gone out, and he relit it with an elaborate gold lighter. 'I've *seen* the expression on your face when you sit under the umbrella talking to Sir Crispin and Julian – I *know* what's going through your mind, *and* your body.'

'You don't – you couldn't,' said Agathe fearfully.

'Don't be a cretin, woman.' He smiled triumphantly, knowing that his next revelation would prove the killer for her. 'I've seen your book – your precious scrapbook. Did you think you could hide anything from me?'

'No!' cried Agathe. 'You couldn't have.'

'Oh but I could and I have. A lovely book, Agathe, so beautifully assembled, and with such affection. I must congratulate you on such a comprehensive selection of photographs of our dear Mr Brooks.' He laughed unpleasantly. 'It's certainly been well thumbed, your scrapbook.'

'How did you find it?' whispered Agathe, shame for herself and hatred for the Toad both rising in her like lava.

'I searched your room, you fool.' He smiled again. 'I had a suspicion you might have something like that – I needed to find it.

You didn't conceal it very well, Agathe. Under the mattress – ha! – very original. Any one of those stupid maids who work here could have found it, even though it was well wrapped up – in one of Julian's shirts, if I'm not mistaken.' His eyes gleamed.

'No,' she said softly. 'No. No, that's my property – it's private – private. You're trespassing.'

'Now, Mademoiselle Guinzberg, I'm going to forget totally that we ever had this little conversation, but only if you go away right now like a good woman and just allow Dominique to get on with her work. If you choose to make a scene, call her parents, or do anything of that kind, I will personally see to it that everyone on this picture, including Julian Brooks himself, gets to know of your pathetic, pitiful obsession with him. Do I make myself clear?'

She nodded, her eyes burning with tears.

'And of course if Dominique's parents ever find out that the very person they trusted to look after their precious daughter is no more than a sick, sexually obsessed *pervert*, you will be undoubtedly thrown off this film in less than the time it takes to shout Action – I do make myself clear, don't I?'

She nodded again, still unable to speak, and rose to leave.

'Not a word of our meeting here tonight will you breathe to anyone, Mademoiselle Guinzberg. And we shall all continue to be one big happy family. Do you understand?'

His eyes never left her as she walked slowly to the door, her shoulders slumped, her head bowed in defeat. Pathetic creature, he thought, feeling an unaccustomed emotion – pity. He would spare telling her about Dominique's roaring affair with Julian – the shock would probably kill her.

16

It was a clear moonlit night when Nick decided to shoot Dominique's nude swimming scene, followed by her seductive dance for Julian. The studio had become terribly excited when they had heard about it. It was breaking so many of the Hays Office censorship codes. Spyros Makopolis knew that in the new and dangerous territory they were entering, they were creating a precedent for future erotic scenes in movies. If the censor passed the scene in *Cortez* – without cuts – it would open the floodgates for other productions to shoot bare-skinned actresses and the public would demand more and more titillating scenes.

After arduous discussions with the Hays Office, with Scrofo, the Frankovitches and with Dominique herself, Nick had finally figured out a way to shoot it which would make it not only erotic and sensual, but would not actually show any censorable parts of Dominique's body. Only in long shots or in silhouette would the outlines of her beautiful body be seen. To be completely safe, the following night they were going to shoot the identical scene all over again, this time with Dominique in a primitive bikini.

Agathe spoke little as Dominique prepared for her first swimming shot. She stood completely and unselfconsciously naked in front of Agathe, who had to avert her eyes while the makeup girl applied waterproof makeup to the girl's rosy nipples. Her breasts were firm and up-jutting, her nipples a dark pink colour. The makeup girl was trying to mask their colour with the sponge so that the camera would not be able to see them from the boat, some two hundred yards away in the lagoon.

Dominique rather enjoyed the sensation of the soft sponge on her breasts, but her mind was filled with thoughts of what she and Julian would do together to while away the time tonight between shots. They both had cabins on the boat, and she knew that as soon as they finalized the first take, and he had glimpsed her glistening nude body rising from the sea, climbing up the side of the boat, he would feel a desperate urge to take her. She shivered at the delicious expectation, already becoming aroused by the thought of their passion taking place so close to where the crew would all be working.

She admired her reflection in the full-length mirror. Her belly was flat and tight, and at the base of her pubic triangle of black hair the wardrobe woman has pasted a small piece of flesh-coloured fabric, not as a concession to her own modesty – which didn't exist – but to protect the footage from the potential wrath of the censor.

There was a sharp knock at the door, and Bluey's voice boomed out, 'How we doin', Dominique?'

'I'm ready,' she said happily, tossing her long black hair over her shoulders and smiling again at her gorgeous reflection. Agathe stole another look at her charge. The girl was exquisitely formed, there was no doubt at all about that. She seemed to have matured in the few months since she'd left St Tropez; now she was no longer a schoolgirl but a ripe young woman in full flower. Agathe felt a surge of jealousy engulf her again as she imagined how Julian would feel when he saw the naked girl for the first time. She shuddered. She didn't *want* to think about that.

The wardrobe woman tied a large multi-coloured sarong around Dominique, who then tripped down the beach to where a small tent had been erected on the sand.

Nick was there waiting to meet her. 'All set, Dominique? You look terrific, darling – how do you feel?'

'Great, Nick, great – I'm so excited, ready for anything.'

'You really don't mind the nudity, you're absolutely sure?'

'Of course not,' she laughed. 'We all look the same without our clothes – it means nothing to me, Nick, less than nothing. I do think it's better for the scene too, more – how-you-say – *erotique, n'est-ce pas?*'

'Erotic, right.' He grinned, admiring and liking this girl's frankness and her refreshing joie de vivre. They'd made the right choice with this one, no question – she was a born star, and her sexuality seemed to gain in power each day. 'OK, now I'm going to get on the boat. Wait in the tent until you hear me call Action. Then you come out slowly – look around you – to see if the guard is watching. When you get to the edge of the water you drop your scarf, and wade out very, very slowly into the sea. All the time you look towards the boat with an expression of anticipation. You're longing to see Cortez. Let me see how you're going to do it.'

She rehearsed for him in the tent, and when he was satisfied with everything he gave her a big kiss on the cheek.

'Break a leg, kid, you're gonna be great, and if you get a cramp while you're swimming, just yell – we've got divers all around – you'll be quite safe.'

'I know.' She smiled. 'I'm a strong swimmer, Nick. Don't forget I live in St Tropez.'

He smiled to himself as he sat back in the speedboat which took him out to the majestic sixteenth-century schooner, whose tall masts towered impressively. If his instincts were correct, this was going to be quite some scene.

The crew were busy setting up on deck, and as he went over to consult with his lighting cameraman, he was accosted by Croft.

'I need to talk to you Nick,' the Italian said in an unexpectedly friendly tone, putting his hand on Nick's arm.

Nick pulled his arm away as if it had been stung, saying, 'OK, let's go down into my cabin then.'

In his small and claustrophobic cabin, Nick nodded towards a chair for Croft to sit in. Ignoring the Italian, he stood with his hands on his hips looking at his script with a frown.

'It's about this scene we're going to shoot,' Umberto began.

'What about it?' Nick's voice was sharp. 'The studio have agreed to this scene in principle, so what's the problem, Hubie baby?' He couldn't keep the sarcasm out of his voice, nor could he bear to look at the abhorrent creature who sat puffing on his stinking cigar.

'I want to know exactly how you're going to shoot it, to protect Dominique's modesty,' said Umberto. 'She's young – she shouldn't be out there flashing her snatch at the crew without a stitch on. I want to know that you're all going to behave like gentlemen.'

Nick raised his eyebrows. 'Since when did you become the moralist?' he sneered. 'Since when did you know anything about gentlemen and their behaviour? I didn't realize you were so concerned about protecting Dominique – I assumed that you had other ideas about her.'

'And what do you mean by *that*?' snarled the Italian.

'Oh, nothing, nothing,' said Nick, innocently turning the pages of his script. 'You've got a cock too, Hubie baby – haven't you?'

'Listen, asshole.' Umberto rose, his huge bulk, enveloped in clouds of cigar smoke, seeming to fill the tiny room. 'Let's not have any more cracks about *me* – I'm still the fucking producer on this fucking epic whether *you* like it or not, you little Greek shit-head. *Here.*' He threw a crumpled telegram on the desk. 'Read that.'

Nick picked up the scrap of paper and read: 'Hays Office most concerned STOP Despite them having agreed to pass nude scene it is essential that any shots filmed, repeat any at all, must have no salacious content vis-à-vis body position or exposure of the girl STOP They unaware Dominique is a minor STOP Be very careful STOP Picture so far is great but we need this scene so get it right STOP Regards Makopolis.'

'I've already had a copy of this,' said Nick, throwing it back at Umberto. 'I've spent all today and yesterday on this boat with the operator, the lighting cameraman and with Dominique or her stand-in. We've carefully gone through every fucking frame. Any time there's the minutest possibility that we might see a flash of tit or any of her other bits, we've always got a piece of sail or some scenery to cover it – does that satisfy your prudery, Hubie baby?'

'What about the crew – will they be able to see any of her body?' Umberto asked.

'Of *course* they'll be able to see her!' exploded Nick. 'But they're fucking professionals, for Christ's sake, not a bunch of peeping fucking toms.' Like you, he almost added, but he badly wanted to get rid of the Toad. The sight and sound of the man always put him into a blinding fury and he had to get to work right away. There was a great deal to be done tonight.

'Well, I'll be there the whole time to see that you do exactly what you're supposed to,' said Umberto, his eyes glinting at Nick like chips of coal. 'And no one had better take advantage of that girl.'

Least of all you, asshole, Nick thought to himself, but all he said was, 'Right, have you finished now, Hubert? Are you satisfied?'

'One thing you should know about me, Nick,' sneered Umberto, his face close to Nick's, 'I'm *never* satisfied.' With that he stalked out, slamming the cabin door.

Nick shrugged and made a couple of notes in red pencil on his script. This was just another typical day with Hubert. Every day he tried to make trouble, and every day he succeeded in infuriating someone in the crew or a member of the cast.

Nick looked out of the cabin's minute porthole which faced the deck and saw Hubert talking angrily to one of Dominique's wardrobe women who was looking back at him with patient irritation. Nick grinned. He'd seen that particular look on practically every one of the crew members' faces. They all loathed Scrofo. He put the Italian out of his mind as best he could and, as he strode purposefully back on to the deck, concentrated his attention on the forthcoming scene.

'Ready boys?' he called to his two camera crews, both set up for different angles on the deck.

'OK – ready, Nick,' they shouted back in unison.

'Right – let's *go!*'

The clapper boy snapped his wooden sticks in front of camera one, then again in front of camera two. The sound operator called, 'Rolling.' Nick then shouted the magic words through his loud-hailer: 'Aaand – *Action!*'

Also on deck, Umberto Scrofo stood out of sight just behind the camera crews, a pair of powerful binoculars pressed firmly to his porcine eye sockets. He didn't want to miss a single second of this spectacle. Naturally, he'd thought Dominique a lovely little creature since the first moment that he'd laid eyes on her, but she had resolutely and continually ignored him. If he ever tried to talk to her, she would only reply in monosyllables and with barely disguised contempt.

As she paused at the shoreline Dominique looked steadily towards the anchored boat. Slowly and with an infinite yet natural sensuality, she unloosed her flimsy sarong and let it fall with a faint whisper to the sand. The full moon illuminated her flawless breasts and gave an ethereal beauty to her whole body. She looked like a dark and less modest version of Botticelli's Venus rising from the waves. She was a divinely created masterpiece, a tender peach, the personification of youthful and feminine perfection.

'*Madonna mia*,' muttered Scrofo, the lump in his throat almost as uncomfortable as the one in his trousers, '*Che bellissima, raggazza – bellissima.*'

He was far from alone in his admiration for the naked beauty who was milking her moment at the water's edge to the very utmost. Slowly, sinuously, she walked into the cool black waters. Pausing momentarily as the ocean lapped around the top of her thighs, she gazed again with a look of undisguised desire at the deck of the boat where Julian was waiting for her.

'My God, what a dame,' whispered Bluey to Nick, who stood transfixed, just gazing at her. 'That's the fuckin' body of a fuckin' angel if I ever saw one.'

Nick didn't bother to answer. The tableau was so exquisite in its simple timeless beauty that he felt he wanted to drown himself in it. Dominique took another two or three steps and, as the water covered her waist, she gave a tiny cry and dived under the surface, to reappear seconds later with her long hair streaming out behind her like black seaweed. She swam impressively and strongly towards the boat. The close-up camera was filming her face and shoulders, but the operator was concentrating on trying not to reveal any glimpses of her breasts.

'Fantastic,' he murmured under his breath to his assistant, who was constantly adjusting the focus as Dominique swam closer and closer to the boat, 'Fan-fuckin'-tastic.'

Julian was standing between the two cameras, so that as Dominique swam within thirty yards of the boat she could see him clearly. She gave him a smile of such devastating innocence, seductively tinged with voluptuous adult longing, that he could feel his mouth becoming dry, and his cock, in anxious anticipation of the delights in store for it later, began its irresistible rise.

Finally she arrived at the rope ladder which hung over the side of the boat, and grasping it tightly she climbed on board. For an instant she stood absolutely still, posing, allowing the cameras to capture the electric sensuality that emanated from her. Then with a passionate sigh she murmured, 'Oh Hernando, my love,' and threw herself into Julian's open and welcoming arms.

'Cut,' shouted Nick. 'Beautiful, Dominique – absolutely beautiful – we don't need to do another one; that was perfection, darling – just great. Relax for an hour while we get set up for your dance – dry yourself off, have a hot drink – we don't want you catching cold.'

The wardrobe woman had already draped Dominique with towels and a terrycloth robe, and she wrapped herself in them, twisting another around her wet hair like a turban. Julian stood close by while her posse of helpers fussed around her, and she felt she could almost see his hardness through the material of his breeches. She shooed away her entourage and stood very still as he approached her.

'Can I buy you a drink?' he whispered.

'You could,' she breathed. 'But I'd rather you made love to me.'

In the privacy of his tiny cabin, neither could control their desperate impatience. Julian sat on the bunk fully clothed, and she stood shaking between his legs – more from lust than from the effects of the cold water – as he slowly unwound the towels from her damp body.

They could hear the crew up on deck preparing for the next shot, and the gentle sound of the waves slapping against the hull. A dim yellow lamp glowed from the table in the cabin, and as the towels fell away from her breasts it bathed them in a warm, golden light. His mouth went to each one in turn, licking and gently biting them until she threw back her head and cried out for him to stop – then his hands caressed her hips as he unwound the towel from her waist, laying bare her buttocks and her sex. He stroked the soft firmness of her muscled rear as his lips dropped down to her silky mound and his tongue found the exact place for which it longed.

She moaned softly as it probed her gently and softly. He now knew well how to please her, and in only a matter of seconds she came, her hands tangled in his thick hair, as he continued to massage her nipples gently with the palms of his hands.

Then she was on him like a wild creature and his cock leapt out at her as she unbuttoned his trousers. It seemed to her harder and larger than it had ever been before. Lovingly she put as much of it in her mouth as she could, rhythmically sucking it until he almost burst. Then she put him inside her, and rode him, gently at first, but gaining momentum until they orgasmed together – two bodies but one flesh.

Bluey went to knock on Julian's cabin about an hour later.

'Is Dominique in there by any chance?' he said in a tone of mock innocence.

'*J'arrive* – coming right out,' called Dominique happily, blowing her lover a kiss, and leaving him lying back on his bunk happily and completely sated.

Nick wanted to rehearse the dance scene, so Dominique put on a leotard to run over it until Nick was completely satisfied that it was perfect. Umberto stood beside the cameras, cigar jutting out from his mouth, saying nothing, but his very presence making everyone uncomfortable and distracted.

The cameras were positioned in such a way that the areas of Dominique's body which were censorable were always masked by parts of the boat's equipment and rigging. It was a highly complicated and difficult shot and it took almost all night to get it. They needed to do more than fifteen set-ups with the three cameras to make quite sure that no mistakes were made.

Dominique was in her element. She found the idea of dancing naked in front of forty men, including her lover, enormously exhilarating. Each time that Nick yelled 'Cut – it's a print – next set-up' she and Julian would slink away to one or other of their cabins. No one disturbed them. Even though everyone knew exactly what was going on, and although lewd jokes and comments were bandied about by the crew, nothing was ever said within earshot of the two principals.

'Maybe we should call her the Submarine,' joked Bluey to the operator.

'And why's that?'

'Because she's always going down,' laughed Bluey, nodding towards Julian's cabin.

Julian was lying on his bunk after the fifth set-up. They'd been shooting Dominique's dance for over six hours now and he was feeling exhausted. Not from the dancing, as all he had to do was watch, but because Dominique was so sexually demanding. Every time they came back down to the cabin, she would want to make love again. She was in such a high state of excitement that it was becoming infectious. All the crew could feel it radiating from her, and almost every one of the men had a pleasurable discomfort in his loins as they watched her, each with his own fantasy.

Her body glistening with water in the lamplight, she leaned against the cabin door, eyeing Julian who was lying back on his bunk.

My God, they'd done it four times already tonight. Surely she couldn't – wouldn't – be able to do it again, he thought – not after all that swimming and dancing. But he was wrong. Her robe dropped to the floor once more, and he could almost see her pulsing to receive him.

'Dominique, don't you think we've had enough for one night?' he said weakly, but only too aware that in spite of his physical exhaustion his expectant cock was rising yet again.

'Certainly not,' she crooned, leaning against the mahogany door, looking like some wanton maiden, with her hair falling shiny and wet around her full breasts.

'I want you to want me again, Julian – I want you again, my love – I want you now.' She was touching herself now, in a way which she knew would drive him half mad with desire. Massaging her nipples gently between her fingers, she then slipped one hand down to between her legs, two fingers beginning to slide in and out of her moist pink sex.

'Of course I want you,' he said, his voice made hoarse with passion. 'I want you too damn much – you're an enchantress, you know that – a little witch, and you're driving me mad.'

'I want you, Julian,' she moaned, still leaning against the door, her fingers now moving so rapidly, and her breathing so fast that he could see that she was about to come again.

He watched spellbound as she did. She cried out his name.

'Je t'aime, Julian, je t'aime, mon homme.' He saw her whole body quiver with her own ecstasy.

'Come over here,' he said huskily. 'My God, what have you done to me, Dominique – what have you done?'

'Nothing,' she whispered, 'nothing at all. Her eyes were wide with rapture as he immersed himself into her once again.

'I've just made you love me – *j'espère* – because I love you, Julian, I always will.'

As Julian walked from his cabin to the upper deck where the crew were filming he saw a man silhouetted against a pile of rigging in the shadows. He paused for a second, his actor's instincts sensing something unusual.

Thinking himself unseen, Hubert Croft was leaning against a furled sail, his eyes fixed on the distant, dancing figure of a naked Dominique. One of his hands was moving fast and furiously in the pocket of his baggy linen trousers, his eyes were half closed and his breathing harsh.

'What the devil do you think you're doing, Croft?' hissed Julian.

The Italian abruptly ceased what he was doing and stared at Julian.

'Well, well, well, if it isn't our Mr Brooks come to check up on his Lolita,' he sneered, seeming neither ashamed nor embarrassed to have been caught masturbating almost publicly. He removed his hand slowly from his trouser pocket, looking at Julian with a mocking smile.

'Jesus Christ, Croft, you're acting like a bloody pervert,' said Julian in disgust. 'If any of the crew saw what you were doing you'd be thrown off the set.'

'Let *not* you be the one to cast stones, Julian old boy,' said Croft, mimicking Julian's impeccable English in his grating voice. 'If any of the men saw what *you* have been doing with that little slut – deliberately flaunting herself in front of them – you would not be thought of any longer as the second coming of Olivier, but rather a pathetic ageing Lothario.'

'I'm not going to bandy words with you, Croft,' said Julian, feeling his face burn. He knew what the crew were all thinking about Dominique and himself. He couldn't blame them, either. 'It's none of your damn business.'

'Oh but it *is* my business,' smirked Scrofo. 'And my dear chap, much as I, the producer of the film, admire your performance on the screen, your performance *off* it proves that you are nothing but a vain and shallow actor, attempting to retain your youth through having repeated sex with that innocent girl.'

384

Oh, sure, thought Julian. Dominique was about as innocent as a basketful of adders. Where she had learned her siren skills he didn't dare think.

'I'm wanted on the set, Croft,' he said tensely. 'I'd prefer not to linger any longer in this conversation. Frankly it's making me ill.'

'Not as ill as Mademoiselle Inès is going to feel when she reads yesterday's *Herald Examiner*,' said Scrofo.

'Oh? And what, pray, is so interesting about that?'

'Read it and weep,' said Scrofo, 'as will your fiancée, no doubt. As I told you before, Brooks, don't throw stones – you'll only get mud on your shoes.'

He chortled harshly as he waddled back to the set, and Julian stood quite still. What could possibly be in the newspaper that might affect Inès? He groaned silently. He knew only too well what it could be: some gossip about him and Dominique. It wouldn't be the first time that he had been grist for the gossipmongers' mill, but, by God, if it hurt Inès . . .

He walked quickly back to his cabin where his makeup man was busily sharpening eyebrow pencils.

'You haven't by any chance got a copy of yesterday's Los Angeles newspaper have you, old chap?' he asked Tim casually.

'Naw, guv, you know I only read the comics,' said Tim cheerily, blotting Julian's sweating face with Kleenex. 'But some of the boys get it, guv. I'll see what I can do.'

'Thanks, Tim, I appreciate it,' sighed Julian, wishing this night were over. Talking to Croft always left him with a sour taste in his mouth.

Tim went around the crew asking for a copy of yesterday's paper, while Kittens was retailing to the wardrobe women, in excited indignation, the fact that she had seen Croft peeping voyeuristically at Dominique's nudity and playing with himself at the same time. Within an hour the entire unit knew what their producer had been doing, and their dislike of him reached new heights.

The following night the whole scene was shot again, this time with Dominique clothed in a series of veils. These worked perfectly well when she was in the water, but as soon as she was out of it, the see-

385

through chiffon clung to her curves in the skimpy bikini underneath in such a suggestive way that Hubert again cornered Nick in his cabin after the very first shot. The crew were then treated to a screaming match between the two men which could have been heard far away in the highest guard tower of Ramona's villa. Eventually the two protagonists emerged, both grim-faced, to consult further with Agathe, Kittens and the wardrobe woman.

It appeared that Hubert thought Dominique's nipples were clearly visible through the flimsy, saturated material, the censor would be forced to use his sharpened scissors, and the scene would be a write-off.

Dominique was summoned away from Julian's cabin where the two were about to indulge in yet another amorous session. She stood sullen and pouting in her cabin, fuming that she'd had to leave her lover, as they fussed around her. Nick was furious but he did see that Umberto had a point. During Dominique's dance the wet fabric rubbed itself against her breasts and excited her already prominent nipples until they became clearly visible from several yards away. It was impossible for the camera not to see them in all these shots unless they could somehow be camouflaged.

'I really don't see what all this *fuss* is about,' sulked Dominique, longing to get back to Julian. '*All* women have breasts, I can't understand why you Americans are so prudish about showing them?'

Everyone ignored her as Kittens and the wardrobe woman conferred in hushed voices. Eventually the men were shooed out of the room while the women performed various experiments to try to conceal Dominique's pert papillae. But the more they pressed on flesh-coloured pads and stuck them down with strong surgical adhesive, the more her nipples seemed to swell, pushing through the material like two acorns.

Dominique felt impatient, hating the whole infuriating performance. She was already in a state of advanced sexual arousal, and having her breasts poked and pushed only encouraged it. She just longed to be back cuddling up to Julian and feeling him inside her again.

Eventually the women were satisfied with their handiwork and

Dominique was dismissed. She rushed back to Julian's cabin where her lover waited, his erection long since deflated. When he saw Dominique's bosoms covered with a curious network of masking tape, Band-Aid and flesh-coloured silk, looking something like a cubist collage, he threw back his head and roared with laughter.

'What's so funny?'

'Darling heart, I'm sorry but they do look strange – like two perfect little peaches all bandaged up!'

'Not so little, thank you very much – I think you're a very rude man,' said Dominique, giving him her most seductive smile. 'And now, since you're not allowed to touch them' – she bounded friskily on to the tiny bunk bed – 'I'll just have to play with this soft old thing.' With that she took some moisturizer from the shelf next to the bed and began reverently massaging the liquid on to his slumbering cock. In no time Julian was back at full stand and he groaned ecstatically as she gently lowered her body on to him once again.

Dominique's sensual dance had excited practically all of the male crew members to such an extent that for the next few nights the whorehouses of Acapulco did a roaring trade.

Hubert Croft had found himself tremendously aroused by the girl's erotic dance. Although he had no feelings one way or another about Julian Brooks, thinking him merely a conceited but handsome actor who had just been lucky, Umberto felt angry and jealous that Dominique seemed so crazy about him. His only consolation was that the whore Inès seemed to be getting what she deserved. He knew the bitch was on the verge of a miscarriage, and it pleased him enormously that her fiancé was blatantly two-timing her with a girl young enough to be his own daughter.

The night following Dominique's dance scene, Ramona's small house party dined as usual on her candlelit terrace. Dominique was extremely tired, as well she might be, thought Scrofo. She excused herself soon after dinner to retire to her room.

Half an hour later, Hubert tapped at her door.

'Go away – please,' the girl called out sleepily. 'I'm asleep.'

'I have to talk to you, Dominique,' said the producer. 'It's extremely urgent.'

'*Merde*,' he heard her mutter as she opened the sliding opaque glass doors to her bedroom.

'What do *you* want?' she asked sulkily, loping back into her room to sprawl sleepily on the edge of the bed. She hadn't bothered to put a robe on, and was wearing just a tiny baby-doll nightdress of sheer white cotton edged with broderie anglaise and cornflower ribbon. Umberto could see her matching panties as she looked up at him with bored resignation.

He never felt quite sure of himself in her presence. She seemed to possess the assurance of an adult, and never seemed intimidated by him, unlike so many others on the film.

'I think that your liaison with Julian Brooks must stop,' said Hubert stonily, feeling the familiar tingling in his groin.

She laughed contemptuously. 'It's none of your business, Mr Croft. Whatever Julian and I do off the set has *nothing* to do with you.'

'But it most certainly has, my dear,' he said frostily. 'Please *don't* forget that you're still a minor, and as producer of this film *I* am the one responsible for your welfare.'

'Agathe is responsible for all that,' yawned Dominique, leaning back crosslegged against the zebra-striped headboard, a challenging expression on her sulky face.

'And she doesn't know a thing about your sordid little affair, does she? You've been very clever, Dominique, very clever indeed. But if Agathe had been aboard the ship last night she would certainly have known about it. Everyone else does.'

'So what?' said Dominique. 'I'm doing nothing wrong.'

Umberto's breath started to quicken, and lowering her eyes, Dominique saw to her dismay a small distention in his trousers. She raised her eyes quickly – *merde*, the pig was getting excited. *Quelle horreur*. She uncrossed her long tanned legs and tried unsuccessfully to pull her nightgown down a little more.

'If you told Agathe about it she wouldn't believe you anyway. She thinks I'm a blushing virgin – just like she is.'

'And of course you didn't allow her on the ship to watch your

388

dance, did you?' said Umberto ominously. 'So she could see your disgusting behaviour.'

'Well that was her idea,' Dominique shrugged. 'She had a migraine or something – she just wanted to go to bed.'

How very convenient for Agathe, thought Umberto. She was obviously unable to bear the sight of her idol making love to this minx. 'What does she think happens when you go into Mr Brooks' locked trailer at lunchtime?' Umberto was genuinely curious.

'She thinks we're practising our lines, of course, of maybe even having lunch,' laughed Dominique. 'Rehearsing – and that's exactly what does happen,' she added defiantly, disconcerted because the fat man's expression had become more intense.

He took a step nearer the bed.

'That's what we were doing last night, Hubie – and you have no proof of anything else.'

'Oh don't I?' sneered Umberto. 'What about these?' From behind his back he produced a large manila envelope which he threw on to the bed. 'Open it.'

Slowly Dominique undid the flap, pulling out several black and white photographs.

Her hands flew to her mouth. 'What are these? Where did you get them?'

'I'm sure you know perfectly well what they are,' sneered Scrofo. 'They are some photographs of you and Mr Brooks which I took on the beach the day you were fornicating together in front of anyone who happened to be passing. *Slut*,' he hissed. 'French slut.'

He suddenly felt totally omnipotent, as finally Dominique looked up at him with genuine fear in her eyes.

'What are you going to do with them?'

'That rather depends.' Scrofo advanced slowly towards her, his huge bulk ominous in the semi-darkness of the room. 'It depends on how nice you are to me.'

'Nice? *Mais, c'est une blague! Non – non!*' Dominique tried to scramble across the huge bed, but despite his size Umberto was too fast for her. He grabbed her ankle and pulled her towards him as she screamed for help.

His gross body pressed her down on to the bed, and he clamped his hand over her mouth. *Merde*, the pig was strong, she thought with mounting panic, as she thrashed around trying to throw him off. To her disgust she became aware that he was trying to unzip his trousers with one hand, as he moaned his litany of lust to her.

'Don't scream, Dominique – just be a good girl, a nice girl, you'll like it, I know how much you like it – you'll like it with me too – I'm good – just as good as Brooks.' She tried to squirm her sinewy body away from him, but he was so heavy that she was pinned like a butterfly to a specimen board.

'Be a good girl now,' he rasped, his mouth close to her ear. 'A good nice little girl, and I won't show the photographs of you fucking Julian to your chaperone – because if I *do*' – his hand tightened sadistically over her face – 'she will make sure that your parents hear about everything that's happened, and you'll be bundled back to St Tropez in disgrace, faster than it would take you to unzip Julian's fly.'

Dominique tried to scream out, but it was impossible with his clammy hand pressed hard over her mouth. She tried to raise her strong dancer's legs to kick him in the stomach before he could manage to force himself into her, but his sheer bulk made it impossible.

Momentarily she lay still, the realization of what could happen paralysing her. Agathe. Would she report back to Maman and Papa? Surely not – Dominique could twist Agathe round her little finger, the woman was always in such a daze.

Umberto continued to drone on in his horrible rasping voice, his small, erect penis pressing itself against her bare thigh. 'Just be a good girl, Dominique – just be good, my dear, and when I've finished I will tear up all the pictures and you won't have to worry about anything any more.'

'No, get away!' she screamed with a sudden surge of strength, struggling more forcibly as a rough hand grabbed at the elastic around her panties and began to pull them down. The pungent smell of his vile cologne assailed her nostrils, and she threw her head from side to side as his bulbous lips drew closer.

At that moment there was a knock at the door and Agathe's shrill voice called out,

'Dominique, are you all right?'

Dominique's eyes widened with relief, and triumphantly she looked into Umberto's bloated face. For a second he froze, then the knock came again.

'Dominique, I said are you all right? I thought I heard you call out? Answer me, Dominique, otherwise I'll call the guards.'

Umberto bent his gross head and whispered, 'I'm going to take my hand off your mouth – and you better say you're all right or *I can promise you that you'll regret it* – right? No tricks now.'

She nodded and gradually he released his hand. After a deep breath of air, she shouted towards the door, 'Agathe, oh Agathe, thank God it's you. I've had such a scary dream – I feel so frightened.'

'Let me in, *chérie*,' Agathe ordered, worriedly rattling at the locked door. 'Right now.'

'No, no, don't come in,' Dominique called, gloating up exultantly at Umberto's face which was gruesomely contorted in anger and panic. 'I'll come out to you – I want to sleep in your room tonight, Agathe. I've had such an awful nightmare.'

'Of course, *chérie*, *viens*, hurry up. I'll take care of you.'

Triumphantly Dominique rolled away from under the Italian's bulk and scampered over to the door, grabbing up a dressing gown and stuffing the photographs into a pocket.

'You haven't heard the last of this,' Umberto whispered hoarsely as she glanced over at him from the door. 'No one ever gets the better of me, you little slut – no one.'

Dominique made no answer as she slid open the glass doors and fell into the security of Agathe's arms.

'Oh Agathe, it was such a horrible nightmare,' she sobbed, tears of relief running down her flushed cheeks.

'Hush, hush, don't cry, *chérie*. I'll take care of you, *ma petite*, come – come with me.'

With her arms enfolding the shaking girl, Agathe led Dominique into her room and locked the door behind them.

Umberto Scrofo listened carefully to his telephone caller, blue jowls creasing into a wider and wider smile, as he heard the news which made him so pleased.

'In Paris, you say – you found him in prison?' He listened again and then laughed, 'French drunks – I've seen 'em – they're all the same. They'd sell their grandmothers for a glass of absinthe. How much does he want?' He frowned when he heard the reply. 'One hundred thousand francs, that's ridiculous – I wouldn't pay him nearly as much. Offer him ten thousand.'

The caller continued to jabber on, and Umberto's demeanour became increasingly ebullient. 'Tell him to call me himself – no, better not – the poor bastard probably can't afford it. I'll call him. What did you say his name was?' Umberto scribbled down a name and a telephone number in Paris, saying softly to himself as he hung up, 'Yves Moray, how very, very interesting.'

Julian had been in a turmoil of guilt since his two nights of frenzied sex during the shooting of Dominique's nude scene. He knew only too well that everything he was doing with Dominique was completely and utterly wrong, but his body recently seemed to be nothing more than a series of raw nerve endings, all connected to his cock, which still swelled expectantly each time he found himself near her.

They had made love for hour after hour in the cabin and now he could barely walk. Last night he'd arrived back at the hotel just as the grey fingers of dawn were creeping over the hills.

When he staggered into the bathroom he started thinking of their lovemaking, and immediately became hard again. He stared at himself in the mirror in shocked self-disgust. He was either superman or on the way to becoming certifiable, and although this amazing virility which Dominique inspired had enslaved him, he knew that he was in the throes of a selfish obsession which could well destroy his relationship with Inès for ever.

He had tried to obtain a copy of the newspaper Croft had mentioned, but no one had it or seemed to have read it, so he dismissed it from his mind, thinking that it was obviously just some cheap ploy to annoy him. Croft was not worth worrying about. He was a low-life whom Julian found intensely disagreeable. He knew Inès disliked the Italian too. She had told him so after Ramona's party. Did *anyone* have a good word or kind feelings for Croft? Obviously not.

In the bedroom Inès awoke from a drug-induced slumber as she heard Julian in the shower. Dr Langley had sent her pills to help her sleep at night, because she was so inactive with nothing to do all day except read, or stare at the view, that to sleep at night had become more and more difficult.

'Are you all right darling?' she murmured when Julian quietly slipped into his side of the big double bed. 'You've been working so hard lately, such long hours, I've been worried about you.'

'I'm fine, just exhausted,' he whispered, a painful pang of guilt hitting him like a physical blow. 'Please don't concern yourself about me, sweetheart, just worry about yourself and our baby. Goodnight, my darling.' He kissed her gently on the forehead and turned over, pretending to sleep.

Inès stared into the blackness of the room. Her finely tuned instincts told her something was wrong. She knew all about Julian's sexual past and the succession of liaisons with every single one of his leading ladies. Surely he wasn't having an affair with a sixteen-year-old girl? Not now, when the two of them were in such harmony together, and she was finally giving him the child that he'd always wanted. Surely he couldn't contemplate doing such a thing – could he?

Although not an analytical man nor one to share confidences, Julian felt he had to talk to someone or else go mad. He decided to confide his problem to Nick Stone, whom he believed to be discreet, and a man he could trust. The day after the dancing scenes were wrapped, filming finished early. Also Dominique wasn't around to bat her eyelashes coquettishly and bewitch his cock into a state of perpetual tumescence, so on the way back from location he asked Nick, 'How about a drink, old chap?'

'Good idea – how about hitting La Perla? We can watch the divers – and I don't know about you, but I feel like diving into several margaritas,' said Nick. He was in high spirits about the film, although his hatred for Scrofo was smouldering away just beneath the surface. He tried hard to control it, but Umberto seemed capable of inflaming his anger with only the slightest provocation.

At La Perla, Julian and Nick sat at a quiet corner table, away from

393

the tourists. As soon as they had ordered, Julian began to unburden himself.

'I don't know what the hell to do Nick,' he said, 'I'm truly up the proverbial shit creek without a paddle.'

Several young muscular Mexican boys were crawling like spiders up the steep rocks behind him as they prepared to perform their famous death-defying dives into the ocean far below, but the two men ignored them.

'I presume you've noticed what's been going on?' said Julian.

Nick smiled ruefully. 'Kiddo, you might as well have stood on the Empire State Building and yelled it out,' he said. 'I guess you mean you and the girl?'

'I certainly do,' said Julian glumly. 'The Girl. I can't get enough of her, Nick. I don't want to, but I can't stop myself. Christ, I'm thirty-seven years old, for God's sake – old enough to be her father. I hate myself for it, but she's honestly bewitched me.'

Nick listened sympathetically, glad that he didn't suffer similar problems with women – maybe that's what comes of being too handsome, he thought. Julian had always been romantically incontinent, but who could blame him with the way women had always thrown themselves at him? 'Do you love Dominique?' he asked.

'Hell *no* – of *course* I bloody don't. I'm *madly* in love with Inès – at least I think I am – that's why I'm in such a bloody state about Dominique. Every time I'm *near* that little minx, I just have to have her. I think I'm going mad – I think I'm going stark staring bonkers, Nick.'

'Of course you're not,' said Nick. 'You're not crazy, Julian – you're a man, just like the rest of us.'

'A man doesn't behave like this,' said Julian bitterly. 'A man is faithful to the woman he loves, especially when the woman is as wonderful as Inès, and lying flat on her back all day long to save our baby.'

'So why *do* you do it?'

'She's a witch – I've told her as much,' breathed Julian. 'A siren; a Circe. She's springtime – she's innocence – and she's unbelievably sexy. Sex with her is *incredible*, indescribably amazing. She's *sixteen*, Nick, and she makes love like an experienced woman. God, I want her whenever I'm near her – she's like a drug and I've become a complete addict.'

They ordered some more margaritas, and watched as the first of the Mexican divers took off like a swallow from the peak of the high rock, hitting the water at the exact moment when the seventh wave crashed into the shallow gully. As the boy's head appeared triumphantly above the water and the assembled patrons cheered and applauded, Julian leaned forward.

'I want to end it, Nick, but every time I manage to make that decision I see her again and this bloody thing' – he pointed angrily at his crotch – 'changes my mind for me, and what's more so does the rest of me.'

Nick laughed. 'Then I guess you do have a problem – I can't really help you. I wish I could. I can only say that every man on this film would give his balls to fuck Dominique.'

'Even Sir Crispin?' laughed Julian.

Nick smiled. 'Perhaps not him, but I've talked to the guys – I've heard what they say about her. It isn't just you, Julian – you're not alone. She's a mantrap, she's like a walking aphrodisiac. Every single guy has got the hots for her, and the more they see her the more they fancy her – and how they envy you! I think she's just sex appeal personified, it's like some kind of gift.'

'That's for damn sure,' said Julian ruefully.

'Monroe, Brigitte Bardot, they're gonna have to look to their laurels when our kid hits the screen,' said Nick. 'I think she'll be the biggest female star that Hollywood's had for years.'

'Yes, well that doesn't exactly solve my problem,' said Julian, 'which is simply that the woman I love is off games until our baby is born, whilst I *cannot* stop being self-indulgent and fucking this nymphet.'

'Listen, Julian,' said Nick. 'I'm not a man of the world, I'm nowhere in your league – I'm just a simple Greek guy who happens to be happily married and wants very much to stay that way. But let me give you a bit of advice.'

'What is it?' said Julian. 'For God's sake I'll do anything that will help me to get out of this mess.'

'There's only one way,' Nick said simply. 'If you really love Inès you've gotta pretend Dominique doesn't exist. You're an actor – you can do that, can't you?'

Julian looked dubious.

'Cold turkey,' said Nick. 'It's the only way.'

Inès sat on the hotel balcony numb with shock. A slim manila envelope, addressed to her, had been placed on her breakfast tray that morning. A wave of nausea had engulfed her when she'd opened it. Blurred black and white photographs, taken with a telescopic lens, revealed a couple entwined on a beach.

There was no mistaking Julian's back, just as there was no mistaking the slim, sensual legs and long black hair of Dominique, her body hidden from the camera by Julian's. Inès was aghast as she read the enclosed press clipping from Harrison Carroll's Los Angeles gossip column:

Mr X, the handsome but not yet divorced matinée idol, has been 'oh-so-close' with the beautiful but very young Miss Y, while they toil together on a tropical location. This column is concerned as to how attractive Miss Z, the fiancée of the former, must be coping with the situation?

Who could have hated Inès enough to send this disgusting loathsome piece of gossip, take these perverted photos? She knew the answer only too well. There was just one person in the world odious enough to want to hurt her so much. Umberto Scrofo.

What was Julian doing? One blissful year together, a baby on the way, a wonderfully romantic life, the most fulfilling happiness she had ever known, and Julian had started to cheat on her. Why? What was he getting from Dominique that he could not get from her? Gloomily she stared out of the window. She knew the answer to that if she knew men. He was getting sex, and plenty of it. But was it just sex, or was it something more?

She mustn't let Julian suspect that she knew of this affair, or behave any differently towards him. Any change of attitude from her would cause him to ask questions that she didn't want to answer. Certainly he had been no less affectionate or considerate towards her in the past few days, even though lovemaking had been forbidden. What did he say about that to Dominique, a girl not quite seventeen? Did he confide in her the truth that his love life with Inès was suddenly nonexistent because of her pregnancy? Or did he lie to her, saying Inès was cold, unaffectionate, frigid, did not give him what he wanted? Inès knew that old routine. Her past lovers had often told her how disappointing their wives were in bed.

Her hands cupped her still-flat stomach. Dominique – young, French, beautiful. Maybe she should take some small measure of comfort in the fact that Dominique was so like herself – Julian had remarked on the amazing resemblance between them.

It was all because of Scrofo that she had not had enough time for Julian. Scrofo, who had made her so involved in his script problems. Scrofo, who had made her life so miserably stressful recently, and Scrofo, who had abused her so brutally as a girl, causing her to suffer the pain of imminent miscarriage. If only she had succeeded in killing him, none of this would be happening.

Inès fingered her lucky bracelet of amber and silver. That loathsome creature was ruining her life. She had to do something about him. But what? He was the producer of her fiancé's movie, he had power and influence, she was just the girlfriend. But she had survived Scrofo's monstrous humiliation before. She would again – she had to.

Without doubt it was he who had sent her the vile photographs, planted that sickening blind item. Could he also possibly have contacted the dreaded *Confidential* magazine too, telling them of her past? Knowing his sick mind, that would obviously be his next step.

A pair of tropical birds was singing outside her balcony, chasing each other around the lush foliage. Beyond the palm trees Inès could see the hard red tennis court, hear the thwack of ball against catgut, the excited cries of the players.

This is a war, but one neither of you will win, she thought. I've been in plenty of battles before and I have come out of them intact. She smiled grimly to the empty room.

You, Mademoiselle Dominique, even though you are more than a dozen years younger than me, and a little sex bomb to boot, will be quite easy to eliminate. Scrofo, however, would be another problem

397

entirely. Until he was out of her life she would never have the secure future she craved.

17

Ramona Armande's dinner party for Dominique's seventeenth birthday was a command performance for all the principals in the cast. Filming had been going well, and everyone seemed to be in high spirits as they gathered on the starlit terrace to toast the girl. But Dominique herself was in a sullen mood. She had been given a horrid shock when Julian arrived with Inès, who had pleaded with Dr Langley to allow her to go to this party. Inès had decided that she must fight fire with fire. Even if that meant a possible risk to the baby, it was better than losing Julian to that pubescent Jezebel.

Julian had expressed guilty surprise when Inès told him that the doctor was allowing her to get up and do a little more, but he was delighted to see how gorgeous she looked when she was dressed and ready. More ravishing than ever – more desirable. He knew that sex was still out of bounds for them but he realized how much he truly loved her.

'I love you, Mrs Brooks,' he whispered as they walked arm in arm into Ramona's marble and crystal palace. 'I can't wait to be married to you.'

She smiled up at him radiantly as they strode into the room, the two of them a perfect picture of togetherness. Inès, pale but ravishing in a Balenciaga sheath of apricot chiffon, a colour which complemented her luxuriant champagne coloured hair. Julian, as heart-stoppingly handsome as ever, in a black voile shirt and white linen trousers.

Dominique drew in her breath sharply and gritted her teeth. Her fingernails cut deeply into the palms of her hands, and she was flushed with fury. How could Julian show up with *her*? Why hadn't he said that he was coming to her birthday party with Inès? She was supposed to be bedridden. *Merde.* This would certainly ruin the party. Particularly since the horrible Hubert Croft who she had tried to keep away from the past several days kept glaring at her with a secret disgusting smile. She shuddered. She hated that man. He was a sick monster, and she wished he was dead.

As for Hubert Croft, he thought himself quite a *bella figura* tonight in his overly tight black silk trousers and his white frilled Mexican shirt. But he too was also extremely surprised to see Inès. Surprised and angry even though she'd been doing exactly what he'd instructed her to do. The six or seven times that he'd ordered her to persuade Julian to choose a particular scene, she had always managed to convince him to do it.

Hubert had been delighted that she was ill, and no doubt tortured by the possibility of a miscarriage. Serve her right, the murdering whore. He'd put her out of his mind recently, concentrating all his attention on overseeing the movie and on keeping the studio in Hollywood up to date on what was happening.

Now here she was once again, the picture of elegance, dressed up like some fashion plate, hanging on to the arm of her film star fiancé, and smiling as charmingly as if butter wouldn't melt in her slut-mouth. His lips closed in a grim line as he observed Inès' perfect composure across the terrace. Surely she must have received the photographs he'd sent? It was meant to be his little joke, just to make her suffer more as she lay in bed day after day. Obviously the joke had misfired, because here she was looking radiant and carefree, and gazing at Julian as if he were Romeo, and she his Juliet. He'd like to wipe that sweet smile off her face. Oh how he wanted to hurt this woman who had almost managed to put an end to him. He fingered his scar which had started to itch again. Well, it wasn't too late – not at all. There was a week left to go on the movie, still time left to give Mademoiselle Inès Juillard a real taste of what she deserved.

Ramona was also thrown into a tizzy. She had a superstitious dread of thirteen people at her dinner table and Sir Crispin had brought his boyfriend, Tony, who had suddenly flown over from London. There was little she could do about it other than cross her fingers, pray to the blessed Virgin and nervously twist her elaborate necklace of gold and amber beads. She had placed the guests with her usual care tonight, with some help from Agathe, who had become friendly and helpful to her in so many ways. Ramona was pleased with her own ability to bring shy people out of their shells.

Ramona drifted off to her winter dining room, where the glittering table for twelve twinkled with crystal and silver. Polished mirror place mats reflected the white lilies and hothouse roses which had been flown in specially on her private plane only that morning from Mexico City. Thirteen for dinner. Damn, damn, damn. She didn't want to make a fuss, but she felt it was a terrible omen. She ordered her butler to set another place, and after a few deft arrangements was satisfied that all would be well, though she hoped that no one else would notice the unlucky number.

Dinner proved a great success, and no one paid much attention to Dominique's barely disguised sulking. The oysters Mornay were delicious, several people asking for more, and the roast partridge, flown in from England, was a triumph.

'I'd like to make a toast,' Nick said, raising his glass of vintage Krug.

'To our new young star. Happy birthday, Dominique – we all love you, darling.' He had been persuaded to come to Ramona's, just this once tonight, by a prettily pouting Dominique. He could hardly refuse.

Inès winced as everyone raised their glasses to Dominique. and an enormous pink birthday cake, ablaze with seventeen long sparklers, was wheeled in. Dominique cut the cake prettily, posing flushed and excited for photographers from *Look* and *Photoplay*. She looked over at Julian, who smiled back at her coolly.

Hubert Croft made a pompous speech in his croaking voice, then Sir Crispin said a few amusing and well-chosen words, and finally Julian was cajoled into speaking. He rose, not one person at the table missing the irony of this situation: Julian and his two mistresses, both hanging on his every syllable. After he had finished a brief simple toast, finding it difficult to meet Dominique's wounded glare, there was a sudden silence. To break the tension, Irving Frankovitch decided to stand up and take the limelight.

'To a young actress of charm, talent and grace beyond her years,' he began. 'We are delighted –' Suddenly, a spasm of pain contorted his face; he weaved slightly and then slumped back into his chair, breathing heavily, his face ashen.

'I'm terribly sorry, but I don't feel at all well,' he wheezed as Shirley rushed over to him.

Suddenly, Inès too felt a wave of sickness, and she had a terrible feeling that if she did not leave the table at once she might embarrass herself dreadfully.

The baby, oh, the baby, she thought as she felt the familiar and agonizing empty sensation deep down in the pit of her stomach. She looked towards Julian pleadingly, and he was shocked at her pallor. Damn. He had told her he didn't think she should come out, but she had assured him that the doctor had said she could. Now she was the colour of chalk and looked on the verge of collapse. He started to help her from the room when there was a piercing scream from Shirley Frankovitch as her husband fell heavily forward on to the table, his bald brown head smashing down on to a Limoges plate of birthday cake with a sickening crash. The entire table was now in an uproar as all the guests started getting up, their faces greenish white, dashing for the bathrooms, some collapsing on to the floor with groans of pain.

Ramona was in a panic. 'What on earth is happening?' she called to her dumbstruck butler, who couldn't seem to move. It was exactly as she had feared. The curse of thirteen at dinner was coming true with a vengeance.

'For God's sake call a doctor,' Nick shouted, unable to control the great tide of sickness which engulfed him.

The stunned butler and waiters all stood rooted to the spot with fear, as if by moving, they too might be infected by this terrible plague.

'We've all been poisoned.'

Inès had no recollection of collapsing, no memory of the drive to the hospital, the trip in Ramona's private plane to Mexico City, or the long, complicated and dangerous operation which had been performed to save her life.

When she finally regained consciousness, it was several days later. She lay in a narrow white room, with tubes and needles connecting

402

her to various drips, and a pale, frantic Julian standing at the foot of her bed.

'Darling, oh, my darling, thank God,' he cried softly, covering her arms and hands with solicitous kisses. Then he held her face between his warm and reassuring hands, kneeling on the floor next to her bed, gazing at her with wonder, sadness and, most of all, with love.

'I thought I'd lost you, my angel. I thought you'd gone.' His tired eyes were tearful, and Inès saw the exhaustion in his face.

'What happened?' She heard her own voice as if from a great distance. 'We were at the party, then I can't remember anything. What was it, Julian? What happened?'

'Food poisoning,' he said. 'We all got it, everyone who was at the dinner. Some had it worse than others. You were one of the unlucky ones, I'm afraid.'

'Where am I?' She looked out of the window, expecting to see palm trees and luxuriant foliage, but seeing only the concrete slabs of a city.

'Mexico City, darling – the best hospital in Mexico. Ramona sent us here in her plane. Oh, God, Inès, you nearly *died*. It's made me realize what a total fool I've been, what a bloody, stupid fool. I'm sorry, darling, I'm so sorry.' He started to weep tears of both remorse and relief.

'Don't, darling, please don't.' She lovingly stroked his hair and touched his tear-stained cheeks. She had never seen him cry before. Then her hands went to her flat stomach.

'The baby?' Her eyes were pleading now, filled with tears. 'I've lost the baby, haven't I?'

He nodded sadly.

'Darling, listen.' He sat on the bed, holding her close to him, filling his voice with optimism. 'Please don't think about the baby – it's tragic, I know, but you're young, you'll have another baby, the doctor said so – many babies.' He put a hand to her trembling lips, holding her closer as she started to sob.

'No, Inès, no,' he said firmly. '*Stop* it. Please don't feel self-pity. It really could have been so much worse.'

'How?' She tried to stop crying, but found she couldn't. 'How much worse.'

'Irving Frankovitch is dead.'

'Oh, God, no!' Inès' hand flew to her mouth. 'How? Why?'

'According to the autopsy it was those bloody oysters Mornay we all ate. Apparently they were flown in from Mexico City the day before, but they were all rotten.' He shook his head. 'God, darling, you can't believe how sick everyone was. I've *never* seen anything like it, but poor old Irving didn't stand a chance. The old boy sort of crumpled up, collapsed in agony and just died in front of us before the doctor could even get there. Sir Crispin got it very badly, too, but he's a tough old bird – he seems to have recovered now.'

'And Dominique, how is she?' Inès tried to keep her voice expressionless as she watched Julian's reaction carefully.

'About the same as the others, I suppose,' Julian replied simply. 'I haven't spoken to her.' This was the truth. 'The only person who didn't get sick was Ramona.'

He wanted to stay off the subject of Dominique. He had been burdened with even more guilt and shame ever since the dinner party. He had seen his weakness for what it was: purely and simply the lure of flesh, the lust of a greedy, selfish lecher who cares nothing for anyone or anything other than himself. An ageing man making love to a teenager. He felt ridiculous and weak.

He despised himself for his affair with Dominique, for allowing it to get out of hand; for stupidly allowing it to become a subject for common gossip. He now realized that he would hate himself for ever if he did anything to hurt Inès. But he *had* hurt her – he could clearly see the pain in her face which she was trying so hard to disguise.

'Why not Ramona?' Inès' voice sounded weak. 'Why didn't she get sick?'

'She hates oysters – never eats them at all,' Julian told her. 'It was a stroke of luck that she didn't – she was able to organize the panicking servants, telephone doctors and arrange the plane for you. God, darling, it was ghastly.'

'It must have been.' Inès' eyes started to close. She felt so tired, but still clung tightly to Julian's hand. 'I don't remember . . . I must sleep now, darling. Do you mind?'

He kissed her pale forehead. 'Of course not. Sleep tight, angel,' he whispered. 'I love you, Inès – so much. I'll be right here when you wake up. I'll always be waiting for you, my love. Always.'

Dominique had tried continuously to contact Julian. She, like the others, had suffered from the particularly virulent bout of salmonella food poisoning, and it had left her feverish and vomiting for twenty-four hours, frail and listless for several days.

The doctors had advised Hubert Croft that it would be unwise to shoot in the tropical heat while the actors were still in such a weakened state. The insurance company in LA had screamed their heads off, but the doctor remained adamant. The only people he would allow to work were Ramona, who had not been affected, and Julian, who had barely touched the oysters so had suffered little. But there were no scenes in *Cortez* which involved Ramona and Julian alone, so the crew and technicians sat idly by in the cafés and on the beaches, drinking beer and tequila punches and playing cards, while the insurance company fumed and Umberto weakly croaked out his instructions and sent long telegrams from his sick bed to the studio in LA.

When Dominique hadn't been able to reach Julian, she had presumed he was just too sick to answer the telephone. But when Agathe reported that he had gone to Mexico City to be with Inès, Dominique was beside herself.

She stayed sobbing for hours in her room, not eating, playing Edith Piaf records of love and betrayal, miserably unhappy that Julian had not contacted her, not even sent her a note, a flower, anything. So this was the pain of rejected love which Piaf sang about. Well, she was certainly experiencing it for herself and she hated it – her heart felt empty and hollow and she had no appetite at all.

Whenever Agathe or Ramona called to see if she was all right, she sent them away, then buried her head in the pillow, weeping until she felt that she had no more tears left. Even Scrofo came to visit once, knocking at the door, but she had screamed 'Fuck off' at him with such a volley of hysterical fury that he hadn't returned.

She had heard from Ramona about what had happened to Inès, and the thought that Julian was with his fiancée made her sick with jealousy. After discovering the name of the hospital in Mexico City she had instructed Ramona's operator to place a call.

When she heard Julian's voice on the crackling line, her knees started shaking.

'Julian,' she whispered. 'Oh, Julian, *mon amour*, is that you?'

'Dominique?' His voice was hushed as he stood in the corridor outside Inès' room. 'Dominique – how are you?'

'Oh Julian, Julian – how *could* I be? I'm *terrible*,' she cried, starting to weep softly into the telephone. 'I've missed you so much, but I didn't hear anything from you – nothing, nothing – oh Julian, what is happening to you – to us?'

There was a long silence before Julian answered.

'Dominique, what I am going to say to you is going to hurt you very much, I know, but I have to say it – I must say it now, otherwise I'm being a coward – and I *am*, Dominique – I've been the most terrible coward and I despise myself for it.'

'What do you mean?' she asked, a feeling of panic rising within her.

'We can't go on, Dominique,' he said. 'We can't – we just can't – it has to end.'

'No,' she moaned. 'No, Julian, you can't mean it – I will *die* – I *swear* it – I'll kill myself.'

'Hush, silly little girl, you'll do absolutely no such thing.' His voice had a stern authoritative tone – almost fatherly, she thought bitterly.

'I was going to tell you properly, Dominique, when I returned to Acapulco, I was going to tell you face to face – not like this on the telephone. But now that you have called, I must confess.'

'Confess what?' she whispered. 'What, Julian, *mon amour, l'amour de ma vie?*'

'Stop it, Dominique,' he said. 'Darling child – and you *are* a child, Dominique – I don't want to hurt you, I *never* wanted to hurt you – I loved you – in my fashion.'

'I know you did,' she breathed. 'I know that – when you made love to me I knew how much you loved me.'

'But it's not going to *work*, Dominique,' he said firmly. 'It *can't* and it *won't*.'

'Why?' she asked. 'You love me – you said it many times. Why can't it work?'

'Because I'm in love with Inès,' he said simply, 'and my life, my future is with her. I know that this is hard for you to understand, Dominique – and God knows I feel like a first-rate bastard for telling you like this, but even before the food poisoning I was going to tell you that it was all over between us. Our affair, my darling girl, must end.'

'No, Julian, it's not true!' she cried.

'*Please*, Dominique darling – *please try* to understand. I know you're young. You're a baby. I'm twenty years older than you. You need to be with someone of your own age. It could never work. I don't want to hurt you but this must be the end.' He could hear her sobs but he continued, 'Please understand, darling girl, please.'

'No,' she sobbed. 'I can't – I won't understand.'

'You must,' he whispered. 'You *will*, my darling child. I know you will. Now be a good girl – go back to bed and tomorrow you'll start forgetting all about me – goodbye, my darling.'

'Never,' said Dominique, tears running down her face. 'I'll never forget you, Julian, how can I?'

But there was nothing more to be heard from Mexico City. The line was dead. Sobbing, Dominique threw herself on the bed, buried her head in her pillow and finally cried herself to sleep.

And some three hundred miles away in a stark hospital room, Inès quietly closed the door, a faint smile on her lips, having listened to all of Julian's conversation.

Dominique eventually decided Julian wasn't worth it. Her pragmatic French brand of common sense took over, and she decided that she had been a complete fool to fall in love with a man the same age as her father. Yes, he had been a wonderful and considerate lover, he had taught her a great deal about sex, but then so had Gaston. Perhaps now was the time to put their lessons into practice.

Two days after speaking to Julian over the telephone she had recovered, and her natural youthful energy returned. She put on her beach clothes, and knocking on Agathe's door, called that she was heading for Caleta Beach to go water-skiing, did Agathe want to come? The door was slightly ajar so she pushed it open wider and saw, to her surprise, Agathe fast asleep on the bed. She was wearing a man's dirty white shirt, an old rag was bunched up under her chin, and a large album crammed with what looked like press clippings and photographs lay on the floor next to the bed.

'Agathe,' Dominique said softly. 'Want to come skiing with me?' There was a groan from the sleeping woman so Dominique shrugged, closed the door and skipped off to the beach.

She was seventeen, gorgeous and a budding movie star. The world was hers for the taking. Young men whistled wherever she went, and she smiled back at them. There was nothing for her to feel sad or down about, nothing, not even Julian Brooks. He was an old man, she was young – young and free and beautiful. She could have her pick of men.

She took one of Ramona's jeeps to drive to the beach. The soft breeze blew her long hair across her face, and she could smell the tang of the ocean and the aroma of tacos cooking in the little beach restaurant. As she came nearer she could hear mariachis playing, and see teenagers dancing and enjoying the glorious day. She parked the car, conscious of the many eyes watching her. Dominique always enjoyed people staring, and she swung her hips in her snug shorts as she walked.

She quickened her stride as she saw a tall, tanned boy with yellow curls looking at her, smiling invitingly with eyes which were bluer than the sea.

'Hi. Wanna Coke?' he asked as soon as she entered the bar. She nodded. When he brought it over to her, she noted with some interest his young, muscled arms and sculpted chest. How firm and deeply bronzed they were. In contrast, she noticed that he had tiny golden hairs like down all over his arms. Very pretty indeed, she thought. How exciting to have those arms around me. He was good-looking too. Not the Handsomest Man in the World but young and sexy and very virile.

'An' then maybe you an' I can go water-skiing?' He grinned lazily, and Dominique smiled back.

'Would you like that?' he said.

'I love water-skiing,' she told him. 'I know *just* the place to go,' and her eyes strayed down to the bulge in his shorts.

*

Agathe awoke just when Dominique closed her door. At first she didn't know where she was, and then it all came back to her. In the week since the salmonella outbreak, she had thought of nothing else.

Fool. She was a fool and an idiot. She had failed to do what she had planned so carefully. It had been a faultless scheme – the perfect murder which she had read about long ago in one of her books in the cellar in Paris, but it had backfired badly. Her plot had killed the wrong person. Agathe hadn't really spoken more than a dozen words to Irving Frankovitch – a nice enough man, now dead because of her ineptitude.

She had bought some oysters at the local market some days before Dominique's birthday party, and had hidden them in a secret place just outside her room. The day of the party she had helped Ramona and the servants set the table and had supervised the staff as they brought in the first course of oysters Mornay. Unknown to them, she had inserted an eyedropper into the rotting oysters and dripped a tiny drop of their poison on to each fresh oyster. One of the bad ones, however, as well as some slightly poisoned oysters, she put on the plate intended for Inès. The Mornay sauce, Agathe assumed, would disguise the taste of the rotten oyster, and Inès would die soon after she swallowed it.

But Sir Crispin had unexpectedly brought a friend, and Ramona had not consulted Agathe about changing the place settings. Irving Frankovitch had eaten the oysters meant for Inès. Agathe's *soi-disant* perfect murder was ruined.

She had bungled it badly, very badly indeed. It was Inès who should have died . . . Inès the whore . . . the murderess . . . the traitor . . . the enemy slut. Agathe's hatred for her was so intense that it was almost like a burning coal in her chest. She moaned, clutching Julian's tattered shirt to her lips, sniffing the cotton fabric, trying to find a taste of him, his scent, his essence, his sweat.

Where is he now? She thought. With *her*, in Mexico City, planning their wedding day, the birth of their baby, their life together in London? *No!*

Agathe sat bolt upright in Ramona's silky, lime-green-sheeted bed, staring at an enormous painting of some huge butterflies of all shades and varieties. She was trembling violently, both from the

409

after-effects of the self-inflicted food poisoning and from pure hatred. She looked around the silk-panelled room decorated with every species of butterfly imaginable. Her heart was beating so fast she thought it would burst, and she pounded her fists on the mattress in an uncontrollable fury.

First the woman had been Inès Dessault. Then Inès Juillard and within the next few weeks she would be Inès Brooks – Mrs Julian Brooks. 'No . . . no.' Agathe was crooning softly now, feverishly turning her amber rosary around her neck. 'It can't be. It can't happen. She will *not* marry him. She cannot. She *will not*.'

Two people now seemed to be in possession of her psyche, each battling for supremacy. There was Agathe Guinzberg, the proper chaperone, the spinster ballet teacher – polite, quiet, well-mannered and prim. And then there was Agathe the devil, the woman who slaked her lust for Julian Brooks every night on her bed, in the green onyx bath, on the floor . . . whispering his name, rubbing herself fiercely with his shirt, kissing his photographs, moaning, with infatuated madness.

She could not stop herself any more. Just the thought of him made her moisten and ache until only the rough touch of his shirt could ease the burning between her legs.

Last week, when she had sat on a canvas chair next to Sir Crispin, watching Julian laugh, studying the tiny beads of sweat on his muscled chest, right there in the chair she had felt the waves rise within her. She could almost feel him entering her as she squeezed her thighs together tightly until she reached a plateau of pleasure which had been unknown to her a few weeks ago.

It was as though a dam had burst inside her. She couldn't stop. Six, seven, eight times a day, whispering her love's name, she reached more and more tumultuous orgasms. But once – oh, God, just once – she wanted *him* to make love to her, to fuse that magnificent body with hers. She yearned for that.

Agathe was still technically a virgin and had only a vague idea of what a naked man even looked like, but last week, she had even stolen one of the phallic-shaped candles Ramona kept for her winter dining room, and now this, too, was used to pleasure herself.

Thirty-one years of frigidity exploded into lust as Agathe found herself on a merry-go-round of erotic enslavement without a partner to satisfy her. Julian belonged to her. He was her destiny – her man – she had to win him away from Inès. He had to know how much Agathe loved him – how they were meant to be together.

Despairingly, she did it again now, almost viciously – chafing, hurting herself with the blue shirt which was not much more than a tattered rag. Afterwards, exhausted, she tried to think. She *had* to think, she knew she must try to end this obsession with Julian – his face, his body, his eyes, his cock which she had glimpsed once, outlined by yellow bathing trunks when he was playing ball in the water with some of the crew.

She knew that what she was doing and what was happening to her was a sin, but she was no longer in control of herself.

She rang for some coffee and papaya, and while unsuccessfully trying to read the *Acapulcan News*, she thought again of how her plan had failed. It had been a good plan – an excellent plan, but the next one had to be absolutely foolproof.

18

There were only a few days of shooting left, and Inès began to feel better both physically and emotionally. Although saddened by her miscarriage, she was assured that she could have more children, and there was the consolation that the experience had brought her closer to Julian again. He had confessed his affair with Dominique, apologizing so profusely and so fiercely that Inès forgave him. Now she could visit the set to watch him work again, and she went every day, trying not to be intimidated by Scrofo and his cold, deadly stare.

Much to Scrofo's chagrin, the sexual electricity between Julian and Dominique had fizzled out completely. He had tried to cause a chasm between Inès and Julian by sending her the scandalous photographs he had bribed a local photographer to take the day Julian and Dominique had gone to the island. The pictures were excellent but his ploy hadn't worked, for Inès and Julian were still together. Stupid bitch, she had forgiven him. To take a man back into her bed when she knew he'd been fucking another woman, she didn't deserve to be happy.

Scrofo followed Inès one night when she took a solitary walk along the beach, away from the shooting; then he cornered her.

'You think you're safe now, don't you – whore,' he said, his eyes gleaming a sulphurous yellow in the humid darkness as he grabbed her arm, holding it too tightly.

'Let go of me, Scrofo,' Inès said calmly, realizing that no one was around to help her.

His grip became more vice-like as she repeated, 'Please let me go.'

'I'll let go of you when I'm good and ready, whore,' he hissed. 'You got my little present, I presume?'

'If you mean those filthy photographs – yes, I received them. And I tore them up,' she said coldly.

'Of course – of course you did. You didn't want to look at snaps of your fiancé making love to his under-age paramour, did you?'

'Look, Scrofo, why are you doing this? I did *everything* you asked of me.'

In spite of herself Inès felt hot tears stinging her eyelids. Still weak from surgery, she detested this man so much that the mere touch of his hand filled her with loathing.

'*Every* scene that you sent to Julian I persuaded him to do – for weeks I did that, Scrofo. Surely that's enough for you?'

'No – it'll *never* be enough,' he croaked. 'It's a small price to pay for *this*.'

He pushed his great neck closer to reveal in ghastly detail the puckered scar tissue. She could almost see the surgeon's stitches in his flesh.

'*You* did this, bitch, and you must be punished. I need to punish you much, much more – and you will be when the magazine comes out. You certainly will be.' He laughed triumphantly. 'That will make you squirm.'

'What magazine?' she asked.

'Ah, that's *my* little secret,' he gloated. 'But the whole of America, in fact the whole of the world will see the pictures of Dominique and your fiancé fucking each other – censored of course,' he sneered. 'Then the whole world will know about you and your whoring past.'

'How will they know? How – what have you done?' cried Inès. 'Whatever I did to you . . . Whatever happened was *years* ago. Can't you forget it, Scrofo – leave me in peace? Why do you need to do this now? Why?'

'I can *never* forget, slut – never,' Scrofo said savagely. 'But it isn't just me who's contributing to your downfall. I have an expert witness to your sordid past. One who knows you well. Better than Julian – better than anyone, in fact.'

'Who?' breathed Inès. 'Who is this person?'

'Yves Moray,' chortled Scrofo, relishing his moment of victory. 'Your ex-pimp. Your ex-lover – the one who deflowered you. My people found him in Paris last week.'

'No, it's not possible,' whispered Inès. 'You couldn't have.'

'Oh, but it is, it's very possible. The world is really a very tiny place,' sneered Scrofo. 'Look at us, Inès my dear – who would ever think that you and I, who met in such unfortunate and squalid circumstances in Paris, would be here together in beautiful Acapulco making a film?'

His brutal hand held her arm so tightly that she could feel the bruises his fingers were making.

'Where did you meet Yves?' she asked, her voice shocked into a thready whisper.

'Oh, I didn't meet him – I didn't even see the man. It all happened quite by accident, a fortuitous coincidence for me. He was arrested in Paris for fencing some stolen jewellery. At the police station he was babbling on in an alcoholic stupor and pleading his innocence – his complete innocence – of the theft, but of course he was such a pathetic drunken bum that no one believed him, so they threw him in a cell. And guess what, Inès?' He leaned his face close to hers, leering with vindictive glee. 'There was a photograph of you and Julian in a magazine that another prisoner had, and poor Yves started bragging that he knew you. In fact he knew you extremely well – because *you worked for him when you were fourteen years old!* He said he was your pimp and you were his little baby whore, and he taught you everything he knew.'

'No . . .' sighed Inès. 'It's a lie.'

'Oh no, my dear – it's no lie,' said Scrofo, relishing his power. 'One of the prisoners happened to be an old army acquaintance of mine, a Signor Volpi, who knew that I was producing a film with Julian Brooks. He contacted me and told me the whole fascinating story, and then I phoned your old boyfriend Yves. Of course he told me everything. It's amazing what a drunk will do for a few hundred francs,' he remarked contemptuously. 'Well, the rest, as they say, is history. It makes a wonderful story, Inès – rags to riches, tart to movie star's wife – and then *fini.*' He looked at her pityingly. 'Enjoy the short time you have left with your fiancé, Mademoiselle. Because when he reads the truth about your whoring past, your life with Julian Brooks will be finished.'

On the way down to the beach from his trailer, Nick was stopped by the harsh sound of Scrofo's raised voice. What was Gourouni doing now? Who was he trying to intimidate? He drew closer into the shadows to watch and listen, silent as stone. Scrofo obviously had some sort of sick hold on Inès. Nick heard the vicious blackmailing threats and his lips tightened in anger. Scrofo was vermin. He didn't deserve to breathe the same air as decent people.

Nick was just about to go over and help Inès when he heard Bluey's voice yelling on the loudhailer from further along the beach: 'Nick, where the hell are you? We're ready for rehearsal, pal, get your butt down here pronto.'

At that the Italian released his grip on Inès' arm, pushing her away from him so violently that she stumbled and fell to the sand.

In Nick's mind Inès suddenly became his mother, cowering on the ground while the monster Gourouni towered over her – ready to kill. The tableau was so real, so terrifyingly graphic that Nick wanted to scream out at the top of his lungs. Nick was going to kill the murdering slime now. He had to.

As he started to race towards them the tableau suddenly dissolved. Inès had clambered to her feet and run down the beach and Scrofo had turned, laughing, strutting off in the opposite direction. Nick's hand clawed at the knife in his pocket and he started to follow Scrofo.

'Nick! For Christ's sake where are you? It'll be dawn soon. Hurry up.' Bluey's amplified voice brought Nick back to the present. He shook his head as if to clear it as he watched the squat figure of Gourouni disappear into the night, then he walked rapidly down to the rehearsal, with more loathing than ever in his heart for Scrofo.

The following evening in the production office at Scheherazade, Scrofo attempted to tell Nick and Bluey that Inès had been a prostitute. Bluey looked at him with disgust.

'That's a helluva thing to say,' he spat. 'You've got a dirty mind, Hubie baby.'

Nick, however, suddenly became violently angry.

'Listen, you suet-faced prick,' he roared as he gripped the Italian's fleshy shoulders and pushed his face close, 'don't you ever, *ever* talk about a lady – *any* lady – like that around me, or in front of *anyone*, do you understand, you motherfucker?'

Suddenly Umberto was genuinely terrified as Nick's hands were now round his neck, his voice hoarse with hatred as he squeezed the adipose, scarred flesh of Scrofo's throat.

'You filthy scum,' he bellowed. 'You *dare* to talk about whores. *You're* the whore, you lump of shit. What you did to those people. What you did to them . . .' His voice started to crack as his grip tightened, and Scrofo's eyes were beginning to pop out of their sockets, his face turning crimson.

The vision of his mother filled Nick's brain. Her quiet beauty and goodness snuffed out by this bastard. He was going to kill him now, at last. He'd rid the world of this filth.

Nick's eyes were closed and his hands, clamped around Scrofo's neck, began to squeeze even harder.

Bluey could see that Hubert was losing consciousness.

'For Christ's sake quit it, Nick. He's not worth it,' Bluey screamed as he tried to pry his friend off the wilting Italian. The transformation of a man who was usually so controlled in spite of all the difficulties on the set, calm in emergencies, hardly ever losing his cool, was as alarming as what he was actually doing.

'*Stop* it, Nick, for God's sake stop it! You're only hurting yourself,' Bluey yelled. 'Get hold of yourself, man – you must.'

Nick released Scrofo's neck as Bluey's voice penetrated his consciousness and slumped into the chair, his breathing shallow, his face still contorted with rage. Bluey realized that Nick could have killed Umberto if he hadn't intervened – and the Italian thought so too. His pudgy hands gingerly massaged his scarred and now bruised throat where the livid red marks of Nick's fingers were imprinted.

'Jesus, kid. Jesus Christ, slow down,' Bluey said and quickly poured him a stiff scotch.

Nick tossed it down, his burning eyes fixed on Scrofo.

'Get out of here, you fucking pig,' Nick spat, his voice hoarse and shaking. 'I'm making a fucking movie. I'll do what the fucking studio tells me to do on the set but don't *ever* talk about that woman or *any* woman in front of me again or I'll squeeze your fat neck until your eyeballs come out of your head. I mean it, pigface – get out of my sight. *Now*.'

Bluey poured another whisky as Umberto, badly frightened and quite the opposite of the *bella figura* he fancied himself, nervously slunk out of the office. I will have my revenge, he thought. When these idiots see what comes out in *Confidential* they will realize I am right about the French slut. They'll know she's a murdering whore. That will be my first revenge on her. After that – who knows? His mind boiling with ideas about how to hurt and ruin Inès, he limped off through the dark corridor to his room.

'I hate that motherfucker,' Nick breathed. 'It's only a matter of time before I kill the bastard.'

'Hey, hey, kiddo, *quit* it, will ya?' Bluey tried to sooth Nick. 'We all know he's a complete asshole – a phony who knows as much about the movie business as my left testicle. Don't let him get to you. You're doin' great. The studio loves the dailies, you're keeping your head above water and the picture's on schedule and even on budget. We've only got a few days left. You're a whiz kid, so calm down, will ya?'

Nick nodded, the whisky clearing his head a little. 'Gotta get some sleep, Bluey.' He pulled his worry beads from out of a pocket and swung them morosely while he gazed out of a window at the sliver of new moon palely reflected on the still, black water. Then he picked up his bulky script, and walked decisively to the door. 'I'm sorry, Bluey. It's a good thing you stopped me. I was out of control – I was gone, man, gone.'

'Get to bed, kiddo,' Bluey said. He looked worried. 'Big scene tomorrow. You gotta give it your best shot. Forget Hubert, Nick, for God's sake forget him.'

'I can't forget him, Bluey – I've seen that face too many times. I've seen it in my dreams and in every fuckin' nightmare I've ever had.'

'What are you talkin' about, man?' asked Bluey. 'You only met the motherfucker a few months ago.'

'Oh no,' Nick said harshly. 'He's haunted my life for more than ten years.'

'Jesus.' Bluey was silent as he stared at Nick's grim face. 'What has he done to you, kid? Whatever he did it couldn't have been that bad?'

'He killed my mother,' Nick said simply. 'He killed her and I'm going to kill him.'

19

Inès had been undecided about whether or not to watch Julian and Dominique shooting their tenderly erotic final love scene. The two actors had not worked together since Dominique's birthday party, and when they saw each other again there had been a noticeable coolness between them. Inès had heard through the gossip grapevine that although she now had a new boyfriend, Dominique was still furious and hurt that Julian had ended the affair. Inès understood how the girl must feel; Julian had not conducted himself at all well.

'Do you want me to come to the set tonight?' she asked casually as she lay back on the bed in the twilight dusk, watching Julian prepare to leave.

'It's entirely up to you, darling.' He found it difficult to meet her eyes. Julian was in a quandary. He hadn't spoken to Dominique since he terminated their affair, and felt like a cad because of only explaining the situation to her on the telephone, but the circumstances had never seemed right to face her directly. He had been working hard on the exhausting battle scenes, and in his free time had thrown himself into his reconciliation with Inès. They had been utterly inseparable as he comforted her over the loss of their baby.

He was secretly dreading his lovemaking scene with Dominique. It was tricky enough to have to simulate making passionate love to a girl with whom you had recently ended a blazing real-life affair, but even more galling was knowing that he had not behaved at all like a gentleman towards her, and he was angry with himself.

Now the thought of Inès watching their fervent kisses and caresses embarrassed him.

With her natural intuition, Inès understood completely. 'Darling, don't worry,' she said, smiling. 'I'm expecting a call from the doctor in Los Angeles. The results of those blood tests should be in. I think I'll just stay here, drink margaritas and watch the sun set.'

'No, I really think you should come, darling. Yes, yes really I want you there,' Julian said firmly, moving next to her on the bed, gazing into her glorious eyes. 'Please come, darling. I need you. You know it's over between Dominique and me, you do believe me, don't you?'

'Of course I do. All right, I'll come with you,' Inès agreed, brushing a strand of hair off his forehead, then kissing him lovingly. 'I'm not worried about you and Dominique. And I'll stay well in the background. Don't worry, my darling, I won't make a fool of myself, I promise.'

Julian gave her a rueful look as he picked up his script and blew her a kiss.

'I love you, Inès. You're magnificent. I'll see you later.'

Inès stared at the closed door for several minutes, trying to analyse how she really felt about watching Julian and Dominique making love. Did she mind? Did it bother her, knowing that the whole crew would be watching her reaction? The odious Scrofo, who had gone to such pains to blackmail her, gloating – looking at her for any signs of weakness.

She shrugged as she sauntered into the bathroom. It didn't bother her any more. She believed that Julian was completely over his infatuation. If his verbal assurances were not enough, his passionate declarations of love, even though lovemaking was still forbidden, reassured Inès that he was hers, and hers alone. As far as others were concerned, she really didn't give a damn what people thought. If they chose to gossip and tittle-tattle, she would be above all that. The only person who made her skin crawl, whose very presence in a room made her squirm with loathing, was the sluglike Scrofo. She had to do something to stop this terrible story coming out in the magazine. She had tried hard to talk to Scrofo the day after he'd threatened her, begging him not to print it, but he had merely laughed, telling her, 'You have a couple more months of the good life left, Inès. The magazine is holding the story until just before the release of *Cortez*. It will be great publicity for the film – huge coverage. Make it an absolute sure-fire box-office blockbuster, don't you agree? Those pictures of Julian and Dominique making love – so sexy – so wonderful – everyone will race to see the film. We'll be a runaway hit.'

Sickened, unable to reply, she had walked away. There was still some time left to stop the story from being published, but it would be common gossip in Hollywood long before that. As soon as Julian heard he would question her. Of course she could lie, but she would tell the truth, the whole sickening ghastly truth. Inès shuddered.

Next week, as soon as she and Julian arrived in Los Angeles, they were going to be married. The final decree had been issued, and she would be Mrs Julian Brooks at long last. She had to stop Scrofo from printing the truth about her in that magazine. She had to – but how?

Agathe sat beside Dominique in her small, stuffy trailer by the water's edge. She was going through tonight's dialogue with her, but her heart wasn't in it.

On the sofa was a week-old copy of *The Hollywood Reporter*. The lead item in the gossip column had caught Agathe's eyes the instant she sat down:

Wedding bells will ring out at last for Julian Brooks and the lovely Inès Juillard. The happy couple will tie the knot next week at the home of Spyros Makopolis after an arduous three-month stint in Acapulco on *Cortez*, the legendary Julian's first American film. Congratulations to the two of them.

A white-hot flame was burning in Agathe's head and she couldn't concentrate on anything Dominique was saying or doing.

Makeup girls and hairdressers bustled around the young star as she sat having pancake applied to her chest and shoulders. She seemed as usual to have no modesty; she was bare to the waist, calmly allowing the body makeup girl to paint her exposed flesh.

She had few words to learn except 'I love you' and 'My father will never understand'. Kisses and burning passion were the main ingredients of the scene tonight as Cortez and the princess would be rolling around naked on the sandy beach in the moonlight. Dominique had been given a flesh-coloured body stocking to wear to save the censors' blushes. Her nude dance scene had been approved by the Hays Office but there was still a limit to the amount of licentiousness which they would allow on screen.

Dominique thought about how it would be to make love with Julian again. Always during their scenes together he had wanted her afterwards, and their combined passion had rocked the flimsy walls of the trailer. But Inès had never been around then. Now she was on the sidelines watching all the time, never taking her eyes off her fiancé. Dominique sighed. There was little chance of a reconciliation with Julian, she realized. But she had seen the flash of desire in his eyes when they had kissed during rehearsal, though it had gone as quickly as it appeared and he was again the ultimate professional – the actor – coolly removed, pleasant, trading japes and jokes with the crew, polite and considerate towards her. Dominique knew she had lost him, but after all she had Frankie. Her new boyfriend was a member of the crew, American, young, blond, a most attentive suitor and a good lover. Not as good as Julian but certainly younger.

Agathe, her own passion for Julian still raging, couldn't have cared less by now that her young charge was having an affair. Nothing mattered to her any more. She tried hard to act as normally as possible around the crew, hoping that no one would notice that she was thinking about Julian all the time. No one did.

There was a knock on the door and Frankie loped in, a broad smile on his face.

'Oooh!' Dominique said, pretending to be shy and half-covering her breasts. '*Méchant garçon.* You surprised me – give me a kiss.'

They kissed lingeringly, neither noticing that Agathe had slipped out of the trailer as soon as the boy entered it – she needed her fix. A glimpse of Julian, maybe even a word from him, it was all that she lived for these days.

As the new moon slid behind a puff of darkened cloud, a lone figure sped quickly down the hundred or more stone steps that descended at one side of Scheherazade. The guard dogs were silent; the figure knew at exactly what time they were taken on their rounds, and had timed the arrival at the cable car perfectly to avoid the watchdogs and their handlers.

Swiftly the figure squatted by the side of the wooden carriage and, removing a few small tools from a pocket, made some slight adjustments to the machine's gear box. It took only a few minutes; then, with a furtive glance around, ears strained for the slightest sound, the figure disappeared into the thick tropical foliage which surrounded the vast estate.

Now, as the moon reappeared from behind the clouds, it was reflected in the small puddle of amber beads which had been dropped behind the padded seat of the wooden cable car.

They had decided to shoot Dominique and Julian's love scene on Ramona's private beach, well away from the prying eyes of Acapulco tourists. Part of the beach was brilliantly lit by a dozen arc lamps, which were placed around the area on which the stand-ins for Julian and Dominique were lying on the sand entwined in each other's arms.

Nick paced up and down nervously, a cigarette hanging permanently from his lips, talking to his lighting cameraman and to Bluey. Sometimes he glanced over to where Scrofo stood, half concealed behind an arc lamp, as usual speaking to no one but occasionally staring over at Nick with hatred.

Nick stared right back at him. How could this man have become such a monster, he wondered. What in his childhood had created such a sadistic beast? There had to be some reason for his venom, for the evil that seemed to radiate from him. He looked over again, but Scrofo was gone.

Nick shrugged as he went over to where his unit bustled about chatting quietly. They were all thankful that for once the Toad was not hanging around the set to irritate them. All the crew, and most members of the cast, had suffered from Croft's foul mouth during the past few months. All of them despised him, and few made it a secret.

Shirley Frankovitch's reports on his acumen as a line producer had been totally exaggerated. The charm, diplomacy and respect she had glowingly talked of were all sadly lacking. His knowledge of the mechanics of film making was rudimentary, and his alienation of the crew and the actors was remarkable in its totality. Things were always more calm on the set, and certainly Nick was easier to work with, when the fat Italian wasn't around.

Further down the beach Julian sat in his canvas chair wearing a light seersucker robe over his flesh-coloured bathing suit. He flicked through the pages of his dialogue casually, looking up as Inès came to sit beside him, smiling as he put his hand lightly on her shoulder.

The moon shimmered on the flat ocean, with only a slight tide disturbing the shoreline as Inès put her hand on his, and they both stared out at the moon.

One of Romana's houseboys suddenly appeared and tapped Inès on the shoulder, handing her a scribbled note.

'Excuse me, darling,' she said. 'The doctor's calling from Los Angeles. I must go up to the main house to take the call.'

'I hope the results from the tests are OK,' said Julian.

'I'm sure they are.' Inès smiled. 'I'll be right back, darling.'

Julian blew her a kiss and admired her slender body as she walked across the beach to the cable car.

It sat at the base of the jagged rocks, its plain white wooden frame strangely out of place against the splendour of the exotic, sumptuous surroundings.

Inès got in and pressed the third button. With a shuddering creak the ancient contraption started its gradual ascent up the side of the steep rocks to the house. It seemed to be going much slower than usual, Inès thought, it shook and trembled all the way up, and there was an odd sort of rasping sigh from the pulleys as they dragged the groaning machine up to the third level.

The third floor was in complete darkness. Inès stepped from the cable car on to the white marble floor, her flimsy sandals echoing hollowly as she made her way to the main production office.

The room was pitch black. Inès shivered even though it was a humid night. She switched on the light, went over to the telephone, and told the operator to put through her call from Los Angeles.

'There's no one on the line for you, *Señora*,' the operator said.

'But there must be. I just received a message that my doctor was calling,' Inès told her.

'No. I'm sorry. No one has called you at all tonight, Miss Juillard. It must be a mistake.'

Puzzled, Inès replaced the receiver and sat thinking for a moment before she went to the door. As she reached it she saw in the hallway the shadow of a horribly familiar squat figure strutting slowly between the marble pillars of the terrace. She stopped. The last person she wanted to see or talk to was Umberto Scrofo. She did not want to be cornered by him again. Not at night, in the empty darkness of the villa.

Suddenly Scrofo stopped in his tracks, turning around swiftly as if he had heard something. He was like an animal, Inès thought, he had the instincts of a beast.

She could smell his cologne, that foul, cheap scent which seemed to hang in the humid night air like a noxious vapour. Even the odour of his body lingered after him.

After a few seconds Scrofo continued on his way, obviously heading for the cable car. Inès saw him press a button, then heard the familiar loud creaking as the machine began its laborious, strained descent.

The funicular had not gone more than a few feet when there was a harsh rending noise, a cacophony of screeching wires and pulleys exploding out of their sockets, and a hideous animal scream from Scrofo as the white wooden carriage was ripped from its moorings and began to fall down the sheer cliff.

Inès ran to the cable car's top landing and to her horror saw the funicular smashing its way down, down, down to the bottom of the rocks. All the way Scrofo screamed in terror. Inès could see as if in slow motion the hated bullet head, the great yaw of a gargoyle's mouth opened in the agony of his inevitable death as he plummeted to the ground.

Scrofo tried to hang on until the last impact. When his body was thrown twenty feet through the air, it landed on the rocks like a smashed doll. All that he had managed to clutch for support was a small row of broken amber beads, and the tiny crucifix which hung from them.

Epilogue

For over a year the whole of America had been bombarded with hype on MCCP's latest, greatest and soon to be released blockbuster, *The Legend of Cortez*. It was a rare newspaper or magazine indeed which had not featured some story, photograph or article on one or other of the principals in the movie. *Cortez* mania gripped the nation, and MCCP was crossing its corporate fingers that the publicity machine had done its work well enough to guarantee that every box-office register would be working overtime.

Although the new stretch-version Cadillac was fitted with the latest in air conditioning, the hot Californian night still made the air hang heavy inside the perfumed darkness of the car. There were six of them in the limousine – Nicholas and Elektra Stone, Dominique with a handsome escort, and Julian and his wife.

She was concerned that the excessive and controversial publicity which he had received might adversely influence the critics. Julian was being hailed as the greatest English actor since Olivier, and his name had become a household word long before most of the American public had even had a glimpse of his talents. Hubert S. Croft's death and the scandal of Inès' past had been universal gossip for months after the incident. The death of the Italian producer was as juicy a piece of news as anyone had heard for years.

Julian held his wife's hand, smiling at her reassuringly. He had seen a rough cut of the movie, and although self-critical to an extreme, he realized that his performance had been electrifying. He had brought to his stereotyped role a swashbuckling magnetism, combined with a sensitive naturalism, which had been nurtured and polished on the London stage. The word was out in Hollywood that he was about to become as big a male star as Gable. The stacks of

427

offers which poured into his agent's office ensured him a place in cinematic history, but his thoughts, in fact, were less on tonight's premiere than on his next challenge. He was going back to his roots to star in *Coriolanus* on the West End stage. He felt that he'd already spent enough time on the Hollywood scene, even though the result so far had been just two films, but he had only two more pictures to make for MCCP. When those were finished their baby, David, would be almost three years old, and they had decided to settle down in one place to give the child the security of an ordered life.

'Did David mind that you didn't stay with him until he went to bed?' Julian asked.

'Oh no, darling. I think he must somehow have realized how important tonight is to his daddy.' She thought lovingly of month-old David's beautiful smile as she handed him to his nanny after giving him his bottle. Julian was her life, but David ran a close second, and she adored her two men passionately.

She sighed happily. She felt she was a lucky woman.

'Oh, look.' Dominique pointed excitedly to a small art-house cinema they were just passing on Sunset Boulevard. '*La Città Perduta* – wasn't that Hubert Croft's Italian film?'

Everyone peered through the tinted windows of the limousine to where the flickering neon sign spelled out the names of the cast and that of Umberto Scrofo as producer.

'Honey, don't remind us of *him* – that's all over and forgotten,' Dominique's escort told her. 'It's yesterday's news.'

Nick stared out blankly at the cinema. Hubert S. Croft, Umberto Scrofo. The man whose ghastly image had haunted him for so much of his life. Dead now, but the memory of him would never die. Nick could never forget the horrors of those war years on Hydra, the countless atrocities which Scrofo had committed culminating in the brutal murder of his mother.

'It's a year ago tonight,' Nick said quietly.

'What is?' Dominique asked.

'It's one year exactly since Scrofo died.' Nick's voice was so soft that the others had to strain to hear him.

'Oh my God, so it is, you're absolutely right,' breathed Julian. 'God, only a year.'

'As far as I'm concerned that bastard finally got what he deserved,' Nick said harshly.

'Poor Agathe,' Dominique muttered. 'I wonder what she's doing now?'

'Rotting behind bars in some Mexican jail.' Julian's voice was uncharacteristically unsympathetic. 'She was a madwoman, completely certifiable. If Croft or Scrofo, or whatever his name was, hadn't died that night, it would have been Inès for certain.'

'And all for the love of you, Julian,' Dominique teased. 'All for the love of you.' She flashed him her sultry gamine smile as she snuggled closer to her escort.

There had been several men in Dominique's life in the past year. As an eighteen-year-old star with a brilliant future, she was more gloriously sexy than ever and revelled unashamedly in her sorceress' ways. She smiled at Julian, who smiled back uncomfortably. They were friendly now but she knew she would never get over their passionate romance until he belonged to her again. How could she? It had been the ultimate and perfect love for her – and she wanted it to happen all over again. It was a once in a lifetime affair, never to be forgotten.

But something which none of them would ever forget was that night – that terrible night in Acapulco exactly one year ago.

When the Acapulco police arrived at Ramona's villa Inspector Gomez had begun his slow interrogation of each of them about Hubert Croft's 'accident'. He strongly believed it to be murder, and questioned everyone with painstaking care. By the time he turned his attention to Agathe, the woman was trembling violently, her face shining with sweat, and she was wringing her hands in a frenzy.

Before the Inspector could question her, she fixed her eyes on Inès and crooned softly, 'It's all her fault. She made me do it – didn't you, Inès?' Her eyes seemed to burn into Inès who was suddenly dry-mouthed, unable to speak. 'Yes you did,' Agathe spat. 'You forced me to do it. I killed Hubert Croft. *I* did,' she hissed. 'But I didn't mean to. I meant *her* to die. She – *she* should have been the one who ate the poisoned oyster, not Irving.' She took a step towards Inès, who stood absolutely still, rooted in shock. 'Inès Dessault –

Inès Juillard, the *whore*. She should have been in the cable car.'

'What? What did you say? Why did you kill him?' said the Inspector, scribbling furiously as the others watched Agathe's transformation in amazement. The mouse was turning into a she-wolf, and it was not a pretty sight.

'Because of *her*!' she screamed, saliva flecking the corners of her lips, her eyes wide and bloodshot. 'The enemy whore – why didn't you die? Why – why? You should have. I planned it so well – so perfectly.'

Dry keening sobs racked her emaciated body and her hands became claws as she suddenly tried to pounce on the spellbound Inès. Two burly policemen grabbed her by the arms, trying to hold her as her sobs became heaving cries of pent-up rage and frustration.

'The wrong person died. Hubert wasn't a saint but he didn't deserve to die like that – the filthy slut should have died. I arranged it for *her*. Why didn't she die?'

Julian was stunned. Whore – Inès? Enemy slut? What was this demented woman saying? His arms tightened around Inès, who was staring at Agathe, a faint flicker of recognition dawning in her eyes.

Oh God, Inès thought. Another one – another creature from the past come to destroy my life. But who was she? Inès desperately racked her brains to try to recall when she had known this woman.

Agathe screamed hysterically, 'You didn't know she was a famous Parisian prostitute, did you, Julian? Did you?' She laughed, her face a mask of hatred.

Inès' face paled and she felt the rigid body of Julian moving away from her. Then suddenly she remembered.

'Oh my God,' she whispered. That wispy, strange girl she had seen only once or twice at the cash register of L'Éléphant Rose during the war. She had never even seen the girl's face properly, but now she remembered all the stories they'd told about her. Those years of privation when the Jewish girl was hidden down the cellar; how her hair had turned completely white; how when she got out she had despised not only the enemy but all the girls who fraternized with them.

Inès took a step towards the babbling woman whose face was a twisted mask of pain and vengeance. She seemed barely human now. 'Please stop, Agathe,' Inès pleaded. 'Don't. I beg you, *don't*! *Please*. Why are you saying these things? They're lies. You mustn't do this – you *can't*.'

'I can – oh, but I can and I *will*.' Agathe's smile was vicious, her laugh a crone's cackle. 'Now that *he* knows what you were – what you *are* – he won't want to marry you any more – will you, Julian?'

Suddenly she burst away from the restraining grasp of the two policemen and rushed towards Julian, crooning, '*Mon amour – mon amour*.' One skinny arm clamped itself around his neck, while the other yanked feverishly at the knot of his robe, trying to pull it open.

'My God, Agathe, what the hell are you doing? Stop it!' Julian was strong, and he held her at arm's length in a tight grip, staring into her demented eyes.

'Tell me what you meant about Inès,' he said, his voice steady and menacing. 'Tell me, Agathe.'

Inès sank on to a couch, hiding her face in her hands. It was over now. All over. Now the truth would finally be known. To her lover, the man whose child she had carried – whose wife she was going to be. It was finally finished. Her whole life lay in ruins around her. Julian would never forgive her for her past and her deception. How could he?

'Yes, yes, Julian, of course I'll tell you – I want to tell you *everything*.' Agathe licked at her dry lips, her eyes darting gleefully between Julian and Inès, revelling in the attention of the whole group who were riveted to her every word with horrified fascination. She was centre stage finally, now they would watch *her*, listen to *her*, while the arms of the man she worshipped held her tightly.

'Paris. It was Paris – at the night club L'Éléphant Rose during the war – she fucked them – all of them – the Boche, the Gestapo, the SS, the Italian pigs. Soldiers, officers, she didn't care who she did it with. She danced with them – she laughed with them and she let them *all* fuck her. Do anything with her. They gave her money which she threw around, showing off to everyone. She loved the life of a whore, didn't you, Inès?' She glanced over at Inès' slumped figure and with a contemptuous laugh, continued, 'Then one night she went too far. She killed a man, with his own razor, she cut his throat.

At least she thought she did – didn't you, bitch?' Again, she looked towards Inès huddled on the couch, the humiliation of having her past laid bare rendering her mute and immobile.

'*Who* – who did Inès kill?' Julian's voice sounded hoarse, cold and tired. Inès could tell now as he looked at her that he hated her. Her dream was just another nightmare.

'*SCROFO!*' Agathe screamed. 'Umberto Scrofo – the Italian General, the fat one with all the medals. The one who called himself Hubert Croft here. She was his girl – his doxy. He made love to her *many*, many times in Paris. Then she tried to murder him – but you didn't succeed, did you?' She sneered at Inès. 'What a pity for you, whore. You didn't succeed just like I didn't succeed in killing you – but maybe I've done something even better. I've *ruined* you, and your precious life with Julian, because he's *mine – MINE!*' With that she lashed a bony hand across her dress, tearing off the buttons to reveal small shrivelled breasts.

'Kiss me, Julian! *Mon amour.*' Eyes closed, she tried to squirm closer to him, but Julian held her away from him, an expression of disgust on his face.

'I've been waiting for you, *mon amour*, my Julian,' she cried despairingly, her eyes now open and pleading. 'Waiting, my love. I know you want me too, it's our destiny to be together.'

As Agathe tried to press her writhing body against his, the Inspector signalled to the two policemen, who grabbed her, pulling her away from Julian. Ramona put her shawl over Agathe's half-naked body, her eyes mirroring the pity she felt for this poor wretch, and the rest of them turned away in shocked embarrassment.

Julian stood quite still, his tanned face ashen.

Nick went over to him. Unable to find anything to say, he put his hand comfortingly on Julian's shoulder. Dominique drew closer to the two men, her childlike, inquisitive eyes riveted to Inès, who still hadn't spoken.

Ramona was comforting Shirley, who was weeping quietly. 'Irving, my poor, poor Irving. That mad bitch killed him too, that bitch. Oh, Christ.'

The rest of the cast and crew stood stiffly like extras in a crowd scene, huddled in the background, staring at Julian, Agathe and Inès

432

in fascination. They sensed that something even more dreadful was about to happen in this frozen tableau. All the principals were silent except for Shirley's muffled sobbing, and the faint sound of waves sighing on the shoreline was the only background noise.

Then Julian spoke in a dark, threatening voice which sent a shudder through Inès. 'Is all this true, Inès? Is what Agathe said the truth?'

How could he? How *could* Julian ask her that question in front of everyone? Couldn't he leave her with even a shred of self-respect? Inès had waited to find the man of her dreams for many years. Now he stood before her with dozens of people as witnesses, about to denounce her for what she had been, and for what she had done in what seemed a former lifetime.

Julian asked the question again, his voice even icier than before. The electrified silence of the onlookers intensified his theatrical presence. He was centre stage – the leading actor – and all the supporting cast seemed to be waiting with bated breath for the inevitable drama to unfold.

'I asked you if what Agathe has said is true, Inès?' he asked for the third time, his voice raised. Inès could hear the suppressed rage, see it in his posture, his attitude. His fists were clenched, his eyes narrowed, his regal head proud. The king was demanding obedience from a subject.

'Answer me, Inès!' he roared authoritatively. 'Say something.'

Inès raised her head to look unflinchingly into Julian's cold eyes, struggling to keep her face impassive. She had too much pride to cry, though her throat ached with pain. The man she loved was demanding a public confession from her, demanding that she reveal her past to him – to all of these people – because of what he considered to be *his* divine right.

Slowly Inès rose to her feet and the crowd held its breath in anticipation. There was silence as Inès stared defiantly at Julian, a slight breeze stirring her dress. He took an angry step towards her, roughly brushing aside Nick's restraining hand.

'I said *answer* me, Inès, I want the truth. *Now.*'

Inès' voice was only slightly louder than the whisper of the breeze. 'Julian, oh Julian, the camera isn't turning. You don't have to perform now.'

'How dare you!' The power of his voice caused the sleeping parrots in the trees to awaken and raise a cacophony of screeching. 'Don't *preach* to me, Inès. Answer my question. That's all I ask of you.'

'Not here – not *now*.' Her eyes never left his face. 'No, Julian. No. I can't and I won't.'

She turned, light as gossamer, and walked swiftly from the great marble hall into the welcoming darkness of the night, the tears that she had held back almost choking her.

Nick grabbed Julian's arm as he tried to follow her. 'No, Julian, no, let her go. She's right. This isn't the time nor the place. Leave her alone, you must.'

Weeping with despair, Inès began slinging her clothes into suitcases. One of Ramona's drivers waited outside the hotel. She was leaving Acapulco. Leaving Julian. Leaving behind her perfect future. She was going – to where? She didn't know; she knew only that she had to escape. Hastily she pulled off her silk dress, putting on a skirt and jacket. She snapped her suitcases shut, oblivious to the pieces of stray fabric which trailed from their sides, and rang down for a porter.

The door opened suddenly and Julian walked into the room. He had changed out of his robe into trousers and a shirt. His face was pale, his eyes full of pain.

They stared at each other. He looked down at the closed suitcases, at her travelling clothes, at the defiant expression on her beautiful face.

'Why are you leaving me?' he asked.

'Why?' She smiled weakly. 'Oh, you know why, Julian. It's true what Agathe said – not all of it – she exaggerated – but I *was* a prostitute in Paris, and I *did* try to kill Scrofo or Croft or whatever he called himself.'

'My God.' He shook his head and sat down heavily on the bed. 'But why, Inès? Why in God's name did you never tell me before? You must have known that one day I'd find out?'

'I just hoped that you wouldn't. I suppose I didn't think you could bear to hear the truth. Yes, I was a whore,' she said quietly, 'but only

434

because of circumstances. You see, my mother had been one, and probably my grandmother before her.'

She looked at him but his expression remained enigmatic. She sighed.

'It was an easy, almost normal way of life to me, Julian – I was very young when I started, an adolescent, and I really knew no other life. Perhaps I was too greedy; maybe in London I should have stopped being a prostitute, taken a proper job in a shop or an office, and found a man, any man, to marry. I shouldn't have cared whether I loved him or not. I should have just married him for security and to have him to take care of me.'

She looked at him, her eyes huge with tears. 'That's how it's supposed to be for a woman, isn't it, Julian? No one said you had to be in love to be married – but to me, to marry someone I didn't love, was an even worse kind of prostitution.'

Julian said nothing, his face still expressionless as Inès continued, 'I loved you so much – I *do* love you so much, that I couldn't run the risk of probably losing you. I know you, Julian. Don't forget that. I know how you think, how most men think. You have double standards regarding men and women. You would have left me if you knew, I know you would. You wouldn't have been able to bear what people would have said, the malicious gossip, the scandal and all the whispering that would have gone on behind your back.'

'No, Inès.' He took a step towards her and she thought she could see tenderness gradually coming back into his face. 'It isn't true. I would have understood, and I would have forgiven you because I *love* you. You are – you always have been, always *will* be, the only woman for me in my whole life. Don't you know that?'

She stared at him uncertainly. 'But my past? Doesn't it bother you – surely you must mind?'

'Mind – mind? Of *course* I bloody mind, you silly little goose. But what can I do about it? Nothing. It happened, it's part of what has made you the person you are, the woman I love, the woman I want to marry and spend the rest of my life with. Inès, you forgave me for Dominique – a far worse thing. How could I not forgive you, my darling, how could I?'

'But you were so angry in front of everyone – it was so humiliating. I was mortified, Julian.'

'I'm sorry, my darling. I'm truly, truly sorry. What more can I say?'

He stood up and took a step nearer to her. She could see the soft familiar look of love in his eyes and the colour coming back to his face.

'I hate myself for hurting you, Inès. You've been hurt too much in the past.'

His arms reached out for her and she found herself wanting to melt into their safe refuge.

'God knows I've been a bastard to you, worse than a bastard.'

'It's all right, darling,' she murmured. 'It's all forgotten.'

'None of it really matters to us any more,' he whispered, taking her in his arms, and the breath left her body in a great sigh of abandoned relief.

'It's all forgotten, my love. All over now.'

'Thank God,' Inès breathed. 'Thank God, everything's out in the open. I'm glad you know the truth, Julian. I think our life together would have become impossible if I had always had to pretend.'

'You're right, my angel.' Julian smiled lovingly at her. 'You're absolutely right, it's never any good to pretend. That's only for actors.'

Long before their limousine arrived at the theatre, the occupants could see the dozens of searchlights criss-crossing the thick blackness of the sky and hear the excited shrieks of the eager fans in the bleachers greeting each arriving celebrity with approval.

'Here goes,' Nick said, adjusting his black bow tie. 'This is what we've all been waiting for. It's sink or swim time, boys and girls.'

The women took out their powder compacts to check their perfectly made-up faces for the last time. All of them were silent with their own particular thoughts of what tonight's premiere would mean to each of them.

For Elektra it meant that Nikolas would finally achieve his lifetime's desire: to be an important director in the American cinema. He had expunged the memory of Gourouni from his mind in the past year and was filled with optimism about the future.

Dominique was being hailed as the brightest new star in Hollywood, and the studio were considering casting her opposite Julian in his next film.

Inès smoothed the folds of her ice-white velvet gown. Turning her perfect profile away from her husband, she looked out of the window into the night, the encroaching cheers of the fans suddenly provoking thoughts of the past. She thought how lucky she was – so very lucky. Luck had saved her from the vengeance of the Gestapo after the incident with Scrofo. If it hadn't been for luck, she too might have lived those years of torment that Agathe had endured, which had slowly driven her mad. If she had been forced to exist in that cellar, would her life have been any different from Agathe's? Could *she* have remained sane?

Inès really couldn't blame Agathe for what she had tried to do. The ravages of war and evil had created a certain kind of madness in almost everyone who had survived it.

As the white limousine drew up outside the brilliantly lit theatre, the crowd's cheers built to a tumultuous crescendo.

'Ready, darling?' Julian gently squeezed Inès' white-gloved hand.

'Ready,' she said with a brilliant smile. 'Ready for anything, darling.'

From the darkness opposite Dominique looked across at them and a sly and secret smile flickered over her beautiful face. One day, she thought, one day soon, Julian, you will be mine again, I know you will. I can feel it in my bones.